to
MR.X
*who went to Outland
in a small aeroplane
on Wednesday
week*

Naomi Mitchison was born in Edinburgh ████ ████ and
educated at the Dragon School an█ ████████ ██llege
Oxford. As a member of the H█████████ ██ ██ father was a
noted physiologist and ███████ ███ ███ genetic
scientist and essay███ ██████ ████ █aomi Mitchison
has been equ██████ ██ ████████ one of the foremost
historical nove█████ ██ ███ ████ ██eration.

In 1916 she marr██ ███ Labour politician Dick Mitchison,
later Baron Mitchison, QC, and during their years in
London she took an active part in social and political
affairs. Her career as a writer began with *The Conquered*
(1923), a novel about the Celts whose approach antici-
pated similarly imaginitive reconstruction from later
writers of the Scottish Renaissance. Further novels were
set in ancient classical times, most notably *The Corn King
and the Spring Queen* (1931), which drew on her interest in
myth and ritual and the writings of J.G. Frazer. *The Blood
of the Martyrs* (1939), brought her hatred of oppression
and a perennial concern for human decency to a tale of the
early Christian movement. Naomi Mitchison returned to
Scotland in 1937 to live at Carradale in Kintyre, and her
novel *The Bull Calves* (1947) deals with the years after the
Jacobite '45 and the Haldane family history at that time.

In a full life of cultural and creative commitment Naomi
Mitchison has known and corresponded with a host of
fellow writers, including E.M. Forster, W.H. Auden,
Wyndham Lewis, Aldous Huxley and Neil Gunn. There
are over seventy books to her name, including biographies, essays, short stories and poetry. Her entertaining
memoirs have been published as *Small Talk* (1973), *All
Change Here* (1975) and *You May Well Ask* (1979).

Naomi Mitchison

THE
CORN KING
AND THE
SPRING QUEEN

With a new Introduction
by the author

CANONGATE
CLASSICS
29

First published in 1931 by Jonathan Cape, first
published as a Canongate Classic in 1990 by
Canongate Publishing Ltd, 17 Jeffrey Street,
Edinburgh EH1 1DR. Copyright Naomi Mitch-
ison 1931. Introduction copyright Naomi
Mitchison 1990.

The publishers gratefully acknowledge general subsidy from the Scottish Arts Council
towards the Canongate Classics series and a
specific grant towards the publication of this
title.

Set in 10pt Plantin by Hewer Text Composi-
tion Services, Edinburgh. Printed and bound in
Denmark by Norhaven Rotation.

Canongate Classics
Series Editor: Roderick Watson
Editorial Board: Tom Crawford, John Pick

British Library Cataloguing in Publication Data
Mitchison, Naomi, *1897–*
The corn king and the spring queen.—
(Canongate classics)
I. Title
823.912

ISBN 0-86241-287-0

Contents

Introduction

To write an introduction to a book which has been written some sixty years back is rather like introducing one's grandmother. So, at least, I suppose I know how my grandchildren might feel. I look at my book, half reluctant, half eager, turning the pages—could I really have written that, amn't I on dangerous ground, trying to assess it? I write differently now, perhaps better, perhaps not. But I know that by now I am a very different person with different ideas of the world, above all writing for a different audience, probably more critical, themselves leading more interesting and varied lives than those readers two generations back. What will the new ones think of this old book?

But then I take a gulp of the old vintage. I find myself remembering, only too well, the moods and problems, but also the delight, of writing this book which you are going to read. But my brain-child has run away; now it belongs to its readers rather than its writer.

Now let us look at the story of this book. It begins to happen somewhere on the edge of the Black Sea. You will not find Marob on any map, but for you and me it is real. The people who lived thereabouts are vaguely called Scythians; one of the few things we know about them is that they made astonishingly beautiful objects, mostly bronze. You can see a few in the main museums of the world, but most and probably the best are in the Hermitage Museum in Leningrad. We judge a civilisation by what its people do, what they think if they put it into writing or speech, but also by what they make. When we look at their artefacts there must be constant interpretation, just as there should be when we do the same with present cultures. Some of these may have been going on for hundreds, perhaps even thousands of years, but have only lately been touched by what we think of as our own superior culture. Yet are we always quite certain of our superiority?

What earlier people thought about, how they dealt with love and hate, joy and disaster is often hard to understand if they are far across the bridges of written or remembered history. Yet, if their remaining artefacts are beautiful across the sea of years, something can be adduced about them, some understanding can be made.

Yet none of this was in my mind when I first made contact with Marob in a sailing boat off Plymouth, watching the waves and not attending to what Julian Huxley was telling me about the minutiae of the ocean population. But it grew into a force behind my writing, page after pencilled page in those notebooks I carried with me and dropped on to floors or into mud and took with me on long, uninterrupted, Underground journeys, sometimes round and round the Circle, totally unaware of my fellow passengers, because I was not really there, but far elsewhere. You might have thought I was worrying about politics or about which shop to go to for something I wanted, or indeed, that I was deep into a love affair. But no, no, I was being one person or another in my book, becoming them in turn as I wrote about them and they seemed to be sitting beside me.

In the late twenties and early thirties, the *Cambridge Ancient History* was coming out volume by volume. I gobbled them up, even decorating some volumes with pasted-in photographs of buildings or statues. But I had to find out more, I had to get closer, behind the answers to my questions. I got into exchanges with Professor Adcock and some of the other historians who were writing it, above all William Tarn, who seemed to be in tune with my ideas, so that everything he told me fitted in. As often as not I asked questions which they couldn't answer or only with an additional *perhaps*, or occasionally a *probably*. But I think most authors are rather pleased to answer the questions of readers who have clearly absorbed what they are asking about. There were other books of course, including my dear old *Golden Bough*, and so often—but any writer knows this—something, a sentence in a book, a tree, the expression of someone passing, a cloud across the moon, will set the instrument ticking. One will grab the nearest pencil and write.

So, over the months, my picture of the edge of what we call civilisation built itself up and beyond that the fuller picture of what was happening in the centres of Mediterranean culture, yet always keeping an eye on what the historians, or, for that matter, the contemporary authors, wanted us to believe. Plutarch, for instance, had very firm ideas of how his biographies should be regarded and what lessons could be learned from them for a later era.

So the pictures gathered and gathered. Something that began with one girl, for the moment myself, playing with little crabs, on a beach—but of what sea?—who happens to be able to work magic, turned into a whole country and culture of people with, almost touching them, pages of real, admitted history. When this became so pressing that it had to be written down, I got on with it, checking all that could be checked. It became an elaborate, even exhausting, story. Sometimes I turned aside to write something different, or the real world with its pains and anxieties broke in, and the story of the book went dark for a time. But it always came back.

The main picture became clear: how these people who lived on the edge of the real Mediterranean culture, but not too near and with a comforting background of custom and magic to help them with their problems of health and happiness, their food supply and their social habits, came into touch with other ideas, more akin to those we ourselves know. The book follows those who leave Marob and what happened, both to them and to those left behind. As the story gathered and coloured the individual people became more clear to me: the Chief of Marob, his witch-wife and her brother who makes the beautiful things, those bronzes. I saw them struck by another set of ideas and carried away into the last phase of Hellenic culture and into an understanding of the ideas of philosophers and politicians.

Now the story had shifted into the revolution in Sparta, led by the last of the Kings. At the time of writing that seemed very relevant to what was going on in the real world of the early thirties. I would wake from my book to watch these realities and see each in the terms of the other. My book, by this time, was based on real, documented history, but all the same, how we look at history depends on what we want to find. If a bit of historical guessing, even by an accredited historian, did not fit my story, I disregarded it or found holes in it. There are newer historians, even in the unpopular classic stage, who cast a different light on some of my characters.

So, readers, remember that my account of what was happening in Sparta or Athens or even Egypt, is all based on real history, but the view was moulded by what I—and many another person—was thinking in the Europe of those days, with Mussolini and his fascists in Italy and already the shadow of Hitler in Germany. If I was writing this book now I might treat my characters and my story differently. But I cannot be certain, even of that.

We know certain historical facts, for instance about King Kleomenes of Sparta; the picture of him in this book by this storyteller allows these facts and perhaps throws light on them, and yet may be misleading. We try to imagine what went on in other people's minds, and what we think they might have said or done, beyond the secure facts. Here and there it is just possible that I may have guessed right. This is the best that an author dealing with real people, either in fiction or biography (and can one draw a complete line between them?) can hope to do.

So my story which I hope you will be following, leaves Marob and the world of magic in which anything can happen, for the Mediterranean civilisation on the way to modern times and modern ideas and religions. Real people take their places in my book: Sphaeros, a known minor philosopher, and then King Kleomenes in Sparta with his wife and children and much that is known about Egypt at that time, and others who are at least names in history books. They were real people with real lives, apart from me and my alien language. But the dead cannot complain if I have got it wrong.

Events really happened, but must have looked different to those who wrote about them, starting with writers much nearer in time than ourselves. So, readers, in this tangle and mirage, good luck to you. Watch what Erif Der and Tarrik the Corn King did for the Plowing and the Harvest and then follow them across the Mediterranean, a big jump towards today. Be with them, and so, with me.

Naomi Mitchison

Foreword

The things in this book happened between the years 228 BC and 187 BC. Some of the things really happened, and some of the oddest things are said to have happened by Plutarch and others who call themselves historians. The place called Marob is not historically real, but people on the shores of the Black Sea, and thereabouts, made very beautiful things, of the kind which Berris Der made. For the rest, I have tried to deduce a place, from a good deal of evidence of actual ideas and happenings in all sorts of other times and places. As between Marob and Sparta or Alexandria, it is very doubtful whether, at a distance of more than two thousand years, one can ever get near to the minds, or even to the detail of the actions, of the people one is writing about, although they are in a way nearer to one than one's living friends; it is scarcely possible that Kleomenes of Sparta was really at all like the Kleomenes I have made, though I doubt whether, in the present state of knowledge, anyone else's idea is inherently more probable—it is all a game of hide-and-seek in the dark and if, in the game, one touches a hand or face, it is all chance; so Marob is just as likely, or as unlikely, as the rest of the world.

At the beginning of this book there is a family tree of the Spartan royal family during the time I have written about it. There are no names recorded for the children of Kleomenes and Agiatis, but I have given them ancestral names which seemed to be likely.

I think this is all.   Naomi Mitchison, 1925–30

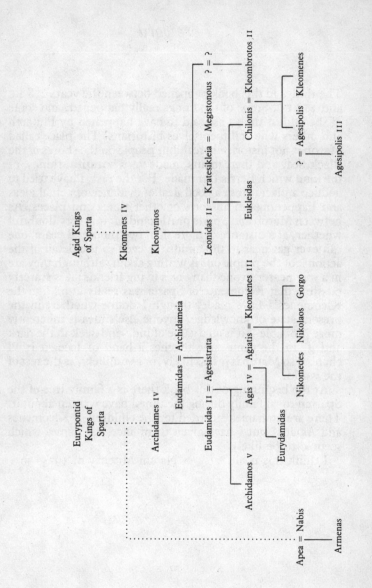

Agid Kings of Sparta

Kleomenes IV
Kleonymos

Leonidas II = Kratesikleia = Megistonous   ? = ?

Chionis = Kleombrotos II

Eukleidas

? = Agesipolis

Agesipolis III

Kleomenes III

Kleomenes III = Agiatis

Nikomedes Nikolaos Gorgo

Euterpontid Kings of Sparta

Archidames IV

Eudamidas = Archidameia

Agis IV = Agiatis

Eudamidas II = Agesistrata

Eurydamidas

Archidamos V

Apea = Nabis

Armenas

PART I

Kataleptike Phantasia

Lavender's blue, dilly, dilly!
   Rosemary's green;
When I am king, dilly, dilly!
   You shall be queen.

Call up your men, dilly, dilly!
   Set them to work;
Some to the plough, dilly, dilly!
   Some to the cart.

Some to make hay, dilly, dilly!
   Some to cut corn;
While you and I, dilly, dilly!
   Keep ourselves warm.

PEOPLE IN THE FIRST PART

People of Marob
Erif Der
Her father, Harn Der
Her mother, Nerrish
Her eldest brother, Yellow Bull
Her next eldest brother, Berris Der
Her younger brother, Gold-fish
Her younger sister, Wheat-ear
Yellow Bull's wife, Essro
Tarrik, also called Charmantides, Corn King
    and Chief of Marob
His aunt, Yersha, also called Eurydice

Greeks
Epigethes, an artist
Sphaeros of Borysthenes, a Stoic philosopher
Apphé, Yersha's maid

Men and Women of Marob, Greek sailors
    and merchants

ERIF DER WAS SITTING on a bank of shingle and throwing pebbles into the Black Sea; for a girl, she threw very
straight. She was thinking a little about magic but mostly
about nothing at all. Her dress was pulled up over her knees,
and her legs were long and thin and not much sunburnt yet,
because it was still early in the year. Her face was pale too,
with flat, long plaits of hair hanging limp at each side, and
her ear-rings just shaking as she threw. She wore a dress of
thick linen, woven in a pattern of squares, red and black
and greyish white; at the end of the sleeves the pattern
ended in two wide bands of colour. It had a leather belt
sewn with tiny masks of flat gold, and the clasps were larger
gold masks with garnet eyes and teeth. Over all she wore a
stiff felt coat, sleeveless, with strips of fur down the sides,
and she was not cold in spite of the wind off the sea.

A crab came walking towards her over the shingle; she
held out her hand, palm upwards, so that the crab walked
over it. Erif Der laughed to herself; she liked the feeling
of its stiff, damp, scuttling claws on her skin. She picked it
up carefully by the sides of its shell and made it walk again,
this time over her bare foot. A cloud came over the sun;
she threw two more pebbles into the sea, sat up and put
her shoes on, then walked back towards Marob harbour till
she came to the high stone breakwater; instead of going
round with the road, she climbed up it, by way of a chain
and ring and some wave-worn places in the stone; she was
always fond of doing elaborate and unnecessary things. On
the other side, she jumped down twelve feet on to another
shingle bank, but she was not at all an easy person to hurt;
air and water at least knew too much about her.

She went on more quickly now, and up into the town:
she felt as if her father was calling her. Soon she was passing
the Chief's house, straight in front of the harbour, looking

square on to the sea, east and a little north, with thick stone piers and small windows. Erif Der wondered if she would like to live there, and thought not, thought it would be cold, thought particularly that if she ever did have to, she would do her best not to have Yersha there too. As she was thinking this, Yersha herself came out of the main door with her hair done high and her mantle caught up on her shoulder, Greek fashion, and two armed guards following her. However, Erif Der was hurrying a little and did not choose to be seen or stopped, so Yersha looked the other way for a full minute, and when she turned again there was no one in sight; that was annoying for Yersha, who hated being magicked at all, even as little as this, and suspected it was done by Erif Der—who was much too young to have any powers really, besides being the daughter of Harn Der, besides going about alone like a street-girl, besides having been chosen to dance with the Chief at Plowing Eve and having—Yersha suspected—spoken with him of more matters than the plowing and the Courting dance! It had been occurring more and more to Yersha, in this last year, that her nephew, the Chief, had not told her exactly all that he had been doing and saying every day. That was bad enough, without having children like Erif Der, who ought to be kept at home and made useful, working magic on her! Yersha hated magic: she could not do it herself, because of the quarter of Greek blood in her that made things too plain and too real to be twisted about in the Scythian way.

Meanwhile Erif Der went on, along the main street of Marob, and across the flax market to her father's house. Harn Der was standing in front of the hearth, jabbing the fire with the shaft of an old boar spear, so that quantities of smoke poured into the room, which was dark enough already. He was a short, thick man with hair and beard that bristled out all ways at once, and a leather coat and breeches. Erif Der stopped and blinked and rubbed her eyes. 'Well, father,' she said, 'here I am.' Her father left off stirring the fire and the smoke cleared; when her eyes stopped tingling she could see that her brother, Berris Der, was there too. As usual he had a hawk on his shoulder; equally as usual, he had something in his hands to play with, this time a strip of soft copper that he was bending and unbending, so that sometimes it looked more like a cup, and sometimes more like a flower, or a snake, or a bracelet. Berris Der was three years older than she was and they were not always interested in the same things; but still they smiled at one another rather more consciously than as simple relations. The girl came and stood by her father. 'Well,' she said again, looking at the fire rather than at him; 'you wanted me?'

Harn Der frowned at her. 'You have to see and to know that it is time for your part in this,' he said.

Erif Der swung her foot uncomfortably, and the corners of her mouth twitched a little; all at once she looked much younger and less magic. 'Still I don't know how!' she said. 'Father, are you sure it has to be me?'

'Little fool!' said Harn Der, more gentle in voice than in words, 'I shall be Chief of Marob before the end of the year, and remember, that will be you.'

'But it's so hard,' said the girl, 'first to marry him, and then to magic him, and then to unmarry him. I think I shall go wrong somewhere.'

Harn Der answered, smiling to himself a little: 'What are you afraid of?'

'Myself. My own power.'

'You should go and learn power instead of sitting on the beach and doing nothing—like your mother.'

The girl's mouth and bright eyes twisted into sudden laughter: 'Much you know of learning magic, father!'

'Would I use you if I knew myself, little vixen? Go, get on with my work! What was the use of Plowing Eve if you will not watch your furrow?'

'Ah,' said Erif Der lightly, shifting to the other foot, 'I can tell you that. I think the Chief knows.'

'I never told you to think!' said her father, 'besides— it's not so. Tarrik is a fool: he cannot know.'

'All the same—' she said, then shrugged her shoulders. 'Well, perhaps he doesn't know. Perhaps he is a fool.'

'He is not that, then,' said Berris Der suddenly, 'he is the one of you all that knows what I am looking for, and if father's plan was anyone else's plan I should be well out of it! And remember, if you hurt Tarrik, I shall be out of it!'

'Oh you, Berris,' said his father, 'if you don't want to know you shouldn't listen. And—for the hundred and

first time—we are not going to hurt Tarrik. I know as
well as you that it would be no good in the end: so long
as he is Corn King. If I did not know it, couldn't I have
killed him twenty times over and been Chief by now?
But that would have been for my harm and the harm of
Marob as well. I am not going to hurt the corn. As it is,
the Council will see that he goes, gently, for no one hates a
madman, and then they will put me in his place and Marob
will not be divided against itself.'

'But I shan't have to stay married to him?' asked Erif
Der anxiously.

'Of course not. You will be the Chief's daughter: to
do whatever you and we choose. But listen: when I said
Tarrik was a fool, I meant a fool in the way you thought
he was wise. He does not know of the plan, still less that
you are part of it. And as to the way Berris thinks he is
wise, whatever that may be, it will not alter, and when I
am Chief, Tarrik can work with Berris and they can both
talk about beauty.'

Erif Der shook her head, but said nothing and went over
to a chest by the wall; she took out a coat of brown fur, a
shade darker than her own hair, and put it on instead of the
felt one, which she folded carefully and put away. Then she
took a gold bracelet out, and tried it on her arm, first above,
then below the elbow, pinching it into place; when it was
high on her arm the sleeve hid it, but then, whenever she
lifted her hand, it flashed out wonderfully. 'Which is right,
Berris?' she said. Her brother frowned at her and walked
out; she hesitated, changed the bracelet to the other arm,
and ran after him, caught him up, and walked beside him,
a pace behind.

Harn Der looked after them, scratched his head, and after
a little walked out into the flax market; he found one of his
own farm people, who had been sent down to Marob to buy
new milk jars, and was going back with the big red crocks
slung over his shoulder; he said that everything was doing
finely, the wheat well up, the flax and hemp high for the
time of year, and there were two fat calves ready to be killed
and sent down whenever they were wanted. Harn Der was
pleased, thinking of his crops and his beasts; no one in
Marob had better land than his, few had so much of it;
and all good, sheltered, and well watered, away from the

sea, but not so far from the town that the inlanders, the Red Riders, would ever come and raid it. In a few weeks he would be going down there with his wife and children, to live all summer in great yellow tents, with the birds and the beasts on the plains all round him, and the sun shining and the crops growing.

But it was more than land he had, and better than gold. Every one in Marob knew him and thought of him always as wise and strong and a ruler of men; the elders had seen him at war, seen him guarding their land against the Red Riders in the days when Tarrik was only a child. A great archer was Harn Der then, and a great horseman; you could see the yellow tassel of his helmet a mile away across the fighting, when things were at their worst, and then back it would come to you and you would know that everything was going to be right and the Red Riders beaten and driven out of the fields you loved. That was Harn Der, and that was Harn Der's eldest son, Yellow Bull, who was making himself new lands out of the swamps to the south of Marob and had built his house there, not in the walled town. Harn Der sighed, and went home again moodily, thinking of his sons and all he was doing for them.

Berris and his sister were out of sight by now; they were walking fast and Erif Der was out of breath and a little angry. She took an odd-looking, small wooden star out of the front of her dress and held it for a few yards, then stopped for a moment, panting, and touched her brother's hand. 'It's very hot, isn't it, Berris?'

'Yes, I suppose,' said Berris vaguely, slowing down, and took off his coat as he walked and trailed it from his hand till it dropped. 'Very hot,' he went on, and began pulling at his shirt, and, 'very hot,' his sister echoed, looking at him gravely. He pulled the shirt over his head and his felt cap dropped off with it; there was a brown line at the base of his neck where he stopped being sunburnt. The belt went with the shirt; he started just a little at the chink of the clasps falling on the road, but he was looking at Erif Der. Still walking slowly, he stepped out of his loose trousers. 'So hot,' he said again, and there was a film of sweat on his skin. He pushed back the hair from his forehead, and suddenly behind Erif Der there seemed to be a face staring at him, two, three faces. He stared back at them. They were

opening their mouths to say words to him, his sister faded
and they came real, and all at once he noticed, first, that
he was really quite cold, and then that he had nothing on
and all his clothes were straggling in little heaps down the
road where he had dropped them.

He stood and swore at the starers till they ran—they
were all poor men, and he, in spite of everything, Harn
Der's son. Then he went up to Erif Der; she had her
mouth tight shut and her cheeks pink; she tried to look
him in the eyes again, but he was too angry for her now.
'Pick up my clothes,' he said.

'I won't!' said Erif Der, getting pinker.

'Yes you will,' said her brother, and got her by the two
plaits. She screamed and hit out at him, but he swung her
away by her hair. 'Pick them up,' he said.

She went and got them without a word, and threw them
down at his feet; she was too sore and angry to cry. 'You
beast, Berris!' she said, 'I'll make you sorry for that!'

Berris recovered his temper with his trousers. 'No, you
won't,' he said, 'I can always pull your hair and you can't
always magic me, so it won't do you any good in the long
run.' She kicked his coat and said nothing. 'Little goose,'
he went on, 'what did you do it for? Suppose Tarrik had
seen?'

'Well, let him!' said Erif Der. 'Let him! Then no one
can say he didn't know what I can do!'

'Oh,' said Berris, 'so that's what you're after. My belt,
please. No, pick it up. Pick it up! So you want Tarrik to
know?'

'Tarrik does know! I'm going home. I shall tell father
you hurt me!'

Berris caught her by one arm: 'Baby! You come with
me to the forge. Come and blow the fire for me. Erif, I'm
making something—something exciting. A beast. Come
on, Erif.'

'Is Tarrik going to be there? Is he? Let go, Berris!'

'Very likely. Erif, you are shiny when you're so cross.
There, that's better. Are you coming?'

'I won't answer till you let me go.'

He dropped her arm. She rubbed it against her cheek for
a moment, then nodded and went down the street towards
the forge.

Berris Der unlocked the door, taking a little time over
it, because he had made the lock himself and was proud
of it: the key was like a little stag with mad horns. He
left the door open and unfastened the shutters from inside.
Erif Der went to the fire and raked away the earth that had
been banked round it the evening before: it was still alive
and stirred redly under her breath as she fed it with dry
chips. She leaned to the bellows. 'Why have you got to do
that?' asked Berris. 'Can't you make the fire obey?' Erif
Der shook her head: 'I don't know enough about fire,' and
she turned her back on him to get a purchase on the bellows
handle. Berris was at another of his own locks now; it
was on a great oak chest, bound with forking straps of
silver-inlaid bronze. He took something out, and laid it
carefully on the embers, which throbbed white and red
with heat under the bellows. After a time he called her
to look.

She stood away from him, watching. There was a small,
queer, iron horse, twisted and flattened, biting his own
back; he was angry and hammer-marked all over; his
mane shot up into a flame; his downward jammed feet
were hard and resisting; the muscles of his body were
ready to burst out. Berris Der laid him on the anvil and
began hammering to a rhythm, one, two on the horse,
three with a solider clink on the iron of the anvil. The
horse twisted still more; fresh hammer marks beat out
the old—the substance seemed less and the movement
more; every moment he became less like the tamed horses
of fenced pastures; and more like something wild in the
mind, beaten madly by the violences of thought. The glow
died out of him. The blows stopped suddenly; he was back
in the fire, and his watchers at work, thinking of him. Then
again the anvil. Berris chanted in time with the hammer,
tunelessly: 'Horse, horse, horse.' At a point of the fantastic
he stayed, the hammer half raised. 'Well?' he said. She
came nearer, tracing the horse shape half unconsciously
in the air with one finger. 'I see,' she said. 'I expect
he is the best thing you have done?' 'Yes, but how do
you know?' 'Not any way you'd like. Ask Tarrik.' Her
brother did not answer, but stayed still, his lips pursed,
watching his queer little horse as it lay there with the light
on it, the centre of the forge; he made the movement of

touching it, but could not really, because of the heat in the iron.

There was a tapping on the open door of the forge; Berris looked round, half angry at being disturbed, half pleased at having someone fresh to admire his work. Erif Der stepped back one pace and sat down on the floor beside another chest which stood between the fire and the window. 'Come in!' said Berris, smiling at his horse; 'come and look.'

A man came in out of the sunshine and stood beside Berris, one hand on his shoulder. 'So!' he said, 'you have something new?' And he stood with his head a little on one side, looking at it. He was older than Berris, tall and graceful, with long, broad-tipped fingers, bare legs, and dark, curly hair; he was clean shaven and his eyes and mouth showed what was going on in his mind. His clothes looked odd and bright in the forge: a short, full tunic of fine linen, light red bordered with deeper red, and a heavy mantle flung round him, one end caught in his belt, the other over his shoulder and hanging thickly and beautifully from his arm. He had thin sandals on his feet and moved cautiously, afraid of knocking against some hot metal.

'What do you make of it, Epigethes?' said Berris Der, speaking shyly in Greek.

The other man smiled and did not answer at once; when he spoke it was gravely, paternally almost, though he was not so very much older than Berris. 'Very nice,' he said.

'You don't think so!' said Berris quickly, flushing, frowning at his horse. 'It isn't!'

The Greek laid a hand kindly on his shoulder: 'Well, Berris, it's rough, isn't it?—harsh, tortured?'

'Yes—yes—but isn't that, partly, the hammering?'

'Of course. What have I always told you? You must work on the clay first till you get out all these violences. And then cast.'

'But, Epigethes, I hate clay! It's so soft, such a long way from what I want. And then, there's the time it takes, with the wax and all—and when it's done I've got to scrape and file and chip and fill in nail holes!'

'I know, I know,' said Epigethes soothingly, 'but you can always come to me for the casting: any time you like. I would tell my man, and you would have nothing to do but leave the model with him.'

'Yes, but—' said Berris again, and then suddenly, 'Oh, it's more than that! Whatever I did, you wouldn't like it! I can't make my things right, I never shall!' He looked down at the shape on the anvil; he hated his little horse now.

Epigethes sat down on the bench; still he had not seen Erif Der. 'Berris,' he said, 'I'll make you an offer. I can teach you, I know I can teach you! You have the hands and eyes—everything but the spirit. There—forgive me, Berris!—you are still a barbarian. No fault of yours: but I can cure it. Come and work with me for six months, and no one will know that you are not a Hellene born.' But Berris Der was getting more and more gloomy; all the joy had faded out of his horse; he saw nothing but its faults, its weaknesses; he lost all pride and assertion, could not hope to be anything but a failure; he shook his head. 'No, but I promise you!' said Epigethes. 'I swear by Apollo himself! And all I ask is what you can give me easily, this pure northern gold of yours, the weight of a loaf of bread, no more. And not coined, not to spend on foolishness, but to use as an artist, to make into beauty! Like this, Berris'—he put his hand into the breast fold of his mantle—'and I am sure you could do as good if once you had the spirit.'

Berris bent over to look. It was a gold plaque in low relief, a woman's head bowered in grape tendrils, with heavy, flowing lines of throat and chin, female even in the gold, and exquisite, minutely perfect work on the grapes—those vines that had been worked on over and over again by generations of Greek artists, till they knew for certain which way every tiniest branchlet should go. But it all meant something different to Berris Der, something worshipful, the impacted art tradition of Hellas: for a poor barbarian to stare at and admire, but never to criticize, oh no, not criticize. He took it in his hands; how different it was from his horse, how well Epigethes must have known just what it was he wanted, and exactly how to get it! And he would be able to make things like this, if once he gave himself up to the Greek, gave his hands and powers as tools for the other to work with. He would make—as one should, one clearly should!—soft, lucid shapes, nature beautified, life in little, sane, unfantastic.

He went to the chest again and took out something else, half of a gold buckle, beaten into a gorgon's head, full face, with staring eyes. He passed it to Epigethes, rather roughly. 'Is that better?' 'But of course!' said the Greek, surprised, holding it up to the light. 'No one need be ashamed of this. The style is coming; why, it is like a boss on the big vase I am making now. You will be an artist yet! When did you make it?' Berris Der looked at the ground. 'I went to your house a week ago,' he said, 'when you were with the Chief. I saw your vase; I measured the heads on it. This is a copy.' And he snatched it back and shoved it into the chest, trembling a little.

'Why not?' said Epigethes, 'between friends? You cannot do better than copy me for the next half-year. It will train your eye, and everything else will follow. Come again when I'm there: any time. I doubt if your Chief wants to see me again!'

'Tarrik! Why not?'

'Oh,' Epigethes smiled, a little self-consciously, 'I'm afraid he does not care for my work. I thought he might, having some Hellene blood himself. But no: you, the pure Scythian, you are more nearly Athenian than he.'

Berris was sad, he wanted to justify the Chief—and yet—'I wish he liked them; but perhaps he will some day. Me more Athenian . . . Oh, do tell me about Athens again!'

Epigethes laughed. 'Some day you shall come there with me and see all the temples and theatres and pictures and everything! You shall fall in love with all the goddesses and try to pick the painted roses, and you will forget that you once twisted iron into ugly shapes.'

'Oh, I wish I could come!' said Berris, 'I do so long for Hellas!' And he coloured and looked out of the window, thinking what a barbarian he must seem. But about Tarrik—'Why did the Chief not like your work, Epigethes? How could he help it? What did he say?'

'Oh, he said a great many things, foolish mostly. But it makes difficulties for me. I had hoped, if he cared for my things, laid out some of his treasures on these—perhaps!—more lasting treasures, I might have been able to stay here for a long time, teaching you some of it. But now—well, I am not a rich man.'

The Greek glanced at his plaque again, then folded it up in a square of linen and put it back. Berris Der went over to the wall and unlocked a tiny metal door, heavily hinged, that opened with a certain difficulty. Epigethes turned his head tactfully away. Berris took out a solid lump of gold, about the size of an apple. 'I meant to work on it,' he said, 'but you—you are worthier. Take it. Oh please, take it!'

The Greek shook his head. 'How can I? My dear boy, I can't take your gold like this.'

But Berris held it out to him imploringly. 'Oh, I do want you to stay! It's mine, my very own, do take it!'

Epigethes seemed to make up his mind. 'Very well,' he said, 'if you will come and take lessons from me.'

'Oh I will!' cried Berris, 'and you shall teach me to be a Hellene!'

'If your Chief will let me!' said Epigethes, feeling the golden lump with his finger-tips.

'I'm sorry about that.' And then Berris had a brilliant thought: 'Oh, Epigethes, you must go to my father. He'll buy your things—after I've spoken to him. And my brother, down in the marshes, I'll take you there. Will you start teaching me soon?'

'Tomorrow if you like. Walk with me to the corner of the street, won't you? Let me see your keys, Berris; you made them, I expect? Still crude, you see.'

They walked out together. When they were quite gone, Erif Der got up and went over to the anvil; the horse was nearly cold; she stared at him with lips pursed, poked him here and there, turned him over. Then she shrugged her shoulders and went back to her corner. She had a handful of little metal scraps, bronze and copper and iron; she arranged them on the floor in patterns. Or perhaps they arranged themselves, while she sang to them, a tiny, thin song in the back of her throat.

Berris Der came back to his forge looking very grown up and determined. He took up his tongs. 'Blow the fire!' he told his sister. She began, then stopped, one hand on the bellows. 'You aren't going to change your horse?' she asked. But, 'Blow!' he half shouted at her, 'I want it hot, melting hot!' And he threw on more wood. She started blowing, with long, steady strokes from the shoulder; twice she spoke to him, but he did not answer. He took his biggest hammer, a great, heavy, broad-headed thing, and propped it against the anvil. The logs flared and glowed and crumbled into white heat; the little iron horse lay there till he was red all over, and the girl's back ached from the bellows. 'So!' said Berris, and she stopped, and straightened herself with a sigh of relief.

He took the horse and laid it on the anvil; he looked at it with cold anger, and then began to smash it with the big hammer, all over. The red-hot sparks flew round him, thick and low, scorching his leather apron and shoes; he hit anyhow, with a blind, horrible passion of hate against his own work, grunting at his efforts sometimes, but saying no word. He did not stop till the iron was black again, and shapeless. Then he took it up with the tongs and threw it clanging into a corner of old cast-off scraps. Erif Der watched it go; she was back again in her old place on the floor.

Her brother went to his chest and stood beside it, taking out one thing after another, mostly half finished; he handled them and frowned or muttered at them, and put them back again. At last he unwrapped the Gorgon's head buckle, and found a piece of gold, roughly beaten out, and compared the two; he was copying the head exactly on to the other half of the buckle. He took them both over to his bench, right under the window, and began to measure and make tiny marks on the gold. They were right under his eyes as he sat upright with both elbows in front of him on the bench to steady himself. He took his magnifying crystal out of the soft leather roll it lived in, and peered through it, counting and placing the tiny balls of filigree. But he seemed clumsy at his tools; his hands were shaking after all that violent hammering; he dealt unlovingly with the things. Once or twice other men passed the window and looked in and spoke to him; he answered crossly, covering the work with his hands. Sometimes there was sun shining on him, but more often not, as the day had turned out cloudy after all.

Chapter Two

BY AND BYE ERIF Der felt that someone was watching her; she looked up, rather cross at having been caught. Under her eye-lashes she saw Tarrik lolling against one of

the door-posts, quite quiet, with a bow in his left hand. He
had a squarish, smiling, lazy face; the oddest thing about it
were his bright brown eyes that looked straight into yours.
He was clean shaven about the chin, but in front of his
ears and on his cheek-bones near the outward corners of his
eyes, there were little soft hairs. He was brown and red as to
colour, as if he lay out in the sun all day, and let it warm his
bare skin while others were working. Like Berris, he wore
loose shirt and trousers, both of white linen, and a white
felt coat embroidered with rising suns and a criss-cross of
different-coloured sunrays. His belt was all gold, dolphins
linked head to tail; it had a rather small sword hanging
from it on one side, and at the other a gold-plated quiver
of arrows, a whistle, and a tiny hunting-knife with an onyx
handle. He wore a crown, being Chief, a high felt cap,
covered with tiers and tiers of odd, fighting, paired griffins
in soft gold; his hair, underneath, was dark brown and
curly; on his upper lip, too, it was brown and quite short,
so that one saw his mouth, and, when he laughed, as he
often did, his white, even, upper teeth.

The girl looked quickly from him to her brother; but
Berris was tap-tapping on the gold, with his back to them
both. Tarrik smiled, tightened his bowstring and began
playing with it, till it buzzed like a wasp. She frowned
at him, not sure whether he mightn't be laughing at her,
treating her like a baby, when really it was she who had
all the power. She put her hand to the wooden star under
her dress.

Then the tapping at the bench stopped and Berris called
her to blow the fire again; the gold was getting brittle, he
had to anneal it. As he got up, Tarrik made the bowstring
sound sharply again. He slipped off the stool and gave the
Chief his formal salute, right hand with bare knife up to
the forehead, then went over and took Tarrik by the upper
arms and shook him with pleasure at the meeting. Tarrik
grinned, and let him, and Erif Der took the opportunity of
getting to her feet and taking out the wooden star. 'I didn't
know you were coming,' said Berris. 'Oh, Tarrik, I've had
a terrible day! I thought I'd made something good and it
wasn't!'

'How do you know?' said Tarrik, and his voice was as
pleasant as his smile. 'Let me see it.'

Berris shook his head. 'No. I killed it. Wait, though; let me get this hot now, or it will crack.' He took the gold and put it carefully on to the fire, gripping it lightly all the time with his wood-handled tongs.

Tarrik leant over to look. 'Yes,' he said, 'that's bad. You'd better melt it down, Berris.'

At that Berris coloured, but still held the buckle steady in the flame. 'Suppose,' he said, 'suppose you know nothing at all about it?'

'Has our handsome friend Epigethes been here? Has he?' asked Tarrik. 'I thought so.' He looked across the fire at Erif Der, blowing the bellows, with the bracelet on one arm and the star tight in the other hand. He began to sing at her, very low, in time with her movements, a child's rhyme about little ships with all kinds of pretty ladings. And still she was not sure if he was laughing at her or making love to her. The fire on the forge between them nearly stopped her from working on him.

The gold was hot and soft by now; it would not crack. Berris Der took it out and across to the bench. 'It's bad, it's bad, it's bad,' said Tarrik, leaning over, 'it's like a little Greek making a face.' And suddenly Erif Der found that she liked Tarrik. That was so surprising that she nearly dropped the star; because she had never really thought of her own feelings before. There was she, Harn Der's daughter and a witch; so of course she would do everything she could for her father and brothers. And there was the Chief, who was to have the magic done on him, to be her husband for a few months—because that was part of it—but never, somehow, to get into her life. But if she liked him it would all be much harder. Quickly, fear came swamping into her mind; she wanted to stop, to run away. She began to creep out, very quietly, slinking along the walls of the forge. But Berris wanted his gold heated again; he called her to blow the fire, angrily, because he was working badly and because he hated Tarrik to tell him so. She went back, her head in the air, pretending to herself and every one else that she knew exactly what she wanted. But while she blew she got fuller of panic every moment. If she could not run, at any rate something must happen!

Tarrik was talking to Berris Der very gently, spinning his bow on its end or playing a sort of knuckle-bones with odd

pieces of wood. Most of the time he was abusing Epigethes,
quite thoroughly, with maddeningly convincing proofs of
everything he said. Sometimes Berris wanted not to hear,
to be too deep in what he was doing, and sometimes he
answered back, violently, trying to stop it. 'He's the first
Greek artist who's ever had the goodness to come here,'
he said, 'and this is all the welcome he gets! You—you
who should have some feeling for Hellas—you haven't
even the common decency to be civil to him the first time
you meet. And you don't even manage to frighten him, you
just make a fool of yourself—and a fool of Marob in all
the cities of the world.'

'Not if the corn we send them stays good,' said Tarrik,
rather irritatingly.

'Corn! You used to care for beauty. But when beauty
comes to us you won't even look.'

'And you won't look beyond a pretty tunic and a Greek
name. Well, I've got a Greek name too, call me by it and
see if you don't pay more attention to what I say.'

'You fool, Tarrik!'

'Charmantides.'

'You—God, I'm over-heating it!' He snatched the
buckle out of the fire and back to the window.

Tarrik followed him: 'But if you do—isn't it bad and
getting worse? Berris, look at it, look at it fresh, what's all
this nonsense here, all this scratching, what is it about?
There's no strength in it—oh, it is a bad little buckle!
What else have you made?'

'Nothing, nothing—I never have! All the beauty goes,
the beauty goes between my eye and my hand! Oh, it's
no use!' And suddenly he saw how bad it really was and
dropped the hammer, let go of everything, and sat with his
hands fallen at his sides and his forehead on the edge of the
bench.

'Stop!' said Tarrik. 'Get up! Listen to me. I'm being
Charmantides now. I'm just as good a Greek as Epigethes
and I don't want to be paid for my lesson. I'm good Greek
enough to know it's not something—something magic,'
he said, looking round, a little startled, as if that had not
been quite the thing he meant to say. 'There's no use our
copying Hellas; we haven't the hills and the sun. You
know, Berris, that I've been there, I've seen these cities

of yours, and I would see them again gladly if I could, if I were not Chief here. And they are not so very wonderful; they are not alive as we are, and always I thought they were in bond. They pretend all the time, they even think they are free, but truly they are little and poor and peeping from side to side at their masters, Macedonia on one side, Egypt and Syria the other. Hellas is old, living on memories—no food for us. Turn away from it, Berris.'

'Then you think my buckle is as bad as all that?' asked Berris mournfully, bringing it all, of course, to bear on his own work.

'Look for yourself,' said Tarrik. 'Take it as a whole. You don't know what you want. Is it a copy of life, less real, or a buckle for a belt? Which did you think of while you were making it?'

And so they might go on talking for hours and nothing would happen. Erif Der stood at the side of the forge, hands gripping elbows, her eyes full of reflected flames. 'Tarrik!' she said, loud and suddenly, 'is that all you have to say?' Both men stopped and turned round and looked at her. The light of the forge flickered on her cheeks and long plaits and the front of her throat, coming up, pale and soft out of the rough linen of her dress. Her mouth was a little open; there was a pattern round her feet. Berris stayed by the bench, but Tarrik dropped his bow, and came forward two steps. Aloud, he said, 'Erif Der, I love you, I want to marry you.' He reached out towards her, but she was in a circle of her own and would not move from it; only he could hear her breathing gustily, as if she had been running; his own hammering heart sounded plainer still.

She did not answer him, but Berris did, with a question: 'Do you? Will you marry her?'

'No—yes,' said Tarrik, his hands up to his head, pressing the crown down on to his hair, half covering his ears.

Erif Der threw up her hands with a little cry, loosing him. 'I did it!' she said, 'I did it, Chief! Well? Am I clever?' She stepped out of her circle.

'Why did you tell me?' said Tarrik softly. 'When will you let me go?'

'But I have!' she cried. 'Now say—say what you really want!'

'I want the same thing,' said Tarrik and pulled her over to him. She ducked, butting at him, clumsily, childishly, with head and fists, and got kissed on her neck and face and open mouth, maddeningly, and found nothing to shove against, nothing that would stay still and be fought; so that suddenly she went quiet and limp in his arms, and, as suddenly, he let her go. She had trodden on Tarrik's bow; the string snapped; he picked it up. 'Witch,' he said, 'I shall go to Harn Der, and then I shall marry you.'

'I give my leave,' said Berris hastily, 'and so will father.' But no one listened to him.

'Very well,' said Erif Der. 'Now listen, Tarrik. I will magic you as much as I please and you will not be able to stop me!'

'Go on, then,' said Tarrik, 'but there are some other things I shall do that you will not be able to stop.' She smoothed her plaits and stroked her hot face with her own familiar palms. 'You'll see,' she said, and went out. But it was all very well when Berris pulled her hair; next time it would be Tarrik, who was much stronger. She knew her magic depended on herself and could be as much broken as she was; never mind, the sun had come out again, the sea smell swept up the streets of Marob, fresh and strong. She went back to the flax market, half running; father would be pleased with her, she must tell him quick. And how soon could Yersha possibly be got out of the Chief's house?

Tarrik and Berris Der were still talking. When she had gone, they had dropped back at once to where they had left off, Berris wondering, startled at the way it had come, thinking of his father and not liking to talk about it to Tarrik, because it would have been bound to be all lies. But Tarrik felt wonderfully light, leaping from one thing to another in his airy mind. He had always been rather like this; he knew how it angered the Council and Harn Der, but now it was all marvellously accentuated. He knew that he was free, that nothing mattered—not Marob, not the corn, not the making of beauty, nor his own life. He went on talking seriously, as he had done before, but every now and then laughter rose in him like a secret wind, and shook his mouth while he was speaking about art to Berris Der. By and bye it became too much and he got up, saying he would go to Harn Der later that day, but must go now to the Council. 'Yes,' said Berris, startled, 'because of the road? I should have thought of it—oh, go quick!' He pushed the bow into his hand and hurried him out. Tarrik went out of the forge and down the street with a kind of swaying, dancing walk, as if he were trying not to bound into the air at every step.

As soon as he was out of sight, Berris took the half-made buckle and melted it down, with some filings he had, and ran it into a plain bar. He would have done the same with the other buckle, but at the last moment he stopped, he could not bear to kill so much of his own work in one morning. Then he damped down the fire, hung up his leather apron, and saw that everything was locked up. He knew he should be glad that the plan was working and his father would be Chief so soon; but yet he felt heavy and sad, partly because of Tarrik, and partly because of his own failures, and partly because there had been so much magic going on round him for the last few hours.

Tarrik was worse than usual at the Council. To start with, he was late—not that he was often anything else, and anyhow they could always get on perfectly well without him—but still, unless he was there, none of their doings had any sacredness: they were only, as it were, parts of his body.

Today they were talking about a great plan that had been started the year before by Yellow Bull, the eldest son of Harn Der, who lived south in the marshes. He had gone over all the ground, punting himself through those queer, half-salt, weed-choked channels that spread inland for miles, alone in a flat boat, living on snared birds and eggs and muddy-tasting fish. He stood before the Council now, a rough-skinned, wild-eyed young man, wearing mostly fur, very eager to have his plan followed, very bad at explaining it. He wanted them to make a secret road through the marshes, building on piles between the islands, digging deep drains towards the sea, and making strong places here and there with walls and towers. There was firm ground a few feet down in many places, and their draining for the road would leave acres of dry pasture, where neither horses nor cattle had ever grazed before. And there were great, wild islands, that needed only to be cleared to get them new lands, where they would be free from attack for ever, out of the reach of the Red Riders, and beyond . . . Yellow Bull did not know himself how his road should end. It went on and on, getting less real every mile that it went. Whenever he dreamt, it was this: of pushing and winding among endless reed-banks, with the smell of rotting stems always in his nostrils and the mud bubbling among the hidden roots. And his road would follow Yellow Bull through the reeds with great armies marching on it; and yet he would be alone. But Yellow Bull could not tell the Council his dreams, he could not say how much he wanted the road.

And the Council could not decide if it was worth while. Harn Der thought it would be, but saw all the difficulties and dangers there must be. It would take a lifetime, and all the labour there was in Marob—lives and years. The Chief had been more interested in this than in anything that had been before the Council since the Red Riders had been beaten behind the northern hills four seasons ago. He had been most eager to keep it a secret for Marob, have some hidden and guarded entrance, and let no stranger in on to it. He had asked and thought about its end.

Today Yellow Bull and those who cared about the road had hoped to get orders from the Chief; for this, in the end, must be his doing; they had no power to bring such a change to Marob. They had told the Chief, and he had promised to be there. Now there was no sign of him. Even his best friends were angry. At last he came, not by his own door, but from the main road, with a broken-stringed bow in his hand, enough to bring bad luck to anything. He came quite slowly, as if he had not kept them waiting long enough already. Yellow Bull stood with his hand and knife up at the salute, looking very fine and strong and rugged. Harn Der looked from one to the other, and thought very well of his son; and he was not the only one there to think that.

In the very middle of the Council room there was a great, ten-wicked silver lamp, hanging down on a chain. As he passed underneath it, the Chief suddenly ran three steps and jumped, swung forward on the lamp and dropped off. It scattered oil all over the ground on its swing back, and the Council looked shocked and horrified, but none more so than Yellow Bull. Tarrik, on the other hand, took his seat as if nothing had happened, and smiled pleasantly at the Council. They signed to Yellow Bull to speak again; he began, nervously.

It was after this that Tarrik became quite unbearable. He simply sat there and laughed, shatteringly; no one could speak or plan with that going on, least of all Yellow Bull. Only for a few moments did the Chief recover. It was when Harn Der spoke of the end of the road, how one day it might come through the marshes and out to a new land, a seaport perhaps; one of the others had taken this for a danger, opening a way to attack from the south, not the Red Riders, but ship-people—Greeks even. Then Tarrik had spoken, suddenly, bitterly and reasonably, to say that the Greeks were no danger that way—swords came from the north and the north-east; no one need be afraid of Hellas; they had been beaten too often now. The danger was that people should still think them great and wonderful, still do what they said, not through fear of war, but through fear of seeming barbarian. 'Let us be what we are!' said Tarrik, and seemed to cast out the Greek in himself. But no one cared for him to say that; they must not have their relations with the south disturbed, they must keep their markets, the flow out of corn and flax and furs and amber, and the flow in of oil and wine and rare, precious things, the pride of their rich men, the adornment of their beautiful women—and besides, something to look to, some dream, some standard. Harn Der thought of the Greek artist his son had spoken of, made up his mind that the man should be encouraged, and considered what to buy, a present perhaps for Yellow Bull to take back with him to the marshes and his young wife, who must be lonely so far from the city and everything that makes life pleasant for women.

The Chief most likely saw that he had pleased no one again; he went back to laughter or silence. Disheartened, the Council began to break up. Then suddenly he said: 'I must see where the secret is to hide. Yellow Bull, take me to the road.' 'I will, Chief!' said Yellow Bull eagerly. But again Tarrik was laughing.

They went out. A slave came in and mopped up the spilled oil, with a timorous eye on the Chief, who still sat in his chair, still laughing a little from time to time. It began to be near evening. With the room empty and windows unshuttered, there was always a little sound of waves, light in summer and loud in winter, coming up across the road from the harbour and the stony beach.

Tarrik, whose name was also Charmantides, got up and went through the house to the women's court, to find his aunt Eurydice, who was called Yersha by the Scythians. Her room looked partly over the sea and partly over the gardens, where there were lawns of scythed grass between great rose hedges, carved marble seats under apple trees, and narrow borders of bee-flowers and herbs round fountains and statues that came once from Hellas. But Yersha who was Eurydice sat at the other window, watching the sea. She had been copying manuscript; there was pen and ink beside her, and half a page of her slow, careful writing, and now she was quite still, beside her window. Along her walls there were chests of book rolls; above them their stories were repeated in fresco, black lines filled in softly with tints of flesh or dress—Achilles in Skyros, Iphigenia sacrificed, Phaedra and Hippolytos, Alkestis come back from the dead, horsemen with the thick, veiled beauty of a too much copied Parthenon, women with heavy eyelids and drooping hands and lapfuls of elaborate drapery, all framed in borders of crowded acanthus pattern that repeated itself again and again on the mouldings of doors and windows. The floor was of marble from Skyros, white streaked with brown and a curious green, the couches and table of citron wood and ivory, with worked silver feet. There were a few vases, light colours on a creamy ground, with palely florid borders and handles, and one or two marble groups, a swan or so, and the little winged, powerless Erotes, like mortal babies.

She turned from her sea-gazing and smiled at him. 'Charmantides,' she said, 'come and talk to me. Tell me why you did it.'

'Did—which?'

'Just now, at the Council: laughed, dear.'

He stood beside her fingering her pen. Why had he laughed? It was gone now. Gone. He shook his head. 'I am going to marry Erif Der,' he said, and felt her breath and thought both check a moment before she answered.

'I see. And that was why you were laughing? I am glad you are so happy.'

He looked down at her, standing there by the table, making ink patterns on his finger-nails with her pen, and wondered what to answer. He did not think it was happiness that made him laugh, he was not the least sure what were his feelings for Erif Der, except that he wanted to get possession of her; he knew that she was somehow dangerous.

His aunt knew that too. She went on: 'Have you spoken to Harn Der?'

'No,' he said.

'To Yellow Bull, then?' He shook his head. 'But surely you've seen someone besides the child herself?'

'She's not a child,' said the Chief.

'All the more reason, then, that she should not answer for herself. But—Charmantides—you know I have tried to be a mother to you, since your own mother died. I think you have loved me. Why did you not tell me about this before?'

He began to elaborate the patterns on his fingers interestedly. 'I didn't know.'

'Are you sure? Not at Plowing Eve?'

He smiled: he liked thinking of Plowing Eve. Yes, she had been the best Spring Queen whom he had ever led through the needful dance—and afterwards, how the men had enjoyed themselves. . . . But he had not thought of marrying her then. 'No,' he said truthfully, 'it was only now.'

'Then, if it was only now, surely you see that this is not natural, not right? Surely you know, Charmantides, the things she can do. This is magic and done for some purpose of hers or her father's!'

'Very likely,' said the Chief, 'perhaps that was why I was laughing. But I am going to marry her all the same.'

'Why?' said Eurydice. 'Oh why!'

'Because I like to,' he said, and looked out of the window. Cloud and sunshine swept over the sea; and below him on the beach was Erif Der, standing on a bollard, her fists clenched over her breasts, looking up at the Chief's house. Abruptly Tarrik began to laugh again. 'I am going to see Harn Der,' he said, and went striding out, his white felt coat swinging stiffly as he went.

As he walked along the streets of Marob, the men he passed saluted him with drawn knife at the forehead, and any girls who were armed did the same, but most of the women just lifted hand lightly to eyes, looking at him softly from under long lashes, hoping he would turn their way, the truth being that they and all the younger men liked Tarrik far better than old Harn Der and the Council, who would rule them for their good, but for no one's pleasure. Still, it depended on little, it would come and go, and Tarrik could only be young once. He certainly enjoyed himself, and had broken very few hearts for long; most of his loves were married by now, and not at all angry with him, still looking softly even. There were several possible children, but none quite proved or at all acknowledged. At any rate Erif Der knew as much about it as anyone.

Tarrik answered the salutes and glances more or less; but he was not thinking about them. Nor, for that matter, about what he was going to do now. He was making a charming plan for killing two birds with one stone; actually, that is to say, killing one of them, and as to the other, well, Yellow Bull was an extremely worthy young man—in spite of his having such a ridiculously red, scrubby face! A knot of girls at the street corner giggled to one another with speculations as to why the Chief was laughing out loud all by himself; but this time they were wrong. He stopped at a window and called up: 'Oh, Epigethes!' The Greek leaned out, his face changing to suspicion and some fear when he saw it was the Chief. 'Will you come and ride with me?' Tarrik shouted up. 'Down south, to see Berris Der's brother. In three weeks? We will talk about art, Epigethes.' There was something about this that terrified Epigethes. 'But I shall be busy, Chief,' he said. 'I have been given work to do by your nobles. I am an artist, I have no time for riding.' 'Ah yes,' said Tarrik, 'but I command you. Remember you are in my country. You know,' he went on, happily watching the Greek getting more and more frightened, 'I am a barbarian, and if I were to lose my temper—I can take it, then, that you are coming when I am ready?' And he walked on. Then after a few minutes he stopped and blew three times with his fingers in his mouth, making a curiously loud and unpleasant whistle. Almost at once a shock-headed man in a black coat ran up to him. 'See that there is no ship in my harbour to take Epigethes away,' said Tarrik, laying a finger on the man's arm.

By the time he came to the flax market it was almost sunset; people were going home to supper. A small boy was sitting on the well curb in the middle, singing at the top of his voice and kicking his bare heels against the stone. Tarrik came and sat beside him. The boy looked round and gave a mock salute, and went on till the end of his song; then, in the same breath: 'Are you coming to supper with us, Tarrik? You must!'

Tarrik pulled his hair, gently and affectionately: 'Nobody asked me, Gold-fish,' he said. 'I want to see your father, though. And I'm going to marry your sister.'

Gold-fish slid off the curb and stared. 'Has she magicked you?' he asked.

'I expect so,' said Tarrik. 'Does she ever magic you, Gold-fish?'

'Can't magic me!' said the small boy proudly; then, truth getting the better of him, 'At least, she won't try. She's horrid sometimes—I did ask her. But she wouldn't be able. She magics Wheat-ear: easily.'

'Will Wheat-ear do magic too, when she's grown up?'

'No,' said Gold-fish, 'she's just plain. She's my special sister.'

They went into Harn Der's house together; supper was ready on the table. Erif Der and a woman-slave were lighting candles, but when she saw it was Tarrik, she bade the woman run and get the great lamp and tell her master. Meanwhile she went on lighting the candles herself, and, though her face was steady, her hands were shaking.

Harn Der came in with the lamp carried behind him; the slave went out, and then Erif Der with her little brother. 'Harn Der,' said Tarrik, 'best of my councillors, I am come to ask for your daughter Erif Der to be my wife.'

For a time Harn Der said nothing. At last he spoke. 'My son Berris told me what was in your mind. It is not a thing to be lightly thought of or spoken of. All Marob will be either better or worse for your marriage, Chief. I cannot answer alone. I have here some of the Council: with your leave, I will call them in.'

'Call them if you like,' said Tarrik, rapidly and crossly, 'if you must make it an affair for Marob! But remember, I'm going to have Erif.' Harn Der did not answer this, but went to the door and called. Ten of the Council came in, oldish men, the best and most trusted by every one; a little behind came Yellow Bull, awkwardly, playing with his sword hilt. They all had gold chains and brooches, and long cloaks of embroidery with fur borders. Tarrik thought with pleasure how hot they must be. He stood beside the table, pinching one of the candles; the warm, sweet wax gave, half reluctantly, under the pressure of his fingers, and he thought of Erif Der. 'None of you will oppose my marriage?' he asked, with a kind of growl at them.

One of the older men spoke: 'The marriage of the Chief should be a matter for the full Council.'

'The full Council can pretend to give me leave tomorrow,' said Tarrik; 'meanwhile, I want it settled. When shall I have Erif Der?'

The elders coughed and fidgeted. Why should their Chief treat them like this? Yellow Bull flushed angrily. Harn Der spoke with a certain impressiveness: 'If the Council see fit, my eldest daughter shall be the Chief's wife. I cannot think that there is anything against her in blood or in person.' The others assented. He went on: 'But it would be less than right if this were not well considered or in any way gone into hurriedly. Let us not speak of marriage until autumn.'

'Autumn!' said Tarrik. 'Six months! I want a wife and you tell me to wait till she is an old woman!' He banged his hand so hard down on to the table that one of the candles fell over, and looked round savagely at the Council. 'None of you remember what it was like being a man; but I am a man and I am asking for my woman!'

'Gently, gently,' said one of them. 'Remember, Tarrik, we are not powerless. You cannot be Chief alone. Harn Der, she is your daughter—what do you say?'

'She is fully young yet,' said Harn Der; 'she must make her wedding-dress first. Let the betrothal be when the Council wills. In summer we must all go to our lands, she with me to mine; after harvest—may all go well with it!—we will have the marriage.'

He looked hard at Tarrik, and Tarrik back at him. 'What does she say?' asked Tarrik.

'It is not for her to speak. Tomorrow the Council will find you a lucky day for your betrothal.'

Tarrik walked straight to the inner door and called: 'Erif Der!' After a moment she came, her eyes on the ground. She had changed her dress; the new one was made of some fine, Greek stuff, a very delicate, silvery linen web, crossed again and again with dozens of colours, yellows and blues and greens, and sometimes a metal thread, copper or gold, that held the blink of the candles. It stood out lightly all round her; her plaits hung forward from her bent head into the hollow of her breasts; her coat was of white fur, very short. She went and stood between Harn Der and Yellow Bull; just once she looked at Tarrik, a glance so quick that no one but he saw it. 'Are you going to marry me when I choose?' he said. 'Erif Der, answer me!'

But her voice was little more than a murmur. 'I will do what my father chooses, Chief,' she said. And the Council nodded and whispered to one another: she was a good girl, as they would wish their own daughters to be; there was nothing odd about her.

'Very well,' said Tarrik, 'I'll let you win—this time! I thank you for allowing me to be your Chief still!' And he turned and went out into the sea-damp evening.

Harn Der wondered why he had said just that last thing; it was queer. . . . But no one else had noticed particularly; the Chief was always bad to deal with when he was crossed. Some of them stayed on for supper with Harn Der; they spoke of the marriage, hoped that the Chief might grow less wild, saying he was worse than a wild-cat to deal with now and would some day bring harm to Marob. And then they praised Erif Der for looks and modesty, and she waited on them and made little magics over their food and drink, and was amused to see one trying to shake out of his glass a spider that was not there, and another startled at his butter turning pink. When they were all gone, she and Berris went out too, and left her father and eldest brother together. 'I did that very well,' said Harn Der. 'I was not so ready that anyone might think there could be a plan, and not so cautious that they might remember it against me when he is not Chief any longer.'

'But what will happen to him?' said Yellow Bull. 'Will he be magicked enough not to care whether he is Chief or not? Otherwise he will be dangerous.'

'Ah,' said Harn Der, 'I have been thinking that too. Well, we shall see—alive or dead.'

'Yes,' said Yellow Bull again. 'I know you don't quite

believe in what you tell Berris; but still—he did promise to come and see my road.'

Chapter Three

YELLOW BULL HAD ridden on ahead to warn his wife they were coming and bid her get her best food ready for them, and now Tarrik and Epigethes were quite alone in the afternoon, with the track stretching across the plain as far as they could see, in front and behind. In the distance, on the right, there was a flock of sheep grazing, but no shepherd in sight. Every now and then a large hawk would come circling near them, and sometimes they roused hares or grass rats from the tussocks beside their path.

Tarrik was riding a young horse that had never been properly broken; it shied at its own shadow and had already tried to bolt with him twice. But he was such a brilliant rider that it only made the day pass more amusingly, and now the horse was answering better to bridle and knee than it had in the morning. Epigethes was on the whole a bad rider, and out of practice; he was very stiff and sore, and far from Hellas. They did not talk much. Tarrik had started several conversations, but after a short time they always seemed to drop, or else something unpleasant would creep into them, a hint of too absolute power by the Chief, or Epigethes showing rather too much of that fear that was whispering painfully all round his heart, all the time, that had been there ever since the day the Chief of Marob had called him from the street, and afterwards he had tried to find a ship that was sailing . . . but there were none. He would have gone anywhere, to Olbia, to Tyras, north or south, given up all his plans; he offered fantastic prices; but no one seemed interested in him. And now—now this unknown fear was coming closer, he tried to keep his mouth and eyes still, knowing that this terrible Scythian would see any least movement, knowing exactly—so hard it is being even a bad artist—the slight flicker of pleasure that would go over the Chief's face, watching his own pain.

Every mile or so they passed great patches of wild-rose bushes, very sweet, and covered with butterflies; they were going downhill almost imperceptibly. By and bye they began to see the spreading of the marshes in front of them, the deeper green of reeds, the steel blue of still waters curving among them. Soon they were near enough to be tormented by the mud-happy gnats and gadflies, their horses swerved and started and kicked and tried to roll. Epigethes was thrown once, and picked himself up with an aching head, and the feeling that the ground was getting softer and beginning to smell queer and rotten. There were plants with greyish, swollen leaves, and sometimes they saw the tracks of wild boar crossing their own way. They had to go carefully, keeping to the raised path; once they crossed a plank bridge and saw fish moving slowly over the black mud below them. Then the ground lifted a little to an island, and some large elm trees with cattle grazing under them. And over the ridge was Yellow Bull's house, facing south over the unknown country, tarred wood and reed thatch, with byres at one side, and store-houses at the other.

The earth in the yard was not yet summer-hard, but at least they could pick their way dry-shod between the worst of the mud; Yellow Bull brought them into his hall and helped them to pull off their riding-boots. They could smell their supper nearly ready and even hear the hissing and bubbling of roast meat over the fire in the other room. In the meantime the women brought them water for hands and feet, and such wine as there was in the house—not good, but at least it drove the fear a little further from Epigethes, and helped him to talk and laugh and look about him.

Yellow Bull's wife, Essro, was a small, pale-skinned woman, with eyes that seemed too big for her face; she lived mostly indoors, so as not to have to look at the marshes. She had always been good at domestic magic: her milk stayed sweet in hot weather, her stored apples never rotted, a bushel of flour went a long way with her. But she was easily frightened; she never tried to work magic on people, least of all on her husband, and the farm slaves found her easy to cheat. It was only very timidly that she dared say words over her own hair, even, to stop it falling out in the autumn, when there were mists creeping over the whole of their island, and she longed most for Marob town.

She waited on them at supper, very nervous of Tarrik; once she dropped a milk-jug and screamed, not very loud, but enough to hide the gasp of sheer terror from Epigethes. Afterwards she brought in torches and candles, and more wine. Yellow Bull drank little, but the others had their cups filled and refilled.

Tarrik had a strong head, but very much enjoyed getting drunk. He never got to the stage of completely losing control of his body, except at the three great feasts of the year, when, as Chief and Corn King he had led the rest in this, as in everything, and even then it was a drunkenness not even mostly of the wine and corn mead. But an hour or so of fairly steady drinking would just give him the necessary feeling of unreality, of separateness, of being able to stand apart and observe, and be free of mere human emotions.

And Epigethes found it was doing him all the good in the world; the fear retreated right into the back of his mind, till it was scarcely more than the tiniest black cobweb on the clear mirror of his perceptions. He began to feel again a Hellene among barbarians, amused at their odd habits and manners and clothes. Yellow Bull asked him if he was stiff with riding. He was. He wanted to explain that riding was not truly Hellenic, that it was better to run beautifully and exercise one's own body rather than a mere brute's—he sketched a few gestures, of running, disk-throwing, wrestling—a swimmer, even, with one arm raised for a perfect side-stroke . . . he grew a little mixed in his movements. But Tarrik woke up out of his detachment, brought spirit to body, to speech: 'You swim?' 'But of course,' said Epigethes loftily to the barbarian. 'And dive? Wonderful! Our northern rivers are too cold.'

Epigethes tried to explain, tactfully—oh ever so tactfully, as befits a Hellene—that it was not because of the cold that no one practised swimming here, but because of their ridiculous clothes that muffled them up, kept them pink and modest like women, hid their riding bow legs. He, on the other hand, was proud of his body, would strip and swim and show them. Yes, that was it, they were all admiring him now, rightly and properly, as they should. . . . And then, somehow or another, there was night air falling coldishly and sanely on his face, damp grass underfoot, and that spider's web of fear suddenly obscuring the mirror. . . . When he turned, the house was out of sight, they must have come a long way already. The moon was up, shining on water at each side, sleek mud, willows, flowering water plants. Words began to collect in his head: 'Is this really the best time?' spoken quite calmly, with a little laugh—yes, that was better, a little laugh to pass it off. 'Tomorrow morning, say? Why, I'm half asleep, and I'll bet you two are the same.' But somehow they went on.

'My road,' said Yellow Bull suddenly; all three stopped. They were on a high bank, with a gentle fall on one side to tangled marsh, and on the other a creek, with a small boat moored in it, quite still. They went on a few yards; the bank ended abruptly, crumbled almost under their feet. There was nothing in front but a steep slope of mud, nine feet down, and then black water with only its surface reflecting the moon, just rippled, gurgling faintly as it mouthed its way past the mudbank, eating into it all the time inch by inch. 'Now you shall dive beautifully,' said Tarrik, standing on the edge with the moonlight catching the clasps of his coat and belt.

Epigethes looked backwards once. He could not run away; he did not know the path, and Yellow Bull did. Besides, he was too drunk—or had been—to get the full power out of his legs; it was a hard thing to be a Hellene and know that. And, after all, he had never been such a good runner as he pretended—only, in his head, among all the other shapes, the shape of himself as the athlete. He took his clothes off slowly; the web was matted all over the world now. For a moment he stood, stripped and rather beautiful in the moonshine. 'Now, dive,' said the Chief. Epigethes looked from him to Yellow Bull, but the other Scythian was quite impassive, in shadow; he seemed to have no eyes, nothing to appeal to. The first filming of a cloud began to cover the moon, the water looked worse. He gave one great, tearing sob, and dived.

In the dimming light those two on the bank could hardly see, yet plainly hear, the bubbles coming up out of the mud. But after some ten minutes the cloud passed from the face of the moon, and the water moved clearly below them; it was all as it had been, without Epigethes. Yellow Bull picked up the clothes and belt, and looked across at the Chief. 'You meant him for my road?' Tarrik nodded and turned and began walking back; suddenly he stretched his arms and laughed aloud in the night. 'I was thinking of your sister,' he said, but Yellow Bull frowned and went on solidly.

When they came back to the house, Essro was sitting upright at the table with two candles between her and the door. She looked at them coming in, and shivered, and went away. Yellow Bull put the things down on the table; there was a purse fastened to the belt, with two or three drawings and measurements in it, a list of names, and at least a dozen keys, some made very lightly of wire. 'What were all these for?' said Yellow Bull. 'Not all his own, surely!' 'No,' said Tarrik, 'but we shall find locks for them,' and he took them and put them into the pockets in his own belt. Then he stirred up the hearth fire and began throwing in the clothes. 'The brooches—take care!' said Yellow Bull, trying to pull them out of the stuff; but Tarrik threw them in with the rest. 'You can rake them out tomorrow,' he said, 'they'll be dead too, then.' The next morning Tarrik got up and rode off, very early, while Yellow Bull was still dreaming about his road. The other horse stayed on the island; it was not really a very good one.

Tarrik rode straight north and then a little inland, keeping clear of the town. Sometimes there were crops, but more often pasture, or just rough land with scrub that was no use to anyone. Where the ground rose, there were sometimes a few trees, but all the forest lay right inland, four days' riding from Marob; wherever there was a river, there would be swamp at each side of it, and he had to go carefully, marking the trackways and fords. As he got further north and east, the land was better, the soil sweeter and dryer. For nearly half a day he rode through the blue flax fields, seeing how well up the plants were, strong stemmed and clean. Sometimes there were tall patches of hemp, and later on that day he came to food crops, rye, barley, and some wheat. All the fields were guarded by children, in case anyone's beasts strayed. Here, again, everything was looking strong and healthy in the sun; the blades were broad and deep coloured, the ears were big already. As he passed, Tarrik thought of himself as Corn King and was proud of what he and earth and sun had done among them; then he thought of the Spring Queen and the dance they had acted together in the middle of the ring on Plowing Eve; if that was to come real, he felt, so much the better for the corn. He rode slowly, so that all the lands he passed should get something from him, and slept securely at noon

in beanfields and did not count the days that went by as he
went north towards Harn Der's land.

Sometimes there were orchards, fenced in with turf
banks; the apples of Marob were in those days the
sweetest in the world. In one or two places there were
figs and pomegranates, very carefully grown and sheltered
from the north. But these were only near farms or camping
places, and Tarrik was keeping clear of these, except at night
when he took supper and the best bed from the nearest place
he saw, once as it happened a small and very dirty farm
where he was half eaten by lice, and once the great tent of
a landowner come out from Marob for the summer, one of
his own counsellors, who had skins of good southern wine
with him, and oil for washing, and clean linen. It was later
on the same day that he came to Harn Der's lands, which
lay on the two sides of a very flat valley, with a stream going
down from pool to pool in the middle and a wood of limes and
oaks half-way up one slope. Here Tarrik slept the night, with
the food and wine he had taken from the last place, under a
lime tree, his saddle for a pillow. Leaning back against it,
he could see through the tree trunks to the far slope, and
the lights of Harn Der's camp: the fires like big yellow
stars, and at night the great peaked tents glowing faintly
and queerly from the lights inside them. He did not sleep
very much, partly because of the violent sweetness of the
lime flowers, shedding layer on layer of scent about him,
partly because he started dreaming of the bubbles in the
mud and Epigethes wriggling formlessly like a white slug
underneath, but mostly because, after this, to keep himself
from seeing it again, he had begun to make pictures of Erif
Der over there on the far side: of chasing her and catching
her and handling her and playing with her all over, till
by morning there was nothing for it but to ride and get
her, herself. He cantered down and through a deep pool,
splashing himself all over, but not much cooler by the end
of it. They were only just stirring in Harn Der's camp, it
was still so early.

In the half dark of the women's tent, Erif Der turned
over sleepily. It was days since she had thought of Tarrik,
but this morning, as soon as she woke, she found he had
come into her head. She did not want him there; she sat
up and peered about. At the far end of the tent she could

see someone moving, her old nurse probably, reknotting
the plaits of her sticky grey hair. But Wheat-ear, next her,
was still asleep, charmingly curled up with her fists tucked
under her chin. Erif Der blinked across at her small sister
and called in a whisper; but Wheat-ear did not stir, so it
must be little after dawn yet. Somewhere, right above her
head in the great hollow dome of the tent, there were some
big flies buzzing about, knocking against the sides; she
could not see them. Someone slipped out past the curtain,
and for a moment there was a breath of cool morning air.
Erif Der pulled the blanket over her head and tried to go
to sleep again.

The children had always loved this summer life, riding
out, or driving in the big carts, singing and shouting, all
in clean, light clothes to match the flowering plain. They
had left winter behind; the house that had been getting
dirtier and stuffier day after day for eight months, would
stand open and be smoked out and scrubbed and painted
with bright colours to welcome them again in autumn. They
could eat the last of the old stored fruit and honey, be done
with salt meat and the hard winter cheeses. Soon the sweet
grass would be waving wide ahead of them, there would be
fresh things to do and smell and eat and look at; suddenly
they felt twice as alive.

For the first week or two they were always just mad,
running about and rolling and playing, riding the colts and
splashing in and out of the stream. Then they would settle
down to summer. The women would find the best pool for
their half-year's washing, and a smooth slope for drying and
bleaching; the men would be hunting, rounding up the
young cattle and horses and branding them; Harn Der
would ride gravely all about his fields and have long talks
with his farm-people; and the two little ones, Gold-fish
and Wheat-ear, made themselves a house of branches and
took all their food there, and got more and more difficult
to chase back to the tents at night.

Berris Der found that he was apt not to think about
making anything for weeks at a time; he flew his hawks and
hunted, and raced with the others on half-broken horses, for
miles across the plain. Then suddenly, something would
come into his head and he would begin drawing frantically,
convinced that this was the best he had ever done. He had

been like that the day before; now he was still asleep, among a litter of charcoal sticks and odd bits of linen with drawings all over them. He had seen two grass-cocks in their spring plumage, sparring with one another out on the plain; now he was making them into a pattern, with the sweep of their raised neck-feathers to balance the flare-up of their tails and spurs. Bronze, he thought of it; but that must be cast. He had been wondering what Epigethes would make of it—never mind, it was good! When he was back in Marob, he would go on with his lessons; he could, for that matter, ride back easily any time, stay a few days, and work with the Greek. It seemed less attractive now, but still, he could not drop it all till autumn. Epigethes might not be able to stay. Mentally, he cursed Tarrik for that. Here, at least, things would be better when his father's plan came off: art would come into its own in Marob, and he would be the one to see to it. So he went to sleep, and dreamed of his cocks fighting, and the odd noise their bronze beaks made, clicking together.

By and bye, when the sun was up and only the shadows very dewy still, Erif Der, who had been half asleep, threw off her blanket and ran out, barefoot, in her linen shift. The servants were all busy, making the fires up again, cooking, bringing in the milk-pails. She sat down in the sun, outside the women's tent, and began combing her hair; she liked doing this, for it was a comb she had magicked so carefully that it never pulled. When her hair was quite smooth she began plaiting it again, flicking it in and out of her clever fingers, admiring herself. She thought she ought to go on with the weaving of her wedding dress, but decided not to, there was no hurry on a day like this. She stretched herself, dropping the plait, breathing in huge mouthfuls of the sunny air, half thinking of getting Berris to come hunting with her; she loved hunting, much better than making wedding dresses. She began to wish the Red Riders would come again, just a few, so that she could shoot them.

Then she heard two or three sharp voices, and looking up to find what was the matter, what they were all pointing at, she saw Tarrik riding through the camp on a very beautiful, very nervous horse, that shied, terrified, at the fires and great tents. Tarrik himself was looking very big. She got to her feet, and found that for some reason her heart was thumping violently and painfully; she put both hands over her breast to quiet it. There was a little buzzing in her head and finger-tips. Tarrik came up close to her; she was fascinated by the twitching, jumping body of the horse, the pawing of its hoofs on the dry turf. Quite still herself, she watched intently Tarrik's hands on the reins, with an acuteness, an accuracy of vision that might have been her brother's. The grip shifted to the right hand only; Tarrik leant over and picked her up like a rabbit; she felt the linen of her shift tear all along the seam, and screamed. But by that time she was on the horse and Tarrik had loosed the reins; she held on to the mane with both hands, half across its neck, her balance all wrong, with nothing in her mind but the flying ground, the danger. Then Tarrik pulled her up, shifting back in the saddle himself, so that she had a little room, and holding her tight against him.

They were out of the camp; for a minute or two Erif Der was too dazed to tell which way. All down one side she was sore and bruised; she was being treated as a thing, not a person! Tarrik was saying something; she squared her shoulders and butted her head back sharp against his chin; he squeezed her so hard that she almost cried, not quite, though. She began to work her free hand in under the other that he held so tight against her, under her shift, finger-tips groping for the star. She felt its chain, the pin that fastened it, one point. She was all screwed up to get it, the words she must say were on her tongue; she was as clear headed as possible.

It pulled up, into her fingers. And then Tarrik caught her hand in his and jerked savagely; the chain bit into her neck, then broke, but she still had the star. His hard, terrible fingers were digging it out of her palm. She bit his other arm, got hers free, and reached back for his face, his eyes, something to go for. He got her tight again, wrist and face, bruising her lips with his arm-bones, and his other hand tore out the star and threw it away. Her teeth closed on saltish linen and skin and muscle, and she threw herself sideways with a kick against the side of the saddle. They hit the ground both together, rolled over half a dozen times. After that, she was almost too done to struggle or fight him any more.

By and bye Tarrik, beginning to realise how black and blue he was himself, asked her if she was hurt. She shook her head sullenly and sat up. Tarrik, not having, on the whole, had much to do with virgins, did not really know how much hurt she was likely to be, quite apart from falling off a galloping horse. Still, he was not very happy; he did not like her looking grey at the lips. She got to her knees, and began slowly to look at all the tears in her linen shift; it was torn right down the front at one side and she pulled the three-cornered piece up quickly over herself and held the top edges together in her fist. But there was nothing to fasten it with; she let it go to rub her fist across her eyes; after all, it was silly to mind if Tarrik did see her breast now. She didn't think she could ever mind anything after this—he seemed to have broken all the clean, sharp edges of her feeling for ever. He rolled back his own sleeves to see her teeth marks and a little blood; she had bitten his neck worse, though. The horse had come back, and whinnied to them questioningly from the top of a ridge. She tried to stand, but failed altogether; he caught her and stopped her falling; together they looked at her ankle. 'You must have come down on it,' he said. She nodded; it was beginning to send shoots of pain up her leg, the under side of her knee, drowning everything else. 'I'll get some water,' said Tarrik. 'What else?'

She looked at him. 'If I had my star,' she said, and watched him run off down their track, and presently stoop and pick it up.

He brought it back. 'You'll magic me, too?' he asked, still keeping it tight.

She held out her hand. 'Oh, give it me!—Tarrik.'

'But will you?' She began to cry hard, partly at the check to what she wanted, partly at the softness of his voice—getting at her, trying to stop her hating him and all the violence and pain that was part of him. 'Will you, Erif dear?' he said again. 'I don't want to be turned into a bear.'

'I can't,' she said, sniffing, 'it's too difficult. I haven't learnt.'

'Well, anything. I don't want to be magicked. Will you not, Erif?'

She said nothing for a moment, then; 'Not just now.'

He gave it to her. She fastened on to it, leant forward, and touched her foot all over with it. The pain went further and further back, till she scarcely felt it, only, behind it and coming into consciousness now, the deep bruising of her thighs. He bandaged her ankle as she told him, with a bit of his own shirt. 'Now I want the star back,' he said, and opened her hand and took it.

'I can do magic without that,' said Erif Der.

'You can't ever magic the Greek bit of me.' She said nothing. 'Not even when we're married. Can you?'

'I haven't tried,' said Erif Der, 'but I will. And I do hate you, Tarrik.'

He put on his crown again, caught the horse and lifted her on, then went to its head and led it back towards the camp; neither of them said anything more. When they were in sight, he took off his felt coat and gave it to her; she found it hid a good deal, but smelt of him. Harn Der came out to meet them, with Berris; both were armed, but she was afraid they were not going to do anything. Tarrik left her and went forward by himself to speak to her father; she could not hear what they were saying. Berris stared at her, questioning with his eyebrows; she put out her tongue at him. By and bye Harn Der came up and stood beside her. 'So you're a woman now, my daughter.' 'And you don't care,' she said, 'how I'm hurt, how I'm dishonoured.' 'Well,' he said, smiling at her, 'you were betrothed. It's nothing to make a song about. Go to your mother, Erif.' He went back to the Chief, and Berris said: 'It serves you right for magicking people.' 'Well, who told me to?' said she furiously. 'Oh, of course,' said Berris, 'but you know you like doing it. You think you're clever.'

She leant forward and hit the horse on the neck, and sent it clattering off towards the tents, nearly throwing her. She called for her mother; the foot was hurting again, it wanted magic. The women helped her into her mother's tent, saying nothing, because they saw she was angry, and knew what she could do to them if she chose to use her power. The old nurse brought her clean clothes, her best, and warm water, and olive oil, and soft woollen towels to wash with. Then at last came her mother, Nerrish, so small and quiet and shadowy in her grey dress, that she was hardly there.

She sat beside Erif, holding her hand, crumbling something over her hair, while the girl cried solidly for ten minutes. Nerrish knew a great deal about people and a great deal about magic, but it had worn her out. She felt very old, she could scarcely deal with her children, hardly ever thought of the younger ones. But she would give what she had to this elder one who was most like her, whose life she could best see into. After a time Erif fell asleep, and while the sleep was at its heaviest, her mother and nurse undressed her and washed her, and saw to the bruises and the twisted ankle, and dressed her again, and plaited ribbons into her hair, and discussed between themselves, in very low voices, the doings of that curious, savage creature man, and how one should deal with him and overcome him. Then they moved a little brazier of burning charcoal close to the girl's head, and Nerrish laid some large, flat leaves on it. The smoke rose and hung and spread itself upwards along the walls of the tent; Erif Der lay and slept, breathing easily, the colour coming back into her cheeks.

Meanwhile the horse had found its way back to Tarrik, and stood, with twitching ears, blowing into the palm of his hand. He had just said to Harn Der: 'Three days ago I killed Epigethes,' and was watching to see what would happen next. Harn Der said nothing at all for the moment, but breathed heavily. Berris, though, had heard. 'You haven't done that,' he said, 'Tarrik!' And then, seeing it was true, covered eyes with hands in sheer horror.

Said Harn Der: 'This was—unwise.'

'Yes,' said Tarrik, and began laughing as he had that day at the Council.

'Why did you do it, Chief?' said the older man.

But Tarrik went on laughing and then suddenly kicked backwards like a vicious horse at a clod of earth which exploded under his heel.

And Berris groaned: 'Are you mad?'

'He was bad,' said Tarrik, and stopped laughing and walked from one bit of scattered turf to another, tramping on them. 'He was bad. His things were bad. Rotten. Rotten roots. I like sound things. Sweet apples. Hard apples—like yours, Berris.'

'My things!' said Berris Der. 'Oh God, you should have killed me—I don't matter. But he . . .' And his voice trailed off into silence, overwhelmed with the loss of Hellas.

'The Council will think you mad, if they think no worse,' said Harn Der again.

But Tarrik bent down and was lacing his shoes. 'I shall want clean clothes,' he said. 'Burn these, with hers, and give them to your fields, Harn Der.' He spoke now in the voice of the Corn King. They would be very careful to obey him; next year the crops would know.

He took the clean linen and went off by himself to the stream. All this time her star had been round his neck; when he lifted it, he found it had blistered his skin underneath in a star pattern. So while he washed, he put it under water to get cool, downstream from where he was. He also found that where her teeth had gone through the skin on his arm, there was still bleeding; it would not stop for cold water, or burnet leaves, or dock. After some hesitation he touched it with the star. Then it stopped at once. Tarrik knew no more about how magic worked than any other of the men, but it interested him immensely; that was perhaps the Greek part of him, not taking everything for granted. He dressed and walked slowly back to the camp; the star was on his neck again, but well wrapped in leaves, so that it should burn them first. It was the middle of the afternoon by now, very hot; he thought he could smell the lime grove, breathing its sweetness towards him from the other slope, a mile away now.

When the fire in the brazier had burnt right out, Erif Der woke up again, slowly, in time with some singing of her mother's. Moving her eyes and hands a little, she found, comfortingly, that she was wearing her best clothes, and remembered after a time what had happened. She was no longer a virgin: she settled down to that, with a certain pleasant relaxing of all her muscles. She had been hurt: that was all cured. By Tarrik: who cared what Tarrik did?—he would not be Chief much longer. But Tarrik had her star. She sat up suddenly. 'Mother, oh, mother!' she said, 'he took my star!'

'Well,' said Nerrish softly, 'do you mind?'

'No,' said Erif, 'perhaps not. But what shall I do for some things?' And she put her mouth close to her mother's ear, and whispered.

'The power is in you,' said Nerrish. 'Listen! I have done without things for years now. Have you ever seen me eat lately? No. And as for my star, I threw it into the sea last winter. I will tell you something, because you are more to me than the rest: soon, quite soon, I am going to turn into a bird, a wise bird with rosy feathers. After I am buried, I shall creep through the earth, all little, till I come to an egg, and there I will rest for a long time. Then I shall come out to the rose-red bird flocks. Look, Erif, my baby bird, it will be soon!' And she spread her arms and the grey stuff wavered about her as she hovered a moment in the dim light of the tent.

'But are you going to die, mother?' said Erif, and her lip trembled.

'Yes, perhaps. And he will be sorry'—she nodded towards her bed and some of Harn Der's gear hung up beside it—'but you will know better.'

'Won't you tell him?'

'No,' said Nerrish, 'he is a man, he would be afraid.'

'Some men aren't afraid,' said Erif musingly, and reached down to take hold of her own slim legs; as she did it, her plaits with the coloured ribbons fell forward. 'Oh, mother,' she said, 'oh, my lovely hair! These are your very own ribbons that came from the other end of the world!'

'Yes,' said Nerrish, laying her cheek for a moment lightly on the smooth roundness of Erif's head, as a mother wild duck does with her soft babies.

Erif was stroking and purring over the bright, lovely colours, the rainbowed shining silk from that other end of the world! 'Oh,' she sighed, 'I must go out, I must show them to Berris. Every one must see me!' As she stood up, her mother slipped a stick into her hand, a long, smooth thing of ivory, carved into narrow leaf-shapes, and a fruit under her hand. Half consciously she leaned on it, and took the weight from her foot; her mother knew it was dangerous to disregard a pain that was no longer felt: it might come back.

Outside the tent, the sun was blinking bright. She stepped out, with her high head, her white dress woven with coloured, fantastic lions, her coat of thin linen bordered with kingfisher feathers, her turquoise belt and ear-rings, and the brilliant shine of her plaits. Slowly, leaning on her long stick, she passed the groups of servants, the fires, pale yellow in sunlight. Wheat-ear ran up to her: 'Oh lovely, lovely!' she cried, and danced round her big sister. Further on, Erif saw her father with Berris, and, rather to one side, Tarrik in clean clothes, standing by his horse. They all stared at her, and she wished there were more of them. Tarrik came up to her, a little uncertainly. 'I have your star,' he said, 'you beauty, Erif!' And he suddenly kissed her hand. 'I'm wearing it now,' he said again, with a kind of challenge. 'Go on, then,' said Erif kindly, disconcertingly, and looked him up and down, and touched his arm, and then his neck, his cheek, and his lips with cool, baffling fingers. He stood quite still, feeling them trail about him. 'And I have your coat,' she said. 'Burn it—for the fields,' he said earnestly. But she answered, low, 'Oh, no, Tarrik. You don't know everything,' and went past him, to her father, the Spring Queen, quite grown up.

Harn Der drew her aside admiringly. 'He has killed Epigethes, the fool! Was that your work, Erif?' Fortunately Erif was much too pleased with herself at the moment to look as startled as she felt. 'It begins,' she said. 'If it goes on,' said Harn Der, 'there will be no need for you to marry him.' 'No,' said Erif Der, and made a childish but fleeting face, and walked away.

In the meantime Tarrik had mounted; he rode past Berris, then drew rein and turned again, and held out something in his hand. 'I got these from Epigethes,' he said, 'after he was dead; he left them. Look, Berris.' Berris looked, and looked again, and frowned. He took them into his own hand and peered at them closely. 'These are copies of my keys,' he said. 'I worked on them too long not to know.' 'And those?' Berris shook his head, beginning to look horrified; these were the keys that locked up his precious metals and stones. There was only one use that could be made of a duplicate set. Tarrik jingled the others gently in his hand. 'Copies of somebody else's keys?' he said. 'Well, Berris?' 'Yes,' said Berris, with a dry mouth, trying to speak ordinarily. 'Yes, Tarrik, I see.'

Chapter Four

SLOWLY AND JERKILY the ox-team was dragging back the great cart; every jolt went straight from axle to floor-boards, and through the thick, black carpets, and shook Erif

Der till her teeth rattled. She and the other women in the cart talked in whispers, and nursed their hands, scored across and across with arrow-heads for dead Nerrish. Wheat-ear was there, and Essro, and four or five older women, cousins or aunts, and the nurse, tired out with wailing round the grave. Erif Der herself was wondering whether her dead mother had yet started that journey, a little angry with her for having died just then, when her daughter might be needing her so badly. She frowned across at Wheat-ear, who was crying, more from excitement than anything else, then, finding it had no effect, pulled the little sister over to sit on her knee where she would not feel the jolting of the cart so much. By and bye Wheat-ear quieted down and began sucking her thumb, as she still did after any passion; unconsciously, Erif Der held her a little more closely, musing over children unborn. Once they came through a wood of ash trees, and the broad, dry leaves blew about, some falling into the cart; there were not many left on the trees now, for it was late autumn.

The cart came to the town of Marob, jarring along the deep ruts from street to street, and so to Harn Der's house, where the funeral feast was held. The men were there already; they had been drinking, and some had cut their cheeks as well as their hands. Her father was covered with a black blanket, only slit in two places for his eyes and mouth. Tarrik was there, with his high crown showing over every head; but no one spoke to him now unless they had to, and Erif Der noticed with an odd calm how much thinner he was getting every week. When he sat down at the table, the man on each side of him edged away, till there was a space both ways; he looked straight in front of him, white rather than flushed, pressing his thumbs into a piece of bread. After a time, Erif Der left her sister and came slowly over and sat down at her husband's right hand; she heard his checked breathing deepen, and felt him stir a little on the bench beside her. One or two of the men stared at her; but she knew the Chief was not unlucky—only magicked; how should she be afraid of what she had done herself?

Every one was hungry after their long ride or drive in from the burying in the plains; they ate without talking much at first—boiled mutton passed round hot and steaming in the three-legged cauldrons, with garlic and beans and salsify, and stewed fish, and soft, sweetish strings of seaweed. Tarrik ate little, though; obscurely, that began to worry Erif Der, and she put bits from her own plate on to his. She could not eat either, but this was partly because she knew that soon her father was going to talk to her, urge her, put his will in place of her own. While she was still a child that had not mattered; but now she was a woman, four months married. She sat up very straight and lifted her head, heavy with the weight of the stiff cone and veil she wore. People were staring at her as well as at Tarrik.

Suddenly it seemed to her that there was an unwarrantable amount of unhappiness in the room; not much for the dead, magic woman, except perhaps from her father and the old nurse; but for all sorts of other things. Tarrik was unhappy, of course, because she had magicked him, because he hated not being favourite with the people any longer, and he hated having done anything badly, failed so completely as he had that twice when he had been in her power; and because she had disturbed the sure base of his judgment. And Berris Der was unhappy; she did not quite know why, but there was some fight going on inside him, where sometimes one side won, and sometimes the other. He sat forward with his head on his hands, looking like he did after he had broken the little horse. The people who stared so at Tarrik were unhappy too, because they knew something had gone wrong with him, with the Corn King, and they thought of their seed corn rotting; and yet they still did not know what to do. Uncertainty, that was it, thought Erif, that was what made people unhappy. And she herself? No, she was not unhappy, she was not uncertain, she had her hand on the plow. Angrily, she began to eat again, picked up a bone and cracked it between her strong back teeth.

It was dark before the funeral feast was over. They bolted the shutters and heaped the fires up; there was a rising wind that might turn to storm before the night was out. One by one the guests went away, with their coats drawn tight about them and their fur caps over their ears. Tarrik was one of the last; he stayed on, as if he had been hoping for something; but Erif Der said she must stay this night in her father's house, for the last things to be done, and bade him go home, out of the death circle. He took up his great cloak of white fox fur, and the gold scales along the edges jingled stupidly. After a moment she followed him to the door, but he was riding home, and did not turn his head once to look for her. She could just hear the sea now, a low continuous dashing on the beach, filling all the air, coming up past the houses; she thought the weather must have broken for the year.

The children were in bed and asleep by now; she kissed them and talked for a little to Essro, and then came back to her father and brothers. Such of her mother's things as had not been buried with her were laid out on a table beside the hearth; they had to watch that night in case she came for any of them. Harn Der had taken off the black blanket, and lay back in his chair, tired and yellow-looking. She sat at the other end of the table, the brothers at each side; they said over together certain words, and then stayed still. For a time no one spoke; Erif began to think of her mother again, and wondered if it would really be so terribly frightening if she were to come back. Whatever she had felt, love or indifference, she had always been able to trust her mother utterly while she had been alive; but now she was dead one could not be sure; she might be different, changed into something cold and waxen and hurtful. It was this that was frightening. She shifted a little in her chair, clutching the arms and sweating lightly; her father broke silence at last, and they were all glad.

'Your work is nearly done,' he said to her, 'but you must go on to the finish. A step backward now, and all would be to begin again.'

'Yes, father,' she said, 'I know. I have done my best for you.'

'Only twice,' said Yellow Bull, and bit the end of a finger-nail.

'Twice, that you saw!' she said indignantly, 'but you don't see everything, Yellow Bull! And what a twice—Midsummer and Harvest! He did the words backwards and the Dance wrong, he—'

But Yellow Bull interrupted her, a little nervously: 'Well, better not speak of it!—not—not till next year's corn is up.'

Erif Der leant forward: 'I have not hurt the corn!'

she said. 'I tell you again, I went myself that night with his crown and the sacred Things! I built the Year-house again, by myself. I am Spring Queen, it is in my hands too! If there is any bad luck it is not my doing, but yours, Yellow Bull—you, who won't believe me!' She stopped, with tears in her eyes: it had been so terrible doing those Things alone, letting the Powers sweep through her, standing between bare Earth and Sky, with the sun in one hand and the rain in the other, knowing that her own magic was nothing beside this stolen Godhead. But none of the others understood; they could not imagine it. She had done it twice, and the second time was the worst, at Harvest, when she had gone alone to the stubblefield and bound herself difficultly with straw, and then gone back at midnight to the door of the Corn King's house and spoken herself the right words to the sleeping actor in the Corn Play; it had seemed to her that years had fallen on her, that she was an old woman, worn out like her mother. And this was all the thanks she got from Yellow Bull! Berris leaned over and patted her knee; she blinked the tears out of her eyes and stared across at her father. 'Well,' she said, low, 'what am I to do?'

'Finish!' said Harn Der, 'the Council are ready. They know me and they know my son'—he looked at Yellow Bull who was still worrying at his broken nail—'and as for the people, they would give him up this moment if they saw another Corn King. Erif Der, we count on you.'

She knew she wanted to say something, but could not think what it was. Berris spoke for her. 'But, father, what good will she get from all this? She is Spring Queen now, she has all the treasure of Marob if she chooses to call for it: suppose she doesn't like to give all that up?' And he glanced from her to the others, and back again; he was wondering a little what sort of Spring Queen Essro would make when Yellow Bull was Corn King.

'I will give you anything you like, Erif,' said Harn Der, 'and your marriage shall be undone at once. You shall still have what power you choose—after all, you have more power now than any of us.' He laughed, a little nervously. 'In a year you will have forgotten all this. There is nothing to make you not forget, Erif?'

'No,' she said sharply, 'I am not going to have a child—yet.'

'All the more reason to finish quick,' said her father.

By now all Marob was asleep except these four; they could hear nothing but the wind, and the wood-fire burning quietly beside them, and their own movements and voices. They dropped to whispering. Berris wanted to talk about a new idea of his, the way certain curves, running into certain other curves, gave him a feeling of sureness in the heart; but he knew his father and brother were not interested, and Erif Der was too deeply absorbed in some pattern of her own. Tarrik would have listened; Tarrik would have put it into words for him. But he could not talk to Tarrik these days without feeling such a traitor to all friendship, such a brute-beast, that he could not work for hours afterwards. He began to puzzle out the practice of his idea, not as an animal or a flower, but just as lines in the air, not bounded into a flat surface or the solid edges of wood or metal, but passing through one another like the cracks in a great crystal. As night wore on, it grew more dreamlike, less fixed, less possible to remember, and when the others spoke, their voices followed the curves, cutting each other's paths, light for his sister and darker for the other two.

At dawn they were all awake still, and nothing had happened; the pile of things lay there in front of them, no smaller; the dead would not return. The slaves brought them in food and drink, but this time no full plate or cup to stand aside in case One came for it. Essro strayed in too, gentle and anxious, and sat by Yellow Bull; Erif Der went to the heap and took two or three small things of her mother's, an embroidered coat, a pair of shoes, and a little box full of cowrie shells, some painted red, and small loose pearls. She pushed back the shutters; there was rain blowing past on the wind; she reached out her hand and it pricked her coldly, stinging the fresh scratches, and all at once she felt as if her heart was being pricked and pierced, and she began to cry bitterly, as she had never yet done in all the week since her mother had died. So she ran out, and back in the rain to the Chief's house by the harbour, where one was never out of sound of the sea.

For three days that storm rose, beating in from the Black Sea, till all Marob felt salty with blown spray; then it lulled suddenly, but left the beginnings of winter behind it. There were scarcely any leaves left on the trees in the Chief's garden, and the few late flowers seemed too much battered to revive again for any sun. Erif Der put on a long felt coat, lined with reindeer pelts, and walked in the garden with her box of cowries. She made a face, sometimes consciously, sometimes not, whenever she passed one of the Greek statues; the half-draped marble nymphs looked cold and silly. Before she had made up her mind what to do with the shells, she met Eurydice, whom she still thought of as Yersha, walking in the garden too, with her favourite maid Apphé, who was a hunchback, but pure Greek. Erif Der hated seeing Apphé; it frightened her to think of people being like that; she liked funny, twisted things made by her brother, half beasts and half men, but not living flesh. She tried not to show how uncomfortable and afraid it made her, because she hoped Eurydice did not know yet; but if and when she did, Erif thought, this much of her own power would go. Eurydice motioned the maid to go on; as she passed Erif Der stiffened, but did not draw back. 'Are you sorry that the summer is over?' she asked Eurydice.

'Summer is not over yet,' said the elder woman decidedly, and beckoned Erif to sit down on the seat beside her.

'It seems like winter,' said Erif softly; 'look over there at the clouds—so grey—'

But Eurydice, who was not Yersha in her own garden, would not look up higher than the things she knew. 'Child,' she said, 'I am not going to play games with you. And I do not think Charmantides will play games with you any longer.'

Erif Der spilled out the cowries on to her lap. 'I like playing games,' she said. 'Will you help me to thread these shells, Aunt Yersha?'

But Eurydice's lips tightened, and she swept the shells on to the ground and caught Erif Der by the shoulders and shook her. 'You have bewitched my Charmantides!' she cried. 'Take care! I can see if he cannot. I tell you, if you hurt him, I shall hurt you more!'

Erif Der, cramped against the corner of the seat, pushed out at Yersha, her hard, hateful hands and face, but could not get free for a moment. 'I have done nothing!' she said. 'I am Queen, not you! What do you mean?'

'I mean,' said Yersha, almost spitting into her face, 'that whatever you can do to your own barbarians, you cannot magic a Hellene!'

Erif Der got loose. 'I shall tell Tarrik,' she said. 'I suppose he used to like you once, Yersha—before you got so old.' She stooped and began to pick up her shells. Eurydice stamped the heel of her sandal on to the girl's hand, and crushed one of the cowries; it seemed more adequate than words; an arrow scratch tore and began to bleed again. But Erif Der laughed. 'Even suppose what you said were true, Aunt Yersha, how much Hellene are you?—in winter?' But Eurydice turned and walked quickly up to the house, calling her maid in a high voice, careful not to look up at the sky, in case there were any clouds after all.

Among the cowries, Erif Der picked up a hairpin of Yersha's, and laughed again; but her hand was sore all the same, and she wished she was out of the Chief's garden and standing alone on the seashore in the cold, or down in the forge with Berris, making things—and not magic. She went over to one of the fountains and sat cross-legged on the ground beside it, dabbling her fingers and frowning; then she began threading the cowries. In a way she was glad that Yersha hated her as much as she hated Yersha: it was all simpler. When it came to an end, as it would soon, Yersha would be in her power. She thought of all sorts of amusing things that might be made to happen to her, with all the lively imagination of a young married woman against an old maid. Yes, Yersha would be sorry for stamping on her hand: quite soon now. And Tarrik?

As she sat there, Tarrik came out of the house; he had been talking with his aunt, and, in a way, he knew that she was right. He knew he had married a witch and must beware of her; he knew she was working against him somehow; and yet he could not quite connect her with anything that had happened, least of all Midsummer and Harvest. The more he tried to remember, the less certain he was of what had happened; some cloud had come over his mind, and she—she could take it away if she chose. Yet it had been his own doing at the beginning, and he was Chief and Corn King and whatever he did was right. Make her be different, then. He went over to the fountain; she had a long string

of odd shells and she was playing with them, pulling them
along the ground and pouncing on them like a wild kitten.
He could not see her as quite grown up, nor, somehow, quite
plainly; he rubbed his eyes. And he should have got used
to his wife by now. Used to her and tired of her, he thought
savagely, remembering his old love affairs, and stood still,
considering her critically. Then he pulled off her fur cap
and threw it away, and rubbed his hands in her hair; it was
wonderfully soft and full of little ends; it tangled round his
fingers. She reached up gently and caught his wrists, but he
shook her off and picked up the string of shells and broke
a twig from the bush beside him and began pushing it into
the long, smooth slits of them. He let them slide from one
hand into the other, and then began to coil them round
his neck, with the two ends hanging loose over his coat in
front. 'You like taking my things, Tarrik,' said Erif Der,
still sitting cross-legged, leaning a little against his knees.

'Yes,' said Tarrik. But how to make her different? 'I do
what I like with you,' he said again, and pushed the sleeve
back from her arm and ran his hand along it. Then he took
off one of his own rings and put it on to her middle finger.
'That's for you, Erif,' he said. Women like to be given
things. The ring was too big for her: it was a sun-ring,
a topaz in a claw setting, warm from his skin.

'Who made it?' she asked.

'It comes from inland, from the north,' he said. 'Do you
see, Erif, it is really a sort of dragon?'

'No Greek could have made that,' she said.

'No.'

'We make better things than the Greeks.'

'Yes.'

'Tarrik, you hate the Greeks, don't you?'

'Yes. No. Erif Der, take your hands from me!' He
stepped back quickly and a loose end of the cowrie chain
swung against his sword hilt, tinkling. He twitched at it,
and it broke: the shells came showering down between
him and Erif.

She gave a little cry: 'Oh, Tarrik, you are worse than
Yersha!' and began to pick them up again hurriedly.

For a moment the clouds seemed to thin. 'She spoke to
me just now,' he said, and then, 'Erif, I am in danger! I
know I am as much Corn King as ever, I know I have the

power still! But they think not, they think—oh, I can't tell what they are thinking! I will make them believe in me again. You are my Queen, the Spring Queen, Erif; you must help me. You must! If you don't I shall hate you: I do terrible things to the people I hate, I kill them in horrible ways, I hurt them for hours. I don't want to hate you, Erif, I love you—' Suddenly he stopped; he was saying things he had not meant to say. Was she changing?

'You are mad,' she said. 'You are mad, Tarrik!' and got to her feet. She had put the cowries somewhere, into her dress, perhaps, between her warm young breasts. He put out a hand for them and then checked himself, only keeping a grip of the woollen stuff of her dress, holding her so that she could not go away unchanged.

'When the snow comes,' he said, 'they will have the bulls in, and the racing. I shall fight the bulls, Erif! Then they will see I have power, they will know I am Corn King and Chief of Marob!' He let her go.

'Yes,' she said gently, 'do that, Tarrik. Then it will be over and you will not be unhappy any more.'

'I will not be unhappy any more,' he repeated; and suddenly picked her up in his arms, picked her right up off the ground and kissed her as if he would never be done. In a little he felt she was kissing him back, her arms were round his neck, soft and strong and straining. He took her into his house. Women like to be given rings.

Eurydice, up in her own room, called the maid Apphé sharply to draw the curtains and light the lamps. 'I feel so sad when the good weather is over,' she said; 'when the sea is rough: no ships, nothing! Oh, shall I ever get away, shall we ever go south, Apphé? Light the big lamp—yes, and more wood. And bring me my mirror. Oh, I am not so old. If I could get to my own Hellas I would still be happy. How happy I should be.'

'But I know it will come, my lady,' said Apphé; 'let me read your hand again. Look, you see, the sure line, the travel line, isn't that certain?'

'You've seen that often, so often, Apphé, and so have I. But it never comes. How could it? Charmantides will not leave Marob.'

'Unless anything were to happen to we-know-who,' said the maid.

'Yes,' said Eurydice, fingering the edge of her silver mirror, 'unless he were free.' And then: 'I wish I knew what truly happened to that artist—Epigethes; he was to have made me a jewel-case. How he talked! Athens, Corinth, Rhodes. . . . What do you think, Apphé?'

'You know what they say, my lady—'

'Not a word of it true! He denied it—to me. How could Charmantides— ? My sister's son!'

'No, my lady.'

'And yet—all this last year—Oh, Apphé, it surely cannot be winter again already!' She twitched the drawn curtains back; yes, there were real clouds, and that leaden, restless sea.

When it was nearly dusk, Erif Der, who had been lying back, half awake, half dreaming, suddenly sat up—so suddenly that Tarrik woke and blinked and swung over an arm to catch her; heavy and warm, it rested on her a moment before it slipped off again as he settled to sleep once more. She got up softly and soberly, and picked up her shoes and dress from the floor, and put them on, and splashed her hands and face with water that had sweet herb leaves soaking in it. She smiled at Tarrik lying there; she could see the mark on his chest where her star had burnt him, and his strong, bare arms that had held her so firmly and yet so softly, and the dark curly hair in his armpits that smelt of hay and summer and sun. She moved a step towards him, and then shook herself and tiptoed out, and down the stone stairs and out of a side door on to the road, and so to the beach. Eastwards, out to sea, it was black and wild looking, unquiet still after the storm; the only light was inland, over the tops of the houses. The snow might come soon, any day now. And, 'I will do it!' she said aloud, stamping on the pebbles, 'I will! He shan't change me—not this way! Let him go to his bullfight and end it!' And then she began to run, plunging breathlessly across the shingle till she got to sand; while one is running hard there is no time for regrets, for changing one's mind, for softness and love. When she stopped it was full night; she stood between low cliffs and a sea of hollow black and the lightless grey of foam-caps, unending. As she looked out,

she thought she saw something, a spark, a tiny light, far
off, hardly in sight. It was late in the year for a ship, late
and bad weather; she could not be sure, sometimes it was
there, sometimes hidden. She climbed half-way up the cliff
to see better, but night was almost come, the wind pulled
at her dress, she was cold and cramped, and if she stayed
longer, they would miss her in the Chief's house.

She went back more slowly, not at all afraid of the dark;
she was making plans for magic now, to put something
between him and the bulls, so that neither eye nor hand
should do what he wanted of them. This bullfighting would
be all the barbarian part of him, that she could bewitch
easily, as it had been before, for the two Feasts. It would
have been a different matter magicking him over anything
in which the Greek part of him counted; but she had been
lucky. She knew it. Carefully she thought out the things
to do. He might be killed by the bulls; they were always
savage, coming in from the plains. She frowned to herself
and went on faster; she would not let him be killed, only
make him do it badly—so that people saw—and then
her father could get his way at last and leave her in peace.
Or would it be better, better for every one, if he were to
be killed, dead and forgotten? He would rather be killed
than lose his power—if one could ever judge for another.
And she herself, she would forget him, surely she would.
Times like today were meant to be forgotten; she would
be free again, to start another life of her own, not his nor her
father's. She took his ring and threw it hard out of sight, out
to sea; and then thought what a fool she was; she might
have used it. Never mind, she would use other things. She
suddenly remembered Yersha's silver hairpin that had come
so opportunely to her hand, and laughed aloud and ran on
again till she was back at the breakwater.

She scrambled up, lightlier than ever, and stood on the
top, swaying to the wind; by the harbour wall she saw
Berris holding a lantern, and called to him. He came,
startled. 'Where have you been, Erif?'

'Talking to the crabs,' she said. 'And you? Won't you
make me something? Do, Berris! I'll come and blow
for you.'

'Later,' he said. 'I can't work just now. Oh, Erif, what
are you doing to Tarrik?'

'Doing what father wants.'

'But not unless you want it yourself,' said Berris, low and eagerly. 'Father is not a god—nor Yellow Bull. They never think of beauty, they—oh, Erif, I wish I were well out of this.'

'Do you?' said Erif. 'You're a man, you can't make up your mind. I can. I'm happy.'

But Berris pulled her over by the sleeve to where the light streamed squarely out from a house window. 'You don't look it,' he said. 'Erif—I'm frightened of you when your face is like that!'

Chapter Five

BERRIS TOOK HER back to the great door of her own house; the guards lifted hand and sword to their foreheads as she went past, and did not look at her directly; it was no part of theirs to wonder why the Spring Queen of Marob had gone out at night with no servants, no coat, and nothing on her head. Erif Der tossed her plaits back over her shoulders, and grinned at them for the fun of seeing them not take any official notice. Then she kissed her brother and went on alone. She found Tarrik in the Council Hall, sitting in his great chair, with his chin on his hands. 'I am thinking about the secret road,' he said. 'You can tell Yellow Bull. I wonder if it will ever be a danger. What do you think will have happened to Marob in ten hundred years, Erif? Will they be our blood, the Chiefs, then?'

He looked at her softly, with those smiling, bright eyes of his. And she looked away, because if she had met them and smiled back, she could not have gone on keeping secrets; she would have told him everything, put herself into his hands, into his mercy and love, done anything he bade her, been a good wife to him, niece to Yersha. Oh, if she could start life again! 'I can't think so far ahead,' she said huskily, through stiffened lips. 'I hate the time when I shall be dead! I hate countries I shall never see! I hate stars! I hate things that men have no power over!'

She threw herself down on the floor and hit her head with her knuckles; Tarrik went on speaking from somewhere above her: 'But time is our own making, Erif. Even time so far off. I wonder if there will be any Marob then, or any Hellas. Athens has been going on for hundreds and hundreds of years, but I think she is almost dead. And the other cities of Hellas too. Nobody knows how long Marob has been here; people don't think about that; I don't often. And I don't really care much what's going to happen, either. Erif, do you love me?'

'Yes,' said Erif. Oh, anything not to have to talk just now!

'I never minded if the others did or didn't,' he said. 'I expect they did. I always got what I wanted and no one was any the worse. It helped the Corn. In five months it will be Plowing Eve again. I wish I knew what happened at Harvest; I cannot remember it better than a dream, and yet I was not even drunk. At Plowing Eve my head will stay clear, though. Will you help me, Erif?'

She answered 'No,' but with her face on the floor, so muffled that he did not hear or heed.

'Ever since I was a man, I have known that I was truly Corn King,' he said. 'It is a queer thing to have power. But you have power too. So has Berris, but differently. The Greeks used to have power, but it is lost now. Yellow Bull thinks he has power. So does the Council. I am seeing without a cloud now; Erif, why is that?'

But before she could make up an answer, something had happened to drive it out of both their heads. The Captain of the Chief's Guard came running in. 'Chief!' he shouted, 'there's a big ship blowing in north of the harbour—her mast's gone and she's nearly on to the shingle!' They both jumped and ran, Tarrik giving orders as he went. At the door he turned and shouted to her: 'Erif, stay here!' But that was the last thing Erif Der was going to do.

The night was quite different now. A yellowish full moon had risen out of the sea and torn through the clouds to the north-east; even when their jagged edges streamed across it, the puzzling, diffused light went on. Over the hissing and grinding of the waves came other noises; men's voices at top pitch, and sometimes on the back of the gale heart-tearing sounds of timber breaking up, the screech and crash of the strained wood, and sharp improbable sounds there was no time to guess at; and crackling of the bonfires they had lighted high up the beach, and neighing of the sea and fire-maddened horses, and women crying to one another behind; and again and always, the sea. There was no chance of launching a boat, but the men were wading out with ropes tied round their belts, legs braced against the surf; things were passed from man to man, inshore and up to the bonfires, to be helped back to life if they had breath in them at all. Erif sent a dozen women off to the Chief's house for wine and warm clothes; she could do that, anyhow! Tarrik was nowhere to be seen, and for a time she was so hard at work among the half-drowned sailors that she did not think of him; he would be somewhere. They seemed to be half Scythian and half Greek, perishing with cold and wet and four days of storm and desperate struggle against it before the sides began to strain and gape hopelessly, and at last the mast snapped and killed three of them. They had a hold full of corn from Olbia, the last of the season; and they had left it too long. They gulped down hot wine and huddled themselves in the dry clothes, calling each other by name as man after man was passed up, and asking where they were, thankful to have come on a town and friends and food and rest after that terrible four days, and the storm ending too late to save them.

Tarrik was down in the sea, stripped to the waist and covered with oil for warmth; he was head of one line, as far out as he could keep his footing on the battered shingle. The light from the bonfires on the shore lay out on the surface beyond him as far as the third or fourth wave, so that he got some warning of anything coming in and had a moment to brace himself and take it. Sometimes a man clinging to a plank or swimming weakly in the trough of a wave, sometimes a cask or chest or bit of a mast, once a horrible, heavy strip of torn sail that tangled round his legs and pulled him over into the surf. Further out, between him and the moon, he could see the black, jagged outline of the wrecked ship, heaving and pitching as she broke up.

For more than an hour, though it scarcely seemed five minutes, he had been extremely efficient and enjoying every moment; he was shouting at the top of his voice and using every inch of his strength and skill; his side stung vividly where a splintered plank had grazed the skin; his eyes were used to seeing quickly in the half-lit dark, his arms and shoulders to heaving weights; he had beaten the sea! But now no living thing had come in for nearly ten minutes; he began to feel the cold at last. One more look out to the wreck before he turned. And there was a man moving on the black against the sky. He yelled out, though he knew it was no use against this wind. But the man had disappeared. For a minute or two he held himself hard against the battling waves, peering out ahead, then at last saw the black smudge on a tearing water crest that meant something coming in. He moved to the right, shouting back to the man behind to be ready, leaning against the weight and struggle of the sea. Then over the top of one great blinding wave the swimmer came at him head foremost, and both were rolled over and over and into the next on the line, one of the guards; he stood firm and held Tarrik, who heaved himself up, choking and cursing, one arm round the man from the ship. 'Are you the last?' shouted Tarrik, as soon as he got his breath. The man gasped yes, clinging to Tarrik's bare, slippery shoulder. He was small and light, soaked and streaming like a bunch of seaweed; an open cut on his temple was bleeding steadily, smearing his face with pale blood. Between them, Tarrik and the guard helped him in through the fierce shove and suck of the shallow water, and up to the bonfires. And so Sphaeros the Stoic came to Marob.

Erif Der had clothes and hot wine and food for them all; she saw to the graze on Tarrik's side, and odd cuts on his arms and hand; furtively, she kissed his cold back as she helped him on with a shirt. Yellow Bull came up, wetter and wilder looking than one would have thought possible; he had been head of another line of rescuers. 'That was fine, Chief!' he shouted, and then suddenly caught sight of Erif and remembered and checked and buried his face in a huge cup of wine. But Tarrik was far too excited and happy to notice the change in Yellow Bull, or even see that, for the moment at least, every one was round him again, talking and cheering, forgetting that he had ever been unlucky.

But Yellow Bull drew his sister aside out of the glare of the fires. 'What have you been doing?' he asked. 'Wasn't this your time?'

'Yes,' she said, 'I suppose so. I forgot. It was so exciting. I'm sorry, Yellow Bull.'

'Father will be angry.'

'I know. But—you can tell him there's going to be another chance, quite soon, at the bullfighting.'

'He's going to try that, is he?'

'Yes. So you see, then—It will all work out. Yellow Bull, let tonight alone.'

In the meantime Tarrik was giving out the rescued sailors to the chief men in his town, to keep for the moment, anyhow. Time enough tomorrow to see what should be done with them. Nearly all had been saved, not much hurt, including the captain, who kept on talking to anyone who would listen about his insurance. When they had been allotted, all the other things, barrels, rafts, bedding, and whatnot that had been washed up, were heaped at one side and left under guard. Tarrik found the little man he had saved last sitting quietly by the fire, trying to tie up his own cut head; he was managing it very neatly, but his hands were shaking still. 'What in hell were you doing to stay so long?' asked Tarrik suddenly.

The man looked up. 'I knocked my head; they thought I was dead and left me. It wouldn't have mattered.'

'No,' said Tarrik, amused.

'But you see, when I found I was alive after all, the impulse was too strong for me. Besides I am still hoping to finish my journey.'

'Where were you going?' Tarrik asked, in Greek this time.

'To Sparta, to King Kleomenes. I am his tutor.'

'What do you teach him?'

'Philosophy.'

'You had better teach me; I am a king too.'

'I do not know if you would be a good pupil; if you are, I should be glad to teach you. But Kleomenes needs me.'

'I have been to Greece, but never to Sparta; they say it is a rich place, where a few have all the power, and most are poor and unhappy.'

'It is like that now; but States may become better. Who are you, King, and what is your country?'

'I am Tarrik of Marob; but my name is Charmantides as well.'

'You are partly Hellene, then?'

Tarrik hesitated a moment, looking the philosopher up and down. 'I do not choose to think myself Hellene,' he said. 'I am a barbarian.'

The little man laughed pleasantly and openly, half shutting his eyes. 'Good!' he said. 'Now we have something real. I do not think Hellenes are good and barbarians bad, Tarrik of Marob. I think we are all citizens of one world. I think, too, that you have seen the worst sort of Hellene. Isn't that true?'

'Perhaps. They were not citizens of my world, anyhow. What is your name?'

'I am called Sphaeros of Borysthenes. You see, I am not quite a Hellene either.'

'You will come to my house,' said Tarrik. 'The blood is getting through that bandage. Does it hurt?'

'Not much. It is of no consequence, anyway.'

'Perhaps not to you. But I want you to teach me, I want you alive!' He called: 'Erif! Look: will you make the blood not come?'

Erif Der laid her fingers over the red patch on the bandage, then after a moment took them away sharply, and spoke low to Tarrik: 'Who is it?'

'Sphaeros: a Hellene: a teacher of kings. Make him well for me, Erif!'

She frowned and began muttering words and making little movements. Tarrik looked on anxiously, wondering what was the matter. Sphaeros sat quite still, feeling a little weak, only just sometimes lifting a hand to wipe away a trickle of blood from his neck. 'I can't,' said Erif Der suddenly, 'I can't! It doesn't work on him!' She jumped up and called to the women for a bowl of water, needle and thread, quick. Then she undid the bandage. 'This is the other way,' she said to Tarrik, and took his sharp little hunting-knife and cut the hair all round the wound, and then sewed the edges of it together, with her lips pressed up firmly, and eyes fixed on what she was doing. Sphaeros twisted his hands between his knees and shut his eyes, but said nothing, only gave a little gasp when it was all over. Tarrik gave him a cup of wine; the bleeding had stopped; Erif Der turned away and made one of the women pour water over her hands till they were clean.

The next day the Council met; they had to decide what to do with the ship's crew and the few passengers, a merchant with his clerk and two servants, and Sphaeros. The natural thing was to take them as a gift from the sea, and, after due thanks, enslave them or hold them to ransom. Three generations ago this would have been a certainty; but these were degenerate days. The Council discussed other possibilities. The Chief was being curiously reasonable, hearing both sides and then giving his own opinion, in a way that made Harn Der and his eldest son rather anxious. However, they comforted themselves with the thought of the bullfighting later on. Erif Der might have her own ways, but they could trust her to be loyal to her family.

In the end it was settled that such of the crew as had any money should have a sum fixed to be handed over in spring, whenever a ship came to take them away; the others would have to work for their living, and there would be correspondingly larger sums for the captain and passengers to pay. 'But as to the Greek, Sphaeros,' said the Chief, 'I will pay his now; he is my guest.' Any cargo, wood, baggage or provisions washed up from the wreck were to be distributed.

When the Council was ended, Tarrik found that his aunt had asked Sphaeros up to her room and was talking to him. Sphaeros sat on the edge of a chair, looking displeased and faintly uncomfortable; he had already refused offers of money, clothes, books, and exclusive friendship as between Hellenes in a barbarian country, from Eurydice, always with politeness, but still firmly. 'I am honoured,' he said, 'but, as you must see, I cannot commit myself yet.' He was a little curious to know more about Erif Der but was too discreet to ask. He had always liked Scythians, rather romantically, perhaps, but then he was more than usually sane and clear-headed over other things. He liked the hardness, the violent living of these riders and fighters, the carelessness of pain. The contrast in his mind was between them and the rich Greek—the kind of life that he saw reflected in this room of Eurydice's—rather than the Wise Greek. The Wise Greek was so very rare, thought Sphaeros: one thought one had found him, but how often one was disappointed. And it seemed to him that this strong, questioning, bare-breasted Tarrik was a Romantic Scythian. But so far he could not quite fit in Eurydice. At any rate, it gave him no pleasure to eat caviare and white bread from golden dishes on an ivory table, and hear rather second-rate poetry read aloud. He did not really mind in the least that his clothes were slightly torn, and discoloured and shrunk with sea water; in fact, he had not noticed. His sandals were borrowed and on the large side, but he did not even know who was the lender, so he could not possibly fret about returning them.

Tarrik leant against the wall, with his thumbs hooked into his belt. 'You're going to stay with me all this winter,' he said, 'and teach me.'

'But I must go to King Kleomenes as soon as I can,' said Sphaeros. 'There will be small ships sailing from harbour to harbour still; I can work my way south.'

It suddenly occurred to the Chief that he really had someone to deal with this time. 'You won't go till I let you,' he said. 'I have the power here, my philosopher.'

'Yes, King of Marob,' said Sphaeros, 'but you cannot make me teach.'

'I can kill you the moment I choose—and I will if you don't do what I want.'

'Yes, and how well I shall teach then!'

But Eurydice came between them, distressed at this scene between her Charmantides and a real Hellene philosopher. 'This is all nonsense, of course! Charmantides, you mustn't be rough. This delightful Sphaeros is *my* guest.' And she smiled at him, feeling that there was something to be said for being a respectable age—though not, of course, old!—at the moment.

But Sphaeros did not respond properly; he had a hand on Tarrik's arm, and was looking up at him earnestly. 'King!' he said, 'I will tell you why Kleomenes of Sparta needs me, and then you will let me go to him. I do not think you are truly the sort of king who kills people without reason.'

Tarrik, unused to this particular form of flattery, blushed and said: 'Well, we shall see. Tell me, anyhow.'

'It's a long story, it begins before you were born, King.'

'At supper, then. Oh, I shall get Berris!'

At first Berris refused to come to supper, with all sorts of excuses; but in the end, of course, there he was, with his eyes fixed on the Hellene. They sat round, more or less Greek fashion, Eurydice in a high-backed chair, waited on by her own maids; Tarrik half lying, half sitting, always very restless, on a big throne with red cushions; Erif Der beside him with her proper crown, five spikes of

silver, lightly engraved with stags and lions that had star
sapphires for eyes, and a heavy patterned dress that fell
over her feet. Sphaeros was on Tarrik's other side, head
propped in hands, lying along a couch of cedar lattice, with
small cushions, and Berris beyond him on another couch,
but sitting half up, clasping his knees, eating by fits and
starts. They had a long and large supper, with quantities of
meat, stewed and boiled and roasted, and fish, and raisin
pies, some good wine and much bad, wheaten cakes and
run honey and cream.

Eurydice only spoke when she had something to say
which appeared to her to be really noble—or witty—or
revealing a heart which yearned for Hellas; this made her
conversation rather fitful. Tarrik kept on thinking, quite
rightly, that she was at her best when alone with him. He
talked rather little, because he was hungry and at the same
time happier than he had been for months. Sphaeros was
naturally rather silent, and tonight he was tired too, but
knew he must tell his story well enough to convince the
Chief. So, during supper, Erif and Berris Der talked at one
another most of the time, across the others, sparring like
two pretty game-cocks. They talked Greek out of politeness,
and hers was bad, but fluent and very funny, whether on
purpose or not. They ended by throwing bread balls at one
another and Eurydice disapproved; but Tarrik joined in,
and then Sphaeros, not out of any sense of compliment to
his barbarian hosts, but in all pleasantness and seriousness.
Only then in the middle of it, Tarrik suddenly took up a
half-loaf and threw it at his cup-bearer and shouted to them
to clear the food and bring more wine. He pledged them all
in a skull cup, one of the chiefs of the Red Riders that he
had shot himself as a boy ten years before. 'And now the
story,' said Erif.

Sphaeros sat up on his couch, so as to be able to face
them all, and shifted his head bandage where the edge was
catching his ear. 'The beginning of the story is away back,'
he said, 'in the time when the Spartans did something that
no one else had ever done with their eyes open—or ever
will, I think. They turned their backs on the beauty that
was ripening in Hellas, in their own hearts too. They said:
"We will not build temples, nor make statues or paintings
or music, we will have no poets here. We will make life

hard and bitter so that only the strongest can bear it, and these shall be our citizens."'

He stopped for a moment, just long enough for Berris to ask 'Why?' The others were all quiet.

'Why?' said Sphaeros, half to himself. 'Because Sparta is a hot green valley, a garden where flowers blossom too much and die; they had to climb out of it, to live on the peaks in the cold winds. They made themselves the strangest State in the world; strong and free and caring not at all for death, no man for himself but all for the others, for Sparta. By casting out the beauty we know, they made a beauty of their own.'

Tarrik began to fidget and frown. 'Sparta is not like that. I have been to Hellas—I know for myself: no traveller's tales, my Sphaeros. I tell you, if there was any luxury, anything rare and precious and sought after, they had it in Sparta.'

'Yes,' said Sphaeros, 'but that came afterwards. It seems that no man and no State can live on the heights for ever. Sparta became too powerful, and the doom of the conqueror fell on her: gold and silver flowed down into hollow Lacedaemon and rotted the very roots of their greatness. These things, rather than the riches of the spirit, came to be what they cared for in Sparta; men strove for them only. In that moment the Good Life left them and was gone. Now gold follows after gold, and with it land and power, houses and cattle and slaves; more and more of the lands and riches came into the hands of a few men; and those of the citizens who dropped behind in the gold race must needs take to trade or farming to get their bread, and so they lost the good Life, and had no more leisure for the Training, the Eating-together, and all those matters without which no one can have citizenship of Sparta. A time came when all the riches in the State belonged to scarcely more than a hundred families, and of these many were unbelievably rich, though some had mortgaged their land and were deep in debt, and had nothing but the appearance of riches. The rest of the people worked for them, and were humble and slavish through debt and anxiety and poverty, and there was no happiness.'

Tarrik was listening quietly now, and so were the others, more or less. Only Eurydice was bending over a piece of

fine embroidery, and seemed at least as much interested
in it as in the story; her hands were still very white and
beautiful, and they moved over the sewing like big moths.
It was rather dark in the hall, in spite of the torches all
round in rings on the wall, but one of the maids knelt
beside Eurydice, holding a lamp just so high that it shone
round and softly on those hands of hers. Berris kept on
looking at them, and for a little while Sphaeros found them
a certain interruption in the thread of his ideas. But by and
bye the room faded, and he was away in another country,
among the dead that he had known and loved.

'Well,' he said, 'the story comes nearer: to fifteen years
ago. Sparta has always had two kings, and in the days I am
telling you about, one of the kings was called Leonidas. He
was an oldish man and he had lived much in Syria with King
Seleucus and the great lords there: there was no luxury or
pride that he did not know or practise. He had a daughter,
called Chilonis, and two young sons; they had only to ask
for a thing to get it. I know his house well; it was all
plastered with gold. He was the sort of man who could
not bear a straight line or a plain wall; everything must
be twisted and tangled and gilt and coloured till one's eyes
ached. Every corner was crammed with statues and fat gold
vases like old men's bellies and life-size pottery peacocks
painted and glazed, and goggling black slaves he'd brought
from Antioch, smelling of fat and scent; and everywhere
there were soft carpets and lamps running over with sweet
oil, and food and drink enough for an army. And there he
was in the middle, this old Leonidas, always grabbing and
hungry for more, never satisfied, never happy, as rough as
any peasant with it all. His wife was a tall, proud Spartan,
who kept herself away from him, and the daughter was
married to her cousin Kleombrotos, a decent enough young
man; she, woman-like, hated all this violence and luxury
of her father's and would tell her little brothers stories of
Sparta in the time of the Good Life; and they listened
to her. Leonidas loved her, perhaps because she was so
different, and it was she who persuaded her father to ask
me to come from Athens and teach the two young boys,
Kleomenes and Eukleidas. So for a time I went and lived
in his house, among all those vain riches.

'But the other king of Sparta was called Agis. He was

not wise, and never free from desire. And yet—if I could have loved any man—' He stopped again, with a little gasp, so vividly had Agis come into his mind. But two of them at once said: 'Go on.' He moved a little sideways on his couch and went on. 'Well, it is all a long time ago, and the world goes on still. Agis was young—little older than Berris here—and gentle and kind-hearted as a girl. He had been brought up with all tenderness and no sparing of money or love, by his mother and grandmother, and early married to a wife who was as beautiful as she was good, Agiatis the merry-minded, only daughter of the richest man in Sparta. He had these three women always by him, giving him of their best.

'Agis grew restless in the heat of summer and went up into the mountains of Sparta, and he stayed there alone for two nights. Then he came down and looked with new eyes at his country, and he saw how evil the times were, and he knew so clearly that there was no doubting it that he must bring Sparta back to the Good Life. So he cast away all pleasures and softness, all the graces and sweetness of his young life, and followed the old rules. The three women loved him so much that they did not try to hinder him. And gradually the rich young men of Sparta began to give up their pleasures too, and do as he did. But King Leonidas thought him a fool and said so to me; I kept my thoughts to myself, for I wished to go on teaching Kleomenes.

'Now Agis, having seen that he himself could lead the Good Life, planned to make it possible for all Sparta. In this State, the power lies not with the kings, but with their counsellors, the ephors, and in these days the ephors were rich men ruling in the interests of the rich. But Agis procured matters so that his own friends should be the ephors, among them his uncle, Agesilaus, whom he trusted: for he was young and without experience of men and their foolish and evil wills. Then, through these ephors, he proposed his new laws—the freeing of the poor from debt—the dividing up of all the lands into equal lots for all the citizens—and the granting of citizenship to those not Spartiate who yet had free minds and strong bodies and a will to serve the State. All the people were gathered together to hear these new laws, utterly surprised for the most part, and dumb and fearful as men are of any new thing. Then

Agis stood up among the ephors, with downcast eyes and wearing the rough Spartan dress. He spoke very shortly and simply, saying that his life was not his own but theirs, and if they would have the new laws, so would he. And with that he gave them all his own lands, which were very large and fertile, to be divided up, and six hundred talents of coined gold, which was almost all he had, and told them that his mother and grandmother and all his friends would do the same.

'Then, as it came real to them, the people went mad with excitement and admiration and love for their king. And suddenly Leonidas saw that it was no mere boy's game and that if it went on all his lands and riches would go too, and then and there he turned on Agis with bitter blame and anger. After that the State was divided into two, the poor and young following Agis, and the old and rich, Leonidas, who bribed and persuaded the Council of Elders to reject the new laws. But Leonidas was not the winner for long; the ephors attacked him, and his son-in-law Kleombrotos, eager to do as Agis had done, claimed the kingship, and he had to fly from Sparta. Some would have killed him on his way over the pass, but Agis heard of this and forbade it. The boys went with him, and so did Chilonis, for she was one of those who would rather be unhappy than happy. And I went north to Athens to be with my teacher Zeno, for I was sick of rich men and their ways. Only I promised Kleomenes to come back one day.

'Now Agis had all the deeds of money-lending burnt in the market-place of Sparta, and so far freed his people. He would have gone on at once to the division of land, but Agesilaus his uncle had other plans: he was a man with many debts and much land; now he was free of the debts, but hoped to keep the land. Agis did not understand this; he was too young to believe the worst of people. So he went marching to the wars, leaving half his work undone. Still all would have been well, but that the general of the Achaean League, whom he went to help, was jealous of him, and would not let him win a battle. These things happen and there is reason in them if one could see it. His army was all under the old discipline and he himself was the youngest there; they loved him, he was a flame to them, he would have led them to victory. But in the end there was nothing for them to do, and he had to bring them back ingloriously, and found that all was in disorder in Sparta, because of Agesilaus, who was still ephor and was using his power to oppress the people and get everything for himself. He treated his nephew Agis and the other young king as foolish boys, and gave out that there was to be no dividing of the land.

'Then the people turned fiercely on those who they thought had tricked them, and sent to Tegea and brought Leonidas back in triumph. Agis knew that his army was utterly his and would fight for him, even against the rest of Sparta. But he would not let the army save him because that would have meant killing others of his fellow-citizens. Kleombrotos agreed. The two young kings fled for safety to the most sacred temples, yet I think most likely Agis knew that he was choosing death. Kleombrotos was saved by this same Chilonis, his wife, who stood between him and her father, and went with him to banishment, just as she had gone before with Leonidas. But Agis was not to be forgiven.

'His enemies tried to persuade him to come from the temple; he would not listen to them. But again he was trapped by his friends—by his own pure heart that would believe good of anyone until, too late, their evil was proved. They lured him out of his refuge and dragged him to prison. Leonidas and his followers among the elders came there to accuse the king, to show some pretence of justice. He stood before them, bound and smiling, and happy because of the things he had tried to do. They sentenced him to death; there was such a glory about him that the executioners dared not touch him. It was those one-time friends who dragged him to his place of death!

'But now his mother and grandmother had heard. They rushed about the city, stirring up the people, reminding them of all he had done and hoped to do. They came clamouring round the gates of the prison, saying it was for them to hear and judge him. That only brought him a quicker death. The officers of the prison wept for him, as once they did in Athens for Sokrates. He bade them not to mourn for him dying innocent and unafraid. He gave his neck to the noose.

'Then these friends who had betrayed him, came out with

fair words to the women, saying that there was no more danger for Agis. They brought in first the older woman, his grandmother, and killed her. Then his mother came in, thinking to have him in her arms again, and they were both lying dead. "Oh, my son," she said, "it is your great mercy and goodness which has brought us all to ruin." And they hanged her too, till she died.'

Sphaeros stopped suddenly and looked round at the Scythians. Eurydice's white hands were quiet now, Tarrik was leaning forward with his hand on his sword. The other two were both in tears. Said Erif: 'But what happened to the other, his wife—Agiatis? Did they kill her too?'

'No,' said Sphaeros, frowning a little. 'They did not kill her. She was heiress to her father's estates, so Leonidas married her by force to the boy Kleomenes. She hated that; she had a little baby, and besides, she had loved Agis. She did all she could to keep herself his, and his alone: she hated Leonidas. But she was in his power—as all Sparta was then.'

Erif Der drew a breath of pity. 'Poor dear, oh, poor dear! Was she very unhappy?'

'I think so,' said Sphaeros. 'The baby died very soon: and Leonidas was not kind to her. But my Kleomenes was gentle, and, as soon as he was old enough he began to love her so much that in time she loved him back. But she never forgot Agis, he was always in her heart, and by and bye she found that her husband was the one person she could talk to about him. I was in Sparta again some three years after this marriage (between-times I had been home again, in Olbia) and Kleomenes told me, as if it were something quite new, the story of Agis. He was all in a passion, flaring up and then crying like a child over it: he wanted to know what I thought of Sparta, as it was now under his father, a worse place than ever, rotten with luxury and idleness and the evil wills of the rich. He swore to me then, if ever he was king, with my help he would change it all and make it a place where men could be wise. And I swore too, that if, when the time came, he still needed me, I would come. Nine years ago his father died, worn out with desires and the vain image of pleasure. Kleomenes was still little more than a boy. He is a man now. He has written to say that at last he needs me.'

'I see,' said Tarrik, and got up, and began walking about the room, fidgeting with his crown, his belt, the edges of his coat. At last he came to a stand in front of the philosopher and looked hard down at him for a minute or two, as if he were trying to see through the man's eyes into his mind and heart. 'And so it seems as if you must go,' he ended his sentence.

'Yes,' said Sphaeros gravely.

'You may have difficulty in finding a ship.'

'I know. His letter did not reach me till late in autumn. But you will help me, King of Marob.'

'Yes,' said Tarrik, 'I will help you.'

Chapter Six

E RIF DER LEANT OUT of her father's window and watched them driving the bulls into the flax market. The openings of the streets and the house doors and lower windows were barred across, because of the half-wild beasts pouring in, tossing heads and tails, brown and white in the sunlight, not angry yet, but ready to be. From housetops and windows half Marob was watching. Snow had fallen the week before and been cleared away; now it was a lovely, sharp, windy morning. The well-head in the middle was covered over with hurdles to make a raised refuge place for the branders and killers. They stood about on it, some ten or twenty young men who wanted to show off to their girls and friends, all gay with coloured knots and leather fringes to their coats and boots. Tarrik was among them, standing right on top of the hurdles, with gold and red ivory scales sewn all over his clothes and the long, plaited whip hanging from his hand to the ground; he jerked his arm up and cracked it out over the bulls' backs. Most of the people shouted back at him, ready to give him his chance and let him show he was Corn King again. But Erif Der started, clinging to the side of the windows; she waved her hand to him, with something tinkling between the fingers; she was very white, and after a moment looked back into the room as if she were going to fall. Yellow Bull came close to her and whispered: 'You are sure—this time?' She glared at her brother and said nothing. Harn Der, wiser and perhaps more anxious, pulled at his arm and got him away, right out of her sight.

They left her alone; she had worked out every-thing—everything except what the bulls would do: that she must leave to chance. She wished she could stay still now, frozen, unthinking, unpicturing, instead of being horribly alive to it all, in the middle of this magic that she had made herself, and that she knew was well made. She gathered it up against Tarrik and let it go; at any rate, she was in her father's house; why need she feel that there was any change between last winter and this?

The bulls were beginning to get angry now, swinging their great heads and bellowing; but so far they had kept clear of the men at the well-head, knowing the sound of whip-cracks and the gadfly bite that always followed. The people watching all round began throwing stones and shouting. One of the bulls charged suddenly, horns down, at a house wall, but then at the last moment swerved aside and came blundering back into the herd. Two women in the window above him screamed, and one of them called shrill to a boy among the branders, who yelled back and shot out his whip-lash and flicked the flank of the bull, angering him. In another ten minutes the show was at its height; the old bulls were being killed and the young ones branded with this year's mark. Blood ran dark and bright in the gutters; people and beasts alike were smelling it, and the singed hair and flesh. They got mad. The boys on the top of the flax stores were throwing down balls of tow that they had set on fire. One of the branders, not quick enough, was caught before the others could come to his help with their weighted whip-handles, and had to be carried into a house with his arm broken. But nobody minded except him: it was all part of the fun. Only Erif Der was not really looking, not enjoying it properly as she always had in other years; her father came softly behind her to see what she was doing, but she did not turn round, and he went away again with Yellow Bull to the other room. Yellow Bull wished he had been bullfighting too this year: it would have been, somehow, fairer. But his father had wanted to be quite sure of having him safe; he saw that this was wise, but all the same, it stopped him from getting any pleasure out of the show.

Tarrik had waited till there were a dozen bulls at once charging about the market, clatter and thud and grunt of their wild, hot bodies, the weight and danger behind their sharp horns and stupid, savage brains. Then he marked his beast, jumped clear and threw out his coil of rope with the stone on its end. It went snaking out, low after the bull, and twisted round his hind-leg. Tarrik braced himself gloriously, with eyes and ears open for another brute to dodge. As the strain came, he heaved himself back on the rope, feeling his strength and godhead burn down through muscles of arms and back and legs to his quick feet hard on the rammed earth of the market-place. The bull fell, kicking with all four of its hoofs like knives, and he was on to it and banged it between the eyes with the bronze knob of his whip. The shouting all round rose to a yell for him; he heard his own name and thrilled to it, and stuck his knife deep into the bull's throat folds. It quivered immensely and groaned; then its eyes glazed and it died. Tarrik jumped on to its ribs and stamped on the warm, foam-streaked hide, cracking his whip and shouting shrilly as he felt the blood trickling down his hands. Then he began showing off to Marob, playing tricks, jumping over the brutes' backs and under their noses, roping a young bull to be branded, scoring the neck of an old one with his knife point to madden it; he was all barbarian.

From a broad window, not too high above it all, his aunt was watching; sometimes she felt herself almost swamped in the waves of savageness bursting all round her; she nearly got to her feet and yelled too. But still she could stop herself, look away, ask Apphé whether she had remembered the gold thread for the embroidery. She wondered if she would always be able to stay so beautifully calm; every year, as she grew older, she enjoyed it more. Sphaeros was sitting beside her, and he watched, but he did not seem as if he even wanted to yell; the lines on his face showed, his clasped fingers fitted together; he had not spoken much, nor even answered her questions with at all a courteous fullness, all the morning. Perhaps he was shocked, in spite of admitting it all intellectually: the Scythians of Olbia had never played this savage game.

Then Erif Der, sitting in her window, began to sing in a high, shaking voice. No one could have heard over the din in the market, but Tarrik seemed to be listening. He stood quite still where he was, with his rope trailing on the ground; one of the bulls, charging blindly, just missed him; the other bull-fighters shouted at him, ran towards him—and then stopped, all shaken with fear at something in his face. They saw that his bad luck had come again, the blight on the Corn King: this was how he had been at Midsummer and Harvest.

Erif Der shut her eyes; she did not choose to see it happen. It was better, if one must think, to go right on into next year when it would be all over, and this house her house again. Then her mind split into two; one half worked quite free of the magic—the most living half; it darted about, hovering over faces remembered; her father telling her their plan, making her feel a grown woman fit to act with the men; Yersha walking blind into a magic net made fast with the pin of her own hair; Berris, unhappy, not wanting to make things; Tarrik. Tarrik. Tarrik. There he was, solid, at the end of all the paths that darting mind could take. Deliberately, with a great effort, she blotted out that half of the mind, shoved it down and under till she was poised again on a tide of magic, flowing out on the thin music of her song, to do what she wanted. She dared to open her eyes; all this boiling in her mind had taken incredibly little time. Tarrik still stood there, clouded, and yet—it was not finished.

For the first moment, Eurydice had not understood; she thought he was showing off again, and leant back, smiling half apologetically at Sphaeros. But then, when everybody else had seen, she saw too. She caught her neighbour Hellene by the arm, with a kind of soft, whispered shriek: 'Look! She's killing him!' 'Who?' said Sphaeros quickly. 'Erif Der—that woman—oh, what are you going to do?' 'Make him think,' said Sphaeros, and slipped the heavy cloak over his head and off, and put one knee up on the window-sill, blocking her view, so that for one moment she only saw the hard jut of muscles in his arm and shoulder, wondered dizzily at a middle-aged philosopher being like that, heard a yell of something—horror or admiration—go up from the crowd, and fainted.

Sphaeros saw it was only twelve feet to the ground, and jumped easily, his hands just touching the ground as he sprang up again. He watched his line among the bulls and took it. Twenty years ago he had been a brilliant runner and proud of it; the pride was gone, but that same body was ready to do what action he willed. He called to Tarrik by his other, his Greek, name. 'Wake!' he cried, 'think!' And as he got there, Tarrik shuddered from his feet upwards and turned to him. They were almost touching when an old bull charged. Tarrik, coming alive, heard the loudening, sudden bellow, and saw the lowered terror of black horns coming at them. The cloud lifted.

The bull knocked Sphaeros over sideways, then dropped its head and spiked him in the armpit with one horn, roaring. Tarrik threw his looped whip over the other horn and dropped against it with all his weight. The bull, over-balanced, slid round on its forelegs with a wrenching grunt, and came down on one knee and the looped horn, which broke off short. Sphaeros' body had fallen across its neck, so that Tarrik stabbed behind the shoulder, falling forward on to the knife hilt to get it through to the beast's heart. Already half his mind was racing off into questions; but in the meantime he did exactly what he meant to do, and all Marob shouted for the Corn King.

Erif Der had seen. Back came her magic on to her own head, with shock on stinging shock, till she could only cling, rigid and speechless, to the window-bar, fighting against her own clouds. At last she tore the beads from her neck and wrists; they lay on the floor, faintly smoking in the sunshine. She stared down at them, panting. Her father and Yellow Bull came in. She had seen her brother angry before, but never Harn Der. She thought they were going to hurt her. In sudden terror she tried to turn the clouds on to them, but it was no use: she only span dizzily in her own magic till they took her by the shoulders and shook her. 'What have you done, you little fool?' said Harn Der. 'Look at that!' and twisted her round by the hair to look at the flax market and Tarrik's triumph. 'Trust a woman!' said her brother bitterly, and then words became inadequate and he kicked her ankle as hard as he could.

But all the branders and slaughterers had come shouting up round Tarrik, keeping a space open and safe for him. The bull was quite dead. It had seemed to Sphaeros as if he were rushing off somewhere, on the clear path at last, away from the world, the thick air of passions and arguments, into some simple, fiery place, from which the movements of the stars were all plain. Only his arm was holding him, pulling him back, with immense tension and pain; if once his spirit could make the supreme effort, tear itself away regardless of any hurt, he would be able to lose himself in that fire of truth and understanding. For long ages he struggled to bring his will to bear on this sure Good, and then without any pause he was looking up at Tarrik's face between him and the sky, noticing the flecked brown of his eyes and the tiny drops of sweat crawling down his forehead and nose. 'Truth,' he said, clearly, in Greek, 'truth is—a fire—God—Charmantides, my truth—' and so came back, dejected, into the tangle of unfriendly arms and legs that seemed to be his body. Tarrik put an arm under him, gently, and nodded to one of the others to pull, biting his lip, because he hated the sound of a friend in pain, and knew it would be bad, getting the horn out. 'Don't strain!' he said, 'go soft—we shall do it quicker so.' And obediently Sphaeros the Stoic relaxed into their hands, into heaving, alternate waves of pain and faintness, for some ten minutes, while they got him loose from the horn and bound up his shoulder with soft rags, and by and bye took him out of the flax market into a house. He found then that he was crying, making small noises like an animal, and he stopped himself, concentrating his mind instead on the problem of breathing without hurting his poor body too much. Tarrik was standing beside him, twisting knots and loops in his whip-lash, and then pulling them out again. 'You saved me then,' he said dispassionately, into the air, as it were, over Sphaeros' head, and then again, 'you risked your life to save me.'

'Yes,' said Sphaeros at last, hoping not to have to say any more.

But Tarrik dropped on the floor beside him: 'Is it because I am king? No. But why? Would you do it for anyone?'

'Of course,' whispered Sphaeros again.

'But do you not care for yourself at all? Sphaeros, Sphaeros, how are you so brave?' He bent closer, staring into the white face and eyes half shut: he could only just catch the sound of those faintly moving lips.

'Good,' they whispered, 'to do good,' and fell into the shape of laboured breathing again.

'Is it because you are a Greek?' asked Tarrik again, very eagerly. 'Are all good Greeks like you? Is it—could I see for myself? Was I wrong? Is it like this in Hellas after all?'

But for all Tarrik's wanting to know, and for all that he was Chief of Marob, he could get no answer at all out of Sphaeros then, nor for another half-day and night. But his mind had come awake and cloudless, and gone south, searching down a secret road—towards Hellas.

When Erif Der screamed, the odd part of it was that she screamed for her mother. It was not the sort of thing that either of the men expected of her, and it made them angrier than ever. Yellow Bull would probably have beaten her solidly with a stick, particularly as she started by hitting back at him and even getting in one good tug at his beard before he had her hands tight. But Harn Der would not have it: he was too deeply angry for a fleeting violence like this. He told her quietly that she had ruined everything, her father and brother, her family, Marob itself, how she was nothing but a woman after all in spite of the trust they had put in her, and the way he said it made her wince and quiver away as if he had spat in her face. She had a lump in her throat that stopped her explaining. She just said once: 'It was the Greek—' but they did not choose to heed. They treated her at once as a naughty child and a wicked woman, and she, with her own hostile magic to deal with as well, had nothing to do but take it.

Outside, the bullfighting was over for that year. The young bulls had been driven, branded and exhausted, to their winter byres: the old ones had been killed and the carcasses taken away for salting. The crowd had almost gone. Dumb and aching in her spirit from all this unanswered anger, Erif Der turned and jumped out of the window. Air and earth were kind to her still; she fell unhurt, but with Tarrik's clouds so wrapped about her eyes that she stumbled into pools of blood and knocked herself against a corner of the hurdles on the well-head. She went home to the Chief's house: for once she felt utterly lost and baffled and unhappy. As she passed the forge, she looked in, and there was Berris leaning over his bench, making a chain of triple rings. He looked up vaguely, his face changing to astonishment as he saw her. Then she ran.

All the household were scurrying about with excitement: Sphaeros had been carried in and was lying on the great bed in the guest-room. She stood in the doorway for a moment, listening to the laboured heave of his breathing. Though it was all his doing, she did not, somehow, hate him. For some time she sat on her own bed, with her hands clasped in her lap. It was odd that Tarrik should be alive after all that afternoon. From minute to minute she was struggling inwardly with her own magic; the clouds were on her so badly that there seemed to be nothing to do but acquiesce and wait till it was over, as it must be some time. She wished Tarrik would come; she wanted fantastically to have somebody's arms to creep into and take shelter in from herself. She groped out for a shirt of his and held on to it, until he should come himself. But instead of the Chief, Eurydice came in, with the maid Apphé behind her.

'Well, Erif Der,' she said, 'I think even our Charmantides must see now.'

Erif Der gathered herself up to meet this with some of the lies that had been her daily sport with Eurydice—for months now. But her tongue was slow and she could not help looking at the hunchback maid leering at her from behind. 'I don't know what you mean,' she said at last, rather wearily, 'and if I did, I don't care!'

'But you will care,' said Eurydice, 'all in time. And how did your dear father like it?'

'If you think you've found out anything that Tarrik hasn't known for half a year,' said Erif, low and savagely, sitting sideways on the bed, screwing her eyes up, 'go and tell him! Much he'll thank you for it, you double-clever Eurydice!'

But Eurydice was bending over her, looking down into her clouded, miserable soul. 'I have seen him looking like this,' said the aunt, 'yes. . . . So you can be hurt too: of course. These things are in your nature. Well, child, I am glad to know it.'

Erif Der jumped up and hit out at her; but the same thing happened to her that would have happened to Tarrik with the bulls. Her right hand jerked up with all the fingers out as if something had suddenly pulled at it, and a bluish and buzzing flash blinded her for a second. 'Oh,' she said, very softly, 'so it would have been like that.' By now the clouds had hidden Eurydice; she was left alone inside herself, and there she was thinking that this was what Tarrik had escaped. From behind a thick curtain, she felt that Eurydice was laughing and going out, and that the hunchback maid had gone with her and left the room calm again. For herself, there was nothing to do; she lay down and slept.

Tarrik came in and held a lamp close to her face and looked at her; her shut eyelids screwed and twitched and she whimpered in her sleep. He had meant to wake her, to hit her suddenly in the face so that she would wake in a fright and answer any questions. But he watched a few minutes, thinking it over, and at last decided not to. He felt strong enough now to stay uncertain and not make judgments. He lay down beside her, pulled the blankets over to his side, and he slept too.

Nothing more happened for a few days; the fine, late autumn weather that had come after that storm lasted on, though any evening it might break, for good this time. Eurydice copied poems and embroidered, and re-read Pythagoras without understanding him any more than usual, and smiled to herself, because it seemed to her that what she wanted was going to happen at last, and she believed, of course, that it was good. Erif Der stayed very quietly wherever she happened to be; she had come out of her clouds, and now she was very angry with her magic and would not touch it for the time being. She had left some of her beads in Harn Der's house, but she would not even go and fetch them. She thought they could look after themselves; besides she would rather lose them than see her father or brother again, or even know what they were doing. One day she went and walked along the shore, to the place where the cliffs began to heighten; there was a spring of fresh water there, just at the top of the shingle, icy-cold to her feet, but she liked drinking from it, cheating, as it were, the salt of the sea. There were still occasional timbers being washed up from the ship that had been wrecked; she pulled one up, with horrid naked-looking barnacles dangling from it, and took some of them back, and shoved them in through the window of the forge for Berris to see. But Berris Der did not like them very much; he was after something fresh, something which could not be interpreted through any natural form. He was not sure what it was, only he knew that it was in some way intellectual, a beauty of the mind rather than the eye.

As for Tarrik, it was as if part of him had suddenly been let loose. He went about with his eyes shining as if he were in love with a new girl: Sphaeros was teaching him philosophy. He had never done anything with that part of his mind before, and he admired himself enormously for the lucid and quick way that it was going. It had set to work on a whole new series of problems, and was tumbling about them like a puppy. Sphaeros found it restful, while he was still lying down and in some pain, to be able to give these very mild first lessons in the unreality of the physical universe, and to watch the disintegrating effect of the discovery that after all tables and chairs are only one sort of reality and that a not very interesting sort, on an intelligent mind which had never considered tables or reality before. Tarrik's barbarian world of colour and smell and solidity broke up deliciously about him into a new freedom, a universe of appearance slithering round his head, a sense of time being within himself, not a mere black and white blinking of nights and days. For nearly a week, he revelled in this, while Sphaeros, gradually getting well, regarded him and waited for the reaction.

It came, of course. His underneath mind had gone on working, following ideas to their conclusion, and then disconcertingly presenting them at odd moments in the shape of disturbing emotions. Tarrik woke up in the middle of the night and found he had lost his grip on everything and was left quite unrelated to life, dithering in the middle of this world of appearance, alone, alone. He turned over and caught hold of Erif Der. She was half awake, alone too, but in a different way. Her world was real enough still; but it had turned against her. She could not get far enough out of her own unhappiness to sympathise with his; wearily she let him kiss her and hug her close and tight. But it was less than no good, a mockery by stupid bodies, when their souls were withdrawn, each into its own void, too far away to make much effort, even to break through into ordinary life again.

They turned away. Erif began to try and recapture part of her world again; it seemed to her that the ring of safety

Sphaeros had unwittingly made round the Chief was not protecting Yersha. After a time she went to sleep, thinking of ways and means. But Tarrik lay quite still and astonished, almost afraid to move in case everything disappeared. If this went on there was no meaning in being Chief of Marob. He clutched for support at his godhead, being Corn King; but that seemed to be gone too; he was not even much interested in wondering what would happen to the crops. At last he quieted down to formulating a set of questions to ask Sphaeros the next morning.

He had forgotten that there was to be a gathering of the soldiers that day, and he had to be dressed up with crown and sword, bronze rings on neck and arms, and a round gold shield like the sun. He was angry and impatient, and knocked down one of his men, who had scratched him with the edge of his breast-plate. It was only when they brought his horse that he calmed down and mounted, and went out through the square seaward door of his house. The men were drawn up between the house and the harbour in a great mass, roughly divided into squares, after the universally admired fashion of the Macedonian phalanx, but without the Macedonian discipline. Almost all had bows, and nearly half were mounted. When he came out they all shouted and waved their bows, and the horses reared and kicked, and everything got into a tangle. He scowled at them, considering that they must at least be treated as real, and gave orders, cursed them or praised them, and had up the headmen and captains and told them what they were doing wrong, sharply and definitely, as befitted the Chief. They loved him for being like that, and thought the curse was well off him; at least most of them did. But Harn Der had many friends, and they had come to certain conclusions and had decided to stay by them. Yellow Bull had brought his men to the gathering, and had come up with the other captains to see the Chief. Tarrik caught sight of him, rather at the back, and suddenly called him forward. 'How is the road?' he said; 'I am not forgetting it, Yellow Bull. Give me time.' Yellow Bull thanked him awkwardly. Nobody else seemed to be thinking of his road; it always made him feel a curious love for the Chief when he talked of it, as if they were sharing some secret.

Sphaeros was trying to write; but the Chief's house was

not a really quiet place, except in Eurydice's rooms, which he was always doing his best to keep out of. When Tarrik came clamouring in, he sighed and gave it up in despair. 'Yes,' he said at last, 'this is the fear of Chaos, which is the first step to knowledge. I can cure you of fear.'

'Can you?' said Tarrik; 'it is something real after all?'

'It must be, or there would be nothing to know. Unless there were some standard, one could not even know that one does know. It is certain that the mirror image is less true than the thing itself, that the straightness of the rod is more proper to it than the crookedness we see in it when we look at it through water; so there must be degrees of unreality, until at last one comes down to certain appearances which are so undistorted that one may take them to be sure. It is these that seize upon the mind, and are in turn seized upon and turned into security: the Kataleptike Phantasia. They build the wall against unreality and the fearful place where a man may lose himself.'

'Yes,' said Tarrik, twisting a pen between his fingers until it broke, 'and what then?'

'If you have time and will listen,' said Sphaeros, 'I will try to explain.' Then he showed Tarrik how it all hung together, this fear of unreality and a rushing on nowhither without reason, and uncertainty, and unfulfilled desire for happiness that in itself is unobtainable; and he showed how man's will may be weaned from desire and folly, and made to go the way of nature, of things-as-they-are, not crossing the purpose of life, but going always with that reason that governs the movements of the stars and all the universe—through your own helping making yourself one with God.

'Yes,' said Tarrik suddenly, 'that is how I help the sun to grow the corn!'

Then Sphaeros spoke of the wills of kings, and how they, above all, should follow the good; and he talked of choice and duty, and the ways that are always open before any action. And he told Tarrik stories of kings, the wise and the unwise, and what came to their kingdoms. So they went on, day after day.

Tarrik found he was quite able to split himself into two people; one a Greek, who was an interested, if not always consistent, Stoic, with a vast amount of moral and philosophic curiosity which had never been satisfied before; and the other a barbarian god-king, who made the flax and wheat grow in a very small place called Marob, which nobody had ever heard of except wholesale merchants and ships' captains, whose beginnings had been odd and dubious and something to do with his dead father and a ceremonial feast, and whose end was better unthought of for the moment. This was all very amusing. But Tarrik was distinctly aware of Harn Der and the possibilities of something unpleasant. However he was fairly clear that his luck was back now—if all went well at Plowing Eve. And he had given orders to his guard, whom he knew to be faithful, to follow not too far behind when he went out. If it came to anything open, he backed himself against Harn Der and half the Council. As to Erif— well, she was queer and unanswering nowadays. He began to look about for something better, but only half-heartedly; for the moment his mind was not on women.

And then a small trading-ship came into harbour. She was a squat, patch-sailed creature, that every one knew; she used to trade up and down the coast, even in winter, from one small harbour to another, never getting far out, or taking risks. She was going south now, and would probably fetch up at Byzantium in about a month if the weather was possible. Sphaeros said: 'I must go.' And he went down to arrange with the captain.

Tarrik knew not only that Sphaeros must go, but also that he would. He did not say anything at once, nor did he follow his first impulse—to have the captain strangled quietly, or the ship sunk. He considered what was the Good, and when Sphaeros came back from the harbour he said: 'I think I might go to Hellas again.'

'Why?' said Sphaeros.

'In case there are more men like you,' said Tarrik, and the philosopher, in spite of himself, felt a curious glow of pleasure at the way of Nature here.

'But how can you leave your kingdom and your people, Charmantides?' he asked.

The Chief seemed to think it not too difficult. 'I shall give my powers to two others,' he said; 'the power over my people to one, and the power over seed-time and growing-time to a second. And I shall be back by summer. I want—'

he said, suddenly shy and looking away from Sphaeros, 'I want to see Kleomenes and Sparta!'

Sphaeros nodded. 'It could be done,' he said, 'but— think it over. Be sure of what you are doing, and do not be led by appearances or any sort of pride. I do not know if the Hellenes you make pictures of are even like the real Hellenes. I do not even know what Kleomenes is like now he is a man.' And Sphaeros sighed, with the knowledge that, whatever he was like, it would not be the eager-minded, strong boy he had said good-bye to that day in Sparta.

Tarrik had gone back to his old habit of talking things over with his aunt. Erif had been very good to talk to at first, but lately she had only made him feel a stranger, alone with her. He went to Eurydice's room now, and sat down beside her on a cushion; she stroked his hair and wanted to kiss him, but thought he might not like it much. He looked up at her. 'You're tired,' he said; 'your eyes—you can't have slept!'

She was so pleased to think he was noticing her looks again! 'Oh, it's nothing,' she said; 'I have not been sleeping well, that's all.'

'Why not?' said Tarrik. 'Would you like more music? Shall we see if anyone has a daughter who can sing?' He brightened up at the thought, and Eurydice smiled inside herself—or rather would have smiled but for this pricking, pinching feeling that had lasted over from her dream. There was something very unpleasant about the dream; she could not quite remember what; it seemed—ridiculous!—as if it had been about two-legged pins walking all over her, hairpins in fact. She shook it off; she was too old to have idiotic fancies. What was Charmantides saying now? 'So you see, aunt dear, I think it would be a reasonable thing to go.'

Reasonable! What long words the boy used nowadays!

'Yes,' she said; 'I have been wondering if this was what has been going on in your head these last days.' And that was true; she had wondered.

'It would be for six or seven months,' he said; 'till midsummer (may all go well with it!) and then—I shall be satisfied.'

'Hellas!' she sighed, and then, 'dear, shall I come with you?'

'No,' he said; 'not in winter. Perhaps—in spring, if you wanted to. Yes. You might like to join me then.'

'Spring on those hills!' she said, flushing a little. And then came another idea: 'Only—someone must take care of things when you are gone. Well, I must do that; it will be just like when you were a little boy, Charmantides!'

'Yes; but remember, Aunt Eurydice, I am not sure yet if it would be good. I must be clear it is not my own desires—oh, I must talk to Sphaeros again!' He jumped up and went out again, and walked up and down the garden, trying to make up his mind. Only he found that a big bough had fallen off the elm at the end, and this made a new way of climbing up—so he did climb up. And the serious course of his thought was somewhat broken.

He did think of consulting Erif that night. But she put it right out of his head. He found that she had made one of the guards bring in five crabs from the beach, and they were all in a ring on the floor, with the hungry, attentive look crabs always have, and they seemed to be watching her doing a dance for them in the middle of the room. He liked watching her dancing as well, so he sat down between two of the crabs, and waited very happily till she was finished with the first part of her dance, and, ignoring the original audience, began another for him. Very soon it was with him as well as for him, so much so that he felt it would be a waste to look for a new girl yet. He wondered just a little why she was so particularly delighted with herself, but he had better games to play with her that night than wondering, or even serious conversation.

But Eurydice was having bad dreams again, a very nasty, tangled kind, with hairpins walking accurately across them. 'Apphé,' she said, 'what can the matter be? I can't think!' Apphé, who was arranging a scarf across her shoulders, looked round crookedly and caught her mistress's eyes in the mirror. 'Can't you, my lady?' she said; 'I can. . . .' Eurydice shifted and gave a little gasp: 'Of course. And I never guessed. Well, Apphé, this time—I've come to the end of my patience. These tricks . . .' She twitched her dress down impatiently, looked critically at herself in the mirror, and beckoned to the maid to follow her out and across the Chief's house to Erif Der's big, yellow-walled room at the other side.

Erif Der was still in bed, lying with one arm under her cheek, and poking the torpid crabs. 'Oh,' she said, 'I wanted someone to take my crabs home. Will you tell Apphé to carry them down to the beach carefully, Aunt Eurydice?'

For half a minute there was an uncomfortable trickle of silence through the room: then Eurydice deliberately picked up one of the crabs and threw it against the wall: it was the smallest of them, and it was broken to bits. 'So,' she said.

Erif Der sat up suddenly, her face crimson with rage; she looked like a small child in her short, blue shift. 'You—you—' she gasped, 'get out of my room!' She picked up Tarrik's dagger and held it with the hilt against her own breast and the point at Eurydice's; then she got off her bed and moved forward.

'Take care!' said Eurydice sharply, 'you little savage!'

Erif Der looked at the remains of the crab, and then across at the other woman. 'How did you sleep last night?' she asked.

'You admit it, then!' said Eurydice. 'I thought so! Listen: Charmantides knows. He is sick of you. He is going away, and while he is gone I shall take his place. And I shall teach you yours.'

They were nearly at the door now, Erif Der still coming on with the dagger. 'He is not going!' she cried.

Eurydice turned and looked very bitterly at the girl. 'Ask him,' she said.

Chapter Seven

ERIF DER SAT DOWN again on her bed, and wondered if it was true. Supposing it was—it complicated things. She had decided that she was probably going to have a baby, but no one else knew, unless possibly Essro, whom she had asked, as casually as possible, about signs. But that was not so very important if—if this other thing was true; she would not want to tell him. By and bye her women came in to dress her. She never liked that, but the great cone and veil were difficult to put on for herself, and she had to wear them today for the feast after the Council meeting. Her father would be there; she might have to speak to him and Yellow Bull. Her dress was of thick felted wool, so stiff that it stood right away from her feet; it was embroidered all over with spirals of yellow cord, and she had a ring on every finger. That morning she looked rather pale, so they put her on some colour—a round, red spot on each cheek. There was nothing to do till the feast-time.

She sent the crabs down to the beach, and then she took the queen's keys and unlocked the treasure-room and went in, with lighted torches to stick in the sockets on the pillars. All along three walls there were bronze-bound chests, and hanging above them dresses and armour sewn with jewels and flat gold scales, and strung like onions from the rafters gold-faced skulls made into devils and guardians, with coral drops dangling from their necks in the way blood does when it is cold and sticky. There was another big, standing devil, too, in the middle of the room, facing the door, with black glass eyes and real teeth, and strings of tinkling egg-shells between his hands and the walls. But he would know the queen's keys, and Erif Der need not be afraid to touch him, nor to stand with her back to him, rummaging in the chests, choosing herself a new wand of tapered jade and a necklace of jade and lapis lazuli, very heavy and cold, to wear at the feast. When she was done, it was time to go to the hall, with all her women behind her, holding up branches of silver and coral and peacocks' feathers.

All rose to their feet as she came in and took her place at the north end of the table, with Tarrik at the south end. She sat in a very high chair, with steps and a pointed back of streaked marble. On the steps at each side was a girl child, one with tame doves sitting on a green bough, the other with a double flute, and a soft, monotonous tune to play, something to fill the deeps of Erif's mind while she was talking in the shallows. Round her were women, wives and daughters of the chief men in Marob, stiff and not very real in their hard, embroidered dresses, with the coloured cones on their heads, banded with gold and jewels. Yersha sat in a chair much like Erif's; she had powder and paint thicker than usual to hide the black rings round her eyes and the slight shrivelling back of tired lips. It seemed also as if she were finding it hard to keep still, as if something was suddenly pricking her from time to time.

Erif talked to the women and saw that the food and drink were plentiful, and graciously took and praised the small customary gifts they brought her, gay-coloured flowers made with waxed threads and silver wire and beads: because it was thought that this was a bad time of year for the Spring Queen, and she must be helped now, or she would not help Marob at Plowing Eve. While they were still eating it grew dark, and even when the lamps and torches were all alight, she could scarcely see down the table as far as Tarrik. She could not, at least, tell what he was talking about. He seemed excited, though, leaning forward, beating on the table, throwing himself back to laugh, open-mouthed. Sphaeros was close to him, little Sphaeros whom she half liked in spite of everything, and her father and brothers, all very fine and glittering. Once or twice Berris, who was nearest, had tried to catch her eye, but she always looked away in time. But if only she knew what they were talking about! This going away . . . She noticed, interestedly, that her heart was paining her, heaving suddenly outwards and then caught again, as if a hand were squeezing it. At first she thought that this must be someone else's magic, and angrily set her own on guard. But it was only herself.

At the end of the feast, as drink and talk and music began to break down the set pattern of behaviour in every one's mind, the men and women moved about, laughing with each other, though nothing more, because it was the Chief's house. Erif sat on in her chair, between the two girls, grimly, thinking that this way her father would have no chance of whispering. Sometimes she could hear Tarrik's voice—she listened for it. He had got up, was walking about, kissing any of the girls he fancied, lightly and easily. She wondered whether she minded this or not; on the whole perhaps a little—a very little. It was the other thing she would mind: if he went really away so that she could not even see him!

Berris came down the side of the hall, walking along the bench, just under the torches. The big room fitted itself together into a pattern, a criss-cross of yellow light in fat wedges, a layer of people's heads, moving and tiny, a layer of glow, hardened here and there to torch or lamp, and a last, most beautiful layer of hollowness and faint shimmer, and the great cross-beams reaching up into darkness and the heavy night pressing on the roof tiles of the Chief's house. The square heads of the men, the pointed heads of the women, ranged themselves exquisitely under his eyes; and there at the end was his sister, up in her big chair, pretending to be Spring Queen, with her white, smooth child's forehead, and soft lips. He came towards her quietly and leant over her chair before she was aware of him. She was much more startled than she ought to have been; her eyes went narrow and then wide with fear. 'It's only me,' said Berris; 'I haven't seen you—for days. Tell me, is it true Tarrik is going away?'

'I don't know,' she said very softly, looking straight in front of her.

'He was talking—and every one else—this evening. But he's not sure. It's as if he were doing it half against his will. Well, Erif, I suppose that's you?'

'Tell father what you like,' she said. 'Is he glad?'

But Berris shook his head. 'We do not talk of this now. I go my way by myself. Only—take care, Erif, I think father is doing without you now.'

She turned her head quickly, the shadows shifting across her face. 'Doing—what? Berris, who else is with him?'

'Tarrik knows the Council better than I do,' said Berris, low. Then: 'I wonder if he is really going to Hellas—again.'

'You would like to go with him, Berris.'

'Yes.'

'And so would I,' said Erif surprisingly. 'I should like to know if it is really Epigethes or Sphaeros.'

'Yes,' said Berris again, 'but you would hate not being able to magic them, Erif, whichever it was.'

'Magic,' she said, sitting there, still and small, 'my magic! I can't help myself. I can't be sure what's going to happen any more than you can when you start thinking of a golden beast.'

'Can't you?' said Berris, very close to her. 'I thought you had more power than mine.'

Erif looked down and round; suddenly she saw Apphé standing quite near to the other side of the throne, her head cocked like a hunched bird over her thick, brown-clothed body. 'Yes,' said Erif, rather louder, 'I have got more power—as much as I choose to take.'

But Berris went out of the hall, unsatisfied, back to his forge. He often slept there now, rather than at his father's house, sometimes with a slave-girl he had bought that autumn, an odd little savage, Sardu, brown and supple, from far north-east, beyond the Red Riders' country, with a flat, bony face and sidelong eyes, very black. Now that Erif was with him so little, he made this girl blow the fire and sort the sweepings from his bench; he used to draw her often, and taught her to sing his own songs, which were too bad for anyone else to hear.

Erif Der managed not to speak to her father or Yellow Bull; she and her women left the feast long before the men, who stayed very late, talking and drinking, so that she scarcely woke for Tarrik's coming. In the morning she wanted to ask her questions, but he was sound asleep, warm and satisfied looking. She got up and half dressed, and pulled back the shutters from the windows. It was calm and snowing lightly; but the snow did not lie yet, or scarcely at all, only here and there in the road, but not on the beach or the breakwater. As she looked, she saw a covered cart jolt round the corner and stop. Essro stepped out of it, looked round hastily, pulled the shawl over her ears, and ran towards the door of the Chief's house. Erif left her plaits half finished and ran too. They met in the half-dusk of the second hall. Essro's women came behind her, carrying baskets; she seemed more fluttered than ever. 'I'm come,' she said, with a short, anxious gasp, 'I'm come—with the things you asked me for, Erif—the herbs!' Erif, acutely aware that she had never asked Essro for any herbs, called her own maids to come and take the baskets and entertain her sister-in-law's people; then took Essro by the elbow and led her along to the little room at the head of the stairs. 'Now,' she said, 'tell me.'

Essro went close to her; there were still a few snowflakes not quite melted on the ends of her hair. 'If Tarrik is going,' said Essro, slowly and distinctly, 'let him go at once.' Erif felt suddenly sick and quivered down on to the floor, half lying; she did not answer. The other woman knelt beside her. 'What is it?' she said. 'Surely you knew?' Erif nodded, one hand over her throat. Essro pursed her lips, took the knife from her girdle, and touched Erif with the hilt, here and there.

The Spring Queen sat up, with the flashing smile of one

child to another. 'Thank you,' she said. 'Your magic: it never hurts you, Essro?'

'No. But perhaps it will. I am not so clever as you, Erif. Are you better?'

'Yes,' said Erif, then all at once: 'That was—you know—Tarrik's child.'

'Oh!' said Essro, clasping her hands, 'oh, they don't know that!'

'Who don't?' said Erif sharply. 'Essro—where did you get that message?'

'From Yellow Bull. Oh, I must go home!'

'But why? Essro, stay! Was it—is it—is Yellow Bull warning Tarrik because of the road? Because Tarrik gave him a sacrifice? Is father going to do something?'

'Yes,' said Essro, with shifting, panicky eyes, 'tell him! And—oh, Erif—shall I tell them about the baby?'

'No!' said Erif, and put her hand for a moment on the hilt of Essro's dagger, 'if I need help I will go to you and your magic.'

'Help?' said Essro, trembling, trying to go away, and yet always gentle.

'Yes,' said Erif, 'help. A secret road.'

Tarrik sat about, sleepy and strong, while his men dressed him; every now and then he stretched himself largely and yawned, with the colour-stitched white linen of the shirt loose round his neck and wrists. Then they had to stop and stand aside till he was ready, one holding his boots, another with fur coats over his arm for the Chief to choose from if he liked, spotless soft fox and deer pelts, with clean linings of scarlet or black. Tarrik took one at random, knowing they all suited him. He was rather angry with Erif for not being there when he woke; he wanted to talk to her about his plans—if she was in a mood for talk. Even with Sphaeros to advise him—and, now he remembered it, how little positive advice Sphaeros ever gave!—he had been unable to make up his mind about which course was the wisest. He was somehow afraid that if he went it would be merely a flight from uncertainty: Harn Der, and Plowing Eve, and his wife. Suddenly, without noticing how un-Stoic he was being, he made up his mind that he would ask Erif, and if she really wanted him to stay he would stay—because then something would be certain!

He went to the window, as he did every morning, and held out his hands eastwards to the risen sun, which, even behind clouds, as now, must know his brotherhood. Then he sent one of the men to find his Queen and ask her if she would come to him. She came at once, in a long, plainish dress of grey wool checks, and the fur of her coat bordered with heavy silver tissue. He thought it made her look old till he saw how wonderfully glossy her plaits were, hanging over it, and how clear her pale skin showed above the tight, round neck of the dress. 'Erif,' he said, 'I thought of going to Greece with Sphaeros.' She nodded, facing the fact but not his eyes. 'I want to see the King of Sparta,' he went on, 'and learn if there are not other ways of ruling besides mine.' He took her hands and pulled her gently down till she was sitting on his knee; she put her arms round his neck and hid her face in the hollow of his shoulder.

'You mean to go—soon?' she asked, sorting out her words so as to get no trace of feeling into them.

He tried to look at her face, but she clung tight, with hard wrists and fingers and her forehead butting into him. 'Quite soon,' he said, 'if I do go. Erif—shall I?'

She felt his live, powerful heart beats under her cheek as she lay against him; for a moment she could not bear to separate herself from them. Tarrik was almost sure he would not have to go, and was glad. He put his arms right round her, for his, for certainty. His lips bent to her round, soft head, the baby hairs at the back of her neck that would not stay in any plait. She did not move; only she said: 'Yes, you should go.'

The voice was very soft, and yet so clear that he was quite sure he had heard right. He tried once more. 'Erif, do you want me to go?'

It was she who was startled now; she had not thought there was all this on his side of it; he almost got the no out of her. But at last she said: 'Yes, Tarrik.' Then she went quite still again, afraid of the time when his arms must loosen and let her go.

This being so, Tarrik said he would go the next day. He stirred himself and every one else to prodigious energy. They swirled round Erif in a sea of life and action. She was just left in the middle of it, half dead and small and useless. Tarrik summoned the Council. He seemed mad

enough now to justify them all. 'My aunt is to have the
power of the Chief,' he said, and Eurydice came in and
stood beside him, stiff and tall and smiling thinly; she gave
almost every man in the Council the feeling that she was his
aunt too. Harn Der was not badly pleased; this would not
be too difficult to deal with. He could not think that there
was anyone nowadays who would not rather have him as
Chief than Eurydice. But who was to be Corn King? Till
he knew that, Harn Der was not prepared to say anything.
Tarrik was speaking of what had to be done while he was
away, urging the Council to look on his aunt as himself,
advise her well and obey her orders, remembering that he
himself would be back by midsummer. At last he ended:
'As to the Corn King. I lend my godhead to Yellow Bull,
son of Harn Der. Let him come to me and take what I give
him an hour before dawn tomorrow. And I give him full
leave to take a tenth of men and money from Marob for
the secret road. And I warn him to do this soon.'

For a moment this was too much to believe. Harn Der and
Yellow Bull and their friends could not help staring at one
another before the shouting started; it seemed impossible
to be so favoured. Tarrik put his hand on to his shirt over
Erif's star, and looked at them all with a very clear vision.
Then he smiled and sat down. It suddenly occurred to Harn
Der that perhaps this was all Erif's doing, and for the first
time for weeks he was pleased with his daughter.

Tarrik did not even go to bed that night. Erif Der lay
alone, waiting for him; after about three hours she fell
asleep. But he was not in the house at all: he was in
his other house, at the far end of Marob, where he was
no more Chief, but Corn King and god. It had been
cold going there, and very dark, with a few snowflakes
falling out of nothing. Inside it was still cold, but airless,
choking under the low stone roof. He took his own clothes
off, as he had to, chewing bitter berries all the time,
and put on the long, red robes, straight from neck to
ankles; the stuff was damp and harsh against his skin. He
shivered and put on the head-dress and mask, dark polished
squares of jet and carbuncle and onyx, the blood-red coral,
the upright corn ears, the Single Eye on his forehead.
He went into the inner place; the guardian, an old, old
woman, crouched in a corner. He stood over her and

passed his hand three or four times in front of her face; she slept.

Tarrik took another mouthful of berries, and lighted the lamp over the stone. He did not much like what he was going to do; but it was only till midsummer, and besides he was a pupil of Sphaeros. He tried to think of it all in Greek, but there were no words for half of it. At any rate, this would be Yellow Bull's pay at Plowing Eve. He took down the Plowshare, blew on it, and wrote in the mist his breath had made. He did the same thing with the Cup and the Sieve, and he undid certain very important knots in the Basket. Last of all he took off his head-dress, and ran a tiny nail into it, so that it would just scratch the ear of the next wearer. He took great care not to touch the point of the nail himself. When that was done, he took off the red robes and got into his own clothes again; it had all taken a long time, and they were cold like a deserted nest.

The next two hours he spent with his head-men at the real, the Chief's house; they were making him up bales and chests of precious things to take with him. He would come to Hellas as a Power! There were twenty he had bidden make ready to come with him, young men, strong and faithful, all free and of the noble blood of Marob. He gave them everything they wanted, armour and money and fine clothes. They were all sad at leaving their horses. But it was not to be for long. When he came back, he would know how to be a real, Stoic king.

Yellow Bull came as he had been told, an hour before dawn. He and Tarrik went together the way the Chief had already been. They talked about the secret road and how much could be done on it, even in winter. 'I will make a good road, Chief, I swear I will!' said Yellow Bull. 'Yes,' said Tarrik gently, 'I am sure of you.' They were close to the other place now; in a few houses people were stirring; they could see a sudden line of light behind the shutters, the first thin fighting against the night. Yellow Bull suddenly found his eyes full of tears. 'Nobody else believed in my road,' he said, 'and now—' But Tarrik laid a hand on his arm, and there they were at the door.

Half the town was down at the harbour next morning, with much lamentation. Many of them had brought presents for the Chief to take with him. He had very wisely decided that it would be better to go in the trader rather than in his own state ship, which was much faster and very beautiful, but would not stand continuous bad weather. He walked quickly, with one arm across Sphaeros' shoulders; they both wore long fur coats and thick boots. The Chief had left his crown for Eurydice, and he was bare-headed, but had a fur hood to put on later if he wanted it. He and his men were all in a bunch together, full of movement and life and warmth under their heavy coats. The Spring Queen and her women came separately from the great door, chill and downcast, to say good-bye. And the Council, with Berris Der and a few others, waited on the breakwater for the Chief to pass. There was not wind enough to sail by, but the rowers were ready; the sky was low and grey over the ship, and the sea grey and scarcely rocking against the harbour walls.

Berris had only heard that morning. The evening of the feast he had not taken it very seriously—he was thinking of his sister. And the day after he had ridden away into the country to draw trees. He had found elms and limes and ashes standing on the bare plain, and he had been so fascinated by the tangles of their black arms that he had stayed there till sunset; and after that he went straight back to the forge, not to his father's house. He still could not quite realise that Tarrik was going. All these last months he had seen very little of the Chief, but somehow the assurance that he was there had been enough. It seemed to Berris that when he had made something supreme he would show it to Tarrik and everything would be right again. In the meantime he was not sure what he was after; he had done scarcely any solid work, only sketches and a little jewellery and ironwork just to keep his hand in. Since he had found out the truth about Epigethes and the wire keys, he had gone back entirely to his own mind for form and pattern, but now, while Sphaeros had been in Marob, the Hellenic ideas had come softly back and ranged themselves before him, vague and straight and beautiful. For certainly this Sphaeros hated the house of Leonidas in Sparta, and it seemed clear to Berris that it must have been full of just the kind of things that Epigethes liked: that he had liked himself ever so long—nearly a whole year—ago. But what did Sphaeros like? He never could make out, and found it quite impossible to believe what the Stoic assured him was the truth: that these things did not appear to him sufficiently real or important to give him any very great pleasure one way or the other. Now Tarrik and Sphaeros were both going! He stood on the edge of the breakwater, watching the slaves go past with all the things the Chief was taking with him; every time a man went by it seemed as if a bit of himself were going too.

The Chief was talking to his Council now. It occurred to Berris that probably he had the loudest voice of anyone in Marob. Or was it only that he did not care how much he let himself go? The men were all on board now; the ship was only waiting for Tarrik. He was saying good-bye; they gave him the salute, knife and hand. And last, Erif.

She did not know what to say; she wanted to show him some sign. Because love is so much an affair of giving yourself away, by word, or look, or touch. But here, in the middle of this crowd—she had not even told him about the child. If she had: well, if she had he might have stayed. And she wanted him to go: out of danger. 'Till summer,' he said, 'till the fine days and the warm sun, Erif!' And questioned her with his eyes. But she could not answer. Only she put her hand up on to his breast, hurriedly, clumsily, in under his coat and there was the hard flat lump her star made below his shirt. 'Look for me here!' she said. 'It will tell you—if I live or die. Tarrik, I will be faithful to you!' He looked down at her hand, then straight at her face; he held her at arm's length, searching, searching. She dropped her eyes. 'Give me something!' she said low, then, as he hesitated, not knowing what would work, she pulled the onyx-handled hunting knife out of its sheath. 'If this clouds,' she said, 'you are in danger.' She dared not say more, for fear of saying too much. They kissed each other under the eyes of the crowd, a bad, short kiss. Tarrik turned to the sea and the ship.

He saw Berris Der standing on the edge. 'Good-bye, Berris!' he said, holding out both hands, smiling. But to Berris it seemed quite impossible to say good-bye all in a minute; he had far too much to talk about. 'Good luck, Berris,' said the Chief again, 'good luck and good-bye!' But, 'Oh,' said Berris, 'I'm coming too!' And he jumped on to the ship and Tarrik jumped after him, shouting: 'Cast off, cast off!' And so they went to sea.

Erif Der fainted into the arms of two of her women. A very proper display of feeling, every one thought. When she came to, she refused to go back to the Chief's house and her quiet room. She went instead to the Spring-field, that place of her own that she had just as the Corn King had his. It was barred now, and lightless, till winter was past, but she went in and stayed there while it was day, and came out a little happier; she had done what she could to give Tarrik a good wind and fair weather for his journey.

Harn Der was partly horrified and partly relieved at what Berris had done. It was a foolish and dangerous thing, but, on the other hand, in some ways it made their plans easier if they had not got someone with them who might suddenly change sides—Berris had been as uncertain as all that lately. As it was, he had always wanted to go to Greece, and now he was going. Artists are difficult people to have in a family. And about Erif. 'I wonder why she fainted like that?' said Yellow Bull thoughtfully.

'She may be going to have a child,' said Harn Der.

'Essro ought to have told me.'

'Women like their own secrets, my son. But—if she is—well, I think it must be dealt with. If Tarrik is to go, no use not doing it thoroughly.'

'Will she mind?' asked Yellow Bull, doubtful.

'She married him with her eyes open. She has no business to mind. Better for her to get clear of it all. And even if she does mind, it will have to be done; she must know that as well as we do.'

'Better not speak of it to her.'

'If she had done what I meant and worked her magic better it would never have happened. But women are like that, even the cleverest.'

'Yes. Father, it is a queer thing being Corn King suddenly like this. He took me to the House—. Is it strange for you too, your son being God?'

Harn Der rubbed his fingers through his beard; he had not got that sort of mind. 'No,' he said, 'not very strange. I shall not feel it strange when I am Chief, either. I give Yersha about four months.'

'Yes,' said Yellow Bull, 'and there will be a Council

meeting tomorrow, father? I can start at once on the secret road!'

That evening Eurydice was looking at herself in the mirror; she wore the crown of Marob, and she thought she looked like a man. She felt like a man, at any rate, full of power. This was her time. And then she thought of Charmantides, and how pleasant it would be if he were to come back from Hellas this summer with a wife, some charming, modest, well-born girl, so that there should be more Greek blood in the line of the chiefs of Marob. A girl who would be a little frightened of the north, the cold and the snow and the savagery, and who would come to her aunt for protection and kindness and love. . . . If a messenger were sent out to assure him that Erif Der was dead. If she was really dead. It would be for every one's good. Erif Der and her magic dead and done with.

On the ship, out of sight of land, Tarrik had supper early among his friends, with Sphaeros on one side and Berris on the other. He loved them both—and all this company of men, free and singing and his own to command! He was happy and very tired. Not long after it was full dark, he stood up and bade good night to them all, and to Berris. 'I'm glad you came,' he said, 'it was you I wanted all the time. God, I am sleepy—I was doing things all last night. Take anything you want from my stores, Berris—anything. If I'm still asleep, come and wake me at sunrise. We shall be that nearer Hellas. Good night, Sphaeros, and good dreams, sleeping or waking!'

Erif Der was alone in the Chief's house. She had all the lamps alight in her room, and the shutters open too; it was still enough for that. She sat on the edge of her bed, undressed, with a fur rug pulled round her, clutched under her chin. There was no one in the room, nothing to hurt her. But still she sat there, quite quiet, watching and listening, very white.

PART II

Philylla and the Grown-ups

I had a little nut tree,
Nothing would it bear
But a silver nutmeg
And a golden pear.

The King of Spain's daughter
Came to visit me,
And all for the sake of
My little nut tree.

NEW PEOPLE IN THE SECOND PART

Greeks
Kleomenes III, King of Sparta
His wife Agiatis, widow of King Agis IV
His children, Nikomedes, Nikolaos and Gorgo
His mother, Kratesikleia
His stepfather, Megistonous
His brother, Eukleidas
His foster-brother, Phoebis
His friend, Panteus
Philylla
Her father, Themisteas
Her mother, Eupolia
Her younger sister, Ianthemis
Her younger brother, Dontas
Her foster-mother, Tiasa
Therykion, Hippitas, and other Spartiates
Deinicha and other Spartiate girls
Panitas, Leumas, Mikon and other helots or
  non-citizens, their women and children
Aratos of Sicyon
Lydiades of Megalopolis
Spartans, Argives, Athenians, Megalopolitans,
  Rhodians and others

People of Marob
Kotka, Black Holly and other men of Marob

IN A FIELD NEAR Sparta there were three children with
bows and arrows shooting at a stone mark, roughly painted
as a man with a shield. It was winter—you could scarcely
call it the beginning of spring yet—and the grass had been
cropped close by the beasts. At the high end of the field were
twenty old olive trees, lifting grey, beautiful heads to any
sun there was; through them a goat-path, trodden hard,
led down from upland pastures to the city. All round the
field there was a stone wall, and beyond, on three sides,
the still jagged mountains of Sparta.

The two younger children, a little girl and a still smaller
boy, were looking crossly at their big sister; they wanted
to play, and she was making it into work. They were chilly
as well; she had made them leave off their warm cloaks,
and the cold crept up their bare arms and legs, and under the
thin wool of their indoor tunics. 'A real bowman,' she had
said, 'mustn't let anything interfere with his shooting.' And
when they protested that they weren't real bowmen, she said
then they mustn't shoot with her bows and arrows: so they
had to be. But she'd always been like that, and it was worse
than ever now she was maid of honour to the Queen.

They had to shoot in turns, standing a long way from
the mark, so that they hardly ever hit it, which was dull,
and they had to watch their arrows and find them, and
between times they had to stand quite still and not drop
their bows. It was unbearable; by and bye the little boy,
Dontas, rebelled. 'You said it was going to be a game!'

His big sister looked at him scornfully. 'That was only
to get you to come,' she said, and her nose tilted at him.
'This is much better than a game.'

'It's not!' said the others, both together, and the small
girl suddenly began to cry: 'You've cheated us, Philylla!
You said we were going to like it and we don't!'

'It's better than any game,' said Philylla in an excitement which somehow disregarded them. 'It's real! We're all real Spartans now. I'm teaching you.'

'We don't want you to teach us, do we, Dontas?' She appealed to the boy, who nodded, frowning as hard as he could. 'You aren't grown up any more than me, and besides we're Spartans already!'

The big one tossed her head and made a comprehensive face at them. 'That sort of Spartan—very likely! That pay other people to do their fighting for them!'

'Well, you can't fight anyway,' said the boy rashly, 'you're only a girl, Philylla. I'm tired of playing with girls.'

Then he bolted, but not in time. Philylla suddenly losing the temper she had so admirably kept till then, jumped at him, and caught him almost at once, and shook him and hit him with her fists. 'I'm not a girl!' she said; 'you shan't call me that! I'm a soldier! I'm a Spartan! I shan't ever let you touch my bows and arrows again!'

The boy squealed and kicked, ineffectively, because his feet were bare; the little girl encouraged him shrilly from behind, but was too cautious to let her hair come within grab of Philylla's long arm. This went on for a minute or two, till Philylla suddenly felt she was being a bully, and let go.

Dontas broke away a yard or two, then stood, with his face red. 'Keep your silly bow!' he said. 'When I'm a man you'll be married and you won't be allowed to do anything!'

'Baby!' said Philylla bitterly; 'cry-baby, go home and play!'

The small girl, afraid it would start again, pulled Dontas back, whispering to him; elaborately not saying good-bye, they took their cloaks and went trotting off towards the town.

Philylla picked up her bow, talking to herself out loud. 'I won't marry,' she said; 'the Queen won't want me to. I'll be a soldier.' And she began to shoot again, from still further off. She stood solidly with her white tunic pulled up through the belt to clear her knees; she had grey eyes and a small, obstinate mouth and chin, and her hair was tied up tight on the top of her head in a knot that overflowed into jumping, yellow curls. When she hit the mark, which was not always, she would suddenly boil over with a terrific, secret excitement; she sprang straight up into the air and yelled: she had killed an enemy! The headless arrows made a little click against the stone; she wanted a louder noise and thought she would ask the Queen to tell her father she could have a spear. A spear and a horse . . . and never get married, never want men making love to her like all the other sillies of maids of honour! She was nearly the youngest, but she knew the Queen liked her better than almost any of them; and she—she wished that stone was one of the Queen's enemies, one of the people who said horrid things about her. There!—she'd hit him full in the heart.

After a time the King and Panteus came down the goat-path out of the hills; it was a safe place to talk secrets in, and Kleomenes had plans in his head enough to set all Sparta by the ears. Even now, Panteus was only just understanding; but he was excited, so wildly excited that he kept on stumbling over stones and olive roots and talking in jerks, not finishing his sentences. The King was excited too, but he showed it less, hardly at all unless to a person who knew him very well, who could see that queer, blind, blazing look behind his eyes, and the corners of his mouth twitching a very little with the force of the images that were tearing through his mind. They both stopped at the edge of the olives, suddenly aware of the child below them, shooting and shouting all by herself in the field.

Each smiled at the other, secretly, a moment's check to the unbearable torrent of their excitement. The King put his hand up to his mouth and gave a hunter's call down to the child. She jumped round to face it, still and startled, the bow held tight to her breast. Then with her free hand she swept up the loose arrows from the grass beside her and ran towards the olives, her eyes on the King, wondering what was happening now. He looked tired, she thought, leaning one way on his long spear, with the other arm round his friend's neck. Both had tunics of fine wool, deep red, wine-coloured almost. She remembered the stuff being dipped by the Queen's women, the first day she came to the house; the bitter smell of the dye, the maids of honour making faces at it behind the Queen's back, and Agiatis herself with the red dripping off her arms, down from the elbows, a tiny smear on her neck. . . .

'Well,' said the King, smiling at her, 'what are you doing that for?'

She looked down, fingering the bow, not wanting to answer.

Panteus helped her out, asking gravely: 'Are you a soldier?'

She nodded. 'The Queen lets me. And—I do really try!'

'I saw that,' said Kleomenes, 'but don't your friends come with you?'

'My brother and sister were with me to begin with; but they wouldn't go on. They're babies.'

'But the maids of honour?'

'Oh no! They won't start, they're grown-up!'

'And you're just half-way between, so it's all right?'

Philylla suddenly got shy and couldn't answer him; she thought that was it, but didn't want to say so. He was a grown-up too!

Again Panteus came to the rescue: 'May I look at your arrows?' he said. She handed them over silently. 'You don't always hit the mark, do you?' She shook her head and he picked out three or four of the arrows. 'These aren't straight,' he said. 'Look. Where did you get them?'

She was almost crying but could not bear them to see; she took the arrows and broke them across her bare knee, ducking her head over them so as to hide her eyes.

'Who made them?' said Panteus again.

'I did,' she said at last, scraping her finger hard along the bowstring.

Panteus was really unhappy; she was so like a boy, standing there among her broken things. 'One always makes a few crooked ones at first,' he said. 'I did. There's nothing to cry about.'

'I'm not crying,' said Philylla indignantly, and turned round to the King. 'Sir,' she said, 'I want to tell you—if I can ever help you, do say! The Queen—she said I might speak if I saw you—and—she told me what you're doing, how everything's going to be splendid again! Some of them don't like it, but I do, and—I do wish I could help.'

'You may yet, Philylla,' said the King gravely, 'and thank you. We shall want every true heart. Now, run on and tell the Queen we are coming.'

'I will,' she said, and ran, her thick cloak in one hand, dragging out behind her, strongly, like a flag. Her heart was full of mixed pleasure at her own daring in speaking to the King and getting that answer from him, and shame at having made bad arrows, and the man thinking she was crying. Yet he was a good man, he hadn't laughed; and the King had looked tired. She had noticed that; she was beginning to know about grown-ups. Only, did he think she was crying . . .? Hot and cold, hot and cold, Philylla ran down the goat-path, back to the Queen, whom she loved.

But those last words of hers had sent the King and Panteus racing back to the overwhelming thrill of their plans. Only first Panteus had asked who the child was, 'because she seems like part of the new things.'

'Philylla, daughter of Themisteas,' the King answered. 'My wife chose her. In three years she will be breaking hearts all round her.'

'She doesn't think of that yet,' said Panteus, and then again they looked at each other secretly, flashingly, because in three years Sparta was to be all different!

The King sighed a little, saying to his friend: 'I wish Sphaeros was here. He should have got my letter.'

Philylla found them all out in the courtyard, and stopped a moment, feeling it all so poised that she must not break into it, however gently. The King's mother, Kratesikleia, was sitting on the step, telling stories to her grandchildren; she had been very tall as a young woman, but now she was much bent, though it was somehow softly, as though less with age than with much stooping over cradles. Her hair was done high in a shining silver knot; below it the skin was finely wrinkled over the strong bones of her face. Her eyes were black and bright like a bird's, and her hands very small; she used them a great deal in talking, and they always impressed her hearers. Even now the children were looking at them rather than at her face, as though the story came from them. There was a great red cushion behind her, and she leant forward from it as if she were going to leap out of the picture, or so it seemed to Philylla, into that tremendous, obsessing future that they all kept at the back of their minds.

The two youngest children sat crouched beside her, listening hard. The baby girl was quite still except for her cheeks and lips sucking at her finger, and a rhythmical curving and straightening of her toes, as if some current of thick air were passing over them. The five-year-old boy had a hovering smile and his dark eyes looked far out, as though he were meditating some mischief—again for the future! Those two were like their father and grandmother, but the eldest, who was almost more than a child, who was nearly eight and would go to his class—if—if the classes were started again!—he was like his mother, with thick, silky-soft hair, lighter than his sunbrowned skin, and clear grey eyes, and lips that shut firmly over any secret. He saw Philylla coming in and smiled at her silently; they were great friends.

But it was his mother that Philylla turned to. There was almost twenty years between them, but yet the girl felt there was no separation for them, none of the natural aloofness between two generations. It had all flowered in this last six months; the Queen was more to her now than her own mother could ever be again, or her own sister for that matter. The thing had happened completely.

Agiatis was standing sideways to the others, with a piece of embroidery in her hands, the edge of a purple soldier's cloak for her husband. She was still one of the most beautiful women in Sparta; perhaps it was partly this that made the twenty years seem such a small thing. Her hair, that Philylla loved to comb and plait when it was her turn, was almost covered by a close net of blue and silver cords. She wore the Dorian dress of plain wool, summer-bleached white, her own weaving. There were no ornaments at all; even the shoulder brooches were only silver, worked in a dullish pattern, and her ear-rings the same. Philylla admitted to herself dispassionately that Agiatis had very little eye for clothes, but then they didn't interest her nowadays—why should they?—and it didn't matter, for she was the right height and figure to look splendid in these simple things. Only: the child wondered for the hundredth time why they had ever called her Agiatis the Merry-minded. If one knew her well, of course—but just to see her and speak with her, it was the last thing one would say. Fifteen years ago she might have seemed very different, but surely not so different as all that! She stood there now, in her own house, looking at her own beautiful children; and yet she looked sad. Sad, but not minding it, Philylla thought again, and then suddenly jumped and shook herself, and ran into the court with her message.

The picture broke at once into movement and noise and the present, but Agiatis was smiling now, the special, very soft smile she had for Philylla, that deepened again into something even more essential when the child spoke of her husband and Panteus. 'And I told him!' she said, her eyes bright and cheeks pink with running, 'about wanting to help. I think he was pleased.'

'I'm sure he was,' said the Queen; 'there aren't so many to say it. Not among the women, at least.'

'No,' said Philylla slowly, thinking of the other maids of honour, 'they are silly, aren't they. I don't know why.'

The Queen smiled at her. 'You will though, Philylla. When things turn simple, women have to give up much more than men. Because they live in shadow, by mystery.'

'I see,' said Philylla doubtfully, not seeing, 'but they won't be when I'm grown up, will they? I don't like it!' And unconsciously she moved further out towards the middle of the court, full into the winter sunlight.

It was not every day she could go out into the fields and be a Spartan in her own way. The next morning she had to be indoors, with the others, weaving. She did not like this much; for one thing Agiatis always wanted them all to sing the old weaving-songs while they worked, but none of them liked to except Philylla, and she had an uncertain ear and more uncertain voice; so she was never allowed to sing. They talked instead, the elder ones about love and clothes, and occasionally politics, the younger ones about food and lessons and games and one another. And both the sets had, of course, that particular source of interest or annoyance, Agiatis, the Queen. The thing she was trying to do now was to train them for the dances again: as if anyone wanted even to think about those horrible, dim gods now! Two or three of the older girls were talking about that now, under cover of their looms, all rather horrified. 'What does she think the good of them is if they aren't real!' That was

Deinicha, a pretty, spoilt girl of sixteen, with fluffy hair and her finger-nails pink and polished. 'It's not right. If she goes on, she may make them come real. And Artemis—' 'I know. Some of the little ones like pretending they're doves or bears; they may make up some goddess of their own to fit the songs to, nothing like the old ones anyhow! But I can't bear playing with these things. They've had too much power. And besides, if—if one has any feeling—one doesn't look there for help!' The other nodded and made a sign with her hand, something un-Greek enough. The Spartiate women imported their gods in the same ship with fine muslins from Egypt, or scents and hair-wash from Syria. At home in Hellas there were only charms, and little godlings for luck in love or housekeeping.

They went on to talk of their perennial grievance, the clothes Queen Agiatis made the girls about her wear, their own weaving even, as if there were no such things as trade and good money in Sparta and lovely stuff over-seas, patterned and delicate, for soft skins and subtle colouring. But she wouldn't even let them have powder, let alone all the possible small hints they knew they could use so cleverly, the lengthened line, the different tinting, that gave mere nature the mystery and attraction of art. It was all very well for her, with her husband and children and no one daring to laugh at her whatever she chose to look like. But her poor maids of honour, wasting all their best years at this extraordinary Court, while their sisters and cousins were enjoying themselves, and getting lovers, and living a life that you could call life! Well, the only comfort was, it couldn't last. Or . . . could it? One of the helot women came in, with a huge grin and her arms full. The girls all stopped and ran up to her or looked round the corners of their looms. 'Who's the lucky one?' they said, and one or two blushed and giggled self-consciously. But the woman, with as nearly a wink as was consistent with their dignity as the Queen's girls, went over to the little ones and dumped her things on the bench beside Philylla, who was so really surprised that some of the others thought she must be acting. 'Oh!' she said, 'are you sure? It's not my birthday! Did mother send them?' 'Oh yes!' said the woman, chuckling, and nudged her. 'There you are, my lamb!'—it was a tablet, stringed, and sealed with red—'now you write something pretty back.' But Philylla was more interested in the presents than the letter. There was a great bunch of violets, sweet ones, blue and white, mixed with pink sprigs of daphne, and a rush box of honey-cakes sprinkled with cinnamon, and a bunch of arrows. She looked at them for a minute—they were light, but real grown-up ones with bone points; and last of all, in a cage of withies, a smart and glossy magpie, long-tailed and bright-eyed, that hopped towards her. Now the point of this, as all the older girls knew, but Philylla didn't, was that a magpie was the one fashionable present just now from admirer to admired. They were usually taught to say some special phrase, not always very proper. The others all crowded round. 'Take him out, Philylla! What does he say? Pretty bird, then, pretty bird!' The magpie was very tame and friendly and sat on Philylla's shoulder as she stood there, stiff and pink with pleasure and some pride, but he didn't say anything, only whistled, cocking his jolly head at them. 'But who's it from?' they clamoured. 'Who is he? Why haven't you told us, sly thing?' 'But I don't know,' said Philylla, dreadfully confused, fingering the tablet. 'Read it then,' said Deinicha. 'Read it aloud, there's a love.' They all tried to peep over her shoulder, and she couldn't bear to open it there in the middle of them; she wanted to run away by herself. 'But read it!' they cried at her, so excited that they were nearly pulling it out of her hand. She wriggled up to the wall and jerked at the seal; it was quite easy to read—she had been rather afraid it might be difficult. It was quite short. 'Panteus to Philylla, greeting! Here are four things. Tell me which you like best. I think it will be the one I hope.' She rubbed it out quickly with her finger; but still the others had seen it and repeated it to one another. They were more than a little surprised and jealous. 'Panteus! Well, you're flying high! Lucky little minx! How did you get your claws into him? What does the King say? Panteus indeed, why didn't you tell us?' 'But,' said Philylla, 'I can't help it! I really and truly didn't know. I've only just seen him.' 'You must write a letter back,' said Deinicha firmly, 'and no baby nonsense, Philylla; you've got to do us credit—though you've done very well so far!' she added handsomely. Philylla looked at the things again. Clearly it wasn't the flowers or the cakes—though they were very nice!—it must be the arrows: because of what he had said about her own. And they were lovely arrows, a whole dozen of them, with stiff goose-feathers to make them fly. She would be able to shoot all sorts of big beasts now, deer even. But all the same she did love the magpie.

She took the tablets and began to write slowly. 'Philylla, daughter of Themisteas, to Panteus, son of Menedaios (she was going to do it properly!), greeting. I thank you with all my heart for the four things. I think you want me to like the arrows best. They are beautiful and straight and I will shoot with them. But I do like the magpie too.' She thought a moment, then decided to be really truthful, and made the last sentence into 'I like the magpie best.'

Deinicha took the tablet and read it, then shrieked with laughter and fluttered her hands. 'Philylla, you baby, you weren't going to send that! Do remember you're thirteen years old and one of us! Rub it all out—we'll tell you what to say.'

'I won't,' said Philylla solidly.

'But—my dear child—what will he think of it? You'll never keep him! You must put something in— well, a little pretty. This is the sort of letter you'd write to a brother. Poor things, one must give them a little encouragement!'

Philylla hugged the tablets to her, very red and uncomfortable, feeling partly that Deinicha must know what one ought to do, and partly that, after all, if it was really true that Panteus liked her, it was her own affair. 'He doesn't want to be encouraged.'

'Oh, is it as bad as all that—?' They all giggled.

'I hate encouraging people!' said Philylla, stamping. 'You're making it all horrid. Take this and go!' She turned and half shouted at the helot woman, shoving her out. Then she ran to the bench and her things. 'If you talk about it any more, you shan't have any of my cakes!' The rest subsided laughing at her behind the looms, and whispering to one another. She was fondling the magpie, and talking low to it, soothing her hot cheeks with the cold black and white of its wing feathers, offering it a bit of her cake; and the tame bird flirted with her, hopping from her shoulder to its own cage-top, and back, whistling its odd, half-human tune over and over again.

That evening she came to the Queen with a thick garland of violets on her own head, and two in her hand, one for Nikomedes, the eldest child, who could scarcely keep it on his head for wanting to take it off and smell it, and the other—if she would!—for the Queen.

'Where did you get them, lamb?' said Agiatis, surprised, stooping her head to be crowned.

Philylla explained. 'And I may keep the magpie, mayn't I? I do love him! I'm afraid we ate all the cakes; there were just enough to go round.'

'Yes, of course keep him. But—sweetheart—are you old enough for all this?'

'All what?'

'Well,' said the Queen, smoothing Philylla's hair between her finger-tips, wondering how much to say or leave unsaid, 'why did Panteus send you the presents?'

Philylla frowned and tried to get it clear to herself. 'Because he wanted to show me he really thinks I'm grown up, in spite of having talked to me in the field as if I was a cry-baby!'

'You haven't spoken to him before?'

Philylla shook her head. 'I've seen him often, of course—with the King.' Then, suddenly bold: 'Do you love him too?'

Agiatis sat down on one end of the bench, clasping her knee and leaning forward, suddenly very young looking, so much so that Philylla felt, quite rightly, that for all intents they were the same age, and sat down too, quite close to the Queen, so that she could reach over and stroke her arm. Agiatis said suddenly, 'I do love him. You see, Kleomenes has been very unhappy—I'm telling you this just for yourself—first when he was a boy, with that horrible father, and afterwards too. I couldn't make him happy at first, because my heart was shut up with the dead ones, my baby, and Agis. That's all come straight now, but it meant that when he was just growing up I didn't help him. At first he had Xenares—you've seen him, haven't you?—I never liked him much, he hadn't the fire, the courage, he tried to hold back the future. That came to an end, as it was bound to, and then he'd only got me; and I had the children, I couldn't give him what he needed, could I, Philylla?'

'Yes,' said Philylla, a little uncomfortably, wriggling her feet together, 'I mean, no.'

'Then, when things were just starting, last year, Panteus was brought to us by that lame cousin of his. He hadn't ever done anything but games and hunting, but all the rest was in him, waiting. Kleomenes talked to him, and he came alive. That was just before the beginning of the war, and once they were out, facing the League, Panteus showed he was a born soldier. So then, he and Kleomenes fell in love with each other and he's made Kleomenes happy at last, and so I love him too.'

'And so do I,' said Philylla, 'and I'm glad—oh I'm very glad he sent me the arrows and the magpie!'

Chapter Two

THEY WERE SITTING round the mess-table, King Kleomenes at the head, his friends and officers at each side. They had been speaking of the war with the League, and plans for the spring, a month ahead, when roads would be good for marching again. 'If I knew what Aratos would do next,' Kleomenes said, for the third time, nursing his head, crouching angularly forward against the table, 'if I could make sure I had no enemies but him and his Achaeans! But supposing he were to get help from somewhere else—from Egypt—or Macedon.'

'We've got to leave that out for now,' said Therykion, from two down the bench, a tall, nervous man with a short beard. 'Aratos has nothing to offer them. They don't look his way—or ours. Take it in Hellas alone. That's what counts.'

'That's what's real. The other places are only—appearances. Yet perhaps appearances will kill us all before we're ten years older!'

Therykion shook his head gloomily, and drank, out of old habit, though this rough wine they had at the mess was very different from what he had been used to a year ago. None of them spoke for a time; all had enough to think of these days.

Then Hippitas, who was sitting at the King's right hand, looked up. He was rather older than the others, and lame from an old wound, but he was always one of the happiest of them, and extraordinarily gentle, with blue eyes that he blinked a great deal and a country burr in his voice. It was he who had first brought Panteus, his first cousin, to see the King and hear about the new things. 'But look,' he said, 'everything is very different from last year. We never thought it would be so simple. Three-quarters of the country will be for us whatever we do. You can go as fast as you like, Kleomenes.'

'Yes!' said a fair, rough-looking man from the far end of the table. 'I speak for my people, Kleomenes. Get on with it!' This was Phoebis, half-helot and not a citizen—yet. But he was the son of the King's old nurse; they had been brought up together as young boys. He was as brave as any of them, and, if possible, even more anxious for the change in Sparta.

Gradually the King unstiffened; he began to poke the dry walnuts in front of him more hopefully. 'Well,' he said, 'this much for tonight. Now—a song before we go.' His eyes travelled round the table till they lighted on Panteus, and stayed. 'You,' he said, very tenderly, so that every one looked up, smiling at one another, because this love of the King's was, as it were, their own Spartan flower, the sign of the new times, and every one cherished it and watched it grow.

Panteus stood up and came slowly over towards the King, who took off his own garland and crowned him with it. All shifted a little towards the song, except Therykion, who was afraid of music or anything beautiful, anything that might possibly tempt him out of the straight path. Panteus picked up the small lyre and rubbed the strings of it softly, thinking what the King would like from him. He was three years younger than Kleomenes, and not so tall, with blue eyes and rough, light-brown hair that grew low on the middle of his forehead and curled and tangled over his ears. He had an extraordinarily compact, strong body, that seemed of itself to know the way of things, to run and jump and wrestle without his mind being quite aware of it. Like the rest of the younger men, he wore the short tunic, one loom's-width of wool doubled, pinned at the shoulders, and belted with the edges loose and open at the left, hanging forward from the brooch as he stooped to the lyre, so that the skin of his side and thigh looked wonderfully pale and beautiful against the deep red of the stuff. He sang them old songs, in the mode they knew and liked and thrilled to now, 'Swords Tomorrow,' 'The Barberry Bush,' 'You go my Way,' and so on, then a very early thing, ten lines by Tyrtaeus, that had become less a song than a symbol of past turning future, and then a last, even shorter one, of soldiers waiting before a charge, as they themselves might be soon. His voice just filled the room, very sweet, and unelaborate as a shepherd on the hills.

Then suddenly the King stood up, tall and thin, with his long neck and jutting brows, and the frown that stayed as part of him, even when he was smiling. 'Good night,' he said, 'good night, friends.' They went out by twos and threes; as they pushed back the leather curtain from the door, great waves of frosty air blew in and shook the flame of the lamps and chilled the room. Outside it was starry—a calm, deeply arched sky with that familiar closing inward and upward of mountains on each horizon, the valley of Sparta like a cup to hold so many stars. The King's brother, that much younger and less assured, less complicated, stopped a moment. 'Are you sure the ephors are going to send you, Kleomenes? Suppose they don't want the war?'

'That will be all right, Eukleidas,' said the King.

'But—' the brother began. And then, 'Well, I suppose it's got to be your way, Kleomenes,' and he went out too, after a worried and questioning kiss.

Panteus waited easily, as if his body were asleep and his mind only half awake. Suddenly both came alive, his eyelids lifted, his hands turned inwards towards the King.

'Look!' he said, 'I wanted to show you this.' It was the letter from Philylla.

Kleomenes read it laughing. 'Well,' he said, 'you've got your answer!'

'But she didn't mind, did she?—about the arrows?'

'Dear, you'll have her falling in love with you if you don't take care. Don't you see from her letter? She's got as far as speaking truth to you, and that's a long way for a woman.'

'She's not a woman, she's a child.'

'She's a little bit of a faun. Hadn't she got prick ears, Panteus? No, but truly, Agiatis loves her, and I trust Agiatis to see into people's hearts. Why don't you take Philylla out and teach her to shoot properly? Teach her to throw a spear and ride.'

'Kleomenes, is she as much of a boy as all that?'

'You would teach my girl if she were older, Panteus. Perhaps you will if—if things go right. And I know Agiatis thinks Philylla could do all this, if she had the chance. But her own father and mother—well, we know Themisteas. Catch him and Eupolia having their daughter taught to be anything but a pretty softy!'

'But they let her come to Agiatis?'

'Yes, but they didn't know what Agiatis is like. People don't. You do, Panteus.' He took hold of the other's shoulder and pressed it gently.

'Yes,' said Panteus. 'Shall I ever have the luck to marry someone like her, Kleomenes?'

'There aren't two of her, any more than there are two of you. Your wife will be the lucky one, Panteus.'

'I don't think so,' said Panteus seriously, sure to the bottom of his soul, as is perhaps right in love, how much less good he was than his lover. 'Besides, that's a long way off.'

'Yes,' said the King looking deeply at him, and seeing after a time that he was shivering, partly with cold, took half of his cloak and wrapped it round, over his friend's shoulders and bare arms.

It was three days later that a Hellespontine merchant ship put into harbour at Gytheum, after a long and anxious but not very adventurous voyage. Tarrik and his Scythians had stayed at Byzantium for the worst weeks of mid-winter and there changed ship. Even on the way south, after that, they had delayed at a dozen small ports, kept in by contrary winds or the fear of them, often turning back maddeningly at the harbour mouth. Their captain had attended to every possible omen! But here at last they were. Before it was light enough even to guess at the coast-line, Sphaeros had been on deck, standing with his books and change of clothes all done up in a bundle under his arm. By dawn they were fairly near in with Kythera behind them and the two sides of the great bay gradually closing in on them and the great ridge of Tainaron rising to the left and Taygetos far and high ahead of them, misted and silvery in the first light; it was not different from ten years ago. The Scythians were all dressing up, putting on armour and swords and elaborate bows and quivers and necklaces and bracelets and fur-cloaks, and their best coats and breeches sewn with gold and silver, so that they jingled proudly and fantastically about the ship. Only Tarrik, who had been there before and remembered or guessed a little about it, had put on nothing but a plain shirt and trousers and coat, white linen bordered with white fox fur; the only gold about him was a belt-clasp in branching leafwork that Berris had made on the voyage, and a narrow circlet of gold on his head. He was not armed either, except for a small hunting-knife insignificantly tucked into the side of his belt.

He had told the others that this was the best thing to do, but none of them chose to follow his advice, and after all, they were free nobles and could dress as they wanted. Only Berris was much as usual. He had been so thrilled for the last few days, while they were touching at one after another of the Greek Islands and getting nearer and nearer to the country of his dreams, that he had not thought about things like clothes; as far as he considered them he felt ashamed and inappropriate with his barbarian things—the solid stuff of coat and trousers, the thick boots and childish ornaments. He wanted to slip quietly ashore and creep into the heart of Hellas unobserved.

They had to wait about by the harbour for the best part of that day while their things were being unloaded; a good deal stared at, but still, nowadays there were so many odd foreigners going to Hellas that no one was really surprised. Probably they had come to hire officers for some infinitely remote war of their own. In the meantime the only problem was how much money was to be extracted from them here at Gytheum—before these robbers of inlanders could get at the pickings! Sphaeros managed to look after them to some extent, but a few insisted on making purchases. All of them could speak Greek fairly fluently and they liked showing it off. Two of the most sensible were sent off to hire riding and pack-horses.

That day they got about five miles, and filled the whole of the country inn. They were all excited about different things—the heat in the middle of the day already, the clothes, the food, the women, and the fact, which is always, somehow, so surprising in a foreign country, that even the smallest children could speak this difficult language. Berris had seen odd and brilliant flowers growing by the roadside—crocuses and irises and cyclamen—and the air had been intensely clear between him and the purple hills. These were the first really jagged and violent hills he had ever seen: the ranges west of Marob were low and thickly wooded all over.

It seemed to Sphaeros that Sparta was unchanged, so far. It was just as he remembered it—a rather disgusting place where wealth was the one real standard. Gloomily he thought that it would take more than one man, even Agis returned from death, to move this mass of a population gone bad. But as they got nearer the city of Sparta itself, things began to look better. He had seen one or two young men going about with a certain proud simplicity of dress and bearing, carrying spears. Perhaps he could ask one of the mule-drivers who they were.

'Oh, the King's friends!' said the man, adding rather resentfully, 'When you're rich enough you can afford to pretend there's not a penny in your purse!' But all the same, there was something in his manner, Sphaeros thought—a touch of hope or pride, or nothing more than respect, but at least as if something was happening in Sparta.

When they were within sight of the Brazen House, Sphaeros asked Tarrik and Berris to go on with him dismounted, leaving the rest by the roadside with their horses and baggage. Before they had walked half a mile, they were all three violently nervous. With Sphaeros it was mostly physical; his mind was almost calm, and so was his outward appearance; he could notice with amusement the thick beating of his heart and the curious spasmodic contractions of his bowels, but except for an occasional deep sigh, he was in complete control of his breathing. The other two kept on looking at each other. Tarrik had been very reluctant to come, dismounted, without any armed following: how would this king know he was a king too? But still—if Sphaeros said it was the best way, well, he would be a Stoic and walk! So long as Sphaeros was quite right about Kleomenes being a philosopher too. But clearly, Sphaeros could not be quite sure. It was a comfort to be armed. He tried to make up his mind what to say to the Spartan King, something that would show who he was, short and decisive, but it was very difficult. He frowned and smiled, and frowned again, turning over the words, and stared stiffly ahead of him when children called after him in the roads, and did not really see any of the things Sphaeros pointed out to him.

Berris, on the other hand, was seeing everything, with a terrific hunger for detail and colour; he was full of a confusion of images, whirling round with them, only one still and central point of criticism saying: 'So this is Hellas; now—is it as good as all that?' This was worrying him desperately; he wanted to lose himself among fulfilled hopes, to find what had led him so far; and here was the clear air, here the beautiful outlines of mountains in an afternoon of winter sunshine. Here were a few at least of the Hellenes, the people living under Grace, the strong unhampered bodies, poised so after centuries of war and games and delight in all loveliness. But—Berris Der had not found it yet. And this King would perhaps talk to him and he would not be able to answer him properly. He wanted to be let alone and allowed to be clear water, for this dust of appearances to fall through and settle. Only kings were dangerous cattle, one had to answer them the way they wanted to be answered; he would have to wake up and think about that, or else Tarrik might be the sufferer. He pulled himself together, and said something in Greek to the Chief.

At the door of the King's house, Sphaeros stopped for a couple of minutes, making sure that his mind was prepared for anything. Tarrik stood beside him saying nothing: he thought this was probably some ritual. Berris looked at the bronze knocker, which was very large and much worn, so that he could hardly make out the design, but it seemed to be a lizard with all its lines hardened into a form for metal. For all its age and roughness, he thought it was one of the best bits of work he had seen in Greece. Sphaeros, noticing him, smiled and said: 'That belongs to the King's house; it has always been there.' And he lifted it to knock, shouting for someone at the same time. They stood back for the door to open.

'I have come hoping to see the King,' said Sphaeros.

'Who are you? Strangers?' the man said, looking from Sphaeros to the barbarians and back again.

'I am a philosopher. I was the King's friend—once.' After another long look, the man led them along into the outer hall and left them there with a couple of strong-looking armed helots on guard.

It was a square, darkish room with four doors, and not too clean. In each corner there was a large bronze vase, cast and rather badly finished, with jagged-looking holes for the rings to go through, and a stupid and very much elaborated egg and dart pattern round the bulge; one of them had dried bulrushes in it. There were also two or three glazed pottery lamps, shaped into fattish sphinxes, and a trophy of arms, not very interesting. The walls were more pink than red, with a black stripe near the bottom, and imitation pillars painted at each side of the doors. Berris grew more and more depressed; he thought of home, of his own forge, and the clear live shapes of his own things, fire and anvil waiting for him, and the little girl Sardu sorting his tools and putting them away in their leather roll. He thought of Erif Der, her pale face and grey eyes between the plaits. He thought of the harvest—the heavy, gentle heads of the garlanded cows; the little fir trees stuck about with apples and coloured knots; the striped reeds of the flax-pickers; the thick blue and scarlet dresses of young girls running on the snow of Marob. His eyes wandered round the room again, and at last caught Tarrik's and stayed there. Tarrik was laughing, but that made it no better. The helot guards looked at them suspiciously, their hands on their sword hilts.

After about ten minutes, when still nothing had happened, Tarrik began to fidget and suggested to Sphaeros that kings were sometimes difficult to see and he had plenty of Greek money with him. But Sphaeros shook his head, beginning to be rather unhappy. Then, after another time of waiting, a girl came into the room from one of the side doors, with a great bundle of folded linen across her arms. She looked at them over the top of it, hesitated and stopped.

'Is it the King you wish to see?' she said with some dignity. They were so pleased at anything happening that they all said 'Yes!' in the same breath. A little confused herself, she smiled at them, prettily, mostly at Berris, who seemed to be more her own age. And suddenly Berris knew that everything was all right, and he had come this long way to Hellas for no vain hope.

As he realised this, he heard Sphaeros speaking, and saying who he was. The girl hugged the bundle of linen tight against her; her eyes were big and bright; she spoke in a whispered cry: 'Oh, you're Sphaeros at last! You've come to make us good again and bring the King's time! Come—come to Agiatis.' Berris, watching every least movement, saw her try to get one arm away from the bundle, and jumped forward himself and caught the linen as it slipped. She thanked him with a word and half a stare at his funny clothes, and took Sphaeros by the hand and led him through. The guards saluted her. They went down the passage and into a light, open court. Tarrik was the one of the three who looked about him now.

By and bye Kleomenes came, grave and hurrying, and took Sphaeros by both hands, then quickly bent and kissed him.

'Now,' he said, 'I shall know what I am doing. Oh, Sphaeros, I see so crookedly sometimes!' Then he became aware of the other two and frowned terribly. 'Why are these barbarians here?' he asked.

Sphaeros, seeing Tarrik elaborately pretending not to hear, stood back so that the two faced one another across his shadow: 'This is Tarrik, King of Marob, Corn King of the Marob Harvest, who is also called Charmantides. Without him you would not see me here. I was wrecked on his coast, and he took me into his house and was my pupil as you were once. He brought me here in all honour and knowing that King Kleomenes of Sparta would use him and his men no worse than he used me.' He laid some emphasis on 'knowing' because it was something real to him, an idea and a word not to be used lightly.

Kleomenes saw this, and for a moment he hated Sphaeros, first for bringing this barbarian and complicating what he had thought of as clear, and second for doubting him and his behaviour. His neck swelled, and the veins on his forehead; his eyes seemed to darken. Tarrik kept quite still, measuring his own height and strength against the other king's. But suddenly the Spartan's head jerked back, his hand out. 'Welcome to my house, King of Marob!' he said, with something surprisingly near sincerity.

Tarrik answered quickly: 'Good words, King of Sparta. I take your welcome—I and my men—to a well-heard-of house! And if you need help, money, or swords, we will be your friends and allies.'

Kleomenes looked sharply at him: 'How many are you?'

'Twenty, and all free; some are my cousins. All young too.'

'Mm,' said the other king, 'I might find a use . . .' Then suddenly: 'Where is Marob?'

Tarrik found it hard to explain; he had never exactly thought of this; Marob had always been, as it were, here, in the middle: other places, somewhere away north or south. Besides, if he knew about Sparta, then this other king ought to know about his country! But Sphaeros began to tell the whole story; it was better to have it clear. The three of them drifted off, Tarrik apparently admitted. But Berris had not been quick enough, nor for that matter quite bold enough, to follow his Chief. He stayed where he was, looking about him, enjoying the sunshine on his face and hands. The girl he had seen came up quietly from behind and made him jump when she spoke.

'Who are you?' she asked.

He assembled his Greek as quickly as he could under the child's disquieting eyes; he saw now that she was younger than he had thought at first. 'I am Berris Der,' he said. 'I came from Marob with my king and Sphaeros.'

'Is that your king?' She pointed. 'I see. He looks very fine. Are you his friend?'

'Yes,' said Berris.

Philylla nodded sympathetically. 'What kind of man is he?' she asked. Berris was not at all sure how he ought to answer. He began tentatively: 'He can kill bulls and shoot through a man's eye a hundred paces off. And—oh,'—seeing this was the wrong thing—'Sphaeros has been teaching him all the winter, and they read a great many Greek books! He is called Charmantides sometimes—his great-grandfather was a real Hellene from Olbia!' Philylla was too polite to laugh outright, but she grinned a little, and he grinned back appealingly. 'Words mean such different things!' he said. 'What kind of man is your king?'

Philylla looked at him hard and took a breath and said solemnly: 'He is going to make our country great and wise and free. He never thinks of his own pleasure, only of that. And the Queen is the same, only more.' Suddenly she remembered that he could not know who she was. 'And I am Philylla, daughter of Themisteas. I am maid of honour to the Queen. Till she comes I am your hostess.'

She stopped short; it seemed to be Berris's turn. He would have liked to say something impressive. 'My father is one of the Chief's councillors at Marob,' he began, 'and no one can give him orders but the Chief, the King, that is.'

'Yes,' said Philylla, 'foreigners always have to obey their kings. We are free in Hellas.'

'But your king—'

'Oh, that's different. Our king is a citizen like the rest of us under the ephors. If he told us to do something that was bad for the State, or unworthy, we would not obey him. But that won't happen with King Kleomenes!'

Berris tried to think of something comparable to say about Tarrik, but couldn't manage it. He said: 'I'm a metal-worker. I make things out of brass and gold.'

Philylla drew back a step: 'You said you were a noble!'

'But I *am*! I work because I choose. I draw beasts and trees, and sometimes I carve, and sometimes I model in clay.'

'Oh, then you're an artist!' said Philylla, slightly mollified, but still looking down on him.

'I'll make you a gold bracelet if you like,' said Berris, 'with any pattern you say! Shall I?'

She blushed, not sure for one thing whether he was asking for an order or suggesting a present. 'The Queen doesn't want us to wear many ornaments,' she said. 'Besides—oh—do you like being in Hellas?'

'I came here because I was an artist,' said Berris, finding the Greek came easier, 'to see everything. People always told me that there was no art outside Hellas, so I had to know.'

Philylla had not considered art much yet; she looked quickly all round the courtyard and for the first time really noticed the marble groups of Laughter and War—coloured marble they were, and very expressive, given to Kleomenes by his father and much admired. These, of course, must be art. 'Yes,' she said proudly, 'everything pretty comes here. I expect you'd like to look at the statues and things. They're very beautiful, aren't they?'

'I am sure I shall find some beauty.'

'But haven't you yet?'

'Well—not much. Not made beauty, anyhow.'

Philylla led him squarely in front of the war group, which was particularly tangled. 'There! Now, what do you think of that?'

Berris looked at it and wanted violently to be truthful—and then smash it. It had no centre and no balance; it was all twisted and none of the twists were in the right place. There was no sense of marble about it, no sense even of the original clay it was modelled in. Berris felt himself getting swollen with annoyance and the inability to express it properly. At last he muttered: 'It's very nearly perfectly ugly,' and left it at that.

Philylla stared at him, hardly able to believe her ears, but his clenched fists and scowling eyes told her the same thing. She chucked back her head, saying indignantly: 'I think you're mad!'

Berris had a moment of wondering guiltily whether Tarrik would have allowed him to be so truthful on the first day, then he looked from the statue to Philylla and didn't care. 'I will make you see for yourself,' he said; 'you know, you don't really like it either.'

'I don't think it's important enough to like or not to like! It's only silly made-up stuff. But if I chose to, of course I'd like it. It belongs to the King and it cost as much as hundreds of barbarians!'

Berris was so anxious to justify himself that he hardly noticed that. 'It is important!' he said. 'What is the good of anything else if there's no beauty? Philylla, what can there be to like about that ugliness?'

'It's about war, it makes me think of soldiers and swords and victories. They are the things that matter. We only make statues of them just to be reminded. The statues aren't anything by themselves. Of course they aren't!'

'But—but—is that all the praise your artists get?'

'Artists!' said Philylla, with incredible contempt. She could not at the moment think of anything scathing enough to say. At last she said: 'You haven't even got a sword!'

'I thought strangers did not need to go armed in your State,' said Berris bitterly, wishing he could knock her on the head, make her understand somehow! 'See this,

Philylla, daughter of Themisteas—I'm a better artist
than the man who made that statue. You set me anything
to do, with sword or bow, on foot or riding, and I'll show
you you're wrong!'

It was quite a minute before Philylla answered. 'You are
going to war under the King,' she said very seriously. 'You
are to kill one of the generals of the Achaean League. You
are to bring me back proof that you have done it.'

'And then?'

'Then I'll believe everything you tell me about your silly
statues.'

'Very well,' said Berris, quite happy again, 'that's agreed,
isn't it, Philylla?'

'Yes,' she said, suddenly nervous. 'Oh yes! But I had
better bring you in now. The Queen will want to see you.
Are you—are you going to tell your king what you've
promised?'

'Of course.'

'And if he forbids you?'

'He won't.'

'But he may. And he will be very angry with me. But I
don't mind. You *are* going to do it, aren't you?'

'I am.'

'Then we're friends?'

'Yes,' said Berris. And then all at once: 'I've got two
sisters at home, one older than you, I think, and one
younger.'

'I'm going to be fourteen. How old are your sisters?'

'One's seventeen. She's the Chief's wife, and she can work
magic.'

Philylla stopped and turned round: 'Magic! Oh, how
lovely! Can she make charms to get people to do what she
wants? Oh, can she tell fortunes?'

'She can make stones dance, and men and women invisible. She can make the waves follow her along the beach,
and the sky change colour.'

'I don't believe you. No one can do that, not even the
priests in Egypt. Can you make charms yourself too?'

'No, but my chief can. Only not here. He's Corn King
in Marob. He makes the flax grow and the corn. Whatever
he does, happens to the crops. So he has to do special things
sometimes.'

'Sacrifices? Our kings have to do them. But it's for war and good laws. The slaves do them for the crops here!'

'Yes, but—' said Berris, wanting to explain fifty things at once, and then they came through into another court. And there was Tarrik, who had found a convenient pillar to lean against while he listened and smiled; and Sphaeros explaining and asking questions and walking about as he did it, unconsciously gone back to childhood, making patterns with his feet on the marble chequer of the paved floor; and the King and Queen of Sparta, hand in hand, standing beside the round raised basin of clear water that reflected that bright, almost spring-like sky.

Chapter Three

THE CHIEF OF MAROB and his people were housed in some of the very large and much decorated guest-rooms that King Leonidas had once ordered to be made, round an old court at the back of the King's house: that was years ago when there had been some very particular visitors from Macedonia to receive and impress. By now the plaster and paint showed signs of wear and decay, though Agiatis had seen to it that there should be enough cleaning and touching up to keep them very magnificent. Nothing of the sort would be made nowadays, of course, but still she and her husband thought of it all—when such things occurred to them—as very fine and adequate for the guests of the Spartan State.

She had given Sphaeros an even better room, close to their own. It had a vine painted all over it, with red grapes and yellow baskets in low relief, and winged babies, grape gathering or asleep. There was one that always reminded her of her own dead baby. Philylla, spreading a coloured quilt on the bed, looked round and saw Agiatis staring at the wall quietly and solemnly, with her lips a little parted, and knew what it was, and wondered for the hundredth time which of the two kings whose children she had borne, Agiatis had loved best. And then suddenly she found that old wonder changing into a new one, about the barbarian who had spoken to her so oddly about beauty: because, of course, the babies and the grapes were ever so pretty, and she'd always liked them and always would, and anyhow what he said hadn't meant anything, couldn't have, only she'd have to try and believe him—if he kept his promise.

Tarrik was quite decided about not letting Sphaeros see any the less of him now that they were in Hellas. The position became gradually clear to him, though not to Berris nor most of the others. On the one hand there was the King and his friends, those odd and silent people with some intensely interesting business of their own, in whose completion he and his men might be called upon to share, though they were so completely shut off from its preparation. He could feel that they could never be friends, he and Kleomenes, they would never talk together about kingship and all the things he had learnt from Sphaeros, learnt easily because of his own partly Greek mind, and that he had come all this way to know more of. So far, he was angry and rather hurt. He was prepared, at least he had thought so, to be looked down upon by these true Hellenes; but only for ideas imperfectly worked out or concepts scarcely realised—something that could be remedied; not, certainly, like this, as a simple matter of course.

Then there was the rest of Sparta. They did not seem to look down on him, and yet perhaps they puzzled him more. Because, in a way, they seemed more Hellene than the King's friends. The elaborations and distractions of their lives were more what he had expected and half feared, yet knew he could very quickly get into the way of dealing with, seeing that money was the one thing needful: beauty could so easily be bought.

Not that Tarrik was taken in for long by this beauty. Even if he was not a craftsman himself, he had the clear eye and ready scorn that he had learnt from Berris and the metal-workers of Marob. He and Berris used to laugh together immensely, and not very secretly. It pained Sphaeros, who could not see why his pupil should value his own idea of beauty higher than courtesy to his hosts. Neither had much importance, but one was at least expedient.

The Chief's other friends were, on the whole, delighted with this second half of Sparta, which received them so well, asked them to banquets where the food was excellent, the wine better still, and the general air of magnificence far surpassing anything they had ever come across. They drew on the common store to buy themselves slaves, horses, fine clothes, and all other necessaries for the life of pleasure, and thought well of their Chief who had brought them to it.

It was odd how definitely they thought of him as the Chief now, the leader in war and council, and not as the Corn King. At the same time they forgot all about the blighting and unlucky things that had happened to the magic part of him, the God in him. He was a man here like the rest of them, governing them through the force of that manhood. There were no gods in Sparta, no gods at least that did things, only vaguely remembered, faintly and formally recognised shadows of what had been; or if, after all, there was anything more, it was hidden from the people of Marob.

During the voyage Tarrik had looked from time to time under his coat at the star. Since the day he had taken it, Erif had never had it back, nor, for that matter, asked for it; but it seemed like part of her still, some part that was virgin in spite of him. It was always warm to touch, and in any dim light it shone a little so that one could see the veining of the wood wavy across it. In daylight Tarrik could only see the glow by hollowing his hand round it and looking in between his fingers. He liked doing that, as if it were Erif herself he held there, tiny and still and his very own, as somehow she had never quite been in her real body. But since they had come to Sparta the star had gradually got cold, till now it was no warmer than the heat of his own skin made it, and the light had faded too. It was so gradual that he could not believe anything had happened to Erif Der; it seemed more as if the magic had lost touch with her. So he asked Berris what he thought.

They were outside, at midday, sweating and excited, and the light was quivering down in white sheets edged abruptly with the oblique shadows of houses. The pink smoke of fruit blossom still lay all about the plain of Sparta: the brilliant flower colours were still unfaded by the sun; they had not seen or imagined the pale drying of the summer grass. 'I wonder,' said Berris, screwing up a spray of sweet leaves against his nose, 'what is the real reason. I don't think anything can be wrong with Erif; she's never ill. Unless she was going to have a baby?' But Tarrik shook his head. 'Well then, it might be there's a sort of gap coming between you that the star can't bridge. Perhaps she's gone back to father and Yellow Bull.'

'Why should she?' said Tarrik sharply, and clutched so hard at the star that the chain snapped with a little ting and the broken end flicked up against his neck.

'I don't know,' said Berris rather unhappily, and picked up the chain. 'I don't know what she told you. I hadn't seen any of them much since the bullfighting. They would talk, and I'd got things to work out. But supposing Erif is just where you left her, could it be you? I mean, if you didn't care—'

But Tarrik said: 'I do care.'

'Oh well, I suppose you know, Tarrik, and I suppose that girl you're after now is just to remind you of her!'

'Oh, that young woman! She's just to see how much the Greeks can stand of us after all!' And Tarrik grinned, relaxing his grip on the chain. 'But it's no good trying the Queen's girls, Berris. That bare-legged crew of hers won't have anything to do with savages like you and me. You'll never have that Philylla girl of yours!'

'I don't want to,' said Berris, a good deal hurt, partly because he had never considered Philylla like this and partly because he was a little ashamed not to have. He went on: 'But, Tarrik, about the star. If it's not her and it's not you, mightn't it be the place? Look—look at the light there is on everything, every single grass blade so all over seen that it couldn't hide a fly! Look at those flat walls, just spread out blank for the sun's patterns to go on! All these sharp things completely seen, Tarrik—I mean, it's not a magic country.'

'No,' said Tarrik, 'I believe that's it. Magic won't work here, just as it wouldn't with Sphaeros. But I shan't lose my own, I can't! Not the magic that's in me! Berris, I can make the corn grow still!'

Berris said: 'You've given that to my brother now.'

'Yes, but after—if I'd lost it here and couldn't do it any more!' For a minute he was rather badly frightened and Berris, watching him, couldn't find a word to say. They both knew what happened to the Corn King when his godhead began to fail; the thing that had happened to Tarrik's father; the thing that would happen to Tarrik if he had the bad luck to get old—not be killed first by the

Red Riders or drowned in a storm. Only it had always been a very long way off before; now it grinned between them. With an effort, Tarrik broke past: 'Nothing can happen to me! But that must be it about the star, Berris. I wonder if Erif can tell about me. I wonder if she's finding that the knife has gone dim too. You know the King wants us all for his war next week?'

'Oh, but does he!' said Berris, and fell to thinking.

The next week, then, they all went off, marching against the Achaean League.

Philylla went home for her fourteenth birthday. Her father had two houses, one in the city of Sparta itself, and one in the country, a low white house beyond Geronthrai on the top of a foothill, looking west across the broad crop-patterned valley towards Taygetos. As it was spring and rather lovely up there, the family had left the city and gone over with several ox-carts of essential furnishing and provisions with them. They went for miles through their own estate; the tenants and cultivators, slave or half-slave or free, came out of the farms as they went by, and their daughters brought bunches of flowers or anything in the way of food or drink that it was thought possible the noble owners might not despise too much. Dontas was riding and maddeningly pleased with himself; he charged the flocks of geese and sent them flapping and cackling and hissing out of his way.

When they got to the farm, Philylla's mother, Eupolia, went into mild hysterics over the bareness of everything before the hangings they had brought were put up, and Themisteas walked off to look at his stables; his racers were mostly kept up here out of harm's way. Philylla had all the country servants crowding round her, saying how she'd grown, how pretty she was, what a lucky man it would be who'd get her. The big, soft-eyed country woman, Tiasa, who had been her wet-nurse, came up through the crowd and kissed her and brought her over to a seat under the furry first peepings of vine leaves. Philylla shut her eyes and began breathing in the queer, shiveringly alive country smells, of green things pushing and growing, and tight, rustling corn sacks and meal sacks, of old wood and hot dung and places where honey had dripped. Her foster-mother was feeling at her with big wise hands that knew what they wanted, touching at all the soft, very sensitive growing points of her body. Waves of feeling poured over her as she waited, shut-eyed, centering, centering. . . . And then she jumped up, one spring on to her feet, another on to the bench, and looked down at the smiling face and big breasts of her foster-mother. The smells still clung about her tongue and widened nostrils; the rustling and cooing and bleating, the always remembered lilt of the country voices, struck like deep bells on her ears. She shook herself and stuck her arms out into the sun. 'What is it?' she said.

Tiasa answered: 'Time will show,' and stooped and kissed her feet between the thongs of the sandals. But already Philylla was thinking away from it all to her own time, the King's time.

She could usually bully her small sister and brother into at least not contradicting her, but the grown-ups were maddening! She couldn't help sometimes trying to tell them, and then they either disregarded her or laughed at her. She knew she didn't always explain it properly, and often she got too excited to be clear; or else she didn't quite know herself exactly what it was she wanted so much to happen. And sometimes they did listen for a minute or two, but then they always ended by producing all sorts of silly reasons against it and against the King and Queen. They said: 'Experience shows us—,' 'When you know as much about human nature as I do—' 'When you're my age, Philylla—' As if there was anything good about being old! Philylla knew that the new ideas ought to work, and when she was told they wouldn't and couldn't, but the only reason seemed to be that most people are greedy and lazy and selfish, she just got too angry to bear it and ran off into the store-room and hid behind the big oil jars and cried. She wanted somebody else to come and cry with her and agree that the grown-ups were silly, and solemnly vow and swear never to become like that themselves, however old they got. Sometimes she pretended Agiatis was there, but she knew the Queen was too patient and gentle ever to hate properly, as she hated. Sometimes it was one or another of the maids of honour who thought as she did, and sometimes it was one of these other two: Berris Der, that she could explain it all to and who would listen; or Panteus, who would explain it all to her. She didn't know which she would rather have. Panteus would be rather frightening; he was too near the King. They were both away now, with the army. There were going to be battles. It was unfair that she couldn't be a soldier!

It was the week after her birthday and she was beginning to wish she could go back to the city at once instead of staying at home for the three more days she had. Everything seemed to be going wrong; she had been rude and then violently apologetic to her father and mother; she hadn't wanted the presents they gave her for her birthday, the dresses and jewels and combs; she was afraid of losing her new ear-rings, and Themisteas laughed at her for wanting a horse of her own, though he said she might have one of the racers and let it be entered in her name—but not to ride, oh no! She usually slept like a dormouse, but that morning she couldn't. She dressed and went out into the court; no one was about yet—even the slaves slept late. She looked round and bit her lip and undid the lower bolts of the gate; then she pulled up a truss of hay and got on to it and undid the top ones. She heard the man in charge beginning to wake up, so she pulled it open just enough to slip out and run. It was early yet. Across the valley the far mountains were all bathed and gold in the dawn sunlight, but she and her mountains were in shadow still. If she had got that horse she would have galloped down and across the valley till she met the light. And it was, there was nothing for it but to wait until the sun had come over the top of the great range behind the house. She went quickly down the slope and out of sight.

Out of a thicket of low bushes she ambushed the dawn flowing towards her across the pastures; it was infinitely satisfying to jump out on to it and leap about in the dazzle. Only she was cross with herself for forgetting to bring anything to eat; that wasn't being like a soldier. Still, over the next ridge was her foster-mother's farm; she broke herself a big stick and went on, humming and chanting odd bits of things in the way that was so annoying for every one except herself.

Good! they'd been cooking at the farm. She smelt food and cows; there would be milk. She walked without knocking into what seemed a very full room, rather dark after the bright morning outside. Tiasa and the other women all ran round and began touching her; she noticed suddenly that she was as tall as a grown-up now, taller already than some of the helots. There was nothing she was afraid of. They brought her pig's tripe and bread, and tipped her a bowl of warm milk from the frothy pails. They murmured and stroked her yellow curls, put their fingers through the rings in it. On a low bed in the corner that she had not seen at first was a woman with a young sprawling baby half wrapped in soft rags. She took her bread in her hand and went over to look at them. There was a young man sitting on the edge of the bed stroking the woman's legs and feet. He did not move. Philylla glanced at him out of the tail of her eye, but her foster-mother ran over and shook her fist at him: 'Get up, you dog!'

The man looked round and grinned and spoke across her at Philylla: 'There won't be any of that soon!—not when we're all masters, me and him and him. We won't stand up for you—but for your pretty face!'

Philylla gasped as if she had been ducked, but held up her hand to stop Tiasa from answering for her. The man was half standing now and staring at her, leaning up against one of the house posts; there were two or three others—she couldn't quite see how many; dark and laughing, they waited for her. The woman on the bed waited, her bare, soiled toes cocked up and still. She said: 'What makes you speak like that to me?' Tested, her voice was adequately calm.

'You know,' said the man.

She began to feel rather queer; by saying that the man had brought some sort of community between them; it was as if he had dared to touch her face. For a minute she only wanted to smash that community; she heard her foster-mother stirring with shocked and angry eagerness just behind her; and further behind were all the powers of life and death, of prison and torture and abuse when the abused has to stand silent with his hands folded and neck meek. The combined inheritance from father and mother boiled and tossed through her against the helots. Then her own lifted and calming hand stayed her, gave time for the image of Agiatis to come. She felt her blood ebb back into an even flow. She said: 'You mean, the New Times.' The helots nodded and murmured and came closer, four young men. Suddenly she gave a little funny sigh and dropped her hand, palm outward; in her own mind she had allowed the community. Then almost immediately she had the experience of pride such as she had never known as a Spartiate by herself. She lifted her head: 'How did you know that I—follow the King?'

'Panteus told Phoebis, and Phoebis told us.'

Now smiling and steady she took stock of them. They were tall, broad, three with thick beards, the other younger. She thought she could never have looked at a helot before. She said: 'Why aren't you with the army?'

'We aren't soldiers, we're only farmers!' They laughed.

Her head jerked back to a return of anger. 'There won't be room for cowards in the King's time!'

Before any of the men could answer the woman on the bed swung herself half up on to her elbow: 'You call them cowards! What have you had to face yourself, my lady?'

'Well, I know I wouldn't be a coward!' said Philylla, suddenly childish again.

The man who had spoken first leant over to the woman: 'Don't you tease her,' he said.

'She isn't!' Philylla said. 'As if she could!'

Her foster-mother at her elbow spoke comfortably: 'That's right, my lamb! Whatever people may say, there'll always be master and servant.'

But Philylla was not happy. She stood in the middle of the farm-room with the people looking at her, waiting; to cover her embarrassment she finished eating the slice of bread. She wished anything else would happen, a cow jump down the chimney or something.

Then one of the other men began to talk. He said: 'A hundred years ago my father's fathers were citizens, like yours. Then there were wars and bad seasons and accidents and too many children. They couldn't pay their share of the mess. They stopped being citizens. But by blood I'm as much a Spartiate as you, Philylla, daughter of Themisteas. Your father gives me orders now, though; so of course you have a right to call me a coward.'

Philylla felt herself blushing; they had left a large hollow space for her to fill with her answer. She swallowed the last piece of the bread chokingly. Her voice was only a loud whisper. 'I didn't know about that.'

But the man went on as if he had not heard. 'So now I am the same as the slaves; they are my brothers.'

Suddenly Philylla found her voice again. 'All right, then—will you all be the King's soldiers in the New Time?'

Something seemed to break and begin to grow clearer. 'We hope so,' said the first man.

'Oh dear,' said Philylla, 'I wish I could be too. I'm sorry.' It was not clear whether she was sorry for being only a girl or for having called them cowards, but the room seemed less full of strained breathings. She moved forward and held out a finger uncertainly towards the baby.

The man sat down again on the end of the bed and began again stroking the woman's feet. 'That's my baby,' he said, 'and my woman. She likes having my babies.' Embarrassed as before, Philylla dropped her finger. The woman was staring at her boldly. She was a solid, handsome woman; her hair was long and greasy and fastened back with big copper and coral pins; she made Philylla feel dreadfully young. The man said: 'She wants me to put another baby into her. Well, that's easy done. When we have them we keep them; they work on the land. There's no fuss about splitting up the estate between them! It was all very well for you, my lady Philylla, being the eldest, but what about your little sisters?'

Philylla didn't understand; she looked puzzled. She heard her foster-mother say: 'Ah, be quiet—' and then the man again: 'Don't you know there were three more of you who weren't allowed to grow up?'

For a moment nothing happened; nothing was conveyed to her mind. Then several things at once rushed out of memory into the front of her consciousness, things she'd heard said and hadn't attended to—horrid things! 'Ooh!' she went, moaning like a little funny bird, 'ooh—oh!' She felt Tiasa's arms round her and the voice she knew. 'There, there, every one does it—' and then the man being scolded. She sat down on the edge of the bed; she could smell the milky, live smell of the woman and her baby just beside her; she felt her hand held and patted, she did not even try to draw it away. She didn't listen to what anyone was saying. At last she looked up and shook herself and said: 'Let's talk about something else. Tell me if you have any news later than mine.' Suddenly she was a general holding an important council with her subordinates.

'They're all up by dirty old Megalopolis,' said the younger man, 'but Aratos won't fight. He dodges about and keeps out of the way and wears out our people trying to catch him. But he's an old man and our King's not old; the young one will catch up in time—as he did before in the same game—and won! They say there's little love lost between the generals of the League. I don't know, but Aratos is a Sicyon man, good enough at buying and selling, whether it's stuff or his own friends! He's no soldier. When he hears an arrow his heart goes flop and his eyes turn up, and when he sees a spear he's got to go quick behind the first tree to empty himself!'

'I've heard that too,' said Philylla politely, recovered from the shock she had been given, 'and I can't see why the Achaean League stays so strong with a man like that at the head of it.'

'Ah, there's money behind the League,' said the man wisely and vaguely, shaking his head. 'Egypt. Black men. Crocodiles.'

'Oh,' said Philylla, 'Egypt is a very civilised place. One of the dresses I had for my birthday was made of Egyptian muslin; there's a sort of plant they have that grows wool like a tiny sheep. Did you ever hear that? It's quite true. They must have lots of money. But swords will win in the end!'

'Swords and the King's will.'

Now Philylla would have gone on quite happily being a general and a sort of grown-up. But suddenly her foster-mother interrupted them: 'You and your King Kleomenes! He gets round you all like—like a woman! As if things were ever altered this way. He's no better than all the rest, bless him. Shall I tell you something about him?'

'If you've got anything interesting to tell,' said Philylla, rather annoyed, 'but I don't expect it is. The King's a black bull—the silly stories all round him are flies. We don't listen to the buzzing.'

Tiasa sat on a stool and put her arms round Philylla, who by habit had come to stand between her knees. Thick looks passed between them, the dizzying half-way from love to anger. The woman began her story. 'Ever since the very beginning there have been two kings in Sparta: one for peace and one for war; one to come and one to go; one to be steady, one to be ready, and two for the brothers of Helen. Your Kleomenes is king of one line. Agis was king of the other. After Agis died—'

'Was murdered.'

'Well, well, poor lad, it's all the same to him now; well, after that his baby son was king of that line. But the baby died, as babies do, even the ones that are wanted most. Then the king was Archidamos, Agis' young brother, who'd fled away in the bad times. Your Kleomenes sent for him to come back, and back he came out of Messene.'

'I know this story,' said one of the men. 'It is not true.'

'All the better if it's not,' said the woman, and went on. 'He hadn't been back a month before he was murdered one fine night between moonset and cockcrow. Little enough was said about it; you'd have thought there was only one king in Sparta, and that one Kleomenes. Whoever had done it they were never caught, and never much hunted for that matter. And no one else has come home to claim the kingship on that line. But I've had it in my mind it must be a sight easier for Kleomenes if he's got all these high and mighty ideas that you children talk so big about, if he hasn't another king beside him who might have respect for the laws and get in his way.'

Philylla laid her hand over the woman's breasts, with painful knowledge of the complete intimacy there had been between them not so long ago, with a queer vision of herself tiny and ugly, sucking, slobbering, at the brown nipples, helpless in the big hands. She said: 'If you were not my foster-mother you would not dare to say this to me.'

'But I am, lambie, so I do dare. It's good for you to hear something else sometimes.'

'As if I didn't hear it at home! Listen: you must not say these things. Not ever again. Kleomenes never did that deed. I swear it. I know.' She turned to the men: 'We will not have it,' she said, 'we stand for the King and justice and hard living and truth!'

'Yes,' said the man who had spoken to her first, 'and now you must go back, or else they will miss you and send to look for you. It would be a pity if they found you here. Good luck, Lady Philylla!' They crowded round then and kissed her hands, and all at once she was a queen—a queen like Agiatis!

Chapter Four

AT THE END OF the battle of Leuctrum, the Marob people went back to their own quarters, half a dozen tents in a little walled enclosure of fruit trees. The green almonds were swelling already, beginning to weight the twigs; Berris had never seen them before. He was dazed and very unhappy. It had all only just happened.

He had shut his imagination and gone among the spears. Tarrik enjoyed that, but he didn't. It had been a muddling, scrambling sort of fight, in and out of ditches, putting one's horse at loose stone walls—then who was quickest at the far side, you or the other man—losing touch with one's friends in back gardens with ridiculous smug rows of cabbages and beans or sunk lanes between the stony little cornfields, not sure till the last moment whether the man galloping towards you was friend or enemy. Then he and the Chief, and perhaps a dozen others from Marob, collected in a patch of waste ground where the garden rubbish was dumped; there was a shed for a wine-press at the far end. One of the others had a helmet full of water, and they all drank. The place was covered with some sort of vetch, pink and white. There was a great noise and they got their horses in hand and a bit of the battle came at them, a sort of ragged cavalry charge. They shot off arrow after arrow at the horses, brought down three or four who broke up the line behind them, and then met the rest on their spears. As it happened, Berris was opposite the leader, and quite by accident managed to kill him, he was not very sure how. And then a prisoner, a man from Megalopolis, told them that it was Lydiades, their own leader and one of the two most important generals of the League. Immediately Berris remembered his promise to Philylla.

He had dismounted to look. Lydiades was not quite dead, just moving a little all over, but unconscious and beyond speech. The spear had gone through his chest, but he did not seem to be bleeding much, outside at least. He was a noble-looking man, with clear skin and his neck set rather beautifully on to his shoulders. Suddenly Berris became dreadfully sorry; he had spoilt something irreplaceable. He knelt beside Lydiades and looked at the horrid smashed hole his spear had made. He tried to close it up, to make it seem as if it hadn't been done. That was no use. Lydiades died. Over the body he found himself looking across at one of the prisoners, who was kneeling too, his face so twisted with misery and anger that Berris found his own face was twisting in sympathy. 'Tell me,' said Berris.

The man said: 'He was the best—the best of us all! He had power over us for a year; if he had chosen to stay tyrant he could have, for no one else loved glory and splendid things as he did. But he did not choose! He threw off the tyranny of his own free will, gave us back our liberty, let us join freely the free Achaean League. He was braver and more generous and higher hearted than anyone else, and now the old dog Aratos, the son of Klinias, has let him be killed.' The man broke down into fits of weeping. Berris looked once more at Lydiades, noticing the beautiful proportions of his arms and legs and the way he lay tangled up with his splendid armour. The shield and helmet were heavily and tortuously inlaid with golden comets and gorgons. In the near presence of that dead man, their owner, Berris did not quite like even to think his inevitable opinion of them.

King Kleomenes was told. He was angry and upset for two reasons: first, because Lydiades, though his enemy, had also been the great influence against Aratos in the councils of the League, and Aratos was the only part of the League he really feared; also he had always thought of Lydiades as being in some way and in some future a possible ally, and Sphaeros had thought the same. This was part of the second reason too, and the rest was simply violent regret that a man like Lydiades who had also been influenced by the Stoic philosophy and had at least done one action worthy of a philosopher king, should be dead like this in a skirmish. He bade them bring the body over to his quarters, and put on it a purple cloak of his own, and so sent it back in all honour to Megalopolis, whose tyrant it had been once and since then the first of the citizens. He sent with it an escort of half a dozen citizen prisoners; they had seen his grief and the gesture of the cloak, sincere enough too. Things like this were as good for Kleomenes in the eyes of men as many gifts would have been.

It was Hippitas who came limping over to the Scythians' tents and told them all this. They were angry, and Tarrik made up his mind to go straight home, not stay any longer in this Sparta, where nothing was happening the way he had meant it to. Hippitas soothed them down; his own opinion of them had got much higher from what he had seen himself during the fighting. He did not think the King really blamed them, and a good many of the Spartiates, including Therykion, had a quite different idea and were delighted at the death of one of the two great leaders of the League. Tarrik was partly appeased, but not altogether; Hippitas went to find Sphaeros and ask him to go and see his former pupil.

Sphaeros was with the King, so Hippitas waited in the sun. He had taken off his armour and washed after the fighting, and now he had nothing on but a loose linen tunic; under it he could feel the good sweat that the heat brought out trickling freely down his body. He was glad the battle was won; he was glad he was not too old to like his own body. When the King's time came and Sparta was itself once more, everything would be better still. It would be a good thing if Sphaeros went rather soon to see the barbarians and tell them to be sensible; he himself was not clever at that kind of talking. He went over to the King's tent. There were two of the large, common water-jugs standing in the shade of it; he drew his hand caressingly across their cool, damp flanks. He could hear the King's voice inside the tent, but did not distinguish any words. Panteus was on guard at the tent door with a long spear, Macedonian fashion; he frowned and motioned Hippitas away with his left hand. Hippitas went back past the jars, where he drank, and sat down again on a stone a little way from the tent, so that he would see Sphaeros coming out; he found a fresh clove of garlic in his belt and began to chew it.

Inside the tent there was a mattress covered in the day-time with fine fox furs; it had a couple of rolled-up blankets and some cushions, not very clean. There were three carved oak chests, bound and hinged with bronze, and two bronze rings at each end for carrying them. There were a few folding chairs, bronze and painted leather, and a trestle table with the top inlaid for playing various games. On the table were a set of tablets, as well as a roll of Egyptian paper with pen and ink beside it. Sphaeros sat at one end of the table and King Kleomenes at the other. Panteus at the door could hear everything they said.

Sphaeros looked unhappy and old and puzzled. Kleomenes was staring at him with a small, fierce smile that showed his very white teeth. 'Well?' he said.

Sphaeros began fingering the ends of the pens. 'I must ask you this,' he said. 'After Archidamos came home to take his place as your fellow king, what happened?'

'What have you been told happened?'

Sphaeros sighed. 'You know as well as I do, Kleomenes. Have you got to be mocking me all the time?'

'Very well,' said Kleomenes, 'if you want it you shall have it. I think I know what you have heard. It's mostly true. I knew he was going to be killed, and I could have stopped it, but I didn't. You might just as well say straight off that I killed him myself. There you are, Sphaeros, there's your pupil.'

'How do you justify yourself for that, Kleomenes?'

'Have I got to justify myself? Well, if you wish it—I wouldn't for most people. I asked him, then, to come back from Messene after the child died; I thought we might even work together. But when he came and I saw him I found he was frightened. Agis let himself be killed because he was too gentle and good. This brother of his was gentle, but he was not much else. He would have hampered me, whether he wanted to or not; he would have asked for mercy and compromise when there is no time for them; when they have been tried already and failed. It was a pity to have to kill him; he would have done plenty of things well, but being King of Sparta—just now—was not one of them.'

'So you are King alone. The two lines ruling side by side have come to an end after six hundred years.'

'Have I got to tell my teacher not to think he is sorry for a thing he doesn't really mind about in the least? As if it matters that the double kingship is old! You'll tell me next that the Twins have put a curse on me! I am King alone and perhaps my son will be that. Or perhaps it may seem better to go back to what used to be. It is wiser not to be too sure of one's wishes, and above all not to put them into words.'

'If the baby had lived?'

'I suppose you are asking me if I would have killed him, Sphaeros? You may even think I did. No. He would not have hampered me; he would have worked with me. He was the son not only of Agis but of my Agiatis. That last day I stayed with her by the cot till he died.'

'I see,' said Sphaeros, and stayed silent and greyish for a time.

The King beckoned Panteus over from the door of the tent. He came and stood by the table, trailing his spear a little so that it should not touch the linen roof. The King took his other hand and swung it a moment, mockingly. 'Sphaeros thinks I'm a bad pupil. We oughtn't to have done it!'

'Sphaeros has only been here a few months,' said Panteus, more gently and seriously. 'He does not believe enough in the New Time—his own time, really.'

Sphaeros looked at them both and spoke to Panteus. 'You, his lover, do you think this was a good deed?'

Panteus did not answer for a moment; he looked down along his spear. Then he said. 'I will try and tell you how it all seems to me, though I am not sure if Kleomenes agrees. At least I know he doesn't, because we have often talked together of just this. I believe that a man must think a great deal about what is good, by himself walking in the hills and with friends in the long nights of talk when it seems only an hour between midnight and dawn. When he has thought and talked much and has a plan in his head for the Good Life, then he can act, and if he has thought rightly, his action will be right. And it seems to me also that Kleomenes is this man.'

Sphaeros said: 'I do not think it is possible for a man with a life so full, with a wife and children whom he loves and spends himself for, yes, and armies and a kingdom, to stay still and think enough to be sure of rightness. Even Zeno my master was not sure.'

Kleomenes said nothing; his eyebrows moved on the steep bony ledge of his forehead, his face twitched between laughing and frowning. Panteus went on: 'It seems to me as well that two actions may be different, though both, in appearance and outward circumstances, are alike, according to the mind of the man who does them. A thing that is bad if it is done with great care and forethought, yet out of a mind that is unsure of its rightness, may be good if it is done simply and calmly out of a sure and calm mind. Just as, if one's body is well trained and good in its own bodily way of awareness and strength, one can trust it to move as it should. I see where my spear should go, and there it goes: simply. And Kleomenes has his mind at ease like that because he knows the good he wants. Archidamos had to be killed. But it was done simply: just that nothing else was possible.'

Sphaeros said: 'It would have been terrible for you, loving him, if you had thought he had done a really wrong thing.'

'We could not have gone on loving each other then.'

'And because that is impossible you must find for yourself some way of being certain that what he does is not wrong.'

Panteus looked at the King, not even touching him. 'I do not think it is that,' he said.

Suddenly Kleomenes pounced like a fox on the first idea before it had trailed away out of the tent. 'I do not myself consider that Panteus is right. He does not allow enough for the future. In his idea there is thought in the past and action in the present, but he does not show you the future pressing on me, on all of us more or less, like an unborn babe, forcing us to action for its sake, not for our own. Archidamos was a sacrifice for the future, as many others may be before I am done—as I may be myself.' He shivered and sank into himself; Panteus' hand went to his shoulder; the great spear shaft was a strong thing for him to gaze at.

Sphaeros got to his feet. 'At least, I understand, for any use that may be. You have gone beyond my teaching, Kleomenes. I hope you have not gone beyond truth.'

Kleomenes said: 'I am not as sure as I used to be that truth is so utterly the worthiest thing to seek, nor that it is only of one kind. All the same, I think I have been a goodish pupil in that sense. By the way, Sphaeros, I have not told Agiatis about this one thing. It would have hurt her unnecessarily, though I think she would have understood my reasons. And she has been over-much hurt already.'

He looked hard at Sphaeros, who nodded and went out.

He was tired and would have liked to rest and think it all out, but Hippitas was waiting for him, and insisted that he should go over at once to see Tarrik of Marob and stop him from doing anything stupid.

Tarrik, however, had calmed down quite satisfactorily. His men had taken several fine horses with gilt saddles and scalloped and painted bridles, and now they were playing dice for them. Tarrik himself was eating pickled octopus, which he seemed to like very much, and a Spartiate captain—the son of one of the ephors—was sitting beside him. Sphaeros thought they must be talking about women. Berris was not there. When Sphaeros came in, Tarrik looked up, quite pleased, and shouted to them to bring another plate and olives; his Spartan friend grinned and said: 'Well, how's the philosopher cock and all the philosopher chickabiddies?' Smiling, Sphaeros avoided answering him, refused a helping of octopus which in any case he did not much care for, and asked Tarrik if he was still angry. Tarrik shook his head: 'My mind is back in its right place. They can say what they like now. But there was an hour or two when I didn't do my teacher much credit!' A quick spurt of laughter bubbled out of Sphaeros. He said: 'My pupils are always so kind about blaming themselves, not me!' And then he asked after Berris Der. The Chief said: 'Oh, Berris! He's in love. That makes everything worse. Who? It's plain enough: that Philylla girl, one of the Queen's maids. But he'll get over it. We do!' He sounded rather defiant. That was because it was still worrying him that the star on his breast was quite cold and he was a very long journey from Erif. Sphaeros nodded, but, in the presence of this other Spartan, made no comment.

After that battle nothing very much happened for some time. There was a great deal of feeling in the Achaean League that Aratos, with the main body of the army, had not supported Lydiades and the cavalry, and had consequently lost them the battle. Some said it was deliberate treachery, others that it was just his usual dislike of actual fighting. Finally, they said they would give him no more money, and if he wanted to go on with the war he could pay for it himself. And so, for a time, he did. He was an odd little man; he did not care much for other people, but he cared immensely for his rather unexciting political ideals, for the Achaean League of free cities—oligarchies, of course. He had read Aristotle. He saw that the only chance for the Greece of his time was for the cities to bind themselves together as securely as possible. All the little states had been romantic and inspiring in time past, but that was before the days when Alexander's generals and their successors for nearly a hundred years had made rich and powerful kingdoms out of the barbarian nations: Egypt, Macedonia, Syria, Cappadocia, and so on. As it was, he had to get help, sell himself here and there, but never completely. He had very few friends, but he had one son and he kept a diary. Some day, it seemed to him, this would be published and read, and people would do justice to him, that is, if he was successful. He cared a good deal about the opinion of the world, but did not care whether it was to be his own world, or some future one. Again and again his feeling about Kleomenes was pure annoyed anger at this bad luck which had thrown up, after so many generations of mediocrity, a Spartan king who had to be reckoned with and to whom this future approval might go from those who did not understand. And all these revolutionary ideas of Kleomenes made him look like something very grand to that large number of men in every one of the free cities of the League, who, naturally, were not included in the oligarchy. All the same, thought Aratos, reason would win in the end and certainly reason was on his side.

Tarrik suddenly decided that he wanted to see Athens, and see Athens he did, with Berris and half a dozen others; they went round by sea. Athens had been under the Macedonians up to a few years ago, though not very painfully so. However, it was now free again; the foreign garrisons were gone and there was a fairly full democracy. It was Aratos who had bought off the Macedonian general, for he had a curious intellectual passion for the place, but somehow the Athenians had rather disregarded him and his League. Not that they had any sort of liking for Kleomenes of Sparta, but that was hardly to be expected.

Athens was perfectly accustomed to strangers. Tarrik and his friends found a whole programme of sight-seeing almost inevitably mapped out for them. The time before, when he had been to Greece as a boy with his Aunt Eurydice, they had lived in Corinth, a rather secluded life among oldish people, with a visiting tutor to give Charmantides a good Greek accent and a grounding in ancient history. He had visited Athens for a few days, but somehow the only impressions he had got of it were of his tutor taking him firmly to places of historical interest and making him stand still while he was being lectured to, or else of meeting some other old Scraggy and then the two of them would have endlessly dull conversations while the boy dawdled about and yawned and was not allowed out of sight. He still remembered a sweet-stall they used to pass—always so unkindly to pass! He tried to find it again now so as to buy masses of sweets, but it had disappeared and had to be left as part of the geography in the slowly enlarging Platonic Kingdom of the Unattainable.

There was no denying that they found it exciting. There was the sense of the sea all the time: it kept the mountains back, that had been walling them in all along the horizon, day after day, round Sparta and Megalopolis. And then there was so much actual beauty. At first they could hardly see the trees for the wood; it was difficult to get more than a tangle of impressions, and when it came to pictures and statuary, the guides who had been introduced to them were sometimes rather tryingly reminiscent of Epigethes. Berris was rude to them and was suitably snubbed, and finally he went off on his own and hunted down the things that pleased him and afterwards dragged Tarrik off to see as many as possible.

At first he had been distressed at finding nothing but a naturalistic convention, or at least one that tried to be. Marble and metal alike made soft and plastic, treated like flesh or as clay, not allowed to take their own proper forms. He had not discovered any of the cold, logical lines and masses that he looked for now. The only thing he liked for a long time was the brilliant colour, deep yellow and red and black caught up in the fierce light that came on to everything. If marble was to be treated as they seemed to enjoy treating it, the only thing to do was to pretend it was something else and cover it with paint—but even that was not done by the more modern sculptors.

The actual pictures amused him very much. He had seen very little of the sort before, and he loved finding out what could be done with perspective and grouping. There was

one he particularly liked by Philoxenos of Eretria: a huge
battle-piece, with Alexander and his generals, the whole
background filled up with great pikes, straight and slanting,
twenty feet of wall striped with these painted Macedonian
sarissas. Another by the same painter had palm trees used
as a background in much the same way. It was not more
than a few days before he managed to make friends with
a young painter, a pupil from one of the famous studios,
who was doing the back wall of a colonnade that had been
given to the city by a group of rich citizens; it was to go
alongside the new fish market, and was being painted with
groups of fisher boys pouring the catch out of nets. Then
he had a delightful time learning the technicalities of design
and material. Soon he was helping to mix the colours and
clean the brushes. It all had to be done very rapidly before
the plaster dried, and in the end several square feet of that
Athenian colonnade were painted by Berris Der with the
great sturgeon that they catch in the landward part of the
marshes south of Marob.

He found his way about the older stuff too, and with
his young painter friend rediscovered some of the archaic
things which were just becoming fashionable again with the
more advanced groups. There was plenty of three and four
hundred year old sculpture stowed away in the backs of
temples, too sacred to be destroyed though too old fashioned
to be shown. They got leave to draw and measure it and
then produced statues of their own with as much of the old
conventions as could be worked in nicely. All this amused
Berris; none of the Athenian artists whom he met seemed
to him serious about their work, as he had been serious
about his; but it was a good change for him and he
learned all the time, for they were competent craftsmen.
He had done hardly any work on marble or stone before and
enjoyed finding out about it, watching the way it chipped,
fascinated by the new surfaces he could make.

Once, rather cautiously, he had asked if anyone had
known a man called Epigethes. The name seemed vaguely
familiar to one or two, and at last someone thought he
remembered a rather inferior person of that name, who
had been turned out of one of the great bronze-casting
studios for stealing another man's savings without adequate
excuse, and had then had to go and make his living among

the barbarians. Berris said no more; he felt infinitely grown up now. He could not imagine how he could ever have been so silly and unsure of himself as to fall down and worship anything that smelt ever so little of Athens—now that he had seen the real thing! Now that he had seen hundreds and hundreds of Greek pictures, vases, sculpture and metal work, every form of art, and could compare, and say what was beautiful and what was a copy and bad at that. Now that he felt sure of his craft. Tarrik reminded him that this had happened before and that sooner or later he always became unsure and transitional again, but Berris did not think these precedents held any longer. Perhaps he had been like that as a boy, but he was a man now. Altogether he enjoyed himself very much for three weeks.

Tarrik had been less happy. He was looking for something, a wisdom, a way of life and action and government, and he did not find it in Athens, even though they were friendlier than in Sparta. He went to hear various philosophers, sometimes with introductions from Sphaeros, sometimes on his own, struck perhaps by something he had heard by chance in the street or theatre. But he never got much out of them. Instead, he would go off with the younger and sillier of his nobles, and such of the Athenian youth as were attracted, and spend a great deal of money and over-eat, and either go to expensive actresses or else make elaborate and giggling plans for climbing over garden walls and kissing respectable citizens' wives. When Tarrik was being deliberately stupid, he was worse than anyone. And he did not make any friends. At last he said they must go back.

Between the battle of Leuctrum and their start for Athens, Berris had not managed to see Philylla and he had not liked to write to her. He was not sure how she would take the fact that he had killed Lydiades. But once they were back, he decided that he must see her and tell her all about Athens. It was a few days before they met; he was getting impatient. When he did see her, he stopped her and said: 'You promised you'd let me talk to you about beauty if I killed a general of the League. You know I've done that for you, and now you're trying to hide!'

'I know,' said Philylla, 'that in a way I am to blame for Lydiades of Megalopolis being killed. But I haven't been hiding, and I keep my promises. I can't stop now, because we are all going to put down the linen for bleaching. But I'll meet you this evening when the others are singing.'

'But don't you want to sing?' asked Berris, suddenly quite shy and afraid he was being a nuisance.

'No,' said Philylla definitely. She did not want to say, least of all to a Scythian, that the others refused to have her when they were singing, because she would insist on trying to sing too, and there had been rather a fight about it, but there were more of them than there was of her. 'At the top of the bleaching-ground,' she said, 'after supper.'

Before going, she told Agiatis, who was a little nervous. She said: 'Beauty is a dangerous thing to talk about, a dangerous goddess—you know we kept her in chains in the old days?' 'Oh yes,' said Philylla, 'but you know, darling, I can look after myself. It's not as if he was a man, he's only a silly boy. And if he tries to kiss me I shall run down the bleaching-ground; I know where the pegs are and he doesn't, so he'll trip over them and come down on his nose.'

Berris, however, did not try to kiss her; all he did was to catch hold of her wrist and emphasise his points by hitting it against his knee. This embarrassed her a good deal, but as it would have embarrassed her still more to make him let go, she allowed him to keep it. She did not in the least understand most of what he said, although by now his Greek was quite good and very fluent. At first, while he was taking some trouble over making things clear and considering her rather than what he was talking about, it was easy enough; but then he began on technicalities and went on as if he were talking to himself, and when she tried to stop him and make him explain he got impatient. She did not much like it, either, that he was always talking about Athens. She tried to get him back on to subjects that she considered interesting, but it was no good. Just a little of what he said stuck, enough, she found afterwards, to make her uncomfortable, not sure whether after all she did really like any of the things she used to think were pretty, whether she had ever looked at them, really looked at them—what Berris Der called looking! Naturally, she wouldn't admit it at first, but when she had to, that was what it came to.

As they sat there talking the sun dipped towards the level

of the mountain tops; dimly peaked shadows spread all across the land and up towards them. They were sitting on the ground under a low pomegranate tree with the squares of bleaching linen wide out on the slope below them, held down with stones or pegs. Philylla's magpie perched on a twig and sometimes whistled; she shook the branch and pomegranate flowers fell and lodged themselves a moment, brilliant scarlet, between its glossy shoulders. Berris began to talk about his sister, and now Philylla listened altogether. He told her about the women's magic of Marob that was handed down from mother to daughter, how bad witches were drowned and even their babiest daughters were drowned with them in case the thing had been taught already, and he told how good witches were allowed to do all sorts of things just like men: could walk alone in the fields and carry knives, and if they chose to marry they made the best of wives, because they were too much interested in magic to want lovers. Suddenly he said: 'If you were in my country, Philylla, you would be a witch.'

'Would I?' said Philylla inadequately, and blushed. Then she said: 'It must be sad for your sister to be left alone now.'

'Yes,' said Berris, 'I wish I knew what she was doing just this moment! She will have plenty to see to, because she is the Spring Queen and she has to make things start. She has to walk among the flax fields with the other chief women of Marob and all the witches that can be found. I don't know what they do; it is a woman's magic, but they make the flax grow long and tough.'

Philylla said: 'Do you really believe that, Berris Der? I mean, of course, I know there is some magic, and people can tell fortunes, and I once saw an Egyptian myself who could swallow fire and pull live pigeons out of an empty bag, but all this about the flax! It's the sort of thing the slaves believe in here, only of course all of us know that the seeds just spring when the time comes and there's rain and sun for them. I wish you didn't believe in that kind of magic, Berris!'

'But I do,' he said. 'I've seen it happen. I know my sister and I know Tarrik, and they aren't pretending about it. They are quite certain they do it with the magic that is in them, and I can feel it all about them too.'

'But what happened before your sister was married to—to Tarrik? Who was Spring Queen then?'

'Well,' said Berris, 'whatever girl the Corn King chooses to dance with at Plowing Eve is Spring Queen for that day—and it's the most important day in the year. And then, for the other things, any girl he goes with has a little bit of the Spring Queen's magic put into her with him, and that lasts for a month or till her child is born if she has one. So there's always some woman who's got enough of it to do the things.'

'You are a set of savages,' said Philylla, and got up and began talking to her magpie.

Berris was still thinking of his sister when he heard his name being called over and over again. For a moment he did not recognise the voice. He looked down the bleaching-ground; it was beginning to get dark. He saw Tarrik at the bottom of the slope with his arms spread out oddly, and called to him. Tarrik came stumbling up.

'Oh,' said Philylla, 'he's treading on the linen!' But she said no more because almost at once she too saw that there was something wrong.

Berris began to run down to meet him and then checked and stood shivering. 'What is it?' he said. 'Oh, Tarrik, what has come on you?'

And Tarrik said: 'She's dead!'

Berris started trembling from head to feet. 'I was just talking about her,' he said. 'Oh, Tarrik, she can't be! Oh, Tarrik, it's not true! Who says so?'

'Eurydice has come from Marob, my Aunt Eurydice. She says Erif is dead. My wife is dead.'

'Oh, Tarrik,' said Berris, 'I did so want to see her again!' And he stamped and choked and stuck his fists into his eyes. Tarrik looked at him blankly and said nothing. Berris said: 'What are you going to do?'

Then Tarrik said: 'Erif is dead and my magic has gone out of me.' And he turned away from them and ran up a little winding, stony path that started between the pomegranate trees and went on towards the hills. Berris looked after him, getting smaller and smaller among the shaking bushes.

Philylla had been standing by, horrified and inadequate. She went over to Berris and touched his hand. At the touch he collapsed on to his knees at her feet and began sobbing and whispering frantically his sister's name. She began to stroke his shoulder with little dry touches. 'Poor Berris,' she said. 'Oh poor, poor Berris!' But he did not notice her at all.

Then the Queen and Panteus came up towards them. They watched her for a moment, then Agiatis beckoned. She left Berris and went over to them. She came up to the Queen's shoulder now, and she was still growing fast. Berris did not move. 'Poor boy!' said the Queen, and squeezed Philylla's hand. Then she asked where the other had gone. Philylla pointed up the twisting path, and saw Panteus look quickly at the Queen. 'Yes,' she said, and then to Philylla, 'that was the path King Agis took when he went up into the mountains and came down to me in the morning with the idea of the New Times in his head. That was the path.'

Chapter Five

AS THE PATH WENT almost steadily uphill, Tarrik's running settled down into a gusty walk. Night fell entirely and he bruised his feet on stones and tore his hands on bushes. Ahead of him always was the mountain wall in different shades of darkness. He did not look behind him to see the widening horizon, the greater space of sky. For a time the physical effort of his running drove thought out of his mind, and he was almost happy. Then thought and images crept persistently back, bringing with them so dreadful a grief and longing, and such darkening of the spirit that if there had been a precipice in front of him he would not have hesitated to step over it. He beat his hands against his face, he kept on hearing his aunt's voice, telling him, so kindly. Yet that was more bearable than hearing Erif's voice saying good-bye to him, as he did if he listened more inwardly still; for now he could detect all sorts of tones of longing and unhappiness in it; he was desperate that he could never now alter that.

By and bye the path disappeared altogether; he crossed a ridge with boulders and deep, dampish hollows between them; when he stumbled his fingers felt flower stems. He dipped into a hollow of utter blackness, then came up again, sometimes through scrub and sometimes over scree or bare rock. It was much colder. He got up to the level where snow had been earlier that year. He wanted the night never to end; he could not bear that dawn should come, light and beauty, without her; and the night seemed to be going on. Now by the queer gusts of chilly air that came blowing along the hollows, and by the sight of the jagged top against the stars, he felt he had come very high, out of reach of the valley. He had never been up a mountain before; it seemed to him that Hellas lay well below him now, left behind. His legs and back ached. Suddenly he lay down and slept for about half an hour without dreaming.

He woke out of peace to abrupt and shocking realisation of what had happened. Before he could put up any guards, his mind and heart received the full impression, and he sat up and yelled at the echoing cliffs with rage and misery. His hands tore at his hair, at his coat, pulled at the neck of his shirt. He was a wild beast. Then something very odd happened. For he felt a spot of warmth on his breast and he looked down, and there, under his torn shirt, was the star glowing with the same light it used to have before he came to Hellas.

Then he leapt on to his feet and shouted and shouted her name. 'Erif! Erif!' he shouted, and the rocks echoed and the stars quivered and the wide night lay unchanging round the mountain tops and the Corn King of Marob felt himself filled with magic and godhead again. So, shouting or silent, he climbed again through the night and the coming of dawn, and when the sun was up he was on a very high col between two peaks, and there were odd mountain lilies growing all round, and he could see eastwards to a broad rim of sea, silver and dazzling and unreal, but growing bluer and realer every moment as it dipped away from the sun.

Berris Der went back to the house. At first he avoided Eurydice, but yet, after a short time, the longing to know grew stronger than this pain of seeing her and hearing the thing definitely. She had come by ship to Gytheum, as they had, with a very presentable following, all of whom she had put into more or less Greek dress. She did not very much want to see Berris. She did not at all want to see him! All the same she had to. It was made easier by the fact that when she told him in detail about his sister's death, he merely cried and asked no questions. She was distressed about Tarrik; she had not thought that after this long absence without witchcraft working on him, and for the matter of that after his wife's dubious conduct in autumn, her nephew would mind so much. Now he had run off, the gods alone knew where, without even waiting to hear her other news or to ask why, when he had appointed her Chief in his place, she should have left Marob.

Berris found out later that day and the next morning from some of the others; though, being Yersha's people, they had no particular liking for him. But gradually he discovered that what had happened was that the Council of Marob had got thoroughly bored with Yersha, and about the beginning of spring had said so, refused to obey her any longer, and appointed Harn Der Chief. Yellow Bull was already Corn King by Tarrik's appointment. He had gone through the ceremonies at Plowing Eve with his sister, Erif Der, for it was still she, and not Essro, who was Spring Queen, and every one was satisfied. The weather had not been very good afterwards, though it might be better later in the year. That was about as far as Berris Der got. Yersha's people had orders not to tell him certain important facts about his sister. All he could gather was that she had gradually got ill, with bouts of mild fever, and at last died just before they left. This would account for the bad weather in spring.

Berris heard this and drifted off. He could not imagine Marob without his sister; he did not care about the crops. He did not even pay much attention to his father being Chief. Harn Der usually got what he wanted. He began to draw and for a time managed to forget. He was not satisfied with his drawings. Abruptly it appeared to him that he was drawing very badly, and that all his ideas were other people's. Then there was nothing to do.

Tarrik came down from the hills in the evening. He appeared suddenly in his aunt's room. He said: 'Are you sure?' And Eurydice answered that she was sure indeed. Then he asked for the rest of the news and listened to it in silence, not seeming much surprised or altogether attentive. He said: 'So Harn Der thinks he is to be Chief now. That's stupid of him. How soon before you left did she die?'

'She was only just dead, my dear boy. Then—I was forced out. I could see to nothing; they scarcely gave me time to get my things together. We shall come back, though—and meet force with force. And, Charmantides'—she laid a hand on his arm and looked into his eyes—'are you grieving much for Harn Der's daughter?'

'No,' said Tarrik.

A weight seemed to lift from her. 'You know,' she said, 'that after you were gone she played her wicked tricks on me? She was more of a witch than you ever knew. Charmantides, my dear, you must marry again; some pure, good Greek girl whom we shall be able to trust. You do not mind my saying this?'

'No,' said Tarrik again. Then he went and found Berris. He said: 'Well, Berris, did you know your father wanted to be Chief?'

'Yes,' said Berris, not bothering about it.

'I knew too,' said Tarrik, 'and I suppose she did. Now listen, Berris: we shall fight one more battle for King Kleomenes and see if he will talk about the right ways of government even once. Then I am going back to Marob in time for harvest, and perhaps in time for midsummer, and, as your father is Chief, I suppose you will go too.'

All Berris said was: 'Will you wear mourning for her, Tarrik?'

And for the third time Tarrik said 'No.'

Berris looked at him and said: 'What happened when you were on the mountains, Tarrik?'

But the Corn King could not or would not answer. He sat alone in the room and Berris went out and wandered about the city, walking in the full sun till his head ached.

Philylla saw him go out; she watched him from the end window of the long store-room, where she had gone to fetch more flax for the looms. She would like to have said something, but she could not think what. This that had happened to him was beyond her experience. Deinicha, running up to see why the flax was being so long, caught her at it and asked if she was falling properly in love at last and wasn't it nice. She felt quite sympathetic. Philylla said rather angrily: 'Can't I look out of the window without you all thinking I'm in love!'

'Not with that face!' said Deinicha. 'Did he wave his hand nicely?'

'Of course he didn't!'

'Oh bad, unkind Panteus not to wave his hand at poor little Philylla!'

'Well, it wasn't Panteus I was looking at, so there!' said Philylla and began picking up the bundles of dyed flax, leaving Deinicha very much regretting that she hadn't peeped quick at the beginning to see who it was, and also astonished at the baby Philylla having already acquired two strings to her bow.

On their way down they met the King's mother Kratesik- leia, and the man whom she had married for the sake of the State—to bring him into the right ways of think- ing—Megistonous, a grave soldier, thickly bearded. His only son had been killed in an earlier battle against the League; he was an extra but rather sad grandfather to the King's children. Philylla, rather unreasonably, did not like him much; he seemed to her to be out of the picture and a bore.

He had only ridden down to Sparta for a couple of days; then he went back to the northern fort, Orchomenos, which he was holding against any possible attack. This time the Marob people went back with him, and Eurydice hired a house for herself and lived there in a curious state of happiness, refusing to think of the outer world and her life of so many years, and gradually getting to know a number of rich and elegant Greek ladies, and absorbing herself into their lives and tastes and ways of thought. She had, of course, brought her maid Apphé with her, but somehow she felt she did not want to see so much of her now, so she got herself other maids with new ideas about dress and manners, who did not remind her by voice or gesture of anything unpleasant, which was now over and should be suitably forgotten. And Apphé had a nice long rest.

Sphaeros managed to evade her almost entirely. He spent most of his time with the King and the dozen other chosen ones, working out plans and trying to show them all how these plans might or might not fit into the Stoic scheme of life. None of the others had such a grasp of abstract things as the King, except perhaps that queer, nervous creature Therykion, to whom no philosophy brought any calmness of spirit. There was much that Panteus was in a way too happy to understand fully; he was country bred and he had not the scepticism about appearances that comes more naturally to someone who had been brought up in a complicated place with pictures and literature. All the same, if ever the thing should happen which would wake him fully to life and show him that everything could not possibly be done either simply or happily, then he might be able to think. As for Eukleidas, the King's young brother, he listened and understood up to a point but not beyond; when they were boys, Sphaeros had thought there was little to choose between them, but since then Eukleidas had dropped behind.

Philylla heard as soon as anyone about the defeat at Orchomenos. She was playing marbles with the King's children on the earth terrace outside the house which had small, decorated flower-pots set regularly all along its edge. Nikomedes, the eldest, was a good shot; sometimes he beat Philylla when they both rolled their marbles against a chalk mark on the same flower-pot; he had made some tiny wooden bridges for them to go through, as well. The little one, Nikolaos—Victory for the People—was playing, too, and cheating firmly and openly, so that even his brother had to laugh. As for the baby girl, who was called Gorgo, after a remote and famous princess of her line, she tumbled about and grabbed the boys' marbles; but Philylla didn't mind because she rather loved picking her up, fat and fierce and wriggling, and running away with her to the other end of the terrace. Kratesikleia, their grandmother, sat in the shade writing a letter on her knee, which was to be taken to her husband at Orchomenos.

The day before, Philylla had taken her courage in both hands and asked her mother about those other three children who had not been allowed to grow up. She felt as if she did not know her mother at all, and it had been a difficult thing to talk about; even now she only knew the bare facts. There had been two girls born after herself, both of whom had disappeared; but the third one had been kept. Then came the hoped-for boy. Another girl, born after Dontas, had not, of course, been wanted. If there had been a second boy he would have been kept too. It was bad luck having so many girls; it was bad luck, really, having so many children at all. Most women, however much they were married, only had one or two; their bodies seemed to know what was wanted of them. Had it been like that in old days? Well, perhaps not. Perhaps this was because aristocrats always married inside their own state, their own cousins usually. It was the only thing to do. But Philylla would remember that racehorses and dogs, when they were bred much together, tended to be less fertile. It was a good thing.

Philylla had been rather frightened. She hated being frightened. It was too difficult even to try and realise what her mother had felt; she was talking calmly enough about it now. It was the usual course to take. One was spared a great deal of trouble. It was, of course, better for the others—better for Philylla! That was dreadful. If she had children herself—suddenly she wondered whether the New Times, breaking up the great estates, making less distinction between rich and poor, would make a difference. If so, which way? If the New Times came before she was married she would have less dowry to bring her husband—or none at all? She wondered if Panteus would be her children's father. She would like a child, but the father was not so interesting. It would be rather nice if it was Panteus. She would be that much nearer Agiatis and the King—for always and always!

She knelt, with finger and thumb now intent on the game; the marble rolled, span along the earth, went slower, hit with a satisfying little jerk against the flower-pot. She was pleased. Of course she knew she was an older person playing with the children, but still she did like doing it properly. She even rather liked beating Nikomedes, who would be King of Sparta one day. Then Agiatis ran out. She did not look at the children; she was along the terrace beside Kratesikleia, who had dropped her tablets. 'They've taken Orchomenos!' she said. 'Aratos came up in the night and attacked. Dear, Megistonous is prisoner, but we'll get him back.'

Kratesikleia picked up the tablets again. She said: 'How many were killed?'

'About three hundred, I'm afraid, counting the paid soldiers.'

'Oh, those! How was it, do you know? Did we put up a good defence?'

'Most brave, the messengers say. It was a night surprise. Every one thought Aratos was fifty miles away.'

'Megistonous should not have allowed himself to be surprised. I suppose they will let me ransom him. He is wanted here, or will be soon. He could not have found a worse time to be taken prisoner. Is he wounded?'

'They say not. Dear granny, you must not get anxious about him.'

Kratesikleia smiled and patted the younger woman's hand: 'My lamb, I shan't sleep any the worse. You've been married to two men and in love with them both. I've been married to two men and not the least in love with either of them. Leonidas gave me the boys and Chilonis, and he wasn't as bad as you used to think, and Megistonous and I have a very proper respect for one another, but as far as that goes we are quite as happy when we are not in the same place and I am sure Aratos will have the sense to treat him well.' She turned suddenly with a snap of her black bright eyes, so that the other jumped. 'Philylla, you are listening! Yes, I can see it! Well, take my advice, and don't fall in love with your husband, it will save a great deal of trouble.'

Agiatis protested: 'Don't listen to her, Philylla! And will you tell the children about this? Say it will be revenged, and soon. The King says Aratos will not try to push south—he has not got the army for it. And the moment things are settled here, we will attack him and make up for it. If the men at Orchomenos had been all Spartan this would not have happened. But that will be changed in the New Times!'

The Queen and her mother-in-law went in, and Philylla told the children. The two eldest understood a little and got angry and stopped playing for a few minutes. Then they started again, only shouting rather louder than they had before. Philylla rather thought the Scythians must have been in Orchomenos. Megistonous had very few Spartan troops and a good many hired ones—he had paid for them himself, as a gift to the State—Cretans and Italians, men from the Greek colonies and roughish, dark people from the native Italian cities which, it was said, were beginning to get prosperous and powerful, one most of all—Rome! A big, walled city among marshes, always fighting. That was what was happening now in all these outside countries that nobody had ever heard of fifty years ago. But, she supposed, they would all disappear again, in time, when she was older.

Yes, she was sure the Scythians had been in the fortress. She did hope they hadn't all been killed. She frowned and began to remember, attentively, the things Berris had said.

Now that he was not there and perhaps never would be there, she thought of the answers she ought to have made and began to put together a theory of her own about beauty, or rather, against beauty, recognising, as Agiatis had, its inherent dangerousness. She thought of what really mattered to her and it seemed that two things did matter: the first was people, those warm, immediate people she knew and admired and loved; and the second was her country, Sparta—that country, not so much now as in the future, but a quick future; soon, soon, when it was as she and the others wanted it to be! Beauty, as Berris had explained it to her, came into neither of those things except accidentally, as, for instance, the Queen was beautiful and the mountains were beautiful. But it was not really a part of either of them. Trying to remember scraps of philosophy, what she had overheard and what the Queen or even the King had told her, she got to closer terms still with her ideas. Then it seemed to her that what she looked for both in people and in the State was goodness certainly, truth perhaps—she could not remember whether Sphaeros said they were the same thing!—but not this matter of beauty. She saw beauty as an alarming, violent, destructive power, Aphrodite the Untamed, caring for no standards but its own. She understood at last the thing which the Queen had told her: how in old days the Law-givers had driven Beauty out of Sparta for the sake of the Good Life. Already she foresaw conflict if it was let in again, though she was too young to put any form to it, and she was angry with beauty for upsetting things and angry with Berris Der for having talked and having given her these troubling thoughts where such a little time ago she had been quite clear and calm. It was no use wondering if he was dead. She gave her mind to the game again. She was not going to let Nikomedes beat her!

Later she heard that several of the Scythians had been killed, but that the Chief, Berris Der, and a couple of others were prisoners. As soon as they were arranged, Eurydice would send the ransoms. There was a certain amount of misunderstanding about this, and one letter went astray, but it would be got together and sent off. In the meantime Tarrik was practically unwounded and none of the others were much hurt. Berris had been stunned by a falling stone and had a nasty couple of days, but now he was all right.

Eurydice was trying to make a plan to ransom Tarrik without Berris; that was natural enough. She felt languid and yet very much alive during this very hot weather at the end of the summer. There was no wind to stir the warm air between the baked, golden brown mountains on either side of the plain of Sparta. A man was making love to her, a Rhodian merchant, younger than she was, with sliding dark eyes. She knew it was mostly, even perhaps wholly, for her money, but she did not care. She watched them bringing in the harvest, and he sat at her feet and sang and played on a very sweet-toned small harp which she had given him; the ivory of its base was engraved with the judgment of Paris. She asked him to advise her about the ransom; she was only a woman with no kind, strong man to help her!

In the meantime things happened with a certain rapidity in Sparta. Megistonous had been ransomed quickly without bargaining; he was an influence among the older people and Kleomenes wanted his help. Agiatis had terrible, vivid memories of young Agis preparing for his new laws and changes fifteen years ago. She prayed at his tomb, asking his spirit to help them, and made vows. Philylla, knowing what it was the Queen wanted, made vows too. The feeling of something about to happen grew very strong; those of the Queen's maids who were with her in heart watched and listened and whispered; the others either laughed at them or were frightened. Philylla and one of her friends invented a secret password and a kind of sign language which made it even more exciting. Yet when it really happened, they only heard hours later, for the plan the King had made was quite quiet, as well as being quite effective.

The King had been marching up and down, harassing Aratos and the League at one point or another, and bringing up provisions to the further garrisons. His army was tired out and thankful when at last he let them settle down in camp, a day's march north of Sparta. Then he himself with those he could trust and the best of the mercenaries, went south to Sparta, and had four of the five ephors secretly and quickly killed while they were at supper. Phoebis, who was a lawless man, did this, and with him Therykion, who felt that, having gone this far with the King, he must seal himself in blood to go further. The next day every one in the city went about very quietly or stayed at home. The King and Sphaeros had drawn up a list of eighty men who were against them and had power enough to show it. He gave them till nightfall to get beyond the boundaries of the State; they went at once. Then in the evening he called a meeting of the citizens, and at the same time sent Panteus and Therykion back to tell the army that the thing was accomplished and they must accept it.

Kleomenes was standing on the raised plinth underneath the bronze Apollo that had been in the market-place at Sparta so long that people had ceased to notice it. He himself stood in the same sort of attitude as the statue, drawn up to a tensity that must bring violent disaster on someone, and as he looked at them his shut mouth grinned with a beginning of triumph, and for a moment it looked alarmingly like that other very early metal smile. When the crowd was quite quiet he began talking to them, no louder than would just carry to the edges. Between sentences he slowed himself down, remembering how Sphaeros had again, for the twentieth time, warned him against speaking too fast. He tried to fix his eyes on some one man among the crowd, but that was not at all easy. It was so intensely important for him to get not only one, but all.

Kleomenes had taken weeks of thought about this speech to the citizens; it was to be the supreme justification of his way of action. It was a terrible thing to kill the ephors, the magistrates and representatives of his State; he did not try to say it was not. But desperate times need desperate remedies. In the old days Lycurgus had made his revolution without bloodshed. But now he, Kleomenes, was doctor to a State far worse diseased than the Sparta of Lycurgus. The time-old and native ill was there: riches and poverty together in one body, a hot and a cold fever. But now there were ills come from foreign countries, with names that should not be known in Sparta, luxury, usury and debt. For these he must be surgeon as well as physician. As for the ephors: he and his advisers (and here many who were listening knew that he meant the Stoic Sphaeros), wanting to understand certain things that had seemed to them very strange, and strange perhaps to many others as well, had searched through the store of tradition and law and memory handed down from father to son, which was the history of their State; and it had come to them that the ephors had gradually taken more and more power both from the State and from the kings. So long as all had gone well the ephors were their own excuse. But he asked the citizens to think back to fifteen years ago. He said that and stayed silent for a moment, trying to pierce through into the crowd in front of him, the citizens of Sparta and a good many others who were not truly citizens, but wished to be and were going to be. The man he had fixed his eyes on at first seemed very much excited, but the crowd was on the whole orderly, and it was still not convinced. It looked him in the eyes and frowned.

He turned a little and Agiatis his Queen came from beside the statue and stood by him, all in the dead white which the sun shadowed into a queer, hollow blue. She was very white herself and not altogether like an ordinary woman. She held their son, Nikomedes, by the hand; she was the past and he the future. But did the crowd know that? Kleomenes said: 'There is something so strange and sacred about the Kingship of Sparta that, whoever holds it, he has so much of sacredness about him that even his enemies in battle fear to be his death. But the ephors, out of their pride, thought otherwise. They banished one king, my cousin Kleombrotos, husband of my sister Chilonis. He died in exile—their doing. His children have been brought up by exiles. They killed another king. They killed Agis, the gentlest and best the gods have ever given you, murdered him without hearing his defence, because he tried to let you have back your oldest and most nearly divine way of government. I am not ignorant that my father Leonidas was one of the contrivers of this murder. He is dead. I take the best way to purge his spirit of the murder by avenging the murdered man. Yet I say this: that if Agis were alive now he would be very willing to die again for the sake of his laws, and he would say that if, because of his death, his laws were made real in Sparta—and they shall be made real, through his death and now through the death of the ephors whom I have killed to make the circle full—then we should be happy, and on his death day there must not be lamentation but gladness and remembrance and praise! I say this for him, as he would say it for all!'

Panting, Kleomenes took her by the hand, Agiatis the merry-minded, the mourner for Agis. She had made no movement either of sorrow or gladness, for she was a Spartan woman, but now she stood beside the King and she looked very beautiful. Kleomenes thought that the crowd in front of him was larger. There were more all about its edges. He had lost sight of his first man, but he thought they were all catching fire a little, and suddenly he took a glance up and saw from below Apollo's thin, terrific grin, and knew the god of old Sparta was shooting arrows for him. He went on: 'I will do all that Agis would have done, and because I am older than he was, I will do more. I will build up a Sparta that shall not only be secure in the goodness of a good State, but shall through that be the standard and leader of Hellas. Now the first thing towards this is that the land shall from now on belong to every one, and not be the slave of a single owner. Then debtors shall be made free of all their debts. Then all those with brave and free hearts, whatever they may be now, shall be made citizens, and it is they who will save the city. Then those of us who love our State with action as well as words will give her all we own. We will do nothing by halves, the time for that is past. Citizens, it is my privilege and honour as your King to be first to do this!'

He called by name on ten of the oldest and most respected citizens and asked them to check off the money and promises as they were given in to the common stock. He gave his own partly in coined gold and partly in written deeds. Every one looked on in the kind of hush that is made up of intense whispering. Then Megistonous, his stepfather, did the same. He had lent a certain amount of money, and had the bonds for it. Kleomenes bade light a fire and Megistonous threw in his bonds. Then one after another his friends came with their money and bonds and deeds and promises. The stock and farm implements would go with the land and be divided up with it. Then there was a little pause. And then the thing happened which the King had waited for. The crowd moved, and one after another men came forward, nervous or stolid or wildly excited, and gave away all their possessions to the State, most by promise before witnesses, but some going home to their houses to get the actual money and deeds. And now there were bursts of a glad noise, the shouting of men suddenly full of a great hope.

All night this went on. The women joined in. Agiatis threw into the common lot the golden bracelets and necklaces which Kleomenes had given her when they were first married. Fifteen years ago when Agis had done the same thing she had thrown in his love gifts too, for she knew he wished it, but she had cried about them for nights afterwards. This time she knew she would not regret them at all. Kratesikleia threw in hers too. From her own people and from Leonidas she had necklaces so heavy that she could scarcely wear them now, chains dangling gold acorns and leaves and lily buds, valued by their weight alone, and snakes with ruby eyes and twenty different precious stones along their backs, double and treble bracelets with sun-rayed knobs sticking out of them, and crescent ear-rings or ear-rings of gorgons' heads dripping pearls from their grinning mouths. She had liked them well enough as a young woman; they were less becoming now.

Word went back to the King's house; they were all waiting for it. Philylla stood twisting her hands, wondering what her father Themisteas was doing, longing for him to have been persuaded but hardly daring to hope he had been. Suddenly she said: 'We must go out and give our things!' and she ran to the chest where she kept her dresses and jewels. Half the other girls ran too—they had to do something! It was difficult; they did like their pretties. Could they be sure that all the other girls would do the same? It was all very well for grown-up married women; yes, and it was all very well for Philylla, when every one knew the Queen was going to give her Panteus. The ones who had fewest things loved them better, but also this would level up and stop the ones who used to have more from crowing over them. Some of them understood and were glad for their things to be consecrate, though it was to a strange god. Others just had to shut their eyes and gasp and grab. But that, for the younger ones at least, made it all the more marvellous. Philylla and most of her friends weren't old enough to be ashamed of feeling like a band of heroines. They ran out of the King's house, the Spartan girls, and into the market-place, with gold and silver and ivory and precious stones in the skirts of their dresses.

The crowd parted for them. They came and heaped their things under the eyes of the King and Queen. It was like a dance.

At the end Philylla looked up, a little dazed, and saw her father quite close to her. She ran to him and threw her arm round his neck. 'Oh, father!' she said, and then again in another voice: 'Oh, father!'—for she thought she saw—

'I've done it, my dear,' said Themisteas. 'I'm most likely a fool, but I'm not a coward and I can't see a brave thing tried and not be in it myself! I don't know what your mother will say, but we've got to give the King his chance. It's a good job you're pleased, my lass, anyway!' And he kissed her.

'Have you given up everything, father,' she whispered, 'everything?'

'They seem to have taken my land,' he said, 'so I may as well finish it off. Besides, by God, if this means that we get an army that's some use, then it's worth it! I'm giving him all my horses for his cavalry. But don't blame me, Philylla, if you ask me for a dowry some day and don't get it.'

'I won't, father,' she said, very seriously.

After that she stayed by the Queen and watched. It was all tremendously exciting, though nothing so much so as her own giving up. She saw the King's friends all about and suddenly asked the Queen if Panteus was there. But Agiatis said that he had been sent to tell the army. So he had not seen her and her friends come out of the King's house and throw in their things. All at once she felt a little tired. It was late; everything was going on by torchlight. The Queen and her maids went back and then to bed. The New Times had come.

But the thing went on steadily. Kleomenes never let it slack off nor allowed for a moment that the most difficult part was not still to come. The raw material was under his hand, waiting to be put into form. He and his friends, and Sphaeros most of all, had the plan of it almost worked out. Every one had to work, the men in defence and government of their State, the women in its maintenance. Much of the old life was brought back with a fresh violence. Beginning at the beginning they started the classes again. Nikomedes was eight. He went, as kings' children had always gone in time past, out of his mother's hands to learn hardness and discipline; he was shy and terribly excited; he went for a long walk with Philylla and told her about it. He was longing already for the adventure of making friends.

The eating-together was insisted on for all citizens, and no foreign cooking or hot spices to make the black broth go down. The new citizens were chosen and enfranchised, men of all classes, even the poorest. Later on there might be still more enfranchisement. Men went off to see to their lots of the divided-up land. Even those who had been banished were given their lots, for Kleomenes was set on having them back as soon as things were running well; he was not going to waste any Spartan blood. Very often an arrangement was come to with the old owner, about the standing crops at least, and it made a difference what sort of reputation he had got in the old days for his dealing with the under-folk.

Everywhere there was great activity and with it a curious order and decency of life, for no one had much time to spare from this absorbing and fascinating work of renovating and making beautiful their state. Many of those who had at first been most reluctant became interested, and by and bye enthusiastic. Men were making new contacts and friendships with others who had looked on the same life from a very different place. There was less bitterness and gossip and jealousy because they had stepped into a wider and more generous world. Perhaps they might get tired of it sooner or later, but at first most of the young ones, anyhow, were all for the King and his times.

Kleomenes had remade the whole of his army, letting all except the best of the mercenaries go, and training his new brigades to use the great Macedonian pike and be less hampered by their shields. They drilled and played war-games in the fields about Sparta, and the King encouraged the daughters and sisters of the new citizens to go out and see them, for he was working for the next generation as well. There was plenty of singing and laughter, and catchwords going about. The young men who had been most subtle and agile-minded and had invented the oddest amusements for themselves in old days, were angry and bored with it at first, but then found they wanted to be among the leaders, too, and turned their minds to that. Philosophy was fashionable enough in the Spartan army, and the poorer men, for whom it had been a luxury which they had never been able to afford, put a new liveliness and sense of reality into the old philosophic tricks and games and set dialogues.

The King was constantly busy. His friends all had their hands full. Sometimes he did not see Panteus for days at a time. Agiatis saw less of him, too, but she was busy among the women: they took longer to be talked over and persuaded—the good for them was much less obvious. But she was so glad that he was getting his heart's desire at last that she minded very little, and tried not to miss the nights when he had been desperately unhappy and depressed, and had given her the joy of calming him and making him hopeful again. It was early autumn and there had been no rain for months. In dust and sun the New Times went on.

Chapter Six

REVOLUTIONS ARE always awkward for foreigners who happen to find themselves there. Eurydice fled over the hills into Messenia and her Rhodian merchant fled too. There was a ship of his at Pharae, and he urged her to come. But Tarrik was still in prison, and she had not yet been able to arrange what she wanted: to ransom him without Berris. However, she had managed to stop any of the other Marob people from doing anything on their own; it was certainly her place to act. She had in the meantime sent a smaller sum, which would allow the prisoners to make the necessary arrangements for any small comforts or extra food which they would be sure to need. So she settled down again in Messenia. Her house had a vineyard behind it and now the grapes were ripe, the solid, unpruned bunches of wine grapes that were like single fruits to hold in the hand and that bled warm red juice on to face and neck as one bit into them.

It was a good year for the vines. There would be wine for the new Spartan armies to drink to Kleomenes. The carts of grapes went creaking down the street of Sparta. Therykion stood back into an angle of wall to let them pass. He was tired because he had been doing a night march with one of the new brigades and seeing to it that the various officers knew what they were about. Now he was going to report on it to the King. When the carts were by, he went on, frowning; he was not sure that he had a uniformly good report to make; he wondered how this new stuff would face real war, rear-guard in a losing battle, say . . .

Panteus came loping along towards him; he had a bright blue tunic with a black edge. He ran with an amazing amount of spring, as though he were always on short turf. He stopped short, with a last bound, beside Therykion, not panting at all, and said: 'Where are you going?'

'To Kleomenes,' said Therykion, 'with reports; or Eukleidas, I suppose. Sit a minute, Panteus, I want to ask you something.'

'Very well,' said Panteus, 'I've got my people up in the hills—sweating. I'm going to have a great hunt for every one next week; it'll do them good and please the farmers. Can you let me have any hounds?'

'Yes, any I have now. Listen, Panteus: what about Eukleidas?'

'Well—he's been made the second King. I don't know what you mean.'

'You do know. You know Kleomenes ought not to have done it. There have never been two kings of the same line, let alone two brothers.'

'I don't think it matters,' Panteus said. 'Plenty of odd things have happened lately; odder than that. I like Eukleidas. And there's no "of course" about it, Therykion. He and Kleomenes aren't much alike. Why do you want us always to stick to the past?'

Therykion said: 'We are always pretending to. And this is what it comes to! Panteus, did the King believe all that about the ephors having stolen the power in times past?'

Panteus laughed. 'Why bother? Therykion, these are the New Times. For God's sake let us accept them with our arms open! Oh, by the way, I've been asked about those Scythians who were taken prisoner at Orchomenos. Are they still in prison? Megistonous doesn't know. He's got some scheme about Argos now and won't talk about anything else.'

Therykion shook his head; he didn't know either, and didn't care. He had not been at all interested in the Scythians.

Just then Phoebis came up to them; his hair was sticking up in tufts and he was grinning. He said to Therykion:

'You look as if you wanted cheering up. Have you heard the story about the goat?'

'Yes,' said Therykion with a snap, and turned away with a jerky, raised hand.

'Will you come to my autumn hunt?' said Panteus. 'I'm putting my whole brigade to it.'

'Do I look it!' said Phoebis, extremely gaily, and went on.

'I suppose that means yes,' said Panteus, 'in our new laconic manner. Good old Phoebis.'

'Phoebis,' said Therykion suddenly, 'has got quite intolerable since he's been a citizen.'

'No,' said Panteus, 'no. You're tired, Therykion.'

'I know I am. God help me, I can't tell how things are going to work. But I wish Phoebis would comb his hair sometimes, or even wear a clean tunic!'

Panteus put an arm round his shoulder gently. 'We both mind that,' he said, 'but not so much. Here's Sphaeros. He'll tell you it's only appearance if you want to make really sure.'

Sphaeros came over to them and Panteus repeated his question about the Scythians. Sphaeros looked worried and wrinkled at once. 'Yes,' he said, 'they're in prison still and I can't get at the woman Eurydice. It's her business to ransom them, but she keeps on delaying for some reason, and now she's run off to Messenia. Who asked you, Panteus?'

'Another Scythian, a new one. Some sort of a servant. He couldn't speak Greek very well.'

Sphaeros said: 'I'd better see him, poor thing. I can speak his own language. He is probably frightened. You know, Tarrik was their good genius as well as their king. Perhaps things have seemed to them in Marob to be going wrong without him.'

'The Queen told me his wife was dead,' said Panteus, following up some train of thought of his very own. 'I wonder if he was fond of her.'

'He was,' said Sphaeros, 'though she was a queer creature. I heard all sorts of stories about her. I did not think most of them were very credible, though; at least, not now and here. Marob was a curious place. Panteus, do you know where your Scythian was lodging?'

'You'll run into him sooner or later; he was funny

enough to see a mile off! Sphaeros, aren't you glad about everything—on the whole?'

Sphaeros drew himself upright, but he did not come beyond Therykion's shoulder; he looked up at them both and said: 'On the whole—yes.'

It was then that Panteus pointed and said: 'There!— that's one of the Scythians for you. Riding! I wonder how he's managed to get a horse. It's not so easy nowadays.'

Therykion said: 'It's a woman.'

Panteus said: 'She rides well.'

Sphaeros, who could not see as far as they could, waited, screwing up his eyes, till the rider was nearer. Then he said: 'It is Erif Der.'

She trotted up, waving a hand to Sphaeros, and dismounted. She was wearing black linen breeches and a green coat with feathers and antlered heads of black linen cut out and sewn on to it. Her boots were green leather sewed in black with criss-cross patterns. Her head was bare and her face and neck had burnt very red from the sun. Sphaeros thought, first, that her plaits were scanty and rather darker, and then that her body was thicker and her face thinner. She held out her hand: 'I am glad I found you, Sphaeros!' she said, in still rather halting Greek. 'Now things will be easier. Where is Tarrik?'

'A prisoner,' said Sphaeros, 'somewhere in Achaean League territory. So is your brother. I believe they are both well. Tarrik was told you were dead.'

'Who told him? Eurydice?—I suppose she's called that here. Ah, she thought I was! But it was an appearance, Sphaeros.'

Sphaeros said: 'It is good that it was only that. Now, here are two friends of the King of Sparta—Therykion and Panteus; the Queen of Marob.'

They bade her welcome. Her Greek was improving at every sentence. Panteus asked how she had got the horse. She said: 'I am not very easily hindered about things like horses, even here. I saw some horses in a field and met three girls with them. I asked them to lend me a horse and one of them did.'

Panteus was looking carefully at the horse and its harness: 'Of course!' he said, 'it is one of the King's horses. But still I don't understand how you got it, Lady of Marob.'

'I told the girl I came from Marob and I was a witch—Sphaeros doesn't believe that!—and she said she would have been a witch if she had been my sister, and she let me have the horse for today, because I was tired and I had to find out about my man. She was younger than me with very bright eyes and hair, and she looked as if she were in the middle of something very exciting. She had a bow and arrows and a bird that she talked to.'

'That was Philylla, daughter of Themisteas,' said Panteus. 'She can shoot well now.'

'I can shoot, too,' said Erif Der.

Sphaeros said: 'Tell me what you have been doing all this year.'

She sighed and made a queer, strained little face. 'I'd like to tell you some time, Sphaeros,' she said, 'when I've got Tarrik back.'

'Are you going to get him yourself?' asked Sphaeros. 'Have you the money?'

She smiled again. 'I don't waste money,' she said.

Erif Der had come from Marob with only half a dozen men and no women. She had also brought some of her brother's finest tools which she knew he would be sure to want, though she was equally sure that he would be so pleased to see them that he would forget to say 'Thank you' to her. They were his goldsmith's tools mostly, and especially the magnifying crystal, which had been left him by his uncle, who had first taught him the craft, and which was certainly hundreds of years old. He would like having that in his hand again.

She got her men housed in Sparta and asked a certain number of questions. Then, still with the horse she had borrowed from Philylla, she went north towards the cities that were members of the Achaean League. Every one there had their eyes on Sparta, Aratos most of all. At first he had thought that the revolution in Sparta would have shaken things up and given him his chance of a not too expensive victory, but soon it was clear that the new Spartan armies were an infinitely more powerful weapon for Kleomenes than anything he had had before, and besides, now that he was free from the ephors and their traditional cautiousness, he could do what he liked. And what he liked, Aratos well knew, would be nothing short of the leadership of the

Achaean League going to Sparta and himself. That would mean two things, and one would be the end of Aratos. The other that this Kleomenes might take it into his head to start revolutions in some of the other states. There were some who would welcome him too: the riff-raff, of course. But Aratos wondered if he could be sure even of the respectable poorish people. It was unfair that Kleomenes should have made himself so popular. Ptolemy would send money, but no soldiers. Aratos began to look somewhere else; a very safe messenger took a secret letter to Macedonia and King Antigonos.

Meanwhile Tarrik and Berris Der and the two others, Black Holly and Kotka, were in prison and getting more and more gloomy as the days went by and nothing happened about the ransom. Midsummer was past and now harvest would be past as well. The others were not so much disturbed about this, for they remembered that Tarrik had made another Corn King before he went, and they supposed Yellow Bull was working the corn magic, and Essro would be his Spring Queen. But Tarrik himself knew what was likely to have happened to Yellow Bull and his magic, and he was very much distressed when he thought of the Marob fields and the bad things let loose on them. The star on his breast had gone dim again, but he found it was possible to go back in memory to that night in the hills above Sparta. Though he was not certain and dared not say anything hopeful to Berris, he yet did not despair of seeing his wife again; but he got very, very tired of waiting.

They had been treated fairly well. For the first few days they had all been chained except Berris, who was obviously too ill to walk; but in these wars it was generally recognised not to be a good thing to be too unfriendly towards the mercenaries and foreigners; they might be on one's own side next time. Tarrik was angry that his Aunt Eurydice was taking so long about the ransoms, but supposed it might be due to what he vaguely heard was happening in Sparta. They were actually in prison at Argos, but none of them were very sure where it was in relation to Sparta; they had been marched there through puzzling hill-roads. The four of them had a fair-sized stone room to themselves with mattresses and blankets. There was no window, but the door was only an open framework of iron bars. It looked out into a small courtyard with a plane tree in the middle, and they were allowed to be there all day. It had a gateway out of it, but there were always armed guards who were severely punished if they were caught taking bribes from the prisoners. There were seven other rooms opening off the courtyard and other prisoners in three of them. A few of these were Tarentine mercenaries, who told Tarrik and his friends about Italy, shifting the centre of the world still further west and away from Marob. They all played dice with one another and any other games they could think of, and tried to get the guards to tell them what was going on outside.

At night they were locked into the rooms again, but two guards were always left in the courtyard. It was hot and difficult to sleep: some sorts of flies preferred the sun, but others came out at dusk. Berris usually lay nearest the bars; he could overhear one of the guards—a Thracian who spoke very bad Greek—making clumsy love to a town girl he had brought in. The other guard was a Greek of sorts. Berris had drawn things in charcoal all over the walls of their room; he was unhappy because the next people would rub them off. Being unhappy about one thing reminded him of the other things. He thought of Erif Der and how she used to blow the forge fire for him, and all that they had laughed at together which no one else would ever laugh about in the same way. He began the painful picturing of her: her face pale between the plaits, staring at him, staring out of the darkness, the dark of earth, her lips moving. 'Berris,' she said, 'Berris.'

Immediately, between one breath and the next, he realised that this so much alive image was not his making, was not an appearance at all but the thing itself. She passed him in wire and pincers. 'It looks an easy lock,' she said. He got to work while she crouched against the bars. He was too intent to ask questions, but pure gladness made him clever. 'So,' he said, 'so!' The door creaked. 'Wake the others,' she whispered. 'I can see Tarrik! Tell them to follow and not to speak.' He woke them all. Tarrik was dreaming already, fidgeting at the hot star. Kotka began to ask questions and had to be stopped. They slipped past the half-open door. She had a dagger for each of them. Tarrik touched her hand and nodded, then slid his eyes round questioning towards the sentries—he could only see one, the Thracian, standing close up to the wall and his woman. She shook her head. 'I killed the Greek. The other I've dealt with. Come.' The Thracian and his girl were staring straight at them as they went past in the starlight, and Tarrik heard him say to her: 'Look at those shadows by the wall; one would say they were men.' And then they were back again at their kissing and giggling.

She led them down a quite empty street and turned into another, across a small square with a dripping fountain and a party of men laughing behind light-chinked shutters as they stepped past. She turned again into a yard full of the rustle of roosting hens and pigeons, took a ladder and climbed a wall. The moon rose above the town; they could see fairly well. At the other side of the wall was a deepish jump into bushes, but they all did it. Then down a zigzag path to a shed and five horses, one better than the others which she mounted herself. They rode some way without speaking. Gradually Tarrik came abreast of her till their knees touched. After a time she said they could stop now. They were among hills in coldish air and seemed to be miles away from anywhere.

She sat down on a bank in the moonshine and Tarrik sat beside her; they could see one another's faces very well. Berris came closer. Kotka and Black Holly tied up the horses, whispering, and then came and sat down too. There was bread and cheese in a bag by one of the saddles. Berris was watching how her hands and Tarrik's began groping towards each other, touched, started away, and then came together again. All speech was between the two of them, as though they had been in bed together. Berris listened and a certain jealousy of Tarrik kept coming into his mind. The other two would have found it queerer to have been overhearing if the whole nightful of events had not been so improbable and touched with the woman's magic of Marob that made them feel as if they were in two places at once, there and here. Kotka was married himself and his wife was a witch.

She told first how she had got to Sparta and come straight from there, and what they were to do now. She looked for quite a long time at the scar of an arrow graze on Tarrik's wrist. She asked him about the fight at Orchomenos and the other battles. She asked what he and the King of Sparta had said to one another. She asked what he had thought when he was told she was dead. She asked what women he had made love to in Greece. She did not seem to want to answer anything herself. At last it seemed as if she had to, for Tarrik was holding both her hands and asking insistently what had happened at Marob.

She said: 'Yellow Bull is dead.' Looking aside, she saw Berris horribly startled, as she had known he would be. But the Chief said nothing, only stiffened a little. 'You killed him, Tarrik,' she said, rather stating a fact than asking a question.

'Yes,' he said gravely, after a moment, 'I killed him.' The others breathed and stared and stayed very still on that Greek hillside.

'Well,' she said, pausing as though she were going to make some judgment, some statement of her own feelings perhaps, but then went on, 'he died at the beginning of summer. Then there was rain and rain and blight on the corn. The flax was all beaten down too. I do not think there will be much fruit and the bees could not get out to make honey. It was a bad season for fishing. And in June I had a child.'

They both cried out at that, her husband and her brother, and Tarrik jumped to his feet, head up and eyes shining at this beautiful, startling thing. He had never known how splendid it was to be a father! 'Erif!' he said, 'a child—a son?'

She looked away from him, away from this unbearable glow of his happiness. 'Yes, a son. And they killed him.' She looked up again through the moonshine, in time to see Tarrik shiver and half shut his eyes and grow cold, and Berris drop his face into his hands. Now they had taken some part of her own pain on to themselves. But Tarrik—she went on more quickly—'my father did it thinking to finish with you and yours that way. He said he thought I wouldn't mind. He said he thought I was on his side.'

'But you did mind?' said Berris softly.

'Yes,' she said, dry-eyed, 'I minded. I was not on his side by then. I was on your side, Tarrik. I am now.'

He took her hand in his, looking down at her, then knelt close to her with the other hand on her neck. 'But weren't you before, sweetheart?'

'No. I magicked you. I said I would and I did. I tried to kill you, just as Yersha told you I did. But that's all past. And was, long before he was born.'

'What was he like?' said Tarrik.

'I don't know. I only just saw him. He seemed to me . . . lovely. Then they took him away. Oh, Tarrik.' She suddenly grabbed hold of him and her lip trembled horribly. He took her in his arms, extraordinarily gentle. It was not quite real to him, and all that just awakened paternity turned back to comfort Erif. It was as if she were his little daughter who had been hurt.

'Was it so bad?' he asked, kissing her hair.

She nodded. 'When I knew—when they told me—I think I nearly died. I would have, but for Essro; she helped me with her magic. She had a child just before I had.'

'Was your magic no use then?'

'No. You see, it goes with me. And I was so weak. I haven't told you, Yersha tried to poison me before she went.'

Tarrik let go of her suddenly. 'Yersha—Eurydice! No! Erif, are you sure?'

'Oh yes!' She even laughed a little. 'She'd been trying for a long time, months, I think. I didn't understand at first; I thought it was your baby that made me feel so ill. But after she'd gone somebody told me. Just before she had to go out of the house I very nearly died; she thought I would quite. She hasn't meant to tell you lies, Tarrik!' And again she laughed and shivered. 'So you see, between that and your baby—Oh, my love, I did want to give you a child!' The laughter broke and passed into deep, bitter crying, partly the pain of all she remembered; the tiny things that no one could ever know, that she could never tell, not even to Tarrik; the silly dreams and wishes of any very young mother over her unborn first child, all unfulfilled; and partly anger at the life and effort and agony wasted; and partly pure, cold hate of those who had done it, for herself, for Tarrik, and for her son who was dead and could not even hate.

She leapt on to her feet, clutching, gasping for air and freedom from pain, the pain which had smouldered in her for weeks, waiting till she could tell, and now was out and smothering her. She stood with her back bent over, her face

to the moon, stiff and quivering. Tarrik stood away, afraid
to take her in his arms, she looked as though she would
break so easily. Berris was stroking her foot; she was not
likely to feel it through her leather boot, but it was a certain
comfort to him. He was dreadfully sorry for her and he,
too, felt old and protective. He could not understand about
Yellow Bull. He wanted to ask more, and about what their
father had said and done. He wished she would stop and let
him ask. The others understood that there had been a bad
magic about. The Corn King and the Spring Queen were
together again, but this was how it was. They shifted down
towards the horses and wondered what other evil things
had happened in Marob. They wanted to ask questions,
too, and they did not like being so long under the white
glare of the moon. The horses snuffed among the bushes
but could find little to eat; Erif Der's horse had gold on
its bridle. At last Kotka and Black Holly, watching from
below, heard no sounds, and after a time they saw the two
dark shapes of the Corn King and the Spring Queen blot
together as Erif got nearer and nearer, and at last ceased
from consciousness of either pain or gladness or anything
but rest and Tarrik's arms round her again.

Two days later a shepherd sighted them riding down into
the valley and cried the news to his mate further south; so it
got to Sparta, and all the rest of the Marob people rushed out
in their best clothes to welcome the Chief. They had heard
all that had happened in Marob from Erif's men, and they
were very anxious to get home as soon as possible and make
their Corn King put things right immediately, at least make
next year's crops begin well. Tarrik said he would start in
a week, but first Erif must say good-bye to his aunt.

Berris alone was very doubtful about going back. He could
not tell what was going to happen to his own immediate
family. All his father's plans would have been upset by
Yellow Bull's death—in whatever queer way it was that
Tarrik had brought it about. Harn Der himself could not
be Corn King; he was too old or would be in a few years;
it was not worth while. And Gold-fish was too young. He,
Berris, would not take it if it was offered to him by all
Marob! He had his own cunning, the magic of his own
craft, he would not take anything from outside. Besides,
would it be like that? It seemed more likely that Tarrik

would come back to his country as saviour and welcome to every one and have it all his own way from now on. Erif had gone over to his side. That was very likely a good thing, and anyway his father's fault. But what would happen to Harn Der after Tarrik's triumph? Erif would see that no harm came to the children, her small brother and sister, but she might not choose to stand between Tarrik and her father. Whichever way it was, Berris Der found he would not be able to meet his father with either love or hate entire. He thought he would not go back till the thing was settled one way or the other, but he put off saying so to his sister until she had come back from her errand.

For Tarrik had given her the life of his Aunt Eurydice, his aunt who had brought him up from childhood and been in many ways a mother to him, with even a mother's jealousies. It was just. He told his men all that had happened and they agreed. Erif and Kotka, with twenty others, rode over the pass into Messenia. Tarrik stayed in Sparta, getting ready to go, intent on thinking only forwards.

The day before his wife was due to come back he told Sphaeros, who was horrified. He did not much like Eurydice, but equally he had a certain prejudice against Erif Der; she was the kind of person who disturbed life and made it run counter to its natural and divine order. She made stresses and violences, and as she grew older would make more. He was not now certain how much he believed that it was she who had bewitched Tarrik at the time of the bullfighting, though certainly when he had leapt into the flax-market he had believed it absolutely and acted in accordance with his belief. But it seemed to him that she made it impossible for Tarrik to act as a king, who was also his pupil and a Stoic, should act. He was doubtful how much the love of women was compatible with a good life. Agiatis was different, perhaps; her influence was for calm; she had learnt to master herself and change turbulent passion into kindness, and she was kind not only to one, but to all. Sphaeros, in his middle age, used to suffer most annoyingly from indigestion. He disregarded it, of course, and ate sour bread and black broth with the rest, but Agiatis used to make hot and comforting brews and get him to take them by saying that she knew she was a silly woman, but it would give her such pleasure, and smiling at him very nicely. Nobody else noticed at all.

Erif Der came back the next afternoon, tired and heavy-looking. She was less beautiful than she used to be, but Tarrik had not noticed that yet. He went out along the road to meet her and Sphaeros went too, for he was anxious to counteract, if he could, the passions that would almost inevitably be roused in his pupil, the thought of blood, the thing which should be hidden, brought up to the surface of the imagination. Erif dismounted at the side of the road and came over to them; Kotka followed her. It was a piece of stony waste ground beyond the houses, half covered with crawling dusty plants of the bitter cucumber. She began popping the little green gourds with the toe of her riding boot, watching the yellow juice squirt out. Tarrik found himself unable to speak, unable to ask how Eurydice had died. When the last of the cucumbers within reach of her boot was popped, she said, without looking up: 'I didn't kill her after all.'

During those days she had been gone Tarrik had managed to steady himself against the horror of the idea of his aunt's death. Now the idea was taken away and he overbalanced into indignant anger and said: 'Why not?' Then he saw Kotka looking at him with his mouth open, idiotically surprised. He flung up his hands and plunged away across the dusty land.

Erif Der looked after him. 'I knew he'd do that,' she said, miserable and helpless, biting her lip.

Sphaeros had stayed. 'Tell me what stopped you,' he said very kindly.

'I told her everything that had happened,' said Erif. 'I told her Tarrik knew I was going to kill her and had let me go to do it, and that hurt her through and through, yes, just like poison. And then Kotka brought in the man, her Rhodian.'

'He went soft under my hands,' said Kotka.

'So after that I thought,' said Erif, 'that she had better marry him and go away and never come back to Marob. So I suppose she will. Then we went away.'

Sphaeros nodded. 'But can you not tell me what it was—what principle, what idea—that told you to spare her?'

'No,' said Erif, 'I don't know. I just did. After all, she hadn't been able to kill me, though she took such a long time about it, and it wasn't she who killed my child. That will be different. I tell you what I did do, Sphaeros, on my way back. I found Apphé and killed her. I've always wanted to do that. She was a nasty worm with legs. Kotka held her arms and I cut her throat. It was nice. Do you think Tarrik is angry with me for not killing Eurydice after he gave me leave?'

'No, no,' said Sphaeros. 'You poor, unhappy children! But how could any of you hope to get what you seek out of Hellas?'

'I never thought we would,' said Erif. She looked round into the hot, cloudless sky that now, after all these rainless months, seemed to have dried all bright colours out of the earth, leaving it as brown as the world was before there was any grass or trees or friendly beasts. She rubbed her dusty hands on her coat and smeared the sweat out of her eyes.

'It was my fault,' Sphaeros said again. 'I should never have let your Tarrik think he could get any good of it. He persuaded me . . . against my judgment . . . that he and Kleomenes might be friends. It seemed possible in Marob, but I should not have allowed myself even to consider it.'

Kotka brought up the horses and told two of the men to dismount so that Tarrik and Sphaeros could ride. He was glad they had finished with Greece. Tarrik came back and mounted and rode on sharply, but Sphaeros said he would rather walk. He waited until the dust from the riders ahead had settled, and then followed them, more slowly.

Chapter Seven

ON HIS WAY BACK Sphaeros met Phoebis, who was on the whole sympathetic about the Scythians and how little good they had got out of Sparta. He himself was rather distressed and indignant because some of the Spartiates who had been friendly enough to him and his likes before they were citizens, were now not nearly so ready to consider them brothers. Sphaeros soothed him down. 'It'll pass, Phoebis,' he said, 'after the next battle! And I know it's none of the King's own Mess.'

'No,' said Phoebis, 'but I'm the only one who's in that, and the others mind more than me. They'll get their own back some day, or their sons will. I'm half and half, but some of them are pure helots, though we all pretend not to think so—except the King, who does dare look straight because he's an eagle! And they've been kept down all these years and years, oh, beyond time, Sphaeros! And now they've got their rights. It's like strong wine.' He scratched his head and grinned. 'Well, we've all got something wrong with us. There's our poor Therykion gone and fallen head over ears for a pink-and-white boy who can't run across two fields!'

'I heard that,' said Sphaeros. 'One hoped he might have been able to choose more wisely at his age: if one must fall in love, as you all seem to do whatever follies you can be certain it will lead you into.'

'Some people are fools,' said Phoebis. He laughed and felt better. He quite liked Therykion, but thought him fussy about his beard and nails and the hang of his otherwise very plain tunic. 'Panteus is the lucky one,' he said. 'Everything he touches goes right. I do like it when he sings. He and the King have got each other's heart for keeps, and when she's old enough he'll have Philylla, who's the same for the Queen or as near as makes no difference. She's a picture, isn't she, Sphaeros?'

'I suppose so,' said Sphaeros. Phoebis had hold of his arm and was walking him along rather fast. He stumbled once or twice. 'Is she gentle, do you know? When I'm there she scarcely speaks, but I have seen her racing about the fields by herself.'

'She's gentle and wise,' said Phoebis, 'and she knows something about my people. She doesn't mind the smell of cows and pigs and old thatch and garlic. She'll give him children. Sphaeros, did you know I was married? Well, I am. I married young and I married back, too. None of your fine useless ladies! She looked after the goats on the farm next ours. I've got two boys.'

'Does it hinder you?' said Sphaeros.

'No, it helps me. Because of the children. She'd stick to me too, whatever happened, even if the King was beaten in the end, as Agis was, and my citizenship was taken from me.' But that was a thing Phoebis didn't care for thinking about. He let go of Sphaeros suddenly and jumped over to the side of the road where there were bushes with milky-blue flowers, the kind that had been sacred to Hera in old days. They made quite a good garland flower, and Phoebis picked a whole bunch of them and began knotting the twigs together with a handful of stiff grasses. He made a pretty, straggly sort of crown and wanted to put it on Sphaeros. He was rather ashamed of having said so much and wanted at least to turn it into play, but as Sphaeros was extremely firm about refusing to put it on, he crammed it down over his own forehead and gay eyes, and then went rushing off, while Sphaeros went on towards the King's house.

He asked to see the Queen and waited. They brought him a bench with cushions into the front room, but by that time he had got out his tablets and was writing on them and not in a state to notice whether he was standing or sitting. One of the maids of honour went to find the Queen. There was a big, cool room at the back of the house, whose only windows opened into the covered walk round a courtyard full of green plants and the trickle of a fountain, so that they could not let past the dusty glare of the unveiled sun or the heat on the roads. The ceiling was made carefully of reeds, though there was a big rafter in the middle with two hooks on it for a rope swing, which was now looped back; the walls were blue and the floor had lately been sprinkled with water. Agiatis lay on a couch along the wall with the little girl tumbling about her feet. She was looking merry enough then, and soft and pretty as a young, new-married wife. Philylla had been reading to her, but now she had stopped and was talking about the nice baby Gorgo, whose mouth was full of her own silly curls and who wriggled and squealed with laughter and brightening eyes as her mother's strong toes tickled her. Philylla said: 'I do wish you'd have another baby, Agiatis. I would love to see you with a tiny fat baby.' She came and stood beside Agiatis and touched her breast gently with one finger and patted the edge of her white dress which the little princess had tugged down off her mother's shoulder. 'Oh, Agiatis, I would love to see you suckling a baby! Did you feed them all yourself?'

Agiatis laughed up at her. 'Yes, these ones,' she said, 'they were dears. It was what Kleomenes wanted. But I didn't with my first one. Nobody thought it possible or fitting for the Queen. But it's a sweet thing to do. You will, Philylla.'

Then Sphaeros was announced and Agiatis sat up straight and held the little girl in her arms, jogging her to keep her quiet. Philylla went over to the corner of the room and got herself distaff and spindle and would have gone out, but Agiatis called her back, for Sphaeros had just asked if she knew that Phoebis was married, and this was a thing that Philylla knew more about than she did. 'I've ridden over there,' said Philylla, 'oh, four times anyway. The place is full of bees in spring, tearing in from the hillsides. I always have bread and honey there and sometimes butter, for they've got cows: two more since the dividing up of the land. It's a big farm; all his people live there. She's nice, Sphaeros. Her name's Neareta. I think their own names matter a great deal to people of that sort; perhaps it's because they don't belong to one another the way we do. Her voice is rather thick and country, and she's getting fat, but I can see she must have been a lovely girl when he fell in love with her. And strong! she told me she could carry a big nanny-goat on her back, in those days. She's wonderful with animals now; they don't seem to mind what she does to them. And they've got two little boys.'

Sphaeros, used to estimating pupils from the answers they least thought he was attending to, on the whole thought that Phoebis was right about Philylla. He said: 'I want you both to be kind to the young Queen of Marob who came here to find her husband and is sailing off with him in two days.' And he told them all he knew about Erif Der and how he wanted the Scythians to go back to their queer outer land with not too bad an idea of the Greeks.

Agiatis listened and nodded and kept the child still, and Philylla listened and held the distaff in her armpit and set the spindle twirling with her clever, unconscious fingers. She had been curiously startled to hear the Scythians were going so soon. Why hadn't Berris Der told her? He was her property and he'd got no business to run away. Then she felt ashamed of herself and the thread broke, and for a moment she did not hear what Sphaeros was saying. She would be nice to this Queen, of course she would! Hospitality was a sacred thing. She had been right to lend her the horse at once without question. Then Sphaeros went out and Agiatis said: 'He is going to bring this little barbarian Queen to see us. I wonder what she'd like to have said to her. You've seen her, Philylla. How is one to talk to her?'

'Oh, she's just as nice as a lot of people,' said Philylla. 'Besides, she's a witch.'

Agiatis burst out laughing. 'You silly dear goose, you don't believe that?'

'She told me so herself,' said Philylla, 'and so did her brother. They ought to know. And I think, as well, that I understand the sort of way women can be witches.'

Agiatis sighed. 'I think I did when I was your age. One feels full of power, doesn't one? But it never lasts, sweet; not if one lives a full woman's life. One's giving too much all the time. Now, run and fetch me my comb and a mirror.'

Philylla went to the door of the King's house to meet Erif Der and bring her in. Erif was very nervous and hot, running with sweat in her best clothes, one of those stiff felt dresses embroidered all over with sets of toothed concentric rings in every colour. On her head was the heavy felt cone, and round it the very elaborate Spring crown that she had brought away with her: flower sprays with improbable blossoms and little animal running in and out, gold and coral and various enamels. Her hair was plaited with the queer patterned Chinese ribbons, and there were rings on all her fingers, most of them solid, hollowed amber. Philylla tried hard not to seem surprised and took it all in. Erif Der thanked her for the horse, which Kotka had led behind her as far as the door, for she could not possibly ride with that dress. Philylla said it was sad that she must go away so soon without seeing anything. Erif answered that her brother would do the seeing for her, as he was staying on. 'Oh,' said Philylla, as unconcernedly as possible, 'isn't he going with you, then?'

'I wish he was. But he won't.'

'Why not?' Philylla dared to ask.

But the answer was not very exciting after all. 'He is afraid of what may happen when we get back. He doesn't want to see it. He's not really brave.'

'He fought for Sparta and killed a general of the Achaean League!' said Philylla, almost too eagerly.

Erif, though, did not notice the tone. She said: 'Almost anyone can kill people in a battle. They don't have to think. It's all coming at one at once. But Berris sees things that are going to happen so clearly that he can't imagine any way round them. Then he runs away. That's being a coward.

And in the meantime someone else is sure to use his forge and break his tools and go to bed with his slave-girl.'

'I didn't know he had a slave-girl,' observed Philylla.

'Oh yes—Sardu. A nice little brown thing. After he went I used to practise magic on her sometimes. She didn't mind. Philylla, do you like my brother?'

'Oh—yes,' said Philylla.

'I'm glad. He gets stupidly lonely when his work isn't going just as he wants it to. He and I used to do things together a lot. I thought we always would. But everything has been different to what we meant. Philylla, what shall I do when I see your Queen?'

'There's no ceremony here. She's just like anyone else—only, I mean, of course, she isn't! She's Agiatis. Just go in.'

She stood aside at the door, and after a moment the Queen of Marob went into the cool room, and the Queen of Sparta, all in white, with only a white cord net over her hair, got up from the couch and took her by both hands. Erif Der looked straight at Agiatis, into her calm eyes, and forgot what she had meant to say and half absent-mindedly tilted up her face like a child's to be kissed, for she was not so tall as Agiatis, though taller than Philylla. Agiatis kissed her hot, damp cheek; she was amused and rather surprised, though she was used to younger women falling suddenly in love with her, and after a minute or two she thought she liked this odd Scythian Queen in her very curious and uncomfortable-looking clothes. She asked her what she thought of Sparta. The truth was that Erif, prepared even more than Berris to be impressed by things, had found very few of them that she liked at all, even less since the revolution and the new fashion for an authentic simplicity and Laconic bareness of life. She said: 'I have never seen such high mountains. They look closer than they are. But it is very hot.'

'And the people?' said Agiatis, smiling.

Here Erif Der had got a very definite impression, starting from the first day when she had met Philylla with the horses. 'They look as if something were going to happen,' she said.

'Something *has* happened,' said Agiatis, with a curious, rather sad pride.

Somehow it was the sadness that Erif Der caught. 'Yes,' she said, 'Sphaeros told me. Your baby died. Your eldest son. And I suppose you have never forgotten.'

Agiatis said nothing for a moment; she had not been thinking of that at all just then, at least it seemed to her that she had not been. She remembered what Sphaeros had told her about this other Queen. 'One does forget,' she said, 'one can, if one is wrapped round with love as I have been and as, I think, you will be. Lady of Marob, my dear, you've got your man back safe.'

Philylla had taken up the distaff and spindle again. Suddenly she found herself saying, with all the cheerful obviousness of discovery: 'How funny it is that women can make friends with one another so much faster than men! It's because of the way the same things seem to happen to them all.'

After a moment of translating it to herself, Erif Der began to laugh, and said: 'That's the kind of thing my brother says!'

Agiatis was rather embarrassed until the laughter came. It was so ridiculously like her dear and sometimes quite baby Philylla to arrive at the remark in this way. Was she ever going to grow up? Grown up and silent and observing and doubtful like a real woman? No. The Queen said: 'It's just as well women can do it quickly. We haven't as much time to waste as the men.'

Erif said: 'May I spin for a minute with your distaff?'

Philylla brought it over. 'It's a thin thread,' she said; she was proud of her fine spinning. 'Take care or it will break. It's sure to if you start it with a jerk.'

Erif Der twisted the spindle too hard, and of course the thread did break. Philylla picked it up. 'Shall I make the join for you?' she asked.

But Erif Der said 'No,' and laid the two ends on the palm of her right hand. 'Now watch.' And under the eyes of the other two the threads groped and wriggled like white worms and came together. 'There!' she said, and dropped them off her hand. The spindle swung from an unbroken line.

Philylla stared and came nearer and ran her finger down it. Then: 'What's that red mark on your hand?'

'Oh,' said Erif, 'that's a drop of blood,' and she stooped and wiped it on the under side of the hem of her dress.

'Why?'

'I had to make the thread alive so that it would come together; so it had to bleed where it was wounded.' And she began spinning properly. 'I think you will find this is a strong thread now,' she said, 'a very strong thread. I am doing my best with it.'

'Yes,' said Philylla, 'I see. But if it was me I'd like to be able to do it with people.'

Agiatis, though, was rather horrified. Later, when Philylla was taking Erif Der back to the door of the King's house, she picked up the thread which the Queen of Marob had spun and tried to break it. But it was certainly very strong. Then she thought of burning it, but she was not quite sure whether that would be a good thing to do. Later on it disappeared, and she thought it was wiser not to ask Philylla what she had done with it or whether she had woven it into some dress of her own.

Two days later the Scythians left Greece. Kleomenes, when reminded of it, went to say good-bye to the Chief of Marob who had fought for him, and made a real effort to be understanding and courteous and helpful, more because he knew Sphaeros wanted him to be than for any other reason. So Tarrik went away with the feeling that after all there was something in Hellas, and, though this time he had just missed it, perhaps one day it might be easier, and if there had only been, say, a week quite to spare with nothing important happening in it, he and Kleomenes might have made friends. But now he was very doubtful whether he had learnt enough even to try and be a philosopher king by himself. It would be easier to make the crops grow again in Marob and the women have plenty of boy children.

He was not bringing much away from Greece, except some rather fine weapons, a good many barrels of wine, partly for himself and partly as presents or bribes for when he got home, and several little linen bags of flower and vegetable seeds. He also had two or three seedling almonds in pots; even if they would not fruit in Marob, he wanted their blossoms for the Spring Queen. The others all had lots of things. Sparta, after the revolution, had been an admirable place to buy works of art in, pedigree dogs, jewellery and dresses; it would have been silly not to take advantage of it. Kotka had a set of small vases with curly ears and coloured wax stoppers all full of the latest and most fashionable perfumes of the western world for his wife. Black Holly had a pair of over-lifesize bronze wrestlers. Tarrik told him that if the ship were in danger they'd be the first to go overboard, and Black Holly was less annoyed than he might have been because once he had bought them he found that he liked them much less than he had meant to; they seemed squashy. But all the same every one hoped that the Corn King's ship would be lucky. Philylla had seen how much Erif Der liked her magpie, and had sent out and got her one to take home. It talked very well and with a certain impropriety, but luckily none of the Marob people were sufficiently up in the subtleties of the underworld to appreciate it fully, and Erif began teaching it phrases which had to do with the Spring Plowing; she thought it might be useful.

Sphaeros rode with them all the way to the coast, trying to think of the absolutely right thing to say and feeling curiously guilty. He said, and meant, that he hoped he would see them all again. Berris said good-bye at Gytheum too, and rode back, half depressed and half immensely elated, for now he could see what sort of a man—and by this he meant what sort of an artist—he would be by himself with no influences except those of Hellas. The first thing he did was to accept an invitation to go out hawking with Panteus, who was quite friendly, and some of the older boys and young men of his brigade, who were being trained in the new-old discipline. Berris loved hawks: the feeling, even over a gloved wrist, of those tense, strong claws clutching and balancing. He had always had them in Marob and he was expert at dealing with them and drawing them.

They went off into the hills in the very early morning when the light was loveliest. By and bye Kleomenes joined them, with his wife and most of her maids of honour. Some of the birds that were brought down were sent back to the King's Mess; others went to the brigade. By the afternoon they had killed enough, and though it was still the full heat of the day, Panteus made his boys show off to the King, wrestling and running and throwing hunting-spears and high-jumping over thorn bushes. The girls ran off to get leaves and any flowers there were to make crowns for the winners, and then ran back as fast as they could to see those boys and young men stripped and active. It was all happening in rather a pleasant rocky valley with a piece of flat field in the middle of it. This had once been plowed, but now it had been let go out of cultivation and the wild stuff was all over it again. At one side of the flat ground was a fairly deep ravine, quite dry now, but the beautiful plane trees that grew out of it showed that there would be water again in another month or two. On the other side were more trees, mostly the low, golden-green pines and between them dark prickly undergrowth with red berries. There were little goat-paths through it, and at their edges larkspur and crowds of violet-scented butterfly cyclamens. The girls picked lapfuls of them to mix in with their crowns, and made themselves necklaces of them and the pretty, strewn feathers of the game-birds. Most of them climbed up into the pine trees which grew slantwise with low boughs, and hung the wreaths as they finished them on to the warm, resin-smelling twigs. Up here in the branches they could see admirably and point and make their comments without being too much seen, and giggle and jump their swinging trees about when someone leapt short into a thorn bush or was thrown in the wrestling and came down on a stone.

'It's the one thing we didn't get in old days,' said Deinicha, expertly weaving a long supple heron's feather in and out of her fluffy hair to make a crown nearly as shining as silver. 'Oh my dear, they're going to have boxing now! I do hope nobody's going to get hurt!'

'I hope they are,' said one of the other girls, more truthfully. 'I do love it when they really get angry and go for one another and the blood comes. I feel as if it was all for me!'

'Well, it's not,' said Deinicha, 'so there! Look how they're sweating! There's Philocharidas, he's my cousin. It's doing him all the good in the world, anyhow; you never saw such a stupid as he used to be in old times. Never looked one's way once. Always reading and playing the flute, of all silly things, when it was perfectly easy to hire a really good professional. But now! Holy Mother, he doesn't let me alone a minute if he gets half a chance.'

The King and Queen walked together under Philylla's

tree; she dropped a loose chain of cyclamens, strung head to tail, over the Queen's head, then, as they both stopped and looked up, greatly daring she dropped one over the King too. He frowned, and she was rather frightened, but then she saw it was really a play-frown, and in a second he had jumped and caught her dangling hand, so that she was pulled right round under her branch, squealing and holding on for all she was worth with her knees and feet and other hand. Agiatis ran at the King and shoved at his throat and shoulders, laughing breathlessly in defence of her girl, and he let go Philylla to catch and hug his wife and then to put her wreath straight. She looked very young in the dappled light under the tree, just as those September cyclamens looked like spring. Philylla settled herself again in the crook of her branch, rubbing one bare knee where the bark had grazed it. 'Do you like them?' said the King, pointing out to the runners.

'Oh yes!' said Philylla, 'they're lovely. I do like the colour they are now.'

'You like them best with their clothes off?' said Kleomenes grinning.

'Of course,' she said, and then blushed and tried to pull down her short tunic.

'So do I,' said Agiatis. 'You're quite right, lamb. I believe my girls could do as well as some of Panteus' boys, though. I'm sure I've seen you jump better than that, Philylla.'

'I believe I could,' she said, measuring the distance. 'Now they're going to wrestle again. Oh the beauties!' And then suddenly she leant down out of her perch and touched Kleomenes lightly on the neck. 'Oh, sir, do go and wrestle yourself!'

'Shall I?' said the King to Agiatis. She nodded. For another moment Kleomenes stood still, frowning and pulling himself together. The cyclamen flowers looked lovelier and more delicate still on his dark head, but the thin little wreath had snapped already; the petals only clung on by their own twisty lightness. Suddenly he shouted and ran straight out into the middle of the field and threw down his clothes and picked up a handful of dust to rub himself with.

Agiatis said: 'Oh, you are clever, Philylla! It was what I wanted. He's been working too hard making out the plans

against Megalopolis. I could never get him away from it.'
She sat down on a big stone beside the tree and watched
him from under her hand. 'He looks well, though, don't
you think?' she said a little anxiously. 'There's so much
depending on him!'

He challenged the best of the boys, who came up, rather
nervous, and was fairly easily thrown. The King's long
sinewy arms got unexpected and unlikely grips on him.
Then Panteus came. Naked, he was quite a different shape
from the tall, thin-flanked King, much squarer and more
centred and better balanced on his feet, but not so quick
and perhaps not so violently in earnest. His body looked
less hard, still with a certain quite young roundness about
the thick muscles. Philylla gasped with pleasure, watching
them. They circled and closed and strained at one another;
for long periods of time they stood so still that she really got
her fill of the sight. But she knew that all the while they
were heaving, shifting stresses and balances, imperceptibly
altering their grips. The clear air put no barrier between
them and her. She saw Berris Der sitting on a rock a
little way off, watching just as she was; she felt very
friendly towards him, sharing the same beauty. The boys
and young men watched too, in lovely pale-brown groups,
half conscious of their own bodies and the girls in the trees
behind them, setting one another off with long legs and
straight backs and heads up in the golden sunshine against
the very deep blue sky.

The two wrestlers moved suddenly, got new grips, stood
and shoved, felt about with their feet in the dust. Then,
after a new movement Panteus got under the King's arm
and threw him, and every one shouted. Kleomenes got up,
rubbing his hip, where he was going to have a big bruise,
and said something to Panteus which made them both
laugh. Then they dressed and came back, hand in hand.
The winners came crowding for the King to give them their
crowns. They shook the trees as they passed under them,
but the Queen's girls held on and threw pine cones at them.
Berris Der came too, looking very odd and different from
the others in his coat and trousers, apart too in his observing
eyes; it seemed to Philylla that she was the only one who
noticed him at all. The hawks perched heavily, fed and
still, with their heads sunk down into their shoulders.

The boys went back to their brigade. There was no one left but the King and Queen, Panteus, and four or five of the maids of honour, who were playing cat's-cradle with a scarlet thread; the others were playing hide-and-seek among the trees. Berris Der stayed too, for there was no special reason why he should go anywhere else. He was cutting things in the wood of the pine trees, his own name three times over in beautiful Greek characters, and then just designs, letting his knife slice and cut in shapes that seemed to fit with the peeling bark and the light wood. Transparent resin oozed out of the cuts like very slow, very deep grief. The ship sailed back to Marob. It was too late to change his mind.

Philylla suddenly got up from among the cat's-cradle players and walked over to the Queen, who was sitting on the ground where the King had spread his cloak for her. She laid both hands on the Queen's shoulders and swung her lightly about. Strength flowed up through her wrists and arms; she was so strong, she could have picked Agiatis up in her two hands and run with her, carried them all like babies, plucked and bent the tough pine trees. Now it was almost evening; the level light swam between the King and the Queen and Panteus. None of them spoke, but they were feeling very near to one another. Philylla stood over them and said: 'I am very happy. I've got everything I want. I'm living at the right time and in the right place. I love you all.'

There was a queer silence for a moment while Kleomenes and Agiatis stared at one another in horror, as though some god were approaching whom they could not ward off. Panteus got to his feet and stood and looked across them at her. 'Take care, Philylla,' he said. 'Oh, take care or it will be turned against you!' And he held out both his hands towards her.

PART III

What Advantageth it Me?

And there were present the Picninnies, and
    the Joblillies and the Garyulies,
And the great Panjandrum himself with the
    little round button atop;
And they all fell to playing the game of catch-as-catch-can
    till the gunpowder ran out at the heels of their boots.

WITH THE END OF autumn the north wind that blows
softly or strongly all summer through in the Ægean Sea
shifts round to the south. They ran in front of it past island
after island, first dim and misty blue-purple ahead of them,
then as they got nearer an unfolding of barren brown cliffs,
and here and there a valley with patches of green along its
bottom, a harbour, a little town. So, hour after hour, they
coasted along till the island drew behind again, became less
actual, faded and faded till, when next they remembered to
look back, there was nothing there. This way they passed
Seriphos, Paros, Naxos—constellations of small islands,
named and obscure, or almost nameless, just rising out of
a smoothly silvered sea—Chios, Poieëssa, Lesbos, the
mountains of Asia on their right with the sun rising behind
them. The air grew cooler; sometimes there were clouds;
twice a short storm kept them in harbour. At Byzantium
again they changed ships.

During their few days in the town Tarrik sought out the
best known of the merchants who traded with Marob and
got the latest news and rumours from him. It seemed that
Harn Der was well thought of as Chief. There had been
another raid by the Red Riders towards the end of summer,
but Harn Der had ambushed them, killed more than half
of them—they were never kept as slaves—and driven
back the rest, scattering and terrified, into the lost wild
forest and marshes behind the hills. But there was no Corn
King, and, as far as that went, things had gone badly with
Marob. Having found that trade was so poor, the merchant
had not bothered to discover exactly what was happening
in Marob, but after much questioning Tarrik and Erif Der
found out more or less. Yellow Bull had died without giving
his powers to any successor, but Essro was Spring Queen,
and, as Tarrik had done nothing to hurt her things, she had

done her share well enough. Part, at least, of the flax crop
of the year had not been quite as bad as people had thought
it was going to be. Her son, Yan, was a very young baby
still, but the merchant remembered he had heard that the
Council of Marob had seen the child and thought well of
him, discovered certain marks on his body—not that the
merchant knew or cared anything about it!—and it was
at least likely that there were some in Marob who thought of
him as the possible new Corn King. At that Tarrik frowned
a good deal and looked at Erif, but she did not meet his eyes.
She glanced at herself in a silver mirror which the merchant
had hanging up beside his door, and it seemed to her that
she was recovering her looks.

For a time it had been all she wanted—or so she
felt—to be with Tarrik again. She made no plans and
asked herself no questions about magic; she was forgetting
Greece, forgetting all the time when he had not been there.
Even, in a queer way, it was good to be sad, for then he was
so kind to her, gentler than she had ever hoped anyone could
be. Sometimes she thought that, for herself, the pain had
been almost worth while. Yet, if she began thinking that,
she would lose faith with the dead child, the son who had
been violently alive all winter and spring inside her body,
almost talking to her, with little feet and fists and head
pounding against her heart. All that was left of him now
was some part of her; that part must be, still and always,
angry and unsoothed. But, for the rest, she had good nights
with Tarrik.

During the first days of the voyage they had lain on deck,
on the high stern of the boat. When they woke, they woke
sweetly to stars that looked down and were sorry for the
world, as Sphaeros had told them, stars moving in the great
circles that were proof of God. Erif liked stars now; though
neither she herself nor any magic could reach them, she did
not mind; though she could not reach them they did not
hurt her, they were beautiful without pain. She lay with her
head on Tarrik's chest and looked up at them, aware of the
calm sea and the tapering, trembling masts. Tarrik was big
and quiet. He had his arm round her, holding her down
to his body. She had got the peace she had always known
she could get by giving herself up altogether to him. She
had fought against it before, but now she did not feel like

fighting any more. So she could be quite quiet for a time and watch the stars from her place over Tarrik's heart.

> And when in bed there
> You call me sweeting,
> I lay my head there,
> I hear it beating,
> Or sleepy shifting
> On your strong breast,
> Dipping and lifting
> And giving rest,
> I feel the strength in
> Its steady beating
> While minutes lengthen
> To hours heaping:
> I know my life is
> But yours to use,
> To be your wife is
> The thing I choose.

For all she knew that might go on for ever and ever.

At Byzantium they had a big room with a bed raised on steps. Kotka used to bring them supper in there, all the oddest kinds of cakes and sweets and sausages that he could find. He wanted to do all he could to ensure their luck. He would be seeing his own wife soon. Erif got in half a dozen women to put her dresses to rights and make her more from the stuffs which she bought; men used to come from the warehouses with lovely things from all parts of the world and spread them out over the bed and on the steps, and Erif sat in the middle and laid folds of them over her wrist, tried them against her eyes and hair, and bargained for loom lengths to pack into her painted chests. For almost a whole morning these were being shifted and tipped and quarrelled over and carried down the gang plank into the ship which Tarrik had hired to take them back to Marob.

On the ship, Tarrik talked rather little about his plans. The others saw that he had them and left it at that. Some of them remembered, as they got nearer home, the queer things that had happened last year at midsummer and Harvest and at the bull-fighting, but when they discussed them in whispers together they came to the conclusion that whatever bad luck had been on the Corn King then would probably be off by now—had perhaps ended with the death of the child begotten in ill-fortune—and that at any rate if there was any hovering about still they were not going to help it to settle by allowing it in their words and thoughts. Kotka had asked him once what he was intending to do, but had not dared to go into much detail. Erif seemed content not to ask anything.

They were three days south of Marob when a rather annoying and persistent north-west wind began to blow dryly off the land. They rowed against it, but made very little headway. Tarrik was patient for quite a number of hours, but at last, when he got too tired of seeing the same mud-banks with the same low, greenish cape behind them, not altering position when he glared at them over the side, he began challenging the others to fight with him. They were none of them very anxious to take him on, but he threw things at them and called them names and hammered on the irritation that the wind had thrown every one into till they were all angry or sulky. At last Black Holly, who was one of the biggest and strongest, said he would fight. He had the advantage of knowing just where Tarrik had been wounded at Orchomenos and how to hurt him. Kotka searched them both for weapons. A space was cleared in the waist of the ship. Erif sat in the middle of a pile of fur rugs, heaped up between her and the wind, and laughed at them.

They ran at one another like two dogs, and clawed and kicked and grunted and rolled over and over one another and hit themselves against the deck and the spare oars and any corners of things there were. Black Holly ran his nails into the scar on Tarrik's wrist. Tarrik bit off a small piece of Black Holly's ear. Then the godhead came clear; Tarrik became filled with the strength of bulls and rams and growing wheat; Black Holly saw it and whimpered and lost his own strength. In a minute he was down, with his arms pinned to his sides and Tarrik kneeling on him and banging his head against the deck. The others pulled their Chief off. Erif jumped up and went to Black Holly, who was still half lying against someone's knees and feeling his bones to see if anything was broken. She began stroking him and telling him he was quite well, saying it was all play. She put the hilt of her dagger into his hands. He stopped glaring at the Chief and smiled at her instead. In a few minutes every one was quite cheerful, including Tarrik, who swung her off her feet and kissed her; his teeth were all red with Black Holly's blood still, but that would wash. Someone began singing; they all joined in. And at last they seemed to have got beyond that flat cape!

Now Erif had been reminded again of magic. She curled down among her furs and propped her chin in her hands and began remembering. She saw something grey fluttering over the waves, blown towards them. When it was nearer she saw it was a pigeon. The wind tossed it on deck close to her; as she picked it up its wings spread and quivered. She saw that one of its quill feathers was ringed with yellow paint and knew it must belong to Essro, her sister-in-law. She took it below and gave it bread soaked in wine. It recovered, slept, and was then quite tame, as if it were used to being handled by humans.

They were nowhere near a town, but in the evening the wind dropped a little and they got into shoal water, sheltered by mud-banks, and anchored. After midnight, when Tarrik was asleep and the whole ship very still, Erif woke. She pulled up the wick of the lamp to make a bigger flame and went over softly to the bar where the pigeon perched, asleep too. She looked at it hard; she listened; she put out her hand and felt it; she was almost sure it must have come on purpose. She cut herself off from every one on the ship, even Tarrik, and laid herself open to anything that might have come with the bird. She heard its heart beat, tiny and distinct and very, very quick; she knew that in its sleep it thought it was stretching its wings and curling its little claws in flight. For a moment she got its sleep vision of an air world, all a-flutter with possible dangers. But she could not get beyond it to Essro or anyone else.

After an hour she was very cold and her eyes ached with the unsatisfied strain. She pushed down the lamp-wick again and felt her way back under the blankets to Tarrik. She half meant not to wake him, but in the end, holding her cold hands and feet against his warm body, she got impatient at being left alone and woke him to take her back out of magic. The next morning she asked a question which she had managed not to want to ask yet. She said: 'What are you going to do about Yellow Bull's son?' He said: 'There cannot be two Corn Kings in Marob, but I'll see when we get there.' And he began talking of other things. Erif, though, was almost sure he had made up his mind. Then it appeared to her that the bird's coming on board was after all an accident of the wind; the poor creature no doubt saw the ship while it was being blown over the water and struggled to get to safety. There was no purpose of Essro's. The purpose would be her own.

All that day the wind dropped. Erif wrote on a thin piece of linen: 'Hide with your baby. Danger from us.' She tied it round the bird's leg, fed it well and let it go. For a few minutes it circled uncertainly, then seemed to get its bearings and made for the land. She turned from watching it and found Tarrik watching her. 'Were you doing magic?' he said. Then: 'For me this time?'

'I never know what it is going to be in the end,' she said, 'and what I was doing then wasn't quite magic. It was more real, I think, not an appearance.'

Tarrik said: 'Your magic is not an appearance, Erif. You are not to say it is.'

The bird was almost out of sight. 'Why not?'

'Because I tell you not to, little witch! Because I don't want to hear any more about appearance and reality. Because I've left Greece and I am going to be King of my own country.'

'I liked Sphaeros,' said Erif, 'by the end.'

'I never said I didn't like him. Or any of it. But that's over. When you say your magic is only an appearance, Erif, you mean that mine is too—my power over the seasons! And you are not to say that.' He shook her.

'Very well,' said Erif, enjoying being scolded as she would have enjoyed being out in a storm. But she couldn't all the same help saying: 'It's not very safe to say about anything that it's over. Is it, Tarrik?'

A few days later they rowed into Marob harbour, a little after dawn, and made fast to the rings. They had seen, when they were close to the harbour mouth, a great crowd all along the breakwater sand walls, but as they rowed in the crowd dispersed, and by the time they had thrown out mats between their sides and the stone quay and then tied up, there was no one left except three or four of the inland traders who were nothing to the Chief of Marob, and some slave girls who would never be noticed either way. All the same it was probable that they were being watched from the houses. Tarrik came up into the bows by himself in full dress as the Chief, white felt embroidered with metals and colours; but he was bare-headed because the Corn-crown was still in Marob. He stood quite still at the prow, looking towards the town, quiet and bright and just the same between grey sea and a sky so very pale blue, only lighted by the strengthless, November sun. When he had looked he turned his back on the town and sat down on a coil of rope.

After a little, Kotka beckoned to one of the inlanders, a squat, hairy savage who traded in furs and resin and sometimes amber. 'Where is Harn Der?' said Kotka.

The man grinned; he did not like Harn Der, who had killed a great many of his cousins, the Red Riders. He said: 'Harn Der is gone.'

Kotka gasped a little and looked up at Tarrik for a sign, but the Chief stared out to sea beyond the harbour mouth, and his face was hard. 'Where?' said Kotka.

'Away, in his winter waggons, with all his household, and food for six months.'

'Much good that will do him,' said Kotka. 'We shall track him and catch him like a beast.'

'Perhaps,' said the inlander, but he looked north into the whitish and chilly sky, and Kotka too, following his look, thought it very likely indeed that the snow would come within three days and there would be no tracking anyone.

Erif Der made a sign to Kotka. He said: 'Where is Essro, who was the Spring Queen?'

'Gone,' said the man. 'Gone too. Suddenly.' Then he said: 'I have a present for the Spring Queen who comes back.' He took three very fine ermine skins out of the breast of his coat. 'Tell her: from the inlanders.'

Kotka took them, a little disdainfully, though he could see they were beauties. 'Oh, these,' he said, 'from the inlanders: very well. But—take care!—not from the Red Riders!'

The man went back to his friends and seemed to be telling them all about it. Someone else came down on to the quay. It was Kotka's wife, the witch Disdallis, with two small children beside her, a boy and a girl. She was very fair and she wore a stiff dress of crimson felt with branches and hearts of crushed turquoise sewn on to it round the hem and waist. The cone on her head was crimson, with turquoise dangles, and her ash-fair plaits were tied with the same colours. She hurried stiffly down the quay to the ship, waving her fingers at Kotka. He was going to jump ashore to her, but she cried to him to wait till she had strewn some small things she had brought with her on to the stone which his foot would touch first. He called to her: 'I am going to the Council. If they want the Corn King back they must say so, and quick.'

Disdallis motioned that she could not speak for a moment, then put down the last of the things and said: 'Oh, they'll want him. Things have gone badly wrong this year. Now, jump!' She held out her arms.

Kotka jumped into Marob and gave her and the children a thorough kissing. She went nearer the boat. Erif leant over and they touched hands. 'Do they want me too?' asked Erif.

'They do,' said Disdallis, 'and we do. We like Essro, but some of us did not help her so well as we would have helped you.' And she reached up a sprig of flowers made of coral and scented wax.

Erif knew she was speaking for the witches of Marob. She fastened the sprig on to her dress, and said: 'Do you know where Essro is?'

'Yes,' said Disdallis, and looked at her straight. Then: 'Midsummer and Harvest went wrong. Essro did her part, but she had no one to dance with. There was rain during all the end of the summer; in some places the corn sprouted in the ear. We shan't have more than enough to keep ourselves over winter. There was none for the ships to take. Last week there was a fire in the flax stores and a great deal was burnt. And one of the wells in the middle of the town has turned brackish. You, Erif—are you ready to begin everything again?'

'I want things to do at once,' said Erif, and stood up and stretched herself.

Kotka and his wife went up off the quay and the ship waited. Tarrik still sat on the coil of rope with his back to the shore. He did not even answer Erif when she spoke to him, nor would he eat. By and bye Kotka came back with most of the Council. Tarrik had his back even a little more turned than before. The Council saw that he was as bad as ever, and that it was on purpose. But they also knew that they must have him back; they could not, for the sake of the land, afford to be proud. They spoke, one after another, bidding him welcome to his own place. He did not answer. The first speakers had tried to hint at terms and compromises; they hoped to get something more reasonable to deal with than the Chief who used always to laugh at them! But the later ones, more wisely, had said nothing about things of the sort. It began to be rather terrible that he would not turn round. They did not know what his face would be like. Kotka stood behind; he and his witch wife were smiling.

The Council whispered together; some of them went back. In a short time they had got hold of most of the rest of the people who mattered in Marob. Also they had made a wide and splendid pathway out of the most beautiful carpets and shawls in the place for the Corn King to tread. They appealed to one after another of the nobles who were on board. Each of them looked out and answered that the Chief was angry because of some different thing, but mostly either to do with their conduct towards him and the Spring Queen, or else to having let Harn Der escape now. The Council consulted again. They brought and showed the Corn-crown of Marob. They sent up to the town for a white bull which one of them owned, and sacrificed it on the quay-side in a noise of horns and drums. Then they smeared its blood on their own throats and foreheads; it was for them.

Tarrik was watching the sky. It was nearly evening now. All the afternoon the sun had been behind clouds, but there was a clear belt above the horizon. The sun was almost down to it. He waited, smelling the bull's blood. He had eaten nothing since dawn and he was hungry. Now in a moment the sun would come clear over the western sea. He rose slowly to his feet and turned. As he looked down from the ship on to the people of Marob, they felt a warmth, a happiness they had not felt all day. They saw him in a golden haze, backed by the sun. He was coming down! The men threw out gang planks; the Council rushed to kneel and steady them. From the stern of the ship the Spring Queen came out. She had washed her hair the day before, and now it stood out over her shoulders and under her crown in a mane of soft lightness. They took hands and walked off the ship together and straight up into the Chief's house without saying one word to any of the Council.

For many days after that both of them had plenty to do. Erif went to the Spring-field, her place, and lighted such candles as she was allowed at this time of the year. Under one of the flower-pots where, later on, she would sow flax seed, there was a pigeon's feather and a written message, which must be from Essro, saying she had gone to the house by the marshes and would trust to the snow all winter. Erif would have stopped the danger by Spring! It also said: 'I never meant Yan to be Corn King. Tell Tarrik it was the Council.' That was just like Essro! Erif found everything in good order at the Spring-field, but Tarrik had to spend many nights and days in his place, getting things straight again, for Yellow Bull seemed to have done some queer things in his last two months, as though he had not been able to think very clearly. The plowshare had a curious dent in it now. Tarrik thought he would have to make or have made a new one. He wished Berris was there to do it.

The third day after they were home the snow began falling and went on steadily for a fortnight till the drifts were piled high against the outer houses. In the town it was trampled down hard and the households got out their sledges. The bullfighting had happened just before they landed; more than usual had been killed and salted down because of the shortage of fodder. All the boats were hauled up on land, including the ship Tarrik had come in. Things had ended at Marob for the year.

Harn Der and the children had vanished. They must have gone at least twenty miles every day before the snowfall; they might be anywhere. Erif Der would have liked to tell her small sister about things, tell her about love even if she did not understand yet; Wheat-ear would have sat quiet and looked soft and wise. And it seemed a long time since she had played with Gold-fish. But she would not think about her father, not till the moment came to do so once and for all and then no more. She hoped they had plenty of food. It would be dull at first in the waggon camp, but when the snow had settled and firmed down over the land they would go about in their sledges and laugh at the silly trees half buried. Essro and Yan had vanished too. Yan had been a quite small, funny, sleepy baby. He had been born a few weeks before her own, and she had liked him because she was going to have a baby too. Only better, only dearer. He must be big now.

It was warm in the Chief's house. Erif found she did not like her old rooms. She took what had been Yersha's, but cleared out everything, dropped the vases smash out of the windows and then was sorry, and had the walls painted over the pale frescoes with stripes of blue and red. There was a certain amount of books and clothes left, which the Chief's aunt had not had time to pack and take away with her. Erif did various magics with them and then waded out into the cold sea, and threw them out as far as she could and bade them not to come back. She thought that the result might be weakened by its journey through the water to Rhodes, but still there would almost certainly be something to remind Aunt Eurydice of Marob! She would try to find out next summer. Erif had never mixed her magic with hate before. Even when she had done all those things to Tarrik there had been little real hate in it; she had thought there was at first, but now that she had got experience of the real thing she understood that what she had felt about Tarrik was only the same kind of tussle there had been when she and Berris had quarrelled as children and had sometimes been days pulling hair and calling names before they had kissed and made it up. Besides, with Tarrik, she had been so interested in seeing what happened. She had done it for fun, as perhaps magic should be done. Real hate was a queer, tricky thing. She did not like it much; she was not certain that it helped her magic at all. It had at least made her ashamed to tell Disdallis or any of the other witches who were friends of hers and who might have taken a share in what she was doing to Yersha's old clothes.

During the first weeks she had gone about proudly and gaily with Disdallis and the others, all going arm-in-arm over the trodden winter snow in their jolly winter clothes, singing the noisy cold-weather songs, stamping and clapping their hands and laughing, helping the laughter of Marob. They were glad to have the Spring Queen with them again; she was glad to be part of them. But this magic she made on Yersha was not a laughing magic: it separated her from them; it was malicious. When they were all together she spoilt it. They did not know why it was happening, but often they did not want her. Often the witch girls of Marob played their games alone or only let Erif Der come in because she was the Spring Queen. She, feeling it, had sudden moods when she spirted out hate against them and against magic. She wanted to be separate. She would have liked to be in Greece again talking to Philylla and Queen Agiatis, liking it and yet free of their life—light as a leaf. Yet that only came on her from time to time during the winter and it did not distress her much until later. So long as she was right with Tarrik she was essentially right with the world.

During the first month Tarrik had to see to rationing the corn and also had to make certain that there should be crop seed next year for anyone with land to sow in. Some of the Council were not altogether pleased, as they had managed to collect a surplus, even in such a desperately bad year, out of their very wide lands, and they were considering profits. But most of them approved what Tarrik ordered. Of course, the Corn King himself had never any land, except the house and garden. If he had he might have neglected other people's. But he could always take what he wanted in the way of food-stuffs. This winter he took his usual share; if there was any over it would go in feasts for the whole of Marob. But he gave very fine gifts for it. Nobody but Erif knew how much emptier the treasure-rooms were than they had been. It seemed to her that he was taking a great deal of thought about how to be King, but she did not say anything to him by way of comment, because he might have suddenly begun to suspect himself of having been influenced by Sphaeros and the Greeks. He had one or two people killed during the first few days, but it seemed rather unnecessary, and he did not behave with the rest as though he were going to go on being suspicious or afraid or likely to do any more killings. He was very anxious to know just how far the secret road had gone and said that he would take it further himself next year. The worst of it was that Yellow Bull had been bad at explaining what he wanted done, except quite immediately. He kept most of his plans in his head, and such as were written down would all be in his house by the marshes.

The little almond trees Tarrik had brought back with him from Greece were put in Erif's room and watered.

They stood on the top of a chest. Inside the chest were the clothes she had got ready for her baby. The almond would bloom again. Erif Der would bear another son.

Chapter Two

THE SNOW HAD MELTED almost everywhere, uncovering the ever-green leaves and the very young leaves and the brown, soft hummocks of earth, rested and sweet after the winter. If you went outside the town and listened, you heard water all round, trickling and soaking away towards the sea. If you listened better still, as Erif listened, you would hear the murmur of the great waters fretting and foaming among mud islands and channels far to the south. She stood beside Tarrik and watched him pressing his hands into the cold sticky clay. He liked it. She felt an absurd, mild annoyance at his absorption with it. 'Tarrik!' she muttered impatiently, 'Tarrik, stop, get up!' He looked at her with smiling, possessive eyes, and spoke softly and thickly as though the stickiness of the soil and the early spring fogs were clinging about his tongue and lips. 'Plowing Eve! We will make a good furrow, Erif!'

It was always the same, year after year, as winter began to loosen and soften, and Plowing Eve got nearer. People came out of their houses more and talked more, looking at one another, men and women, with sudden discovery, and felt a growing and brightening of the senses, keener sight, smell, taste, hearing, touch, not quite a falling in love and yet comparable with it, as though perhaps it were a falling in love with the young, young spring, the incredibly pale and remote and maiden season, still wrapped about with snow. Children felt it as well. Fewer people died at that time of year. They watched the comings and goings of the Corn King and the Spring Queen, looking for signs of the godhead that was ripening in both of them, and getting into touch with it themselves.

Tarrik was used to it and expected it, and yet every year it was equally exciting. They began to give him odd and traditional foods, and hid away all his coats except those of red and yellow. He began to feel extraordinarily strong and gay and sure of himself. As he walked through the streets he would suddenly bound towards people, women mostly, and touch their faces or hands. Even if they had been looking ill or unhappy before, their answer to him for the moment would be laughter and happiness. Childless wives put themselves in his way; often they had luck afterwards. It was good to be able to do that. In his security and confidence he said one day to the Council that he would not care now if Harn Der came back tomorrow; he would not so much as frown at the old man with no power. Of course, no one quite took what the Corn King said at these times as anything binding, but all the same Harn Der's friends looked at one another and felt it was something to start on.

He went to his own Place and did various things there. The new plowshare had to be made by the best of the metal-workers, a friend of Berris, a man so much interested in his actual craft that he was scarcely interested at all in the directions which Tarrik gave him. Most of the time while it was being made, Tarrik hung about the forge, handled tongs or bellows, helped with the cooling. He knew a good deal about the smith's trade, but had never taken the trouble to go through with making any big thing—and small ones bored him. He found himself talking a great deal about Greece. It was odd, but he did not try to stop himself in anything that came naturally to his mind or body just before Plowing Eve. Though he had put out of his thought as much as possible of the people and ideas, yet some of the things stayed, the things Berris had shown him in Athens, and the mountains, and the dry, deep summer colours everywhere. So he talked and talked, and sometimes the man who was working on the plowshare listened to him, and sometimes he was too deep in his work. The snow outside reflected quantities of light into the spark-jetted cave of the forge. When the plowshare was finished absolutely rightly, Tarrik wrapped it in a piece of new linen and took it back by night and in silence to its place.

In the morning of Plowing Eve, every one went up to the fallow field in their best clothes. There were thick clay jars standing about, filled with a brownish drink that was made out of fermented wheat and only used on feast days. As it was rather nasty it was usually mixed with honey. Early in the day it had been raining, but by the latter part of the morning it had stopped, and the clouds rose and parted. The people stood and sat and lay about the edges of the damp field, with the coloured rods standing upright in it for the plowing marks. They got drunk, but this stuff, instead of making them softly drunk, as their usual herb-steeped mead did, made them drunk and hard and excited. After a time, in one and then another and another part of the ring round the field, the excitement grew and flared to a point, a violence, but, instead of wanting to fight, the man would want to shout, would begin shouting for the Corn King to come, for the plowing, for the year to begin. The shouting ran in waves, round and round. They clapped their hands on their thighs. The shouting took rhythm, became a double song of men and women, deep and shrill. It beat across the fallow field, and on to the plowshare at the side of it.

Now it was noon. At opposite sides the ring parted, huddled back on to itself as the song dropped to satisfied eagerness. From the south came the Spring Queen, with her eyes straight and held, unseeing, unsmiling, past men and women she knew well, brushing by her friend Disdallis, more apart than a bride, and so into the middle of the field. She sat down quietly there and hung her hands over her knees and dropped her head forward on to her wrists. She had a white dress with hundreds and hundreds of little coloured wool flowers fastened on to it all over by long wool stalks. As she walked slowly over the fallow field she was almost shapeless with the hanging mass of them, dropping over her fingers and down from the hem nearly over her feet. Her hair hung behind her in a tight single plait.

From the north end of the field came the Corn King, leading his white plow-oxen with painted horns. He himself wore a curious garment, long strips of coloured stuff over his naked body from neck to knee, belted at the waist, but splitting everywhere as he moved. Tarrik, wearing it, knew that his body was all shivering with no more than this between it and the March wind. All round the ring every one still wore furs and felt. Yet it was scarcely cold that he was. He did not look towards the Spring Queen, but yoked his oxen to the plow and began to drive them along the outer edge of the field. The ring of people were singing and dancing: the plow went in a square, inside their circle; it moved slowly past them like a knife-blade scraping along flesh. In the dance they too began to move slowly round the field, slower than the plow. Birds hovered, crows and seagulls, but did not dare to settle in the furrow for fear of the people. Tarrik pressed on the plow-beam, in, in to the hard, sticky, reluctant earth. After he had made and closed the full square about the field, he did not plow it all, only went parallel with his first lines and then suddenly inward on a sharp turn just as his immanent godhead and the sight of one of the plow marks might move him. After a time he began to talk to the Spring Queen in the middle, over his shoulder, in a loud, impersonal voice.

He talked about the plowing. He said: 'This is my field. Mine.' He said: 'Other things are mine. Everything I think of is mine, everything I name. Under the plow. They go under. The plow is a ship. It goes through thick water. It is bringing gold to Marob. I am the plow. It is my body. It is hard and strong. It leaps on the closed sod and plunges through. Soon comes the seed.' And every time he said one of these things the crowd would sigh after him: 'Plow hard! Plow deep!'

At first the Spring Queen said nothing. She seemed asleep. Then she raised her head a little from her knees and began to answer: 'Though you plow the field it is not your field. Why should the field hear? The closed soil has no pleasure of the plow, and cold and hard it will be to the seed. Why should the spring come?' But the people of Marob cried at her softly from the edges of the field: 'Spring Queen, be kind, be kind!'

So they went on until the middle of the afternoon. Tarrik was the plow, the seed, the warmth and force of growth. Erif was the hard, fallow field; the cold, reluctant spring. The words they said were in no set form or order, only, on every Plowing Eve since the beginning of Marob, the same kind of loud, unhurrying talk had gone on between the sweating Corn King and the still, shivering Spring Queen, with the same implications behind it. It would go on happening for countless years longer. This way, in Marob at least, the food and wealth of the people was made to grow. It was better not to make the talk into a plain repetition, a formula; the life might go out of it. Now as it went on the people divided up more and more, the women shouting at the Corn King to plow deep and hard, the men calling on the Spring Queen to be kind.

Tarrik had done all this at Plowing Eve since he was

a boy. And afterwards, if he thought about it, he could never understand how he got the strength for the whole day, the plowing and dancing and shouting. When it was over he always slept dreamlessly and deliciously, yet not for longer than usual. He remembered that for the first few years he had been afraid, when the day came, that he would not be able to go through it rightly; but he always did. Now he had no fears. Only it was difficult to wait through the morning, after every one had left the Chief's house and gone up to the field, to wait there by himself, doing nothing, getting more and more aware of the smell and texture of the brown earth of the fallow field lying ready for him. He did not think of the day when he would begin to feel his strength go. Why should he? It was no part of him yet. As he plowed and talked and pressed and ached and held hard for the plow marks and felt the furrow opening and the wave of earth turning, the dark, torn clods and crumbs tumbling and settling, he knew that the Spring Queen was in the middle of the field and he was coming towards her. He had forgotten that she was also his wife, Erif Der.

This was her third Plowing Eve. The first time she had been a young girl, proud and confident and sure of her strength and her magic, deeply excited, but yet underneath always herself and her father's daughter, working for the moment with the seasons and with Tarrik, but ultimately not surrendered and prepared to work against Tarrik whenever she chose, later on, although at the moment she was doing the thing she liked, for fun. Last year it had been with her brother, Yellow Bull, and it had all seemed wrong and twisted. There had been something very queer about his plowing; even the oxen had noticed it, and she had seen at once through her half-shut eyes. And she was ill then, full of pains that suddenly took her and swept away everything else. She knew that she had fainted once or twice during her wait in the middle of the field, and once or twice she had heard herself speaking as she became fully conscious again, and was only thankful that the godhead was still with her enough to move through her senses. When she had realised that, she had let herself go into a sort of dim condition in which it possessed her and did and said the things for her, and she could look on and bear the pain that she thought

then was coming from Tarrik's child, but was really the
poison with which Yersha was trying to kill her.

This time she was relaxed again to her own godhead, but
without pain. The child in her had not begun to stir yet. It
was still tiny, a little queer worm at the base of her body,
sending small messages of shock and disturbance. But also
it was security. If everything else about her was appearance,
if she grew so uncertain of her own existence that it became
no difficult or unlikely step between life and death, then
this thing which was her and yet not her, anchored her,
nailed her down to some kind of reality. It was good to
feel secure, good to be part of the seasons, budding and
ripening with them.

She raised her head a little to give another answer and
saw that the plow-oxen were quite near, that the fallow field
was almost plowed. Suddenly Erif Der was unreasonably
and beautifully glad. Her voice, as the crowd was hoping
it would, grew louder. She was the spring and she would
come with flowers and small leaves and lambs and a growing
child. The plow came again across her field of vision and
then turned inward towards her. She did not know at all
how violently she was shivering. The painted horns of the
oxen swung together and apart. She saw the Corn King's
eyes over the backs of the beasts. The plow came at her.
The singing stopped. At the last moment she leapt to
her feet, ran under the horns of the oxen, between their
panting flanks, and leapt the plowshare itself as it made
the last furrow right through the centre of the fallow field,
tearing apart the warmed, flattened grass where she had
been sitting.

At once the singing began again, men and women together,
and the ring swept inwards, nearer to the middle of the field
and across the first belt of plowing, so that their feet trampled
stickily into the brown, turned sods, the flesh of earth. 'The
spring is awake!' they cried. 'Awake! Oh, awake and truly
awake! The year is beginning again!' Then bagpipes took
it up, then small drums. Then men ran into the centre with
poles and planks which they fitted together into a booth,
raised a little away from the ground and about ten feet
square. Long sticks twined with ivy and stuck with red
and yellow wool roses went up from the corners and were
bent and tied together overhead into a kind of canopy. It

took an amazingly short time, just long enough for Tarrik
to throw himself on the ground, into his new furrow, and
lie there with his eyes shut and allow one set of images to
die out of him and another to take possession. The Spring
Queen stood at the other side of the booth while they sang
at her and threw sharp, heavy corn ears, left over from
last year; some of them like tiny arrows hit her face and
hands, others stuck in her hair; they pricked her flesh to
movement.

When the stage was finished, all hammered together, the
voices stopped, but the pipes and drums went on. The Corn
King and the Spring Queen went up on to it and stood facing
one another. Then they began a dance of courting. In that
confined space it was necessarily very formal and curtailed.
Sometimes even they were quite still for long moments in an
attitude of gazing, the Corn King pressing back the wrists of
the Spring Queen from the ends of her long arms stretched
straight over her head, leaning over and close to her, staring
down into her eyes. Sometimes one or both of them span
round and round. When the Spring Queen did this the
wool flowers on her dress flew out in a curious widening
shower, and then, as she stilled, folded themselves back on
to her. Sometimes the Corn King just jumped, by himself,
as some sorts of birds do, showing off to their mates. The
strips of stuff that he wore were always jumping out and
apart. Underneath he was earthy with clay of the furrows
over his nakedness. He felt it everywhere, clay that had
been cold now warm against his body.

The drums and bagpipes went on continuously, and the
sharp, hollow handclapping from the crowd. They span in
the blast of noise. The dance became the climax of the
courting between Corn and Spring. He leapt at her. She
gave at the knees and all along her body and fell on the
floor of the booth, not painfully, for she was all slack to
it. Then before the eyes of all Marob he jerked the strips
of stuff sideways and away from himself. For one moment
all the growers of corn could look on the hard and upright
sign of the godhead on their Chief and Corn King. Then,
still to the squealing of pipes he threw his hands up like a
diver and all his body curved and shot downward towards
her. She did not feel his weight because of the tension in
her own skin from head to heels. In the convention of the

dance and in a solid noise of drums the Corn opened the Furrow, broke into the Spring, and started the Year.

It lasted only long enough for this final idea of the dance to get into the minds and bodies of the Marob people. By some curious process, and in spite of the movements he went through in this sacred mimicking of life, all desire of doing it in reality and not only in the dance had left the Corn King. It did not come into his intense but limited consciousness that the Spring Queen was a woman, partner and satisfier of a man's desire. He was not himself a man seizing in ultimate necessity on woman's flesh, but a god making plain his power. Being now this image himself, he was satisfied with an image. Later on that day, as always, the actual thing would happen, but he did not even consider it; he was not yet the person who would be and do that.

Drum and pipes stilled. Suddenly all the people of Marob rushed at the booth of the dancing and at the Spring Queen, lying still and with her eyes shut on the floor. They began to pull the flowers off her dress, snapping the wool stalks, one flower for every household. As they surged round and over her with small rustlings and tuggings, her body quivered and leapt again and again. The Corn King turned her over for them to pluck the flowers from her back. Her shut eyes rested on her hands, damp with sweat that slowly cooled and chilled. He stood back; she was the sacrifice. During the dance her hair had come unplaited; it lay in tangles round her head. People trod on it. The most eager ones would stoop and pull out one of her hairs to go with their flower. Each had a piece of new white cloth for wrapping. Folding it up, hiding it away, satisfied, under a belt, or in the breast of a coat, one after another the householders stepped back and climbed down off the stage. At last all had gone.

The booth was taken to pieces just as quickly as it had been put up. Girls dressed bridally in green and white, with very large hats like inverted peg tops, led the dishevelled Spring Queen away to a covered cart and laid her on a deep pile of furs. She went to sleep almost at once and did not wake, however bad the long jolting back to Marob was. She scarcely stirred when they carried her out, back into the Chief's house. Here they undressed her and smoothed her hair, cutting out and keeping for luck the entangled corn ears, and put her to bed and took turns to stay by her with a light through the evening and night. But she slept very soundly and softly, with her fingers clasped unstirring under her chin, and did not turn over in bed even once.

In the field the Corn King took off his belt and ducked out of his odd, ragged dress. The men brought warm water and poured it over him, rubbing off the clay till he was clean again. Then he put on fresh clothes, coat and breeches of red stuff sewn all over with little plaques of gold, tiny rayed suns, and the same on his boots. He wore a crown with spikes; below each spike stared out a rounded and ringed cat's-eye stone. By now it was sunset; the red light was reflected separately in every one of the flat pieces of gold as he moved or breathed. He was taking the power and glory of the day into himself. They brought him wine, and honeycomb on a golden dish. He took a piece of the honeycomb in his mouth and crushed it between tongue and palate. The golden honey oozed over his lips and down his throat. The dusk of evening closed over the plowed field, but the Corn King himself was the sun now.

Torches were stuck all round and others were carried, whirled and tossed about. Trails of sparks blew across the evening. Half the men of Marob formed themselves into the eight spokes of a wheel, of which the Corn King with the honey in his mouth was centre and giver of motion. They began to sing and wheel. The inner ones turned slowly, the outer, who were all the younger men, bounded hand in hand, stumbling and recovering and leaping in the furrows, knocking down the thin gay plowing marks when they met them. The Corn King was, at the same time, turning slowly and moving step by step onwards along the edges of the field, so that the circle should roll round it, sungates, touching it everywhere. As the spokes of the wheel tired and dropped panting, others from the crowd sprang in and joined hands and made them up again. By now all had drunk deeply of the wheat brew and eaten much honey with it that made them thirsty for more drinking. The torches were seeming to roar and flare behind their eyes now. The wheel throbbed, expanding and contracting. The plowed field rocked and leapt under their feet with pain and pleasure of its plowing.

As the sun ring went on and began to come back to its first

place, a good many of the women left the crowd and slipped off homewards, among them most of the young wives and quite young girls. It was thought no dishonour to stay in the plowed field this day of all the year, and no husband or father could well complain, but all the same they might mind, and one does not want to hurt those one loves. Still, quite enough women stayed for the men to be able to work their own and only magic and help the Corn King to help the year. Among these women, too, the bowls of drink were passed round, and dizzily, too, for them the wheel span on towards their waiting bodies. They sang to welcome it and stirred up the torches and waved red and yellow ribbons and stamped. The wheel swept through its path to the end and slowed down and broke up sweating and panting. The hub of it, the Corn King, the sun himself, stood in a furrow with his arms stretched out; anyone who looked at him could see that his eyeballs were swinging still from side to side, and clearly he could not see much. But that came right. His arms lifted a little, his shoulders squared back, his gold scales glittered, and he grew bigger and fuller of heat and power. He threw up his head and laughed. Then he went forward among the women and made his choice. The night of Plowing Eve had begun.

As it went on and on and the magic of the men was let loose over the plowed field, so Tarrik lost more and more of his godhead. It was fun, it made him laugh in great bursts that every one heard. It started the year well; it was easy. But it had not the sacredness of the sham thing. Between times he began to remember other sorts of ideas. He began also to try and count up how many more times, with the best of luck, this would happen. It only happened once a year: twenty—thirty times more perhaps—three or four times beyond that with any luck. But once you look at a thing and see it is finite, how very little that extra three or four times matters! He used not to mind, used not to think of himself as anything apart from Marob, which went on for ever. It was the Greek part of him standing up in his heart and whispering. The Corn King would always be there, but Tarrik only for a few more years. No, no! Woman, make me forget, rub against me, light fires to burn up all this useless thought!

Towards midnight he encountered Sardu, the little,

brown, wriggling, biting slave girl, whom Berris had been
the first to have. Harn Der had not taken her with him,
and now she belonged, more or less, to one of the other
metal workers. She was useful in a forge and knew just
what to do and why; Berris had knocked all that well
into her. She was useful for Plowing Night too. She did
not expect to be spoken to, but Tarrik did speak to her.
He said: 'Do you ever dream about Berris?' Sardu giggled
and shook her head. He said: 'Some day Berris will come
back. I wonder what he'll make of us all then. I wonder
if he'll want all this. Perhaps he'll have found something
else that's more real. What is he going to think of me,
Sardu?' But Sardu adored Tarrik; she pulled open the
sweat-streaked linen to kiss and bite his flesh. He rolled
half over, pinning her down; he looked into her black
eyes, iris and pupil equally black and blank and bright;
the eyes where Berris had looked but left nothing of himself.
He said: 'Will you always do just what I tell you, Sardu,
whatever it is?' And Sardu whispered brokenly that she
would, she was his bitch.

Gradually the torches burnt down and smouldered out.
The full moon of Plowing Night cruised slowly over them
and then sank into films and layers of cloud. Men and
women got to their feet and breathed cold air and left the
well-plowed field. Everything would go right this year. His
luck had come fully back to the Corn King.

Chapter Three

DISDALLIS STOOD IN the doorway of her house, waiting
for Kotka. The main stem of the vine, knotty with pruning,
crossed above her head. A bird twittered by with a long straw
in his beak. The sound of the sea was washed pleasantly up
towards her. Kotka came down the street with an eagle's
feather in his cap. They went in together. The house smelt
of stored food and the end of winter. She said: 'Why does
Erif Der not want me to come and see her in the Chief's
house?'

'I can't tell you,' said Kotka. 'You want to find out
very difficult things! Why don't women want to see other
women? Well, has Tarrik been making love to you?'

'No!' said Disdallis. 'And if he had I think Erif Der
would want to see me all the more. If there's any one woman

rather than another that Tarrik has just now, it's that little wretch Sardu, though what he wants with a creature that's been handed round half Marob—! Can't you find out anything about Erif, Kotka?' She rubbed her head against him, trying to make him wake up and be less of a solid, stupid man.

'Tarrik said,' Kotka began, 'that she was—not playing your game any more, Disdallis.'

'Oh,' said Disdallis the witch, 'I wonder if it turned on her once, her magic. Well, Kotka, I'm going to see her whether she wants me or not.'

Kotka was anxious; he pulled her towards him. 'No! You must be careful. Tarrik has been like a bear ever since Plowing Eve.'

'Sulky?'

'Yes, and angry. He's done—oh, bad things, Disdallis; cruel things! I won't have you in danger.'

Disdallis sucked her nail and thought. She said: 'Does anyone say anything about Essro and her baby?'

Kotka began squeezing her throat between his fingers and thumb, half in earnest, half laughing. He said: 'If you think you're going to play at who's to be Chief of Marob—yes, or you and Erif between you!—you'll have to reckon with me, my girl!'

Disdallis blinked and removed herself and smiled at Kotka. She did not suppose he would ever, for instance, really beat her, but she hated being even roughly handled, and she knew he knew it! All the same she said: 'They say the Council has advised Tarrik to kill Essro and Yan.'

'They say!' Kotka mocked at her. 'You silly women! Nobody wants Essro killed.'

'Oh! Just Yan. So that they needn't ever have to change their minds again about who's to be Corn King! The lazy, stupid old men! Oh, Kotka, I said them, not you! Don't, don't!'

But it was spring now. Kotka was quite as ready to kiss as to hit. Disdallis wondered whether he was still thinking that the Chief had been making love to her. She had on the whole kept out of the way just in case that should come into Tarrik's spring-wild head. If it did, Kotka could not do anything about it. With the Corn King, that was that, and husbands had to look the other way. But all the same he would hate it. And even when he hit her, Disdallis did not want to hurt Kotka.

In the evening she went to the Chief's house in an old green dress with a milk yoke over her shoulders. The two pails clanked and swayed. Every one looked at the milk, not at her. It did not seem to them odd that she should sit down and wait in one of the Spring Queen's rooms. People passed her. By and bye Erif Der passed her, alone. She looked at the milk, too, but it did not hold her, and her eyes jerked up to the face. After a time she said: 'Why?'

Disdallis said: 'Dearest, what has made you like this? Why don't you play any more? Is Tarrik unkind?'

Erif's eyes seemed to blur. She said: 'No,' and then sat down beside the milkmaid. Others in the room now saw that it was Disdallis, Kotka's wife, whom they had been told not to admit. However, the mischief was done, and now the Queen motioned them away, out of ear-shot. 'No,' she said again, 'not to me.' She laughed a little. 'He's unkind to Sardu, but she likes it! So do the others. He's not been after you, Disdallis? No. That's all part of Plowing Eve, and this spring's difficult, perhaps. But he's done other things. To the slaves, you know; or to strangers, or almost anyone.' She put her arms round Disdallis and whispered: 'I don't like him to touch me after that. Once or twice he got his hands all bloody. It's as if he were wanting to show someone or something that he can do anything he chooses. The Council are frightened of him. They like having a chief who frightens them.'

'Kotka doesn't.'

'No. Nor Black Holly. Nor any of his friends who were in Greece with him.'

'And Essro?'

But Erif Der said nothing. She looked at Disdallis angrily and miserably. She cried out: 'You know I said you were not to come!' Disdallis dipped her fingers in the milk and began to dab it on Erif's hand, but the Queen drew it away sharply. 'You are not to try things on me!'

'It can't hurt,' soothed Disdallis. 'It's my very own magic. I understand it. It will not turn on either of us.'

Erif Der said loudly and challengingly: 'It is better to have no magic! It is better for a woman not to be a witch!'

Ash-fair Disdallis looked at her and could not answer.

After a time she said again, but more softly: 'It's better to be one of the others, just one of Marob, not separated. Things wouldn't matter; Marob goes on. If we are witches, we are ourselves, standing all alone. Outside things matter and we have to find out which are real and the ones we must deal with. And I have found out that the things which do matter and are real are the bad things, the cruel things! Much good magic is to me!'

'But the other things, the good ones—the things that make us happy,' cried Disdallis. 'Why not choose them?' Her eyes moved round the room, looking at the fire, the beautiful furs, the gay coloured carpets, the two little almond trees in frail and lovely blossom beside the unshuttered window, and the March sun streaming in all round them, squaring a pool of quivering light on the clean flag-stones of the floor, while above in the rafters a still more dancing and paler pool came from the same sunlight reflected out of the small waves in the harbour.

Erif looked too. The things stayed stockily all round her. She put out her tongue at them; they didn't alter one bit or come any closer. Ashamed, she shut her mouth hard. 'They don't choose me,' said Erif.

They heard Tarrik's voice in the next room. Disdallis jumped up, slipping her shoulders under the yoke, and turned sideways to the door with her head bent, looking down into the milk. Tarrik did not notice her. He went over to the little Greek almond trees; he stretched his hands at them, clawed, as if he would have torn off the blossom, and then jerked himself away and moved towards Erif Der. While the Corn King and the Spring Queen were looking at one another, Disdallis slipped out. Erif Der said: 'Tarrik, I must know now! What do you want with Essro and Yan? Do you want to kill them?'

Tarrik said: 'You are not to think about these things. I will do what is best for you. When I see you I want not to have to think of them.'

'Why won't you tell me, Tarrik?' said Erif, then, with a half-laughing, half-bitter shakiness: 'I suppose you tell Sardu!'

Tarrik laughed. She began to cry. It was uncomfortable to cry now; it made her feel sick, a sick, dizzy weight along her back, up into the roots of her brain, her throat, her palate. She went pale with crying.

Tarrik suddenly said: 'I wonder what a woman four months gone is like inside. I should like to cut one open and see.'

Erif stopped crying, choked on a deep breath. She did not know whether fear or anger or horror had got her most; she only knew that Tarrik, as he was now, meant it quite seriously. It was the sort of thing he did like. At last she said: 'What is the matter with you, Tarrik? Why has everything gone wrong?'

He said: 'You see that too?' Then: 'There is nothing wrong with me when I am god. I can feel the seed-corn sprouting now all over Marob. But that will come to an end, as it did with my father. I shall be killed, and parts of me will be eaten. They will perhaps be eaten by that queer little thing in your belly, Erif.' He shivered and said: 'Every year the corn springs again. It is cut down. The seed is stored. After the plowing it is thrown into the dark earth. The earth holds it, buried and forgotten. But it comes alive again. That is the game we play at harvest. But where does Tarrik come in? I am tired of playing the game for the corn, making it go on, the food of Marob, making Marob go on, but leaving myself out. And you. I leave you out. Women die. They die in childbirth, Erif. Often they die! Why must it always be the corn and never us? I want to play a different game.'

But he was walking up and down the room all the time he was speaking. Erif had not really heard, only the parts about herself. She thought that perhaps death was now five months away from her and coming steadily and inevitably nearer. She wished Tarrik would take her in his arms. But he did nothing of the sort. He took a painted jar up from a shelf; it was a jar from Olbia with centaurs painted on it, a Greek story, but very un-Greek to look at, and rather fine. 'We die,' he said, and dropped it out of his hands, 'like that!' And he put his foot on the shards and began grinding them into the floor. Erif gave a little scream. She had liked the vase. He had just opened his fingers and dropped it quite deliberately, watched it drop and crash.

Later, during that evening, Erif reassembled her neglected magic. She made a spell with beads and cowries and a smoky fire that left blackish traces afterwards on the green-painted rafters of the room. Then she sent for Sardu, and Sardu walked into the pit. Erif was quite kind; she did not really dislike Sardu, though she thought she smelt. It was always possible to recognise her smell on Tarrik—something slightly disgusting. But, after all, what could you expect from a slave girl? Besides, Sardu really belonged to Berris still, and Erif was not going to damage her brother's property. The girl stood in the middle with her eyes running a little, staring at the spell which was laid out on a table between her and Erif and answering the questions which she seemed to think it, or perhaps Tarrik, was asking her. Erif found out, quite easily, that the Chief was going to send or go himself south, as soon as the ground was firm enough, and that would be any day now, to have the baby Yan killed, and, if necessary, his mother Essro with him. Sardu went out again with her hands to her forehead. She did not know quite what had happened during the last half-hour, only that it had been unpleasant, and that now her eyes and the whole inside of her head ached with the smoke of that fire.

The next morning Erif Der saw Kotka coming away from the Chief, looking angry and miserable as he so often did now. He tried to avoid her, but she called him over. Instead of asking questions, as he had feared she would, she said: 'Tell Disdallis it is no use trying to pick up spilt milk.' Kotka said he would and was pleased. He knew that this was likely to be something to do with his wife's magic, and was glad they were this much together again. He went home, and the Chief went to the Council, and Erif went to the stables and had out her strong, quiet, pony mare. She waved the guard back when they would have followed, and they obeyed her because it is foolish to cross a pregnant woman when one of her moods is on her. She had food with her and there was a great blanket under the saddle which did to sleep in at night. As always, there was a small bag of corn tied to the pommel. She was afraid they would track her sooner or later, so she rode the pony through sheep and then down the muddy bed of a stream. She went south across the plain, very visible and going slow because of the soggy ground, but still no one saw her. That was partly luck and partly her own doing. Up to that time she had been sick most mornings and often in the afternoons as well, but during this ride she was only sick once and that was because she had not wrapped herself up properly one night and woke rather chilled.

On the last day she came in sight of the house under the elms, and brisked up the pony. She rode down through sallows, knocking up clouds of sweet golden pollen; fat shining leaves were unfolding out of the mud. But between her and Yellow Bull's farm was a brown mile of floods. Westwards the sun dropped towards red reflections. She rode a few yards through the water, splashing, and suspected it was nowhere deep, but she grew nervous, and the pony, feeling it through her, refused to go on. She felt shaken and sick. At last she did what she had not meant to do. She crouched in the brim of the flood among the muddied grass stems and stirred the water into ripples, talking to it all the time; the ripples went off towards the island with the elms. She sat in the saddle and waited. Before it was quite dark two of Essro's servants rowed over in a flat-bottomed boat. Erif stepped in and they tied the pony behind. 'Essro sent you at once,' she said contentedly, glad to think of the fire and dry bed waiting for her. But the men frowned at one another. 'We saw you—didn't we?' said the elder of the two.

Essro stood in the doorway, one clenched hand over her heart. 'It's only you, Erif!' she said. 'I thought—at least, I didn't think—come in!' They had supper of salt fish and cheese and grain that had been damped and begun to sprout and was then boiled with herbs. Erif told her sister-in-law how things were. Yan slept in a wicker cradle between them, a great, pink, happy lump of a boy, ridiculously like Yellow Bull. 'I'm still nursing him,' said Essro. 'You see, I don't expect I shall ever have another, Erif. But I give him food as well. He has got four great teeth and he stands up like a man. I wish—oh, I wish he were big, Erif! Then he could talk to me.'

'I'm going to have one in summer,' said Erif.

'I thought so. Are you glad?'

'It would be much better,' said Erif, looking sulkily at Yan, 'if we hadn't ever started being glad or sorry. We could just have had children, or been killed, or fallen in love, or whatever it was, and that would have been all right and we wouldn't have asked questions about it.'

'You couldn't have lived like that, being Spring Queen,

could you? And none of us who are witches can, because we're ourselves. We can't be only Marob. The Corn King has to be separate too. Yellow Bull was, when—when he was that.' Then she went on nervously: 'Erif, it doesn't make any difference between us, all that's happened, does it?'

Erif laughed and patted her hand, but did not answer. It was very comfortable in the house among the marshes; she didn't want to talk.

The next morning, though, they began to consider seriously what to do. Essro had been quite cut off all winter, first by snow and ice, then as these melted by marsh and floods. But the floods were going down. They walked round the island on slime-coated grass that smelt as though it had been half choked. The water was down even since the day before; at one side they were almost joined to the mainland; anyone could have walked across. The winter lake was beautiful; it lay in long soft curves, caressing the shapes of the land, except in one place, away across on the right, where it was broken and changed by man's work and led into long ditches beside a raw, straight dike of earth and hurdles, the beginning of the secret road. Essro peered northward over the shallow, hurrying flood water, screwing up her eyes; she was rather short-sighted. There was no sort of security in them now, beyond another day or two. Erif turned round suddenly and found that Essro was crying. 'They'll come,' Essro said, turning her wet eyes towards Erif; 'they're going to come. It's no good. They're going to kill my Yan. We can't do anything. I may as well give him up first as last. You can't possibly help me.'

'Don't be a fool, Essro!' said Erif sharply, feeling that she herself might very easily get infected with this woman's hopelessness. 'I—I—oh, they shan't kill your baby! What good am I if I can't see to that? It's something real.' She took Essro's arm and walked her back towards the house, away from the smell of marshes. Then she said suddenly: 'Why not the secret road?'

The next day they started. Essro's men rowed them along the dike below the level of the empty road that was to bring Marob to new places. It went from island to island and often there were wooden bridges laid on the tops of piles with flood water sucking them over or bobbing viciously at them with drift wood. Beyond the end of the road Essro took out a roll of drawings which Yellow Bull had made month by month, showing the lie of the islands and currents, first from one point, then from the one next farther on. He had marked their way in red, which Essro said he had got by pricking his arm with his sharp pen. With the help of these they got from island to island until they felt they were out of reach. They had poles and felt for two tents, with blankets and cooking-pots, flour, meal, cheese, salt fish and meat, and a goat which would have kids the next month, so that there would be plenty of milk for Yan if his mother ran dry, as she was likely to soon. They had fire in a charcoal pot and kept it carefully dry. The boat went slowly after the first day. No one talked much. Erif Der felt very well. At last they came to a high island with willows in small leaf rising out of it. There seemed to be no wild boars about, or other beasts that would be a danger. They cut a clearing and camped.

Then every day things got greener. Hourly the lovely rushes crept up, till inch by inch they had made a live curtain round the island. As the floods dropped the marshes were sheeted gold and pink; it was impossible to look at one single flower, there were so many! Where the great channels of water still flowed, year-long draining the wet lands, they were blue and shining and reed-edged. The air was full of larks. The rank, ungrazed grass grew where some day the secret road was to bring the flocks and herds of Marob. Essro had given up that dreadful northward peering for danger and busied herself about the camp, painted the tents with dyes made out of one or another juicy stem, and tamed a willow wren to come down and feed out of her hand. The men shot duck and sometimes swans with their bows and arrows, and cooked, and cut down trees, and sat about, and sang songs, and told stories. Yan ate all the flowers he could. Erif was well and happy. It was all quite different from what she had expected, and much easier. In that first moment of saying: 'The Secret Road,' she had pictured herself with Essro and the child stealing and hiding about marsh ways in a small boat, holding their breaths, chased. But instead everything was calm and green and growing. It was her own spring. Had she made it, down here in the marshes beyond Marob? She did not know or care. Yet by and bye, as it went on, as the earliest flowers began busily to drop their petals and turn to the building up of seed pods, the Spring Queen began to think uneasily of the other spring which she had left deserted and which would be needing her.

The she-goat had kids. They killed and ate one, and its milk went to Yan. The men caught fish; once or twice they set nets and caught the salmon running up from the sea. Then one day there was a heavy rainstorm, with wind. It cleared up the next day to a pale gleaming morning over sweet-smelling bruised reeds and dripping bushes. But some of the stores were soaked, including most of the flour and meal; the goat had broken her leg. Essro looked at it all, rubbed the wet oatmeal through her fingers. This was the stuff Yan needed now. She looked from it to Erif. And Erif suddenly said: 'I must be off, Essro, back to the Spring-field and the young flax and my work in Marob. Send Murr in the boat with me and he will bring you back stores and news. That will be best for every one.'

That same day they started. Murr was the strongest of the men. He punted the boat through the marsh channels. Sometimes they were deep, and he had to stoop right over the pole, and when it came up dripping black mud he stretched and grinned and ran it up between his hands for another heave down. As it plunged again, the marsh gas came hurrying up through the water in great bubbles like eyes. Sometimes it seemed as though the channel was shallowing off to an end, but the grass field which Erif thought she saw, opened and parted and pressed down under their prow, and the water crowfoot flowers bobbed under water and streamed past her, drowned, drowned, only to rise again behind them, shaking and dripping.

Erif Der lay in the boat and trailed her fingers and looked at rushes and reeds and water-beetles and buttercups and crayfishes and moorhens and dragon-fly grubs crawling up the stems to wait and dry and split their fat sides in the sun. She saw water-rats and herons and big docks and marigolds and a great many grey or transparent or bright-spotted fish, and thin wavy roots digging into black mud and a continuous life of little marsh creatures; and sometimes she saw the man Murr punting, looking down at her, grunting, shoving, shining wet hand over hand along the leaping pole, his head dark against the sky. He had a pleasant-shaped head. As the day softened into evening, Erif drew a blanket up over herself; she felt the water so very near beyond the thin planks of the boat, and the brushing of the leaves of the water-plants under the keel, and the faint splashing of the pole. Murr's head was outlined now against a sky of lemon green that brightened moment by moment with stars, but between them was slowly fading into grey. Her eyelids sank, heavy as her body. The Spring Queen slept.

It was the same all the next day. They landed and ate cold porridge in a friendly way. She spoke to him about the things all round, the beasts and the flowers. He brought her a bird's nest. She took her shoes off and paddled among mud and reeds and short water-lilies. The fat water-lily buds pointed and strained towards the surface of the water. They had air inside them. Why? She broke one or two open. They smelt like a more delicate sort of mud. The soft mud rested her swelling body; her white ankles were too small for the body, a silly stalk for it to balance difficultly on, until they were buried, rooting into the mud. Murr found scented rushes and cut some for her to lie on. She thanked him and they went on.

They had Yellow Bull's drawings with them. When they were not sure how to go they bent together over them to look and point; but Murr was certain he would know the way back quite easily. He had the feeling of it in his head, the place where his mistress was waiting for her stores. When there was any difficulty about the way, it was always Murr who was right. Soon Erif was leaving it entirely to him. It was more comfortable so, too.

That evening again she went to sleep as the stars came out, but by and bye the moon rose and woke her. They were in a barer part of the marshes now, salter too perhaps. She dipped a finger; the water tasted faintly brackish. Round her mud islands shone whitish, with a few trailing plants; it was very warm and still. She could hear the duck flighting, but was too deeply sunk in this stillness of night even to turn her head to look. After a time Murr shipped the punt-pole; they were in a current that drew them very slowly on. The moon was behind her now; he could not tell by any gleam of her eyes whether she was awake or asleep. He slid to the bottom of the boat with his face an inch or two from her feet. His breath touched her feet, then his lips. Her cold toes spread and curled against his warm cheek; the mud had dried on them to a fine, dark powder. Slowly, slowly, he began to kiss, up from her ankles. Still he did not know for certain whether she was awake or asleep. She did not know either. She could not move. He was beginning to creep over her. In a moment she would start awake. Why was her heavy body so calm and so aware of what was wanted?

She did start awake, half awake, into his arms. He held her, clung to her, looking up, praying to her. 'Spring Queen,' he said, 'Spring Queen, be kind, be gentle, be merciful! Let the spring come!' He had taken the words of Plowing Eve; they had made him eloquent and in a way impersonal. He was not Murr; he was the crowd, the whole people of Marob longing for the spring. Why not, then? Why not let him come? Spring Queens must be kind.

Tarrik would mind; Tarrik would be hurt perhaps. Tarrik did the same thing because he was Corn King. He must learn to understand and not be hurt.

Now Murr was urging her again. He had her dress open from the neck. He was mumbling against her breasts: 'Let me come! Let me come! There is a child there already: nothing will happen. I cannot hurt you. Spring Queen, take me, take me! No one will know.'

She felt herself stiffen a little, rise a little out of his soft, fumbling grip; he was afraid of her. But could Tarrik mind? For, after all, the child was his. Because of the child she herself was his whoever else came into her. Could the child mind? No, no; no one would be hurt. And why be unkind? Why be unkind to the man and to herself?

The man panted and clutched at her dress. She felt him hot and leaping a little against her. 'Be quick!' he said. 'I must! No one will know.' Then, quite accidentally, his fingers caught in and pulled a loose piece of her hair. She hardened suddenly into a stiff violence; she caught his throat with both hands and knocked him off her, flung him against the side of the rocking boat; a little water splashed in. With an effort she righted it. He lay there crumpled with a darkening face, his mouth half open, licking at his own hands. He had been afraid of the Spring Queen. He had lost his woman. He began to cry and abuse her softly under his breath. She bade him pick up the pole again and keep silent. He obeyed her, trembling a good deal. Neither of them slept any more that night.

The next day there was sun still on the marshes, but the Spring Queen was tired of them. She said nothing to Murr except when they landed to eat—but he ate nothing. He took a mouthful of porridge and chewed it and then spat it out. Once or twice she had been going to tell him to make haste, but he saw the look in her eyes and went on at his hardest. He was afraid of her still. They came to the end of the marshes; the low, willow slopes grew clear and unbroken ahead of them. Murr cast about for somewhere to land. They were several miles from Yellow Bull's farm, but that was in case the Chief had anyone there on watch. Just before they landed on to a solider mud-bank it came dreadfully and piteously into Murr's mind how lovely she had been, how soft, how warm, how alone with him in the boat and almost his. Before she could check him he threw himself at her feet, imploring her once more to be pitiful before it was too late and he lost her for ever. But Erif Der stepped out of the boat and walked away, leaving him to tie it up. She was angry with him because her shoes were muddy; he ought to have helped her out instead of grovelling like a grub in the bottom of the boat.

Before they came to the farm she was aware that he hated her. She did not mind, but she was a little alarmed about what effect it might have on Essro. However, there was no reason really why, hating her, the man should be disloyal to his own lady. Thinking this, she said nothing, but watched him. They came cautiously to the farm on the mound under the elm trees. It seemed to be deserted. They went into the courtyard. They could smell something very unpleasant. Erif had to go into a corner and be sick before she could go on. Murr went into the house and came out again rather quickly. He told Erif what he had seen. The Chief had been and gone. Before he went he had killed every one on the farm whom he had caught. After they had been killed they had just been left about. There was some evidence that he had tortured a few of them, presumably to tell him where Essro was. After that Murr went into the byres one after the other. Some of the beasts must have been killed and eaten. Others had been left tied up with no one to feed them. The Chief must have been in a bad mood. Did the Spring Queen want to see? Or the bodies in the house? He could tell who they had been; he had worked with them all—his brother—No, no, Erif did not want to see! She went out and sat on the grass under a tree and tried not to think of Tarrik, whose child she bore, having done this. She sat there for some hours, until late in the evening. She was very hungry, but did not want to go back into the house. At last Murr came out and brought her food; he had a horse for her too. Several of Yellow Bull's horses had been loose, but they knew him and let him catch one of them. He had found goats too, and a ewe with lambs, and there was plenty of corn and meal. By that time it was quite dark. She stared at Murr and wrapped herself up in a blanket and lay down beside the tethered horse. Not for anything would she have bolted herself into one of the farm rooms now. Murr went away and slept somewhere too.

The next day he filled several pots and sacks with food-stuff, went to the bee-hives and took a couple of early combs, as Essro had bidden him, and made two journeys to the boat. Erif rode her new horse and helped to drive the beasts; the horse carried some of the sacks too. They cut fodder for the goats and sheep and tied them tight by the horns to the thwarts of the boat. Then she sat the horse and waited till Murr had punted well out into the marshes. She was not really suspicious, but it was as well to make as sure as possible about everything.

After this she turned the horse north and rode slowly over the plain among grass and butterflies. She wondered what had happened to her own pony mare and hoped Tarrik had not caught her when he was angry and hurt her instead of his own wife. Late that night she saw lights and rode into a farm and was welcomed with awe and without questioning, only the next morning they asked her if she would walk a little through their springing crops. So she went on from farm to farm and by and bye came to Marob town and her own place, the Spring-field. News of her had come, signalled from one stead to another in this fine weather. Her rooms were ready for her at the Chief's house, and a steam bath fragrant with crushed leaves, and the food she liked best.

It was being a good spring. Every one was grateful to the Spring Queen.

Chapter Four

KOTKA WAS STILL DOWN in the south hunting for Essro and Yan. But he knew he would never find them. Disdallis had sent him a message saying in so many words that she had put a spell on him not to be able to see Essro or any track she might make. He had been very angry and puzzled about it. He dared not come back and admit to the Chief that he had been unsuccessful; and he could not tell him the reason for this failure, because that would mean letting his anger loose on Disdallis. And what was the good of promising himself that he would beat Disdallis when he got home? None at all. Besides, it was quite true that he really did not at all want to catch Essro or have the nasty job of killing her baby.

In the meantime the Corn King and the Spring Queen went on with all the things they had to do for Marob. Tarrik said nothing about where she had been, once he saw that she was well, nor anything about Essro. Until he did, Erif would say nothing herself, but stay calm and confident. They had come to a kind of peace and understanding, based on not saying or being aware of a great deal about one another, a pattern of exclusions which made for great courteousness, tenderness even, and which went easily with the life which they must both lead at this time of year when there was so much to do. Yet it was essentially temporary, a breathing space in which they could just continue to live without facing one another, until the child was born. As Erif got nearer and nearer to her time, so she ceased to think and be herself; the self that was Spring Queen took over all her doings, and unless they were something to do with that self, she did not see or hear or feel things very distinctly.

In April Tarrik went to his own Place to undo a very important knot. He put on the clothes and chewed the berries and did what was needed. When it was satisfactorily settled and he was taking the dress off again, turning back from god to man, he suddenly began remembering that earlier night when he had done the same thing after making certain that Yellow Bull should die. Before he could root out the image, he got full into his mind another one that had happened before, Yellow Bull thanking him, thinking about his secret road. He did not mind killing Yellow Bull, but he had also killed the first life of the secret road. He had killed the wanting it which had started it, which had put it into the wish of Marob. Had he? No, because he had taken up the wish himself and gone on with it. What was it, then, that he had done, which was hurting him still? Suddenly and horrifyingly it all came plain. He had killed his brother-in-law, Yellow Bull, and it was black, it was wrong, it was sin! And he could not anyhow undo it.

He dropped the coat out of his hand and cried out sharply and angrily into the dark of his Place. Why could not the Corn King do as he chose! Then he began to reason about it, to follow this queer process which Sphaeros had taught him, the thing the Greeks used instead of magic. He discovered that it was Sphaeros who had put this thing into him, who had even given him the words for good and evil: this sort of good and evil which were to do with him, Tarrik-Charmantides, and nothing to do with the Corn King of Marob, whose only good was the good of the Corn. But why had he got to be split into two? He was a god, he must not be stopped from doing things as they came to him! He stamped, he shouted at Sphaeros who was not there, saying he hated him; saying he was jabbing his eyes out, pulling his fingers off, smashing, killing him! All that answered him was the old guardian woman moaning and rustling her leaves. He hit her, he kicked her face and belly as she sprawled on the ground. It was no good, she was not Sphaeros. When he was gone she crawled back to her stool, aware that a god had manifested himself on her and passed.

He went home, scowling and fretting. On the way he pushed open a house-door and went in and found a man sitting at dinner with his wife and children. He threw the food into the fire and made the man stand up, and hit him, cleverly, in the parts that would hurt most. The woman and children cowered behind the table. After a time the man fainted and Tarrik went away, more satisfied. It was as if he had been hitting this stupid, hateful reasonableness of the Greeks. It was as if he had been killing Yan, the thing which had come for a moment between him and his godhead.

Once or twice again he did that, and once or twice he killed slaves. But every time the satisfaction was less. He grew quiet. He found that, after all, he would have to face the Greeks and their ideas. He would have to face Sphaeros. Fleetingly, he began to get the notion that he would have to tell Sphaeros what he had done and ask if it could be changed by an action of his own, and Sphaeros would say no, it could not be changed, and Sphaeros would look at him—It might be easier to surrender to the ideas of good and evil and be good himself. That possibility crept through him, but it made him cold. If he was to surrender to anything he could not be a god! In his heart, and saying nothing to Erif or Kotka or any of his friends, he wrestled with old Sphaeros the Stoic.

By the end of April there were merchant ships putting in again; of course there was not much to be had before harvest and the big trading markets, except furs and timber and smoked spring salmon. But they wanted to see how things were likely to go this year and whether it was worth while coming back later. Tarrik and the Council received and entertained the merchants, but he was nervous of them and seemed afraid of hearing news from Greece—not that there was likely to be any so soon after winter. The Council thought he was far more sensible and reasonable now than he had been two years ago. He did not go out of his way to offend the merchants or to amuse himself by doing violent and silly things at their expense. They thought, for that matter, that the fit for blood which had come on him after Plowing Eve had probably worked itself out. It had most likely been a necessary thing after all that had happened the year before. The Corn God had to have his sacrifices; who could tell whether it must be men or bulls?

Only, they thought, he was still hungry for Yan, who had, though innocently, tried to supplant him in the godhead. Once he had met Disdallis in the flax market. He began to talk at her, his face near hers and distorted. He asked why Kotka had not yet caught and killed Yan. He began to ask questions. He held her by the arm in a pinching grip. People stopped and looked at them and whispered. When he let her go she screamed and ran blunderingly away. Tarrik looked round at his people, and hastily they moved about and began to talk of other things. Disdallis did not tell anyone what he had said to her. He did not tell anyone either. Nobody knew what sort of thing Tarrik wanted or did not want, that year. When they saw how well their crops were coming up they brought him presents. If they were jewels he would sometimes pass them on to Sardu. The Spring Queen got her own presents and kept them.

Erif did not know what he wanted. Every week she knew less and less what she wanted herself. Vaguely she was afraid even of the baby being born. She remembered what pain it would be—she woke out of quiet sleep and remembered in the dark. Yet in their present separateness Tarrik could not comfort her. In some way she had become aware now that why he wanted most to kill Yan was because his own son had been killed. He wanted to wipe that out for himself and he thought he wanted it for his wife. She had tried to explain to him how foolish this was, but she could not make him understand; her words went past him. For the time, at least, she gave up trying.

One day she was walking along the shore; the crabs looked up at her out of the pools, but she did not play with them. She picked up pebbles here and there, but did not throw them, only ground them together in her hand. She was like a wave passing along the beach, transparent to everything; she saw and heard and smelt, and it all went through her. Nothing was left in her mind. She walked in the shadow of the low cliffs. She stepped over large stones and in and out of salt pools. In front of her the gulls waddled and flopped away. She came round the corner of a rock and she saw Sardu and Murr together on the sand, whispering to one another, too intent to see her or anyone. She came awake, drew back a pace softly, and stayed still. The crabs came out from under tufts of seaweed and little caves of pebbles; they clustered round her heels.

The first thing she thought was that it would be pleasant to tell Tarrik about Sardu and her new man; though perhaps he wouldn't mind, queer creature that he was. Then she looked and thought again. Those two. Why just those two? What was Murr doing in Marob at all? She peered round; it was queer how she remembered the shape of Murr's face and hands—his dripping hands. The two sat inches apart, suspiciously unlike lovers alone on a summer day. She could not hear what they said, but it became suddenly and convincingly clear to her that Murr must be betraying Essro and her child to Sardu, and she, the bitch, would take it all to Tarrik, and get them killed. Erif bent down and began arranging her crabs. They sidled along, under cover of stones and driftwood, till the circle was full.

Erif Der stepped round the corner of the rock. The two saw her and, after one checked movement, a heave up and crouch down, stayed still, regarding her and her circle. The crabs did not move either, except that the stalks of their eyes twisted about a little and the tufts round their mouths were continuously and eagerly astir. Erif looked down at Sardu, the whimpering, flattened creature, her neck exposed. If Berris never came back to look after his own property, what could he expect? A flimsy, replaceable thing like Sardu was not going to be allowed to kill Essro and Yan, whom she had said she would protect. Erif drew her knife, leant forward over the circle, one hand on the rock to steady herself, and stabbed Sardu in the vein at the side of the neck. She said loudly: 'Yan will not be hurt by you!'

Two brown hands jerked up at the wound, fumbled with it, slipped in blood; the back heaved and hollowed, the head dropped sharply and then tossed wildly back away from the centre of pain, tossed back so that its eyes met Erif's, the black eyes deepened with astonishment and something unexplained. The mouth opened in the head and muttered: 'Not—not hurt—no.' Erif Der began to know she had made a mistake; the knowledge dropped swiftly and coldly all through her. She stumbled forward, through her own ring, breaking it, her blind feet just avoiding Murr's hands flat out in the sand. She said: 'You were betraying Yan to my husband!' throwing the words down on to the dying slave. Sardu's eyelids fluttered; she moved her head in a faint negative. 'You were,' said Erif, 'you bitch!' But her voice faltered. Sardu's thirsty lips opened again. 'No,' she whispered. 'Tarrik lets Yan live. Murr was to tell.' She sighed and sighed in her blood and once more she said the name 'Tarrik' and then she died, with Erif's hands groping about, trying to pull together the edges of the wound and undo what she had done.

Erif Der stood up and realised, first that Tarrik had told this to Sardu and not to her, and that Sardu was dead and the message not perhaps given. Then she saw that Murr had crept away through the broken ring. He was afraid of her again! She yelled at him, she had to stop him! He began to run, zigzagging. Furious, she stamped and yelled again, and, when he went on running, threw her dagger after him. It went cling on a stone a little way behind him. He dodged in under the cliff among the boulders and in a few minutes he was out of sight.

She turned and walked back. The child leapt about in her, punishing her, hammering on her; her back ached. She dragged herself along. She wanted to get home the quickest way, lest she should lie down on the pebbles like Sardu and never be able to get up again. She could not even go down to the sea to wash her hands. Everything rocked about. When she got to the Chief's house the women had to carry her in; they took off her clothes and bathed her, hushed and horrified. She longed for complete darkness and quiet; she gasped and lay very still, contracted and faintly shivering. Pains of one sort and another went flitting about her, but these her women could not see. They only saw that the Spring Queen too had, like the Corn King, perhaps had to give herself a sacrifice. One of them, a cousin of Erif's, a girl she was fond of and liked to play ball with in the garden, plucked up courage to ask her what had happened. But Erif only stared and said nothing. They laid her in bed and drew the curtains half across, because the light bothered her eyes.

By and bye Tarrik came in. She sat up straight with her hair wild and much matted where she had been rubbing it about on the pillow. She flung out her bare arms, her wrists; she cried at him: 'Tarrik, I have killed your girl, I have killed Sardu!'

The thing rebounded round the room, from one mind to another. The women knew now what sort of a sacrificial beast their mistress had killed. They clung sickly on to the hangings, fell on to hands and knees at the bottom of the wall of the room, crept and covered their ears. Erif's cousin wondered wildly whether she must run between them, let the Chief kill her if need be—But Tarrik went over to Erif and sat beside her and began kissing her. His eyes were trying to reach hers. After a time she seemed to understand what he was doing.

Murr went back to the house where he had lived since he had been in Marob. Now Sardu was dead, who was the only one that could conceivably have helped him. The Spring Queen had thrown her knife at him; she would hunt him down like a beast. He supposed she was hunting him down now. He did not know if it would be the guards or her own crabs who would be doing the hunting. Either way he would be caught. He got a rope, climbed, made fast, and jumped. Nobody found his body until evening, and then it would just have been buried in the yard, least said soonest mended, only someone told a man who told Black Holly, and he happened to remember that this had been one of Yellow Bull's men. So after a time the news got round to Tarrik and at last to Erif Der. She went across the town to Disdallis, heavy with the news. Disdallis had heard already both about that and about Sardu; remembering what Erif had told her one warm evening of the boat in the marshes, she put two and two together, and when she saw Erif coming to her house guessed them quickly into four. She sent the woman who had been weaving with her out of the room, and had her arms open ready for Erif. After a time Erif looked up from her sobbing and said: 'But why did he kill himself! Why, why?'

Disdallis said: 'He thought you were angry. He thought he would die a worse death if he were taken. But what does it matter? You are the Spring Queen. He was only a herdsman.' She stroked Erif's hair and rubbed her cheek against the Queen's cold cheek.

'I would not have killed him,' said Erif Der. 'I would rather have lain with him.' She went on: 'He was afraid of me. I was unkind to him. I wish now I had been kind. The Spring Queen should be kind.' She thought of the boat in the marshes and Murr's groping hands that were now stiff. She had no definite custom to go on. For it was said that in old days the Spring Queen belonged to all the men of Marob for them to work their magic on. At the new moons of spring she had lain with the householders in green furrows and flax fields for the sake of the seasons. But now this did not happen; since then the Corn King had gathered so much power and violence into himself that he counted for all the men of Marob with the Spring Queen, and because of that, and because he was also the chief, the war-leader, none of them now dared to force her nor even to entreat her except in the name of the whole community at Plowing Eve. Yet there was nothing alien in the thought that the Spring Queen should be taken by any man. If this was followed by anger, that was the affair of the man and the Chief. She herself could not be reproached. Surely she could do nothing but good by being kind! Surely she was making it easier for the rain and warmth to come, for the corn to spring, for beasts and women to breed! Surely she was making peace in the household of Marob!

She should have been kind. Marob wanted it. Her own body wanted it. She had wronged the life behind her body and Murr's. Ah wrong, wrong, the thing Sphaeros had talked about, dear Sphaeros, telling them about the way of Nature and how one should always follow it! Now she was bitterly and deeply ashamed, more than she could ever explain to Disdallis, or to Tarrik. One way and another her body and mind were as bad as Tarrik's now, and besides she had done her bad things more reasonably, less on the impulse of the moment. She was worse tangled than even he was.

Yet, for the moment, she would not consider the tangle; she had not the strength. She could and must wait until her baby was born. Being a woman, she was allowed that much delay, even by her own conscience. Also, she had some tough, non-rational idea at the back of her head that possibly with the birth of her baby, with that terrific interruption and test of life, it might perhaps all be wiped out and made clean again.

Later on her cousin told her that the man had been prowling round the Chief's house for days before, looking up at the windows, hiding and watching. He did no harm, so they had not said anything about him. He looked like a man under a spell. Erif was angry that she had not seen him, angry with her women and with herself. He should have been real enough to see! He had been hers, but Sardu had been the one to find him and talk to him. He had belonged last and most to Sardu. She would never be able to find out if he had talked to Sardu about the boat in the marshes.

Failing Murr, it was Erif herself who went to fetch Essro and tell her that she could come back, that the Chief was no longer hungry for Yan. She rode very easily this time, with Black Holly and his men as well as half her own women. At night they pitched a striped and embroidered tent for her in the middle of flowers. After a time they sent a messenger and Kotka came to meet them, looking very down-hearted. Erif told him the news and said she must have a boat. 'Essro is at the far end of the secret road,' said Erif, 'beyond where it has got to yet.' Kotka looked at her and his eyes widened slowly and he pushed a hand through his hair. 'As you were saying it,' he said, 'I wondered whether she could be there. But why didn't I look there before?'

She found it very difficult to remember her way to Essro's island and went wrong several times. She wished she could summon Murr to guide her back, but she had not that power. She did not think that anyone of Marob had it in her time, though it used to be done not so many years back. But at last she got there and persuaded Essro that it was true and she must really bring Yan home. He had grown tremendously, and howled at Erif when she tried to lift him. He had forgotten her altogether. They left the goats and sheep on the island; it was easily big enough for them. When the secret road got there it would find them or their descendants. Essro did not come back to the town of Marob for a long time; she stayed on at the farm and sometimes got very frightened; she always kept a boat ready to fly in just in case Tarrik changed his mind. She could not get happy anyhow; she had been married young to Yellow Bull and her marriage was in some way the thing she measured everything against. It was dreadful not to be married. Tarrik had broken it and she would not see him again—not yet, at least. And Erif Der thought she was right.

Kotka came back still very angry with Disdallis, because, although of course he was delighted that it had all ended so well, he was not going to stand being interfered with by her. But when he got to his house he found that she had just been sent for to one of the out-grazing herds where there was trouble, the cows refusing, as they sometimes do, to suckle their calves. He followed her there, but arrived when she had already begun the rite, so stayed behind the ring of cattle-men to watch. She went up to one of the calves which was lying on the grass, with sides fallen in and legs sprawling weakly from hunger. Its mother was grazing quietly with her back to it, a little way off, completely regardless of its miserable and now very faint bleatings. Disdallis crouched beside it, opened its mouth, blew down its throat, and spoke some words. Then she stood up and talked to the cow. After a time the cow turned round, walked back to the calf and stood chewing and blowing while it sucked her. The first time it was so weak that Disdallis had to hold it up. She did the same with the other cows and calves, and walked back to the cattle-men with the halter of the heifer which she had been given as her payment. She saw Kotka and smiled at him droopingly, rather tired with her day's work. He asked her again, as he had done before, how she did it; but she could not explain, except that they were home cattle, part of the Marob herd, food for her man and children. That was how her life was joined to theirs and why she had power over them. She did not think she could do it with strangers' cattle. Then she told Kotka how Tarrik had met her in the flax market and what he had said. It was very disquieting, and they went about cautiously for several weeks. But Tarrik did and said nothing more; he was all smiles to them both. By the time they had finished all their talking it was too late for Kotka even to be very angry with Disdallis.

Riders went west and north-west to find Harn Der. The inlanders who came to Marob in trade were told to pass word through the forest that he and his household might come back. The Council were glad that after this bloody and alarming spring, summer had come so well to the Corn King. It would be splendid to have them both, reconciled, for the good of Marob and the harm of Marob's enemies; one against famine, the other against the Red Riders. Erif Der said nothing. She looked forward to seeing Gold-fish and Wheat-ear again. The rest must wait. She would not think about Harn Der until after her baby was born. She would not let whatever it was that she intended take shape until after that.

Just before midsummer Harn Der and his waggons came back to Marob. Tarrik rode out to meet him. The old man was smiling in his beard; he greeted Tarrik with the salute to the Chief and then a hard handshake. He seemed all one piece with his horse, his bow and silver-plated quiver, the axe in his belt, his helmet of gold and bronze, and his short iron sword. His body was only one more thing that he used, as a weapon or for his pleasure. The two children of his body were tall and rosy, perched on big horses. The waggons were full of fine forest pelts, bear and deer and marten and ermine; pairs of stags' horns, painted in his colours, were nailed along the ridge poles, and bunches of boars' tusks and lynxes' claws dangled from the axles. He had a piece of beautiful clouded amber to offer to the Chief, the kind of thing which would be much praised in Marob. Yes, it had been a fine holiday for Harn Der!

But Tarrik had expected this; he was prepared to meet it with an equally elaborate pretence game of his own. What he had not expected was to see Harn Der, in the moments between the smiles and the easy talk look suddenly for a breath old and unhappy and beaten, hurt to the roots of his soul. His power and honour were much diminished, his hopes which he had worked at so long and patiently were unfulfilled, and he could see as well as anyone that they never could be fulfilled now, even if Gold-fish grew up to be another Yellow Bull; his wife and his eldest son were dead; another son had gone right away, perhaps for ever; his eldest and dearest daughter—well, who could say? Not he, not Tarrik, not even perhaps Erif herself. It was a nasty sort of tangle, enough to make a man feel old. Tarrik had meant to tease him, to withhold news of Essro and Yan, make him think perhaps that the one grandchild was lost too; but after a short time he began to feel a horrid and disturbing sense of being himself in some way the same as Harn Der, in trouble too, in a worse trouble than the men of Marob knew. He was angry at not being able to tease Harn Der, but his silly, unsure mind kept jumping into the other man's skin and hurting him from there! So Tarrik found himself gravely reassuring his father-in-law about the health of Yellow Bull's son.

Harn Der went back to his house and waited for Erif Der to come to it. He himself did not go to any but the most public parts of the Chief's house, the halls where the Council and the feasts were held. She did not ask him to come nearer. But she sent for Gold-fish and Wheat-ear and gave them lovely sweets and things she had bought for them in Greece. Gold-fish was nearly as tall as she was now, and he

could ride and shoot like a man and bear pain; he stuck one
of her long pins into his arm to show her. Wheat-ear liked
seeing that; she turned pink and stuck her tongue out;
but it made Erif feel sick. Gold-fish had a hawk of his own,
as Berris used to have; he understood them. These were
the eye-teeth of his first wolf; this was a heron's egg;
he had climbed so high he had almost forgotten what the
ground was like, and the big herons had tried to jab his
face; he had killed a man already, one of the inlanders
who had come thieving round the waggons.

Wheat-ear was getting a big girl too! Erif couldn't
accustom herself to it. The little sister was growing up,
her shape was beginning to change; she wasn't a soft
baby any more, but a long, budding thing, half-way to
a woman. Erif was shy of her till she saw it was mostly
appearance; Wheat-ear was unconscious of it herself; she
thought about the same animals and games and things she
was learning, as she always had; she was not interested in
her own growing up or what might be going to happen in
her mind or body. She was pleased that Erif was going to
have a new baby; she seemed to have forgotten about the
one who had been killed—or, as she must have thought,
died, as babies do. And she liked being in the Chief's house
and seeing everything; she rummaged about in her sister's
big chests full of things and tried on all her dresses that did
not belong to special occasions. Erif Der was quite happy
about those two. Whatever happened they would not be
much disturbed: they were too deep in the life and peace
of Marob to have very much that was their own and separate
and vulnerable.

A few days after Harn Der came back, Tarrik had a
letter from his Aunt Eurydice in Rhodes. When they gave
it to him he did not know whether he wanted to read it or
burn it. He took it with him to a meeting of the Council,
crumpling it down inside his coat. When he brought it out
again he found that Erif's warm star which had stopped
burning him, had scorched a hole right through the thick
Egyptian paper and loosened the thread which had kept it
fast. He read then that his Aunt Eurydice had wondered
whether to write to him all through the bright, cool months
of her Rhodian winter; she had hoped he understood now
why she had acted as she did (and yet she did not hope too

much, for perhaps it was better for him not to understand if he was happiest so—though in heart so far now from her who had been almost a mother to him!). There were wide seas between them, and there should be peace. If he did at all understand, would he force or pray Harn Der's daughter not to go on tormenting her!

She went on to speak of books she had read, objects which she had bought, a garden with a fountain and myrtles, sunnier and stonier than her garden at Marob. And the pale bodies of swimmers: a different sea to the Euxine. She said little of her husband. Tarrik smoothed the letter out and took it to his wife.

She looked at the scorched hole and then read it to herself. 'Well?' she said, and then: 'I suppose you do understand everything she wants you to understand by now, Tarrik?'

'What is happening to her?' asked Tarrik, not answering.

'I'm not sure,' said Erif. 'I suppose—yes, you see she left some of her dresses behind here. It was a wet magic, because of going over-sea. It must really be odder for her husband than for her!' She laughed a little, but not very prettily.

Tarrik waited till that was over and then said: 'How long will it last, Erif?'

'It will probably dry itself out in time, unless I do it again. I have some dresses still. I was not sure how it would work, whether I was being clever enough, but it seems to have done as well as I hoped. I like being able to do things.'

'But are you going to do it again?'

'I expect so,' said Erif Der. 'After all, why not?'

Chapter Five

MIDSUMMER DAY WAS always a kind of triumph, a thing shared between the people and the land, and this good year more than ever. Although, afterwards, life sloped down into longer nights and shorter days, there was no sadness about this feast; the sun would go on getting hotter and hotter for another month; if harvest nights were longer they were warm and starry and better for sleeping out in the fields. The sun had worked well for Marob; every house had jars full of honey already; the first crop of hay had been cut and the second was thickening and deep green. Fleeces had been heavy and clean. The fishing-boats had done well. The inlanders had come peacefully and respectfully with trading goods. Everywhere there were crops and beasts almost ready for the big markets. The year was working up through midsummer to harvest.

There were always a good many foreigners at this feast. They joined in the processions and songs; it was a good thing. They were part of the prosperity. All the Marob families who were out in the plain with their waggons had harnessed up the oxen or horses and come in for the few days round about midsummer. It was always arranged that there should be a market just afterwards. They were all gay and sunburnt and delighted to see one another, pleased with themselves and their neighbours and especially with seeing and smelling the sea again after so many green weeks in the un-salt inland country. The servants they had left behind had scrubbed and painted their houses till the winter feeling had quite gone, and now stood at the doors to welcome their masters back. The winter sweethearts hung about the doors, too, to whistle and throw flowers and watch critically to see whether their girls had grown too fat on butter and fresh meat. And the heads of households had always plenty to talk to one another about.

As soon as the midsummer sun rose everybody got up and began hanging out the garlands they had made over-night; they were fastened across the streets from house to house and in great swags along the sides of the flax market; where the sun struck on them they dried up and petals shrivelled and dropped, but by that time they had been handled and admired and complimented and their gaiety had got into the day; they had become stuff for lovely bonfires! People wore flowers on their heads and shoulders. Children came running back from the fields with basketfuls for every one to take. Most of them brought a few to the Chief's house and played a game of throwing small, tight posies of field flowers up onto the window ledges. The whole place smelt sharp and sweetish of moon daisies and hawkweed and yellow bed-straw and polleny grass.

It was from the Chief's house that the procession started. It went all through Marob, up and down the streets under the garlands, noisily and at great length. It was the best of the feasts for gay noise and colour and the smell of flowers. People had wicker cages full of wild birds, which they let go when the procession passed their own house-doors, for the birds to tell the news of midsummer all over the land. If they were ordinary small brown birds, they had red patches painted on their wings. It was not lucky to shoot those message birds afterwards until the colour had worn off.

First of all in the procession came a great many children with masks of animals which they had made themselves, rats and mice and weasels and dogs and goats and birds. They pretended to worry and eat one another. That was always great fun. Then came a piebald cow with one crooked horn and lots and lots of flowers fastened on to her head and back. Then came the Corn King on foot and dancing, with a long coat, white and striped, and leading a bear cub from the forest on the end of a chain. The bear had been given fermented honey before they started, and it always danced well, at first anyhow; sometimes it snapped, but as it was only a young cub nobody got really hurt, and the Corn King's thick coat and boots kept it off him. No one knew what the bear was for, except that everybody danced at midsummer, and, as bears can be made to dance, why not bears too! Afterwards it was turned loose outside the town, and the boys and girls threw stones at it till it limped away towards the forest.

After the Corn King came the Spring Queen, sitting high on a cart, with every possible colour in her dress, the keys of the Spring-field hanging from her belt, and a high hat with ribbons and flowers. She carried a wheel made of string stretched on a framework of sticks like a spider's web. After her came the rest of the procession, every one in Marob who chose to join in, some with cocks on their shoulders that every now and then flapped their wings and crowed at one another and helped to make a noise too. They joined in at every street; husbands and wives raced out hand in hand and jostled along with the rest. They went by almost all the houses and round the walls and so to the flax market in the heat of the day. Here everybody sat down in whatever shade there was, and the children ran over to the well and hauled up cold rippling buckets of water and passed them round, and then pulled their masks off and splashed one another. Tarrik and the bear both drank, too, and the bear went to sleep. But Tarrik took his coat off and moved into the full sun and began to do the dance of the Year.

He had a basketful of coloured wooden objects rather like roots, which he had to put down at twelve points at an equal distance from one another on the outside of a circle whose centre was a flat grey stone with a cross on it, each of whose arms was tipped with a little feather of three tails. People called these the flax tails and said they were put there when the flax market was started, but that was not, of course, what they really were. At first Tarrik glanced at the stone from time to time, to get his points, but by and bye it became fixed in his head, and he knew where to put down each of the things just because when he came to the right place he knew he must. There were words to be said with each of them and silence while he said them, but when each was properly placed and planted, every one sang the song about the year-house that the Corn King built. The song got one line longer every time and ended with a satisfactory thudding shout of men and women and children all together slam on to the word. After each placing and while he was still on his knees, he fastened up with teeth and fingers a new knot in the rush plaiting of the basket. These would be loosed, one by one, during winter, as it seemed necessary. But the whole basket was full of knots.

Tarrik had done that dance wrong once, when Erif had magicked him; but that did not trouble him now. For the moment nothing was troubling him except the tickling drops of sweat that ran down his face as he stooped or raised himself in time with the rhythm of the house he was building, that was partly in his own body and partly in the people of Marob as they clapped their hands and spun him on in his dance. When he had built the House of the Year he went to the Spring Queen's cart, and she reached him down the string wheel which she had carried upright all this time. He threw it sideways with a queer little grunting cry at the effort and restraint that made it land fair in the middle of his House, over the cross-marked stone.

Then he began running, first slowly, then quicker and quicker, round and round his House, and at the same time everybody else began throwing things in, wheels and flowers and coloured sticks and balls. It was bad luck to miss, to throw too far or not far enough, but very few did. The Corn King shouted to encourage them, called out their names, or when something was not fully in knocking it in with his feet as he passed. When anyone threw right into the centre that was the best luck of all, and the whole marketful shouted at it. Those who had thrown once successfully did not need to throw again, but often they were too excited to stop. Then they were apt to throw things at the Corn King himself instead of into his House. Still, this did not matter much because they were small and light things: flowers and feathers and flax balls flapping and tapping like sunshine itself against his hot, light-browned body. He leapt higher; he made the bear dance again, and the piebald cow. He picked up a child, stripped off her rat mask with one hand and her thin shirt with the other, and ran with her, yelping for pleasure and fright on his shoulder, clinging hot to his neck, her hard little plaits sticking out like sun rays all round her head. The House of the Year was full and all the people of Marob followed their Corn King in the gayest possible dance round and round the flax market, sweeping along children and animals, the old and sick and lame, the lazy and unhappy—all went swinging in!

Only the Spring Queen's heavy cart was left in place, only the Spring Queen stayed out of the dance. This was not her feast, though she and her kindness had helped to bring it about. One by one her women were dragged away by the pull of the dance, half reluctant yet very willing, looking back at her, kissing their hands, laughing. Erif herself looked down and remembered two years ago when she had made it go all wrong and had then come by night and alone and herself rebuilt the House of the Year. People had not known whether to throw things into the bad House which her magicked Tarrik had made, all crookedly, saying the words wrong. They did not know whether it might not be less unlucky to do nothing. She remembered the older men whispering and consulting hurriedly, their coloured things in their hands. They threw them in finally and half-heartedly, thinking the ill-luck would be on the Corn King alone and not on them. Her father had started that idea, knowing almost for certain that it was his daughter's doing, to help his plan. He had said, and then others had said, that there must be a new and luckier Corn King. She had heard Harn Der saying all this, and then seen him throwing in the first thing himself. He was somewhere among the throwers this time, too, but she did not try to see him.

And then she thought that, in spite of what had been done wrong that midsummer, it had made very little difference to crops or beasts. Of course, the people themselves were uneasy enough for weeks afterwards! Perhaps, though, this, as well as the badness of Yellow Bull as Corn King, had made things go wrong last year. Perhaps. No. The autumn had been no worse two years ago. But why? Had she put it right, quite right, afterwards? She felt, thinking of that night alone with the basket and the cross-marked stone, that if it had happened now she would not have dared.

The sunset and the starry dusk hung low and sweetly over Marob. Men and women and sleepy children went back to their homes, still singing, trailing a few flowers, kind arms round soft and happily tired shoulders. The Corn King and the Spring Queen and the cow and the bear went back to their house. The next day people came late and sleepily out of their houses and unhooked all the faded garlands from walls and windows, carried the slack, thick-smelling field and hedge stuff in deep baskets to the flax market, and swept it all together, and with it all the luck tokens which had been thrown into the Year House, as well as the things which had marked the circle, piled them up over the stone with straw underneath to start the blaze, and made a splendid bonfire. Those who had taken cocks with them in the procession now mostly brought them, flat and skewered, to grill in front of the flames on the end of long sticks. The bonfire did not last long, but while it did every one stood about round it and talked loud and cheerfully and made bargains and considered marriages, and great lovely transparent flames beat up through the sunshine in the market-place like the focused heart of summer itself.

Then everything was cleared away, and booths were put up and cattle driven in, and there was a big trading market. Foreigners from the south, Greeks and Egyptians and Phoenicians came with their goods, and the forest inlanders came with theirs. The Marob people made a profit between them, for it was a law that the inland people and the ship people could not trade directly together. There was a rope across the market, and savage foreigners had to keep to one side of it, and ship foreigners to the other, and it was the worse for them if they signalled across it. Old-comers knew and new-comers were always warned three times by some member of the Council. After that market some of the ships sailed, and most of the households went back again in their great carts to the plains for another while.

The year went on securely, wild fruits and orchard fruits ripened. The Spring Queen bore another son to the Corn King, and gave him suck. For the first moment of seeing him she thought he was exactly like her first baby; she thought he was really her first baby come again. Then she knew that this was an appearance, and the new little creature was his own self already and the past was nothing to him. They called him Klint, and also, as the custom was, for the sake of the outside world, by a Greek name. They called him Tisamenos because he had been paid for. Greek and Scythian-Greek merchants who were in the town came to give the Chief their salutations, and they thought it was a queer name, when they thought about it at all, but by now a good many of the Marob people understood.

When the baby was a week old he was shown to the Council, but Harn Der did not come to the meeting. It seemed to him that if he had tried to come he would have fallen over something in the street and broken his leg, or a tile would have slipped off a roof on to his head, or a dog would have bitten him, or some other thing would have happened; and perhaps he was right. He knew his daughter. But the Council were pleased with the baby, and brought him presents. Disdallis brought him a very nice present: it was a bird on a perch made of shells and wax, that bowed and danced to one when one whistled to it.

For a time Erif had horrible dreams almost every night that he was being stolen away by masked stooping people who were going to kill him. She did not know how her first baby had died; she had never asked anyone who might have known. Sometimes she meant to, but she never could. Those dreams stayed with her, more or less, the whole day, though Tarrik sent her musicians and jugglers and the pick of every ship-load from the south. But when she got up and out into the sun the dreams got better and she had good milk for her baby.

Now Tarrik was glad that he had changed his mind and left Essro and Yan alone. He seemed calmer. Even Erif thought so; though her clear vision of him was obscured by her baby's delightful, silly body and dawning mind. But all the same, the dreadful thing had happened to Tarrik. He had become separate from the life of the community. It was only at the feasts and when he was going through the various observances that were laid down for him that he could get away from it, drop this painful, too-conscious self, and become again the Corn God, the dancing focus of other and more diffuse life, not just this blurred, still circle of his own. Secretly he went back to the books which Sphaeros had left him, hoping that, where nothing else would cure, he might get health from what had wounded him.

The books were difficult to understand, and most of them did not seem to have anything to do with what had happened to him. They were about world-cycles very often, and it did him no good to think that what was going on now had gone on exactly the same in an identical universe before and would go on again countless times, just as, so often, he had seen the full moon rise over one special headland. Sometimes they were bits of good examples, things that wise and great men had done when faced by choices and difficulties; but they were never the Marob kind of choices and difficulties. And sometimes they were about God and sometimes about the Elements and sometimes about how Time is to become a real thing in the mind, an idea of continuous motion. They were written in rather grim, formal little sentences like sticks, but not like his own coloured sticks of midsummer. They all looked alike and he had to be very careful or the one stick which he wanted, which he could use to build with, might get past him and be lost. The books of the older philosophers, which his aunt used to read and he used to laugh at, were pleasanter stuff, full of reflections like an open pond in a garden with birds flying over it. This was a dark little river in a long tunnel; he had to grope through it. He found at last books by the Stoic philosophers, Zeno and Kleanthes, which dealt with good and evil, justice and order, and the causes of things. He went on reading.

In the early mornings he left Erif and the baby Klint, who breathed so dreadfully gently that often he had to stoop right over the cradle to feel its breath, dreading with a gripped heart that he might feel nothing, no tiny warmth, and then have to tell Erif! He went up to the long low room which ran from end to end of the Chief's house, under the roof-beam. Below the tiles there was thick thatch for the sake of warmth, but it was carelessly fastened down, since it was only inside, out of the wind. There were a few small windows and the sparrows flew in and out. In one place there was a bees' nest behind a rotted beam; it made all that end of the room smell of honey. There were chests along the middle with spare clothes and weapons and hangings, and among them one or two which were full of books. He sat down and read and thought.

One of the rolls had notes by Sphaeros himself, perhaps for a longer book. Tarrik had often heard him say that thoughts and words should be the same thing, only one was transparent, the other opaque; the thought comes forth and crystallises into the word; dialectic guides it. But all the same Sphaeros did not write as well as he thought or spoke, though Tarrik, knowing him, put more meaning into the phrases than a stranger would have. The book started by an inquiry into the physical world, the nature of that reality which seems at first to be the only reality until the seeking mind brings stresses to bear on it, and the thing crumbles. Then Sphaeros wrote of the intermingling of man with this physical world, so that there could neither be separation of body and soul, nor of man from the air he breathed, the water he drank and which flowed about his body, the fire which warmed him, the earth which held him up and fed him, from the friends and enemies, the whole rest of the universe which made his circumstances. That section of the book ended and Sphaeros went forward, with a curious eagerness that came out even in the writing to the Duty of Man, Duty of the Wise, Duty of Kings. The Thing that makes one know with utter certainty that one has done wrong: the wrong action as a Kataleptike Phantasia, as though one should imagine a man's daemon whispering in his ear. It seemed easy for Sphaeros to think like this, to have this profound sense of right and wrong, and to cling to the right. But Tarrik hated it: he could not see these things immanent in life, not in Marob at least. And surely not in Greece, where everything happened more easily and lightly because of the sunshine. Even the Spartans—even

the King's half of Sparta—did not feel all the time that
actions were right or wrong. He struggled against it, and
yet felt Sphaeros all the time planting it into some willing,
rebel part of his mind.

Then again Sphaeros wrote about the order of Nature and
how one should be part of it. He said that it was difficult,
for, in detail, how could one tell which of two actions was
the more harmonious? He wrote not too remotely but
as though he had known these difficulties himself. The
book was mostly for Greek readers, men and women of
the unhappy city states, which had once worked so well
and allowed the fullest life, but now merely cramped their
citizens up into a pattern that hurt them and the rest of the
world as well. Their boundaries cut right across the natural
course of humanity. None of the Stoics had regarded them.
They were cityless men. Zeno had come from Cyprus, his
parents from further east; he was a little stooping man with
a hooked nose and a great brown beard. Why should he care
for Greek city states? Sphaeros himself had wandered all
his days, and wherever he had gone, he had broken down
boundaries that men had put up, wantonly, as it were in their
own blood stream. Before Zeno there had been philosophers
who preached the reuniting of Hellas. But the Stoics were
first to name the brotherhood of man.

In all this, Tarrik tried to find himself. He felt profoundly
that he had at some point and unknown to himself taken a
step that had landed him dry and lonely outside the stream
of life. He was out of harmony. And now he could not
retrace his steps. Erif Der, his wife, had done the same
thing and he loved her, and he was deeply anxious for her.
Yet was the old Marob life harmonious? Was it part of the
order of nature to work magic, steal sun and rain for your
own seasons and crops, almost to alter the courses of the
stars? He thought not. Perhaps it had been—before
people like himself had begun to question it. Once upon
a time it had been part of the order of nature for men
to eat the enemies they had killed; there was nothing
wrong or abhorrent about it. But now that would be a
pitfall in a clear road. With time and questioning, rights
become wrongs and wrongs rights. The Corn Kings before
him had been satisfied. They had accepted that their lives
should end, as they all had unless they had been killed or

died suddenly when still in their strength, in that last way, in that queerer feast than any they had made part of before. It had been natural; that was their life reabsorbing itself into the life of Marob out of which it had come. But he, Tarrik—Charmantides—he was not satisfied.

Day after day he wrestled in his mind with this, and was very gentle to every one he had any dealings with. He and Erif were kind to one another, like two hurt, lost children in a wood at night. He never spoke of Sardu. There were other women, but he did not pay much attention to them. If a farm had done not so well or one patch in a crop unexpectedly withered, he might be called upon to go there, and if some barren and unhappy woman was using her forces to suck the good out of the soil and bow the hemp or thin the barley ears, it was for the Corn King to intervene. But every day, between times, he was thinking about the books. It seemed to him sometimes most likely of all that he had got the whole thing wrong, that it was not meant for Marob, just as he himself was not meant for Sparta or friendship with King Kleomenes.

One day a letter came from Berris. It said: 'So much has happened that I don't know where to begin. I had no time to write earlier in the year when we were fighting and Kleomenes was leading us to more and more glory and always more certain ultimate victory. We raided the old enemy, Megalopolis, and beat them back like chickens inside their walls. Then we invaded Achaea and utterly defeated the army of the League. I think they would have accepted him as their leader after that; they were afraid. But then chance, that they call here Spoiler of Victories, stepped in. He was hurrying through the heat of the sun to catch up with his fortune, and suddenly something burst in his throat, and he began to bleed. He could not speak for a long time; he just lay in his tent, white. They thought he was dying, and sent for Agiatis. You know he is not so strong as he looks; I suppose he is based on fire, not earth. He got well, but his Fortune had gone by, and perhaps now he will never find her again. For the League lifted its head; Aratos talked them round. I think, and so does Hippitas, who has talked to me more about it than the others, that Aratos is trying to get a promise of help from Macedonia. If so, I do not know what will happen. I do not know whether even this Sparta is strong enough to stand against the outer world. What do you think, Tarrik? I wish to God that Kleomenes had not missed his chance!'

But Tarrik did not think much about it. All that was utterly remote. And Erif only thought of Agiatis going to Kleomenes and nursing him—and he got well in the end! Berris also wrote a good deal about his work and how now, in the clear shining air, he could stand away from it and look, and once or twice about the girl, Philylla, and her father, whom he liked and who had bought an inlaid breastplate which he had made, not his best work, but then no one seemed to like that! Berris Der wondered if his sister herself would, now. And so, reading his letter, did she.

Meanwhile the flax was pulled and laid in its pits; there was much cheese-making and taking of honey; plums were ripe and dropping. Those who understood went out every day to look at the standing corn. With the new moon they began the harvest. And now Tarrik felt from his heart outward that another feast was coming; the books grew less real. He was beginning to think that they must be leading him wrong, that really it was all much simpler and gayer than that. He surprised and shocked the Council by playing one of his old tricks on a houseful of Greek merchants. But the young men laughed and went about telling one another and telling the girls. The next day he burnt almost all the books. Even while he did it he knew he was going to be sorry, but he also somehow knew that he would not himself feel the sorrow at all until after Harvest. So it did not matter.

Chapter Six

ON THE FIRST DAY of the two days of Harvest they reaped the last field in Marob. The rest had all been cut and stooked by the evening before. Dozens of young men turned out in their best clothes with their sharpest sickles to show how well they could reap. A girl, all in her best too, would go behind each to bind the sheaves. Reaping and binding together was counted as the surest sort of betrothal, and if you found a couple sleeping together after that it was the same as a marriage. Sometimes two or three girls all wanted to bind for one young man; then there'd be bitter scolding and quarrelling and often faces scratched and hair pulled out before it was settled, while the reaper either went on, grinning, or else came back to help the girl he really wanted and took the chance of some other young man getting his swathe. Every one was tired by the end of Harvest and very apt to quarrel. It was a lucky year when there were no murders about then.

The smell of the sweating reapers hung pleasantly and excitingly about the field. People brought them drinks and in return picked up an ear or two to mix in with their own seed corn. The Corn King and the Spring Queen waited and talked to their friends and did not yet feel the godhead at all urgent on them. Tarrik had a leash of spotted dogs, small hounds that were used for tracking roe deer in the forest; they jumped about, and their tongues dripped and quivered out of their grinning mouths. Erif stuck poppies into their collars. Her women had fans made of leaves and feathers, and baskets of cakes, which every one ate. The field had a grass bank all round it so that it was easy to sit and see everything.

The reaping went on through the hottest part of the day and at last all was finished but the very middle. Tarrik got up and stretched himself and went across the stubble with the sickle in his hands; it had golden corn ears inlaid on its wide bronze blade. The reapers gathered round him and he looked at them smiling—his young men! He was their elder brother, he had given them the wheat. He looked at the round, firm breasts of their girls, coming back from piling the sheaves. Their sweat-soaked shirts and bodices clung to them; nipples and bellies and thighs thrust themselves at him. He beckoned them nearer to touch long and gently a damp neck or arm; he stooped to touch stubble scratches on a bare instep, smoothed back a clinging, sweaty curl. He wanted them all in his arms, all to kiss solemnly and gently; they understood and touched him back. For the moment they liked him better than they liked their own young men. They would have put their breasts like apples into his cupped hands.

But he moved; he made a sign to the reapers. All at once, with him in the middle, they shouted and rushed on the last of the corn. Hares and mice were hiding in the thick patch; as it went down before the sickles they came shooting out, terrified, zigzagging. But the reapers clapped their hands and threw sticks and chased all the little beasts off into the crowd at the banks, which killed them joyfully. The girls took handfuls of shining, heavy-eared straw and pressed round Tarrik with it. They bound it with ties of itself round his legs and arms and body, made a stiff, tickly straw man of him. Their quick, clever hands caressed him. Some were witches, some not. At harvest all were women. With one after the other, at full length of his straw-shining arms he did a short and rather odd little posturing dance.

Then the Council, all solemnly in their best, came across the stubble towards him, and among them was, as always, the man whom they had chosen to be IT, the actor in the Corn Play of the life of the corn. This choice was their privilege, and, though the Chief was always told beforehand, they insisted that it should be a free choice. This time they had chosen Harn Der. It was to be a token of reconciliation between one half of Marob and the other, a closing of old wounds. There was honour all the year for the man who was IT at harvest. Harn Der was to get back what he had lost. They would see him in his old place again. Tarrik himself had wanted them to choose Kotka, whom he thought he had insulted in spring and whose wife he had certainly gone out of his way to terrify. But the Council had met without him, as their right was, and had decided to keep to their own choice.

Harn Der was dressed in the usual rabbit-skins, dyed a rather unpleasant whitey-green; he looked pale himself between eyes and beard where generally his cheeks showed a fine ruddy branching of veins. He said to himself that there was nothing to be afraid of. Tarrik looked perfectly friendly. His old companions on the Council who had planned and hunted with him and followed him against the Red Riders, they were all urging him on with their faces full of respect and admiration and interest. His honour would come back to him. He tried to think only of being the actor in the Corn Play. Why must his mind keep on groping past that to something else and worse?

Tarrik greeted him in the old form of words and began to transfer the Corn idea from himself to the IT. First he took off his straw sheathings and bound them on to Harn Der. Then he laid his open hands over heart and back and whispered into Harn Der's ear. The Corn King must always thus for a night and a day give up his godhead to another. It was because the actor in the Corn Play must die and lie dead in the sight of Marob before he was brought to life again. As god he could do it, but not as Chief. It would be bad luck. That had been decided at the very beginning of things. One of the Council silently handed over the Corn-cap, the thing of soft leather and gold that had a golden wheat-ear sticking straight out at the top. Tarrik put it on his own head for a moment and then took it off to crown Harn Der. Then he stepped back, feeling curiously light and free, and regarded IT to see how this weight of the transferred godhead was borne by someone else.

Meanwhile the reapers and their girls had been making great round, thick swags of very tightly bound-up corn with poppies and corn cockles and marigolds and spurrey stuck into the ties. When they were made it took two people to carry them, with forked sticks to hold them up straight. These they brought to the Corn King's own place and leant them against the walls outside. Tarrik unlocked the door and gave the keys to IT, who went inside and found the old guardian huddled and quite unaware of him over the tiny fire into which from time to time she dropped single leaves that crackled and smoked. There was food and drink too, good and plentiful, and a lamp if he should want it, so that he need not have to pass too grim a night. Tarrik locked the door and went home gaily to the Chief's house where a feast was being got ready.

Most people in Marob ate and drank well that night; few women need lie lonely and wanting a man. There were a dozen feasts going on besides the main one at the Chief's house. The next morning they woke late and slowly, with heavy eyes and slack muscles, prepared to be sad, to weep and mourn with all their hearts at the Corn Play. Tarrik went to his place and unlocked the door and let out IT, whom he was somehow surprised to see was still the same old, smiling, rather scornful Harn Der. They went back together to the harvest field. Tarrik had a wooden rattle which he shook round over his head with one hand, and a bell which he jangled hard with the other, to summon the people.

They came following, and many carried laden branches of fruit on their shoulders, wild plums and raspberries mostly, but sometimes even boughs from the orchards. Last came the Spring Queen pacing among her women, each of whom carried one of the things she was to use in the play.

As at Plowing Eve, there was a booth set up for the Corn Play, and those who had fruit branches heaped them all round, so that there was a sweet, heady smell of warm juice dripping from crushed fruit pulp, that helped the sad, excited feeling among the people of Marob. For a time yet Harn Der and his daughter were not called upon to face one another again. The IT of the Corn Play lay on his back in the middle of the stage, with a black cloth over him. The audience stood all round, whispering. There was no music for this; it was the most earnest thing in the year. Tarrik himself sat on a raised part of the bank on a scarlet blanket. One of the women carried his baby Klint and tried to make him look at what was going on. But the baby had hardly yet come into the world of sight; he could only just stare without seeing, and smile.

The Spring Queen came to the booth and her women laid the things she would need along its edge. She was dressed in white linen, embroidered all over with blobs and dabs and feathers and circles, bits of metal and glass and precious stones; for now she was not only the spring, but the life of the whole year. She took a breath and moved forward. Two years ago she had acted this same thing. She could not remember who had been IT: so much he had ceased for her to be himself, some man she knew or did not know in Marob, and become instead the other actor. Two years ago she had stepped on to the stage and at once she too had ceased to be herself, Erif Der. The crowd had not existed except as a background of waiting, hoping anxiety; it could not influence her. Why was that not happening now? Why did she still feel the crowd as something critical, broken up into separate men and women who would see things in separate ways? Why was she so much embarrassed by their nearness to her? But she knew why. She knew she was obsessed by something that was for the moment more powerful than her godhead and all Marob pushing her forward to do their work. But it made things difficult. She had to do every step, make every gesture, through her brain instead of directly and simply through her body. So she stumbled. She was aware of people she knew in the audience, aware of Disdallis, most of all aware of Tarrik. She thought she heard the baby crying. She frowned and tried to concentrate. She knew they would see her frowning. She looked for help to the intricacies of her dress, the hundreds of little embroidered patterns that might be meant to remind one of fruit and flowers and birds and people. She had to think what came next in the play, instead of knowing it.

She took up from among the things a polished lump of crystal to catch the sunlight and throw it down in a round dancing circle on the sleeping IT. She could not remember how it should be held, fumbled, almost dropped it. If she had? That piece of glass was the sun. She took a bowl of water and sprinkled rain from her finger-tips. Those were the spring showers, the gentleness of April. But was she doing it right? Even if she appeared to, if she satisfied the audience, was she really? She did not feel as if she had any of that sort of power coming out of her now. So would the seasons miss it?

IT sat up jerkily, flapping his corn-bound arms, stretching his corn-bound legs. The audience gasped with relief. He went through a series of stiff movements, turning about, growing, rising. The Spring Queen took green cloths and hung him with them; then she laid them by, but did the same thing with yellow cloths embroidered with gold. She waved a clapper to chase the birds away. She hoed round his feet. He stood stiff at his full height, his hands above his head. He stared right in front of him. Mostly, she moved below the level of his eyes. He began to dread the moment when she would show herself to him.

But it came: on a sudden cry, a call from the Corn King to his substitute. Harn Der and his daughter took hands, and stamped, and round and round they whirled, leaning away from each other. His beard touched her face and his hands gripped at hers, trying to send her messages, somehow certain that it was the last chance. But she stamped again and changed direction so that her dress twisted suddenly like a snake round her, and then untwisted and flew out; and she would not accept anything from his body to hers. Still in both of them, the thing that seemed as if it was going to happen, had not yet come clear or quite to the top of consciousness.

Then came the great moment in the Corn Play when the Spring Queen takes the sickle and cuts the corn, and IT must die and be mourned for before IT can rise again. Yet every one in Marob had faith that IT would rise! How else could they live?

So the Spring Queen took the sickle of bronze and gold and the people of Marob saw her go to lay it lightly on the throat of the other actor in his green rabbit-skins, and this would be the symbol of death and waiting and winter. But Tarrik, watching his wife, saw that she was not going to do the right thing, and his mind fell back in horror from what he had instantaneously known she must be going to do instead, and he could not move. And Harn Der at last looked his daughter in the eyes and he knew, too, but it was too late to stop her, too late to come out of the Play into real life, to leap aside or at her wrists. And when the Red Riders came again he would not be there to lead the men of Marob to defend the fields they loved.

She drew the sickle with both hands in a deepening wound across his throat, and in the first second, before he began to fall, a bit of his beard dropped off, cut by the razor edge of the sickle. Then the blood sprang at her, and then there was a great cry, not from Harn Der himself, who died at once, silent, but from Tarrik. Somewhere in the crowd there was a bitter voice which said, dropping like a stone into the deep silence of men waiting to breathe again: 'She has killed the Corn Year. IT will not rise again now.'

Then it seemed to her that she, too, might have to die, and angry, groaning noises came at her, and the crowd began to move. But Tarrik got to her first. He leapt on to the booth and flung himself down on his back over Harn Der's body and shut his eyes and said 'Go on!' So she laid by the sickle and took up the winnowing basket and began to shake it about in the next movement of the dance, and as she did this she became quite calm again; she stopped being herself. She was only the Spring Queen in the middle of the Corn Play at Harvest.

The sun was still hot and high above the stubble field. Now the Spring Queen was mourning for the cut corn; her crying voice jerked up and down; she shook her hair loose and over her face, tugged at it, pulled out a wisp to scatter over the body. From her knees up she flung herself about, she cried to the women of Marob to leave husband and children and come and mourn with her. They came, in a long procession, picking up heavy black blankets from the pile that had been made ready for them. They followed her, they went through all the movements of tearing hair and dress, scratching hands and faces with arrow-heads. The pretence grew so real in their hearts that they did weep bitterly and almost felt blood run. For the proper time they wailed their way round the double corpse of the corn.

The next thing was that the Laughing Man came, whose business it was to stop all mourning and raise up the dead corn in laughter and rejoicing. Failing his being IT, Tarrik had got the Council to choose Kotka for this. He wore a grinning mask with black hair sticking up at the top and a blue and red beard sticking out all round. He was naked to the waist and had coloured spots and curliewurlies painted amusingly on his body. He had a tail, and he had long flippers hanging out at the ends of his fingers. Some of the children screamed, including his own two, but the grown-ups liked him very much. He parted the crowd with a peculiar springing bound and a screech of laughter; he flourished himself in front of them. He leapt over to the women and twitched at their loose hair and black blankets. 'Why are you snivelling?' he said. 'What's all this goats'-dung colour for? Who pulled your hair down, my pretties? What else did he pull? Aha, so that's it, my little cry-babies. But didn't he make you laugh, too? Oh, didn't he, didn't he?' And so on and so forth with nothing at all witty or original, but all exactly what was expected of him, with no stopping or hesitation, until the mere rapid piling on of words and jokes got the male crowd worked up into tension that broke down suddenly on all sides into hysterical laughter that would take anything as fresh food.

Then the Laughing Man began his great boast: 'I can

cure anything! I can cure eagles of flying, salmon of swimming, young women of talking, old men and bulls of growing horns, and pigs of jumping over haystacks!' He went on, a great bout of boasting, the boasting of the magic of Marob, the magic of the men and farmers, the harvest laughter that can cure anything, in the end even death. Before this, the women were swept away into playthings with their comic love affairs and comic birth-pains and their amazingly comic bodies, the final and inexhaustible butt of a man's laughter. They clung together, blushing, all in their deepest feelings knocked over, pummelled, on their backs, for the prancing of the Laughing Man. Oh, how he hurt them, how he tickled them, how the crowd laughed at him and them! By this time Kotka had become so much the Laughing Man of this once in every year, had lost his own voice and manner so entirely, that the next day Disdallis could scarcely connect her husband with the things she had been made to listen to whether she would or not—but all the same would she have missed it if she could?—would any of the others?—this tearing naked, this violence, this cold bath of laughter and male boasting! Most of it went over the heads of the young children. He was a funny, jumping man.

But, for Kotka himself, in so far as he existed inside the Laughing Man, it was a grimmish business. For when he did wake IT, was there any knowing which of the two would stand up? Wouldn't it perhaps be the first one, old Harn Der, all bloody and dripping? The worst of it was, the play carried him on right up to the final moment when he bent over IT and said something so finally funny that IT had to laugh and wake up and join in the fun that life was. There was just a second's complete horror before he knew.

But it was Tarrik who woke, Tarrik alone. He raised himself from the thing which had little by little been cooling and stiffening under him. He could not even see Kotka's merry, friendly eyes because of the mask. He could not immediately see Erif Der among the black-blanketed women. All the same, as he raised himself, he was, as it was right that he should be, laughing.

The laughter shook him and shook him. He was not Tarrik any more, he was one raised from the dead in the sight of the people. Oh, it was a good world to be alive in, only to be alive, as man, as beast, as corn!

> Hard is the grain,
> The sun thaws it,
> Without pain
> The rain draws it.
> The sods rend,
> It leaps between:
> At death's end
> The blade is green!

He had been dead, he had lain stiffly in the cold clay, waiting, and at last the thing had come which he was longing for.

With short quick steps he and the Laughing Man led the dance, off and round the booth, catching with their hands at bunches of fruit, squeezing and throwing it, and so across the stubble field. The whole people of Marob followed them, looking to life, not death. Tarrik was smeared with blood on his back and shoulders. It was not blood, it was red clay of winter where the seed had lain. His face was white. So must the face be of one newly risen. Behind him the Spring Queen danced, splashed with the same red. Ah, on breasts and neck! But the dance went on to its finish.

Yet, when it came to an end people did not go home quietly. The men and some of the women stayed. They were desperately anxious and uncertain. Had she spoiled the Year, for then and perhaps forever? Had she? Tarrik said not; he had taken the baby Klint in his arms and was jogging up and down a little as he talked. The Council were standing three deep in front of him. For the first time in his life he was afraid of them. He tried to tell them that it had been only a shifting of life, of focus, from one man to another, a changing of horses on a journey. Everything has to be paid for. Harn Der himself had killed the first child, the New Year. Now, although through another's strength and will, the still newer New Year, the second child had killed Harn Der. But the Chief himself had snatched up the spirit of the corn as it passed from Harn Der; he had pinned it down as he lay over the body it had taken first. He had got it in him now! Everything was all right. They should see. Life would go on. If the Year had been hurt, he swore, even by his child's life, to set it right! The Council seemed fairly satisfied. Slowly they left the field.

Kotka, listening, had understood what the Corn King wanted to have said. He went and spoke to the other men. He had been closest of all to the Rising-up, he had seen; it had been the real thing.

Disdallis did the same among the women, for Erif Der herself did not seem to want to speak. She was not dazed or unhappy or frightened, but more like someone at the end of a feast, satisfied. She had killed her father, and Tarrik had saved her life. Those were both solid things which she could hold on to with a certain security that they could not change much.

But Tarrik went back to his own place, taking the Corn-cap with him and laying it on its shelf in the innermost division. The other things, which Harn Der had worn or touched, were dangerous now; he had them burnt. His own place was still queerly full of Harn Der having been there for the night. He sat down for a time in the smoke, chewing berries and thinking of Harn Der. The body was now in its own house again, watched by its own household, but for a time Tarrik was Harn Der. If anyone had come in they would have mistaken him for his father-in-law, their eyes would have followed their immediate perceptions and tricked them into seeing a whitish beard on Tarrik. But no one did come in. He shook it off. But all the same, Harn Der had been the dead corn, and he himself was the risen corn. How, in spite of all his talk to the Council, reconcile these two things? Circumstances had forced him and Harn Der, his enemy, so much together, that for a time they had been the same. If he had been the corn and Harn Der had been the corn, was he Harn Der? He tried to remember what he had said in the field to the old men who had doubted. How had the baby come in? Which of it all was real?

Towards morning he slept and dreamed that the only real thing was a little round, brittle ball that he held in his hands; and his hands were cold and fumbled with it, and he kept on just catching it again as it slipped. He woke the old guardian to read his dream for him, as dreams that the Corn King had in his own place must be read. She said his ball was the small world he and his wife together made, reflecting all other worlds. And he agreed that it was real, and he knew that something very different would have happened that day but that he loved Erif. But he did not think this alone was reality. And he knew that she, when she came out of the satisfaction with what she had done, which was steeping her now, would also think that it was only one of many hard yet elusive realities.

Chapter Seven

NOTHING OBVIOUS HAPPENED at once, and the weather stayed fair till quite late; but people were frightened of Erif Der. She could see that. They drew away from her at feasts just as they had from Tarrik during the time when she had been magicking him. They wore red beads and plaited the fringes of their coats or ends of their hair into tangles when they had to speak to her. She caught two of her own women doing that, and herself cut off all their hair and sent them home shamed. But other people went on. She began to look out for it, and it was not always easy to laugh. She grew rather madly bored with it and rode south to see Essro; but Essro was just as frightened as anyone else when she heard what had happened, and besides she was inclined in some obscure way to blame herself and weep about it. She was always following Yan and afraid of things happening to him; he tottered about all over the farm and managed to fall into everything there was to fall into; he was rather an engaging baby and beginning to make noises that really meant something. Erif rode back to the Chief's house and people were still just the same; when she passed a doorway there was very seldom now anyone standing in it to wave a hand and greet her. Now, when she was alone, Erif began to be uncertain of herself as Spring Queen. It is always an unpleasant possibility that other people may be right.

In the slack weeks after harvest Tarrik took power over the men of Marob and ordered them south to build the secret road. Essro sent him the plans, but would not see him. During the summer, wood had been cut and tarred for piles and bridges. The old ones were mended and strengthened and new ones were made. The men looked at the fresh islands with expert eyes; the Council came and spoke of clearing, took up handfuls of the rich stoneless earth, smelt it and tasted it and considered what fat crops its first year would give. They were convinced about the secret road now. The islands were to be common land: no single man was to be given the chance of putting a barrier across Marob's road. Following Yellow Bull's plans and pictures, they made ditches to lead away the flood waters and straight dikes of the earth they had channelled out to protect the lower islands. Slaves were set to do the first clearing, cutting away brambles and willows and rank stuff, and making great bonfires of it all; even next year it was possible that they might use some of the new land for hay and grazing.

The bullfighting went off well enough; no one was killed or very badly hurt. All foreigners had left Marob. The snow began to fall. Disdallis was going to have another baby towards the end of winter and was rather gloomy; she had this dislike of pain to what Kotka thought a quite unreasonable degree, particularly for a woman who is bound to get so much of it. She had managed two safe enough already: why all this fuss? At harvest when he was the Laughing Man, he had mocked at her about it. When she was so silly, it made him feel guilty! And why, in the name of harvest, should he be made to feel that? Erif saw a good deal of Disdallis now; the other witch might be afraid of pain, but she was not afraid of the Spring Queen. It was a pity, though, that this winter they could not go racing about together, which was what Erif wanted to do. Erif was glad of the snow. Once it had fallen and stayed and begun to pack into drifts and hard snow roads, there was nothing for either Corn King or Spring Queen to do until signs of thaw came. So all that part of her dropped off and was put away like a doll in a box, and the Chief and the Chief's wife were the same as every one else. It was usually at this time of year that the Council began to feel very independent and told their Chief what they thought of him; on the other hand, it was also the time of year at which least of a practical nature could be done. Erif Der tried to sink back as much as possible into being an ordinary person; she hoped when spring came that people would have forgotten—and she would have forgotten too!

The Chief always gave several feasts at the beginning of winter. Every one liked them. People told stories and sang and played games and laughed a great deal; they were probably very happy, but hardly any of them thought about that; they did not think about what happiness was. Only, it was stupid to be sad and not laugh. If for some reason you could not begin laughing at once when every one else did, if you were feeling winter or death or pain, it was a good thing to go to a feast and have plenty to eat and drink, and hear funny stories and remember and tell others, and see a lot of lights and girls and coloured things to make the blood run quicker. If you had not got enough food in your own house to last over winter, someone else in Marob would be sure to give it to you. If your wife died, court and marry another. If your child died, make yourself another. It was no use trying to interfere with the seasons, with the life of the year. Some lived and some died. As well expect your wheat to be all grain, no chaff!

Gold-fish and Wheat-ear were old enough to come to the feasts. They had almost forgotten about their father, they were growing up so fast. Erif Der was determined to marry Wheat-ear young to somebody sensible who would look after her well, somebody kind and secure, who would give her children, but not too many. She began already to look about for the right man, before her silly sister began to look about for herself and probably saw the wrong one! Wheat-ear would find it very easy to be in love with anybody who told her she was. Erif would tell her so, too.

In the Chief's garden the supple trees bent under the weight of the snow. Their humped branches made quiet, smooth, unsymmetrical animals, fantastic snouts and paws. Berris used always to love them; he found names for the funniest ones. But some people said they were bad devils. All round Marob the trees looked like that; it was marvellous finding one's way through a wood. Going about in winter was so quiet that every one fastened bells on to their sledges and sledge horses, and stuck up in the snow thin saplings with bells on them, so that there would be a nice tinkling noise, even when no people were there. Tarrik had a sledge made of painted oak; it was so well shaped and balanced that he almost always won the sledge races. Tarrik and Erif raced together, crouching on the sledge, yelling to the horses, swinging out at the curves in a hiss of fine snow.

Erif could not go far afield because of the baby, but Tarrik and his men went tearing out of Marob on their jangling sledges and stayed away all day and through the long, brilliant, frosty nights, singing and drinking round great fires of branches that sunk pits into the snow. Sometimes they brought girls out with them and made hot love rolling in the cold snow. But Erif had her own pleasures too.

She had been afraid of adoring her new baby very much during the first few weeks when everything was going well. She remembered too acutely how her love for the other had been smashed just as it was swelling out into full consciousness, and she was aware how much sorer than anything else in the world a broken love can be. She had not dared to be more than friendly with this one, had not dared to look at him softly. But gradually, as she found that people still thought her unlucky, as she grew slowly to believe in it herself, she began deliberately flying in the face of her ill-luck. She said to Disdallis: 'When I was a girl I thought I could get everything. Now I know I can't, and I think I may have done myself harm to the very bottom of my powers, so that perhaps I shall never be able to lead the seasons again. But one thing I will have, and I'll see that I have, and that's my baby!' She picked him up from the cradle for the mere pleasure of his cuddling warmth against her. 'Isn't he nice?' she said.

Disdallis looked quickly and then looked away. 'Is it worth it?' she said. 'Do they make up for the pain? Even you, Erif, you're strong and brave, but you did scream—as if something wasn't having any mercy on you—and they get sick and die so easily and suddenly—if one were to have that   pain   as   well   as   the   other!' She shuddered at the insecurity of it.

But Erif said: 'I've forgotten the pain when he was born. So many things have happened since then. I can deal with pain. Even if I can't at the time, I can afterwards, in my memory.'

'You may be able,' said Disdallis, 'I can't. There are lots of different sorts of people, Erif, even different sorts of women. One thing's real for one of them, and something else for another.' Her voice died down and she contemplated the prospect of her own coming pain, and could get no comfort from the thought that at least there would be several weeks first during which she would not be hurt. Her mother had warned her against going to see Erif, at the moment most of all, and she was sufficiently sure that when the time came and she was whimpering under the grip and relax and tighter grip of the pain whose quality she remembered so well, people would say it came of having got into the shadow of Erif's bad luck. Well, the other women must be given something to say, some excuse for her hating pain so much!

For days at a time Tarrik would be all alive, doing things for fun, not able to walk because his legs wanted to run, violently active and yet in his heart peaceful with the fullness of physical well-being. Then a day would come when he woke feeling sleepy, stretched himself out by the fire half dressed, and lay there till supper, snoozing and blinking, only willing to play very lazily with Erif and Klint. He had always lived this spasmodic kind of life, and as he got older it got more marked. He did most of his thinking during the periods of activity; when he was lazy the only things that went through his head were words and tunes of songs, and friendliness of dogs or women. But when he was out in the snow he thought about the seasons and what would be best for Marob.

One day they had both been out together. The whistling wind had caught their cheeks and noses; the waves were getting up and beginning to roar and drum. It was good to be sure that there was no one out on the sea now. The trampling sledge horses pulled up at the door of the Chief's house. Erif ran in out of the snow. As they heard her come, clapping her hands together, her women ran to meet her, bringing with them the warm air of the house, charged deep with smells of fur and wood smoke and scents based on musk, for hair or body. She threw off her coat where already the white crisp snow was beginning to melt and soak the white, soft fur into tags. They pulled her boots off and rubbed her long white legs with warm oil. She stretched herself and laughed and thought of Tarrik still out with the galloping sledges, the tingle of ripped flying snow against his face, the sense of speed that winter brought. The baby lay in front of the fire on a blanket; he was awake and staring, first at his own fist and then at the bright, steady flaming of the logs. His eyes were blotted and brimming with flames. His fat legs bent and unbent in a steady kicking; they thumped softly on the blanket; when they stayed still one of Tarrik's hounds would stretch across and lick the toes. Erif came and stood over Klint; he grinned very suddenly at her and gave a tremendous wriggle all over. She tossed her head back. 'Silly thing!' she said, but looked softly at him.

By and bye he began to give little panting, eager cries of desire for food and the warmth and tenderness that went with it. Erif's breasts answered to the noise with a pleasant hardening, a faint ache waiting to be assuaged. Their tips turned upward and outward, and the centre of the nipple itself grew velvet soft and tender and prepared for the softness of the baby. She unpinned her dress and picked him up and snuggled down over him on to a heap of cushions. He moved his blind, silly mouth from side to side eagerly. For a moment she teased him, withholding herself; then, as she felt the milk in her springing towards him, she let him settle, thrusting her breast deep into the hollow of his mouth, that seized on her with a rhythmic throb of acceptance, deep sucking of lips and tongue and cheeks. Cheated, her other breast let its milk drip in large bluish-white drops on to his legs, then softened and sagged and waited. For a time he was all mouth, then his free arm began to waver and clutch, sometimes her face, sometimes a finger, sometimes grabbing the breast with violent, untender little soft claws. She laughed and caught his eye, and the sucking lips began to curve upward in spite of themselves. He let go suddenly to laugh, and her breast, released, spirted milk over his face.

Now by turns he sucked and laughed, and she laughed too; his hands patted her, his whole lovely body was moving with the warmth and sweetness. He lay across her belly and thighs, heavy and utterly alive. She picked him up and held him on her shoulder and buried her nose in his neck, in the sharp, dizzying smell of his bodily warmth. He sucked a little at her cheek and lips, the careless beginning of kisses. She laid him down again on the other side; the mutual pleasure of give and take began again. She brushed her face against his new, growing hair; it was warm and a little stiff. She knew it was brownish, but in this firelight it was all red gold, and there were very small goldenish hairs on his face, like Tarrik's, but tiny, tiny, and coming out of this calm, untouched flesh, this freshly soft skin that no anxiety had ever blemished.

After a time he began to look about him, satisfied, or

only turned to her for a moment to nip and laugh. She laid him flat on her knee and he stared at things with wrinkling forehead and wide-open eyes that never blinked and never understood. He stretched his short round legs towards the fire; he was all stretching and growing. The women were away at the other end of the hall. She did not care in the least what they thought about her; in her own mind now she was not unlucky! Tarrik was still out in the snow. She was alone with Klint. She bent her head right down to him and began to whisper to him; he turned to her and half screwed up his eyes into completest brightness, spread his nostrils, pursed or widened his funny mouth, and cooed at her with small musical sounds. She hugged him up to her and he peeped and threw his head back and gave a deep, soft laugh; he was making the noises of a lover too deep in love to speak with words. She hovered with her face over his, breathing in his warm, faintly sweet breath, staring down into his eyes. Suddenly she thrust her tongue down hard between his very smooth, very delicate rose-pink lips. She felt his hard gums and soft cheeks; his tongue laid hold of hers and began to suck strongly. She drew it out again and laughed. Her son laughed too.

Erif loved Tarrik for being her baby's father, for getting her this solid and lasting thing, this pink, fresh, awakening piece of prettiness, this baby man. She loved him as the father of other babies in other years, lots and lots of babies; she saw herself with her arms full of them, standing up in Marob with the Chief's babies laughing in her arms. Sometimes, in their mutual caressing, Tarrik was rather too much aware of this; he caught her looking right through him at someone else—at her children's father when he himself did not want to be that, was not interested in her children, even in the one who was so obviously here already, let alone all the future ones, when he only wanted to be her lover and friend! She wanted to start another baby at once, but he was very anxious that she should be as strong and well as possible at Plowing Eve. He did not know what would happen then, but he thought it might need all their strength to get hold of the seasons. He had stayed in his own place for hours on end, had spent nights there trying to get a true dream, hoping to see into the future, but it was no use. If she wanted another baby he would give it to her—it was hard enough not to when she made love to him!—but he was not very willing when he was away from her and could think about it calmly. Yet it would hurt and anger her if he went to other women now, and besides he did not want to. Just now the flame in him burnt inwards, not out towards plowing and sowing and begetting.

After the winter solstice every one brought him presents, in gratitude for the relief they always felt after the slight insecurity that always hung about for a few days before that when the sun seemed so very unwilling to come near and warm them. They brought him candles to increase his strength and baskets of late apples, or, if they had not any left, apple-shaped balls of honey and flour baked hard and coloured red. Then there was a feast when all the candles were lighted and the apples eaten, and day by day the sun grew stronger, set later, and soon began to rise earlier on Marob.

In the middle of the feast, looking along the table at his friends and companions, Tarrik suddenly wondered who would be IT next year at the Harvest Play. There was nobody he could ask about it and no precedent for it in the past, and after a time it seemed as if perhaps Marob would not find anyone to be IT. He had taken it on himself. The Corn Man had died and risen again as somebody new and unforeseen and younger. The grandfather had died and the father of the grandson had risen. The daughter had killed her father and her lover was brought to life. The old war-leader was killed and the risen one had been mostly leader in peace and games. The choice of the Council had been killed and the Chief alone had risen. Finally, Harn Der had been killed, yet whenever Tarrik went to his own place now to work the seasons or to dream, he had to beware or he would begin to become Harn Der as well as himself. But which was the thing that mattered, which aspect of it was Tarrik to consider in the future of Marob? He must know soon or he would be haunted for ever by the ghost of Harn Der. If Berris had been there, he might have helped; at any rate, he would have been someone to talk to. Or his Aunt Eurydice? No, it was a long way from her and from Sphaeros.

He leant his elbows on the table and looked down it moodily; it was a men's feast. He felt they were watching him, trying to interpret, whispering about him. Let them interpret if they could! He wished them joy of it. His friend, the metal-worker who had made the new plowshare, was there. He at any rate was not thinking about the Corn Play! He was looking at one of the Chief's candlesticks, with his lip out as if he thought rather ill of it. By and bye he drew it jarringly across the table towards him, and the twenty spiked candles trembled and spilled. He leant across to a neighbour, another metal-worker, and said something. Tarrik threw a nut at him.

It knocked over one of the candles. Almost every one gasped and stopped talking; they were in that state of maddening expectancy. Tarrik stood up, furious. He took the two iron candlesticks that were nearest to him and heaved them up, one in each hand, with that momentary, terrific strength that sometimes came to him. He said: 'I tell you, the dead thing rises again! It takes another shape and lives! Spring will come back, the corn will grow, I have been dead and now I am alive!' He waited, waited for the impulse to leap through his arms and crash the candles blazing down. He thought he would kill somebody, make them stop staring at him! They thought so too. They cowered, lifted their hands and ducked their heads. The impulse did not come.

There came instead to Tarrik the image of the burning candle which Sphaeros had used in books and talk: the wax rushing gently up the wick to consume in flame, but there alone to find its true reality. And gently, too, Tarrik set down the candlesticks, so that they scarcely flickered. He stood with his hands spread behind the flames and said: 'I wish you peace and that you may get your best hope.'

Towards the end of winter, on a grey morning, Disdallis felt her pains begin. Late that evening Kotka went over to the Chief's house and found Erif's girl cousin, Linit, and bade her tell the Spring Queen that Disdallis was asking for her and only her. The girl looked at him and said: 'I wish my Queen very well, but I wish Disdallis well too, most of all now. Is what you ask lucky?'

Kotka said between his teeth: 'I'll tell the Spring Queen this!' 'No, no!' said Linit. 'At least—wait. I'll get her now.' She ran in and found Erif, who got together what charms and herbs she knew of, and went hurrying across

Marob with Kotka, neither of them speaking much. She did what she could, but with Disdallis white and screaming or sobbing with utter exhaustion, she did not manage to help much. The pains were too complete for magic to make any headway against them. Once as she held Disdallis taut and writhing, against her breast, she saw some of the older women there glaring at her. She went home hurriedly to suckle her baby and eat a little herself, and when she came back she found they had hung beads round Disdallis' neck and double plaited the ends of her hair. She was so angry that she pulled the coral straight off and threw it at them. Disdallis was now fainting from time to time. They made her eat, but when she did she was sick. About noon, more than a day and a night since the pains began, she gave birth to a dead baby, strangled with its own birth cord. She was almost too ill to understand. She could only sob helplessly and turn her face away from Kotka when he tried to kiss her.

Erif got her to sleep, and when she was asleep made a magic that would keep her asleep, for as long as the pain had been before. Then she went home to her own house in horror and gave Klint back to his nurses the moment she had fed him. She thought perhaps *that* was what she was asking from Tarrik and what she would get from him next time. She wondered shakenly if she was pregnant already, if so how to stop it. The more she considered it the more she became certain that if he started a child in her now something would assuredly go wrong with it. The bad luck would go down from her hands that had held the sickle to her womb that held the child. Tarrik was with the Council discussing a question of mending the breakwater, which had been rather badly knocked about in the last storm, now, or leaving it till spring. She changed her clothes and had a steam bath. At least she could stay at home and rest while Disdallis slept; she would not have to face her dear friend suffering until the next day. She would see Tarrik again first and get strength from him.

She heard Kotka's voice and ran to meet him. Her cousin Linit was clinging to him, trying to stop him coming. He threw his arm up and swung the girl off. 'Erif!' he said, 'when I left her they took your magic things away, took the leaves out of her mouth—her mother did, Erif!—and she woke up crying. Oh, Erif Der, she won't let me go near her!'

'Is she in much pain?' said Erif. He nodded. Erif half turned her head away, covering her eyes and mouth. She could not bear to go back and face it again!

The girl cousin said to Kotka: 'What did I tell you?'

Kotka did not notice, but Erif did. She looked at her cousin. 'You too!' she said, 'you bitch.' She drew her dagger.

Linit said: 'Kill me then, Erif! But I've defended you time and again against a hundred people. My own father and mother. What do you think will happen and go on happening till you get clean? Oh, get clean, Erif!'

She dropped on to her knees. Erif sheathed the knife and looked at her own hands. 'They seem clean to me,' she said, 'and I thought the snow would have cleaned everything. Get up, Linit, I won't hurt you. Kotka, what shall we do?'

He said: 'I laughed at her. About being hurt. At harvest. She'll never forgive me.'

'I expect she will,' said Erif a little vaguely, but trying to think about that, not herself, 'only not yet. And don't be in a hurry to hurt her again.'

'Never!' said Kotka, 'never.' And he shuddered horribly.

Erif did not answer; she got more of the leaves and shells which she needed and told Linit to bring the baby to Kotka's house to be fed. Tarrik perhaps would come there too, when the Council was over. She found the other women in the same room with Disdallis, who was moaning and twitching and very hot. She went straight to Disdallis and put the leaves on her tongue again and began to speak into her ear low and rapidly, and went on till she fell asleep again. She was so intent on it that she did not hear the scuffles and shrieks as Kotka turned the others out of the room. She stroked Disdallis with light fingers, smoothing her forehead to calm and her mouth to a smile. When she moved away Kotka came nearer and looked down at his wife, out of pain for the moment. 'I trust you, Erif!' he said. 'If it was anyone's doing, it was mine. I'll stay here till she wakes.'

Erif nodded and went out and found the other women all in a bunch glaring at her. 'You picked up my shells, didn't you?' she said, 'in your fingers? They'll begin to burn you in a day or two.'

Then she sat by herself on a stool trying to be still and think of nothing till Tarrik came. 'Sweetheart!' he said, staring at her, 'what have they been doing to you?'

'I'm only tired,' she said, 'so very tired. I wanted you, Tarrik.' She told him what had happened. Then: 'I must stop feeding Klint.'

'But I thought—' said Tarrik.

'Yes!' she cried, 'I want to feed him! I can't bear not to! But now I daren't let him take the risk.'

Chapter Eight

KOTKA BURIED HIS dead baby, hurriedly and at night. After that Disdallis got well, but very slowly and half-heartedly; even when she was up and eating solid meat and ordering her household again, she would sit down to spin and then begin to cry, and if no one came in and stopped her there she would stay, sitting and crying, for hours. Erif brought her branches in pale bud, boughs of thorn and chestnut which she had broken off, black and frosty-brittle, and brought indoors and made magics over till she cheated them into belief that the real spring had come, and by and bye they budded for the Spring Queen. But it seemed to Erif that this year the little leaves came more reluctantly out of their hard bud cases and did not seem to spread and grow green as they should have. She asked Disdallis what she thought, but got no help, for Disdallis did not want to talk about it; and in a few days Kotka came to her, very unhappy, and said that it would perhaps be better if she did not come to the house.

'But,' said Erif, 'surely Disdallis doesn't think I'm unlucky! Oh, Kotka, surely she doesn't think it was my doing—what happened to her?'

'She doesn't quite think so,' said Kotka awkwardly, 'but she will if you go on coming. People talk to her—the old ones. And she's not herself yet.' He looked at Erif like a very nice dog; he would have liked to say something to help her but he did not know what.

Erif said: 'Oh, if *she* is going to lose faith—! If *she* thinks it's true—!'

'Anyhow, I don't think myself that you did any harm,' said Kotka earnestly. 'Harn Der wanted killing. You had the right. Tarrik explained it all. I understood.'

'Disdallis understood then!' said Erif. 'She talked to people too; she helped me. Why has she changed? There's nothing new to know!'

'I can't tell you at all,' said Kotka, and then lamentably, what he so often thought: 'It is very difficult for me, being married to a witch!'

'Yes,' said Erif, almost laughing, 'we all ask questions! Well, I didn't want to see her last spring. One has one's fancies. And after all she may be right.'

The snow began to melt. The earth began to show, ready to wake up. Several small things happened to Erif Der. She would not perhaps have paid much attention to them any other year, but now she did, her dreams got full of them. Her pony mare died suddenly and so did the magpie which Philylla had given her and which she had kept indoors and warm by the fire and fed with her own hands. She caught a bad cold, and then her nose bled in the middle of a feast. Half the stock fish in the store seemed to have got wet, and went bad. Klint had spots and cried. She lost various things. She dropped and broke one of the pots for sowing flax seed in her Spring-field. She had to get another made. The first one cracked in the kiln and the second one was a little crooked, but she dared not say so or the potter would swear it had been straight when it left him, and people would talk still more. The time for Plowing Eve came nearer and Tarrik grew excited again and happy, but a long way from her. He came into her room in the red and yellow coats he wore about that time, and his eyes were bright and he did not seem to be able to understand why she should be anxious and unhappy. It was as though he were only aware of the part of her which corresponded with the mood that was on him now. He played with Klint, tossed him and rolled him and felt about in his mouth for teeth, laughed at the little hard gums biting on his fingers, and the baby knew and held up his arms and tried to roll over towards Tarrik when he saw him coming. But he seemed a little frightened of his mother now; sometimes he would cry suddenly and turn his face away. Erif said gaily that it was teeth, but she did not think so. She was very abrupt with him, suddenly

snatching him up and then as suddenly handing him back
at arm's length to the nurses.

Plowing Eve came. The people of Marob gathered at
the fallow field and the jars of drink went round. The
shouting began. Noon came, and the ring parted to let
through the Corn King and the Spring Queen. Erif felt
them watching her, heard a curious, alarming quality in
the shouting, shivered and whitened as she went through,
forced herself on against sickening fear. She brushed against
a plowing mark and heard a little gasp as it wavered, was
suddenly afraid she was not really settled in the middle of
the field, at last dropped her head over her wrists and tried
to breathe calmly and wait and cease to be herself.

But she could not do it. Her senses could not keep still
and let her be. She heard the grunting and plodding of the
oxen as the plow started. The wind blew smells towards her,
the crowd and its drink, then after a time the opened earth.
Her odd dress fidgeted her; she wanted to move; her
hands were bitterly cold. Her eyeballs shifted under their
lids. And then she began to hear the Corn King talking
about the plowing and she knew she would have to answer.
And suddenly she also knew that it was not merely the
reluctance of a difficult spring which she felt. The spring
was not in her at all. She had lost touch with Marob and
Marob's spring. She was not the Spring Queen!

Ah then, then, pretend! Act it until it becomes real.
With a great effort she raised her head to answer. It would
not be impossibly difficult. Yes, the answers were coming
into her mind. She heard the people calling to her urgently
from all round: 'Spring Queen, be kind, be kind!' She
loved them; they were her people; she would not hurt
Marob! She would go through with Plowing Eve and force
the spring to come.

She went on answering to Tarrik's plowing talk. It seemed
to be all right. Yes, it was going to be! Why be anxious?
She was strong, she was well. She was not pregnant. She
had a baby at home and a splendid husband here on the
field; it was all right. The spring would come, the earth
would be young again and covered with flowers. Every year
Marob grew young again. Trees that had been old in dull
and tattered leaves grew young again. Fields that had been
rough and stubbly as an old woman's face grew fresh and

young again. Salt, sad marshes grew young again and made men glad of them. The islands of the secret road would make men glad with their greenness and youngness.

Yes, yes, that was good and that would always happen, but she, Erif Der, she could never turn again and grow younger, no more be a young maiden moving consciously among glad looks! She was growing older every year—every Plowing Eve she was a year older—and soon she would be too old to make any man glad, not any lover, not her own Tarrik. Oh unfair, oh cruel spring to come young and young and again young while women grow old! Oh spring, luring men from their own women, making them see their women old and used against the young green! She heard her voice in an answer to Tarrik, and it was angry and hard. She knew the people of Marob would be hurt by it, would think it meant a cold and late season. She could not help it. She heard the farmers shouting at her, eagerly, violently: 'Spring Queen, be kind!' And suddenly she remembered Murr, who had not had kindness from her but had died and would not see any spring again.

But now the plow was very near. She tried to force her voice to kindness and gladness, raised her head, thought she was not old yet, thought Berris would come back this year. She wondered if the people of Marob were at all satisfied. Ah, now the plow was turning inward. She must run between the horns of the oxen. One moment she stood, waiting for Tarrik to give her courage. She saw in his eyes that he did not know her. They were not Tarrik and Erif; he was the Corn King and she—she should be the Spring Queen. She sprang between the oxen and leapt the plowshare and did not stumble, nor even cry out or turn pale with the pain of her arm that had been grazed by one of the horns.

The thick, surging crowd swept inwards at her. Oh dear Marob, if only she could be part of Marob again, their Spring Queen, oh lost love! She shut her eyes, swaying, wrestling with herself to come and join them. She heard them hammering together the planks of the booth. Surely there was, after all, nothing wrong? She was the Spring Queen, who else could she be? Every one knew she was the Spring Queen wearing the Spring Queen's clothes! She was bringing them their spring, she was quite, quite certain that it would come, that the corn would grow as well as ever. She had done nothing to hurt the seasons! No, she was not anxious, she was not thinking about harvest or anything that had happened! Yes, she was smiling now! She opened her eyes to their loud singing and the prickling of the thrown corn-ears. That singing answered back to her smile, growing louder and gladder. The pipes and drums thudded up from behind the voices. She was going to do the dance well for them!

The Corn King and the Spring Queen went up on to the booth and began the dance. She had only to follow with her body what Tarrik led in. She watched him. She was the gentleness of the spring. He was the strength of the corn. The corn that had been asleep all winter, but now was growing, was rising. Then suddenly a terrible thing leapt into her mind, and buzzed round and round there. Who was the risen corn? The Corn King of today was the Corn Man at harvest, and the Corn Man was Harn Der. The risen corn was Harn Der. She was dancing again with Harn Der. She had killed him and he had risen, and now she could not kill him again, he had got out of his own body, he had risen into another body, into the Corn King's body. He was looking at her through the Corn King's eyes. She fought the image, she tried to tear it out, she looked for help to Tarrik, her lover. It was not Tarrik any longer! From all round the pipes and drums hemmed her in, crushed the two dancers spinning together in one wild, inevitable rhythm. The climax of the dance was coming again. Erif Der saw with horror and terror her own dead father leap at her. She knew with an immediate grip of the moment and what it brought, that when she had fallen ready for him, it was Harn Der who would sweep aside the Corn King's rags and show himself, Harn Der who would plunge down on her, Harn Der who was the image of God and Man and her possessor and master! Her knees, her body, on the point of bending, giving to the fall, the final yielding of spring, stiffened and shook. She flung up her arms against Harn Der and the thing she must not take from him, screamed with all her might against the rhythm, and jumped clean out of it, off the booth, into the furrow ankle-deep, turned her head to see if he was following her and yelled in panic again and rushed into the crowd that parted all about her.

She ran like a hare, screaming and doubling like a hare, across the fallow field. The crowd scattered screaming too, as though her touch would be death. They trampled on one another. She could have caught and clutched on to someone if she had looked, but she was blind with fear, and no one would save her, no arms open to hide her! Then from two different places in the crowd two women ran to risk everything and head her. One was Disdallis and one was her cousin Linit. When Kotka saw his witch wife running, he suddenly trusted her and followed, and had almost caught her up when Erif Der ran into her arms and cowered there. The three of them held her. Linit was in the bridal dress of the Spring Queen's women, but her great hat had fallen off. There was no one else near them, but all round, at a little distance, people gathered into tight, staring knots.

Erif Der looked up and over her shoulder. She let go her grip of Disdallis and rubbed her hands over her face and smoothed down the wool flowers on her dress. She seemed to want to ask a question; the two women murmured soothingly to her. Kotka took her by the wrist and pointed: 'There are the Council.'

'And Tarrik,' said Disdallis. Erif pulled back from her.

'You must,' Kotka said, 'for Marob. Even if they are going to kill you.'

'But they won't!' said Linit. 'You will be made clean, Erif—somehow. And if you don't go to them they'll come and fetch you.'

'We'll go with you,' Disdallis said, 'and perhaps Tarrik will save you.' The four of them walked towards the Council.

Tarrik was in the middle of them, very obvious in his coloured tatters, talking hard. The Council were talking back at him, baying in their deep, old men's voices. A good many had drawn daggers or swords. Kotka loosened his own dagger in its sheath. As they came nearer Tarrik bounded out from among them, knocking up one hand with a knife. Erif twitched and shivered, but the others pulled her along. Some of the older men came after Tarrik, but he turned, whirling up his arms, and shouted: 'I am the Corn King and I tell you I know what to do! Keep back and I'll save your corn. Come on and I'll rot it!' They checked, and Black Holly came crossing over between them and his Chief, slowly, with a sword.

Then Tarrik glanced west at the low sun, and from Erif to the other two women. 'I must do the dance with the new Spring Queen before dusk. Come!' He nodded at Disdallis, but she cried out 'No!' and pulled at Linit. The girl came forward, hesitating two steps, and then, as she faced the Corn King, suddenly confident. 'I will!' she said. 'Change!' said Tarrik. 'Quick!' He pulled at the neck of the girl's dress, tore with both hands and sent the linen ripping down a green stripe from top to hem. Disdallis untied the cord round the neck of Erif's queer dress, loosened it, and pulled it over her head. Linit slipped into it and tied it as she ran with Tarrik towards the booth.

Erif stood naked and slackly staring till Disdallis huddled her into her cousin's torn dress and fastened it tight with her own belt. When she touched Erif's flesh it was so cold that she shivered herself. 'If we could get her away?' she said. 'Before the Council have stopped being frightened,' said Kotka, and picked Erif Der up. She did not seem to be able to hold on round his neck, so he slung her over his shoulder and walked away with her off the fallow field to where the horses were tethered. His own were at the far side, so he took the nearest two and they rode back to the Chief's house. Erif was able to walk now and even smiled a little. The women who were left brought wine and warm clothes and heaped dry wood on the fire, and asked dozens of questions till they found that no one was answering them. Kotka and Disdallis waited, sitting at the opposite side of the fire from Erif, watching her colour coming back. Disdallis held Kotka's hand and he was very glad of it; she had not done that for a long time.

Meanwhile Plowing Eve went on. Corn King and Spring Queen danced, first to the sound of one drum, then to two, then as the pipers and drummers came hurrying back, to the full rhythm of the courting dance. They finished it and the plucking of the flowers, which Tarrik hurried on with cries and curses, just before sunset. There was not one moment for Tarrik to rest or be cleaned with warm water. He had barely time to get into the gold-sewn clothes and take the sunlight into himself, before it sank. Yet that gave people less time to talk. They had to make the sun-wheel and start it spinning. Honey dripped out of the Corn King's mouth and down over his coat. Those who were next him in the centre of the wheel, the older men mostly, the Council and others, felt as they touched him that he was tense, and gripped with such a strength that they scarcely dared come near either of his hands lest it should close on them and crush.

More women than usual stayed for the night of Plowing Eve. It was of such intense importance to make up for anything that might have gone wrong. Both men and women remembered those two queer times when something comparable, though not so bad, had happened, when it was the Corn King himself who had done unlucky things, nearly three years ago now. It was said that so little actual evil for Marob had followed these things because the Spring Queen had in some way made up for them afterwards with the seasons. Had the Corn King and the new Spring Queen done that this time? What had happened had been so much worse. At that moment of all moments in the year! What had she seen? One witch-girl, dared by another, asked the Corn King what was going to be done to the old Spring Queen. He said nothing at all, but was so violent with her that she was bruised for days afterwards.

The Council met the next morning. Tarrik slept till the last moment; he had never been so tired after Plowing Eve before. It had cost him an immense effort to wrap up the plowshare and put it away properly; the dresses must wait. Erif had been asleep when he got back, and in the morning they only had a few moments together while he hurried into his clothes. She told him what kind of an appearance it was that she had seen. He nodded; he was not much surprised. He said: 'I'll do what I can, for you and Marob. I don't know what it will be. I think everything is going to change.' Then he put on his crown and went to the Council.

Erif Der waited and talked a little to her cousin. Disdallis had gone home, and Kotka was standing armed outside the door of the Council Hall, to be ready for anything. She felt as though she had lately been very ill. It had all worked out curiously even. She had magicked Tarrik at midsummer and harvest two years ago, when she was still in her father's power, doing what he desired. Now she seemed still to be

in her father's power: when she went against him it was
she who was magicked at Plowing Eve. Linit said that there
had been nothing wrong with the Corn King to her eyes.
He had led her through the dance. She had seen it often,
so she knew what she must do. Besides—she did not
have really to understand; it was as if something had
taken hold of her and made her do the dance: the music
perhaps, or some violence coming out of the Corn King's
hands and eyes. She herself was quite sure that the spring
would come now.

Tarrik came back from the Council. He went straight to
Erif Der and said: 'It was Marob's will against ours, and
I am part of Marob. They say you must get clean of Harn
Der's blood or die. I said you could get clean. I do not
know at all how you are to do it, Erif.'

She said: 'Is there no way that seems likely? Has it
never happened in the past? Surely other men and women
have found that they could not always be gods!'

Tarrik said: 'They have never thought about it before,
so it has never happened. We two are different from any
Corn King and Spring Queen that Marob has ever had.'

'Whose fault is that?'

'Perhaps it was a thing that had to come one day, or
perhaps Sphaeros did it to us. I thought of that coming
back from the Council. Erif, I thought—perhaps he
might show you how to get clean.'

'Oh, Tarrik!' she said, 'am I to go from you?'

'I do not see how you can ever get clean here, Erif; you
will not get away from your father in his own land. I have
not got away from him, though he is dead and I have risen.
You will come back when you are clean, Erif.'

'Ah, how shall I tell that?'

Tarrik looked at her desperately and then looked away
'I don't know, I don't know! If I did it would be easy!
You shall take my knife again and I will keep your star and
at least we shall see that much about each other.'

'But, Tarrik—' She caught hold of him, flung herself down on the ground and hugged his knees bruisingly
against her breast. It was infinitely worse than their first
parting. There was so much more between them now, so
much solid truth and trust, things that both had done and
both had forgiven, growth and understanding and a very

great tenderness. They were not pulling and straining at one another all the time as they had at first; they were reasonably certain. And there was the baby. She thought of not having him to kiss and hold and play with and watch growing; she had a sudden ridiculous, dreadful feeling that if she was not there to brood over him he might grow up into someone else, not himself. She tried to say so. It sounded silly. Tarrik patted her.

He said: 'Everything will be all right here. I will see to it. Don't think about anything except saving yourself, sweetheart.'

Unreasonably, when he said that, she could not think about herself at all. She said: 'What will happen to Marob?'

Tarrik shrugged his shoulders. 'I shall find Spring Queens.'

She said: 'I know you will.'

He said: 'You will have to show Linit what to do in the Spring-field, or the guardian can tell her. Erif, don't put things wrong there, for her or for any of them. If you do that everything will smash. Listen: they may be Spring Queens, but you're my wife and my son's mother. That can't and won't be changed.'

She said: 'I won't hurt anything or anyone in Marob any more. But even when I'm gone will it be all right? Is your luck straight? Are you satisfied?'

Tarrik did not answer for a moment; they were sitting side by side with their arms round one another; but either could face away and not show the trouble which each separately was in. At last he said: 'I am satisfied for Marob, and that is what I am Corn King for. But I am not satisfied for myself. You know that, Erif. And perhaps the people of Marob will come soon to want each his own satisfaction too. The seasons will not be enough. Then the Corn King will not be enough either. Sometimes I think I have to get ready for that.'

'Get ready?' she said. It had sounded queer and sad; she did not know what it might not mean.

'I must save myself,' he said, 'and then I shall be able to save my people. Sphaeros would think that was a very proper and right thing for any king to say!' He laughed a little. 'But I was very happy most of the time before

Sphaeros came—and you magicked me. Would I have got into this tangle without him and his Stoics? It's like the marshes, Erif, all low and twisty, so that one can never see clear through it. I want a road.'

'A secret road.'

'To get myself and Marob across. I would be very glad to do that before I died. I want to find where we are in the universe. If it is like the philosophers tell us, earth and air and fire and water, all remote and unfriendly, and currents in it moving one whether one chooses or not! I want to find it kinder.'

'And I want to find it in my power!' said Erif, suddenly and comfortingly aware of herself as a witch, 'and I will! We'll save the people, Tarrik.' She looked at him gaily, feeling for the moment strong enough to face anything. But he was looking away.

He said, hesitating, unlike himself: 'I think that even if they want something more than the seasons, the Corn King might be the Risen Corn for them, for their hearts as well as for their fields. But he might have to die first.'

Erif said sharply: 'I don't understand!'

'Nor do I,' he said, 'yet.'

She had another four weeks before she could sail, as the weather was still very uncertain. All the time she was dragged about between counting the moments left, and wishing that this pain of saying good-bye were over. She spent tense hours with the baby, staring at him, getting his image into her eyes, touching him, getting it into her hands, listening to him so that when she was far away her ears would get an inward echo of his laughing and little bird noises, bubbling cries, funny whimperings that really meant something important. She stared at Tarrik till he could hardly stand it. She went about the harbour and streets; but they were not themselves, not true, because people always moved away from her, stopped their bargaining or singing or shoemaking, called their children in. She was never in the middle of the good, familiar crowd.

She showed Linit honestly everything in the Spring-field that she had to know, and made the guardian look at her hard, to know her later. She gave her the Spring-crown. She said she would be back soon, clean and full of power, in a year perhaps, or two years. She was going to be a witch in strange countries! Tarrik asked her who she would take with her and offered her what she would of the treasure. She took jewels and as many bars of gold as she could carry, for herself and, she hoped, Berris. But she would not take any more, and she would not take any women to dress her or men to guard her. It was better to be alone, able to move quickly and suddenly. This business of saving herself might be dangerous, and she would not drag innocent people into it. Besides, when she got to Greece, there would be Berris. And there would be two in Sparta who would be friendly, Philylla and Queen Agiatis. Tarrik, remembering Kleomenes, was doubtful of how far she could count on them. But he trusted Sphaeros.

Disdallis came to Erif and asked to go with her. But Erif laughed and said Disdallis was better at home. 'You will be there when I come back,' she said. 'I shall think of that. You will tell me what has happened.' When Disdallis pressed it she was a little angry. She said: 'You know you think me unlucky, Disdallis! It would be no help to me seeing my own bad luck every time I looked into your eyes! You took a big risk to help me at Plowing Eve and I will not ask it of you twice. Besides, I may be in danger—I may run straight into danger and pain. You must stay in Marob and keep a little peace for me to have when I get back, Disdallis.' Afterwards Kotka thanked her very truly and humbly for not taking his wife away from him. She did not tell him that she had hardly considered that side of it at all, because that would have made him feel uncomfortable, and she did like him very much.

When the time came, Tarrik said he could safely come with her in his own ship as far as Byzantium. Nothing could happen while he was away. The Council were sufficiently afraid of him now. Black Holly and Kotka and the others would look after things. The young crops were beginning to show, and every one felt glad and relieved. Erif had been, in a way, looking forward to cutting clear of everything and starting her loneliness, yet when she heard this she was wildly glad and wept for pleasure of seeing him, clinging to him for a little time yet, of finding some more certainty and strength before she went and it was all lost.

The baby lay in his cradle, half awake, blinking and smiling. She did not pick him up and hug him. She bent and kissed him and whispered good-bye, lightly, lightly. She smiled at Linit and went down to the harbour. She waved a hand from the boat to Kotka and Disdallis on the quay. They went coasting softly south; she did not look back.

At Byzantium Tarrik found a merchant ship bound for Gytheum, whose captain he knew well of old and trusted; he was a man from Olbia, only half Greek. They had three days. They talked of all sorts of small things. Erif bought toys and painted horses for him to take back and give to Klint—later. She bought oddments for all her friends. They pointed and laughed and ate sweets. He came down to the boat with her. She went on board.

She leant over the rail and talked to him; they could just touch hands. Oh, all the words that had not been spoken, the most important parts of life left unsaid! The things they had not said and could not say—they could say them now! But not all jammed into a tiny moment. Oh moment, stay and let us grip you and talk. But the anchor rattled up, drowning their thought, the rowers leant forward for the first stroke. Every one was shouting, hurrying, blotting out the last moment. He stood on the quay. He could touch her ship still. The oars dipped. The stern glided past him. He could not touch it any longer. Now they were hoisting the sails. Now the ship was only one of a group of ships, beyond sound of any farewell.

> You say good-bye;
> You are swallowed up
> Into empty hollows
> Of time and space.
> I want to see you,
> I want to touch you—

Back to Marob.

PART IV

The Patterns of Sparta

Quand je vais au jardin, jardin d'amour,
La tourterelle gémit,
En son langage me dit :
'Voici la fin du jour !
Et le loup vous guette,
Ma jeune fillette,
En ce séjour.'
Quand je vais au jardin, jardin d'amour.

NEW PEOPLE IN THE FOURTH PART

Greeks
Neareta, the wife of Phoebis
Chrysa, a Spartiate girl
Philocharidas, Idaios, Neolaidas and Mnasippos,
  and other Spartiates
Agesipolis and young Kleomenes,
  the King's nephews
Hyperides of Athens, an Epicurean philosopher
Priest of Apollo at Delphi
Philopoemen of Megalopolis
Thearidas and Lysandridas, citizens of Megalopolis
Archiroë, a woman of Megalopolis

Macedonians
King Antigonos Doson of Macedonia,
  and his soldiers

Spartans, Argives, Delphians, Megalopolitans,
  Corinthians, Tegeans and others

CHAPTER ONE

THEMISTEAS STILL HAD his house in the country, the
home farm and the land just round it; that was his lot
after the division, and at least it was small enough now
to let him oversee its cultivation, and curse the helots if
they did not make the best possible use of it. His wife
was unhappy. She could not understand the New Times
and she did not want to, and when she chose to get on
his nerves he was unhappy too, and for the sake of her
comfort and his own he managed quite a number of small
evasions of the new laws. He himself had, for the most
part, to feed at his Mess, except when he had leave, but
Eupolia and the children must have something better than
black broth. Not that Philylla wanted anything better (or
hardly ever!), but Dontas, when he came back from his
class, which was rather lax, and turned a blind eye on
mothers' pets, was the greedy one, and the eleven-year-old
Ianthemis adored her mother and clamoured for whatever
she thought Eupolia might be wanting. It was all rather
grim for them. Themisteas went off fighting again and
enjoyed it, and came back as eager as a boy for his wife.
She, having found the summer months merely dullish and
anxious, was less eager. Once Philylla found her father
behind the pig-stye, chucking a pleased milk-maid under
the chin; the milk-maid ran away giggling and the two
Spartiates looked at one another, and both kept quite silent
about it. Philylla thought it would have made her much
more uncomfortable a year ago than it did now. But even
still—

Philylla was at home for a month. Her mother demanded
her back from the Queen, and Agiatis, wanting all possible
goodwill towards the King and his Times from the old
citizens, had made her go. That morning Eupolia had been
weaving with her, and her foster-mother, and Ianthemis.

Philylla said to herself over and over again: 'It is good practice for me to listen quietly to them teasing me, scratching
at the things I love. I will not say a word back. It is like
the discipline the boys have. I would rather have the same
as the boys, but as I can't, I will make the most of this.'
And she smiled, and stiffened her hands to keep them
from trembling, and thought hard about Agiatis. When
her piece of stuff was finished and folded into squares,
and when Eupolia had duly remarked on how much better
her daughter would have been at weaving if she had stayed
decently at home, Philylla said that she would like to go out
for a little before sunset.

After a time she found her foster-mother, Tiasa, following
her. She glared, but it had no effect. Tiasa came level with
her. 'My lady doesn't like you to go out by yourself, lambie,
with all these wild lads there are about now, and you grown
so tall and pretty.' 'Oh very well!' said Philylla, and turned
off at a right angle along the edge of a cornfield, 'then I'll
go to the home farm and see if there's anyone there.' She
stalked on, still being followed. On either side of her the
young corn was well up. She balanced herself haughtily on
the top of the ridge between. By and bye there was a low
bank of stones and prickles, and then a drop down into the
track that went to the farm.

The heat of that lovely day still stayed among the
lengthening shadows. There were a great many flowers,
mostly small and starry and close to the turf. She would
have liked to stop and pick flowers, and think about all
sorts of sweet and alarming and desirable things. But to
do that she must be alone. She could not allow anyone,
even the most familiar, to peer into the bud of her heart.
Only once, as some incredibly soft breathing of broom and
violets and distant cattle and wood-smoke and warmed
turf came on her, wild air patting on her face and arms,
shifting the light dress away from her moving legs and
body, she stayed a moment and lifted her head to it,
her eyes suddenly heavy and surprised with tears, lifted
her hands to her brimming heart, the deep centre of all
life, and startled herself again, as she often did now, with
the springing out of her new firm breasts against her
own fingers. She went on hurriedly then, brushing her
touched hands through stiff leaves and twigs. Summer was

coming, summer of the New Times. And she was a child of them.

She came to the home farm in that evening light, bewitching everything to a lucidity, a transparence of matter and colour. Yet the farm was just as it had always been; a cow moved through the yard. Tingling, Philylla waited for its bell to sound and break the picture. But oh, lovely, the sound came at last so soft that it mixed in, and so did the distant voices, the trickle of water, the pleasant gabbling of ducks round the corner of the barn. The farm stayed, the light seemed to glow a little more; it lit up for her a beam of oak, the cross-beam of the byre, aged and grained oak, silver as the skin of a very old wood-nymph. It flowed levelly, right under the roof of the byre, settled against the further inside wall! It lit for her a tuft of house-leek on the thatch, the fat and settled leaves edged with their fine red fur; her eyes travelled along the line of the thatching; beyond the farm was Sparta and the mountains that framed the pattern of her life. She could not wait any longer in this excess of joy. It was almost killing her. So she said to herself, and knew, that she would remember this moment all her days and keep it as clear in her mind as it was now. That set her something to do, allowed an outlet for the choked-up violence of her happiness. Very quickly she put it all away in her memory, packed it up neatly as became an almost full-grown woman, and left it there ready to take out now whenever she pleased, a kataleptike phantasia. Quite calm again, she slipped back the upper bar of the fence and vaulted the two lower ones. She left the bar open for her foster-mother, who was just behind her still, and walked forward into the low room of the farm. She smiled and nodded round at every one, but rather blindly, as it was already nearly dark in there, for the small window faced into the yard and away from the sun, and then dropped into a corner.

After a few minutes she saw who everybody was, or heard by their voices. There were the two old people, Tiasa's little bent father and aunt, sitting nearest the fire in the middle of the room, sometimes stirring whatever there was in the pot which hung from the blackened beam above it. And there were two of the men whom she had found there, oh, years ago now, the day she was fourteen, more than two years ago, so that she could forget it, as they had, not be ashamed of herself any longer. They were the two helots, Leumas and Panitas, but now Panitas was a citizen and Leumas had his name down on the next list. He had been wounded early that year and still had his arm in a sling; his woman was sitting on the floor beside him with her knees up and a year-old baby perched on one of them. She swung it and joggled it and pretended to drop it; the baby laughed and bubbled and grabbed at the combs in her hair; no one noticed, least of all Philylla. The woman herself was happy, but she did not know it. She did not think about what she was doing: the nature of her body was to do this. There were two or three others, men and women whom Philylla vaguely knew; they were always meeting at this farm. It was the natural place where three valley paths converged, and besides—Philylla had never asked, but she was almost sure that it was just a little because she herself was one of the Queen's girls, and a friend.

Another was sitting on a stool behind the meal-chest; in a little she rose, a great solid woman in a red dress with loops of yellow hair pushed into a net behind, and a plaited leather girdle, Neareta, the wife of Phoebis. She stood with her hands on her hips and smiled at the men. She said: 'This'll be the end of the fighting, you'll see; all the world's going to join us.'

Leumas said, fidgeting with his sling: 'Does Phoebis say so?'

'Yes,' said Neareta, 'he was home for an hour last week, on his way back with a message. It's the same everywhere, the League's breaking. There'll be no one left to fight us!'

'But then, if there aren't any more soldiers wanted—will it be all right about the next list?'

'That's it!' said another man, a neighbour. 'Will he make me a citizen, Neareta? I'm down on the next list too. It would be a shame—'

'Yes!' she said, 'yes, my lambs, it will be all right. My man says so.'

Panitas said slowly: 'Is he going to divide up all the land all over the world? Then there'll be no more rich and poor; we shall all be brothers! Everything will be simple like it ought to be. There'll be no borrowing. But if there are bad harvests? Someone has to tide us over. What will happen?'

'The King will help us!' said the old man suddenly and shrilly.

But Panitas brushed it away. 'He's no richer than the rest of us now.'

From beside Philylla, her foster-mother threw at them mockingly: 'Yes, it will be fine for you when the corn's blighted and there are no masters to save you! The brothers will all starve together!'

Philylla waited to see if anyone else would answer, then said: 'But the State has money that the rich gave it and put into the care of special magistrates. The gold is there. The King will help you out of the treasure of Sparta.'

'Ah!' said Panitas. Then: 'But all the world? Will every State have its own treasure and are you sure it will all go to help the poor?'

'Yes,' said Philylla definitely, 'Kleomenes will see to that.'

'Oh, Philylla, dear-to-us-all, little wise one,' said one of the other men, very earnestly, 'tell us one more thing and we will believe you. When Kleomenes has put everything right here, will he let be? Will he love his own State and his own deeds and us whom he has made into men well enough for that, or must he conquer the world?'

'Why not?' said Philylla eagerly. 'He could! Perhaps he is the only man who could. A hundred years ago Alexander of Macedon nearly did, but he was not an Hellene, and he was not a Spartan. But our Kleomenes is everything!'

'If he could stay in his own State—' said the man again, fumbling for words. 'It is so little, so dear to us. We know the soil and the crops; we know the shape of the mountains and how Eurotas floods and falls and floods again. What does the rest of the world matter? The Gods would not punish a man, even a king, for making his own State right, but if he wanted the world—if he was taken by pride—'

Panitas finished the sentence, out of the silence. 'The Gods would have him. I say the same. Laconia is a big enough burden for any man. If he thinks it will keep straight without being looked to night and day—! He should have been a farmer, then he would understand.'

'But the whole world!' said Philylla. 'Surely it is right and splendid to ask for everything, to feel one can have everything! Then the power and kingliness come of themselves, and one can do impossible things.'

'No!' said Neareta, before any of the men. 'You may think that, Philylla, because you were brought up to ask for everything you chose and get it at once. You were one of the masters, but we who were under you know; we've learned not to hope for too much. I wish the King would let us teach him.'

'Phoebis should do that,' said Panitas. 'It is his place.'

Neareta sighed a little. 'They all go mad when they are with the King. My man comes home to me, and he's as quiet and reasonable as an old plough-ox; but when he goes back to the King's Mess, there he is again with his head in the stars.'

'Head-in-the-stars came tumbling to a bad end,' observed Tiasa.

But this time Philylla reached over and shoved a hand across her mouth. 'If you like the old days so much,' she said, 'you just tell me and I'll have you whipped!'

The woman's face flamed and she jumped at tight-smiling Philylla and shook her. 'If this were ten years ago,' she said, 'I'd have turned you up over my knee and made you smart, my lady!'

Neareta stepped between them quickly, talking loud to cover anything else they might say. Panitas, laughing, caught hold of Tiasa with: 'Steady, mother! Come and make us some cakes.'

But Neareta was holding Philylla by the wrists with her even, peasant strength. She turned her round to the wall to hide her crying from the men, transferred the grip to one hand and put the other round, soothingly, over Philylla's shoulders. 'There, now,' she said, 'that's a brave lass. You mustn't fight with Tiasa. It was her milk made you grow so strong and clever.'

'I know,' whispered Philylla, 'that's what I hate.' She was gasping and tossing her head back. Neareta opened the door and they slipped out into the yard. Already the evening star was out above the roof, not just a fiery point, but a broadness one could measure, a cool, kind body of light.

'You'll give your babies your own milk,' said the peasant woman. 'Not leave your breasts fine and useless.'

Philylla nodded and pushed her hair back. 'It's strange,' she said, 'to think of that. Wouldn't it be terrible never to have any children! Or supposing nobody ever married me.'

Neareta laughed and kissed her. 'You needn't trouble your pretty head about that.'

'Why not?'

'Them that asks no questions—'

'Oh, Neareta, don't tease me, please! Do you think I'm going to be married?'

'Yes.'

'Soon?'

'Lassie dear, you're only just ready. Don't be hurrying too much; you don't know what you're asking for. It's a sweet time before and there's bound to be bitter after, a little bitter even in the best of marriages.'

'But, Neareta dear, what do you think? What does Phoebis say? He's in the King's Mess.'

'Yes, yes, it'll be Panteus the son of Menedaios, the King says so. Is that what you were wanting, then? You shall have him, my dear. Lambie, what are you crying for now?'

'I don't know,' said Philylla.

Suddenly a man came bounding into the yard; he was full-armed and he carried a spear. Philylla cried out in surprise and greeting and some fear. In a moment she saw it was Mikon, the other man she had met at the farm two years before, whose fathers had lost the citizenship, but who had now regained it himself. He stopped in his tracks, dropped the spear, pulled off his helmet and flung it up in the air by its yellow plume. 'Philylla, daughter of Themisteas!' he shouted joyfully, 'I've good news! The revolution's gone through at Cynaetha and they've divided the land! They've made songs about Kleomenes; they've written up everywhere in black and red, Long live Kleomenes and Sparta. The League's gone to pieces, Aratos is a whipped dog, all Arkadia's coming over! We're treating with the Caphyae now. By the twins, Philylla, he'll get Sicyon itself before he's done. Half the army's getting leave. Phoebis will be back, Neareta. I'm going to tell them in there.' He picked up his helmet and pounded at the door with his spear butt.

'I must go!' said Neareta eagerly. 'The boys will be glad to see their father. Come over and eat bread and honey with us again, my dearie. I always keep the best of the combs for you.'

'Yes,' she said, 'I will. Perhaps father's coming back too. Listen, Neareta, aren't they happy!'—there was a great noise of cheering from the farm, and suddenly a light in the window—'I do love them. And I mightn't have known them at all but for the King and his Times. Oh, Neareta, it is terrible to think how I might have been looking at them!' She shook herself and ran out of the yard again, homewards, delighted to have dodged Tiasa, delighted to have been with those friendly people, delighted to have been admired, and then—how exactly was it Neareta had spoken—about Panteus?

Where the path to the farm joined the main cart-track there was a dark hollow between boulders. Somebody was sitting in the thick shadow at the side of the road; he rose at Philylla and she snatched out her knife. But it was Berris Der. 'I'm back from the army,' he said. 'Your King's doing what he likes everywhere. I've been with him. I've been fighting, Philylla, up in the oak woods in Arkadia. Whenever there was any fighting I was in it. Oh, don't stand like that; say something, Philylla! Do you think I want to spend my life fighting?'

'I wish I could!' said Philylla stubbornly. 'Nobody's made you do it, Berris. Don't let's stand about here; it's dark. Let's go home. Every one will be glad to see you.'

'Are you glad?'

'Of course I am. Have you been making anything?'

'No, how could I? Except some bronze things for the King. Oh, nothing really. Bridle and saddle pieces. But they might as well be good as bad. He said he liked them, but I don't suppose he did. He doesn't really notice.'

'Well, he hasn't time, has he? But I'd like to have seen. What were they like, Berris?—queer beasts still?'

'No. More—patterns. I'll draw them for you to-morrow. Shall I?'

'Yes, do! I like it when you come back and start talking about that kind of thing. No one else does. Will you go on with the statue, Berris? It's still up in the barn. One day when you were away I unwrapped it and looked, but nobody except me has.'

'You dear!' said Berris. 'No, Philylla, don't hurry. Smell

the dust. There's no smell to compare with it in my country, so alive and sharp as it is. And that apple blossom. I was afraid I'd not get back to you till it was all over.'

'It's going to be a good fruit year,' said Philylla. 'Oh, Berris! You know when you talked about lines crossing one another last time? Well, I tried to make that on a dress in different colours.'

'May I see?'

'Well, I suppose so. But I'm very bad at embroidery. Mother always says so. Have you heard from your home at all?'

'No,' he said, 'but I've been having some very queer dreams about it and about my sister. I believe she must be thinking about me. Can I tell you some time?'

'Tell me now.'

'But we're almost at the house. Oh, Philylla, why mayn't I kiss your hand?'

She stood still for a minute, then said: 'Well, I don't see why you shouldn't. There it is, Berris. But I don't think you ought to stay in Greece all your life, even for the sake of the King and his Times.' She ran quickly up to the door, looking round for him to follow, but he would not yet. He seemed to prefer the night outside. 'Do come!' she said. 'It's stupid to stay out.'

But he shrugged his shoulders. 'I'd rather walk about first,' he said, 'and shake it off.'

'Shake what?' she said; and then: 'Aren't you happy?' But he had run down and into the olive grove below the house. She frowned a little and pushed at the ring in the door till she got it open. He might have helped her! It seemed very warm indoors, though she had not noticed that it was cold out. But when she stooped she saw that the bottom of her dress was wet and heavy with dew off the grass. She wrung it out and stood on one leg, feeling up it with the other foot, which touched the warm inside of her knee so coldly and clammily that she squeaked, then laughed and took off her wet sandals and ran through barefoot.

Just as she thought, her father was home and quite as full of the King and all the exciting things that were happening as every one else. 'Where's Tiasa?' said her mother sharply. 'Oh, she saw me back,' said Philylla, saying to herself that even if she did sometimes fight with her foster-mother she wasn't going to get her a scolding over this.

Themisteas was making an excellent supper, as unlike the Mess food as could be contrived with the resources of the house. He leant back on his cushions and dug into a steaming hot stuffed cabbage with slices of bacon all round it; then there was a goat cheese, sweet and brown, cut into the thinnest possible slices, and he still had some reasonable wine left. Philylla was sitting at his feet, sewing up the side of a woollen dress. Her magpie sat sleepily hunched up on the back of the couch. Eupolia had gone away for the moment to see that they weren't wasting charcoal in the kitchen, and then perhaps to sing one song to Ianthemis before she went to sleep.

Philylla passed the bread over to her father. He was not in the least doubtful about anything. 'Sparta's going to come out on top of the world again,' he said, 'and then we'll be able to say that all this has been worth doing. And then the King can stop some of the nonsense.'

'What nonsense, father?'

'He's carrying this equality business of his too far. All very well when it was decent folk who'd come down in the world; all very well for men like Phoebis, who've done something to deserve it. But he's been freeing out-and-out helots, giving some of our land to them!'

'Father, he's come to help the poor and unhappy, the hurt people. He's making them into fine soldiers and citizens.' How it helped her to think and speak calmly, having something to do with her hands, this long row of even stitches.

'My dear, what was good enough for Lycurgos is good enough for me and ought to be good enough for Kleomenes. And *he* didn't have any truck with helots.'

She pricked herself with the needle. 'But the New Times are going beyond Lycurgos!'

'My dear, if I thought so—sit up straight, Philylla, you're sprawling like a baby!—if I thought so for one moment, I'd give him a piece of my mind. No, all he's doing, in spite of what some idiots say, is bringing back the good old Sparta that made us what we are. Time and again he's said so, and so has his brother, a good lad, Eukleidas, though I don't much care to have both kings of the same house. And that's proved by the way the Gods are helping us now, just as they did in old days. Why, he's half promised not to free any more of these slaves if things go well. But he's got bad advisers as well as good. Still, he listens to *me*.'

Philylla, carefully sitting up straight and keeping the little bead of blood on her pricked thumb from getting on to the dress, looked at her father; he had a bit of cabbage sticking in his beard. She thought of Leumas and her friends at the farm, and the next list. She said to herself that of course it was only father, then aloud: 'But the other cities think he's going to help the poor and put down the rich. Cynaetha, for instance. That's why they're coming to him.'

'Let them!' said Themisteas, and laughed and drank. 'They can do what they like so long as they don't interfere with us. I tell you, my girl, I like Sparta as it is. So long as your mother isn't fussing.' He leant over: 'Just tell me, child, how's she been lately? Not so bad, what?'

'Oh well,' said Philylla, 'when Ianthemis got that chill and a fever after it, she was terribly worried, poor dear, because she couldn't get the Egyptian doctor we used to have.'

'That's all nonsense, of course,' said Themisteas. 'Children always get chills, always get fevers, always did! She's as right as rain now. Women ought to know how to look after these things themselves without running after foreigners. Anything else?'

'Oh, she's been talking at me since I've been back. Father, can't I go to Agiatis again soon?'

Themisteas scratched his head. 'You and Agiatis! What'll you do when you're married, child? You won't be able to run to her every ten minutes then.' Philylla said nothing. After a time Themisteas laughed. 'But, by God, if it's Panteus, I suppose you'll be able! Clever little hussy, aren't you! Yes, the King's spoken to me about that. But mind you, I've not made up my mind. There's time enough.'

'And—has he spoken, father?'

Themisteas sat up straight and looked at her. 'Well, I suppose you know how things are with him and the King? You must, living so close to them all, unless you're more of a fool than I take you for. Well, he'll have to get free of the King first.'

Philylla said very low: 'But I don't want that. I don't want to take him from Kleomenes.'

'It won't be taking him. But he's got to grow up, hasn't he? Though the gods know he's a good enough soldier now, and clever enough with men, and the quickest of all to see the right plan when we're going to attack. Why, my dear, Agiatis didn't take the King himself away from anyone, not even that poor creature Xenares, who looks like an old man now.'

'But Agiatis was different. She had Agis in her heart. She didn't want Kleomenes when they were married, and she's never wanted the whole of him.'

'Well, well, no doubt you know something about it! It's a woman's game, and you're nearly a woman. But Panteus can throw a spear further than most—there's your mother coming!—and he'd get a nice couple of boys on you, my dear.' He turned on the cushions and took a good mouthful of cake as Eupolia came in.

She said: 'The young Scythian has come. Shall he have supper with you, Themisteas? Not that I can give him very much. Bread and cheese, and a mattress for the night. Fine hospitality!'

'He gets no better with the King,' said Themisteas, 'and asks no better, I'll say that for him. A good lad. Send him in.'

Philylla bent over her sewing. How lovely, how exciting, how complicated life was! She turned the dress right side out and looked critically at her seam. Eupolia went out slowly; she was wearing her best dress of old days, but the colours had washed out and she had no jewels. Sometimes the girls used to get their mother to wear flowers, but it was never very successful. Eupolia thought flowers should stay in their proper place: for young girls, for men at banquets and supper parties, since they did at least cover up coarser smells, and at processions and such, though artificial flowers were better than real ones and lasted longer. They were not, in place on a wife and mother, a Spartiate woman whose jewels had been taken from her by a pack of fools and dreamers and perhaps worse!

Themisteas nodded at Philylla. 'Time you went to bed, my dear. Young Berris will want to talk to me.'

'What do you want to talk about that I can't hear, father? Other girls?'

'Sst, you little vixen! But he's not one for girls, this

barbarian. Odd, that! I thought they all were. Nor boys
for that matter. Keeps himself to himself and plays about in
the forges. A good craftsman. No, Philylla, it's not suitable
that you should sit with men at supper. You're not a baby
any longer. How would you like it if he began to stare at
you? Ah, that wouldn't be so pleasant. I give you far too
much liberty as it is.'

'More than Lycurgos would have, father?'

'Nonsense! Go to bed, and take that bird of yours with
you. If you meet him in the hall with your mother, curtsey
and bid him welcome and don't stare, and then go straight
on. Good dreams to you.'

Chapter Two

A FEW DAYS LATER Philylla rode back to the city to
be with Agiatis again, and Berris rode with her. She was
laughing a good deal because the path went through what
had almost all been her father's land before the dividing up,
but mostly they talked about the things Berris was making
and going to make. He had seen the embroidery; it was
clumsy in a way, but more in the carrying of it out than
in the idea. It was odd, he thought, to have been able to
put his forms so much into someone else's mind that they
must come out through her fingers, through her own kind of
craft. To put his ideas into her head and nothing else! For a
time he rode a few paces ahead; he could not bear to look at
her, so trusting, so kind—up to a point, so kind. He had
not spoken to her ever directly, but she should know; he
was almost sure she did know how deeply he loved her,
though perhaps it had never come up to the surface of her
thought. No one else knew, though, above all not her father
or the King. Did Sphaeros know? Perhaps. In some ways
he would be glad if Sphaeros knew.

Philylla did not like him to ride ahead when there was
room on the path for both. She called to him: 'You're
knocking up the dust into my eyes!' She bent and rubbed
them on the skirt of her dress, lifting it so that her knee
showed.

She's only a child yet, after all, thought Berris. Then,
aloud: 'You've changed since I saw you first, Philylla.'

'How?' She was interested.

'Your eyes have got more transparent, not just grey and

friendly, but the colour of water over round stones reflecting the sky. Your hair's darker, but it's more alive; there are all sorts of colours in it. Your mind's grown too, Philylla; it's open to more things.'

'I suppose so.' She considered her mind. 'Yes, your sort of things. It's open to you, Berris.'

She smiled at him very beautifully. Behind her head the slope of the land was in full sun; beyond—beyond was it the sea he saw, that small dazzle? She reached a hand to him; he took it and swung it for a moment in the space between the horses, a firm, square little hand. Dare he risk losing that?

They were fairly near the city now; they had passed several people they both knew, and exchanged news. It was all good. The Achaean League was frightened; they had been beaten everywhere, either by Kleomenes or from within their own cities. Surely Aratos could not keep his power over them much longer, even with his snake's tongue and the money he had! Was it true that he had written to Antigonos? The dirty dog, trying to betray Greece to the Macedonian! It was said that one of the chief men in Argos—Aristomachos, who had been a general of the League once, but Aratos of course had been jealous of him, as he had been of Lydiades: it was always the same!—this man had written to Kleomenes. Megistonous had had a hand in it, perhaps; he had always been planning things about Argos. But it would be a queer thing if Sparta and Argos were to be friends again after all the time-old wars there had been between them. That would be a mark of greatness in the King!

Berris turned with a start to the sound of his own name, and Philylla turned, too, with a strong pull at her horse's mouth. It was Sphaeros in a brown tunic, standing at the side of the road and beckoning. Philylla called to him with pleasure, but he did not speak to her, only to Berris. He said: 'Your sister is here. She came to me hoping I could help her, but I cannot, and I doubt if anyone can. At least you can understand what has happened to her. She is lodging here outside the city with people I know. You had better go straight to her, Berris. She is very unhappy and entangled in her mind.'

Berris was very white; he did not seem to be able to

move for a moment. Philylla looked at him and then over to Sphaeros. 'Shall I go too?' she said.

He shook his head. 'Not yet. Later. I will take you back to the King's house.' He signed to her to go on. Then Berris Der recovered and went to the house where his sister, Erif Der, was waiting for whatever or whomever should come to her.

Philylla dismounted, for she would not have Sphaeros walking in the dust while she rode, though he himself would not have minded it. Almost at once she said: 'Is the King going to free any more helots?'

'He has not spoken to me—either way,' said Sphaeros. 'Why do you ask?'

'It has been promised them,' she said. 'It will make terrible unhappiness if the promise is broken.'

'The worst of making promises is that they may go different ways; then one must be broken. People should be able to learn not to be hurt for this kind of good.'

'We've never been slaves, you and I, Sphaeros. (May I put myself with you for a moment?) Freedom might seem so great a good that suddenly it would change over from seeming into reality. Or have I got it all wrong? But, to own oneself! After a whole life of being another man's.'

'Slaves can own themselves.'

'It depends on their masters. If they feel the thing all the time pressing down on them? Oh, Sphaeros, they're so different now! Do you ever go among them?'

'A little.' He smiled and coughed and patted her on the shoulder. 'But some of the masters, as you call them, are not very good at owning themselves either.'

She walked on for a little saying nothing, sometimes kicking the dust out of her sandal. Then she said: 'Do you think Kleomenes will conquer the world?'

'No. That is neither right nor possible. Let him conquer himself. He has not done that yet. Let him, if he can, make Sparta an island where the order of Nature comes not too badly into conflict with the rest of Hellas. Sometimes it almost seems as if that were happening. When I see other cities suddenly deciding to do something wise and rational. But it is and must be slow, and it cannot be helped by violence. You ask if he will conquer the world. Philylla, my child, try to grow up, face things themselves and not their images in your own pretty mirror.'

She could not answer, looked at the ground. At last: 'But I have grown up. I am a woman now.'

'Well,' said Sphaeros, 'you should know what you are doing if that is so. Do you understand, Philylla, that you have tangled Berris Der, taken him away from doing the things he can do, that are right for him? You are pulling him out of the balance that he might just hold.'

'Me!' she said. 'But—I like him so much. I wouldn't hurt him, Sphaeros!'

'It is perhaps not your fault,' said Sphaeros. 'I find it very hard to see how a woman should live rightly. But it is a pity for Berris Der.'

'Do you mean—is he too fond of me?'

'Just that. Love is bound to be a matter of too much.'

'What can I do, Sphaeros?'

'I do not know exactly. Talk with his sister, perhaps. Here is the King's house, Philylla. Go in.'

But she clung on to him. 'Oh, Sphaeros, tell me one thing! You say love is always too much. But must it be? I love Agiatis, and she loves Kleomenes. Surely that's all simple and right and natural?'

'I cannot decide for you, child. It must be in your own mind. But I do not think there is any great hurt anywhere if you go on loving Agiatis. Yes, I advise you to go on. However, I am not a woman and I cannot be certain.'

The first person she met after she had put her horse into the stable was Deinicha. She ran into her with: 'Here I am again! Isn't it lovely to be back! Where's Agiatis?' And then: 'What's the matter with you, Deinicha?'

Deinicha said: 'I'm going to be married tomorrow.'

'Oh good, I'm back in time! To Philocharidas? But that's what you want, isn't it? Oh, Deinicha darling, tell me!' They sat down on a bench with their arms round one another. Somehow it was the first time Philylla had ever been in the position of being kind to Deinicha, who had heaps of friends of her own; and she liked it.

For a little Deinicha just cried, then she said: 'It's *not* about my marriage, Philylla, you little goose. But when this is all happening to me I think I see things very clearly. But

I won't tell you unless you see for yourself too. Philylla, I—I do like you !'

'I like you, though you used to tease me when I was little.'

'You were such a funny little strong thing, always playing games by yourself. And you used to think you could sing – now you don't try. Besides, that was in the old days, a long time ago. I'm different too; aren't I? I should have had a different sort of wedding in those days, with lots of new dresses and scents and jewels and sweets, and presents from all over the world. It would have taken hours and I should have been in the middle of it all. But now he'll just come and snatch me away for a night and then back to the army, and so to me again, and I shall live in the hut on his lot, up in the hills, Philylla, and be thinking of him all day. And then sometimes I'll go home or I'll come back here, but I won't be one of you any more; someone else will finish the pattern on my loom. I'm going to have my hair cut short, Philylla, as it used to be in the very oldest time, and wear a short white woollen frock. Sometimes I can't believe that's really me. I would have hated it so once! I loved fine bright things, thin muslins one could see through, things from Egypt and Cos and Syria. I do still. Only—I've turned round. I won't be separated from life, the life of my State. And in a marriage the man's more than the dress. I can see myself as I was marrying Philocharidas as he was, but I don't see myself being happy.'

'No,' said Philylla, 'he was rather silly.'

Deinicha squeaked with laughter suddenly. 'Silly! We all were. Even you were, sometimes! Philylla, the Queen's going to be my brideswoman and cut my hair.'

'Oh, you lucky! I think you'll look pretty, Deinicha, with short fluffy hair. Philocharidas is a friend of Panteus now, isn't he? I only wondered if Panteus would come with him to carry you off.'

'And carry *you* off? Philylla, will the King really not be hurt?'

'He spoke about it himself to my father.'

'Does that prove it? Oh, Philylla, I'm that much older than you, I see that love isn't always simple.'

'I can see that, too, now. But this ought to be, because of Agiatis.'

'Yes. Go and see her now. I'll stay here for a little.'

Philylla went on, just for a moment wondering why Deinicha had said that last, then puzzled about the King and Panteus, and resolved to find out how things really stood. She heard the children's voices first and ran in to hug Gorgo, the dark, soft curly head, and be hugged herself with great violence by Nikolaos; she wondered if any man's lips or arms could possibly be as nice as these cool lips, these strong round little arms against her neck. She swung them both round by their hands, and then asked him when he was going off to his class. 'Next month,' he said. 'I will like being with Nikomedes. He's been away such a long time!'

She went on to find their mother. She came softly into the room. Agiatis seemed to be asleep. She lay along the couch with her knees crossed and one hand on her breast, the other at her side. Her face was very pale and in this tired stillness of hers every line showed at its full value, lines on her forehead and round her mouth and eyes, a queer crumple in one cheek. Her mouth was a little open. Philylla's first brutal and startled thought was: she's getting old, she isn't beautiful any longer. And then, as she tiptoed nearer and saw the Queen's lovely hair just as it always was, in contrast with this new face, she thought: but that's not it! What can have happened while I was away? And then she whispered in a queer, sudden agony: 'Oh, Agiatis! Oh, my darling!'

It seemed to break the spell, for the Queen opened her eyes and saw her and sat up in one splendid swing of her body, feet clear to the ground, arms out to welcome this beloved. Immediately too her face altered; the lines weren't plain any more, they were lost in smiling and bright eyes and the delight she had in seeing Philylla. 'Little darling,' she said, 'little lamb!' as Philylla jumped at her, knelt on the couch beside her, held on to her tight and fast and snuggled down against her, kissing her face and neck, pressing with her dear body close against the Queen's.

For a minute or two she only clung and kissed and sobbed. 'What is it?' said the Queen, patting her.

'It was you!' said Philylla. 'Oh, my love, are you ill?'

The Queen took her by the shoulders and held her still. 'I think I am,' she said. 'But if I am, there's nothing to be done, no sense in crying, and the King is not to know. Do you see?'

Philylla nodded; then, urgently: 'Where are you ill? What do you feel? Is it since I've been gone?'

'I've had pains in my body,' said the Queen. 'Not much yet. They started some time ago. You only see the difference because you've been away. Oh, sweetheart, don't be so unhappy. I expect I shall be all right again soon.'

'Oh do you, do you truly, Agiatis?'

'Yes, yes! And what would Sphaeros say if he saw you like this? I thought you were a good Stoic! Wouldn't he say you were making it harder for me?'

Philylla leant back against the Queen's arm and looked at her. Agiatis dried her eyes, like a child's, with a corner of the over-fold of her dress. She kissed her mouth lightly and ticklingly till she smiled. 'I wish I knew when you were speaking truth to me!' said Philylla, and laid a hand on the Queen's heart, over her left breast, which was reassuringly firm and cool and gently moved by her breathing. 'You're too clever. Haven't you told the King at all?'

'No. This perhaps his greatest year, and I won't spoil it. I've taken care he shouldn't think anything. You mustn't say a word to him—after all it may be only my own imagination!—or to Panteus because he can't keep secrets from Kleomenes. Promise: both of them.'

'Yes. But I haven't seen Panteus for a long time, not to speak to.'

'Well, you will. You may talk to Sphaeros—he'll be good for you. I told him.'

'Every one tells Sphaeros! Or he sees somehow. I suppose he just doesn't think about himself and he doesn't love anybody, so he can spend all his time watching the rest of the world.'

'And he has no children. Oh, did you see Gorgo and Nikolaos?'

'Yes. Oh, Agiatis—'

The Queen laid a hand over her mouth. 'Ssh! You are not to think of that or make me think of it either! If it did happen they'd have you, and Kratesikleia and one another. They're fonder of you than of anyone. Oh, Philylla, isn't it lovely that you're back in time for Deinicha's wedding!

I've seen so much of her since you've been away. I never liked her so well before.'

'But you don't like her as much as me, do you?'

'You—silly—little—cabbage!' Agiatis took her by the shoulders and shook her, between laughter and a little real anger, till Philylla, breathless and helpless, admitted she wasn't really jealous. One of the other girls, Chrysa, came in with a letter for the Queen. 'Oh,' she said, 'the King will be back for a night tomorrow! Now we shall know what's really happening and how long the League's going to keep us waiting!' She went out with Chrysa to see that the King's things were all ready for him. He always brought back tunics and cloaks full of holes and filthy and left them at home to be washed and mended.

Now Philylla knew why Deinicha had said she would wait in the same place. She went back there. Deinicha said: 'So you've seen for yourself. What do you make of it, Philylla?'

'I wish I'd never gone away!'

'Much good you could have done. Some of the rest of us love her too, Philylla! Sometimes I've hoped it was just my worrying about her—and knowing I was going away—but it's not. Well, anyway, I can leave her with you now. She'll like that.'

The next day about noon, Deinicha bathed in river water and put on the short white archaic tunic, only belted with a red cord and sewn with red half down the open side. She stepped out into the steeping sunlight of the main court of the King's house. Philylla held her hair close to the roots and Chrysa held the ends. Agiatis cut it across as near as she could to the head with the very sharp edge of a bronze spear point, as Lycurgos himself had said that a Spartan maiden's hair should be cut at marriage. It took a little time to do with that clumsy shearing; Agiatis was intent, and the two girls kept their hands very still. And suddenly it seemed to Philylla that perhaps it would not be the Queen who would cut her own hair at her wedding, and at the possibility of that terrible dark blank in her bright picture she shook a little and gripped the hair harder, so that Deinicha cried to her to keep steady. It was an uneven, odd cutting; the hair showed in curious layers, light and darker, cocked up at the nape of her neck; Deinicha patted it curiously and

shakenly and cried rather. Agiatis tied up her shorn plaits
with coloured ribbon and a few corn ears, and together the
two of them laid it and Deinicha's distaff on the altar in
the King's house.

They all stayed in the courtyard, playing games and waiting. They played violent, running games, touch-wood and a
kind of nuts-in-May, where they pulled one another across
a line, and a ball game where they threw a rag-wrapped
wooden ball so that it ran along the tiled roof that sloped
inwards at all four sides, and fell off into the other party's
goal. Nikolaos came and played too, and Agiatis played
sometimes, and Deinicha played hardest of all, bounding
about and shouting, and her short wild hair tossed without
the accustomed weight of its coils to pull it smooth.

Then came the hammering at the door that they were
waiting for. They checked and looked at one another over
their shoulders, but, 'One more game!' cried Deinicha,
wildly jumping at a friend for touch-last. Again they started
off, shouting each other's names, darting and dodging,
trying not to hear the door clang open. Philylla, scudding
across, saw Panteus in armour, for a moment veered his
way, then hesitated and meant to run back. But he leapt
in front of her and caught her. 'Look!' he said, 'it's
pretty.' She turned and stood beside him and saw young
Philocharidas go at a run straight at his bride, sweeping
away the other girls. She stood straight, facing him. Only
when he picked her up she flung out an arm over his
shoulder, gripping at his neck, hid her face against him,
and seemed to let go to what was coming. He carried her
off out of the King's house, and that was another Spartan
marriage.

Most of his friends followed him, shouting, only one
or two of the older ones stayed, and Panteus. Philylla
felt his arm round her and looked sideways and up at
him. He was not looking down at her though; it was
a careless, friendly arm. With a very, very little laughter
bubbling in her throat, she dared to lean back the tiniest
bit against it. Suddenly and alarmingly she smelt the sweat
in his armpit, a clean, savage, startling smell. She jumped
away from it before she knew what she was doing. Panteus
looked at her now. 'Was Deinicha a great friend of yours?'
he said.

'I think so,' she answered.

'Don't you know?'

'She's not like Agiatis. She's just—oh well, yes, a friend. I've liked her much more lately than I did. Philocharidas looked splendid! Is he a good soldier?'

'Not so bad.' He was looking towards the door, frowning a little with his light, level eyebrows. The girls were going out of the courtyard and the hot sun, back to their own part of the house. Agiatis sat on the edge of the step and Nikolaos was sitting on her knee, fingering her ear-rings and whispering something very secret to her. 'I'm going to wait for the King,' Panteus said. 'He won't be long now.'

'Yes, of course—the King.' She was annoyed with herself for having leant against his arm, even if he hadn't noticed it, the stupid! 'Well, I'm going in.'

'Don't go, Philylla!' He looked at her now as if he too were a little hurt. 'Come and sit down and talk to me; tell me what your father says about us all. Don't go till Agiatis does. Did you knock against my armour just now?'

'Yes, I bumped my nose.' But she came and sat beside him.

'I thought you did.' He took off his breastplate, ducking out of it expertly. He had a tunic of red linen that had washed very soft and was loose between the threads where the shoulder brooches went. Good linen. She somehow thought he must like the feeling of stuffs, their special qualities, wool or linen or leather or whatever it might be. He laid the breastplate down quietly on the step beside him and turned round to her. 'Silly to bump your nose, wasn't it,' he said, and kissed it, taking her face between his hands and tilting it up.

'Panteus,' she said, 'what *are* you doing!' And she put up her hands quickly to pull his away from her hot cheeks. And then, as she gripped his wrists, thought, well, why not? Let him be. She would have dropped her own hands as a sign of consent, only they liked feeling his wrists against their palms, bones at the sides and narrow strong sinews underneath her thumbs, and little hairs on the skin, light, rather curly hairs, she knew they were. How had she looked at them so well before? So they stayed still like that and she said nothing more but looked at him and he at her. They both began smiling and it seemed to her that she had never seen anything so friendly as his face looked then. He dropped his hands on to her knee, and she laid hers in them, trusting him. For some time they sat like this. She wanted desperately to ask him what he had meant—*exactly*—and what was going to happen next; she felt it was unfair that he should know and not she. Yet she managed not to speak, not to ask any questions, it was so sweet as it was. She looked at him all the time, sometimes at his face and the place on his temple, above his ear, where his hair was so curly, and she thought that some day she would kiss him just there; and sometimes at his hands, at his fingers that had closed softly about hers, as though she were a flower.

Panteus looked at her too, mostly at those hands and sometimes at her feet, her straight little toes, and a place where the sandal strap had shifted a tiny bit to one side and showed a small strip of whiter, less sunburnt skin. He did not know she was full of questions. He had no answers for her. He was content with the present, a little dazed with it. He did not know what was to happen next any more than she did, less than she did perhaps. He knew himself towards Kleomenes, but he did not know himself towards Philylla, or for that matter towards any woman except his own mother, who had been dead for some years, and Agiatis, who was a part of Kleomenes, mother of the children, a help and comfort in trouble, the best of counsellors, the kindest part of life. This was apparently something different, and in its own way delightful. He thought of her still very much as though she were a boy, although he had known now for a year that the King and Queen meant them to marry one another and have children for the New Times. So they sat side by side for quite a long while, and then he suddenly stretched out his arms and laughed and thought to himself that he was in love with a girl and this was what Kleomenes wanted him to be, and then he stooped and began taking off his greaves.

'Let me!' said Philylla and tugged at the strap behind his ankle and got it undone. The greaves were gilt on the outside, which marked the wearer as one of the King's Mess, and they were edged with a leaf pattern in low relief. Suddenly she said: 'You ought to let Berris Der make you some with a better design on them. I'm sure he would. Shall I ask him?'

'If you like,' said Panteus, 'and if you think he will.' He put them down beside his breastplate.

'Do you like his things?'

'Oh yes, quite fairly. He's a good metal-worker, but he thinks too much about details. Life's not long enough for that—nowadays. Philylla, I think the King will have news!'

Agiatis came over to them, and of course Nikolaos wanted to try on Panteus' armour. All three children much loved him, and thought he was the funniest man in the world, because he played with them seriously and inventively. Nikomedes was old enough to admire him as a soldier and want to grow up like that himself. Agiatis said nothing about the kiss, but herself kissed Philylla very hard, while the other two played and fought with one another. She looked so well and gay again that Philylla felt quite reassured. They went through to the room with the swing where there was a tall jar of martagons, and Philylla fetched Gorgo so that she could play too. Gorgo didn't like swinging by herself, she always tumbled off sooner or later, so Philylla got into the swing herself with Gorgo on her lap, and Panteus swung them both. She felt the give and push of his hands against her every time she swung back. Gorgo wanted to go on for ever.

Then, in about an hour, Kleomenes came. Panteus left them, went straight and simply to the King, and stayed beside him. Philylla took the children out and ran back herself for the news. She saw at once that Kleomenes was angry; when Panteus touched him he jumped and cursed him. He took a letter out of his belt and handed it to Agiatis. 'That's from Aratos, or just as good,' he said.

'It's not signed by him,' she said, smoothing it and looking.

But the King scowled and grunted and sat down on a bench and began reading the first book roll he laid his hands on.

The other two looked at the letter over Agiatis' shoulders. 'It seems to be mostly about me,' she said; then, as she read on, 'and you, Panteus.'

Philylla stamped and choked. 'Oh!' she said, 'oh!'

and almost felt her hands on the man's throat, killing him herself. Panteus rubbed his forearm over his mouth, as though to get rid of some nasty taste, then took her hand and squeezed it.

Agiatis rolled up the letter again before she said anything; she was rather pink, but quite smiling and calm. 'Well, my dear, we Spartan women are used by now to the joke about our leading our men by the noses. That's nothing new. And as to the other things about you and me, just forget them. They get said about women always. And this about Panteus is the old story too. We make a different pattern of life here. Don't be angry.'

Kleomenes looked up, suddenly dropping his book roll as if it had been a spider. 'Sphaeros seems to be writing more and more stupidly. He's getting old. Like the rest of us! What, the letter? Of course I don't care! Besides, I've written back as good.'

'Oh!' she said, and looked away from him. 'I'm sorry.' And Philylla, half-way to clapping her hands, checked herself, puzzled, trying to understand. Then the Queen looked up again and smiled and went over to Kleomenes and kissed him. 'Well, I'm not a man! Now, what's the real news?'

He laughed and stood up. His anger was quite gone, his face had stopped twitching, his eyebrows were still. He stretched himself and said: 'The real news is that the Achaeans are meeting in Argos. They've written to me asking me to come over in four days and meet them. Is that good enough for you?'

The three looked at one another. Panteus said very gladly: 'That means we've won.'

Agiatis said: 'This will put right the time before! The Gods have given you a second chance, my husband.'

He said: 'Yes, I think I shall get the command of the League this time. Oh, I shall be very happy to break Aratos.'

'And then,' said Philylla, 'you'll conquer the whole world!'

Kleomenes said quickly, going up to her and touching her as though she were something lucky: 'I take it from you, Philylla! I will.' Then he said: 'I couldn't rest up in Tegea those four days, so I rode down here, but I must be off again tomorrow early, and you too, Panteus. Some of the Mess are down here. They'll want supper.'

After this he seemed suddenly tired, and his eyes were a little bloodshot. He let Agiatis bring him over to the couch and arrange the cushions, though he tossed them about afterwards, burrowing into them with his forehead. He said: 'I've got a headache. Sing, Panteus.'

Panteus stood and sang, and the King listened with his eyes shut. He sang whole stories of the lives and loves of heroes, to old tunes or tunes he made up himself. Sometimes he walked about the room and sometimes he stood by the King and stroked his head, drawing the pain up out of Kleomenes into his own fingers. At least Philylla thought so. She stayed and watched him and thought she had never heard anything so lovely and envied him for that singing voice as much as she envied him for being a soldier, and loved it and caressed it in her mind with praise. Then she turned round and saw Agiatis was not there, and tiptoed out guiltily, hoping Panteus had not noticed her—hoping he had.

Hippitas and Therykion came in. The King looked up, twitching his eyebrows and the skin of his forehead; he was cured. 'How long have you been singing, Panteus?' he asked.

'Not long,' said Panteus and smiled, but it was dusk now. His cousin Hippitas could see that he was tired, that he had been at work. He went over to Therykion, whom he had not seen for a few days, and took his hand. 'How are things with you?'

Before Therykion could answer, the King did for him: 'As cheerful as ever! I tell you, Panteus, when that letter came, the first thing Therykion did was to say it was Macedon's chance as well as mine!'

'So it is!' said Therykion fiercely; 'and someone has to say it!'

'I've been wondering about Macedonia too, while I was singing,' said Panteus.

'Yes,' said the King, 'but you didn't say it first thing! You three gave me good omens. I don't know about Macedonia. I don't think myself that Aratos can be very serious, he's trying to frighten me with this business of being hand in glove with Antigonos—making sacrifices for him! I doubt if Antigonos will move—it's no use glaring at me, Therykion, I must have my own opinion as well as you. Perhaps I'm wrong. But he's a sick man, coughing his life out now, and, after all, only a Macedonian. I think'—and he looked at Panteus—'I think Sparta could do anything now!'

Chapter Three

BERRIS DER AND ERIF Der sat in two crooks of an old fig tree, a little above the ground. The figs were not ripe yet, but there was shade inside the tree and a pleasant springiness to the grey boughs. Still more, it was a house. They were together in it, Berris and Erif; they could talk in their own tongue and no one would hear. He wore Greek clothes and moved in them easily; his hands could twitch the folds of a cloak right in a moment. Only his belt-clasp and the hilt and sheath of his dagger were his own work; his shoulder brooches were Greek gold and had been given him by King Kleomenes after the battle at Hekatombaeon. She wore a summer shirt, white linen much embroidered, with loose sleeves gathered at the wrist; no coat, but a belt. She was barefoot just now, but she usually put on soft boots to go about in. Her hair was plaited in a single big plait which kept the sun off the back of her neck, and she had a broad felt hat with ribbons to tie under her chin; but this was hung up on a branch beside her.

They spoke with long silences between each sentence. Nothing that was said seemed to be much use. She had come straight to Sphaeros when she landed, hoping he would help, having made up her mind during the voyage that he would. But she found him so much occupied with his friends here and their problems, that he could not turn his mind at all to hers. Besides it was so un-Greek a thing, and so horrible, that had happened, and he had been so long in Greece now, forgetting her barbarian world and the kind of realities that might have to be faced there, that he could not understand and so could not begin to help. Who would?

Berris had been shocked, but not surprised. As she told him, month by month, what had been happening in Marob, he saw it all in his mind. It was not, of course, in the least accurate in detail; he did not group his people

right, inevitably he gave Tarrik the expression he had when
looking at him and not what he had when looking at Erif;
he made his father too young, he made the picture in his
head of the water-ways beyond Yellow Bull's house quite
different, because the ones he had himself seen were to
him the only real ones; but still it was all vivid enough,
and he breathed quick with excitement while he listened.
He did not doubt that his sister had broken the cycle of the
rite, the thing that was to Marob as a man and woman's
cycle of desire and begetting and calm and birth were to
them, each naturally arising from each. Erif Der had put
in something new and it must be met with something that
sprang from it. She had put in death. Must it now stay
there always, and always be fulfilled as part of the cycle,
or could there be such a new birth after it that the thing
would cancel out?

She spoke of what Tarrik had said—very dubiously, for
she was not sure herself of exactly what he meant—about
this dissatisfaction of his, how he wanted more than just the
life of Marob. But Berris understood at once. 'That's why
I must make things,' he said; 'that is me: my own only
life, not part of Marob or Hellas or anywhere, not even
part of Sphaeros' way of Nature; but itself, to live after
me when I am dead. Tarrik hasn't got that.'

'Marob is his work. Marob will go on living through him,
bought by his life.'

'But that's too big. We want some one little immortality
of our own, he and I. Don't you, Erif?'

She slid her hands along the crumpled, twigless fig
branches; at last said: 'A little, small immortality. A
baby! Something as easily hurt as that. Before the child
was born I thought he would be that. Then I found he was
his own and nothing to do with me. When you have finished
making a stone woman or a golden beast, Berris, don't they
come alive on their own and run away from you?'

'I suppose so,' he said. 'I suppose that's why I don't care
when they're done if I sell them and never see them again.
I don't care who I work for or what they do with my stuff,
so long as it's good. It is good just now, Erif! Don't laugh
at me. Though I'm not doing as much as I should—not
big things. It has this to it over a child: the child knows he
will die and sooner or later needs his own immortality, and

makes his own image again, another child; and so on. Each time he gets further away from you. But my things stay.'

'I wish Tarrik could make something if it is all that help to the maker!'

'Tarrik is not a good enough craftsman; he is too lazy. Have the Red Riders been back at all, Erif?'

'No. What was it you said about not doing as much work as you should? Why not?

He shrugged his shoulders. 'Philylla.'

'Ah! So you're where you were. Just where you were, Berris? Haven't you spoken to her? She's old enough.'

'I couldn't ever marry her, Erif. She's a Spartiate and I'm a barbarian. I daren't speak. I should lose what I have.'

'What have you?'

'Part of her mind.'

'Not much for a man to say thank you for! Tarrik wouldn't. But you're more like a woman, Berris. Why don't you try? There's plenty of Greek blood in Marob, one way and another. There were Greeks there once; Tarrik says so. For all you know, you and I may be a little Greek. No use? Well, then, Berris, stop it.'

'How, my dear?' He looked across the tree at her and laughed. 'But I wouldn't, if you did know how.'

'Well, if you think she's worth it—! But why should she despise you, Berris? You're as good as she is and I'm a queen. I've got jewels with me, Berris, sewn up in little bags. No one in Sparta has such things, not now anyway!'

'She doesn't despise me. She's simply different. You won't be able to sell your jewels here, Erif, nor in any of the states that follow Kleomenes. But you shall be a guest as long as you are in Sparta, the guest of the Queen most likely.'

'Well,' she said, curling and spreading her toes against a branch in a tiny quivering patch of sunshine that had come through the leaves, 'I won't stay here long if I can get no help. I get terribly lonely, Berris, even with you. Whenever I see a child I laugh first and then I'm miserable because of Klint, and when I see a man and woman together they ought to be Tarrik and me. I hate sleeping by myself.'

'You could easily get someone to sleep with,' said Berris, suddenly being a brother.

A few days later the news from Argos came to Sparta.

It was Eukleidas who brought it to the Queen. He usually stayed in Sparta itself while Kleomenes was with the army, unless he was wanted to do anything else. He was utterly devoted to his brother and had been since they were boys; he believed everything he was told, and when Kleomenes was kind to him, as he mostly was, felt repaid for anything. He had not married, and, though he would not admit it to his brother, Agiatis knew that it was because he did not wish to complicate the succession yet. If, finally, Kleomenes should decide that he wanted a child of his brother's as the next second king, then Eukleidas would marry and make a nephew for Kleomenes—younger than Nikomedes—twelve or fifteen years younger. That would not matter; it was just as well for the kings to overlap in age. So far, though, he had not decided, and Eukleidas was at least reasonably content with a boy-love; a nice, gentle, well-bred creature who thought him perfect.

He came in hurriedly and very much distressed. 'Agiatis!' he said, 'it's all gone wrong. They won't have him!'

But it was Kratesikleia who flinched and cried: 'My son!' Agiatis got up and began moving about the room, altering the position of a bench here and a vase there; she could listen more calmly so.

'Aratos got round them again with that tongue of his,' said Eukleidas. 'Oh, how I could kill him myself! He made them say that Kleomenes might only come into Argos quite alone without the army. That means he had made them change their minds completely. It was a mockery of their first letter! Kleomenes refused. He has declared war on the League again at Aegium and called up the year-classes. Oh, I hope he will send for me. I want to be fighting again!'

He was almost crying. Kratesikleia patted him on the back. 'This isn't so bad it mightn't be worse. If he can't win by fair words he'll win by force. You'll see your brother leading the League yet.'

'It's all giving time to Antigonos,' said Eukleidas.

'Oh,' said Kratesikleia, 'there's not much to that, surely?'

'Kleomenes isn't afraid,' said Eukleidas. 'I think, in a way, he'd like to see the whole world against him. But I am and so are some of the others. It's the numbers and the money. He has both; enough gold to buy us up twenty times over! We've just not enough of either.'

'What! You've all Sparta.'

'I know, mother. And we have Kleomenes, who's more than all. I'm sending off a messenger to him in an hour. If you two have any letters to add, I'll put them in with mine. Shall I send across?'

'No,' said Kratesikleia. 'That Philylla girl of yours can take them, can't she, Agiatis, my love? Then she'll be able to pretend she's carrying despatches!' Kratesikleia laughed to herself and sat down to write a gay, witty letter to her eldest son, and a less gay one to Megistonous, her husband.

Agiatis had, of course, said that she would be very glad to have the Queen of Marob as guest again; so Erif came in her best clothes, and at once began playing with Gorgo. She told Agiatis about her baby, but she did not tell her exactly what else had happened, because she had seen from Sphaeros how horrible it was to a Greek mind, and she wanted to be liked by Agiatis; but she said that she had done something which had made her unfit for a time to carry on the rites of Marob. Agiatis thought this meant that she needed some ritual cleansing which could perhaps be given by some other queen, as it was between kings and kings' sons in the Hellas of very old times. But she found that was not it. Erif Der was hunting for a bigger purification. Agiatis did not know much about these things herself, but she remembered that her maids of honour used to be always whispering about their gods and godlings before the revolution, so she sent for Deinicha and one or two others of the older ones who were married.

Deinicha herself had rather forgotten it all now, but the others still found it their stay and comfort, and as they spoke Deinicha remembered too, and it was very queer for her. They told of gods in Syria and Egypt and Kyrene, mother goddesses, most of all Isis, the women's goddess, the pure mother, the gentle one who still kept in her heart the pain of earth, who would stand for ever between women and chaos, guide their souls with her hands. One of them had a little coloured image of Isis, the dear and kind one whose crown had not made her unapproachable, with the child on her knees. Not a fierce maiden like Artemis or Athene, but one of the tamed and hurt, one of the group of whisperers, of women-together. Erif Der cried when she held the image in her hands, because she thought of her own baby and how very much she wanted to have him sitting on her lap and leaning back against her breasts; but she did not think this goddess would understand about Marob.

One of them spoke then, guardedly, about other rites, in Hellas itself, rites of resurrection, of sowing in darkness and raising in light, of passing through a gate and being reborn. Erif Der wanted to know more, for it seemed to her that this was somehow like the rites of the corn. But the women might not tell her much, for she was not initiated, and for the most part the initiates might only be Hellenes. If Erif Der could somehow get herself the citizenship of some city, not Sparta of course, but some little, poor city, where citizenship could be bought—? Was it possible for a woman? They did not know.

She and Philylla found it easy to make friends. Erif Der wanted to know more about this creature whom her brother had thought it so well worth while to love even with the pain it was to him, and Philylla was very friendly, first because Sphaeros had asked her to, and then because she did not want to be unkind to Berris, and hoped the sister would be able to show how she could reasonably be kind. And both of them remembered two years before, and magic, and the borrowed horse. Berris himself had gone back to the army when Themisteas was recalled. They were somewhere up in the north, invading Achaea.

All these months were terrible for Aratos. Time after time he had just saved his League. It was incredibly grim for him to think it might go over to Kleomenes and his ideas, how easily his decent, well-ordered cities might suddenly go blind to their own good and then be torn to pieces by the Spartan—oh, worse than Kleomenes himself those ideas of his rooting and spreading in the unwise minds of the common people who could not tell good from bad! One day he might find that he could not talk them over; they would give him the slip, these assemblies, like the female, fickle things they were, and then it would be over with civilisation and the good, the reasonable things of educated life. Anything was better than that. Antigonos was better than that. Macedonia, from whose power he himself had freed Corinth, his first deed as a young man. He had come down from the citadel and told the citizens, oh tired, and oh happy! That was a long time ago.

Yes, anything was better than the class-war which Kleomenes was allowing and encouraging; division of the land, equality—as though there ever could be equality!—sometimes even the freeing of slaves. And over all the horrible taint of Sparta, the brutality, those barking Dorian voices, the great red-cheeked striding women. It was queer, but when Aratos went, as he occasionally had to during his life, among Spartans or Spartanising Peloponnesians, there was always a smell which made him physically sick: the smell of black broth and sour bread and coarse cloth and unwashed bodies. Antigonos of Macedon would protect him and his cities from this, the fair-dealing, gentle, clever king, the kind of man Aratos could understand and deal with, brave as only someone in the last years of a mortal illness can be, ironic in speech and letter as befitted the world in which they both lived. Better to have the Macedonians.

But before Antigonos had quite made up his mind to come, and he did not come without his bargaining, the Achaean League was being battered by Kleomenes. He took Pellene, he and his officers whom he had made as good as himself. There were about twenty of them in his own Mess, and he valued them all intensely; it was a strain and anxiety for him when one of them came in late; that might mean he was killed and lost for Sparta and the New Times. Punctuality was part of the discipline, as he saw it, and they all tried to live up to it, and meet once a day at least under his eye and see him breathe calmly.

It was worst when Panteus was late, as he was today. The King could not eat, and hardly touched his wine. There had been some skirmishing round the walls of Pellene with a force Aratos had sent out to see whether by any chance the Spartans were resting too securely on their laurels. But they were not. And while the Achaeans were being kept off by javelin men from the walls, Panteus and a picked fifty from his brigade, the youngest year-class, all splendid runners and eager for adventure and praise, had gone round a spur of the hills to get them from behind. It was perhaps rash, but very much in the spirit of the times, and if it succeeded was the kind of thing which would bring great glory to Sparta and discourage her enemies. A moral effect of this sort might perhaps mean another city coming over easily. But that was the last that had been seen of Panteus. The Achaeans had disappeared from under the walls, leaving some dead. And then? Phoebis said that one of his men had seen Panteus since. 'You liar, Phoebis!' said the King. This was true, but Phoebis looked hurt and did not admit it. He had known the King longer than any of them and was prepared to lie to him as much as he thought proper.

It worried them all that the King should not eat. Not that it was very tempting. Everything on the table smelt strong of barley and tripe and garlic. Therykion went out and came back in a few minutes with white bread and thin slices of smoked ham, as they knew how to make and cut it in Arkadia, and a leaf of garden fruit, raspberries and a few of the first pears. He had seen them earlier that day in the kitchen of the house where he was billeted, but had looked away himself. He put them down beside the King and went back to his place. Kleomenes ate some of the fruit.

They prolonged supper a good deal, hoping any moment that the missing one would turn up. Mnasippos, a youngish, good-looking man rather spoilt by a sword-cut over his left eye, got up and went out to look for him. Idaios, another of the younger ones, began nervously to whistle a camp song, but Kleomenes growled at him so angrily that he stopped. At last the King suddenly jumped up, startling them all, and went back to his own working-room in the house they were in, which belonged to one of the magistrates of Pellene. Phoebis followed him quietly. Released, the others all began talking loudly and filled their cups again. After a few minutes Phoebis came back. 'No good,' he said, 'but anyway he's keeping in the house. I told them to let me know if he goes out: put the wind up them! The room's all right, anyhow, flowers and all and the best bed. With any luck he'll sleep. But I wish to God I knew where Panteus is! If he's gone and got killed, blast him—! Bad job.'

Mnasippos came back. 'All I can hear is he brought it off, smashed up that raiding party, gave them a nice story to tell Aratos—the ones that got back! Nothing about him. We'd surely hear if he'd been hurt.'

Neolaidas, another of them, said inadequately, simply voicing their anxiety: 'I would hate it if he got killed!'

Idaios said: 'My young brother's in his brigade. He says there's no one like him.'

Phoebis said: 'If anything has happened, it will be nice for whoever has to tell the King.'

'You and I should do that,' said Therykion, looking up. 'You had better stand by him. I will do the talking. I will say—'

'Oh, stop!' said Mnasippos, and banged a cup down on the table. 'He's all right.' They wished Hippitas were there, but he had a javelin wound in his arm and a slight fever after it, and was lying up in the house of a widow woman, who was looking after him as though she meant him to marry her.

Suddenly Phoebis threw up his head, listening, then dashed out of the room. He was back in a moment. 'Yes,' he said, 'it is. So that's all right. Got two boys with him. Don't know who. Good night. We'll damn him properly tomorrow for giving us such a scare.'

The King was doing that already. He had made up his mind while he waited in pain that Panteus' plan was utterly foolish, that he had thrown away life and love for a boy's trick, scheming for a little bit of glory! In the moment of relief after he saw that Panteus was really there, not even wounded, he shot it all out at him, cursing him up and down, with his voice jerking and breaking. 'All right!' said Panteus, interrupting him, trying not to be angry or hurt, 'if it was honour and praise I wanted, I'm getting them, aren't I! Don't you even want to know if my plan did work, Kleomenes?'

The King was silent while Panteus told him, then said: 'You had more luck than you deserved. A mad scheme! How many of your men were killed? Four? And out of the youngest year-class, four of the future that you've killed!'

Panteus put his shield down against the foot of the couch; his hand shook; he was afraid of throwing it violently at something if he kept it. He stood close to the King and said low: 'I'll go to my quarters now, sir; I don't care much for this in front of the boys.'

That stopped Kleomenes. He stood up with a jerk and

said: 'Who? What boys?' Then stared at them where they stood behind Panteus, embarrassed, very close together. The elder one was in full armour, very fine, inlaid in gold on the shield with a design of a baby gripping two snakes. He had the beginnings of a fair beard; there was a spear in his right hand and his left arm was round the younger one, very like him but beardless still. This one had no breastplate and his forearm was bound up and in a sling; underneath he had a tunic of good stuff, woven, as far as it showed, with the same design. They did not speak; they were afraid, tongue-tied. Kleomenes looked at the device of the young Herakles on both of them. 'You must be my blood,' he said.

Panteus stood back, letting them face one another. 'They are your sister's sons,' he said.

'Chilonis!' cried out Kleomenes. 'Are you her boys?'

'Yes, my uncle,' said the eldest one, 'I am Agesipolis and this is young Kleomenes. We have wanted to come to you for months, but mother would not let us. She said you would go the same way as our father and King Agis. But at last she said we might. Besides, I am old enough, for that matter, not to need a woman's advice. We have been with the army a little time now, but we did not want you to know until—until we thought we deserved your praise.'

He looked down at the younger one, holding him close still, and the boy said lamentably: 'We did think this was well done, my uncle! I was kicked by a horse in their flight afterwards and my arm broke. He helped me and bound it up. It took a long time. But he said you would say it was an honour for me!'

Kleomenes went up and kissed them both. 'Forgive me!' he said. 'Chilonis won't write to me or have anything to do with me these days, but she cannot have forgotten me altogether. Did she never tell you her brother was an angry man, unkind, impatient, one who hurts his dearest friends? I am a bad Spartan over this; I cannot stay calm and use few words. And a worse Stoic, for all my teaching. You two must make Panteus your pattern, not me. He is the best part of me; forget what I have said to him. Agesipolis—young Kleomenes—my mind is clear of evil now, I give you your praise! It was well done of you and still better done of your captain. I will write to your mother, and perhaps this time she will write back to me. Will you stay in Sparta now?'

'We hope to.'

'And accept the discipline and the New Times? And me?'

'Surely, my uncle,' said Agesipolis.

Panteus said: 'These boys should have supper now. Come!'

Kleomenes said: 'I have had little enough supper myself. There will be some left here.' He held out a hand to the younger boy, who took it gladly, the other to Panteus.

But Panteus was picking up his shield again. 'I think you were right,' he said. 'It was perhaps rash of me not to have taken twice the numbers. We did it, I suppose, too much for honour and glory and all that. These things are good for boys. But you were right not to offer them to me.'

Kleomenes said nothing, but took his two nephews into the other room. Therykion was still there, writing his diary under the lamp at a corner of the table. Kleomenes presented him to the sons of Kleombrotos and Chilonis. 'They are the two that Chilonis had with her in the temple of Poseidon when my father, Leonidas, came hunting down Kleombrotos, to kill him with Agis. Do you remember that, boys?'

They shook their heads. 'He was only a baby,' said Agesipolis, 'and I little more. Sometimes I think I remember, but that is all. Mother has told us about it.'

The King filled their cups himself and gave them bread and cheese, and cold black broth to the elder one to see if he would take it. He finished it splendidly, and most of the second helping which Kleomenes rather maliciously gave him. Through a spoonful he suddenly remarked that he was married and had a son. He said it with some embarrassment and as if he definitely did not want it mentioned again. Kleomenes remembered that Chilonis, left in charge, had married her son quietly and firmly to a suitable and virtuous wife. Agesipolis had now done his duty and presented his mother with a grandson, who was called after him, still another Agesipolis.

But young Kleomenes, with his broken arm, was tired and sobbed a little, leaning against his brother. Panteus came in and ate his supper standing, hungrily. At the end he collected the boys, taking the older one's spear and shield so that he could help his brother better. 'Come back when you've got them to their quarters,' said the King over his shoulder.

Panteus said: 'No. I'm sorry, but I'm tired tonight. There's nothing you need to see me about.' And he went out.

In about half an hour Therykion said: 'You'd better go after him, Kleomenes. Sometimes even kings must do that.'

'Did you hear what I said to him?'

'No, but I guessed. For all our sakes, for Sparta's sake, Kleomenes, try to keep steady till the end of this. You took the whole burden of the New Times at first. It's lighter now, but still the whole depends on you, and you may have years of it yet, and all Macedonia to face.'

'I know,' said Kleomenes. 'I will try, Therykion. Tell me, what happened about the boy you fell in love with?—I forget his name.'

'He was flattered at first,' Therykion said, rolling up his diary. 'Then he wanted someone younger and gayer. I don't blame him. And he had plenty to choose from.'

The King said: 'I'm sorry. Therykion, have you read Iambulos's *The Blessed Island*? I was reading the chapters about how they land and begin to understand the laws. It is very beautiful, and life gets further and further away from that. You should read it. Well, I must try to make my peace, anyhow. Good night, Therykion.'

He knocked at the door of the house where Panteus was quartered, and after a time a sleepy slave opened it and showed him the way. He went in; it was dark; Panteus was asleep already. But when the King stumbled over his long spear he woke up with a start. 'What is it, Kleomenes?' he said, and his voice sounded horribly strained and tired.

Kleomenes said: 'I was unjust. You had done very well for Sparta.'

Panteus said: 'I thought it was something that mattered. Why did you wake me? I was so tired.'

Kleomenes groped his way across the room. 'Can you sleep on injustice?'

'I could sleep on anything tonight. Those boys ran me

out. I'm too old for running five miles and then fighting. Go to sleep yourself, Kleomenes.'

The King heard, and guessed him pulling the blankets up over his ears and heard the pricking of the hay-filled mattress as he turned over with his face to the wall. He took another step, knocking into the armour, cutting himself a little on something, and stumbled against the bed, and stooped and shook Panteus by his humped-up shoulder.

Panteus turned over on to his back and reached up a sleepy arm, groping for the King's neck. 'What's the matter?' he said. 'Even if you were hard on me I shall forget it tomorrow.'

Kleomenes said: 'A woman would not be hard to you; she would not hurt you, whatever you did to her. And if she did she could comfort you afterwards as I can't. A woman like Agiatis.'

'I don't want comfort!' said Panteus crossly. 'And there aren't any other women like Agiatis.'

'If you were married to Philylla,' said the King, 'she would put it right when I am unjust.'

Panteus pulled the King's head down towards his own and said: 'I'll marry Philylla when the time comes, but if you think I shall let her come between us two for good or for evil—! If she'd been in this bed with me tonight, would I have told her? I can be in love with her for a time, and I shall give her all she need want, but you're as much part of me as my heart and head are. Nothing's going to alter that, Kleomenes. Now, supposing you let me go to sleep.'

For a few minutes Kleomenes stayed beside him, kneeling on the floor, till he could hear by his breathing that Panteus was fast asleep, beyond dreams. Then he turned and went out; his eyes were now so used to the darkness that he did not stumble over anything.

Chapter Four

ERIF DER WAS STILL hunting for help. Philylla told her about the gods of Olympos. She knew them already as names and in art, and in the sense that Sphaeros and others used them in their books, to represent qualities or elements. As gods, they seemed to her to be dead. She was frightened of the smiling statue of Apollo in the market, but knew that Berris would be able to explain exactly how it had been made frightening. She thought that perhaps what was really alarming about it was the power of the craftsman who had made it in the beginnings of Sparta. She and Philylla rode together to the sacred places, Amyklae and Thornax, passing through those rather terrible oak groves which lay round the sanctuary of Zeus of the Dark Woods. At Thornax the image of Apollo was hidden, but at Amyklae she saw it towering over them from its throne of gold and bronze, and ramping, ancient leopards and horsemen: the horrible great pillar of bronze topped by a frowning, staring helmeted face with painted eyes and lips and stiff arms holding a spear and bow. Artemis of the Marsh was a pillar too, a wooden pillar dressed in red with a polished head and long tresses that hid the shapeless neck. A kind of doll that might come alive. Her place smelt rather evilly of blood. Erif Der had bad dreams about them both.

The priestess of Artemis was Philylla's great-aunt; she took the omens for her when she sacrificed, and clucked and nodded her head, but did not say very much. Erif Der stood by Philylla, looking on, and bowing her head when the others did. When they were out of the temple again she said: 'What happens now? Does Artemis help you?'

'Not exactly that,' said Philylla, 'but it turns my luck if it needs turning. It shows I am not careless or proud. Fate has all the Gods in her net. We believe she is Justice too. She cannot be looked at too close, so the Gods come between us and her lest we should see to madness. They show us if we ask them, a little of what is happening, beyond appearances.'

'What did they show you this time?'

'They told me to be careful. If I was careful I would get my heart's desire. They did not tell me which desire!' She laughed. 'This way one does not see far inward, but there are other places. Apollo at Delphi is the furthest looker. He is the youngest of the gods.'

That seemed to be how things worked in Hellas. The other things she had seen at Amyklae were the great bronze tripods made in the days before Sparta had cast out beauty. Also there was the image of a woman holding a lyre that was called Sparta and always hung with garlands. It seemed to them both to be like Agiatis, but perhaps it was romantic of them to think so. At any rate, it was more like a woman than a goddess.

Erif Der had a letter from Tarrik about the middle of summer. He said that the corn was looking good and the other crops much as they should be. Linit was working hard as Spring Queen. He also said that the Red Riders had come again, and he had led the men of Marob against them and had driven them back into the forest; but when things were happening fast, if they were all galloping about and shooting and being shot at, people would suddenly call him Harn Der. He said that the secret road was going on, but Essro still would not see him. Once he had ridden there, and, for fun, carried off Yan on his horse. Essro had screamed for five minutes and then fainted; but Yan had liked it. He was a big, strong boy. Klint was big and strong too. He could sit up by himself and roll over, and he was trying to stand.

She wrote back to him unhappily, but not so unhappily as she felt. She had little to say that would make sense when it got to Marob! Only news of Berris. And King Kleomenes. Battles, always battles! What did they matter either to her or Tarrik? That Sphaeros was no use; nor any of the Gods she had heard of yet. That she had his knife and watched it, but it had gone dull and ordinary. She knew, though, from him, that this was only because of the air of Hellas cutting off the magic there was between them, so she was not anxious. She hoped her star was bright and warm for him, even between him and another Spring Queen!

When harvest came, which was earlier in the year here, Erif Der felt a queer excitement stirring in her; this was the same as her own corn, but dryer and browner, shorter in the straw and seldom as heavy in the ear. 'Do you do nothing for thanks, nothing to make it better another year?' she asked.

Philylla said slowly: 'We don't ourselves. But the ones who are nearest the corn do. It has been in the care of the helots ever since the beginning. That, I suppose, is the power they have; if one thinks it is really anything. It is their feast and we never interfere; that might be unlucky: again if one thinks it is really anything. I am not sure what they do, but I believe there is something now, and something at sowing time.'

Erif said: 'It is very odd that you do nothing yourselves.'
Then: 'May I join the feast? I will not hurt your corn.'

'I will think about it,' Philylla said.

The next day she came in late, riding through the full sun, a brown, slender, serious creature. 'I have asked Neareta,' she said, 'and she tells me you may come to the harvest feast, but you must wear the right sort of clothes. I don't quite know what that means. And, Erif—most of them are slaves still, but I think they will not be soon. Forget you are a queen, because they are my friends.'

Erif Der understood that. She looked at her dresses, the Marob ones, not the new Greek ones that she was learning to wear in the hot weather. At last she chose one that was yellow and red, for these are likely to be lucky colours for the corn all over the world; the coat was embroidered with running horses in threes, and on the back was the flax-tailed cross from the market-place of Marob. She had seen crosses like that, or with hooks instead of flax-tails on the four arms, chalked up sometimes on rocks or old trees. It was hot, but she wore nothing under the dress. She also put on two necklaces, one of amber and the other of coral. Then she and Philylla rode to Phoebis' farm. At the gate Philylla drew back. 'I won't come in,' she said. 'They wouldn't like it. Not even in the New Times! I'll come back for you tomorrow, Erif. Till then, trust Neareta. She knows you are a guest of the King. I hope—I hope nothing will happen.' She kissed Erif and held on to her for a moment as if she were afraid of what might be waiting for her in there. Those two were very fond of one another now.

Erif Der went across the courtyard between the sun-dried dung-heaps. Neareta met her at the farm-door, her arms stretched across it, barring it. She looked the Spring Queen up and down without speaking. Erif turned slowly round so that her dress should be fully seen. Finally Neareta nodded, went up to Erif, undid her plaits and shook them out, then said: 'Come in and welcome!' and stepped back from the doorway. Inside the farm, Erif felt her hands taken by other hands, her hair and dress being fingered. For a minute or two her Greek left her; she could only smile and gesture and in return touch them or their dresses. She had seen nothing like it since she came to Greece. The women were all wearing dresses shaped to the waist and scalloped at the bottom, in all sorts of bright colours, but mostly red and yellow and black with great square patterns all over them, and their hair was loose. She did not see any men yet.

Neareta was head of the feast and she wore a very high, pointed red cap, higher and worn more forward than those of Marob, with one white and yellow tulip-shaped flower made of linen stiffened with wire, on the top of it. She showed Erif the farm, very proudly: her wooden beds full of fresh hay with woven rugs over it, her chest of linen, most of all the things Phoebis had brought her back from the wars one time or another, an embroidered Syrian wall-hanging, a silver lamp, a pair of scarlet leather shoes with gold beads on them, a fine bronze kettle, two looking glasses, one with an ivory back, the other engraved with a plump Aphrodite, several vases, and his second-best suit of armour which he'd had at the beginning of the war. Erif admired everything and came back into the main room; nothing was happening yet. She wondered which were slave and which were free. They were very mixed as to looks, as though the two races did not in practice keep apart very much. In one corner of the room, on a painted shelf, there were some clay images, which Erif took to be gods, a woman holding something in her hand, a man with a mask, a garlanded woman. They were rough things, turned out of a mould by the dozen and coloured with reds and blues that went on anywhere without much rhyme or reason. Erif Der did not like to look at them very long or directly, and she could not recognise them as any gods she had heard of.

'We go out first and meet the men and the corn,' Neareta said to her, 'and dance: you will see how. And then back here for the feast. After that, lady, you may do as you like.'

She looked away from Erif, regarding her big, work-lined hands. Erif said quickly: 'May I be one of you in everything?'

'You will not have to,' said Neareta. 'You are a stranger.'

'Is it a sacrifice?'

'There is a sacrifice,' Neareta admitted. And then: 'There was one this morning as well, but that was for the men alone. My Phoebis gets leave for this always, but he will not let me ask for the boys. They are with their class.

But there are enough men, for most of those who are not free are left for the reaping.'

Erif Der said: 'Shall I do some magic for you?' It was months now since she had done any, but she had suddenly felt that here she could and must.

'Yes!' said Neareta. 'What will you want for it? Is it a blood magic?'

'No, no,' said Erif. 'Only a little magic that I can do by myself.' She made the women all sit on the floor and herself stood in the middle and made a flower grow for them, not a very good flower, for it disappeared several times, but still they loved it; and she cut off the hair of one of them and then made it long again; and at last she made the whole room turn red for a moment as though they were in the light of a bonfire.

The women were delighted and pressed up all round to touch her as much as possible. At first the unaccustomed smell of them was alarming and rather unpleasant, but soon Erif got used to it and enjoyed the solidarity and permanence of it, the smell of earth behind all. Then Neareta called them together and most of them left the farm, though some stayed and appeared to have business there. They went towards the cornfields, the older ones in the narrow, deep-trodden path, but most overflowing into the fields and rough land at both sides. Erif went between two helot women who held each of her hands; sometimes they walked and sometimes they went bounding along and shouting. Then she went bounding with them. After a time they began to hear long shaking yells that came towards them from the far side of the ridge, and then on the crest they met the men with Phoebis at their head carrying the corn-sheaf on a pole. The men were mostly in their ordinary clothes, but with tags of stuff and goatskins swinging about them to make them look gayer. Only five of them, all youngish, were differently dressed; one as a ridiculous soldier in armour of heavily starched and painted linen and a helmet with an enormous black plume, that would only just stay on; another in a white tunic with one garland of roses and myrtle slung across it and a second on his head; another with his head through the middle of a goat-skin that was trimmed all round its edges with scarlet knots; the fourth made up as an old grandmother with shawl and limp and sheep's wool hair;

and the fifth, a quite beardless boy with merry, sloe-black
eyes, in a yellow tow wig of short curls and a short white
woman's tunic. They all had long sticks of stripped hazel.

The women raced and leapt round among the men, every
now and then bounding up to one of the dressed-up ones,
especially the man in the goat-skin, and pinching him or
pulling his hair. In return the men would swipe at them
with the hazel sticks and often caught one before she got
away. But Erif Der, when she understood the game, was
much too quick for them. So, in about half an hour, they
came to the farm. Here they did a play in front of the door,
the actors talking hard all the time, saying whatever came
into their heads.

First of all there was a sham fight between the soldier and
the garlanded bridegroom with sticks; holes were poked
in the armour and there was a good deal of joking about
Kleomenes and Aratos, though much of it was in dialect
that Erif found it hard to follow. Finally the soldier was
killed and then walked off to join the spectators, and the
bridegroom put on his helmet and began chasing the bride,
who fled and giggled, holding up her already short tunic
a good deal higher than was at all seemly, among the
audience. Some of them tried to trip her, others to trip
the bridegroom, and whenever his helmet came off, which
it usually did, he had to stop and put it on again. At last,
however, she was sufficiently well tripped to allow him to
catch her and carry her off, kicking, on to a heap of corn
which had meanwhile been piled in front of the house door.
It struck Erif, even though she only understood half what
was being said, that it was all a mockery of Spartan ways
and customs, soldiers and brides, and it seemed to her that
Phoebis, standing in front with his arm round Neareta,
looked rather uncomfortable. The marriage-bed scene was
extremely funny and prolonged, with much virginal coyness
by the bride, and every one was shrieking with laughter.
When it came to an end there was an equally funny lying-in
scene with the old woman, who finally collected a rag baby
and put it into a basket, where already the corn-sheaf had
been laid, and rocked it vigorously. This basket rather
startled Erif; it was so exactly like the one that was
always used at midsummer in Marob. Then there was a
dance to flutes by all the actors, criss-crossing and holding

hands with the basket in the middle. In the end figure, the four who had already acted ran round the basket holding bunches of corn, while the fifth, the one in the goat-skin, got into the basket. Then the whole thing began again. For the goat-skinned one jumped out of the basket and fought and killed the bridegroom, then threw off the goat-skin, put on the helmet, and chased the bride. Meanwhile the first man, who had been looking on, picked up the goat-skin, and became the next son and successor. The bride had the most strenuous time, but at any rate she could sit on the corn heap during the fight, while she made intimate remarks about the fighters, and anyhow she was the youngest.

Neareta touched Erif Der on the arm and said: 'Come in when you're tired of this. The children will play it for hours.' So after a little she did go in. The main room of the house looked quite different. There were two rods set up in the middle, one with a tulip like the one Neareta wore, and the other with two flat ears coming out at each side near the top. The clay gods on the shelf, she suddenly noticed, had been turned round with their backs to the room. The sacrifice had been made and lay limp and bleeding below the rods, a black goat. Apparently Phoebis had done it, as his hands were bloody. He and Neareta and the other older ones were praying, using some form of words which Erif could not in the least understand. She doubted if they could either, to judge by their faces. When it was over she asked Neareta, nodding her head towards the rods: 'What do you call all this?' Neareta said: 'We call it a Jix, but I cannot tell you what that means.'

The next thing was that food was brought out to the actors and others, and every one sat on the ground and ate and drank. There seemed to be a whole series of tastes and smells here that Erif had simply never met before; some she liked, some not. The sun dropped into a hot and hazy reddish-gold evening that seemed as if it might have been made of the dust of cutting through dry straw and trampling on dry fields. The younger men were mostly a little drunk, particularly the actors. They pulled the girls about and sang rather well. Neareta beckoned to Erif Der and said low: 'You need not join in the next thing, as you are a stranger and a queen.'

'What is the next thing?'

'After work, the feast. After the feast, the marriage-bed. It makes the corn grow next year.'

'So you do that now instead of at the sowing?'

'It would be wicked to do it at the sowing!' said Neareta, startled. 'That would be all wrong. It must be now, because now the corn is cut and killed, so that the new corn-year must be started.'

'I see,' said the Spring Queen of Marob. She stayed silent for a minute, wondering whether she would use her privilege as a stranger to keep out of it. The first thing that she thought was that she was a guest in Sparta, and if she could repay them at all by helping them with this corn-year, she should. And the second thing she thought was that Tarrik was getting plenty of Spring Queens all this time! She said: 'I will stay and help you, Neareta. You know I have power. I will give you some for your corn next year.'

Neareta kissed her and said: 'You will not want anything to happen. I will show you where the spring is behind the house. It is very cold water and I do not think it ever fails on this night.'

The moon swung up, a great silver thing that put out all the stars around him. But inside the farm it was dark and they lighted no lamps. Couple after couple went in, singing or silent. Neareta and Phoebis went in, and others whom she knew or guessed to be man and wife. But these mostly came out again after a short time, while the others seemed to stay, or else the women would come out alone. Erif had purposely sat down in the black shade of a thick bush; the deep yellow and red of her dress had gone dark with the night and she wanted not to be seen for a time.

Then the sweat-soaked linen began to be cold against her. She moved out, cautiously, towards the farm. Most people were already in couples; she was suddenly terribly afraid that her luck was so far gone that even here in Greece she could not be half a couple! Then someone pulled her hair softly from behind and slid a hand over her shoulder and down under her coat. She turned with immense relief into a man's arms. He squeezed her up to him two or three times, as if to see whether she would do. She clung to him answeringly with arm and legs, feeling all the essential parts of him through her dress and loose coat; she had not realised how much she had wanted a man all these weeks of summer.

She did not look at his face in the moonlight, only saw that he was young enough and seemed reasonably clean. They went into the farm, she leaning and dragging for the violent pleasure of being half carried. The moonlight came through the window in a small square that lighted half-way up the rods of worship. There were couples all over the floor, but he seemed to know how to avoid them. He picked her up and swung her down, rough and quick and impersonal. She did not for a moment let go the touch of his body. So that's all right, she thought, relaxing all over from tension into pleasure, and noticed another small square of moon-luminous night sky above the chimney-hole in the middle, and, putting out her hand, suddenly touched the still, naked flesh of a second couple in the same bed. As night went on the couples got rather discontinuous. Erif Der made half of several. She was thinking that in this rite of the helots there was a constant stream of death and life; the dead corn was never reborn, but the new took its place. Perhaps this was reasonable.

Later on in the night, sleepy and almost over-satisfied, she came out to the cold spring, and afterwards went to sleep on the hillside rolled up in one of the woven rugs which she had thoughtfully brought with her out of the house. She did not wake in the morning until the sun was right on her eyes. But she had time to wash her face and comb her hair at any rate before Philylla came to ride back with her to Sparta. She said good-bye to Neareta with every good wish for next year's corn, and Neareta blessed her and kissed her hand. Philylla was glad, for she thought the Queen of Marob must have been kind and friendly with her under-folk. As soon as it was level enough Erif set her horse to cantering. It was pleasant to be, after all, a barbarian!

It was Berris Der who brought them, a week or two later, the news of Argos. Kleomenes had managed to stir up Sicyon and Corinth so much that half the Achaean army went to keep an eye on him. The other half were watching and taking part in the Nemean Games at Argos, thinking it safe enough with Kleomenes a long march away and apparently busy with other towns. However, he got there at night, and with the help of Aristomachos and the rest of his party inside the walls, took the highest quarter of the town, which commanded all the rest, and there he was in the morning when it was time to go on with the Games. This was more than any Spartan king or army had ever done before; even the most discontented at home had to admit that. And again half of his men came back to Sparta, very gay and full of what they had done.

Erif told Berris of how she had helped with the helot corn rites, including the last few hours of it. 'How many did you say?' said Berris, rather badly shocked.

'I don't know,' said Erif, 'nor if they were slave or free.'

'But what good was it?' said Berris. 'Has it helped you to find your reality and get cleansed?'

'No,' said Erif, 'not a bit. But it was fun! And now, even if I am away for a very long time, I will not much mind thinking about Tarrik and his Spring Queens. Didn't you find any girls in Argos, Berris?'

'I didn't,' he said sharply. And then: 'But supposing Philylla comes to hear of this?'

'She won't. She wouldn't want to know, and Phoebis and Neareta won't tell.'

Because of this, perhaps, Berris took special care to be gentle with Philylla, to talk only of art and philosophy and politics, to avoid, if possible, so much as touching her hand. And Philylla thought it was all much easier; either Sphaeros had been wrong or she herself had managed to put it right. She asked him how he thought Agiatis was. It was so hard to tell when one saw her every day. He was very much shocked to hear that the Queen was ill at all. Yes, perhaps she was rather pale, and perhaps rather thinner. But obviously he thought far more of how it was affecting Philylla herself, and wanted to know that. It annoyed her; she did not want to be thought of! She made him promise not to say anything about it to the King, or to Panteus. He smiled and said: 'I wouldn't, anyhow. You and my sister are the only people I really talk to. Except about work.'

'Oh,' she said, 'did Panteus ask you to make him new greaves with a better pattern on them?'

He shook his head. 'No. Though I'd have made them. I doubt if Panteus cares very much what sort of pattern he has on his greaves!—less than the King.'

'Well, we'll have to teach him to care! He loves other beauty—music—so he ought to love this.'

'It isn't an art to be able to sing. I won't try to teach him, Philylla. But—do you often get the chance of teaching him things?'

'Not often. Oh, not as often as I should like. But I expect I shall, Berris.'

'Do you, Philylla? I didn't know. When?'

She looked quickly at him. They were sitting in the orchard of the King's house. She had brought up a lot of garden seeds to sort and tie up in little twists of cloth for next year. He was looking at the ground in front of him. She had a leaf beside her with a few meal worms which she had got for her magpie; she held one out to him, wriggling, and he came hopping for it. Berris still did not look up. She said: 'It's not quite settled yet, but I think my father is going to give me to him.' She put it that way, with an instinct to keep herself and her own actions out of it.

'Yes,' said Berris, 'I'd heard it spoken of, but quite vaguely. It seems most—reasonable.'

She was puzzled. 'Reasonable—yes! Oh, Berris—Berris, be glad with me!'

'Are you glad?'

'Of course. He is the best thing there is in Sparta.'

'And that means the best thing in the world—doesn't it, Philylla? Oh, I know. And when you're married you'll stop thinking about silly things—like my sort of beauty.'

'Yes, I shall stop a little. You see, I shall have other things, children perhaps. But I won't quite stop. I shall talk about it to Panteus.'

'You'll talk about it to Panteus,' he said, 'yes.'

'Oh, Berris, Berris!' said Philylla, and suddenly leant over, spilling her seeds, and shook him. 'Why don't you like Panteus?'

'I do like him,' said Berris, 'as far as I know him. He doesn't like me.'

'It's stupid of you,' said Philylla, disregarding this. 'You ought to like him. Oh, I want you to.'

He changed the subject, back to one which he knew would interest her. 'Why don't you ask my sister if she could do anything about the Queen? She might, you know, be able to help.'

'Oh, might she really?' said Philylla. 'Oh, Berris, I'll go and find her now!'

But Erif Der could not help much. She tried to explain to Philylla that the air of Hellas was bad for magic and that the Queen of Sparta would not accept it. All the same, Philylla dragged her off to try. Erif Der said: 'You were kind to me when I came here first, Queen Agiatis, and I would repay it if I could.' She was frightened of Agiatis, but very much hoped that the Queen would perhaps like her enough to make some use of her. But it was no good; Agiatis refused to admit that she was ill at all, still less would she allow the barbarian to show any power over her. When Erif was gone, she was even a little angry with Philylla. 'There's a funny half of you that believes in magic,' she said. 'But I don't. And I like it to leave me alone. So remember that.' All the same Philylla wanted Erif to give her a charm which she could slip under Agiatis' pillow or somehow get to her without her knowledge. But Erif could not do magic that way, on the unwilling for their own good. Philylla got a charm finally from her foster-mother, but she did not believe in it much.

Agiatis did not like speaking of her pains; that seemed to make them realer. But she had her littlest, Gorgo, with her a good deal. Nikolaos had gone to the class and was there with his brother. She had hoped he need not perhaps go yet, and had even once done what she had not meant to do—it was after a week during which she had slept badly—and begged Kleomenes to let her keep him at home for another year. By then—But Kleomenes had been firm that he must go. 'It's not like you, sweetheart,' he said. 'Be yourself, be a Spartan mother!' So she had been. However, the discipline was not so hard that the two children might not come home sometimes. When they did Nikolaos was very much of a big boy, not wanting to be babied, or sit on her knee. But Nikomedes was gentle and sensitive to her. When she had not got the children or Philylla with her, she tried never to be without something to do or someone to talk with. At worst, a book.

Chapter Five

NOW THINGS WENT on very well for Sparta and that idea of the world. All through the autumn and winter one place after another came over to Kleomenes, sometimes through fear and sometimes through admiration: they wanted a share in the power and glory. Very soon Sparta had gathered in practically the whole of the Peloponnese. The King took hostages and put in garrisons, and when he did that every one came out to stare at the real Spartans as they went by. Sometimes he banished the chief men who had been against him, but that was not always wise. It was still the poor and indebted who were on his side everywhere, but he did not always alter things as much as they hoped. Perhaps when the war was over he would come back and finish his revolutions: when he had conquered the world! For one thing led to another; he never found the right place to stop. He could not at least till Aratos was smashed, and with him all danger from Macedonia, and he himself had command of the whole free League. And when he had got the command? He dreamed awake with clouded eyes; he made the sacrifices that the King of Sparta must make for his army, and they were good. It would be unlucky to think now of setting limits to his fortune!

Some of the others thought the same. They had needed, in the beginning, to set up such an overwhelming idea of Sparta, that now it stood in their hearts like an armed man forcing them on. They had gone back almost three centuries. Let Antigonos of Macedonia come with all his men, let all the outlanders come! They would no more conquer sacred Hellas than the Persians had, even though they found a traitor to let them through the pass. His reward would come to him in time, oh, a bitter one. Sparta stood at the back of Hellas now, as it had then, when the first Kleomenes had thought and planned for her, and Leonidas his brother had fought and died for her, when Pausanias, king too in that line, forefather of their own King, had finally and utterly broken the barbarians at Plataea. The world was repeating itself; this would happen again. Being Spartiate, they were part of it all; they were in one world with the men of Plataea and Thermopylae.

But some were anxious. They saw, part of the time at least, that this was not a full reality. Phoebis was distressed that the lists of new citizens did not go through faster. He told the King plainly that the Have-nots were still hungry, that now again they were growing suspicious of the Haves. Kleomenes said he would see to it in time, but what mattered now was the war; he must see how these new citizens did as soldiers. 'We're doing well enough,' said Phoebis. 'We—we?' said the King. 'You are part of my Mess, Phoebis. That's a different we.' But Phoebis was still anxious; it seemed to him that the King was going cross-wise with his destiny, that pride was getting him, and the world beyond Sparta. He tried to quiet his people when he went home, making promises he was not certain would be kept, unless luck were kind and turned the King back to what he had seen once, and what Agis had seen.

Another thing: Kleomenes did not insist on the can-celling of debts and dividing of land at Argos, because he wanted to take the force out of Aratos' constant image of him as the hurter of cities, the devil he set up always to frighten the careful Assemblies. And Kleomenes wanted Corinth.

He got Corinth that winter. The citizens were finally very eager to let him have it peaceably before he should come and take it by force. The Achaean garrison would not move out of the citadel, so he blockaded it. Aratos still held Sicyon, but little else except the knowledge that Antigonos was now surely coming. The Gods were beginning to move against Kleomenes. But Kleomenes did not admit that at all; he laid siege to Sicyon, and accepted the private estates of Aratos as a gift to himself and Sparta from his own League of many cities.

In the meanwhile the Spartan army was not always fighting; the blockades went on quietly; from time to time they all got home, and home seemed very good. There were many marriages that winter; both men and women were marrying younger and more suddenly than they used, and were less careful about how many children they brought up, now that there was no question about splitting up the estates. The future was as uncertain as it was surely splendid, and they could not attempt to make provision for it; boy children at least were always welcome, to be brought up as soldiers for new Sparta. Many of Philylla's friends were married already. She knew now that there would always be plenty ready to marry her, she need never be afraid of that; but they did not speak to her father, for all knew that she was half betrothed already in the King's house.

Gradually she and Panteus got nearer to each other; they began to speak of the time when they would be married and the children they would have. Often during the winter there would be hours when they would be all together, the King and Queen and Panteus and she, and they would talk and play games, or Panteus would sing, and the war and the future would both stay a long way off for a time; or at least only that one part of the future would show which belonged to her and Panteus. Often, too, there was little speech. She would be doing something with her hands, spinning or weaving or embroidering or making garlands for the men at supper, and her mind was at ease and flowing sweetly, and sweetly showing itself in words, when words were needed, but not unless they were. Agiatis would be doing something too, and perhaps Panteus would be shaping the end of a bow, or perhaps he would be making a doll that nodded its head for Gorgo. They felt the presence of one another and knew that it was a Good.

Kleomenes talked more than all the others. When he was happiest he most wanted to argue and persuade people, to flourish his bright mind like a sword. If Sphaeros came, he argued with him interminably and brilliantly, so that the others could almost see the arguments as javelins flashing through the air, would sometimes themselves reach out a small net of words to catch and hold one of the javelins and look at it closer. But Sphaeros did not come very often. He was wondering what he had done, what thing it was his teaching had let loose. It is terrible for an old man and a philosopher to begin to doubt, as he did. He tried himself to live the Stoic life utterly: not to care what happened, to disclaim responsibility, still more affection, and to shut himself away from the world of appearances, with his ideas. Sometimes he wrote all day and far into the night; he did not need much sleep now. Those who came to him for advice found that he was short with them, unwilling to be a guide through the mazes of the soul: an old man.

Yet, towards the end of winter, a shadow had come over all these good hours together. Kleomenes knew now that his wife was ill and that there was nothing to be done. Yet he would not quite admit it, any more than she herself did. They helped one another at that, and they were brave and gay to one another till their friends, watching them, had their hearts wrung—Philylla and the rest of the Queen's girls, Panteus and Phoebis and Hippitas, Kratesikleia, the old woman who might so well have been taken instead. Sooner or later, now, the thing was bound to happen. Only the children knew nothing, and wondered why their grandmother should suddenly be crying—or Philylla when they wanted her to play! Mother was the only person who was just the same. The two boys came back from their class whenever their father was home from the wars, or for feasts or birthdays. They didn't always want to; it interrupted things they were doing with their friends. Nikolaos said so, but the eldest, the gentle Nikomedes, never did unless it was forced from him by direct questioning—for he was very truthful. Philylla was full of horror and concern for the child when this thing came on him. Once or twice she tried to warn him, but it was impossible; he could not take in what she meant, and she dared not be plain; being a child, he was still protected from the contemplation of future pain. Thinking of him, she thought less of herself, and that was as well. She could not begin to realise at all what life might be without Agiatis. In that sorrow who would there be to turn to?

Panteus was full of future horror too: for the King. He was beginning to brace himself to stand by when Kleomenes had to take it. Often, now, he was moody and silent. He would not smile in answer to any look from Philylla, nor sing to her if she asked him to: that was the thing she loved best in the world, his singing. She could forget anything then, or at least find it turning somehow into beauty. But in these days he would not or could not help her. He did not know that he was hurting; he thought of her less and less. He was going to marry her some time. He had spoken to her father and there could be no going back on that; he did not want to go back on it. But it could wait; there were plenty of men of his own age unmarried still.

One day Erif Der said: 'I have been dreaming about Harvest. Tarrik has not written to tell me what happened. He should have written. I do not know why he has not written. I have sent a letter myself asking him. Soon it will be Plowing Eve again in Marob. I am not clean yet. I cannot get help here, either from your Gods, or the foreign

Gods I have seen, or the Gods of the helots. I am going to Delphi to see if Apollo there can see further and tell me what to do.'

Philylla stayed quiet for a moment. Then she took Erif's hand and then she began to cry, hot, startling tears, falling on to Erif's skin. She said: 'I don't want to stop you going to the God if you must, but oh, please, please, don't go yet. It is going to be so terrible, Erif, and I don't know what to do. I can't face it alone. Do stay with me till—till afterwards. I do like you so much, Erif!'

So what could Erif Der do, being a guest and one who had been so well treated, and having her hand held by this brown hand, having someone so like a young sister clinging to her, but promise that she would not go, not yet, and say that she too loved Philylla? 'But when I do go, Berris must come with me,' she said. 'He's too unhappy, Philylla; his work is less and less good. He can't see any new things in his head.'

'But I've thought some of the designs he has made lately very beautiful!'

'It's the old stuff; he's working it to death. It's the same thing with art and love; they must move and grow or else they die. I know you can't help it, Philylla, it's not your fault. You don't hurt him yourself, but your image does, this pattern of you he's got into his heart. And—I'm his sister.'

'I'm sorry,' said Philylla. 'I wish I knew what to do. I shall miss him badly when you take him away.' Yes, how very badly she would miss him, that whole part of her life! How she would miss his eagerness and his gentleness and the look of him at his work—she'd watched him so often at work!—oh, why had this other thing got to come across it so that he must go away from her? She did not say this to Erif Der; only her tears, which had stopped, suddenly began again.

'You can't do anything,' Erif said, 'if you're going to be married to Panteus. Perhaps it will be better for Berris when he sees you close and secure in someone else's world. When will that be?'

'Oh, I wish I knew!' said Philylla, and all at once felt it was this other thing she was crying for, no less miserably. 'Mother's always asking me and—laughing at me. I wish he and father would get it straight. I can't myself, and somehow lately—But he must think of the King first. I know that. The King is Sparta, and I'm only a girl.'

'It's a pity there's no one else who can be the same for the King.'

'Yes. Except that, I suppose, if there was it would hurt Panteus.' She stopped crying. There was something to think about now, not a hard and unescapable fact, but a problem.

Erif had one arm round her neck; she leant over towards Philylla, digging her chin softly into the soft shoulder, the strong little shoulder. 'Philylla, will you never mind having only half a love?'

Philylla was smiling a little now. She rubbed the remains of tears off her face. She said: 'No. For this is how I see it for the years to come. The more he loves the King, the better lover he is and the more bright he grows—for love is a brightening thing—and the more he shines into my world. Also, through him I have a share in the King and in new Sparta. And again: I love others besides him. I love Agiatis. Ah, how I do love her, Erif!'

'But—'

'Yes, I know. Don't say it! I'll love her then too. And I shall love my children. And then, if another woman came to be as dear to me—Sometimes I think you're that other woman, Erif, and then sometimes you're suddenly like a stranger to me.'

Erif stirred uncomfortably. 'Don't love me like that, Philylla! I shall go home when I can, when I'm clean, and then—well, I may see you again when we're both older. Or I mayn't. I mightn't ever come back to Greece. Let's love one another now, Philylla, but lightly, oh lightly, not for the future, not with a grip on each other's hearts. I'm not in your world. And I am not sure that I believe in your image of love. You have not tested it yourself yet.'

'No. I think I took it from Agiatis. With many good things. I would trust her over the pattern of love, most of all when it is the pattern of Sparta too.'

'Perhaps it's right for you. People must have thought about it for a great many hundred years here, till it's got down below their hearts into the deep places of reason and philosophy. I don't understand quite what you want in your marriage. I think Tarrik and I love only one another—well, hate one another, too, sometimes! But at least it's always towards one another that we're turned.'

In early spring Kleomenes got news that Aratos had somehow slipped out of Sicyon through his lines, that his shadow League had voted to accept Antigonos definitely as their master and saviour, and that the Macedonian army was moving. That same day he let Sicyon go; for an hour his ring camp was running and shouting and striking tents and saddling horses; then it was away with him riding hard ahead of it to fortify the Isthmus of Corinth against the barbarians. He gained a little time because Antigonos, coming south, had to go the longest way. Aetolia, staying rigidly and violently neutral, had stopped him at Thermopylae. That seemed a good omen to the Spartans, and the King, on the strength of it, sent a gift to Apollo at Delphi, by this doing two things—pleasing the Gods, who had perhaps helped him if they perhaps existed, and pleasing the Aetolians, under whose protection Delphi was. The gift was a gold cup which Berris had designed and made for them, charging nothing for his work. It was more elaborate than he quite liked himself, but he knew that was what they would want. It had to be finished quickly and they kept on coming in and watching him at it; he put in some of them, but quite little, so that there was only a typical attitude to show who it was. Apollo sent back vaguely encouraging thanks.

Kleomenes was not going to face a pitched battle if he could help it, yet. He held all the passes, and that was the only thing that was needed so far; Antigonos failed to get through his lines, and fell back towards Megara. That night the King's Mess wore garlands of wild laurel and mountain flowers. They leant over the map and talked loud and pointed and thought joyfully of the barbarians slinking back. They all hoped that if Antigonos was discouraged enough at first, he would back out of his bargain with the League. And they were very possibly right. Only, that same evening, when Aratos and Antigonos were riding north in retreat, both talking gloomily enough, they turned a corner of the road, and there were a dozen men waiting for them, just come up from the sea with thick boots and cloaks, who drew their horses aside and said they were come secretly from Argos. They said that Argos would change sides.

Kleomenes had not cancelled debts or divided the land, and the poor, who had been so quick to believe in him and march about shouting his name were now burning little scarecrows of him in backyard bonfires. Aratos said at once that he himself would take fifteen hundred Macedonians to Argos by sea. He shook hands all round with the Argos men. 'I knew this would happen,' he said, 'but it might have happened just too late. Now we're in time.' And Antigonos, coughing, agreed that this was so, and they had probably won the war already.

Kleomenes thought Argos was safe. The Argos documents and arrangements were all in the hands of Megistonous, his step-father, who was absolutely certain that everything was going well; he had begged Kleomenes not to banish several Argives whom he suspected of working against him. Megistonous was, of course, a much older man; he could not quite be expected to believe in too much revolution. His idea was that it was all very well in Sparta, since it had produced what he thought of as the society of Lycurgos and the army of Leonidas. But other cities were not like Sparta; they had no ancient and simple past to go back to—their beginnings had been most likely under tyrants—so what use was a change to them? Besides, as he said himself, supposing it had the same effect on Argos as it had on Sparta—well, there was not room for two Spartas in one Hellas.

Being an older man, he slept lightly. He woke as Panteus jumped into the dark of his tent, crying out: 'Bad news! Come to the King!' He knew exactly where his spear and shield were, and picked them up quickly and followed Panteus, who threw his cloak over Megistonous, thinking how thin and grey he looked under the cold stars. The King's tent was across a dip in the hills filled with short thistles. It was impossible to go very quickly. Panteus gave him the news that Argos, whose loyalty he had given his word for, had changed sides. Then neither of them said anything till they came to Kleomenes.

The King spoke very bitterly to his stepfather: 'You have probably spoiled everything. I suppose I was wrong to trust an old man—too old and blind to see what was going on behind his back. I will not make the same mistake again. Megistonous, you must go and put it right.'

'I will either put it right or die,' said Megistonous, very much shaken.

'You can do nothing with less than two thousand,' said the King, scowling at an unrolled list. 'I can't spare my Cretans from this hill work. You must take the reserves from Corinth. God, I shall lose Corinth too over this! Panteus, give them five hundred of yours.'

Panteus said: 'My brigade's not strong now. What about Idaios? His men didn't get the same smashing up in the pass that mine did.'

'No time,' said the King, 'he's away on the right now. But he can take over the Donkey's Back from you tomorrow.'

'Very well,' said Panteus. 'Have I an hour to give them hot breakfast before they march?'

The King nodded. Panteus saluted and hurried out. The King and his stepfather were alone in the tent. 'And before you march,' said Kleomenes, 'bring me over all the documents you have about Argos. I will see to them myself in future.'

He jerked his chair straight under the hanging lamp and sat down. Megistonous stood in front of him and said: 'Things may not be as bad as your messenger said. Kleomenes, I will get Argos back for you.'

'I hope you will,' said Kleomenes, 'but—God, Megistonous, you had better try your hardest.' For a moment his upper teeth showed like a wolf's. 'Get me those papers now—yourself.'

Kleomenes sat on under the lamp with his lists of men and money and material. They were beginning to be rather grim reading. He began to mark numbers against the cities who were likely to be influenced by Argos. No more sleep this night! New lists—yes. He called to the guard at the tent door: 'Someone to write! Who's near? One of my nephews—quick now!' He picked up a big waxed slate from the floor by his bed and started doing sums on it, rubbing them out with his thumb when they went wrong, in the way sums are apt to, late at night. The guard came back at the double with Agesipolis and young Kleomenes running sleepily after him. 'I said one of you!'

'Uncle, we didn't know which—'

'Little fools! Agesipolis, sit down and write. I will dictate from the lists. Date it.' Agesipolis rubbed his eyes and sat down cross-legged on the edge of the bed with pen and paper. His young brother went back to sleep again, and did not even hear the news of Argos until the next day. The King dictated three lists, while Agesipolis, who did not know what they were about, got sleepier and sleepier. Then Megistonous came back, fully armed and breathless with the weight of a small chest which he put on the ground in front of Kleomenes and unlocked. Kleomenes said nothing. One by one Megistonous went through the documents: promises, letters, bargains, notes on one man and another, some quite old. Once or twice Kleomenes questioned him sharply, and he answered. At the end he locked the chest again and handed over the key. 'You see,' he said, 'I did my best for Sparta.'

'Quite,' said Kleomenes, 'and failed.'

'I doubt if any of the younger men would have done better,' said Megistonous. By this time Agesipolis was thoroughly awake again. He did not think he had ever seen anyone looking so miserable as the old man did now. He said again: 'At least wish me luck before we go, Kleomenes!'

'Luck! You understand, Megistonous, that if you fail to retake Argos my communications are cut, Sparta is in danger, and I must fall back and let the Macedonian through?'

'Oh God!' said Megistonous, suddenly and sharply, as though something were breaking in him, 'I will not have everything put on me, Kleomenes!'

'I am not going to argue about it,' said the King. He looked down at his lists again.

Megistonous still stood there. Young Agesipolis, watching them, closed his hand so hard on his pen that it broke. He reached for a new one and began to cut it. Panteus came back, also fully clothed and armed. 'All ready,' he reported.

Kleomenes looked up: 'March, Megistonous,' he said.

Panteus dropped his spear clattering, and took Megistonous by both hands. 'Good luck!' he said. 'You'll do it yet!'

And then Kleomenes, as though it were being pulled out of him, said too: 'Good luck!'

Agesipolis wondered again what it must be like being

King of Sparta. As a boy he had always been bitterly resentful that his father Kleombrotos had been driven into exile and so died, and that he himself had no chance of the kingship. He had been angry with his uncle, the son of the man who had done it, his uncle whom he had never seen. Now he was not so sure that it was altogether enviable to be king. He hoped Panteus would see how much work he had done that night! None of the others wrote as clearly as he did; the King had said so himself.

The next day Kleomenes rode down to Corinth, where he found every one very anxious; he reassured them and strolled about, and asked to see a very fine picture by Apelles which he had heard that one of the rich Corinthians had. He explained that all this about Argos was merely an affair of a few rioters. Megistonous would be back in a week and it would be all over. While they were actually with him, most people felt quite confident again; even afterwards, when they talked to one another, things did not seem so bad. There was certainly no sign of Antigonos. Panteus was in command of the Isthmus for that day. He had watchers stationed at every point and a system of signals so that he could be warned immediately if there was any sign of an army coming out on to the piece of flat land between them and Megara. He himself watched for a time and wondered if there was much chance of Megistonous succeeding at Argos. He got some comfort from the very beautiful shape and colour of the mountain Geranea, twenty miles away.

Meanwhile Kleomenes and Therykion and Berris Der went to look at the Apelles. It had been painted for the owner's great-grandfather—an early piece. The colours were still wonderfully fresh. But, of course, it usually had curtains hung over it. Ah, it was an honour to draw them for King Kleomenes! It was, like most of Apelles' earlier work, at least, a story picture, divided up into loose, bowery squares by fruiting vines with birds fluttering among them, grape-peckers. Inside the squares was the whole life of Ariadne. 'Beautiful,' said the King, 'a possession for all time. Fortunate Corinth with such citizens!' With much love and pride, the owner pointed out its special features; here in the distance the palace of Minos, tiny and golden; you could almost count the bricks! Here the shadow of the slipped cloak on Ariadne's wrist. Here in a corner the locust on a twig. Here the leaping Maenad—what vigour! And there Ariadne turning towards the God between tears and smiles.

Berris Der stood back and looked at it. In the first moment he had disliked it intensely, these open eyes, the flesh you almost shuddered from, it seemed so solid, so made for touch, as though it had all the impermanence of the real muscle and skin, which would die and become corrupted—no immortality, no other value given by the painter's own mind to stand between you and the thing itself. Then after a few minutes he began to admire the amazing craftsmanship. He half shut his eyes, trying to get out of his mind the inevitable contexts of all these solid people and animals—that, after all, was partly a matter of the period—and trying to see the thing as he himself saw a picture, as form and colour. He began to get the rhythm of it, the balance of the great groups, the significance of each of those disturbing little rocks, which, when first seen, just worried one with their grasses and shadows and kept the eye from following the swing of the picture. Having seen all that, he looked again at the separate scenes and was suddenly struck with the gaiety of it, the feeling of spring, as though the vines had just fruited out of all season at the coming of Dionysos! Yes, yes; now all these arms and legs and expressions, all that realism which had been so desperately trying at first, dropped back into its place. For once Berris Der felt that he could not have done it better himself. With all sincerity he praised the picture, giving the owner a few new phrases to try on the next eminent person he showed it to. Who happened also to be a king, Antigonos Doson, the King of Macedonia.

It was the next day that Kleomenes got the first message from Argos, saying that Megistonous was killed, and asking for immediate support. Two more messages to the same effect got to him. That night he and his army withdrew from the passes, and immediately lost Corinth, which made haste to open its gates to Antigonos. Indeed there was nothing else it could do.

He marched straight for Argos, hoping possibly to take it in time. After all these months of glory and success he was suddenly anxious about Sparta itself. His brother was there, but with practically no forces, only the oldest year-class who

were not fit for active service with his own army. He had
come so quickly from Corinth that he took them by surprise
and for a moment held Argos again. He sent his Cretan
bowmen down into the streets to clear them. From the
highest part of the city he could watch the red and yellow
of the Cretans in street after street. Neolaidas knelt beside
him, watching too, while the surgeon stitched up a flesh
wound in his arm. The body of Megistonous lay behind
them wrapped in a purple cloak; his own men had got it
away. He had died very bravely, at the head of them.

When the surgeon was done with him, Neolaidas stood
up, holding on to a pillar and facing for a moment the other
way. And he cried 'Look!' And Kleomenes turned and saw
that it was all too late; for Antigonos was coming down on
them from the mountains. In the complete visibility of a
summer afternoon he saw the tiny white paths that zigzagged
down to the further side of the plain beginning to glitter and
crawl with spears and men of the Macedonian phalanx. He
sent Neolaidas quick with orders to the bugles. Retreat,
retreat, they called to the Spartan army in and about Argos.
He had no more than time to get his men away safely from
the walls. They left most of their dead and badly wounded,
though the body of Megistonous went on with them towards
Sparta and Kratesikleia.

Then the whole thing began to fall away from him. The
troops from the allied cities left, sitting solidly at the roadside
while the hurrying Laconians marched by, cursing them but
not able to compel them, or taking the first fork of the road
that would get them home. The Mantineans stayed with
him, mostly because they were afraid to try and join the
League again after a rather evil massacre of Achaean settlers
which had happened when they first went over to Sparta.
The most cheerful people were the mercenaries. It was not,
after all, their funeral. If things looked too bad in Sparta,
they were certainly not bound by their agreements to die
for any king or any revolution!

The Spartans themselves marched on the whole silently.
Sometimes a song would start and go on for a time. Then
it would die out. The walking wounded were helped along.
Agesipolis and his brother had given their horses to two
of them and were marching together. It suddenly came to
Agesipolis what those lists he had written for his uncle had

really been about. They had never been in a retreat before. It was nasty. Hippitas rode past them—he was too lame now to keep up on a long march—and produced an old joke or two which made them laugh now, the mere idea of ordinary life was so welcome. At last they halted in Tegea, for the moment safe. Antigonos would not follow them up so far—not yet.

Kleomenes was beginning to think of plans, or scarcely yet plans, but possibilities, narrow tracks their hopes might creep somehow up. He was welcomed by kindly, silent people in Tegea, and while he took his armour off and washed, the largest room in the house was made ready for the Mess. The smell of cooking food began. One after another they came in and began eating bread and radishes, all there was on the table so far. Phoebis was telling someone about an eagle he had seen—on the right. Was that a good sign? There was a knock on the outer door. One or two turned, wondering what it was, but the King had his map out and was pointing excitedly with a twig. Someone drew back the curtain at their door, and two men came in whom they all knew, slaves of the King's household. They went quickly up to the King and one of them handed him a letter. Then both stood back, very hurriedly, as though they were afraid of him. He opened the letter. It was from his mother. It told him that Agiatis had died that morning.

Chapter Six

HE HANDED THE letter to Idaios, who happened to be next him, and dropped his head forward over the table. His hands, reaching out, crumpled up the parchment of the map. Phoebis and Therykion had both jumped at Idaios to read the letter over his shoulders. Phoebis turned to the slaves and whispered to the one who was left; the other had gone off, even before anyone told him to do it, to fetch Panteus. Agesipolis and young Kleomenes, hungry and thinking they were late, came running in, but checked on the threshold, throwing up their heads questioningly, like young hounds. It was at the noise of their feet that Kleomenes lifted his head. He stared at them for a little time, while they stayed struck still, and then he nodded at them and seemed to be trying to smile. His face had gone a queer yellowish colour, sunburn over white. He looked at his hands, saw that they were spoiling the map, and took them off it, laid them one on each knee. Phoebis went to him then, and knelt beside him and began to stroke and kiss his legs and feet, calling him by funny child nicknames, helot pet names that dated from their childhood together and that he had hardly thought of since then. Every one in the room knew now. Someone was coming along from the kitchen with a clatter of bowls and spoons. Therykion parted the curtains and took them quietly, then the soup as it came.

Panteus walked into the room and over to the King. He said: 'We knew this would come sooner or later. She knew it too. Kleomenes, she will never get the worst news now.'

The King seemed to be trying to answer. They all waited. At last he said: 'We shall want night-guards on the walls here, and an outpost with good communications along the north and north-east roads. It will be important to have a strong garrison in Orchomenos now. Mnasippos, you will take three hundred of your best men there. Therykion, will you talk to the Cretans tomorrow? Don't promise them more pay if you can help it, but do if they will not stay otherwise. I had told them that I would see to it myself. But I am going to Sparta.'

Panteus said: 'I will come with you.' The King began to produce some elaborate reason why he must stay. 'There's no need at all for me to be here,' Panteus went on, as ordinarily as possible. 'Everything will be quite safe now that you have given your orders.'

'Yes!' said the King suddenly, 'don't leave me alone!' He started on to his feet, knocking into Phoebis, and then sat down again. 'Why,' he said, 'this is one of the lessons. I am going to be good at it. She was good at hers.' He began to smooth the map out with his fingers, a little jerkily still. Deliberately he began to control them, one after the other. Phoebis and Panteus sat down, one on each side of him. He started eating, finished his bowlful, and took some wine, like a clever child who has just learnt how to do it in the company of his elders. He said suddenly and loudly across the table to Neolaidas, who happened to be opposite to him: 'It is curious, but I find the worst things are the easiest to bear calmly. I wonder if that is usual.' When there was no answer—for what could Neolaidas say?—he went on reflectively: 'I suppose this is because the occasion is more like one which might be taken as an example of how the good man should act. So one can take this direct example and follow it. Would you say that was how it happens?'

'Yes!' said Neolaidas, gasping, hunting with his eyes for Panteus or Phoebis to help him.

They did, both at once beginning to talk about some more necessary precautions for the safety of Tegea. After supper the King suddenly demanded that someone should play draughts with him. Therykion did that, but the King could not keep it up for long. A deputation of citizens came in, genuinely grieved over this thing, for they were near enough to Sparta to know what sort of a couple Kleomenes and Agiatis had been. Kleomenes made them a Stoic set-speech which moved them deeply. Panteus stood by in case he broke down in the middle of it. At last the evening came to an end, as such evenings do. One by one they went out, quickly or slowly. The two boys stayed till almost the last, unable to move. Hippitas took a hand of each of them to lead them out, hoping they would say nothing. But at the end of the room the younger one turned, pulling his hand away. 'Oh, my uncle,' he said, gasping, and he kissed the King hard. When they were gone Phoebis began to blow out the lamps. 'Get him to bed,' he whispered to Panteus. 'You'll stay, won't you?' 'Yes,' said Panteus.

For an hour or two the King slept deeply. Panteus, tired enough too after yesterday, stayed awake for some while, solidly unhappy about everything—their defeat, and after it had looked for a moment as though they had got Argos again; his own men that he had trained himself for the New Times, so horribly disappointed; and this awful march back along the road they'd taken going out to conquer the world. And then, at the end, Agiatis, the other half of the King. She had been kind to him; he had loved her much and thought her very wise, but now he could hardly grieve for himself at all, it was hurting him so much more deeply through the King. But at last he too slipped down into sleep. After that the King began to wake, coming quietly out of the drowning, dim awareness of some shapeless disaster, over the threshold of dreams into full and sharp consciousness of everything. For half an hour he would face it with no physical stirring, no tears. He could not, perhaps, have spoken. Then, as his body overcame his mind, the things he saw would waver and blur and rock out into blackness again, and for another space of time he was unconscious and gathering strength against the next awakening.

The fifth time, about, that this happened, he saw the room beginning to grow grey with dawn. Slowly his spear-shaft propped against the wall became itself. He watched it, concentrating his outward senses on the strength and straightness of the spear, so that behind them his mind could come to fairly calm decision. The first thing now was to get back to Sparta and comfort his children, and think what power he could raise against Macedonia. Egypt. How? If Ptolemy were persuaded that Antigonos was going to seize all Greece and stay there and aim across the water at the islands, or Asia? Ptolemy might lend him money to stop that. He had helped Aratos against Macedonia in the old days—at the beginnings of the League. Egypt. Egypt. What sort of a place was Egypt? Agiatis had worn a dress of Egyptian muslin in the summer Nikolaos was born. Muslin embroidered with blue outlines of lotuses and wild duck. Gilt Egyptian slippers. The grip on his heart was beginning to get unbearable again.

He looked away from the spear, down along his body. In the growing dawn the hump, the pressure against his knees, gradually turned into Panteus asleep, crumpled up on the floor beside him, head and hands on his bed, one arm up over him, the fingers slackly and vainly clutching: squarish hands, straight-cut nails. He knew very well how much longer his own hands, laid over them, would be. Shoulders sagging away from the bed with the weight of their tiredness. How stiff Panteus would wake from it! Let him sleep, ah, let him sleep while he could. With concentrated slowness, the King drew himself up out of that vain embrace, and Panteus' head and shoulders sank further down on the blanket and the open fingers still held on to nothing.

The King dressed and combed his hair and dipped his hands and wrists into the water-jar. He put on breastplate and sword-belt and greaves. He tiptoed over to Panteus and knelt beside him and kissed his hair and looked long at him, the grim line his mouth had taken now, the wrinkles beginning to come round his eyes. Sparta was hard on them all. He took up helmet and shield and spear, carrying them carefully. Suddenly he wished he had not played this game. He could not ride alone without this one of his two loves who alone was left. He called him in a whisper: 'Panteus!' and waited. But the whisper did not reach through that sleep. No, the King thought, I will face this alone. If I cannot do that I shall know I am weak and worthless and a coward. He turned to the door. But at one little, warning, metallic click the helmet gave against the shield, Panteus woke with a startled sob and swung round from the empty bed to see the King going softly out into the dawn.

He was with him again in a moment. He said: 'Kleomenes, why were you leaving me?' The King said: 'I did not mean to wake you, my dear, I can do this alone.' But Panteus was armed and ready—he had slept fully dressed and in his sandals—and out with the King before the horses were saddled. He brought bread and cheese for them to eat on the way. They rode up and up out of the plain of Tegea while the sun rose fair over them. At the steepest part of the pass it was quicker to walk, leading the horses. Here Kleomenes talked a little about Egypt and wondered what Egypt would want as the price for help. Aratos had sold the Achaean League to Antigonos for his help: what of Sparta would Ptolemy ask? Panteus said that he thought Ptolemy would not want to appear too openly against the other king. It would be better like that. Supplies sent secretly. If they could hire more soldiers and refit their own! Panteus said suddenly and grimly: 'Money is the most important thing in the world!'

After the pass they went on quicker, cantering where they could, down through olive groves and green vineyards and yellowing corn crops, screwing their eyes up against the dust, down past country carts and men who stared and did not see who they were until they were by. They went down the Oenos valley, between steep hills, good for defence or ambushing. On their right was the brown hump of Euas. Panteus, in his mind's eye, was ringing it with palisades, Euas and the hill to the left, little Olympos. They passed the town of Sellasia and then in half an hour came down on to Eurotas, the wide stone scar of its bed with the great river in the middle, drying up with summer, showing the long rock ridges along its course. And so into the market-place of Sparta, past Apollo who had loosed his arrows at the King and was smiling still, and up to the door of the King's house. There were people in the market-place who watched them but said nothing. They knew about this, but they did not perhaps know of the other terrible things that had happened to Sparta.

The King stood in front of his house and said with a sort of horrified amazement: 'She will not come!' And it was apparent to Panteus that he could not lift his hand to the knocker on that door. Panteus dismounted and did it himself. They went in. Kratesikleia came to meet them, an old woman, broken down, her pride destroyed by sorrow. The King looked at her black clothes, taking them in. He said: 'You know Megistonous is dead?'

She said: 'I did not know that, Kleomenes, but I thought he might be. I had a letter he sent me just before the attack on Argos.' She dabbed at her eyes. 'Well, at least I know now. You sent him away in anger, Kleomenes, and he was old enough to be your father. Is all the news bad, my son?'

'Yes,' he said, 'there's little left now except Sparta itself. Is Eukleidas here, mother? I must speak to him.'

'He is here,' she said. Then, as the King did not move: 'Will you come in? She is there.'

He looked at nothing over his mother's shoulder and said: 'If any of her girls are there, tell them to get out before I come. Go and do that first, please, mother.' She went in, going lame up the steps. He thought he heard one of the children crying, poor little Gorgo, perhaps. He might be able to help the boys, but not her. In a minute Eukleidas came out. He kissed his brother and tried to say something, but Kleomenes stopped him, pressing his mouth down against his own shoulder. He said: 'I want to know how much money we have left in Sparta. Then we must talk over plans. We're beaten right back into Tegea, Eukleidas. I expect I have smashed up your life altogether as well as my own. You're a good brother.'

'I love you,' said Eukleidas helplessly. He wanted to say so many kind and useful things!

Kleomenes said: 'I think I will go in now.' He walked away from both of them, towards the women's rooms, almost certain that he was not even beginning to listen for her voice or footsteps. He felt somebody take his hand and kiss it. That must be one of the girls, Chrysa perhaps. But he did not look down. He stopped in front of the door he must go through next, making up his mind to it. There was something on the floor to his right, doubled up, holding on with one hand to the edge of the bench. Philylla. They'd turned her out for him. He said to her gently: 'Come in when you want, Philylla.' And then he raised his hand to the door.

After a while Philylla looked up. That was because someone was looking at her. It was Nikomedes and he seemed all right for a moment because he was making no noise, but then his face twisted up horribly and his mouth opened and he began to cry again. 'Oh, Nikomedes!' she said, and she meant don't. But he thought she meant the same sort of protest against the horrible thing that the world had turned into as his crying was. He said: 'Oh, Philylla!' meaning that she was the only person who really understood. For Nikolaos was too young and could be interested in other things, even today, and his granny was too old; she was only sad, not angry, not aching all over with hate as he was. Why should it have happened to him, when other boys' mothers—'Oh, my poor darling,' said Philylla, 'what *are* we to do?'

He came and sat beside her on the floor. After a time he put his arms round her neck. 'Shall I have you always?' he asked.

'Yes!' said Philylla, feeling she must say it. 'Till you're old enough not to need me.'

For a time they kissed and petted one another, then Nikomedes began again : 'Oh, I do wish I'd been a better boy to her!' he said. 'Oh, Philylla, I remember telling her lies when I was little. If only I could explain about it now.'

'I expect she knew usually,' said Philylla. Then: 'Oh, Nikomedes, I'm wishing I'd never, never said a word to hurt her, or bothered her about things. Oh, I do wish I'd asked her such lots of questions! I've got no one to ask now. I'm lost.'

Nikomedes snuggled up to her. 'Do ask me if they're not too difficult questions. I know quite a lot. Dear, dear Philylla, don't cry so.'

Nikolaos ran out and saw them and checked and stamped his foot. 'Think about something else!' he ordered. Then he flung himself on to Philylla, crying too.

She had them both in her arms when Panteus came. He sat down on the bench opposite her and watched them, unsmiling. At last he said: 'Is the King in there?'

'Yes,' she said, 'alone.'

After a time he said: 'Ought someone to go in?'

'He told me I might,' said Philylla. She reached out her free hand and said low: 'Oh, Panteus.'

He took it, but there was not much reassurance in his grip. He said: 'What about the children? Shouldn't they go to their father?'

'I won't!' said Nikolaos. 'I don't want to look at mother!'

'Neither do I,' said Nikomedes. 'But—does father want me? I didn't know he'd come yet. I thought perhaps he was still at Argos.'

'Nikomedes,' said Panteus, 'listen. You are a king's son and you must learn to bear things that other boys can't and to hear things that other boys don't hear. We've lost Argos. We've lost almost all the towns we had a week ago. The Macedonians have outnumbered us and beaten us. It was nobody's fault, but it has happened. We have to make new plans.'

'But I thought—' said Nikomedes, stammering, horrified, 'I thought Sparta was going to win—now. Father said so.'

'We all thought so,' Panteus said. 'We're all hurt by it. But it's worst for the King.'

'I see,' said Nikomedes. 'Then I expect I'd better go to him. Philylla, will you please come too, in a little?'

'Yes,' said Philylla. 'Brave boy!'

Nikolaos suddenly sobbed. 'I'm brave too, but I don't want to go in yet, Philylla.'

She petted him. 'Yes, you're a big, brave boy, too. Go and talk to Gorgo now; tell her father's come.' When he went back, she turned to Panteus and said: 'That's bad news. What will happen?'

Panteus shook his head. 'I don't know. The King has plans about Egypt. When this is over he'll do something about it.' He said nothing more but sat with his head in his hands.

Philylla got up off the floor and shook her dress out and sat down on the other bench. 'Panteus,' she said, 'I'm very unhappy.'

He looked across at her with his blue eyes, his straight eyebrows twisted with pain and worry. 'I know you are, Philylla,' he said, 'and I'm sorry. I am really sorry. But I can't do anything about it now, can I?' His voice was angry and helpless and appealing, like a child's who can't help hurting you and wants you to understand it's your fault, not his!

'I suppose you can't,' said Philylla. Then she got up and went softly into the other room. Kleomenes was hugging Nikomedes very hard and they were both crying and whispering to one another. Neither of them was looking at Agiatis now, so Philylla went over and sat down by her feet and leant her head against the couch.

The King spent one night in Sparta. All the evening he and Panteus and Eukleidas made plans and he drafted a letter to Ptolemy. The next day they buried Agiatis. Every one who was left in Sparta came to mourn with the King, and the maids of honour who were married and perhaps mothers came from their houses to weep for the Queen. Sphacros came too. His ship had sailed on, suddenly, leaving this lovely and pleasant island, the springs of clear water, the voices of the birds. He must not regret it, must not turn away his eyes from the piloting of his ship. Kratesikleia cut off her hair at the tomb, and Gorgo's short, soft curls. Philylla did not cut her hair. What was the use? Her heart was for the time buried with Agiatis. All that day and for some weeks afterwards she felt curiously cold, though it was the middle of summer. Before Kleomenes rode to Tegea he kissed her and said: 'I know she loved you better than anyone. Tell me if ever I can do anything for you, Philylla.' But she shook her head and said 'No.' Then: 'All I want in the world now is to be of some use to you and Sparta. She knew that.' The King said: 'Later I will ask you to talk with me about her sometimes. Not yet.'

The two boys went back to their class. It was the best thing for them. Nikomedes had suddenly found himself curiously near to his father. He felt very much now that he was the King's eldest son, that he could share in all the hopes and fears and plans, and really be part of Sparta.

He was a little surprised, but mostly very glad and proud. In this mood he could face life again. Kleomenes himself had been wonderfully comforted by the boy, whom he had always thought of as a child, something in the vague future, perhaps, but nothing so far for him. Now all at once he had seen Agiatis again in her son. He looked forward to days with his boy—soon: in winter after the snowfall when there would be no more fighting. He would hunt with Nikomedes, teaching him all kinds of things, talk to him about how to be a king. That was something definite, a fixed point in the future. He and his son had agreed together that they would do this.

Gorgo was with her grandmother a great deal. She wanted to be petted and have stories told her all the time. She did not believe it when they said her mother was never coming back. And then even Philylla went away, back to her own house, and wouldn't promise to come to Gorgo every day—every, every day till mother was at home again.

Erif Der went back with Philylla. It was the obvious thing to do, now that the King's house was empty. Almost all the maids of honour went home or got married except one or two quite young ones who stayed on with Kratesikleia and little Gorgo. Philylla would have found it very hard to face home without the Queen of Marob to ride back with her and to talk to her mother and Ianthemis instead of letting them ask questions. She went to bed early, but she couldn't sleep. She was seventeen now and full grown, and oh, so ready to be kind to anyone who was kind to her! She couldn't sleep. There were no voices in the house, only the noises of the country at night, the ringing of the crickets on the hot hillside, the low cry of a night-jar, a goat suddenly bleating. It must be midnight. She couldn't sleep. If only Agiatis would come to her, even the ghost of Agiatis. She wouldn't be frightened, she would welcome it. She stared across the room. She cried out: 'Agiatis!' But it was Erif Der who answered: 'It's only me.' She felt her way over to the bed. 'You weren't able to sleep, were you? I felt it. Philylla, I can help you; I've got power over that. I'll do a magic on you, a little easy magic, to make you sleep.' She began to stroke Philylla's head and hands;

she sang like a bee. Her voice got farther and farther away. Philylla dreamt about Agiatis. She could not remember exactly what or how when she woke up, but somehow it had made her less unhappy and she could answer back very satisfactorily when Ianthemis asked if she wasn't ever going to get married.

After that smash-up there was no more fighting for a time, though every one stayed ready for it. Panteus was left in command at Tegea when the King was not there himself and practically never got back to Sparta. Occasionally, there would be a raid against him, but not very serious, rather a test of how things were and a way of stopping the Spartan army from having any adequate rest. Panteus was very careful of his men's comfort; he saw that they had good food and that the wounded were looked after properly, and when there was any good news, he gave it to them at once.

Antigonos was consolidating himself politically, making himself popular with the rest of Greece, and seeing that his Macedonians treated the cities in which they were quartered with the utmost respect. Aetolia, Elis and Messenia kept out, and so did Athens, though with great politeness and many speeches and garlands and decrees. The Athenians had never cared very much for Leagues which were not managed by themselves. Perhaps the best move Antigonos made was when he declared to the Assembly of his own new and enlarged League that he was making war, not with Sparta, but with Kleomenes. Not with one of the oldest and most respected states in Greece, but with social revolution and the class war; not with the ephors and the great Spartiate families, the solid body of Spartan citizens who had been living reasonably and peacefully for generations, but with this lawless and murderous King and his creatures and helots! The Assembly cheered and cheered him.

And it had more effect on Sparta itself than the King or Eukleidas liked to think. While Kleomenes had been having his success, while it seemed that at least his revolution had been worth while for the sake of his victories, every one had acquiesced and most had been enthusiastic. Now the party that was against him began to show its numbers and feelings. There was a growing demand for a new Board of Ephors to be elected and take over their old powers. It was too late for him now to exile or condemn. Besides, that was no part of his plan, in Sparta. He was the Head of the State, the property of the State, not a tyrant. Also, this party against him was on the whole a headless thing with no special leaders or speakers, but no less formidable for that—a general, slow movement against his revolution. He felt the women working against him, the women who, as Agiatis had always said, had least to gain from the rules of Lycurgos. Now that she was dead he could not see what they were doing, still less have any influence on it. His mother was too old and too much of an aristocrat to be a good persuader. He got the Queen's girls together, Deinicha and Philylla and those he knew he could trust, and asked them to help him. They did what they could, but the trouble was mostly in the generation a little older than theirs, who had known the other world, and perhaps also in the generation a little younger who would not accept what they were growing up into. It was all very difficult.

Money was short, and he and his friends had no more of their own to use for the State. He had kept some of the oldest gold and silver vessels of the King's household which he considered State property, cups he might have drunk from when the Council of the League came to ask him to take command of them! Now he sent them out of Sparta to be sold, mostly to Athens. They were often very beautiful, engraved with rows of heraldic animals and stiff, soaring Victories with spotted wings, made in the beginnings of Sparta, before they had seen that Beauty was a dangerous goddess. But that was not the kind of thing that people cared for nowadays. They were almost all sold by weight, to be broken up and made into something new. Philylla, very much distressed about this—for she had handled and loved them all—told Erif Der, who bought a few of them; so did Berris when he came back. Kleomenes suspected that there was more money about in Sparta than he knew of; all sorts of traffics and dealings went on. But he could not get hold of it, short of a house-to-house search, including the women's rooms. He could not do that to his citizens; if he did he would probably be murdered—and most likely rightly. Some prices are too high.

Berris Der gave the finest of the cups he had bought back to Philylla, telling her to keep it for Sparta, for the King's children. She did not say much, but she looked happier than he had seen her for a very long time. Afterwards he told Erif what he had done. 'Was it wise of me?'

'Wise, Berris? That depends on what you did it for.'

'I only did it for her. She was glad. She looked at me—oh, sweetly, Erif! What is happening about her marriage?'

'Panteus is up at Tegea. He has not got down to Sparta for weeks except once for a couple of nights when the King was there, and then he was making plans with Eukleidas all the time.'

'I know all that. Tell me something I don't know, Erif!'

Erif said: 'I don't understand the patterns of Sparta, but, as I see it, Panteus is turned away from her, towards the King.'

'Leaving her in pain! Oh, Erif, I would be kind to her if I had the chance! I would never hurt her by word or deed.'

'What a promise to make! As if a man can ever tell when he's hurt a woman. If ever you have that chance, Berris, you'll hurt her just as much as anyone. And you won't know. At least, she knows she is hurting you, and she would help you if it was anyhow in this pattern of hers. But it isn't.'

'I thought—oh, Erif, I thought she was so much gentler to me lately! She talked about my sort of things as though she were very open to them. She made me a crown of myrtle and wild flowers and put it on my head herself; her hands stayed and touched my ears. Supposing her marriage is not going to happen?'

'But it is—unless Panteus is killed. Even then she'd marry another Spartiate. Oh, Berris, my darling, come away before she hurts you any more!'

'But, Erif, if you'd seen how sweet she's been to me lately, how different! She answers to the least thing one does for her.'

Erif said: 'Don't you see? Oh, Berris, you are stupid! Poor lamb, she's got no one to be kind to her now. Her man is turned from her, so she has turned to you. She can't help it any more than a flower can help turning to the sun. Her mother and sister are on the other side; they hate the things she loves. She's very fond of you, Berris! But not the way you want. Either you've got to take this new kindness as the pleasant, pretty thing it is, knowing—really knowing, Berris!—that it can't last, that it's only till Panteus, who's her other half and has been for years, turns back to her. Or else you should go away.' Berris began to draw in the dust with a stick he'd broken, curls and criss-crosses he rubbed out with his foot and then made again, always a little differently. Suddenly it annoyed his sister too much; she snatched the twig away from him. 'Berris!' she said, 'do you understand or don't you?'

Before he answered he got his stick back, after a small fight that ended with Erif being shoved into a bush of prickles, half laughing but a good deal angry. At the end he said: 'Yes, I understand quite well, in spite of being a man. I probably knew already, and just made the other up because I wanted it more than anything in the world. Oh yes, I understand! I'm sorry if you've pricked yourself, Erif, but it was your own fault. I wish I could see why Philylla thinks there's no one but Panteus. Do you see that at all yourself?'

Erif sucked her hand. 'You are a beast, Berris. Why couldn't you choose a soft bush?'

'There aren't any.'

'Well, Panteus is a good soldier. And that's his job.'

'Yes but—'

'Ssh! And he's intelligent and brave and kind, really, though it's inside out now for her, and they both care very much for the same things in the same way, and he's beautiful. But he's not good enough for her.'

'Of course not!'

She jumped straight up into the air off both feet. 'Caught, Berris! Oh, you can't ever possibly see one another true. And she'd so like you to, poor sweeting. Berris, I've seen her through the worst of her time—well, you and I—and now I must go. I'm getting no nearer Tarrik here. His letters make me anxious, even the last one when he sent me the ruby. I think he's beginning to doubt if I shall ever get right, and he hasn't told me yet about Harvest. I'm going to Delphi to ask the God there. Philylla herself thinks that would be wise. It will be difficult for me to go alone. Will you come too?'

'I'll think about it,' said Berris.

Chapter Seven

IN LATE AUTUMN, BUT before the weather broke, Erif Der and Berris Der went to Delphi to consult the God. Antigonos and his army were wintering in Argos and Corinth. Sparta was watching. A little time after they left, another rather terrible thing happened to Kleomenes. Ptolemy wrote promising help, but he insisted on hostages: the King's mother and his children. That was the Egyptian price.

For a good many days Kleomenes could not make up his mind to it. What a trick of the gods, to take them away, most of all Nikomedes, when they were just making friends, when this winter was going to make an island of joy among the troubles for them both! He could not bear to think of his boys in Egypt, taking away their class, their Spartiate companionship, changing over from that to palace life with Ptolemy and his courtiers and mistresses. He wrote again. But these were the only terms Ptolemy would take, and Ptolemy's was the only help he could get. He tried to speak to Kratesikleia, but somehow could not. It was bad enough in his own mind—in speech it would be terrible.

Kratesikleia saw that something was the matter with her son and asked Therykion, who told her with an ironic smile. She went to the King and made him tell her too. She laughed and said: 'So you were afraid to get it out! Kleomenes, you must leave your children in the Gods' hands and trust to their innocence that they may escape. After all, Egypt is not so far. Ptolemy is a Greek, and so are all the people we are likely to be brought into contact with. The children shall read and write, and not of course go about with the common folk, and you shall send someone with us who can practise the boys in spear-throwing and wrestling. Yes, yes! there is nothing so difficult about it. As for me, my two husbands are dead and Agiatis is dead. I am not in love with life. Make haste and put me on shipboard and use my old carcass where it will serve Sparta, or I may die unprofitably at home.' So she started getting everything ready, and chose what women she would take with her, and Kleomenes sent for his sons.

He told them himself. Nikolaos was furious and wept, but was then consoled by the idea of going in a ship to a country full of monkeys and crocodiles. Nikomedes was much more deeply hurt. He did not say much. Only: 'It's a pity. There are all sorts of things here. Father, do you remember saying you'd hunt with me this winter?'

'I do remember,' said Kleomenes. 'Oh, my dear son, we'll do that yet! In a year or two you'll be that much bigger and stronger. We'll have days and days of it, up in the hills together.'

'I would have liked it this year,' said Nikomedes. He had a horrid, blind hopelessness in his voice, the hopelessness of a child who has not seen enough years to believe much in the future.

It sounded to Kleomenes terribly like Agiatis. He was sending her Nikomedes away, uncomforted.

'It's for Sparta,' he said. 'You're a soldier now, going into battle for Sparta.'

'I would rather do it that way,' Nikomedes said, 'but I see you've got to, father.' He rubbed his fists over his eyes and said with a valiant but rather unfortunate attempt at gaiety: 'I expect Gorgo will learn to talk Egyptian just as well as she talks Greek. That will be funny, won't it!' Then he said: 'Can I see Philylla before I go?'

Kleomenes sent for her at once. She begged to go with Kratesikleia to Egypt, but her father and mother would not hear of it, and the King, too, said she should stay at home. She and Nikomedes talked together for a long time, partly about his mother and partly about Sparta, and how Nikomedes was going to go on being a Spartan in this foreign place and to help his brother and sister. They talked a lot about games they'd played in old days. When they went down to Gytheum she came too. Part of the army marched with them; that pleased the children anyhow.

Kleomenes felt miserably that he had sold them just as Aratos had sold the League. He and Nikomedes could now hardly look at each other, it made them both begin to cry.

At Poseidon's temple, Kratesikleia pulled him in with her; people thought she had a vow to make. It was the old helot sanctuary; there were rows of names there of men and women who had been freed. The King looked at them blindly. Kratesikleia's face was wet now with tears in the wrinkles, but she pulled herself up sharply and spoke to him as if he'd been a child still, scolding him.

'When we come out,' she said, 'nobody is going to see so much as a red eye on either of us! We ought to be ashamed of ourselves, doing this in front of the children and every one. There's little enough we can do nowadays, in all conscience, but at any rate we're going to be an example of how Spartans can behave! As for what's going to happen, that's not in our hands and nothing we can do will change it. Don't think too much about it, Kleomenes. Keep your own soul free and I'll try to keep mine.' Then they came out, and she and the children went on board, and the King watched them away. He managed not to cry, but Philylla was crying bitterly. Panteus came away from Tegea for a couple of days and stayed with the King in his very empty house and comforted him and talked about the boys and their future. But Philylla went home again and there was not even Berris Der to comfort her.

Those two from Marob landed at dawn at Cirrha and hired mules after much bargaining and quarrelling with the drivers, who took them for more complete barbarians than they were. Erif had insisted on wearing Marob clothes, white linen with stripes of coloured linen laid on to it in criss-crosses about the skirt, and a short coat. She had it in her head that she must show herself to the God as nearly as possible as she really was. It certainly looked as though she were the kind of person who ought to be over-charged for her mule up to Delphi.

They went gently across a rising plain of deep and ancient olive groves. Erif Der did not like olives, but Berris did; they were ripe now. There were a good many wild birds, but they could not see far on either hand because of the thick trees. Then they took a turning to the right, momentarily getting a glimpse of near and enormous mountains, and as they went the plain narrowed down into a glen still full of the terraced olive groves. Their road began to slope, zigzagging steeply past ancient and knotted roots and built walls and landmark stones. At the end of a zigzag they came out at last between two great plane trees into an open place.

Ahead of them Parnassos went up in flight after flight of great red, clefted cliffs; small trees rooted themselves in the cracks, clinging between earth and sky. Behind them their glen of olives dropped steeply, far deeper than they'd thought it, and rose again at the far side towards other mountains; at its head the range closed in, peak behind peak, distant and blue and very high. And between them and the red cliffs was the shining town of Delphi. On their own level there were low houses spreading to right and left a long way, houses for priests and pilgrims, and shops and stables. From among them one lovely street went winding up, steeply enough for most of the buildings on either side to show clear, the treasuries of the cities of Hellas, each one gay and square and solid and quite small—a god's or goddess's cottage—with leaping ridge tiles and a carved and painted frieze, most of these from quite early times, stiff and smiling battles and rapes and Councils of Olympos. On their walls of white blocks there were lines of names of men who had brought gifts to Apollo. There were statues in bronze and gilt and marble, from the earliest beginnings until now, tripods of inlaid bronze and pure gold, and shields, and pictures under small porticoes; and a very lovely little stream came down with the street, sometimes beside it and sometimes under it, from basin to clear basin, and men and women stooped and drank from it. There were green trees between the curves of the street and a great many young leaves of iris, coming up fresh again after summer, and at the head of the winding road was Apollo's temple, cool and quiet and very much larger than anything else. There were people moving about on its steps, all in white; at the foot of the steps the stream flowed out into its first basin.

The mule boy stopped to let them look, himself turning his back on it proudly, as though it all belonged to him. They found a suitable guest-house and made terms for themselves. Delphi was very full of pilgrims just now; they would probably have to wait for some time. There was nothing to be done that day, but they were up before dawn the next, and in time to see a very pretty sight—one of the sights of Delphi, in fact—the young priests who had been sweeping the temple, feeding the birds afterwards. The sun crept down the cliffs of Parnassos and the birds began to sing and flutter as the new warmth reached to their nests in the crevices and rooting bushes. The priests threw out handfuls of corn, and they came flitting down to the steps and chirped their thanks to the Dawn God.

After that Berris and Erif made their first offerings at the temple and were told when they could come back with another offering and their question. There were a good many priests, intelligent and sometimes fierce-looking men who walked proudly, staring back at the timid crowd of worshippers. No one ever saw the prophetess, the girl-child who was inspired by the God. People said she was just a peasant girl who could not read nor write and knew nothing of the great world; some said that she could go on prophesying until she was old and bent, beyond the age of any priestess of any other god, but others said that the service of Apollo wore her out and she must be replaced every few years.

There was plenty to do during the weeks of waiting. There was a theatre where the sacred plays and dances were given, and between times secular ones, singing and recitations and sometimes even modern comedy, for after all the Muses had it all in their hands. There were all the monuments to be seen, and their inscriptions, some in fine verse to be read, and on certain days one or another of the treasuries would be open. They drank the waters of Castaly as it poured out through lion heads, and bought a handful of the tiny green snail shells that come out of the rock there; Erif thought they might be useful to her one day. And there were many thousands of offerings to the God. After a time it became apparent to Erif that the one thing her brother wanted to see—in fact, what he really came to Delphi thinking of—was his own cup, Kleomenes' last offering in the days of his power. On the other hand, he did not like to mention it directly to one of the priests who showed the gifts. He was so terribly afraid the priest might say he thought the cup was not so beautiful as some others—then Berris Der would cease entirely to believe in Apollo. He did ultimately see it, and thought how much better it was than he remembered it! But it got no special mention from the priest. In the club-house above the temple there were two great pictures by Polygnotos, each with fifty or more figures in it, story-pictures which brought many sightseers. Berris did not think well of them at all, but somehow Erif found them rather interesting and went back to look when he was seeing something else. She also much liked the gilded statue of Aphrodite-Phryne, made by one of Phryne's own lovers. It was a story too, something to fill her mind, though she agreed with Berris that as sculpture it was soft and uninteresting.

In the meantime they made friends with other people who were waiting with questions and formed part of the excited circle when one of them had his question answered. Quite often the God had said something which might be taken in several ways. The priests themselves refused smilingly to interpret, but there were professional interpreters who came round to the inns, as well as all the pilgrims' new acquaintances. Most of them were Greeks, either come for themselves or, very often, for their city or family or club. Sometimes they came singly, but often a whole deputation together; if it was for a city perhaps most of the men who had paid for the offering. A good many of the Greeks were from the outer world, Asia or Egypt or Macedonia. And there were some real barbarians, a kinglet or two from north or east going about proudly, guarded and laughed at. There were Celts with heavy and uncomfortable-looking gold neck-rings that they even slept in, and great bronze pins and bosses on their belts. They were usually made to pay extra, as they were so quarrelsome. There was one Carthaginian, whom they made friends with, a great merchant and childless. None of his own gods could tell him what to do, but he had travelled much and he was most willing to deal with strangers. He showed them a picture of his wife which he took about with him, dark and grave, with big eyes and long black curls, blue birds' wings coming down from behind them and meeting at the base of her neck. She was a priestess herself, he said. One was apt to believe in the Gods at Delphi.

A letter for Erif was sent on from Sparta. It was Tarrik's

answer to her question as to what had happened at Harvest. No one in all Marob, not even Kotka, or any of the Chief's best friends, would be IT, the actor in the Corn Play, so he had to be IT himself; and when he put on the Corn-cap every one thought he was Harn Der and called him that. It was a short, grim letter for Erif after all this time. But Klint was well.

The weather broke. It suddenly turned bitterly cold in Delphi. Parnassos hid his shoulders in mist, and cold winds blew along the glen of olives. Brown sudden rivers poured off the cliffs and down the roads and waterlogged the black earth round the bases of the olive trees. The time came for Erif to make her final offering and ask her question.

She was desperately nervous. She could not have done it at all without Berris. But the priests were used to that, from women most of all. They were both taken through to the room, where one waited and most likely regretted that one's gift had not been more impressive. Erif had simply asked when and how she could be clean again and able to go home. It was better, people said, to make one's questions as short and explicit as possible. The thing had, after all, to go through the mind, and ultimately the mouth, of such a simple vessel. It had been the way of prophecy always. The priests, of course, made sense of what the girl said—they had been trained to it for years. One could never do that for oneself if one were only given the immediate words she spoke.

Berris was a little sceptical about all this, but he did not say so to Erif. He wanted her to get right, and whether the priests were utterly honest or not, he hoped it might work for her. While they waited, he held her hands and talked about how lovely it would be to get back to Marob at last and see Klint-Tisamenos. Perhaps he would come back himself with her. 'If—if—' said Erif, and watched the door where the priest would come in again.

He came in at last with the folded paper and handed it to Erif, a tall, bearded man. She had jumped to her feet and stood holding the thing, not knowing whether to open it yet.

'Read it, read it!' said the priest quite kindly, but a little impatient at the stupidity of many pilgrims. She opened the

paper and Berris read it too, without asking anyone's leave.
It said:

> 'The Mother must meet the Daughter. The Dead
>   must meet with the Snake.
> A House shall stand in the Cornfield, though it cost
>   five years to make.
> Potters will paint their Vases, Poets will string
>   their Rhymes,
> And Kings will die for the People
>   in many places and times.

The priest, seeing the usual and inevitable questions and
exclamations coming, bowed and went out.

She read it again. 'Five years! Berris, it says five years.'

Berris was extremely angry with Apollo for saying that—
which was the only plain thing in the oracle; she was bound
to see it first. He said: 'You insisted on coming here, Erif,
but as far as I'm concerned I cannot see how this God can
possibly know anything about Marob—particularly a thing
like time. What's all this other mix-up?'

'The Mother must meet the Daughter. But I've no daughter!'

'You could always go and have one,' said Berris to himself.'

But she was not listening; she was thinking of the thing
their own dead mother, Nerrish, had said to her in the tent
about meeting again. 'The Dead must meet with the Snake.
Which dead? What snake? Is that about Harvest? It
might be, because of the House in the Cornfield. Oh, Berris,
Apollo must know, because of that!'

'You probably said something to someone about the
corn! No, I don't think that's very clever of Apollo.'

'But what's the third line for? I don't understand it
at all!'

'Nor I. Have you been writing poetry, Erif? I know you
can't paint—even pots.'

'And then—the last one. Oh, Berris, Berris, is it about
Tarrik?'

It was the only line that had impressed Berris at all, but
he did not say so. He said:

'It might be about him or about anyone else. Kleomenes,
for that matter. Or Antigonos: I wish it was! If it's about

Tarrik it's really nothing new. The Corn King always dies in the end, you know as well as I do, and he dies for the next Corn King and the strength of Marob, so I suppose a Greek might say he died for the people.'

She shook her head and folded the paper up again, put it into her bodice. Another priest beckoned to them to come out; the next pilgrim was waiting for the room.

They went back to their inn and all their new friends and acquaintances rushed up to find out what kind of an oracle they had got. There was a good deal of head-shaking and many more or less unlikely interpretations. One or two people agreed that it must have something to do with the Mysteries: both the first and the fourth line would fit in with that. The king who dies for the people might be one of the new kind of gods—Attis, Adonis, a not-Greek. There were plenty of potters and poets in Delphi: would she like to see some of them? Or a professional interpreter? But she thought she would wait. She had it in her mind that something would suddenly happen which would make it clear. Besides, if it was to take five years—! There was time enough. She could not make up her mind to write to Tarrik about it; she was afraid of what might happen in Marob when he heard.

Berris found her rather a gloomy companion. He was unhappy enough himself already. He kept on thinking, almost every night, that perhaps Philylla was just married. He wished now that he had waited till the thing was certain and finished. At any rate he did not want to go back to Sparta again, once having gone through the pain of leaving it. It was Philylla who had first made him fight for Kleomenes and the New Times. Now she was stopping him from fighting. Let her understand that and be sorry. He said this once to his sister in a mood of bitter resentment. She laughed and said: 'Didn't I tell you that you'd hurt Philylla just as much as anyone else if you felt like it!' They stayed on at Delphi all that winter and spring. It was as good as anywhere else. Five years.

Erif had two letters during the winter from Philylla, the first telling how Kratesikleia and the children had gone to Egypt, the second with little news and much anxiety. After that Antigonos moved and it was difficult to send letters to or from Sparta. He took Tegea and then Orchomenos with

great loss to the Spartans. Berris knew that some, at least, of
his friends must have been killed. There was a Macedonian
garrison in Orchomenos now. Kleomenes counter-attacked
against one town or another, but was too badly outnumbered
to dare risk a real battle.

One day when Erif and Berris were walking together a
little way beyond the town, they heard a lot of shouting—the sort of thing which might mean a murder or a
wild-beast show, or the mere fact that someone had dreamt
of a piebald rat running from left to right. They got as far as
the edge of a small crowd and then asked someone. It was
turning into rather angry and violent shouting. The man
said in great excitement: 'It's a dirty atheist coming and
mocking at Apollo, but he won't do it much longer!'

'Apollo is avenging himself?' asked Berris politely.

'We are!' said the man, and picked up a stone and butted
his way head first into the crowd. Berris said nothing but
looked disgusted, and they both turned back. Erif just
happened to see a large flat rock, crying out to be climbed
on to. When she was on the top she looked. Then she called
sharply to her brother to come too.

They were at the back of the crowd. In front of it there
was, just for a moment, a rather nice man standing and
talking. The next the stones got him and he was down.
On the other hand, the crowd was quite small and looked
quite stupid. Erif yelled shrilly from the back of her throat:
'Tarrik and Marob!' and jumped off the rock, her hair
flying and Tarrik's knife drawn in her hand.

'Oh hell,' said Berris, 'Tarrik and Marob!' and he
jumped too and thought on the whole that they would
both be killed almost at once. He had not reckoned with
this crowd and the alarming effect Erif and an unknown
language would have, particularly from behind. In less than
a minute they were all gone except the man. He picked
himself up with his face and arm bleeding. Berris said:

'They'll be back in no time! Oh, Erif, can't you leave
things alone!'

She said: 'I can make a circle, Berris, I know I can. Look
at the knife!' There was blood on the tip of it—from
someone—but the rest of Tarrik's knife was glowing as
it had not since it was in Greece.

'Then that's all right,' said Berris. 'Make a line while I

get the man away behind it.' If she said she could she would
be able.

She made it, with the knife and the green shells and a
few shaken blood-drops. The first people who came back
to finish off their atheist and whoever else there might be,
found her ending it. She went along it again to strengthen
it. Then she invited them to come. But instead, they all
ran to fetch a priest and show him what was being done in
Apollo's own ground. Erif went down into the olive grove
and whistled for Berris, who answered her from a pile of
wood stacked against the wall.

'The man says he's a philosopher,' said Berris, 'and an
Athenian.'

'Like Epigethes,' said Erif. Then she added: 'A nice
lot of good it's done us before, rescuing philosophers.' She
sucked her lip and thought of Sphaeros—dear Sphaeros:
but how he'd changed things for Tarrik and her!

'That's what I thought,' said Berris. 'Shall we just go
home?'

'I suppose not, once we're in it. If they'd said he was a
philosopher! Still—what shall we do?'

Berris said: 'Every one will know it's you and I. They
know your clothes all over Delphi, I should think. We
can't possibly take him to the inn. There'll be a fuss, of
course. It may cost rather a lot. I mayn't even be able to
work it if he really is an atheist and the priests are angry.
Naturally they can't afford that kind of thing on the God's
own territory. You'd better stay. I suppose you can look
after yourself?'

'Yes!' said Erif, cleaning her knife.

By and bye she looked in under the wood-stack and
told the man to come out. He did, crawling. He looked
particularly ragged because Berris had pulled strips off the
bottom of his tunic to tie up the worst grazes the stones
had made. She sat back on her heels and stared at him.
He was quite young—an altogether different kind of age
from Sphaeros.

'No bones broken?' she asked. He shook his head and
smiled. She said: 'You're really rather nice!'

He said: 'So are you!' and scrambled up to her and
kissed her.

She found that rather pleasing, much more what she

wanted than gratitude. She said: 'As you're a philosopher, I suppose you'll say now that you don't really mind whether you get killed or kiss me?'

'There's all the difference in the world!' said the man. 'I should hate to be killed that way too. It felt as if it was going to be most uncomfortable. Stupid donkeys of people—as if they really believed in their Gods!'

'Apollo is not like the others,' said Erif firmly. 'Apollo here, at least. I've had an oracle myself.'

'Poor dear Apollo! If you were a god would you like to spend all your time answering questions about whether two perfectly dull people ought to marry one another—that's the kind of thing half the questions are—when it doesn't make a pennyworth of difference to the world?'

'It makes a lot of difference to them. I don't know what kind of a god Apollo is, but he has a way of getting behind the future.'

'The only way to get behind the future is by hard thought, a more difficult but less expensive process, which my countrymen don't like at all. Am I depressing? Was it a nice oracle you had?'

'Not very,' said Erif Der.

'Then I shouldn't believe in it too much if I were you. You're not a Greek, are you?'

'No, I'm from Marob on the Black Sea. I'm the Queen of Marob.'

'Do you like being queen?'

'Yes,' she said, 'but I can't be just now. I—I am partly a god myself. But something went wrong. So I came to ask Apollo about it.'

'Member of the same club. Well, there's more to be said for that. Are you a kind god when you're at home?'

'With all my power. I make the spring come.'

'What happens when you're away?'

'Someone else has the power. Don't let's talk about that. What's your name?'

'Hyperides. Hyperides of Athens. Long name, isn't it?'

'It's a gay name. The first philosopher we rescued was called Sphaeros: a short, thick name.'

'Sphaeros of Borysthenes? My poor lambs, a real professional! What did he do to you?'

'He taught us how the good man should live.'

'Does that include consulting oracles? Or aren't you good?'

'I didn't ask him. I think he's good himself. I wish you wouldn't laugh at him! He has helped us and hurt us, both.'

'A habit the Stoics have. I'll take him quite seriously. I suppose he said he would teach you to distinguish between appearance and reality? The kataleptike phantasia and all that? That he could cure you of being too much alive? Yes, that was Zeno's game. My master was gentle. He said he would make us more alive, and cure us of death. Oh, not by taking it away, as the Mysteries pretend to, but by facing it: you see, we have our realities too, but they're human ones. Have you ever been afraid of death, for yourself and for others?—the hells and half lives, the child coming back to look for its mother and not finding her—'

'Oh don't!'

'But I can cure you of that. And of fear of all sorts of darkness and pain. My word is a gentle one for all who are afraid and tired and weak.'

'Who was your master?'

'Epicuros the Athenian. He lived a hundred years ago. He was a man who had seen much trouble himself. Women and slaves and children came to him. He was friends with them. I see you're frowning. People have spoken much evil of him. You may have heard it.'

'Sphaeros says he taught that pleasure was a good.'

'He reminded people that happiness is. Why, what is life for except to be lived? To be lived fully with reason and music and a garden, a community of friends who love one another.'

'Ah,' said Erif, 'you allow love in your pattern! Then indeed you're dealing with life. Here's Berris!'

Berris jumped down off the wall. 'I've bought him from the priests. It was rather expensive. I was so sympathetic to them! He's not liked, you know; he can't go back to Delphi. And what's more, I don't think we can. They don't like the idea of your line, Erif, though I told them it was nothing but a trick to stop the crowd.'

'You did, did you!' said Erif. 'Well, I don't mind; I'm tired of Delphi. Let's go down to Cirrha and see if there are any boats going to Marob. I must write to Tarrik soon. Let's take Hyperides.'

'Does he want to come?' Berris turned towards him.

'I should like it very much. Obviously, I'm under great obligations to you both and I'd, of course, do whatever you suggested, but this would be far the pleasantest. Are you husband and wife?'

'No,' said Berris. 'Brother and sister. But she's married!'

'Well, I'm not a professional seducer if that's any comfort to you. I take the thing too seriously. The other reason your suggestion is particularly welcome to me is that I haven't got any money.'

'Why not?'

'I spent it all. Then I thought I'd take to teaching. You saw what an effect my lessons had on the people of Delphi!'

'Mm,' said Berris. 'You know that funny old man with the whiskers who's staying at our inn, Erif? He gave me an order yesterday for some chairs, bronze and leather. I've never done that before, but I've been thinking out some designs. Hyperides, do you think you'd be any good at making patterns on leather? No, I suppose you regard beauty as a thing of no consequence and you wouldn't see that it mattered if you were an inch or so out!'

'Indeed you're wrong! I'd love to work for you. Beauty's a god that a whole city can share. That, at any rate, was the point of the gods in the old days, in Athens anyway. And, of course, I can see that it must be as accurate as a piece of reasoning. Then it has the same value.'

'Only more permanent.'

'Perhaps! That's been a difference of opinion between philosophers and artists for some time. But I'd certainly like nothing better than to be taught something new.'

Three days later they were settled in Cirrha. Erif Der produced her oracle for Hyperides, telling him something of the circumstances—she found him easier to talk to than most Greeks. He frowned and said:

'It's a typical piece of god-stuff—frightening you! But there's very little in it really. Mother and daughter—a nice obvious thing to begin an oracle with—gets the atmosphere. It might be used metaphorically to cover all sorts of events. Almost any two things can be made into

mother and daughter if you apply your imagination to
them. The snake? Oh, that's only the kind of thing every
one says nowadays. When people are too ignorant and
frightened to face life and death, they invent things to
come between. The Gods don't work now, so they make
themselves snakes and kings that die—the last line is all
part of the same flummery. It doesn't mean anything at all
except that Apollo is determined to follow the fashions. The
second line—you're sure to have talked about the corn.
And they've given themselves a margin of time. Then if
it happens earlier you'll be so pleased that you'll make
up an excuse for them. Third line? Oh, that was for
Berris. They saw he was something of the sort, and put
it in thinking they'd hit some nail on the head. Opinion on
the whole thing? A waste of money. *Don't fuss.* I'm not
really unsympathetic, but I'm afraid this oracle business
makes me angry.'

'Don't you believe in it at all, Hyperides? Not a little
bit?'

'Not the least little bit. Sorry.' He grinned at them.
They both liked him so much. Berris found that when he
explained his work to Hyperides it immediately came alive
in his own mind. He was working far better than he had
since the first year or two in Sparta, tackling new problems
and materials and enjoying it. The chairs were going to be
fun, and he would be well paid for them, which was worth
considering, because they had spent a certain amount in
Delphi. Erif had plenty of jewels still, but it always meant
time and trouble before they could be turned into food and
housing.

There was a piece of bad news early that summer,
which shocked not only them, but every one else they
saw. Antigonos had taken Mantinea, and, in revenge for
the murdered settlers of four years ago, had burnt most of
the city and sold the whole of the citizens, the women and
children on the spot, the men in gangs to Macedonia. Not
only that, but the city itself was to be wiped away, out of
the hearts and thoughts of men, for the new Achaean settlers
who were put there decided that their new Achaean town
was to be called Antigonea. A horrible thing, nowadays; it
was a long time since Hellenes had dealt so badly with one
another. Kleomenes seemed to be doing little but hold the

Laconian borders; but it was better perhaps not to think too much about Sparta.

Hyperides produced a good deal of Epicurean theory, while he and Berris worked and Erif looked on or experimented with dyes or wrote to Philylla—against the time when she could find some way to send the letter—or while they all three wandered about through the warm olive groves in the lengthening evenings. As this went on Erif felt a certain lifting of her spirit. For some time she did not know why, for she had plenty to make her gloomy. At last she decided that it was because he talked extraordinarily little about virtue, not at all about duty or conscience, and he used good in quite a different sense to the one she was used to, in a sense that included a number of things that she was very glad to think were good; things of the body as well as the mind, the whole of life. It was more like Marob. Suddenly she thought: if he'd come to Marob instead of Sphaeros, would Tarrik have got so entangled with himself? And the next day she thought again: if Hyperides went to Marob, could he cure Tarrik of whatever was the matter with him, as—she was beginning to believe—he was curing her of whatever it was which she had wrong? At last she said all this to Hyperides and Berris.

Berris did not like the idea of Hyperides going away when he was so perfect to talk to. Yet obviously this thing was more important. Besides, his work was going amazingly well, he hardly seemed to stop to take breath now! He had enough orders to last him all summer. Erif said she would write a letter to Tarrik and send Hyperides with it, and when he got there he could see what he could do or say. Hyperides liked the prospect only fairly. He was happy where he was with the two bright, half-barbarian minds; he wrote to his friends in Athens and they to him. He would go back there one day. And he was not certain how much he cared for the picture of the Corn King of Marob which he had got from the other two. Something fierce and moody and full of queer barbarous passions and customs that led him to do these strange things and think himself a god. But it would, at any rate, be interesting.

That summer they found a ship which was bound that way, for Tyras and Olbia. Yes, it would touch at Marob and consider the flax prices. The two gave him letters and money and things to take back with him, including toys for a three-year-old child. They wished him luck and saw him sail. The ship went all round the Peloponnese and up to Athens before she adventured eastward for the straits and Byzantium. Hyperides was horribly tempted to stay at home with the money and give things to all his friends, most of whom were not much better off than he was. But Berris and Erif were friends too. Finally he decided not even to land. He turned his back on Athens and began writing what was going to be a philosophical comedy of manners. Then they were off again, bound for Marob.

Chapter Eight

ALL THAT SUMMER Kleomenes was extremely busy at home, refitting his army, enlarging it and training it to the limits of confidence and courage. At the same time he had to deal with his political opponents, using all his tact and cunning and knowledge of people, missing Agiatis every day. He freed and armed a good many more helots, making those who could pay for their freedom, for many had savings. He did not care much what happened to his own household. He slept mostly in a tent or under the stars and he did not take long over his meals. He worked all the others as hard as he worked himself. Once or twice he seemed illish, a touch of the old thing, but it passed over. At any rate they kept Antigonos off, and at the beginning of autumn that king sent back his Macedonians, who were beginning to grumble, to their homes for the winter, and settled down himself in Argos, thinking it was fairly safe: Kleomenes must have his hands full. Besides, no one starts a campaign at the beginning of the winter season.

Kleomenes, however, did. He ordered his army to take five days' provisions and marched off north-east towards Argos. Then he suddenly turned to the left by a mountain road and camped that night on the borders of Megalopolis. Before dawn he sent Panteus off with two brigades to surprise the city. He followed with the rest of the army, and by the time he got there Panteus had taken a great section of the wall and made breaches in it. Before the citizens of Megalopolis were well awake, the Spartan army was on top of them. The city was so bravely defended in street-to-street fighting that most of the citizens escaped, though with little but the clothes they wore, into Messenia. But a thousand were taken and the whole town was left in Kleomenes' hands. That was how it was by dinner-time. Panteus and the King had snatched Megalopolis and the army was wild with delight and renewed pride in them and itself.

The King's Mess met just after noon with more laughter and excitement than there'd been for ages. Agesipolis had been in the first attack with Panteus. He described how they had come up along a dry water-course, and as it grew light had seen the walls of Megalopolis coming thicker grey out of the grey and chilly mist ahead of them, with towers to right and left; how the runners with ladders had gone forward quietly; how they'd followed quickly over as at practice times, one at another's heels; how they'd caught and killed the guards before they could wake the town, secured the nearer streets, opened the gates to the others. Oh, the lovely successful slickness of it all! It was always a surprise, in a way, that Panteus was such an exceedingly good soldier. He looked as if he could obey better than command, but when something began to happen he woke up completely, his body was at the service of his intelligence, and when he shouted or signalled his orders the bodies and minds of his men obeyed to the second. He was a good teacher too. Agesipolis understood the reason of every movement—only he himself could never have managed in the middle of a battle to come so immediately and precisely to these competent decisions.

Plundering had been forbidden. No one was to take more than he needed to eat, even. The army found comfortable quarters in empty houses, and lighted fires because there was a coldish wind. There was plenty to loot if the King would let them. But they must not: or only very little. The prisoners had been brought into the market-place and were being sorted out, the men into the gymnasium, which had high walls, and the big temple of Zeus Saviour, where they were at liberty to make what prayers they liked—the women into the temple next it, of Fortune and the North Wind. Rape had been forbidden, too, for the moment. Anyone who was of any importance was brought straight to the King.

He was standing on the steps of the temple of Zeus

Saviour, resting his hand only lightly on his great spear at arm's length, his purple cloak hanging loose to his heel, the red and purple plume jutting up and back from his helmet. Two or three of his friends were beside him, all fully armed, too, and very victorious looking, with dark beards and bright eyes and more high spears to stand up with his. He watched the prisoners going by into the temples, the men mostly with their hands tied or chained. They were being checked off in tens, made to stay still, and then shoved on, often with the intention of being made to look funny by tripping on the threshold or knocking into the ring on the door. Some of them recognised Kleomenes and called on him for mercy. They were not at all sure what the Spartans at this bitter stage of the war would do to their prisoners.

He did not answer, but smiled a little. He was feeling good all over. He saw a girl in a grey woollen dress and red cloak go by among the women prisoners, with her head a little bent, playing a shepherd's whistle. The notes of it hardly reached him; only the tiniest possible sad little defiance. He thought she was playing for the children who came after her and who were just not crying. One of his soldiers knocked the pipe out of her mouth; she snatched it up again, wordless, and hid it in the fold of her dress, and glared, half terrified, at the man. The children behind her began to cry miserably. She looked straight across the steps, past the soldier, at Kleomenes. She had brown hair, parted at one side and held close to her head by a band of red stuff, and straight, thick eyebrows and a straight nose, and her under lip stuck out a little either with anger or near tears. She must have been quite young. Something very odd happened to the King then, because he quite suddenly and seriously remembered his own cold orders about rape. He wanted that girl hauled over to him. The next moment it was out of his mind again; he had looked away from her. But she had got it full in his look back at her. She went on sobbing into the temple, not knowing what was to happen to her, nor to the rest of the free-born men and women of Megalopolis.

Idaios came up the steps in three bounds, shouting that they had taken Lysandridas and Thearidas among the prisoners. The King looked all the satisfaction he felt. They were two of the richest and most important citizens; if he had them he had an obvious place to start. Idaios pointed them out, being hustled along to the steps, their hands chained behind them. Lysandridas was the elder of the two, a rather jolly-looking man in armour—they had both been among the defenders of Megalopolis—but without helmet or weapons. He saw Kleomenes on the steps of the temple of Zeus Saviour and shouted up to him: 'King of Sparta!' Kleomenes passed his spear quickly to Idaios and came down a step to meet them, signing to the soldiers not to hurry them too much. They were both halted just in front of him and a little below. Lysandridas said: 'Now you've got your chance, King of Sparta.' When Kleomenes did not answer, he went on: 'Your chance to do something finer and bolder than you've ever done—even you.'

They looked at one another hard. Kleomenes felt all the implications behind the words: they pleased him. Lysandridas saw he was pleased. They could not avoid meeting one another's eyes with a curious, excited intimacy. Kleomenes ordered the soldiers to unchain them both.

'Thanks!' said Lysandridas, stretching and rubbing the inside of his arm over his sweating face. 'That's better. Well, King of Sparta?'

Kleomenes said: 'Lysandridas, you are surely not advising me to give you back your city after all my trouble?'

'I am,' said Lysandridas.

'But you can't think I'm going to take your advice?'

'I can,' said Lysandridas, 'easily.' He left it for a moment, then said with passionate earnestness of voice and mind: 'Sir, don't ruin us, don't make us enemies for ever! Give us back our city and make us steady and faithful friends and allies. We can be brave on your side as we were brave against you.'

Thearidas said suddenly: 'We know you can be generous enough for this. Buy our hearts and swords, King of Sparta!' He was a little man and he had a sword-cut on his knee that showed the bone through; he had walked very lame and stumblingly because of it, but now he did not seem to notice it at all.

Kleomenes did not answer for a minute or two. Panteus began to speak, but he checked him. At last he said, not very loudly: 'It is hard to trust so far. How can I? I've no margin to pay for it if it fails.' He came down nearer to the two men and looked at them closely. And then he said again, but louder: 'Very well, I'll risk it. May I never get too old to take these risks! Lysandridas and Thearidas, you two can go off to Messenia with a herald from me and tell your friends they can have their city again if they will break with the League and be my allies.'

He nodded at Lysandridas, and was not unpleased when Lysandridas took him hard by the hands and said in fierce excitement: 'Is that all you want of us, King of Sparta? No indemnity? No land?'

'Yes, that's all,' said Kleomenes, 'only your friendship.'

'I think I can promise you that,' said Lysandridas, and turned to his friend. 'Don't you?'

'Yes,' said Thearidas, 'I do. At least—No, you mean it honestly and we'll show them. Can we go this evening, sir?'

It was after supper that evening that the King, considering this day, suddenly wished that someone else had seen him taking this generous risk, offering to save Megalopolis. Some woman. Agiatis. Some other woman, even. He said to Panteus: 'It would be a good thing to let the prisoners know about this offer of mine.' 'I've done that,' said Panteus. 'Men and women both?' 'No; but I will. I suppose the women may be useful with their husbands later.' 'That's it,' said Kleomenes.

Thearidas and Lysandridas and the herald from Kleomenes rode over the pass in gathering darkness and into Messenia. They were very hopeful. The thing seemed almost done. The few people they spoke to that night agreed. A full assembly was called just after dawn. They stood up and told what had happened; the Spartan herald confirmed it all. There were a good many shouts of agreement and for Kleomenes. But they had reckoned without a young man who had been one of the leaders in the defence of the city, almost the last to get away in the retreat; a young man who had to be helped to his feet and held there because of his wounds, a short, thick, eloquent, angry young man called Philopoemen. He spoke against them, violently asking the assembly if it was going to crawl for Kleomenes, bringing it back firm to its old hatred of Sparta, asking if it was not enough that Kleomenes had their city without his having their bodies and minds as well, asking if they had forgotten all they had ever known about Sparta and Spartan ways. The assembly, in a great burst of heroism, overwhelming those whose wives and children were among the prisoners, refused the terms. Let Kleomenes burn Megalopolis! He could not lure or threaten them into friendship. Philopoemen should lead them against him yet!

They drove out Thearidas and Lysandridas and the herald, who rode back grimly and silently to the city. They were hurried along to Kleomenes, who had been waiting, not very patiently, for them all the afternoon. They had to tell him of their failure and Philopoemen's hatred and success. The King heard it all in silence. He said to Lysandridas and Thearidas: 'You can go.' 'But—' said Lysandridas. 'I advise you to go quick,' he said, 'or you may see something you won't like. You can take whatever you can carry or get anyone else to, from your own houses.' He wrote and signed an order. 'And get your wives and children from among the prisoners. It was a pity Philopoemen was too much for you.' He turned his back on them and they hurried out, white and whispering. He gave orders that all the statues, pictures, and everything else of value, was to be loaded carefully into carts and sent under guard into Sparta. His army could then do whatever they liked with the shell of the place. He suggested that they should burn it. Slave and foreign prisoners were to be distributed or sold. Citizen prisoners were to be held for high ransom.

He walked up the temple steps again. None of his Mess were with him, as they all had their various orders to carry out. The doors were opened for him. He went in. The women did not know yet what had happened, only about his offer to save them and their city. They knelt to kiss his hands and the edge of his cloak: grey-haired, solid mothers of families. He told them succinctly what had come of it. It was funny to see them shrivel away in horror and misery. It was probable that most of them would be ransomed, but if they thought that they and their children were going to be sold, let them! It had been done at Mantinea by Antigonos. Well –

One leaf of the temple door had been thrown back for him. The spear of the guard slanted across it. He had enough light to see by. The statues behind the altars were plated with gold: Fortune and the North Wind. He knew what north wind it was, in spite of the lies some of the prisoners had told him: the north wind that had blown a sudden hurricane and beaten down the great siege tower that Agis of Sparta had brought up against them. Lydiades had bidden make the statue in gratitude for the saving of his city. There was a shrine to Lydiades too, outside the temple, with Lydiades painted as a hero with an eagle behind him and a snake at his side. There were flowers on the edge of the stone now. No one had ever made a shrine in Sparta for Agis, though many went to pray at his tomb. He himself had done that. Supposing he took Fortune and the North Wind back with him to Sparta, turned them over to his own uses, made slave-statues of them? It would be pleasing. Yet perhaps that was one of the things it was better not to do, even in anger.

He looked about him for a minute or two, and then saw the girl sitting with her back to a column, her long legs doubled up under her. He walked over, stepping carefully across a sleeping child, and took her wrist and jerked her on to her feet. She did not understand at once. Then she cried out: 'I am a free woman, a citizen's daughter—' By that time he had pulled her over to the door; she beat and clawed with her free hand at his fist clenched like iron over her other wrist, which only closed that much tighter, as though it could and would easily crush through skin into flesh and bone. She cried once: 'Father!' But there was nothing to help her; the other women did not dare; they clutched their children tighter and hid their faces and called in whispers on the gods. Then he got hold of her other hand too; he held them both in his left hand. He looked more closely at her face; it was longish, with high cheek-bones, a sword of a face. Her eyes were grey-green with very thick, brown eyelashes; her hair had a sharp, bright wave in it, glossy like a young horse; her mouth shut tight as she struggled with him. He thought she was extremely beautiful and told her so. She threw back her head wildly, tossing up the bright waves of hair; her long neck fitted square on to the collar-bones. 'You know who I am?' he said. 'You do? Good. You remember what Antigonos did to Mantinea this spring? Do you? Answer me.'

She managed at last to gasp out yes, her hands helpless and limp now from his crushing fingers.

He said: 'Antigonos sold them all for slaves, men one way, women another. I tried to save your city from that. But Philopoemen didn't trust a Spartan. So you can thank him if you don't like everything that happens to you now.'

She said: 'Don't hold me so tight.' Her eyes were bigger and more dizzying to look at when they were full of tears; her cheeks were flaming.

His grip relaxed a little. He passed his own right arm across her quivering shoulders. She seemed more slender and delicately made than—than anybody. He let one hand go. 'Come,' he said.

She followed him, almost unresisting. Half-way down the steps she lifted her eyes to him and whispered: 'Where?'

'To my bed,' he said, and again, very contentedly: 'You are so beautiful.'

The Spartans marched away from Megalopolis as soon as they had destroyed it. The Achaean League was very much disheartened over this, hearing of it suddenly when the generals were all together at a council of war. They gathered so slowly and unwillingly to the summons from Antigonos that he thought it best not to try too much during winter, but stayed in Argos with only a few troops. Kleomenes at once began to harass him there, making constant small raids, with little loss to himself, plundering and spoiling the Argive land with much pleasure and excitement for his own people, especially the new troops, who were greatly encouraged by it all, and shame and anger for his enemies. He hoped to force Antigonos out to fight with him before his Macedonians were back. But the Macedonian king, supported with a curious loyalty by Aratos, would not be taunted out of safety. The longer he waited, the better for him; he had all the moral security of the man with money. Let Kleomenes go on till he grew hollow-hearted with the thought of the empty treasury behind him! Antigonos was carrying on transactions with Egypt. He had made some conquests in Asia Minor, certain towns that went naturally into Ptolemy's sphere of influence. They could be returned—if Ptolemy would contrive to drop those anyhow not very considerable subsidies to Sparta? That would work itself out nicely, between real kings of something more than a stony valley and a few old songs and a hill or two!

Philocharidas was wounded in one of these raids and

came back to Deinicha to get well. Philylla rode over to see them both. Ianthemis, bored at home, wanted to come too; she wanted to look at a man a little younger than her father and a little older than her small brother! But Philylla was so rough and cross with her that she went back from the stables crying; she was not allowed to go to her mother's room either, for there were some ladies there and they were talking about something important—ladies who did not like the King's Times. Ianthemis wasn't sure; it didn't seem quite fair to go against the King now; father grumbled at him, of course, but said he'd got the genius of a leader. No, it wasn't fair. If only Philylla had been a little bit nice to her, Ianthemis would have known which side to be on. But Philylla didn't understand that, so she was not nice. Ianthemis sat on the step and cried till Tiasa found her and said she could come and see the new calf.

Deinicha was going to have a baby at the end of winter; she looked wise and secret. Chrysa had come over too; she was married now and living on her husband's lot. She and Deinicha talked in an almost showing-off way about crops and beasts, and how to get the helots to do what they ought to do. Philylla waited, soreish, and shut them up when they began to turn this domestic talk towards her; whatever had gone wrong she could bear it best if she wasn't interfered with. Suddenly she reminded Deinicha of the small, fierce little girl that their Philylla used to be—and with no Agiatis to make her gentle and happy again.

Philocharidas came in with his arm in a sling. Deinicha made a delighted fussing over him, with cushions and a little charcoal stove—yes, Chrysa could carry it: she knew our men were worth looking after!—and a plate of pomegranate seeds with honey over them and some late winter apples, all the sweeter for keeping. Yes, and Philocharidas could talk just as well if she put one arm round his neck. They kept on seeing one another and smiling, he and she, keeping Chrysa and Philylla out. But Chrysa had her own seeing and smiling to compare it with. She smiled too, in sympathy and as if hearing some note in the chord of her own pleasure. And sometimes Deinicha looked away from her man to Chrysa, and then they were both eyeing and smiling. Abruptly Philylla asked for news of the war.

'It's been great, this show round Argos!' said Philocharidas, willing enough to talk. 'We don't often get near them now, they run so! Last time we took the hill road from Tegea—a stiff road if you've no mule to carry your shield!—and took a short cut into Hysiae before dawn. Not much of a town, but it's less of one now. Beyond that the valley widens out and we had a gay time stalking the villages. One gets supplies. We came down on foot, but by the end of the day we were all on horseback driving in the cattle. We got as far as Lerna, not six miles from Argos, keeping clear of Demeter's Grove. We didn't do much there, for they'd been warned we were coming, and the whole place was as bristly as a hedgehog. We laughed at them a lot and someone spotted a thatched roof, so we shot in some burning tow-arrows. Oh, I think the Lerneans are sure to tell Antigonos that we were naughty boys!'

'Who was leading?' Philylla asked.

'The King's there mostly himself, though Hippitas took the last raiding party—he knows a good cow when he sees her! I expect, though, we shan't be able to go on much longer. There was snow on all the tops last time; it'll be down on to the passes by now. Yes, I suppose the King will want his house put in order pretty soon.' Philocharidas stopped talking then, suddenly. His wife, to whom his voice was, at the moment anyhow, a mere airy continuation of his near body, did not notice, but went on exploring his neck and cheek with her fingers.

But Chrysa and Philylla both did notice. They stared at him, and he made it odder by blushing. 'What's the matter?' said Chrysa boldly.

Philocharidas approached it. 'Will you be going to the King's house now?'

'I don't understand,' said Chrysa.

Philocharidas turned to Philylla. 'Hasn't your father said anything? Hasn't—hasn't Panteus? I thought— Philylla—I mean: it's Archiroë, the woman of Megalopolis.'

'What woman?' said Philylla stonily. Chrysa had jumped up from her stool, and even Deinicha had stopped fingering him and was breathing quicker.

Philocharidas said: 'Don't be unkind to her. It was no doing of hers. The King took her out of the Temple of the

North Wind. And it's no fault of his either. She's—very beautiful.'

The Queen's girls stiffened. It was Deinicha who said: 'Don't talk to me about beauty!—after Agiatis. What was he thinking of?'

'He wasn't thinking,' said Philocharidas, suddenly annoyed with them and particularly his own wife. 'He was doing something much better!' And he gave Deinicha a squeeze.

But she pushed him away. 'At least he hasn't married her?'

'No, poor thing. She's really his slave. She does everything for him now.'

Another wave of anger went over the three. Philylla said slowly: 'And the King—loves her?'

'Oh, I don't know about that,' said Philocharidas, fidgeting, 'but she really is beautiful. And so young! She loves him. At least she sits in the dark at the other side of the tent and keeps her eyes on him, and the moment he thinks of wanting a thing, she gets it for him. No one else can so much as touch her little finger without her turning on them.'

'Oh, you've tried!' said Deinicha with a sharp laugh, something he had never met in her before.

'No. Little fool!' And Deinicha shifted and cowered under his frown as though it had really been a slap on her mouth. 'No. Archiroë is the King's. She was a free woman, a maid, daughter of a master builder in Megalopolis.'

'And he raped her and she loves him for it. That sort of woman!' It was Philylla who spoke, savagely. She looked at the other two women in turn, slowly, holding their eyes. 'And we—*we* are expected to be friends (I understand you, don't I, Philocharidas, son of Milon?) with this creature. This once-upon-a-time virgin of Megalopolis! We are to spread the sheets for her. Oh, that will be delightful for us.' Her mouth drooped into a heavy fierceness, as her father's or grandfather's might have, swinging an arm up to lash a crouching, dribbling slave.

Deinicha stood up. 'How could he—so soon!' she said. 'Openly. Were we all wrong to think Agiatis was more loved than most women?'

Philocharidas said, angry and surprised: 'It's nothing

to do with that! Why have you got to drag in Agiatis?'
Then, seeing himself outnumbered and his own Deinicha
become a part, not of the lovely couple of marriage, but of
that group of the Queen's girls—cows with their horns
down!—he flung out of the room, his wounded arm as
obvious as possible.

Almost immediately Deinicha began to soften. 'Of course,'
she said, 'it mayn't be as bad as we think. Men do these
things, after all, so lightly. In spite of what Philocharidas
says, I don't think we need take any notice of the girl.'

'No,' said Chrysa, 'no. Why should we? She is nothing
to do with Sparta. She will live in the back rooms and not
show herself. If we are firm to begin with it will be all
right.'

'Besides, he's sure to get tired of her,' Deinicha said.
'And then he will let her be ransomed. So long as she
doesn't forget she's only a slave!'

They breathed easily again. It was, after all, nothing. No
menace to the lovely things they remembered. Philylla got
up and said she must go. She kept on lifting her hands to
her face and hair. She was not disturbed about this any
longer; she did not quite know why she was uneasy. But
no, she would not stay to eat or drink. She must ride.

All along the path between the rocks winter anemones
were holding up to her small stars, blue and scarlet. She
looked at them fiercely and turned her face into the wind,
the snow-flavoured wind off the hills. It blew through her
hair and her dress, cold on her scalp and arms and the front
of her thighs as she rode. Not having eaten with Deinicha,
she was rather hungry now. Why not? Ianthemis came
running out of the house to meet her. 'Oh, Philylla,' she
cried, catching at the bridle, 'he's here!'

'Who? Father?'

'He's home too, but—Oh, Philylla, it's Panteus!'
She was pink and panting with excitement. She tried to
shove a little bunch of welcoming sweet flowers into her
sister's hand.

Philylla dismounted slowly. She looked at her sister across
the horse's back, leaning against the saddle. Ianthemis had
been smiling but now it died out. 'What does he want?'
said Philylla, at last taking the flowers, but crushingly,
never lifting them to her face.

'He and father came together. About your marriage. I heard them say tomorrow. I thought you'd like to know, Philylla; I've been looking out for you the whole afternoon! But if you don't want to know—!' Ianthemis recovered herself and tossed her head, grinning, showing her teeth a little at her sister.

Philylla moved round to her horse's head and led him in. As she came out of the stall, rubbing her hands clean on a wisp of straw, Tiasa met her. 'Tomorrow!' she said. 'Tomorrow, my pretty!' Her arms were warm and freckled over Philylla's wind-blown arms; her eyes gloated lovingly into Philylla's, that slid sideways, looking down, staring at a lump in the clay floor. 'We aren't so ready as we thought,' said the foster-mother, 'not to be clipped and stripped this cold weather. But you'll be warm, sweeting—'

But Philylla pushed her away and went in. Her mother was giving orders to one of the women, whom she dismissed. 'Well,' she said, 'I see you've heard, Philylla. Your father is pleased. I am seeing about the sacrifice to Aphrodite-Hera: be sure I shall do my best for you. And your hair: I suppose you will want that cut? Answer me, child.'

'I—I think so,' said Philylla.

Eupolia looked at her more gently. 'It has come suddenly at the end. But—as you know, Philylla, he was none of my choice, but it is a good family. They do not all share his extreme views. If it had been five years ago—My dear, it's too late to change your mind now, but you will always have your own home to come back to.'

'I don't change my mind,' said Philylla. 'It's all right, mother. Can I see him?'

'No, Philylla, it would not be suitable now. Your father would not like it at all. Tomorrow will be soon enough.'

'Very well, mother,' said Philylla gently, and stood quiet for a moment, as though she were listening to the sound of her own heart.

Sacrifices were made for Philylla, as was customary, and her hair was cut in the fashion of old Sparta. No, she would not think all the time about Agiatis. It was a fine evening, scarcely cold in the courtyard of the house of Themisteas. She waited, with her clipped head and white short dress, and now, oddly, she could only think of the stupidest things: whether she had remembered to speak about her horse's loose shoe; whether she had put back a book in the chest of book rolls; whether there were black or green grapes on the vine at the left side of the second court of the King's house; whether this Archiroë had been told about her. It was curious to stay so calm after a day and night of anger. So calm! When Panteus came she would look him in the eye, out of her calm anger. He would not be able to read there that she hated him for marrying her only when the King had a new mistress and was tired of him. No, he would only be puzzled and worried. But, a few hours later, she would tell him very clearly.

The sun set and the evening star came out, the lovers' star. Let it! She would tell him just like that, out of her cold anger. To hurt his pride. Hurt him as he had hurt her. Panteus, son of Menedaios. Philylla, daughter of Themisteas. He would take her maidenhead; she would take his pride. In a struggle the cold one was always the winner. How cold she was now!

The knock came on the door of the house and she stiffened. The women's voices all round her jumped and throbbed. She raised her eyes to give him that stare. But before it came she suddenly realised that it was quite impossible for her to hurt him, even to try to while he still had those eyes and that smile. She had not remembered what a complete defence they were. She could no more hurt him than she could have hurt a baby of her own! He came towards her and in the meeting of their eyes there was no cold anger but a marriage. As he swung her up in his arms it was as if they had arranged all that, a long time ago. There appeared after all to be no need for blame or anger or explanation. She put both arms round his neck to make herself lighter to carry. But he did not seem to find her heavy; it might have been a thing he was perfectly and beautifully used to. She kissed him where she could reach most easily, just behind the ear on the line of neck and hair, smelling his skin there. As the gate shut behind them and they were out together in the evening, he rubbed his cheek sideways against hers. 'Philylla,' he said. It had all come right.

Towards the middle of the night she woke again, turning herself over slackly, feeling her whole body swayed by this new rhythm of a man's breathing beside hers, slower than hers. The lamp was still burning. This room that she had never been in before, but now whose shadows and angles were all her own for ever! He woke, too, and sat half up, so that his flanks drew level with her head. She slid an arm slowly round him, feeling one set of muscles after another start a little under the soft excitement of her touch; she laid her face close over the hollow of his side between ribs and hip, her lips moving a little against his smoothness and male youth. His hand strayed over towards her head. At last she said: 'Why did you choose just now for our wedding?'

'I don't know,' he said, 'but we were always going to be married some time. I wanted to now. It was right now. I can be away from my brigade now.'

'And the King did not mind your leaving him?'

'No,' said Panteus gently, and Philylla thought she would not speak of the woman of Megalopolis—not yet, not yet, not while they breathed so sweetly and easily together, in this marvellous close quiet after their first violences. She looked up. 'Sing something!' she said, not quite expecting that he would.

But he said: 'Very well,' only pulling her a little further over on to himself, turning her so that she lay face upward, her cheek soft against his belly, her short hair on his, mixing with his. He began to sing a love song. She lay and listened in a breathless happiness. It might have been for a girl or a boy: she could not tell from the words; she did not know or care; she was his wife. Philylla, wife of Panteus. It was low and sweet and very formal as he sang it there to her alone, a grave and tender song:

> O sweet earth all day drinking
>   While it rained:
> My mind's sweet too, with thinking
>   Of my friend.

PART V

Up the Ladder and over the Wall

Dauntless the slughorn to his lips he set
And blew, Childe Roland to the Dark Tower came.
Browning

NEW PEOPLE IN THE FIFTH PART

Menoitas, a Greek merchant, and other Greek
    traders and sailors
Tigru and Diorf, chiefs of the Red Riders, and the
    horde of Red Riders
Tsomla and other men and women of Marob

HYPERIDES, SON OF Leonteos, to Timokrates, son of Metrodoros, and great-grandson of Metrodoros who was the Master's friend: Live well!

I've a hundred and one things to tell you. God, it's such ages since I've seen you all! If you could feel how hard I've remembered you sometimes, you and Menexenos and Nikoteles and dearest Timonoë and the children, you'd tingle all over. Never mind, I shall see you again, and the garden. At least I hope so.

Well, I told you about my two charming Scythians, and how I was going to run errands for them. I can tell you, when it came to the point I didn't feel so gay about it. We stayed a day or two in Byzantium, and I asked them there—for they know all the scandals of the Euxine!—what sort of a man my Erif's husband, this Tarrik-Charmantides, was. They weren't what you'd call cheering! He has the reputation of being very queer and unaccountable, and there were some very nasty stories going about of things he had done to traders, just suddenly for no reason. Of course I quite sympathise with any barbarian who stabs some of these cheating brutes of traders in the back. But the King of Marob went rather further. I suppose it's silly of me, but I have a prejudice against torture, all this messing up of good clean human bodies. And I should dislike having it done to me quite particularly. None of this was very recent, mostly three years ago, in fact; but obviously there's no knowing when he mayn't get taken that way again. So I sailed on, feeling that perhaps I was putting my head into the lion's mouth. The only thing that comforted me at all was the box of toys for the child.

We sighted Marob on a fine summer morning and stood into Marob harbour. How I did look! It was a low, greenish coast, scarcely a hint of rising ground, though I hear there are wooded hills further inland, where the savages, whom they call here Red Riders, inhabit. At first I could not make out much of the town. It does not rise anywhere to the lovely, pale, crowned heights that you and I know in cities. There is no strong high place, no acropolis, no sacred way or rocks for olives. The only building that stood out, besides some great warehouses to the north of the harbour, was a stone house with windows and a roof of the local, rather pretty tiles, and a great square door between towers facing the sea. They told me this was the Chief's house. I suppose Erif lived there always. It was curious to know one was so near to one's journey's end!

Our captain landed with me and took me to an inn where I found quite a number of traders, come, they said, for the mid-summer market; in fact, I have to share a room with a couple, one of them a most trying person—I trust he won't contrive to read this letter!—from Kyrene, called Menoitas, who is persuaded he knows everything about anything, including, of course, the King of Marob, who has, according to him, driven out his wife because he got tired of her, and is now playing about with all the women in the place. This doesn't tally with Erif's own story, and I didn't believe it at first, but now I am not so sure. I should hate friend Menoitas to be right over anything, let alone this, but it looks rather unpleasantly like the truth.

The inn servants are Marob men and women, and some half-breeds. Most of them talk a certain amount of Greek. I believe this Marob was once a Greek colony; I am persuaded of this partly by their own tradition and partly by some worked stones which I have seen in ordinary house walls. But it cannot have been a success, for there is little trace of it left, either in customs or the look of the people, though naturally a good many of them speak Greek and there is a certain amount of intermarriage, among the upper classes, with Tyras and Olbia families. But it seems to me that anyone who comes into this community from outside gets readily absorbed.

I was advised to try and see the Chief as soon as possible. So I washed and shaved and put on my best clothes and with some skill managed to dodge Menoitas, as I did not altogether relish appearing at my first audience with him to give me hints! I took the letters with me, and one of the inn servants carried the two cases of presents and so on.

I went into the Chief's house by that great square door, with my back to the sea and the only way home. They took us across a courtyard with an apple tree in the middle that had coloured strings dangling out of its boughs, and so to a fairly large hall where there were some really fine furs, some of which were kinds I had never seen before, hanging up. Here we waited for some time, and at last a slave in black, whom I took to be tongueless but probably not a eunuch, beckoned us through another square doorway.

The King of Marob was sitting at a table, making marks on a wooden cylinder. He had a curious barbarian crown, three rows of very ridiculous animals on a felt cap, and a white coat and trousers embroidered with the most extra-ordinary coloured higgledy-piggledy. However, I didn't laugh! He is a big, lazy-looking, smiling savage, who may, for all one can tell, be plotting the most horrible things behind his grin. He looks quite incredibly strong, and I could easily believe all Erif had told me about his physical powers. I bowed and offered him the letters. He grabbed them and began reading. I remained standing. Once or twice he looked up over them at me, and he frowned a good deal, presumably about the oracle. I took rather a marked dislike to him then and there. Timokrates, you know what it is sometimes, when one is in contact with this kind of an unmoving, solid piece of butcher's meat—yet, in a way violent, a will that neither reason nor kindliness could get at! Still, of course, I may be wrong. But I hate the bare idea of this thing having possessed Erif Der, not so much physically, but because she wants to come back to him, because he has planted his image, all bloodily, in the middle of her gentle mind.

After a time he rolled up the letters and turned his smile round on to me. In fact, he may conceivably have felt really friendly towards me, for I know the other two had written nothing but good of me during our time together. But I was not inclined to cave in to the smile. We had a short and polite, and, of course, quite meaningless, conversation, as much on the offensive-defensive as two strange dogs! He spoke a good deal about his wife in very fluent Greek, and wanted me to talk about her. I am sure he was very anxious to know on what terms I am with her. He may have been jealous. Once or twice he certainly tried to catch me out over my answers. I think he was disappointed with what I had to tell him, and perhaps felt that it did not tally very well with the letters. But there!—one doesn't feel inclined to let a man, who has done the kind of things Tarrik of Marob has done, into the house and garden of one's friendship. I hope Erif will stay in Greece. It's the right place for her!

A rather lovely girl, not unlike Erif herself, only younger, brought in the child. I noticed that she wore a crown of gold and jewels and a very elaborate dress, and the King seemed very free and easy with her. Also I think she was pregnant, though this may only have been the slouching way in which these barbarian women stand. But it did occur to me that here was possibly one reason why Erif Der was not in Marob. The girls spoke a little Greek, but not much. As a matter of fact, I know something of their language, but I thought it as well not to say so. I gathered that she was called Linit.

The child is a jolly little creature, rosy and curly, more Erif's than his. We took the toys out. I must say, both the King and this Linit girl tried hard to explain to little Tisamenos that these pretty things came from his mother. But I doubt if he took it in. Most of the time he was either dumb or squealing with pleasure and excitement.

At last the King said: 'It is four days to midsummer. Until then I have to work, either here or in my own place. You will wait and see me in the flax market. After that I shall have time. You will tell me all the things you have not told me yet.' I thought that was rather clever of him. He added: 'You shall want for nothing while you are here,' and whistled loud and startlingly for a slave, to whom he whispered. And certainly since then the people at the inn have taken the utmost trouble to make me comfortable, and I gather there will be nothing to pay. If I knew I was going to sail away safely at the end of it, everything would be delightful, but there's a queer feeling about this town. I don't know quite what makes it, but I keep on suddenly finding myself at grips with the most horrible, undefined fear, the sort of thing I thought I had grown out of long ago and would never feel again. I repeat to myself that it is quite baseless and that fear of the unknown is a shameful thing for a reasonable, scientific-minded person to have in his head, but somehow I cannot entirely cast it off. It is partly, of course, that one is so utterly alone here, as far as mental processes are concerned, for none of the traders know Plato from Pythagoras, and if one talked to them about atoms they'd want to know how much a dozen one could sell them for in Alexandria!

I feel least uncomfortable when I'm writing. The play I told you about is getting on slowly; I'm afraid my heroine is a little hackneyed, though. Ask Timonoë to write me a nice letter telling me exactly how she'd answer if she was proposed to by (*a*) by a rather dirty cynic, (*b*) by an elderly tyrant with several other wives, and (*c*) by a nice young man, say me—or you, if you'd rather!

Well, to go on with my adventures. The King sent one of his courtiers to show me round the place, a really very decent young man called Kotka. He asked me to his house, where I met his wife, of whom Erif has spoken sometimes. But she did not say much to me, or produce any magic, as I rather hoped she might! Kotka talked quite a lot and enjoyed showing off his Greek. He seems to be devoted to the King, but of course it is early days to tell how sincere this is. I can't help suspecting that he might have a different story if one got to know him better. I've talked to him far more about Erif and Berris than I did to the King! He showed me some fine metal-work which he had, clasps and cups and quivers and decorations for saddles and sledge yokes, in which I could see the cruder and more barbaric beginnings of the art over which Berris Der has such mastery. They design from animal forms much more than he does (though he told me, I remember, that he used to himself at one time) and sometimes they are just too fantastic and illogical—for me, at any rate. I wonder if Berris has finished the inlaid table that I left him at work on.

The traders at my inn have been telling me something about this midsummer festival. The extraordinary part about it is that they half believe in it themselves. I had rather a heated argument with Menoitas and some of his friends over this. They were amazingly superstitious themselves, to begin with, continually talking about omens and vows and prophecies. I tried to put the rational point of view to them, quite gently, of course, milk for babes!—but they were genuinely shocked. I have been trying to make out just exactly what does happen at midsummer. There seems to be a procession with flowers and children dressed up, all very nice and innocent as far as one can make out, and then some kind of ceremony in the big market-place here, at which the King dances and sings, and the crowd performs some kind of religious rite, throwing stones and sticks about and into the middle of the square. I asked friend Menoitas if he meant that they actually stoned a sacrifice, but he said not, at least he did not think so. I am not sure how much the Greeks are allowed to see. He tells me that the object of all this is to encourage the sun, whose power now begins to decline! I do find it quite illogically annoying that any Greek should have so little idea of elementary physics as to suppose that the sun can be influenced. However, we all know the sun has been the centre of several very respectable and long-lived religions. In fact, our old comrades of the Stoa are a little bit mixed up with that—Divine Fire and what not! I do love to think of the distance the sun is from us, that lovely remoteness, the cool depths of space.

I gather that after this midsummer day affair every one is wildly excited, including the children, and the evening ends in a savage and erotic dance. I understand from Menoitas that I shall have the utmost difficulty in sleeping by myself on midsummer night. He certainly won't try to avoid destiny over this, but I rather think I will! The next day there is a bonfire in the same market-place and everything is, as they say, 'cleared up and burnt.' I suppose I should be less suspicious about it all, but that this Tarrik, this Corn King, is in charge of it. I have an impression that everything he touches will be somehow made horrible.

I wonder if there will be a sacrifice.

I wonder if I shall have to speak.

Farewell.

Letter Two

HYPERIDES TO TIMOKRATES, Live well ! I am sending this letter by a ship which is sailing tomorrow. You will see that it is written on odd scraps of paper at different times. At any rate, I am alive!

I AM A PRISONER in the King's house. I think he is going

to have me killed, probably by torture. That will not last for ever, and in the end I shall have the whole of time to myself, with no pain and no fear.

I have found paper and a pen here. I am writing in case—oh, I should like to explain! After all, it is my only immortality, and my play is not finished. I think, by what they said, that it will be some time yet before they come for me.

On midsummer eve the people in our inn made garlands, which they hung up in the morning early. I stayed indoors and listened to what was being said, which they thought I could not understand. It is incredible how full the world is of ignorance still! The sun is a dead and fiery body made up of the whirling together of atoms. It is far out of reach of earth and earth's air. The moon shines by the reflected light of the sun. The universe turns for ever in a spiral; earth and sun and moon and stars turn harmoniously within it; no man nor god nor force of any idea or passion can change the movement of the universe. I repeat that. Here and now in the King's house. The sun is a dead and fiery body, far out of reach of earth or any doings of man. It cannot be touched by the King of Marob, nor by any other mortal.

The procession began to go by. The inn people joined in, all except the slaves. As it seemed unlikely that there would be any dinner for some time, I joined in too, and so did the rest of the Greeks and half-Greeks. But they were just as full of it as every one else, and utterly refused to listen to me, saying that it would bring bad luck on the midsummer market. They sang all the songs, which were, as a matter of fact, quite gay, though rather tuneless and interrupted by rattles and children banging sticks together; and they made what appeared to be the suitable gestures, not always very polite. There were a certain amount of savages too, the inland fur-traders who had come down to Marob with bundles of skins and amber and resin for the midsummer market. They sang loudly, without, I think, understanding the words. Finally, we all got to the flax market, and every one stood round and the King began his dance. There was a most lovely clear blue sky with a few very tiny clouds on it. I suppose I shall never see that again. Nor my own sky between Hymettos and the sea. Athens. Athens. Athens. All that I mean by Athens.

Well, they said the King was the sun. And I began to talk about astronomy. I told everybody what really happens. I became angry and talked louder. I was mad because they would not listen to me. I spoke in Greek to the traders who tried hard to stop me, and then suddenly I began to speak to the Marob people themselves in their own language. I was surprised myself that I could speak it so well, with such fluency and command of idiom. They were surprised too for a few minutes. The King was running round the thing in the middle of the market. He ran straight at me and knocked me over with his hot arms. I think he was looking for a sacrifice. I think I am the sacrifice. When they come back for me I shall still speak to them about astronomy and the nature of the sun and the laws of the universe.

Erif and Berris, my friends, what a place you have landed me in. You don't know. Perhaps you never will. It does not alter the fact of our friendship. Timokrates, have I done well? Have I followed Epicuros, our master, who first understood that science, showing the laws of nature, also showed a unity and harmony beyond all superstition and all the horrors and follies which men have made for themselves? Timokrates. It helps me to write your name. It makes our friendship come stoutly into my mind. Timokrates. The garden at Athens. The light there. The leaves of the plane trees. Timonoë. Remember me, Timonoë. Timokrates, Menexenos, Nikoteles. There is no way of getting out of this room.

I AM GOING TO write this when I can. The sight of the words makes me feel not too utterly lost. When I heard them coming for me I took up the whole roll of paper and the pen and hid it in my tunic, buckling my belt hard over it. Black Holly said: 'You fool, to speak against the Chief's power! You are to say it is all lies and madness!' I shook my head and said: 'It was all true.' Kotka said, urgently and more gently: 'The Chief bears you no ill-will, but he cannot have these things said in Marob. It will break up our life. Even if it is true in Greece it is not true here.' I said: 'Truth is not a matter of place.' I saw Black Holly draw his dagger. But Kotka said: 'You can tell us other truths, only not this. That's hard for a Greek, but you must. Sphaeros did not hurt Tarrik's kingship; you are not to either.' I said: 'I will not deny science and my master.' Black Holly said: 'There's only one cure for pride!' He was going to cut my throat. I was thankful that it was to be a rational death like that with no secular or religious torture. But Kotka said: 'No, the Chief must decide.' So they tied my hands behind my back and shoved me into a still smaller room.

I was there that evening and the whole of the night, in great discomfort and not, of course, able to write. I was not hungry, but very thirsty. I slept a little, and the morning came. I wished Black Holly had killed me, because I thought I was likely to get a worse death from the Chief. Then there was violent shouting and screaming and other noise. I began to smell smoke. First smoke and then flame went past the small window of the room. The walls were stone but the roof was wooden, so it would catch and then fall in on me. Sparks blew in. I rolled to the far side of the room, choking and slightly burnt. The smoke got thicker. I felt the edges of the paper against my skin. I thought that would be burnt too. Then someone cut the rope. It was Kotka. He said: 'The Red Riders are on us. Up and fight, you Greek!' The roof had caught by then. If Kotka had not remembered me I should have been burnt to death in a few minutes.

I scrambled up and got out somehow into the street at the back of the Chief's house. I picked up a spike of some sort for a weapon and stopped a minute to breathe and stretch my arms. Then I ran towards the loudest noise.

I will say at once that the Red Riders had ridden up during the festival when every one was in the town and attacked the market, hoping to plunder both Marob and the southern traders. They managed to set fire to some houses and in the confusion took away goods and money, but they were being beaten out of the town even when I joined in. I was in a doorway most of the time, banging the legs of the horses and the riders when I could get at them. I had a piece of board for a shield. Then I think I was knocked over and perhaps stunned. The next thing that I knew was gradually becoming aware that I was slung over a saddle and that my head and arm were hurting abominably. Upside down like this I vomited several times against the horse's legs. It was like the end of the world.

I am not very certain of the next several days. At night
the jolting and the worst of the pain stopped, and I suppose
one ate and drank. There were horrible noises and smells
all the time. Then one day I found myself in a skin tent
and the Chief of Marob was sitting beside me. There was a
loud drumming and that was a thunderstorm on the tent;
the rain-cooled air filled it. I sat up. The Chief said: 'Are
you well enough to listen?' Then he explained. We are
prisoners of the Red Riders, and so are a certain number
of others. But the Red Riders are killing them a few at a
time in honour of their gods. They are tied on to an altar
and certain parts of their bodies, including finally the heart,
are cut out by the priests. We have not seen this, but we
have heard it. He and I are separate from the others. He
thinks they mean to use us for some great occasion. We
are well treated, but each of us has an iron fetter on one
ankle fastened to a longish raw-hide rope, and that to the
tent-pole. We have no knife and our tent seems to be in
the middle of the camp. There is apparently nothing to be
done, for the moment at least, but I have smoothed out the
paper and made a kind of ink with fruit juice. I asked the
Chief if he would like a piece to write on, but he said no.
I do not think he can settle down to write. He knows his
house was set on fire and he is horribly anxious about the
child. He has not told me yet how he came to be taken
prisoner. I am not at all sure how much he wants to talk to
me, but he has been kind. My arm is a mass of bruises still,
but the bone does not seem to be broken. He had several
arrow wounds, which are healing well. I have dressed those
he cannot reach for himself. He is sitting on the other side
of the tent now. Both of us are, of necessity, growing very
disgusting stubbly beards. Still, there's no one to kiss! I
should be glad enough to tell him now about Erif and how
her mind is towards him all the time and how she sent me
really to try and help him. But I do not know whether to
speak. I think, though, that he will be a goodish companion
in any misfortune.

The two chiefs of the Red Riders are called Tigru and
Diorf. Tigru at least is even more revolting than the rest
of the savages. He is short and rather fat, with light eyes
and his front teeth filed to points and great ear-rings. Such
women as we have seen are very fat too. A Marob woman

would always kill herself sooner than be carried off by these savages. Diorf is taller and squints.

THERE IS STILL NOTHING to do, or if there is anything it is Tarrik who is doing it, not I. But I am going to write down some of this that is happening between Tarrik and me, because, whatever darkness comes, it is good that friendship has been. For some days we did not talk. I was still suspicious of him because he is violent and I believed him cruel, because he does not think like me, and I believed he did not think at all, because—I suppose most of all—he is Erif's husband and I did not want him to be loved by her. And he of me because I was a Greek, an Athenian, a fellow-citizen of Epigethes (he has told me about that and I pride myself that, having worked with Berris Der, I understand), a fellow-philosopher of Sphaeros, and—again most of all!—a friend of his Erif. Then, through sheer force of loneliness and anxiety, we began to talk, roughly at first, each trying to defend himself against the other, but gradually leaving that behind.

He said one day: 'Plenty of people will think this was your doing, bringing bad luck on the midsummer market. Quick work! But I'm certain your friend Menoitas will say so.' I said: 'Menoitas is sufficiently stupid and uneducated to think anything. He is not my friend. I gather you don't think so yourself?' He said: 'I'm afraid you're not an important enough philosopher for the seasons to pay you much attention!' And he showed his teeth at me a little. I said: 'Of course I am quite utterly unimportant, but you admit I was right?' 'Right?' said Tarrik. 'Right to talk like that! If you had been I wouldn't have jumped on you.' I: 'But you at least don't believe this pack of nonsense about your being the sun!' Tarrik: 'It's not my business rat-hunting after little scraps of truth. I know that what I do works.' I: 'By coincidence, sometimes.' Tarrik: 'No. Because—But why should I tell you, Greek!' I shrugged my shoulders; I was a little angry. I did not think I wanted to know at all. They brought us in our supper of roots and milk and boiled horse-flesh.

It was the next day that Tarrik spoke again. I am ashamed that it was he and not I who spoke first. He said suddenly: 'I work the Year in Marob, because as the Corn King I am wholly a part of the life of the place. It is not only that the people believe in me, but I am not separate from the grain and the cattle and the sap creeping up the green veins of the plants. Whatever I do goes out like a wave to the rest of my place. It is all one. It is all the way of Nature.' I knew that last for a Stoic phrase; it was queer at the end of the other thing. It set me suddenly loose to ask the question which I suppose Erif would have wanted me to ask: 'That is you as Corn King. But I believe there is another part of you which is separate—which cannot look at things in that mystic way?' He said: 'Yes. Worse luck for me! But the thing that matters is being Corn King. When the alarm came this time I was in the flax market. They were on the western side of the town, where my Place is. I went straight there to guard my things. I had not enough men, and two arrows went through the soft part of my arm, nailing me to the door. That was how they got me. But I am inclined to think that I saved the sacred things, the Corn-cap, the Basket, the Wheel, the Plowshare of Marob. I went there, you see, not to my son.' He threw back his head and gasped, and I said again I was sure no harm had come to the child. 'If anything has,' he said, 'I would sooner be dead than alive and needing to tell Erif that—But half of them would have died for him, Kotka or Linit.' I think I feel almost the same about that little Tisamenos. Erif has talked of him so much. Besides, he was a nice little boy. One doesn't care to have small children hurt.

I think, by the way, that I understand also about Linit, the Spring Queen. She is, as I supposed, pregnant, which means to these people that their seasons will be fruitful, but she keeps herself reserved from Tarrik apart from his existence as Corn King and regards herself as the formal substitute for Erif Der. When she comes back, Linit will marry and have much honour. Yet this Corn King and Spring Queen are kind and tender towards one another, as the relationship demands. It seems to me rather complicated, but I am allowing Tarrik to convince me. After all, if he can, why not?

I do not know if I am helping Tarrik at all. I can see how he has been hurting himself just as Erif said, and how it has led him to cruelty. I started by trying to get him back out of this, out of magic and Stoicism to the first principles of science. But now I find that the magic part of him does not admit my reasoning. He says, in effect, that this kind of truth does not apply to his world. It is only a pattern of half-life. Have I been halving life up to now? It is very difficult to believe that of oneself, but it is perhaps good practice to try to! If only I knew if we would ever—Ah, no use writing that.

I HAVE NOT WRITTEN for three days. At first I was feeling an acute depression, partly for obvious reasons and partly because I was thinking out this business of Tarrik and Marob, so that at least if we are to die we can die clear headed and in more or less the same communion of ideas. Now I believe I have it ready to set out.

I do not know how mankind began, and I doubt if it is much use speculating on origins, but I know more or less, from history and observation, how they have been for the last several hundred years, and how they are now. I take it, very tentatively, that the thing could perhaps be put into a formula of approximately this kind.

It is natural for men to live in communities and painful to them when these communities break up. The closer the community is, the better for the general happiness, for there they have a unity ready provided for them, easy to accept, hard not to accept. They need never question: they need only live. And death is not a severance from the community, but merely another facet of it.

Yet, as men's minds grow, they have to question. And as they question and become different one from another and want to be still more different and to lead each his own separate life, so the community breaks up. The people in it are no longer part of a unity and harmony that includes their friends and their dead and their unborn—a unity in time—and no longer part of the earth and the crops and the festivals of the community—a unity in space. They question the gods, and the gods crumble and fade and are no more help. When this day comes a man must stand up for himself and face the truth as far as he knows it, and be no more helped by his citizenship and his sense of being part of a better whole. And it will be well for him if he is a strong man then.

Now in general this comes gradually, and from generation

to generation men have time to grow up until they are old enough and brave enough to wed with the naked truth and perhaps beget wonderful children on her. They can save themselves from the chaos and fear of being cityless and godless. The foolish ones invent for themselves new gods, each a god and saviour for himself. But the wise ones recognise this as a folly, and the only comfort and substitute they make for themselves is the love and trust of their friends and the excitement of the hunt after knowledge. Very often too, when men suddenly separate out like this, there is a change in the government of a State. It was because of this, I think, that we got democracy, in Hellas at least.

But here in Marob there is and has been a close community in which, I suppose, all were to some extent happy, because all were to some extent in communion with the others, though even so I am not sure of them all, especially of the women, about whom it is always hard to tell. There were two who were the keystone of the community, the Corn King and the Spring Queen. Then through, as is usual, a combination of circumstances, but mostly because the Greek modes of thought, and especially those of Sphaeros the Stoic, had suddenly come on them, these two began to question, and, before they understood what was happening or could retrace their steps, they were out of their community and had to stand up unhelped and face a world of apparent chaos and pain and contradiction and moral choices which, being so thoroughly disturbed by old Sphaeros, they could not deal with.

I do wonder if Sphaeros knows what he has done, and, if so, whether he regrets it at all!

I THINK I AM BEGINNING to be able to explain all this to Tarrik. But for these things which have happened to us both I could never have done it, but now I have imaginative good-will towards him, and I can get into his mind. He does not set up barriers against me. I am doing what Erif asked me to do. I am being faithful to my friends.

We have talked about her a great deal and about how she is to be saved. It seem to us that only some very beautiful and terrible event will shake her out of the solitude where she is, back into the life of Marob, and into Tarrik's life if he has it still. We do not think that she can save herself entirely by any intellectual process. Women can very rarely do that. I do not say that one kind of mind is better or worse than another, but I do know that men and women are different. What I seem to want to do with Erif Der is to bring her back into godhead and magic and superstition. Yet it is not quite simply that. It is just that I want her to be completely herself, and she cannot be herself alone, any more than one honey bee separated from its hive and its flowers can be said to be a true bee at all.

I am beginning to accept all this about plowing and Harvest. I am beginning to see the way in which it is compatible with science. Obviously, Harn Der is dead and ended: there is no more Harn Der. But so long as he is still in the minds of the Marob people and in Tarrik's own mind, his image will be projected on to Tarrik. I am trying to give Tarrik the idea of death as complete sleep and finish, and a cessation from action of any sort, even the kind of consciousness of a sleep-walker. I swear by my master that I am not thinking of that all the time in connection with ourselves! And I am not afraid. Or at least only of the pain. Before it comes I shall have Tarrik standing on his feet.

He has to save himself through his mind. He has begun to tell me what are the things that entangle and horrify him. He said: 'Even if we escape now, yet when I begin to grow old, when other men have peace and comfort and story-telling to grand-children round the fire, they will come one day and cut my throat. They will cut my throat in my own place and Tisamenos will eat me, eat my flesh!' He looked shudderingly down at his own legs and body. I confess I was a little horrified myself, but I said: 'Why not? He will not do it from choice, any more than you did yourself when the thing happened. It is the kind of action which one has been led to suppose is awful and shocking, but only because our ancestors did it once for pleasure, and now our taste is so utterly turned away from it that we are in revolt against our ancestral blood. When you are dead you will not feel or know. It will be all one whether you are eaten by worms or men or fire.' And I said : 'You will be spared old age, the misery and shame of not being able to do accustomed things any longer, the pains of disease and loosening teeth, and no more love, and the distress of seeing your companions in the same state.' I said then: 'What happens to the Spring Queen?' He said: 'My mother died when I was a child, trying to bring to birth another son, who died too. But the custom is that there are always new Spring Queens, so that it is very seldom that any woman is still Spring Queen when she grows old. Yet,' he said, 'I think Erif would mind dying that way less than I do.' And then he said suddenly: 'But after all, I wonder if you are not right. Perhaps there is nothing really so bad about it.' If he can go on thinking that!

Is it stupid of me to be glad all the same that this is not going to happen to Erif Der?

But it is not that alone. He is up against the whole idea of the death of the individual. I wonder if I can explain to him that it seems less difficult to me now, since I have got this notion of a close community so well into my head. So long as one is still in one's community! In the Garden. In Marob. There is no such thing as an individual. We are not divided one from another, friend from friend. It is hard to be sure of that when there are sundering seas and wars and poverty. But yet I know I am sure. I will make Tarrik sure too! Before we die.

TARRIK HAS BEEN TALKING to the chiefs of the Red Riders. They came into the tent and stared at us and pointed, as they always do. We are still odd beasts for them. Tarrik is both a strange and a sacred beast. They know he was the Corn King and wonder-worker of Marob. Once they stripped him and looked at his body for signs. He did not resist and they did not try to hurt him, but he could not sleep that night because they had touched him so much. Ever since the first days he has been trying to talk to Tigru and Diorf, really to hold their attention. He has told them that the Marob people would give them yearly tribute of gold and wine and women if they would let him and the rest of the prisoners go. At first I thought he even meant it. But the Red Riders cannot or will not take this in. They are either too stupid or not stupid enough! They did not answer him. But lately Tigru has seemed to attend. He has a Marob girl who was taken this time, in his tent. We did not know about her at first, but now she screams and screams. He would like to get other women. She is the first who has been taken alive for a long time. He came in today without Diorf and said that if Tarrik sent for a hundred women and two hundred head of cattle, and had them delivered at the edge of the forest, he and I would be released. Tarrik said he would like Diorf's word on it too.

Then it became clear that Tigru was speaking for himself, and the other savage was still determined to sacrifice us. Tigru whispered at us greasily. He is taking a risk in going against the feeling of the camp. Tarrik said he would write a letter and Tigru must come back for it after midnight. He said that midnight was his own most sacred time and that an order signed then would be obeyed. That was the kind of rigmarole Tigru could understand. He nodded and went away, oozing a little at the lips with the thought of the women and the fresh meat.

Tarrik says he is going to try and kill Tigru when he comes back and then cut our ropes and try to escape. I will help him over the killing. But we both think that we are almost sure to be caught on our way through the camp. We will have Tigru's weapons and we will not let them take us alive again.

We have said good-bye to one another. We both agree that this chance is worth taking. I will buckle the paper under my belt again. Oh, Erif, I wish you knew that Tarrik and I had made friends!

Letter Three

HYPERIDES, SON OF LEONTEOS, to Timokrates, son of Metrodoros, live well! Oh, my adventures! I will tell you everything from the place where my odd scraps of paper left off.

We lay down and rested, so that we should be as strong as possible when the moment came. We scarcely talked at all: the time for that was over. The camp became quiet, though we heard voices now and then. We listened hard, because we had to find out where the horses were tethered. At last we thought we were sure of the direction. Tigru came in stealthily and fastened the flap of the door behind him. Tarrik stood up, holding the letter, and began to talk, manœuvring so as to get the savage immediately in front of the tent-pole and me. I was in shadow, holding a piece of cloth torn from Tarrik's thick shirt.

Tarrik sprang and knocked Tigru against the tent-pole. He got his wrists at once and fought him hand to hand, while from behind I stuffed the cloth into his mouth. I found afterwards that I had scraped the skin off two fingers on his filed teeth, and later they festered. He was horribly strong. While Tarrik still held him I worked down towards the throat. It seemed to be hard muscles and sinews all over. I could not get at the life in it. I squeezed the whole thing back as hard as I could against the tent-pole, but I did not think I was anywhere near killing him. He made the most filthy choked noises, and Tarrik grunted like a beast with pain and effort. It all took incredibly long, or seemed to. It was more horrible than you would think possible, Timokrates, the feel of that twitching throat! I did not think I could go on holding it much longer. My strength was giving. I trembled all over. Then suddenly I got the impression that something had broken, I still don't quite know what, and the body jerked and then went slack.

Tarrik and I took the weapons and cut our hide ropes. I was slow but he was amazingly quick. For a moment I was afraid he would not wait for me. Then we slipped out. It is very difficult to know for oneself even, still more to write, what happened. But sometimes now when I am just going to sleep I get a kind of flash vision that dates from then of Tarrik stabbing down over a man's shoulder into the great vein. I know I was wounded somehow and he pulled me on. I know he cut through the hobbles of two horses and slashed them into a gallop, holding on to the bridle of mine.

I know we were separated in a wood for some horrible, but most likely quite short, space of time. I know I was blundering on, desperate with panic, half falling off my horse, and Tarrik found me again and we rode all that night by stars we knew in gaps of the thick trees. Twice we drew into a thicket and hid. My forehead was cut and bleeding and he tied it up with a pad of moss. We had no food, but we drank from a brook. Spaces of blankness came over my mind. It was a real and horrible pain to stay awake and balanced. He put his arms round me and held me on the horse while I rode sleeping. We did not dismount till the evening of the next day.

Tarrik knew all the time in what direction we had to go, or if he was ever in doubt I never guessed it. He seemed to take us straight. We chewed leaves and roots and any berries or nuts we could find. He had Tigru's sword, but I had dropped the dagger somewhere, probably in the first galloping off. Somehow I could not begin to realise that we even might be going to live.

Then! Then, Timokrates, a very long way off, at the end of the day, under a darkening sky, I saw a little pale line that was not grass nor tree-tops: the line of the sea; the clear way between oneself and home. And I bent over my horse's mane and fell to weeping with joy and weariness, and Tarrik wept with me because he was to be King again and because very soon he would know whether his child were alive or dead.

From the north-east we came down across the grass plain to Marob, and Tarrik looked at the fields. 'It will be nearly Harvest,' he said, and then he laughed and threw back his stiff beard and said again: 'It is a queer business, but I am done with Harn Der now. The dead has dropped off me. It was, as you say, all folly. I will show the people.' We were riding over a field that had just been cut, over the clean, sharp stubble. 'Harvest,' he said; 'Harvest,' crooning round the word. I did not doubt that the thought of the cut corn had become a solid thing in his mind, a little bright-edged eidolon, instead of the mere idea it was in mine. He looked, himself—how shall I put it?—sun-ripe and golden and full of gifts.

We saw a farm in the distance and went there on foot, hoping to find, as we did, somebody quite stupid who would not recognise the King nor be much interested in strangers. Tarrik did most of the talking, beginning tentatively: 'There'll be fine doings in the town now.' He thought he would be sure to find out exactly when harvest was that way. The slave-girl we were talking to immediately burst out into complaints about having been left behind, and we found that this day was already the first day of Harvest.

Tarrik went on to say what a grim business it had been at midsummer and the girl said anyway they'd got a younger and better-looking Corn King now, bless his heart! 'Younger—' said Tarrik, and stopped. I knew he was wondering if it could be his child. But the next minute it came out that it was Gold-fish, Erif's younger brother. Tarrik was finding it difficult to speak. I said:

'It was a good thing no more got killed at midsummer than were.' 'All the more to get killed afterwards,' said the girl, picking up her spinning again.

That was maddening. We did not know what to say. I asked her to show us the way to the well. Half-way she said: 'I was in town then. Why, I saw Black Holly killed!' The Chief started like a horse, but I gripped his arm and said: 'Ah yes, but the others?' She shook her head. 'But I tell you what I did see,' she said. 'I saw the big horse go by a-gallop, and that poor innocent baby holding on to its mane as gay as a bird, love him!—and the white-faced lady lashing out with her big whip at the ones that tried to catch her!' 'Klint?' I asked quickly, before Tarrik could speak. 'Aye,' she said, 'and I'm glad he's away, for all his father!' Then she suddenly glared at me and said: 'Who are you, anyway, not to know that?' I laughed and said, of course, I was there too and signed to Tarrik to come away. He was holding on to the well curb and licking his lips with the strain of it.

We went back. He said nothing for some time, either in comment or explanation. I scarcely dared to ask. When he spoke it was heavily and quietly. He said: 'I must go back tonight.' Then he began to thank me, not, I think, for anything special, but for just being there when he wanted me. I was—oh, very much moved, Timokrates! After that he gave me directions as to where to go the next day, and after nightfall he rode off himself.

I think I shall tell you now what had been happening while we were away—better than telling you how I stayed awake for hours that night wondering vainly about it and very anxious for Tarrik. It was like this. When Tarrik was taken prisoner and they thought he was killed, the Council of Elders, who had mostly been Harn Der's friends, and had never forgotten what happened, although up to now constrained to think they had, decided to get power over Marob. To do this, they chose as Corn King the eighteen-year-old Gold-fish, my Erif's brother, and said they would make him Chief and war leader as well when he grew older and wiser. But I think they always intended to keep that power for themselves. This was all decided the day after the raid when everything was still topsy-turvy, and they put it into action at once, seizing on the Corn King's

Place and his house itself. There was violent street-fighting, in the course of which Black Holly was killed, and Kotka, wounded already by the Red Riders, was wounded again almost to death. When we came back all these weeks later he was still not able to move.

They meant to have the child either killed or in some way maimed so that it could never be Chief or Corn King. This seemed to them, I believe, a right thing to do for Marob, on the grounds that both its father and mother were proved unlucky. They were afraid for themselves and their food. The girl Linit barred the doors of the Chief's house and tried to gain time, for she would never believe that Tarrik had been killed. The next thing that happened I am telling you as it was told to me without comment. All I can say is that this is a very strange country, and that one has evidence of things occurring here which would certainly be against all the laws of Nature at home.

Essro, the widow of Yellow Bull, whom Tarrik killed, looked down the well in the middle of her farm-yard. The water twenty feet below was like a little dark, round mirror. She saw the face of her sister-in-law, Erif Der, looking up at her out of it. The image stretched its arms as if it were trying to hold something. Then that faded and the image of the child Klint came instead, not as he is now, but as a small baby, as he was when his mother left him. Essro rode north as fast as her horse could go. I have never seen her myself, but they say she is a timid and unhappy woman. I believe she made this long ride in great fear. When she got to Marob she somehow managed, in some woman's way, to let Linit know, and Linit let Klint down to her through a side-window. And Essro galloped away with him through the streets of Marob, and back to her farm.

There are other things that are said here. That Essro, pursued, threw down a thorn branch which grew into a whole wood of thorns between her and the pursuers. That she called into the air and hornets rose up behind her and stung them. That she did even more fantastic and incredible things. All I know is that the Council left her in peace with the child and now she has him with her own son down on the farm by the marshes.

The time, anyhow, went on to Harvest. Gold-fish was put into the Chief's house and seems to have enjoyed himself there, and had plenty of feasts and gave presents to every one. Linit took shelter with Disdallis and helped her to nurse Kotka. When it came near the day of Harvest, the Council chose a man to be the other actor in the Corn Play, one of themselves, a man called Tsomla, a big, bearded fighter. They had already given him Wheat-ear, Erif's little sister (though I suppose she was considered rather as Harn Der's daughter by the Council) for his wife. He waited the middle night of Harvest, as the custom was, in the dark, locked Place of the Corn King.

A little after midnight Tarrik came back to Marob. He knocked in some secret and peculiar manner on the door of his Place, and the old woman who is guardian opened it and knew him. She strewed some kind of stupefying leaf on the fire, and the other actor in the Corn Play went so deep asleep that he did not wake fully for three days. She took his clothes off and Tarrik put them on, and then she looked at their faces side by side and with plucking and moulding of fingers and with dark and pale dyes she made Tarrik look like the man Tsomla. She put white powder in Tarrik's new beard to make it look like the other's, and I think it likely that they also went through certain rites together.

In the morning Gold-fish came to open the door to the other actor, the Corn Man. Tarrik says that at first no one saw that there was anything strange, but as he walked beside Gold-fish in the great procession to the stubble field, Gold-fish began glancing at him and then hastily away, more and more uneasily. But he said nothing and Tarrik went into the centre of the field to do his dance with the new Spring Queen, the quite young girl whom Gold-fish had chosen.

I was among the crowd then, rather behind and quite disguised by my beard and my barbarian clothes. I watched the dance between the Corn Man and the Spring Queen, ending in the rather alarming ritual of death and mourning. And I gradually became aware—but later than anyone else, I suppose, because I was not really part of Marob—that there was a growing uneasiness among the crowd of watchers and worshippers, spreading outward from the young Corn King. I have an idea that Tarrik had looked at him in some rather shattering way from behind the beard and the mask of Tsomla's face.

Into the black-robed company of mourning women bounded the Harvest Fool, the one whose business it is to break up all the sadness and tension with a series of peculiarly crude and school-boyish jokes. Quite often I could not understand the words, but the import was plain enough. The men of Marob began to rock with shrill and nervous laughter. They seemed prepared for anything. The Fool danced over to the black winding-sheet above the Corn Man and suddenly it lifted and Tarrik bounded out, declaring himself with every movement of his body, crying aloud: 'Tarrik and Marob! Tarrik and Marob!' as I had heard it at Delphi in the moment when the stones struck my head.

The first thing that happened (and, in a way, the last thing, for after that there was only one possible issue) was that Gold-fish, the Corn King, howled and scrambled up the bank and bolted. He was found again two days later hiding under a bush and brought back. Every one has been quite kind to him. When that occurred, the young Spring Queen nearly bolted too, but then I rather think curiosity got the better of fear; anyway, she stayed. The Fool had to stay whether he liked it or not, for Tarrik had a compelling grip on him. Then a man near me shouted: 'He is risen again! Tarrik! Tarrik! Tarrik and Marob!' And then voice after voice picked it up and shouted that the corn was sprung, the dead was living, the King had come back to his people. I think most of them believed then, and for all I know believe still, that he had really been killed and was now born again out of the cut and harvested corn. This was partly because of the way they thought he had died, guarding the sacred things from the Red Riders, a death which had in it the seeds of rebirth!

It is very curious, Timokrates, and I wonder what I ought to do, for I cannot help sometimes believing that I am here for the beginning of a new religion. Could I stop it now? Or have I the right to even if I know it to be based on a lie? Is it any use or any good trying to keep Marob away from its gods? Should I or should I not allow myself to be compelled by my philosophic principles to hurt my friends? Anyhow, it is desperately exciting, the most exciting thing that has ever come my way!

The whole of Marob followed their King in a dance of

most pure and wild happiness across the stubble field. I danced with them. It came easily; it would have been hard for me then not to dance. There were a few Greeks there, but not Menoitas, thank goodness, or any of the ones who had been in the same inn with me before. They might have stopped me from being happy a day with the crowd. The Council had no chance of speech or action, even if they had wanted to go against him, which I very much doubt—then, at any rate. I think they were only hoping that this reborn, this stronger and luckier God King, would spare his power and be merciful to them. A few of them, I suppose, realised that he had been a prisoner and then escaped, but even that seemed to mean that he was now completely lucky and in the confidence of Nature. It was almost as startling to escape from the Red Riders as from death. So the Council danced too.

I found that a boat was sailing that night, so I sent off my bits of letters then and there. I went to the Chief's house and slept until late the next morning. Tarrik himself woke me. It startled me to see him suddenly with his beard shaved off, and at first I got the old impression of the smiling, lazy savage. I was embarrassed at speaking to him. Then it became clear that he was the same as he had been when we were prisoners (and, I suppose, the same as he had been to Erif). He told me the news. He had been up and about since early that morning and had summoned a meeting of the Council. He was going to this at once. Several of his friends were dead, killed in the street-fighting, including Black Holly, who had always been someone completely safe and trustworthy. The first tremendous wave of half-religious feeling for him in Marob must inevitably die down; he was not sure of his wisest course. We talked for some little time.

He went alone to the Council, and I shaved my beard too, and had a steam bath, curiously refreshing, especially when they put bundles of mint and tansy over the hot oven before the water is poured on. I wish you could try one! One begins to sweat fairly soon and when the slave begins to rub one down the dirt comes out by handfuls. I had clean clothes too—every stitch clean!—and one of them gave my hair a thorough cut and comb, which I'm afraid it needed.

Since that day the Council have met fairly often. Tarrik did not say what happened at the first meeting, and he does not say much now, but he comes out smiling, like someone who has won a fight. I think it is hard work, but he will do it. He knows he can. There are so many things he is no longer afraid of! I wonder if you think it is quite idiotic of me to get so excited about a barbarian chief. Conceivably it is, but then Tarrik as he is now is largely my doing—or do I flatter myself as a teacher?—and it is fascinating to see how he works! Yes, I think it is reasonable of me to be deeply interested.

He has asked me to stay, and I will stay at any rate until next year. I'm getting on like a house on fire with my play. I seem to have accumulated ideas in all that time away from the manuscript. A new comic character has turned up, and the heroine has really made one or two quite smart epigrams! As a matter of fact I shall probably have to rewrite a good deal; some of the early speeches look simply childish now. And what a lovely lot of new metaphors I've picked up!

One thing I must tell you. That same day, immediately after the Council meeting, Tarrik went to Kotka's house. As we walked through the streets, men and women ran out to touch the Corn King. Some of them cut pieces out of his coat and he pretended not to notice. News of his coming seemed to go half a street ahead of us. Women were throwing coloured cloths and coats out of the windows and made a wonderfully gay and joyful rag-bag decoration. Disdallis herself opened the door of Kotka's house.

Kotka was lying on a couch covered with rugs; he was dead-white and a sunken scar showed up like a streak of red paint across his cheek; it was scarcely healed. The whole room felt and smelt of illness. There seemed to me to be any amount of crocks full of old wives' brews on the table, and I'm almost sure some of the odd things which were lying about the room were meant for charms. The pregnant woman Linit was sitting at the foot of the bed, and Disdallis must have been there too, a minute before. Kotka turned his head towards his Chief, but slowly and in utter weakness; he tried to raise his hands and failed. Tarrik came and stood beside him. The two women stayed very quiet, watching. He had not spoken to Linit, but she did not seem to be demanding it. He stretched his arms, and it did seem to me that when he did this he grew bigger, filled more of the space in the room. However, doubtless this was only a subjective impression. Then he stooped over Kotka and took his hands. He said: 'I have risen. You rise too!' He lifted Kotka's hands, but I do not think he used much force, not enough to lift a man's heavy body, certainly. But Kotka sat up in a series of slow jerks, his eyes held all the time by Tarrik's eyes. Some of the rugs fell off him. A curious flush came and went and came again in his cheeks. Under the lower rugs his legs stirred. Tarrik moved sideways, so that Kotka must slue himself round to face him. The man's legs came over the side of the bed. He stood up.

Tarrik said again: 'Walk. Come into the sun. You are healed. I have made you well.' It was all as simple as that. Kotka took a step forward with one bare, bloodless foot. Tarrik walked backwards, still holding his hands, to some extent holding him up, but not much. Slowly they went out of the room and through another room to the open court at the back of the house where there were pot-herbs and cooped fowls. Disdallis drew back curtains and opened doors, silently, so that there was no check in their walking. I could see that Kotka was trembling a good deal, especially about the legs, but he did not seem to be in any pain. When they were outside Tarrik turned him round so as to face the sun and said: 'Now sit and get warm again. You are healed, Kotka.' Disdallis seemed to be expecting this, because she and one of the men had already brought out a large chair. He sat down in it, not exhausted, but like a man who has walked perhaps ten miles and is glad to rest for a short time. Linit had brought a coat which they slipped over him, for he was wearing nothing but a linen shirt.

After that he and Tarrik talked quite ordinarily about a number of things, and laughed quite often. The women joined in after a time and so did I. It all seemed perfectly easy. When he left, Tarrik said he would be back soon, and for a few days he was there as often as he could spare the time. I usually went with him. The third day Kotka could walk by himself without help; the wound on his cheek skinned over. Now you would scarcely know he had ever been ill.

I wish, of course, that I had been given the chance to

examine him before all this. It is difficult to find out exactly from the women what was wrong with him, except that he had been very much battered about and there were several deep flesh wounds which had not healed nicely. I do not think any bones had been broken, except possibly a rib, which would normally have mended between the fighting and Tarrik's return in any case. But certainly he was utterly strengthless and drowsy, though not able to sleep deeply, and he could not even feed himself. I suppose it was partly acute depression, but I am quite sure that a very great deal of it was physical. And now he is well.

I wonder what you will make of this! It's the kind of thing one must either make up one's mind to or dismiss as a pure invention. Well, I shan't be surprised if you simply put me down as a liar. Obviously, after all, these things don't happen! But I saw it.

There have been all sorts of other excitements, bullfighting and horse-racing and goodness knows what else, and any amount of feasts. Do I like the Marob food? Well, to be quite candid, no! And there's some hunting, which is dull as the country is so flat, and hawking, especially in the marshes, which I enjoy. Oh, yes, and Tarrik took me down to see little Klint at Essro's farm in the south. He was received with extreme ceremony, and Essro welcomed him, wearing the most amazing, stiff, embroidered dress and a cone three feet high on her head, like some very curious goddess come to life. I noticed that she did not touch him if she could possibly help it. They talked mostly about some road which the Chief is having built through the marshes; I gather her ex-husband had something to do with it. Klint was delighted to see his father again, but didn't seem much distressed when he agreed to let him stay with Essro and her small boy—they were great allies, of course!—until the next spring.

You won't hear from me again this year, as the last ships are sailing for Byzantium and the south now, but this screed is long enough to do you for winter! But I'll write again when there's a chance of the letter being sent off, and perhaps I'll be able to send you a copy of my play—I think I shall be able to get it copied here as soon as it's finished. Of course, if you like to talk to one of the libraries about publication—? Seriously, I should be immensely grateful. And anyway, let me know what you think of it. My love to every one. I hope you are all well. I am! And tell the children I'll bring them back some marvellous toys, lovely painted wooden beasts that one can make walk—and a doll in Marob clothes!

Farewell.

PART VI

Dream on, who can!

O the bush, the briery bush,
It pricks my heart full sore.
If once I get out of the briery bush
I'll never get in any more.

O sweetheart, have you brought my golden ball
And come to set me free?
Or have you come to see me hung
Upon the gallows tree?

NEW PEOPLE IN THE SIXTH PART

Greeks
Nikagoras, a Messenian
Kerkidas of Megalopolis
Gyridas, the younger son of Phoebis and Neareta

Macedonians and Others
Alexander, commander-in-chief under
  Antigonos Doson
Demetrios of Pharos
Spartans, helots, Megalopolitans, Macedonians,
  Egyptians and others

CHAPTER ONE

NIKAGORAS THE MESSENIAN looked through the deed slowly, standing by the table, touching the table with the tips of all four fingers. Kleomenes sat, looking away, because if he had looked up it was quite certain that the eyes of Nikagoras the Messenian would have slid over the edge of the paper and met his, and he would have had to respond to them with some impossible cordiality. Yet why, after all, should he have this dislike for the excellent Nikagoras who had sold him the estate, saying he could pay for it after the war? He forced himself to look up at the deed being rolled and tied and placed by Nikagoras in the breast of his tunic, over the heart. Kleomenes had written his name on it. There was his name now next the Messenian's heart! 'Delighted,' said the man, 'delighted to have been of any service to the King of Sparta!' And 'Till we meet again!' said Kleomenes heartily, and the door shut.

He called, and she came in to his hand, his slave-girl, his mistress, lovely, lovely Archiroë in the dress he had given her, the very thin dress that hung and swayed from the tips of her breasts. Her long legs moved under the transparent web like a swimmer's under water. He looked at them with gladness, beckoned her over to stand beside him close, where he could stroke and grip and feel the flesh quiver still as though again and always virgin. Not a Spartiate woman used to commanding and managing. He did not know he was thinking that. His eyebrows arched, his tongue stuck out between his lips, he pulled her about gently, a gentle swing-swong. When he was with her he was enclosed in bodily warmth and ease, the starting out of easy sweat in the pressing and wrestling of love, the sweet smell of hair and armpits, the long, close, dizzy meeting of lips. There was nothing to puzzle and disturb him. She was right for a soldier's woman. He gave her his half of the deed and said: 'I have got you this, for yourself, in case anything happens.'

She looked at him with widening, deer's eyes. How lovely that she still flushed and paled when he spoke to her! She said: 'What is it?'

He answered: 'A farm in Messenia. A dowry. To make you safe, you pretty thing!'

'But you're not sending me away!' Her arms went out to him.

'No,' he laughed, 'but if I die what do you suppose will happen to you? If the other women get you!'

She said sadly: 'I saw them again today. They came to take—to take some of *her* clothes out of the great chest to send to Egypt for the little princess. Your mother had asked to have it done.'

'Which of them?'

'Panteus' Philylla and Milon's Chrysa. I wanted to help them, but they wouldn't let me.'

'What did they say?'

'Unkind things. They said them to one another for me to hear; they wouldn't even notice me myself. I know I'm only a stranger and a slave here.'

'As well I've got you the farm. Agh, you women!'

'We have to be like that,' she said softly. 'It's deep in us. They're jealous. I know; I would be. Have you got to write letters now, my own master, or shall I sing? Shall I play my pipe? Shall I stroke your head? It was a waste to get me the farm. How should I ever want it? If you die, my King, there's nothing left for me to live for.'

'Exactly. That's why I got the farm. Now there is something! Rub down on to my shoulder, Archiroë. I'm stiff there.'

'Turn a little—so, against my knee. Ah, you must keep quiet; how can I do it when you kiss me so hard? What would I want with a farm if you were dead? I should die too.'

'It takes more than that to make one kill oneself, my dear! I want your hair loose. Take the pin out.'

'But wasn't it very expensive?'

'Yes, and I haven't paid for it yet. But there's no hurry. When old Ptolemy starts sending me my money again.'

Her oil-soaked, rubbing hands checked, let slip the shoulder muscle. 'I didn't know he had stopped.'

'That's not one of the things you're meant to think about, pretty. Go lower. Hai, you little bitch, how your fingers walk about me like settling birds! Lower.'

'Keep quiet, then. Don't pull me! What, already? Oh, oh, come then, I'm yours. Ah, you do want me still!'

All the same, it was a bad business that Ptolemy had sent nothing all that spring, nothing but letters excusing himself. He had put up a statue to King Kleomenes. God, when the mercenaries were all leaving because he had no pay for them! They went regretfully, for they were good professionals who valued a brilliant and capable commander. But men must live. So they went over to Antigonos and Aratos, both good generals too, though less daring and sudden and exciting to work with.

It was incredibly hard raising money. He had nothing to pledge, not even Sparta, for, after all, he must always remember that he was not a tyrant, but the head of the revolution and constitutional King by acceptance of the citizens, with whom in the end it rested whether he should remain King and with what powers. Nowadays especially there were plenty to remind him of his position. It was difficult to know where to turn. Young King Antiochos of Syria was busy with his own rebels; besides, he was too far east to have any real interest in Greece. Kleomenes tried to get at him through his own illegitimate brothers, the two his father Leonidas had got, in his worst days, on a Persian concubine, a present from one of the governors of Asia Minor; now they were successful middle-aged courtiers and not prepared to disturb themselves over the distant affairs of their half-brother. So much for Syria. Then there was this new state, Rome, which probably looked on Macedonia as an enemy and might be prepared to help. Kleomenes did not much care to ask help from barbarians, but he had heard that they were sound and well-disciplined fighters. He would put a case against Macedonia, and, with Macedonia, her western ally Illyria, which would make it sound more plausible to the Roman Council of Elders. But Rome had her hands full fighting the Celts up north. It was not the time for Greece yet.

Kleomenes raised what money he could privately, and lived more sparingly than ever. Sometimes he found himself suddenly and simply astonished at how little material good it was being a king. He would speak of that sometimes to Sphaeros, or Panteus or Therykion. The only thing he had was power. Yet after all what else does a man want? What else is the aim of life? What is worth buying? A man asks for power and for love. He had both. And wisdom—? The duty of a wise man—? Let it alone, Sphaeros, all that about right and wrong is sound enough for children, for a beginning, but a man must do the thing that comes to his mind and his hand, and do it well! What about the future? Let it alone, Therykion, I shall see my boys again. Antigonos has thirteen thousand Macedonians and eight or nine thousand League troops who are not all keen—perhaps we can persuade some of them—The Illyrians? Well yes, Therykion, they have a certain reputation. And mercenaries—Yes, my God, I know we are outnumbered—who better. But we've got the name and the fame, both; they're afraid of us still. If we can once somehow, by the kind of chance that good commanders grab out of the Fates' laps, if we can once snatch one victory out of them, get some booty—oh, a few chestfuls would do it!—we'll tempt the mercenaries back again, I'll have the world yet! It's not only numbers that count. We're on our own ground now; we shall have every advantage of position and communications and foraging. Our men know and trust their leaders; in the year-classes every man knows the others; they are all friends together, each confident of the strength and staying power of the man next him whose shield overlaps his body! The Macedonians aren't like that, nor the rest of the League troops. Leaders—old Aratos again. Alexander the Macedonian? Not up to his name. No, Antigonos is the mind there. Demetrios of Pharos? Yes. But he's mostly got his reputation in very different kind of fighting. What, the Megalopolitans and Philopoemen? There aren't enough of them to count. All the same, that's a man I hate, the kind of man the League likes listening to! He wants to smash me. He's young; ah, God, he's ten years younger than any of us! But he won't, the traitor; however much he sells himself to Macedonia. No, Panteus, they won't smash us; not yet!

But at midsummer Antigonos began his invasion of Sparta. He marched solidly south from Tegea which he had taken, and over the pass. Kleomenes took up a position across the Oenus valley, a few miles north of the town of Sellasia and about twelve miles north of the city of Sparta itself. It was a good position, whatever happened. Antigonos halted and foraged and set up tents, and more and more brigades of his army came down from the pass and spread out in front of the Spartans. Each side could see the spears of the others, and a constant glitter of moving armour and little cloaks. The question was, what to do and which army was to do it first.

Kleomenes and his officers stood on the spur of the right-hand hill, little Olympos. There was a continuous coming and going of messengers, reporting and saluting, and finery of gay crests and badges well polished into heartening their wearers to think they were on the winning side. But most of the men who understood the situation were rather markedly silent and constrained. Most of the King's Mess were there, the commanders of the year-classes, Eukleidas who was in command of the hill on the left of the valley, and the captains of such mercenaries as there were. Neolaidas, who was particularly long-sighted, crouched against a rock, looking steadily across and along the valley towards the Macedonians. If anyone climbed little Olympos to the top and then looked over, he would be able to see and signal back south to Sparta itself. There was a big plan of the position, held down by stones, on the ground; the captains of the mercenaries were kneeling over it, pointing with sticks and discussing it with Panteus. They wanted to make quite sure how they were going to be used.

'The left and centre are the holding forces,' said Panteus. 'I'm in command of the centre, right in the valley. We may have to deal with cavalry. It's the only place they can be used. Eukleidas has Euas, the hill on the left; that shouldn't be too hard to hold, even if they try to get round there. The King will be here on the right, behind the palisade. He will have the Spartiate phalanx, and all of you.' The mercenary captains nodded. 'Here and here are the springs, both fairly plentiful. You've seen to your rations. It is probable that the King will not need you to begin with. Rest and keep fresh and give us our money's worth! You'll need to go over the ground yourself.' He hesitated, then said: 'What sort of chance do you think we have?'

'Shouldn't like to say,' said one of the mercenary captains, 'but your King may pull it off yet. This is a nice position; yes, very nice. I take it the Macedonians are likely to have most of their valuables on their own left, where King Antigonos is?'

'Our information says so. Oh, you'll have some overtime due! And you'—he turned to one of the others—'what's the betting?'

'If you ask me,' the man said pretty gloomily, 'we're right up against it. But I'm not a man to go back on my bargain.'

Panteus picked up the map and took it across to another group. The mercenaries began talking to one another in lowish voices. 'This looks like being the end of my job,' said the one who had spoken last. 'If Kleomenes loses this it'll be the end of him.'

'Antigonos will have it all his own way in Greece. We shall be short of work.'

'If they lose this battle most of those Spartiates will go and get themselves killed. Queer, isn't it! Nice young chaps too! We shan't be planning ambushes with them any more.'

Another said: 'When Sparta's lost, the King dies. The Persians only passed Thermopylae over a dead king; the Macedonians will only pass the same way.'

'Kleomenes and the Spartiates are likely to make a vow when he sacrifices, last thing. I want to be there and see. It will be something to tell the grandchildren.'

'But will Kleomenes? That sort of game was all very well in the old days, but now—a man can only live once. Why not make the best of life even if you lose a kingdom!'

'Kleomenes is the people's king. He's got to die for the people. If he'd wanted to live he ought to have thought of it earlier and made peace with the League. It's too late to live now.'

'Ah,' said the first one, 'good thing for us we're not Spartiates! But maybe he'll win yet. He has luck, this King. And it's a lovely position, whatever you say. No, I shouldn't be too surprised if we'd got next year's pay by tomorrow night.'

Several of the Mess had joined Neolaidas, staring out, trying to spot King Antigonos' tent. They whispered and pointed. Phoebis began by looking and then found he could not do it. He had never been so deeply distressed before a battle before; everything was heavy, head and heart dull with anxiety. His eldest son was going to be in this battle, with the youngest year-class. The boy was only sixteen, much too young really, but he had managed to get himself into it. And it was going to be this sort of battle!

They had the map spread out on the ground again. Abruptly Panteus said: 'Even now—what about falling back on Sparta?'

But the King shook his head. 'I don't think I shall be betrayed here. I should for certain there.'

'Yes,' said Eukleidas. 'The ephors' party would have you down, like wolves. All the half-ways will have gone right over against us now—licking the Macedonian's boots! We've got to stick it here, Panteus; it's our only chance. And if we win—Kleomenes, I'll hold Euas for you, or die. That's straight.'

But there were still three days during which nothing happened except raiding parties, mostly sent out by Antigonos to test the Spartan strength at one point or another of the line. It was very hot all the time, even at night, and the armies watched one another, and country people brought news of the numbers and temper of each over to the other. It became fairly clear that the Spartans were outnumbered by about three to two.

On the Macedonian side there were constant councils of generals. They met in Antigonos' tent. He stayed in bed as much as possible, with a light blanket, even in this weather, keeping up his strength. The doctors burnt all sorts of spices round his head, but still he coughed and coughed. When he spoke in that hoarse, whispering tone that they all knew, every one else was silent at once, to catch the low words. His commander-in-chief, Alexander, always saw to that anyhow. He was a Macedonian of the old type. If the young man from Megalopolis wished to go on discussing that surely laboured point about the cavalry, let him do it outside! The King was speaking. The voice of Macedon. So Philopoemen, desperately afraid of his point being missed—and, after all, look at the plan of the ground: is it so stupid, considering the bend of the river?—went outside the tent for ten minutes to discuss it with his friend Kerkidas and two of Alexander's cavalry officers.

Philopoemen had been given the command of the Achaean cavalry by Aratos, who admired him and realised that at this stage, at any rate, he need not be jealous of him. There were only a thousand of them, but they were as good as

Alexander's cavalry, and perhaps understood this kind of
ground better. Kerkidas, a writer and politician, rather a fine
and generous-natured man, led the exiles from Megalopolis.
Only a thousand of them too. He asked young Philopoemen
if he would come and speak to them before the battle, cheer
them up a little if he could and hold out all the hopes there
were—like a flag.

Philopoemen said he would come over that night. Oh yes,
he would speak for them! But if only he could get directly
at King Antigonos! Or was the King too ill to be interested
in such a small matter? Small for the whole battle. Thirty
thousand men in one army! Yet that point of his might
mean the lives of a good many Achaeans and a good many
of the Megalopolis exiles who were down with the cavalry
on the centre. But Alexander, the commander-in-chief, did
not think it was suitable that Philopoemen of Megalopolis,
a mere boy, should trouble the King. Alexander had a quite
intelligible contempt for these much-burnt little towns of
Hellas, towns too smashed up and plundered to give their
citizens decent helmets—what! Did it, after all, signify
if a few more or less were killed? He would take care of
each individual life of his own Macedonians, most of all the
Bronze Shields, the main body of the infantry; that was a
different business. But this Achaean League!—talking
as though it mattered!

There were two or three reports to be put together from
spies who had been sent out the night before to see what
they could discover of Kleomenes' position. Now it had
all been drawn out for King Antigonos to see. He studied
it silently, propped up on many pillows. Aratos sat beside
him on the edge of the bed studying it too. He twisted his
fingers in and out of his grey, thinning beard. At last he
tapped Antigonos on the shoulder and said: 'This seems
to me to be the typical Spartan formation, with the striking
force on the right as usual. We can, I think, be certain that
the Spartiate phalanx is there, on little Olympos. This is the
way the Spartan army has been taught to go into battle for
the last several hundred years.'

'What conclusion do you draw from that, Aratos?' said
King Antigonos, looking round at him.

'It might—I do not yet say that it does—lead one to
suppose that King Kleomenes is too much afraid of us to

dare to take chances. He and his army may be—I do not
say yet that they are—in no state to do anything except
the standard Spartan thing.'

'That is possible, but, as you say, Aratos, not certain.
Given the nature of the ground it seems to me to be an
exceedingly good position; in fact—yes, I think I may
say the best conceivable one.'

'It is a formation that is usually extremely effective against
an ordinary attack. Even with our strength, it would, I think,
be most unwise to attempt anything direct. That is what he
hopes we shall do. He hopes we shall be proud enough to try
the direct method.'

Alexander said: 'I take it you mean to suggest a flank
movement—by me and the Macedonian army. I warn
you: it will certainly be necessary to use the whole of
our forces, all along the line. You Greeks can't leave
all the fighting to us, even if you do all the crowing
yourselves!' He was not going to let this miserable little
Achaean talk about *our* forces—*our* strength!—when
there were only four or five thousand of them in the whole
army, rottenly equipped too, and mostly in reserve because
they'd got so panicked about this Kleomenes! But before
he could think of the really crushing thing to say, his King
had leant forward from the cushions and held up his hand
for silence.

'Naturally,' said Antigonos, 'there is no question in any
of our minds of striking except with our whole forces.
Kleomenes of Sparta at bay is the kind of proposition it
is better to over-estimate. Aratos, you tell me this is the
traditional Spartan army formation. Yet it has from time to
time been beaten in the past. How was that?'

Aratos paused for a minute, then said: 'The other side has
won when it has done something against the rules, something
they didn't expect.'

'Instead of being bolted into a straight attack by the
way they glared,' said Kerkidas, who had come back
with Philopoemen; but no one answered, though Aratos
nodded.

The King bent over the map. He had another fit of coughing that left him exhausted and shut-eyed for a few minutes.
His doctors glanced at the bloodstained bowl into which he
had spat, but the others looked away. It was more tactful not

even to whisper; his ears were amazingly sharp still! All at once he sat up, with a heave which sent a queer flush racing over his thin, exquisitely shaved cheeks. He tapped with a finger-nail on the map. 'We've got to take him on the left flank, round Euas.'

'An impossible march!' said Alexander. 'They know that. It would have to be at night—you cannot expect the Bronze Shields—'

'Impossible is not a word I like to hear,' said the King. 'Now look at the map, my dear Alexander. So—you see? —out of sight behind the ridge—and so—then up from behind. That's King Eukleidas with the light-armed troops and allies—I'm right, Aratos, yes?—we shall give him something to keep him busy in front, and you will smash in from the back. *Then* the whole line can engage. I will take on King Kleomenes myself. It will need careful timing. You will have to flash a signal to me from Euas when you are on the top. The Bronze Shields may consider themselves honoured. Do you approve, Aratos?'

'You think it sufficiently certain that the feint attack can be made at the same moment as the real one? It would be—exceedingly awkward—if the turning column were delayed. Eukleidas is not a fool. Both jaws of your trap must close before he's caught. They are likely to have outposts all down the further side of Euas, let alone that the country people would let them know immediately what was happening. It is quite possible that this is just the move Kleomenes anticipates.'

Antigonos smiled at him with mocking friendliness and said: 'But yet, this is perhaps the last time that anyone will be afraid of Kleomenes!' He went on: 'Kleomenes may have thought this would be our move a few days ago. But I think our last few raiding parties will have confused him fairly completely. I've an idea, though, that the men for this turning movement will be the Illyrians. What do you say to that, Demetrios?'

Demetrios of Pharos looked at the map in his turn. He was glad not to be opposite the Spartan phalanx itself. Yes, that frightened him! He had learnt war first among creeks and harbours and steep limestone islands under Teuta, the pirate Queen, before he had turned against her and gone over, just in time, to the Romans, who, much impressed by his courage and ability, had made him an ally, a ruler by permission of Rome—not that this last thing hindered him much when the Romans were so busy with Gaul in the north and likely to be busy in the south—if all one heard about Carthage was true. Demetrios believed in luck. He was much more comfortably prepared to take on the flank movement against Eukleidas, who was, after all, no one special, only the second king, and that not by birth, but by his brother's doubtful gift, than to have anything to do with Kleomenes of Sparta himself, who undoubtedly used to have, and perhaps still had, an amazing amount of luck. Kings, of course, have their own luck. They are nearer the Gods. The Gods see who it is that makes the sacrifices. Demetrios said: 'I can take this on. My men consider themselves not inexpert at surprises. If there are any outposts we shall be able to deal with them. I will arrange communications with Alexander. He will be doing the front attack on Euas, I suppose? As soon as it is dawn we shall be able to flash with shields; at least one can be certain of the sun!'

In a little silence one of the mercenary captains said: 'Then there does seem to be a chance that Kleomenes and the Spartans will be done in at last! And by God—by us!'

And Aratos said: 'Kleomenes and the army of the revolution. Yes—if They are with us—at last.'

On the Spartan side too there was constant co-ordination of spies' reports to be made. One or two deserters were brought straight to headquarters to be questioned. The King's tent was set up there on a spur of little Olympos, facing left and front, with a clear view across either towards the Macedonians or to the centre in the valley and the opposite slopes of Euas. From time to time the all-well signals were flashed across by highly polished silver shields, or at night by flares. Eukleidas had his own headquarters, and Panteus his. In the intervals of waiting, when everything that could be prepared had been, they did routine things which kept them from thinking. They made lists of provisions and equipment and filled in amounts of what they had taken or needed, one for themselves and a duplicate for the magistrate in charge of the State treasuries. These were good things to worry about. When there was so much evil stuff for dreams in their heads, it was better to dream fantastically of this. The King's compliments, and will Panteus kindly send him a list of helmet straps supplied to his division since the third day of the last month? Dream on who can.

An hour before dawn one of the sentries was relieved and another went on duty for that perilous time. Panteus went the rounds and then knelt in the half dark by a blessedly chilly pool and washed and combed his hair—carefully, carefully . . . a fine corpse . . . all wounds in front. Why think that! The army of the revolution was to live, not to die. Kleomenes, my dearest, if I never see you again. . . . Oh, keep quiet, bit of me, bit of me that I hate!

In that same cool hour Philopoemen had ridden over to Kerkidas and the Megalopolitan exiles. They came round him in a half-circle, closing together so that his voice could carry—oh, too easily! A thousand separate men. It sounded something, but how little the Macedonian king or his commander-in-chief cared!

He spoke with gathering force, saying that now he and they might retrieve the honour of their burnt and beaten city. Megalopolis should be rebuilt—oh, built again on the ashes of Sparta, when that proud and evil place had come to its doom; Sparta, that had brought ruin and despair and exile on them, as in the old days the ruinous Spartan Queen, the destroyer and adulteress Helen! Now, today, if the Gods were willing, flame and destruction would come at last on Sparta and the ideas, the patterns of Sparta. This was a battle for the ideas and patterns of the right-thinking city states, the cities which were now to live each in the harmony of its own laws and ethics and customs, in the peaceful shade of its own guardian mountains. This lovely pattern of cities. He himself would fight and die, if need be, for this. The world would see that this, and not Sparta, was the Gods' choice in Hellas. Before the eyes of the King of Macedonia and all his allies the thing would be made plain. Philopoemen bade them to remember this, he cried out to every man of Megalopolis to have beyond his own individual courage the special and communal courage of being the example, of having all those eyes on them for the utmost glory of their own city and in hatred of Sparta!

He stopped, at the peak of his own resolve for death or honour. Suddenly one of the Megalopolitan soldiers rose up from the hillside in his full armour and spoke: 'Philopoemen, all this is well said, and maybe the younger of us needed to hear it. But we—we fathers and craftsmen, we know already what we have to fight for! You need not show us how or where to hate. We know. Philopoemen, I will say what my hate and shame is, for today I shall have my chance to end it. That King took my daughter, my lovely lamb—from the steps of the altar—my little maid—' And in a great passion of anger, of choked-down hatred, the father of Archiroë threw down his shield and spear and flung up his arms for Philopoemen and Kerkidas and the Gods to witness the undying war between Megalopolis and Sparta.

Chapter Two

TWO HOURS AFTER midnight Demetrios of Pharos marched off very quietly along the bed of the ravine to the right, with no lights and no singing. Just after dawn Alexander gave the signal for the first attack on Euas, the frontal one which was to engage Eukleidas until the Illyrians got him in the back. All along the line every one was ready; an attack of this sort had been expected and Eukleidas, according to plan, retreated uphill behind the palisades, letting the enemy come on; then, when they were on the steep, hot slope of Euas, Panteus in the centre called in his mercenaries and sent them to catch the attacking column in the flank and rear. At the same time Kleomenes and the Spartiate phalanx lowered their spears and charged downhill, down the grass slopes and screes of little Olympos, straight into Antigonos and his Macedonian phalanx, driving them struggling back towards their tents. Here too the mercenaries of both sides engaged. Kleomenes had got the initiative of the battle. If he could keep it. . . .

It was difficult and of the utmost importance for the Spartan army to keep up communications right along from Euas to little Olympos. They had no reserves to fill up gaps and stop a break through if Panteus lost touch with either Eukleidas or the King. Half an hour after the beginning of the battle Panteus got his division swung round, forward on the right as well as the nature of the ground permitted, so as to keep in touch with the King's phalanx; his left was in full action. It looked as if the Macedonian attack on Euas would be smashed.

But then two things happened. Philopoemen, who could get no orders from Alexander, took the thing into his own hands and charged the Spartan centre at the head of his cavalry. Panteus made the only possible counter-move; he recalled the mercenaries to support him, and when they rushed back the Macedonian frontal attack on Euas re-formed and went on. In the river-bed now there was a desperate struggle, Panteus and his division driven back step by step by one cavalry charge after another, first Philopoemen, then Alexander with the regular Macedonian heavy armed horsemen. And whenever a cavalry charge had gone past, the Megalopolitan infantry came grimly after to finish it up. Company after company broke under the spears and horse-hoofs; and through the wounding and killing and screaming and smashing up, Panteus knew all the time that if his division was driven back much further he would lose touch at both sides, the Macedonians would get in between the hills and the pass would be lost. He had only a few hundred cavalry against Philopoemen's thousand. Again, his equipment was not good enough. Spears broke, shields broke, javelins broke, swords broke at the hilt, he hadn't fresh supplies. But the Macedonians had—cartloads. Then the second thing happened. The Illyrian column came up behind Euas and took Eukleidas in the rear.

The Spartiate phalanx re-formed for another charge on the slope of Olympos—quick, quick, before the Macedonians, worse broken up, could get together to take the charge. Now was the time for the break through! The King looked over to the centre; he saw that Panteus was having a bad time, but if he and the phalanx could only drive back Antigonos now, that would immediately relieve the centre—the whole shape of the battle would change! Then he looked right across to Euas. 'My God, what's happening there?' No one could tell for a moment. Then they saw that Eukleidas was trapped and done for. There was no possibility of saving the left. Even while they looked they could see their own men on Euas swept down off the crest, caught on the edge of the column coming up, pressed together, getting fewer, all so tiny, so unlikely from here—not real. The King said quite quietly: 'Oh, my dearest brother, I've lost you now.' That was it. That was the fact. Five minutes ago it had not happened. Now nothing could alter it.

The victorious Macedonians and Illyrians poured down

off Euas on to the centre in the river-bed. Panteus got his men together, retreating in knots from one rock and ravine to another, trying to keep touch. In one of those ravines some of the Illyrians found Philopoemen with a javelin right through both his thighs. They told him to lie still, he would be taken back to the rear and the surgeons, the battle was won already. But Philopoemen made them haul him up on to his feet and in a horrible bloody struggle with his own legs broke the javelin shaft; the pieces were pulled out, someone bound up both the wounds; he grabbed his sword and went on, gloriously, painfully, on to victory for Megalopolis and the end of Sparta!

Antigonos was going to charge now. Keep close, the phalanx! Keep close, hold them. Yes, there are more of them; yes, ten times more; yes, but we're Spartans, we can take it! Don't look at the spears. We've taken spears before. Keep the shield wall locked. Steady! Another two minutes. Who was that man with the cut face who said good-bye to me just now? Damn him, saying good-bye. I am going to live, I am going to live. I knew his voice—well. Who in hell's name was it? Oh, of course, Xenares. Odd. Here they come.

Most of the mercenaries were deciding that they had done quite as much as they had contracted to do. A great many of them had been killed and they had all behaved very well. Now it was time to stop. Those who were left had mostly retreated up the hill. King Kleomenes, if not dead yet, probably would be in a few minutes. He was a fine commander and a gallant man, but they would be getting no more pay from him. Someone else would want them.

Phoebis found his eldest son, the sixteen-year-old, dying, doubled up in the sun, clutching at his wide, slimy wound. A spear had got in under his breastplate, and, dragged out for the next kill, had pulled most of the boy's inside out with it. Phoebis tried to move his son into the shadow of a rock, but he screamed so when he was straightened out at all that Phoebis had to give it up. Failing that, Phoebis gave him water, which would have been a bad thing to do with a stomach wound if there had been any chance of recovery. There was, of course, none. The boy lay very still and looked at his father; he could not smile, but at least he was quiet. Phoebis had to go on. When he came back his eldest son was dead and there were ants on him.

Mnasippos was killed near the King in the second charge. Chrysa's man, Milon, was killed. Themisteas was badly wounded with a spear through his thigh and another through his right shoulder, just clearing the lung. Panitas was killed rather comically by an arrow going through his throat as he was jumping off a rock. Neolaidas had an arrow wound too; the thing shot out his left eye and he spent the next few days alternately getting conscious and then fainting with the pain. However, that was not enough to kill him, though it disfigured him very thoroughly for the rest of his life. Philocharidas was with the centre; he was knocked down and trampled on in the cavalry charge, and left for dead; but he was found later and recovered more or less, except that he could never use his right arm properly again. Leumas was killed. Mikon broke his leg in a narrow ravine and shammed dead when the Megalopolitans came and stripped off his helmet and breastplate. But he managed to crawl away the next night, and escaped. None of the Achaeans were taking prisoners much during this battle. Most of the wounded in the centre, at any rate, were finished off, though when the Illyrians got there anyone who could promise a sufficiently large ransom was quite likely to be able to save his life.

The Macedonian army did not pursue for two reasons. One was that their own losses, especially in the phalanx itself, were very heavy. They had to get into some sort of formation again. The doctors were very anxious that King Antigonos should rest, after the riding and shouting and danger, but it was difficult to insist. The other reason that there was no pursuit was that there was no need for it. There would be nobody, nothing, to stand between them and Sparta now. The thing was final.

A man was kneeling on the top of a rock of the far side of little Olympos, signalling back with a waved cloak. This signal was taken up from beyond Sellasia and passed on to Sparta. There were strict orders that no signals were to be sent down to the city unless for victory. Therykion stabbed the intent signaller in the back and he died at once. Therykion was ahead; the others were following him. Why was he alive after this battle?

The King pulled his horse up sharply to look south into the plain of Sparta. There was blood dripping still from a cut on his cheek. He jerked and twitched every time a fresh drop crawled down his neck. He put out his hand, trying to check Agesipolis, who was crying out now that he must go back and hunt for his brother. But the boy was too badly hurt by a javelin wound to be able to do more than cling on to his own horse's mane; sometimes the pain of the wound stopped him speaking altogether, but more often it sent him rocketing on about young Kleomenes who might be worse wounded—killed. 'Can none of you tell him what happened to his brother?' said the King, suddenly at the limit of endurance. 'For God's sake stop, Agesipolis! If he's dead, he's dead, and that's that.'

Who was coming now? 'Idaios! You've got through! Good. No news of Panteus, I suppose? No. Or young Kleomenes?' 'Wounded and taken prisoner,' said Idaios shortly. Agesipolis cried out: 'How wounded? Where? Who took him? What will they do to him?' But someone snatched at his bridle and held him as he tottered and sobbed and felt the stabbing of his own wound jerking deeper in with the trotting downhill. Kleomenes dropped behind to speak to Neolaidas. He could not help seeing Phoebis riding a little apart and somehow like someone blind.

They came down on to the road and after a time they found that Panteus and a few others had joined them. That was at a short halt at a roadside spring, where they all drank, and Neolaidas was passed over to someone fresh and carried swaying and sobbing in front of the saddle. Panteus said: 'I got them to let me go up Euas under a flag of truce. Demetrios of Pharos was there; his staff helped me. I brought down your brother's body, Kleomenes. There it is.' He pointed over his shoulder to a cloaked bundle tied on to a horse. Kleomenes looked once, then looked away. 'What was it like?' he said. 'Pretty bad,' said Panteus. Then: 'Our people had been killed—in heaps. When the last square on the top of Euas broke. Eukleidas had a sword-cut half through his neck. He must have died at once.' 'And the boy?' said Kleomenes, trying to think calmly, remembering very vividly how it had been the last time he had seen his brother Eukleidas, with one arm across his boy-love's shoulders. Panteus hesitated and then said: 'He was dead over him with several very bad wounds, dead with the most awful face of pain and despair that I have ever seen. I'm sorry, Kleomenes—' He was quite unable for the moment to say anything more. They had lost the battle.

Nearly a hundred of them got back to Sparta that day. The King and two or three others were a little way ahead. It was the hottest part of the day; the heat brought out the smells of tiredness and drying blood. The lips of all wounds cracked and itched. The flies buzzed round them, keeping up with them as they rode. It was still impossible to think. Kleomenes rode without stopping into the market-place. There were a good many men, mostly oldish; many of them, he knew, were the ephors' party, the enemies of his revolution. There were young boys too, and a great many women, pressing their way through. He spoke quickly, before they could begin questioning him. He said: 'One King of Sparta is dead.' He heard the low, murmured wailing running like waves across the women. Then he said, speaking mostly to a group of half a dozen immediately in front of him—men he knew had worked against him lately, if not the whole time: 'I advise you to do what you want to do. Receive Antigonos. Make him welcome. Show him he's master! Yes, he'll put you and your friends into power. You will be a good, little, dependent state—you Spartans!' And suddenly he spurred his horse towards them so that they parted quickly.

Another man said to him: 'And you yourself, Kleomenes?' It was a magistrate, an old friend of his mother's.

He answered: 'I hope to do the best for Sparta.'

'And that will be—what?'

'I cannot tell you yet. I do not know even if it means my life or death.'

The magistrate nodded towards the first group: 'There are some who'd dare lay hands on you to make a present to the Macedonian and save their own skins.'

'I know. But they won't dare: not yet. Now, friend, you should leave me. You had better not let them think you wish me well—if you do. They'll have the power.'

'I wish you well from my heart, King Kleomenes, though you know I thought you unwise. Ah, Zeus, I don't blame you now! Do your best for us, Kleomenes, if you decide to live and hope. We'll wait for you.'

And a quite young boy, the magistrate's grandson, cried out in a cracking voice: 'We'll wait for you years, our King, we'll work for you! We'll go on fighting—' But the older man laid a hand quickly over his mouth. It was not safe.

Kleomenes looked round and saw that the women had come running up to the others, helping them off their horses, taking their heavy armour off and giving them drinks. Panteus was a long way behind still; the body of King Eukleidas was not yet come to Sparta. He dismounted and walked into his own house. Archiroë came to him tenderly—soft arms, soft breasts, and cool, little cool fingers. Curious that these things still existed. What did she want? To give him wine. To unbuckle his breastplate. To take his helmet off. To wash him. To give him food. To give him love. Why should he take it; why should he do what she wanted? He was too tired, too deep in what had been and what was going to be. He brushed her off. She was only a slave. She crouched and cried a little, came nearer and kissed the hand which had knocked her away as though she had been a dog. The hand did not feel the kisses. She longed bitterly to do something, to have the right to do something for him; it was terrible that he would not drink. She began to realise how complete the defeat had been. The Macedonians had won. The Macedonians would come to Sparta and carry her off! The Achaeans. The men of Megalopolis . . . But her man now for ever was Kleomenes.

He leant his arm slantwise against one of the pillars of the house and dropped his face upon his forearm and began to think. Before he could solve Sparta's problems he had to solve his own. The army had been defeated. Most of the citizens, old and new, between twenty and forty, had been killed, and he himself was alive. His revolution was defeated. In a few weeks, perhaps in a few days, everything would be undone in Sparta. There would be rich and poor again, great estates, luxury, usury and mortgage, free citizens working for less than a living wage, boy babies exposed. His new citizens would have the thing they cared for most in the world taken away by the ephors under Antigonos. Sparta was defeated. For the first time in history there would be conquerors in the market-place of Sparta! Before, in the old wars, things had never gone so far. At the last moment the Spartan lion had recovered and sprung. Now after six hundred years it was too late. The barbarians had taken the pass. Leonidas had died at Thermopylae.

Glorious was the fate and noble the doom
Of those who died at Thermopylae.
Their tomb shall be an altar.
Instead of lamentation they shall have remembrance,
And instead of pity, praise. . . .
Their witness shall be Leonidas, King of Sparta. . . .

Ah, ah, and he, Kleomenes, was witness of those that live on after the defeat!

Yet he had been no coward. He had led that first spear-down charge of the Spartiate phalanx, as was the King's pride and due. He had taken the charge of the Macedonians. He had staggered and stood under the shock of their spears breaking against his shield. He had not been afraid. It was not likely that he would have been more of a coward than his brother. And no one could dare to say that of Eukleidas now. Eukleidas was safe from tongues. When he had seen that thing happen on Euas he had known intellectually that the battle was lost. When his own phalanx at last broke, speared down and killed and forced apart by sheer weight of numbers, he knew it deep in his heart. But no spear or sword had got past his skill and armour, and he could not deliberately go and get himself killed. Some men can. He was not that kind of man. On Euas they had been taken in front and rear with no escape. But on little Olympos there had been a way of retreat. It would have been fantastic not to take it. Why should he be fantastic, like someone in a poem simply because he was king?

Yet being King of Sparta was a special thing. He was not a tyrant nor master of courtiers and soldiers. He was only a kind of eidolon, a kind of dream the people had. Without the people there was no king. If the people died the king must die. Yes, yes; but behind and apart from that he was a man and a father of children, a living being with arms and legs and blood and brain! He had not ended.

They had not ended either. Even defeated there was still Sparta, still the Spartan people, the people of the revolution. Certain things were possible. He would go to Egypt and show King Ptolemy, who was, after all, a Macedonian too, to start with, that the balance of power had gone over too much, and now he must restore Sparta against the Achaean League and King Antigonos. He would be able to do that. Leonidas at Thermopylae had done the only possible thing for his time.

Kleomenes would do something harder and more modern. He would live.

Panteus came into the King's house. The King did not see him. The King leant against the column and the flies settled on the cut across his cheek and round the rims of his eyes. At his feet, with her long hair loose and her dress hanging from one shoulder, was the woman of Megalopolis. Before the King moved or spoke that picture had gone very deep into Panteus' mind.

The King did not move yet from the column, but he opened his mouth and said: 'We are going to live. I have come to that decision. It will be bitter, Panteus, very bitter; you do not know yet how bitter people will make it for us that we can be alive. You will think often before the end that it would be easier and more honourable to be dead. It is a bitter cup I am giving you to drink of. We must go to Egypt and be cunning as snakes and foxes for the sake of Sparta. There are ships at Gytheum. We will start in ten minutes.'

'And your brother's body?'

'I will leave that to the people of Sparta. Go out into the market-place and tell them. They will not dishonour glory of that kind. They understand it. Not even those who hated me most will hurt him. They will go through the rites of mourning for their King. The women will do that. So. Then get the others. By the way, where is Sphaeros?'

'I saw him just now.'

'Tell him I want him. He is to come with us. In ten minutes, Panteus.'

Panteus went out. After a time the King heard Archiroë sobbing and felt her hands crawling up his legs. 'My King, my King, my King!' she said. He said: 'Stop it, my dear.' His arms slid down the smooth marble; he stroked her head, the bright chestnut waves; he was going to leave her behind, and his horses, and the dogs. 'What shall I do?' she sobbed. 'You've got the deeds for that farm in Messenia? Good. I didn't think you'd need them so soon. Go there. Be there before your brothers and cousins from Megalopolis come and grab you here, and don't go back to them till you've forgotten me. Oh yes, you will! I know what you're thinking now, but it doesn't last, Archiroë. You've given me some good times, you pretty thing. Give them to someone else in a year or two. If Nikagoras the Messenian comes and worries you for the money, tell him I'll pay—oh, when I can. No, I don't suppose I shall ever see you again. Don't think about it. Still more, don't remind me, don't speak to me! Don't touch me now!' 'Take me with you!' 'No.' She sank down, sobbing. He touched her shoulder. 'Get up. There are some things I must take. Go and see to the spare horses, my dear.'

He went through into the inner court of the house, intent on what he had to get. Not much. He must ride light. Nikomedes would be glad to see him in Egypt.

Chapter Three

THEY SAILED A LITTLE after midnight from Gytheum. They put in first at Kythera, then at Aigalia. They were bound for Kyrene; from there it would be an easy journey overland to Alexandria, and they could wait to hear what kind of a reception they were likely to get from King Ptolemy. It was now two days and a few hours since the battle of Sellasia.

Aigialia was a very small island, the back of a brown hill pushed up accidentally through the flat blue sea. A long way off, on the horizon, were the blue peaks of the mainland, Tainaron perhaps. There were small beaches of coarse sand, and large rocks, and pools full of black and spiky sea-urchins, which the sailors cut open and ate. Kleomenes walked about on the beach with his long legs; his head was a little bent, he dangled his arms, his face was bandaged. Therykion came up to him, and glanced about, but there was no one near. The others were busy, or resting, or on the ship. Neolaidas lay on deck trying to control himself among the coloured flashes of pain that came from the place where his eye used to be. Sphaeros was composing a letter to someone he knew, one of the head librarians at Alexandria. Panteus and the captain were looking at their course on a chart and talking it over. Therykion said: 'Here we go wandering into foreign countries. Only the Gods know what will happen to us. I think, myself, that things will go on getting worse and worse.'

'You would, wouldn't you, Therykion,' said the King, rather absently still.

'I promised myself that the barbarians would not get Sparta except over my dead body. I believe you did too. We made no vows, but that was in all our hearts. It would have been good to die in battle. We would have had songs made about us, as they will be made now for your brother Eukleidas. The boys would remember us. We would have become part of the glory of Sparta.'

'Very likely,' said Kleomenes, 'very likely. I told you all it would be bitter to live.'

'That's gone. But—Kleomenes, supposing we kill ourselves now, here, all of us on this one little island—or if not all, at least you and me!—we get something back, don't we?'

Kleomenes sat down on the sand; it was hot against his legs. For a moment it ran and trickled busily where he had disturbed it. 'Why?' he said.

Therykion sat down beside him. 'There's no point in sailing on,' he said. He looked round at the quiet brown island, the deep colour of the sea and sky, the red sails of the ship making a square, cool shadow. Kleomenes followed his look and tacitly agreed that it was all in itself very pleasant, but for them Therykion was right, and there was no point at all in any of it. A gull rose from among the rocks. Therykion went on: 'What are you going to do in Egypt? It won't be pleasant for your mother to see you as you are now. Kratesikleia is used to death by this time, but she is not used to dishonour. The children will not be glad either, when they are old enough to understand. If you had been going to surrender to any king it would have been better to do it to Antigonos, who is at least a good fighter and a man who keeps his promises. Or is it because Ptolemy put up a statue to you? I wouldn't trust him a yard. Him or Sosibios. But we can trust our own swords, Kleomenes, and our own hearts. Can't we? I can see over to Lakonia from here: our own hills. If we died looking at them it is possible that our souls might go there.'

'Because you are as unhappy as I am,' said Kleomenes, 'there is no need to imagine things that you know are impossible. If we die, we die and are ended: as far as the sun and rivers and hills of Lakonia go, anyhow. If we die we shall never see our friends and children again. That's clear, I think. It is also clear that the easiest possible thing would be just to kill ourselves here and now, and never have to lift up again this intolerable burden of planning and hoping and dealing with strangers and enemies. For one thing, this cut on my face is itching quite devilishly, Therykion. I didn't sleep all last night because of it. I assure you, I should be glad to get rid of it! But I am not going to. I am going to do something much harder. I have run away once; I am not going to run away again.'

Therykion answered slowly: 'That is all more or less what Sphaeros said yesterday to Neolaidas when he was in great pain and asking his servant for his dagger, but I wish you would think of something that is not a Stoic idea, Kleomenes. I know very well that Sphaeros says it is giving up the fight worse now to kill ourselves because we are afraid of hardships and dishonour and what people will say of us, but that is only partly true. It is only the outside, the mere surface and appearance of reality.'

'What is the deep thing, then, that Sphaeros did not see? What do you see as the kataleptike phantasia, Therykion?'

Therykion bent nearer: 'I am not sure if I can explain it. I think—I think there is a kind of beauty which is utterly lost in living and being rational and making plans and having material hopes: even for one's country, even for the New Times, even for Sparta. I think that is at the back of what Zeno and Iambulos say when they write down their dreams of what a state should be. You will not get this beauty for yourself by dying. I know you are right to say that even if we die looking on those hills, they will fade out for ever at the moment of death. But I think that your people and your revolution will get the beauty. I think your dying will put a bloom on them, Kleomenes.'

The King stayed very still. 'You think my blood can buy something, Therykion, that my life and my work and my reason will not be able to buy?'

'Yes,' said Therykion.

There was a very long silence. Then the King said: 'I understand, Therykion. I agree with you in a way. But I am not going to do it. Not yet, anyhow. You see, it is not natural for me to look at things in that way. I can do it for a time through your eyes; but when a man kills himself, then above all is the time he should see clearly and through his own eyes. I have a different idea of Sparta and a different idea of the world. A plain idea with no bloom on it. Only, I think, a good idea. At any rate, the one I have lived for and the one I mean to go on living for. Each man, after all, must do the thing that is right for himself, not the thing that other people say is right for him. You agree with that?'

'Certainly.'

'Very well. I believe I can help my idea best by living, and just plain contriving and scheming. Like a farmer in a difficult year, not like a priest with a sacrifice to make. If ever I come to hold your ideas I will act on them, Therykion. I think, perhaps, you are more like the men of old days, more like Leonidas. In their name, forgive me, Therykion, because I did not die in the battle.'

'If the dead know anything of the living,' Therykion said, 'they see and understand. But, my King, I must act on the way I see life myself. Will you and Sphaeros understand that?'

'I am not trying to stop you if you must, Therykion. This is an odd little island. I shall remember it all my life. This is an odd day. It is like a cover on something. If I only knew how, I could put my finger through it all and tear the sunlight across like a piece of painted paper! Therykion, am I right in thinking that when you were quite a young man you were initiated into one of the Mysteries?'

'Yes. It was altogether satisfying for a time.'

'And this thing you are going to do now will be altogether satisfying for ever.'

For some time neither of the two said anything more. Then Therykion got up very quietly and the King made no movement to stop him. He went a little way along the beach and climbed over a spur of rocks that stood between it and the next beach. Then he was out of sight. In about half an hour the King got up and went over to see. Therykion had fixed his sword firmly between two rocks and fallen on to it. Now he was dead. It seemed to the King simplest and least violently painful to the others to wrap Therykion in his own cloak and put him into a hollow of warm sand and then cover him with more sand. Over it all he made a pile of stones like a small cairn. Then he wiped Therykion's sword clean and fitted it into his cairn, blade upward, and he jammed the stones carefully round the hilt so that it would not fall down for a long time.

After that they sailed again and made Kyrene, and so went along by horse and camel until they got to the boundaries of Egypt. Here they were met by the royal officials of King

Ptolemy. Those of them who were native Egyptians tried to hide the fact under plain Greek dress and a very Greek manner and accent, talking a great deal about Corinth and Athens, where they had seen all the sights and been to the best lectures. But those who were Greek or Macedonian wore Egyptian ornaments and head-dresses, and straight wrapped tunics of yellow Egyptian muslin, and swore a great deal by Serapis and Osiris. They brought embroidered cloaks and bed-hangings for the King, and a set of silver plate for his table, fine horses with gilded bridles, and a leash of the lovely, long-legged Persian hounds to course gazelles for the amusement of the Spartans in the fringes of the desert. They also read to him a long and only slightly patronising letter from King Ptolemy. He listened in silence.

After that they gave him two private letters. One was from his mother, who had just heard the news of the disaster. She wrote very proudly and almost happily about her younger son Eukleidas, who had fallen in all honour on the field of Sellasia. She wrote about her eldest in a kind of hurt bewilderment. She supposed that what he had done was for the best. It was terrible for her to think of the Macedonians in Sparta, swaggering about in the King's house, in her own rooms even! The worst of the women would like them. If she had been there she would have armed and encouraged the best of the women to defiance or death, as Archidamia, the grandmother of Agis, had done when Sparta was in danger once before—but that time they had beaten back the barbarian, the wicked Pyrrhus! Was this generation of Spartans worse than those which had gone before? Yes, she would have fought the Macedonians with roof tiles! He put the letter down. She did not understand yet.

The other letter was from his son Nikomedes, a formal letter of sorrow and welcome, only sometimes showing through love and a great puzzlement. The boy's tutor must have supervised it. He was past thirteen now, able to see things with a man's vision. Yes, a reasonable being, at the age when, in Sparta, a boy would be likely to be singled out from among the rest by his grown lover, perhaps taken up into the hills for love and hunting and teaching and much talk. If he was intelligent and beautiful and gentle to his friends; surely Nikomedes the son of Agiatis would be all that! Kleomenes had been the same age himself when he and Xenares, whose body must, he thought, have been found and brought back from the field of Sellasia, had first met and loved one another. It would be different in Egypt. No hills to go up among, no empty heights full of clear air to run and shout in. So he would have his boy to himself, unshared. Nikomedes would be able to understand what had happened. He would be able to tell his father that he had done right. Yes, he would be old enough to take a hand in it himself, perhaps to advise, to help.

By autumn they were all settled in Alexandria. The boys went on with their lessons. Kratesikleia spent much time with the palace women trying to make opportunities for her son to meet King Ptolemy. And Kleomenes began to get letters from home.

Chapter Four

THEMISTEAS LAY quite still for fear of hurting himself. They fed him with milk and soup and something else that tasted foul and smelt worse. This time he felt strong enough to talk. He raised himself a little cautiously, and after all it did not hurt unbearably. 'It's you, Philylla,' he said, 'my little girl.' His mind tumbled back. 'Are you at home now? For always? Was your man killed too?'

She shook her head. 'No, he lived, with the King. I'm here for the time. Don't think about it yet, father.' She turned her back to him and began pounding up the herbs to put on his wounds.

He thought about what she had said. After a time his unquiet whispering reached her again: 'Where is the King?'

'King Eukleidas is dead. King Kleomenes is at Alexandria.'

'And Sparta?'

'Wait till you're stronger, father. In the meantime, our house is safe. Mother has taken care of that.'

'Why do you speak of her looking that way? Philylla – '

'Never mind how I speak, father. Stay still now, for I am going to undo the bandage on your shoulder. Hold the bowl, Ianthemis. Don't look, silly, if it's going to make you sick!'

More days passed. The slaves carried him out into the court. A few yellow plane leaves blew in and there was a smell in the air that is so lovely after months and months of dry dust and hard, cloudless, glowing blue: the smell of rotting fibres at last; the sweet, sad smell of damp mornings and cooler air. 'How long is it since the battle?' Themisteas asked.

Ianthemis, who sat beside him on the step with her embroidery, answered: 'Twelve weeks, father.'

Themisteas reached over suddenly with his sound hand and gripped her. 'You—tell me! Your mother and Philylla won't. What happened?'

Nervously Ianthemis said: 'But are you strong enough, father? They didn't want you to hear—'

'Hear what? Am I a baby? The truth now, if one of you she-things can get it out! What, is it so bad? Are we all slaves to the Macedonians?'

'No, no, but—Mother and Philylla think differently, I'll try and say. After the battle there was no more fighting. They came for three days. I didn't see them myself. King Antigonos sacrificed and then he went away. They say he had heard suddenly of a war in his own country. He didn't burn anything or steal anything except just enough gold to make things for Apollo at Delos. A lot of people went to him at the King's house, where he lived.' She stopped a minute to breathe, then as she felt her father's fingers tighten on her, scurried on. 'I—I think mother went. At least, I mean, I know she did! And a lot of people were pleased. Mother says he has given us back our Constitution. I know we've got the ephors again. Do you mind, father?'

'The ephors? No! I never felt really right without them. I'd like to know who they are, though. But go on: what about the land?'

'We've got our own land just like it used to be when I was a little girl, only not the house in the city: that's gone. But they've taken away the land that Panteus had, so Philylla has had to come back and live at home. It's horrid for her, father!'

'Stop,' said Themisteas. 'Let me think. Ours . . . as it was. So Eupolia went Macedonian behind my back, and saved us all! What do I do? Don't look so frightened, you little rat! The answer's just nothing. Nothing. The King's gone and might better have been killed as far as I can see. And

Eupolia's saved my estate! Who's seen to all this chopping and changing?'

'There's a Macedonian governor. Mother likes him. He is very kind and polite. He came in once when you were too ill to understand and went out on tiptoe. Philylla ran away that day; she went to the farm and she didn't come back till after supper. Oh yes, and we're part of the Achaean League now.'

Themisteas said grimly: 'I don't see Sparta contributing much army. Tell me again, for I think I have forgotten, the names of all my friends who have been killed.'

She looked round anxiously, but no one was coming to rescue her. She began on the long list of names, repeating them sometimes, beginning to cry herself. Some were as old as her father, but most were young lovers and husbands that should have been! Whatever had happened to Philylla since, she was safely and solidly married and her husband was alive, but where was Ianthemis to find a man now? She said: 'Every one I know is mourning for someone, and Dontas is simply silly because the captain of his class was killed!'

Themisteas stayed silent for a time, considering the list of names, and during this silence Tiasa came into the courtyard with a basket of washing on her head and stopped beside her master. He said: 'It'll take thirty years for Sparta to make this up. Even if you women are willing. Aye, we must find you a man, my little girl, and you must set to work to make boys. Fourteen, aren't you? Well, you can't start too soon with things as they are. If it's all as you say and I have my land back, I'll give you a good dowry. I wonder if your mother has any plans for you yet.'

Ianthemis glanced up at Tiasa, and on her nod of encouragement, ventured to speak. 'I do know mother thinks of someone. He's Chaerondas, the son of one of the new ephors. He's been in Crete, but now he's at home again. I saw him once. He had such a lovely wolfhound!'

'What did he do in the battle?' She said nothing, and Tiasa could not think of anything to say which would help. Themisteas, after a long and uncomfortable silence, went on: 'I see. He's the other side. Well, I suppose I should be grateful to your mother and glad to have my daughter married off to someone who had the sense to see which way the cat would jump. Provisionally, I agree. Now, tell me about Philylla. Aren't I going to have a grandson out of her soon?'

Ianthemis shook her head, embarrassed, and Tiasa answered for her: 'These things can't be done to order, master, not by any of us, and least of all ladies and gentlemen. They don't breed as well as that.'

Themisteas sighed; his wounds were beginning to pain him. He was tired again. He did not want to think of it. 'Poor Philylla,' he said gently, 'she'd have liked a child.'

He shut his eyes. Ianthemis and Tiasa shifted the pillows so as to ease his thigh and shoulder. He was almost asleep. Half under her breath Tiasa said: 'Yes, poor Philylla with that man of hers gone after the King and not so much as a line from him the whole time!'

All the same, a letter did come at last. He said he had not known how they stood, so could not write before. There was deep depression in every line; he did not tell her what to do, only asked her what she thought of doing. He had got the news that his land had been taken away, and added on to the estate of one of the ephors, so he supposed she must be back at home. He wondered if her father was alive. For themselves, they did not know how long they would have to stay in Alexandria; it was difficult to see King Ptolemy. He was old and ill and the minister Sosibios was a difficult and toughish person to deal with. The heir, young Ptolemy, was soaked in women and religion and the writing of verse. The Greeks in Alexandria were a rotten lot all through; not one of them could understand what had happened to the Spartiates and how they felt; people laughed and said it was all right because they were alive, and asked them to parties.

He went on to say that the children were well, but very jumpy. Nikomedes was watching his father all the time like a lover. Krateskleia tried to keep them in too much; she thought very badly of all the boys they were likely to meet, and no doubt she was right, but they were too old for that kind of grandmothering; they obeyed her, but it was hard on them, and they never played games with other children. When the dozen or so who were the King's best friends met to hold a kind of council together—usually after another rebuff from Ptolemy or his ministers—Nikomedes was mostly there too; it was a heavy thing to put on to a boy not yet fourteen. Little Gorgo was sometimes most painfully like her mother now. He saw the children often, for he went to the house most days: a high house in a street in Alexandria, very hot, with balconies. Kleomenes was getting headaches a good deal. Then again, what did Philylla think she should do?

Philylla took the letter over to the home farm; she wanted to brood over it, to see what more could be got out of it, and when she was at home now she felt too angry and unhappy to take in anyone's thought, least of all her husband's. But the farm was safe. Mikon sat on the bench at the door, his leg out stiffly in front of him, slowly plucking a hen; one of the small children, naked and very dirty, was picking up the feathers and putting them into a basket. The other helots had taken on the children and the wife of Leumas; when the boys were older it would get whispered to them that their father had been given freedom and honour by King Kleomenes, and in the end had been killed for him; in the meantime they were slaves again, but they did not understand that yet. Behind the corner of the house two other children were squabbling shrilly. 'Don't move!' said Philylla quickly, for she knew it was all Mikon could do to stand yet. And there were plenty now to order him about and make him stand up for them, obediently and dutifully, on his hurt leg, until they chose to give him his orders and laugh at him hobbling off. For his new citizenship had, of course, been taken away, and the few fields he had been so proud of, and had meant to make his children proud of, too. He was no longer part of the army of the revolution. 'Poor lamb,' said Philylla, 'how is it?'

'Still stiff,' said the man, and then, with a curious but unembarrassing gesture, rubbed his head against her arm. If there were masters and servants again, it would not be so bad to be her servant. She understood that, too. He went on: 'Neareta is here; she's had a letter. Tiasa is quarrelling with her again. I came out.'

'The silly bitches!' said Philylla, suddenly violently irritated, because now she was sure to get tangled up in that instead of being able to think about Panteus and her own plans in the middle of the peaceable farm smells.

'Her boy's here too,' said Mikon softly.

When she gave the door a push from her hard wrist it clattered open. Although she was married she was not at her full strength yet, but getting stronger every month, more pleased to carry weights and shove animals about and give her own orders. A Spartiate woman. How could she bear to live in another woman's house-hold, in her mother's! She must go, go. Set up her own house in Alexandria. It all went suddenly through her mind as she came into the room where Neareta and Tiasa were quarrelling with a close, concentrated fierceness, and the twelve-year-old boy, Gyridas, was sitting in a corner, watching them, and sometimes tossing his head about and shivering. He was very like his father, but a thinner and much sadder Phoebis; it looked to Philylla as though he would never be able to play quite happily any more. He saw her first and jumped up, crying: 'We've a letter from father!'

Tiasa swung round on them with a flap of her big breasts under her tunic like heavy fish. 'Yes, the sort of letter you'd run a mile for,' she said, 'and be sick into the stewpot when you'd read it! And this crazy Neareta's as bad as you—yes, I will say it!—you and your runaway king, stealing off honest women's husbands into God-knows-where—'

Philylla lifted her hand quietly. 'Now, Tiasa,' she said, 'don't be silly. Alexandria is only a few days' journey.' On the spur of the moment she added: 'I am probably going there myself.'

'Ah,' said Neareta, 'I knew you'd stand firm, Philylla!'

But Tiasa gasped and flounced. 'I'd like to know what your mother says to that! As if you'd be let cut off your nose to spite your face. If you can't see reason for yourself, you'll be made to see it, my lady!'

Philylla was afraid of losing her temper and with it all the advantage of her position. She did not answer at once.

But Neareta did. 'It's not your place, Tiasa, to speak that way to a real lady! You're just a slave-woman, aren't you, Tiasa!' And then Tiasa flew at her and there they were at it again, not even arguing, but abusing each other stupidly.

Philylla shrugged her shoulders. Neareta wasn't usually like that. It came of what had been happening to her. They hadn't even got the boy's body home for five days, and then Neareta had to see to it herself. She beckoned to young Gyridas: 'Tell me what your letter said.'

The boy took her hand and they went out of the house together and sat down on Mikon's bench. 'Father wants us to come out to Alexandria,' he said, 'and we're going. The ephors have taken almost all our land, but we've got enough money for the journey, so that's all right. Do you know, Philylla,' he went on, 'they tried to have me turned out of my class—the class where my brother was!—because of father being one of the King's citizens, not the old ones; but the rest of the boys wouldn't have it, and my captain went to the ephors himself. But I'll have to leave it now. Do you think we shall need to stay long in Egypt?'

'When the King comes back to his own again, it will all be made up to you. All that can be.' She thought for a moment of his elder brother, and then again of herself.

'But is it sure he'll come back? Philylla, is it sure?'

She saw Mikon lift his head and look round from the almost plucked hen to her. For both of them her word was certainty. If only she was sure herself!—as she had been as a child, when Agiatis was still there to tell her that the good things were surely true. She said: 'I believe he will come back to Sparta. Or, if he does not himself, I believe the things he worked for will.'

'But he himself!' said Mikon. 'Oh, it must be my King again! If not, we'll have been hurt in vain. I can't'—he stopped and looked round him, then down in a sort of astonishment at his own maimed body—'I can't bear this all the rest of my life. Not after having had the King's Times.' It was a plain statement; the one thing was not possible after the other. Therefore it must happen that the King should come back to his people.

Philylla could not answer any better than she had done already. She turned to the boy again. 'What else was there in the letter, Gyridas? Anything about any of the others?'

'He said everything was going on as well as it could, only that was slow at the best. He said the people in Alexandria were kind, but not like our people. He said he was teaching Nikomedes pole-jumping. I can do that already. He said I would be friends with Nikomedes and Nikolaos when I came out. I expect I will.'

Neareta came out of the house then. She said: 'We'll be going down to Gytheum at once, Philylla, my dear, and we'll just wait quietly for a ship. I've cousins there. He says we'll be coming back maybe in spring. It's then that things come right mostly. And you?'

'I haven't been told what to do,' said Philylla, and her hands closed over the breast-fold of her dress and the hard corners of the letter. 'I envy you rather, Neareta.'

Tiasa stood in the doorway, a country malice in her eyes and breasts. She ignored Neareta and spoke straight at her foster-daughter. 'Still thinking of running away, my babsie-ba? And where does she think the money's to come from?'

Philylla frowned. It had hurt her when Panteus' land and livestock had been taken away. It had been her own little house, where they had been happy. The ephors had taken all the small possessions he had as well. It looked rather as if someone who knew about it had told them. She was markedly silent on this subject to her mother. There was not much about the confiscations in the letter; he could not realise at all completely what had happened while he was away; he would go on dreaming about his land and the house where they had slept together. She said: 'I think you're forgetting, Tiasa, that my father was in the battle.'

'Oh yes!' said Tiasa. 'But he knows enough to lie low and let those who can help him. And he won't be too pleased with a young man who runs off and leaves his wife without so much as a word or a silver piece to click her teeth on! Will he, now?' Philylla waited and breathed and hoped she would be able to think of some reason why this was not true. Tiasa looked round. Neareta and the boy were gone, and Mikon had limped away after them. She came a step nearer and suddenly her voice thickened and softened. 'Aye, there, we know what you've been through. We'll get you out of it yet. Let him go back to his King and stay there! You'll marry another, a good one that'll look your way all the time and stay looking! Don't go telling me that's not what you want: aren't you made of woman's flesh, my sweetie, the same as me? Don't I know! It's hurting you, isn't it, it's screwing round like a knife every blessed minute?'

Philylla made one great effort to throw it off, to give the lie in calm anger to her foster-mother. But as she lifted her head her throat ached with shut sobs, and all at once her misery betrayed her into complete collapse on to this tenderness which was as old as her own body. 'It's true, it's true!' she cried. 'He doesn't love me!' And then she merely let herself run with tears, let herself be kissed and petted and cooed over. She listened, tingling and fascinated behind her wet eyes, while Tiasa stood and abused her husband. The words beat round her and there was just enough truth in them to soothe the pride and love in her which had been injured and which wanted to be angry with him. That part of her was at last being understood; her complaint against life was being made at last. Between these luxurious bouts of listening she cried jerkily with her mouth open and flung out her hands and flapped them against Tiasa's body. Lovely, lovely, to let go!

But after a time this curious pleasure ceased as abruptly as it had begun. The hands went still, the wrenching sobs died down into childish hiccups, she blinked her swollen eyelids and began to look about her. At any rate, she hadn't shown Tiasa the letter, even though her foster-mother had perhaps guessed about it. She said: 'It may be all true enough about me being hurt, but he doesn't understand that. If he did he wouldn't have hurt me. But then, he wouldn't have been a man.'

'That's all very well,' said Tiasa, 'but I can't see you being torn to bits under my eyes just because it's by a man! Now, you listen to me: if you go to him you're going to worse than you left, for you're nowhere with Panteus when it's a choice between you and the King, and you've got to see that. If the King wants him he'll take him every bit, and you for the gutter.'

'No!' said Philylla, 'I'm somewhere. And—and I choose to serve my King too!'

But Tiasa only laughed and went on: 'And you won't have any of your own folks at your back then. You'll be Mrs. Nobody out there among the black foreigners. You won't even have your old nurse to order about!' This time it was Philylla who laughed, but Tiasa went on: 'Oh, my sock-lamb, I'd be cut into little pieces if it was anyways for your good—don't I know my masters?—but I won't go an inch out of my road when it's for nothing but a young girl's silliness that I know best about, as how shouldn't I, being thirty years older than you? But there'll be no one to die for you in Egypt, nor to know you're any way different from that stuck-up Neareta and her little brat of a boy not half so big nor so clever as our Dontas for all he's been put to school with his betters! There'll be no one to stay by you if you're sick nor see you through when your time comes and that man of yours maybe off with the King. What'll you live on if you do get out there? Are you going to beg from the Egyptians?'

'You have forgotten Queen Kratesikleia.'

'Well, so I did, but there's little enough in it! The thing that counts is the heart, and you'll be hit there over and over again, for all the old Queen's in Egypt. Don't you mistake about that. But if you'll stay here—stay and get healed and forget all this—grow out of it—why, don't I know that young spark of your sister's would ten times rather have you, a beauty like you, just plum-ripe for the biting! And he'll keep you well, like wives were kept in the old days, you'll be Mrs Somebody then, not dragging about without a change of linen for all the foreigners to laugh at, but lady of one of the first estates in the land, with a great household to make what you like of, and dresses and jewels—why, Chaerondas could bring up all the boys you like to bear, and that's more than Panteus ever can, now—isn't it, duckie? Just you let me tell Chaerondas you'd be willing to see him—no more than that! Ianthemis can wait a bit—what's she compared with you, my own lovely dove?' Suddenly she threw herself down on her knees in the muck of the farmyard and flung her arms up and round Philylla. 'Do it!' she cried. 'Oh do it, and make your old nursie happy and get happy yourself!'

But Philylla disentangled herself and caught Tiasa hard by the two hands and looked down into her eyes. 'I'll tell you if I need you,' she said. 'Just now—I don't.'

Chapter Five

ERIF AND BERRIS Der came late in autumn into Sparta. Everything had freshened up after the rains; there were clouds on the hills at both sides, but the sky between was blue. Berris was not exactly getting fat, but he did not care how he stood and he was a little soft about the body. His arms, though, were extremely strong and he could twist very tough bits of metal in his fingers. They found that most of their old friends were killed or in exile; there were new people in the same houses. But Berris Der by now had a certain reputation; in fact, people had begun to say that he was not a barbarian at all, but a Greek; that annoyed him rather. He had no difficulty in finding friends or work among the rich in any state he visited.

He had begun portrait painting and was finding it amusing, though sometimes his subjects were not pleased, for he was in an unromantic phase. One of his commissions was a full-length of the Macedonian Governor of Sparta. He did this very competently, and his sister talked to the governor's mother, who was quite a dear old lady. They talked mostly about the gods of Macedonia, who all had Greek names but were rather different in their action, and more particularly about some mountain rites which the nice old thing remembered with a sucking in of lips and wrinkling round eyes. 'Girls will be girls,' she said, 'and we all did it. The best families. These chits of Greeks down here, they haven't the blood. No, my dear. But up in the north we're different, we know how to live. You tell your brother he should take you to Macedonia, you'll find yourself a man there.' She quite disregarded the fact that Erif was married; she liked something she could see and understand. On the same lines, she was cross with Berris because he was not sufficiently accurate in painting the scars on her son's legs. They were honourable scars; once he had a pike-head right through his left calf; he still walked a little lame of it, but not enough to spoil his dignity. Berris, annoyed, made a sketch of the governor with no clothes and more than all the scars, but for safety's sake it had to be burned.

Then one day Erif met Eupolia and Ianthemis at a party the governor's wife was giving. She looked no odder than the Macedonians now in her Greek dress as she came quickly forward to speak to them. Eupolia was quite reasonably pleasant, but Ianthemis was shy and distressed and seemed cross. The girl was thinner and darker than her sister, and her skin was smudgy, so that it was thought better for her to use powder. But behind it her eyes were less guarded than her mother's, so it was she that Erif Der decided to get the news from, after Eupolia, having given courteous replies about her husband's health, had moved on and begun to talk to their hostess. Ianthemis had wanted to follow her mother; she was afraid of being left alone and talked to by strangers, but she was not used enough to parties to finish off her conversation with Erif neatly and quickly, and the thing dragged on and her mother was out of sight and the slaves with cakes seemed all to be at the other end of the room! Erif

Der said quickly: 'Do you ever hear from Philylla now?'
Ianthemis gaped. 'Does she like Egypt?'

'Oh!' said Ianthemis, 'she's not in Egypt!'

Erif was so surprised that she nearly lost her grip of the
talk, but Ianthemis was not enough on the spot to get away
before the question: 'Is she here then?'

'No-oo!' said Ianthemis, and laughed and then looked at
the foreign woman, who was, after all, not a Macedonian, and
decided to tell her—well, something. 'She's at home,' said
Ianthemis, 'and mother sees she stays there! Besides, she
doesn't like these parties.'

'Why is she at home, Ianthemis?' said Erif, smiling as
nicely as she knew how and beckoning one of the cake-girls
over. 'Do tell me. You see, I don't know anything!'

Half won, Ianthemis said: 'Panteus wants her to go to
Egypt. But of course it would be silly. So she's got to be
stopped. Even though she is grown up.'

'Would it be silly, though?' asked Erif. 'Wives have to
obey their husbands first, don't they? And besides—'she
dropped her voice, glancing down at the little cake in her
hand—'supposing all this doesn't last for ever?'

'Oh, you mustn't!' said Ianthemis quickly. 'We don't
ever say that—or think it! Anyhow, Panteus hasn't
ordered her to come.'

'I see,' said the Queen of Marob, and suddenly found herself uncertain of the patterns of Sparta or what had happened
to them now. She realised that Eupolia had rather definitely
not asked her to the house, though at the time she had
not noticed it, because she had not particularly wanted to
go there. Now she did want. She tried the direct method.
'How pretty you've grown, Ianthemis! You don't mind
my telling you so? I expect plenty of people do. I wish
my brother could see you. He's so tired of painting rather
plain governors!'

In a pleasant distraction Ianthemis took another cake;
there hadn't been anything so good to eat in all her life
before! They had paste of dates and chestnuts and some
little greenish sweet lumps—She wanted so badly to ask
whether Erif really thought she was as pretty as her sister,
but somehow she couldn't! She could only say: 'Oh, do
you really think so, how nice of you!' And, flurried, began
on admiration in her own turn. 'Your brother must be so

clever! Every one says so. Did he make your lovely bracelets?' She fingered the lowest of the very fine set which
Erif wore, perhaps rather barbarically, between elbow and
shoulder.

Erif undid it carelessly. 'Oh,' she said, 'they're amusing,
aren't they? He's always making them. Look at the lizard's
head.' She slid it suddenly on to the girl's arm. 'Why,
it's nothing, do keep it! I shall think you hate me if you
don't!'

And really it did look beautiful, and it made—didn't
it?—her arm look almost rather beautiful too! She'd
had so few pretty things since the time father had made
mother give up all her jewellery for the King. Herself, she
hadn't minded then, she was too little, but now she did
mind. She didn't know enough about jewels to tell if this
was valuable at all; probably it was just nothing, as Erif had
said. She blushed and thanked and inadvertently licked the
cake crumbs inelegantly off her fingers, and blushed again
for that.

'And give my love to your sister,' Erif was saying, 'and I
may come and see you both one day, mayn't I? It's such
ages since I've been away.' It was a bracelet Berris had given
her at New Year, his own best work. Well, never mind. At
the end of the afternoon, she got a rather vague invitation
from Eupolia, which she promptly turned into a definite day
and hour.

After the party she went to Berris, who was cleaning his
brushes. She said: 'Philylla is still in Sparta,' and watched
him draw up and harden his mouth and rub the paint still
more meticulously out of the soft brush hairs.

'Where's her husband then?' said Berris.

'Oh, in Egypt, as we heard. But her mother's keeping her
at home. Poor darling!'

Berris did not answer for a time; he seemed to be turning
it over and over. At last he said, very crossly indeed: 'So
you say, Erif, but how do you think you know she wants
to go?'

Erif thought with pleasure of how a few years ago she would
have answered him back, but how now she felt herself merely
a superior player of the not too difficult game. 'We shall know
quite soon, anyhow,' she said, 'because I've arranged for us
to go and see her.'

'Well!' said Berris, 'you are a bitch and no mistake!' But his hard mouth grinned in spite of itself and he went on cleaning his brushes quicker.

Ianthemis told Philylla that they were coming, but Philylla was marsh-sunk in gloom so that she could scarcely turn her head or answer. She had been betrayed by Tiasa, and the whole household was mobilised against her. She had no money and nobody would get it for her. The stables were forbidden, though the young helot groom wept not to be able to obey her. Even her father insisted on giving her long lectures on the uselessness of going on with this: better to submit, as he had. Ianthemis had managed to send off her answering letter to Panteus, which said most solemnly that she would come out to him. Or—was it possible that her sister had betrayed her too? No, no; Ianthemis was a Spartiate where Tiasa was only a helot! She looked out of the high, square window of her room; she could see clouds like fat fishes going by, the beginning of winter. Already there would be fewer ships sailing; she would almost certainly have to wait until spring.

Thinking of that, she suddenly realised what she had been told by her sister. At least there would be Erif and Berris to make life possible during the winter! Berris. She had not seen him for a long time, not since she was a girl, before her marriage. She thought she knew now how unkind she had been. She wondered whether he had been twisted about, forced by the images in his mind into maddening, hot, aching sleeplessness, as she was now most nights, thinking of her man and his body. Sometimes towards dawn she would have been willing enough to have the body alone without the mind or heart. The body, the skin, the—No! what was the use of thinking about it till she was somewhere near getting it! Dreams do no good. She had stopped wondering about Berris. She did not even trouble to change her dress, though when she heard voices, she did come straight through the courtyard to them without needing to be fetched.

She kissed Erif and made much of her, but she was distant with Berris, deliberately putting barriers between her self of now and the self which Berris used to know. The talk was all quite formal. She sat between her father, who was delighted to see Berris again, and her mother. She noticed that one of the embroidery threads on her mother's dress was loose, and had caught round a bronze leaf on the chair leg; when Eupolia got up it would all pull together—the little yellow wool bird on the wine-coloured stuff would wrinkle and shrivel and become shapeless as the thread of its body jerked out—the warp and weft of the groundwork would be suddenly strained on as never since its weaving, snap, snap. She made no movement to warn Eupolia.

Ianthemis sat on her mother's other side; she had not quite dared put on her best dress, but she was in white with anemones in her hair, and she wore the bracelet Erif had given her. She was very silent, but she kept on glancing sideways without turning her head at all towards Berris. She wondered if he was looking at her with his painter's eyes. She put her arms and her body into what felt like poses. Would mother let him paint her? Could it be done, perhaps, as a present for Chaerondas? Meanwhile Eupolia talked pleasantly to Erif, skirting round difficult subjects, but near enough for her to try and test what this woman thought and whether she would be a suitable companion for Philylla.

Erif took up the challenge and played. She had to persuade Eupolia that she was harmless and assure Philylla that she was a friend. All the time part of her was feeling over towards Philylla, trying to say: 'We are both separated from the men we love, let us be sisters'; trying to say: 'I will help you, even though you cannot help me.' But the upper part of her mind was light and laughing. She told them about Hyperides and how she had sent back toys for her little son, and how she had got a letter back from the Athenian, written just before midsummer, saying how well and pretty her boy was and how hospitable every one was in Marob. She hoped to get another letter soon, sent on from Kirrha, but she and her brother had been moving about so much. Yes, they were going to stay in Sparta all winter. Where better to stay nowadays than Sparta? At this she saw Philylla sigh and shift and turn back pitiably into herself, but Eupolia smiled and was satisfied. So far, so good. She would put it right easily with Philylla.

Berris had started by being extremely uncomfortable; he had looked once at Ianthemis and seen his bracelet on her arm. Erif had told him he probably would, and he approved her action, but still he did hate seeing it there! He was seized with a sudden desire in his finger-tips to touch the thing again, and that had been made impossible for him! But he liked Themisteas; they had always got on well together. They talked about the battle of Sellasia, but technically, without any political opinions. If these seemed like appearing, Themisteas glanced aside at his wife and suppressed everything. Berris found himself half the time talking down to the older man. Now he himself was successful, with a security quite apart from birthplace or property, something in the minds of men and in his own mind. Yes, he had got almost enough praise now not to care about it! Even the Spartiates, Themisteas and Eupolia, recognised the quality in him, even though they did not care much for the external products of it. They were polite to him and a little bit frightened—and, in spite of themselves, a little bit honoured! Suddenly Berris, the successful one, had a wild impulse to stand on his head and wave his legs at them and shout!

But, feeling this impulse, he had flung his head up, and there was Philylla looking at him from under her brows, and all at once he was struck down to earth, into the net, and he was not successful any more. Oh God, what was everything if he had not got her! It was no use; he could say to himself as much as he chose that he was free of her; he could go and make love to slave-girls and models and pretend it was the same thing; he could tell a tart in a brothel at Kirrha about this calf-love of his and listen to her laugh at it and offer him better goods. All that muck had gone down to the roots of his passion, had dunged it into strength, now it had borne a blinding rose, now he was a grown man and deeply and bitterly in love with Philylla!

All the time, he went on talking to Themisteas. He told them amusing stories about his adventures, the houses he had been into, the things people had said about his pictures. He asked after the animals. Themisteas told him excitedly about the new litter of hound puppies; he gripped the arm of his chair and half raised himself, then winced and sat back and told the girls to run out and get them. Ianthemis jumped up and Philylla followed her; in a few minutes they came back with an armful each, and the great bitch sniffing and whining behind them. Ianthemis thought, thrillingly, that she was bringing an offering to a great painter, and she did hope her father would think of giving him one. She had the pick of the bunch snuggled into her right elbow; at least the grooms said it was. She ducked her head down and rubbed her cheek on it. Philylla was not thinking about dogs at all.

Themisteas took the whole lot of squirming puppies on to his own knees, and handled them, fingering round their blind, sucking muzzles, their broad paws, laughing delightedly when the needle-pointed claws pricked him through his tunic as the puppies padded over him. Berris and Erif leant over and admired and shoved them back when they tried to tumble off. The bitch sat on her haunches with her head on her master's thigh and stayed so, unmoving, gazing dumbly and darkly at her babies. Themisteas scratched her gently behind the ears and crooned to her, and wondered aloud whether he would ever see these hounds running. His leg was the devil to heal, he could still only hobble about.

Now the mistress of the house clapped her hands and a boy brought in a jug of new wine, with apples and walnuts and thin wheaten cakes. They all nibbled and drank from the pretty, eared cups of black pottery. Themisteas still kept the puppies on his knees and fed the bitch with cake.

Philylla sat down again, leaning forward with her elbows on her knees and hands clasped in front on them. She would have enjoyed being alone with the puppies, or even with them and her father, or perhaps Ianthemis. But now every one was talking and laughing and interrupting the soft babiness of them and stopping her from listening to their funny, tiny squealings and growlings. Berris and Erif weren't going to be much good to her after all. They'd gone over. She had hoped that Erif, anyhow, would remember. Berris, anyhow. Erif. Berris. She had hoped that much of friendship! She stopped listening to what they were saying; it was not interesting at all.

They put the puppies down on the floor, Ianthemis reluctant to let go of the lovely silky rolls of fat on their backs. She squatted among them, tickling and playing with them, shoving them towards their mother's teats or pulling them off. Oh, how nice, father was offering one to Berris Der! He would have his pick. Oh, was he going to choose the right one? She held them out to him, trying without words to get him to take that one, but he didn't seem to understand; he wasn't as interested as he ought to have been. He chose quite a good puppy, but not her special one. It would be ready for him by the middle of winter.

Now it was time to go. Eupolia got up from her chair to say good-bye very cordially. Philylla was watching. There! the thread had caught. All in a moment the embroidered bird was twisted and tortured into shapelessness. Her ears were so keen to it that she caught the sound of the wool thread snapping. Her mother frowned a little and glanced down and appeared not to notice. A slave was sent running to fetch the guests' mules to the door. They went. 'I like that boy,' Themisteas said. 'It will be pleasant to see something of them this winter. He cheers me up. You must ask them again, my dear.' 'Certainly I will,' said Eupolia.

The two mule-riders went back to Sparta. They both had stiff felt cloaks with sleeves, thick enough to keep out all but the heaviest rain. When they were half-way a shower gathered and began to fall, and the land responded immediately with a cloud of damp-stirred plant and earth smells. Berris turned up his face to catch the rain; he had not spoken much. Erif's mind was still back with Philylla. She said firmly: 'We've got to get her out of that. She'll fret herself to death.' But Berris did not answer, and suddenly his sister rather regretted what she had said.

Winter went on; the two were often at the house of Themisteas. It had been difficult for Erif to see Philylla alone—Philylla herself had not seemed anxious to make opportunities—but gradually she had pieced the situation together. As she did so she began to waver and be uncertain of what she ought to do. For it seemed to her by no means sure that Philylla's ultimate happiness lay in following Panteus. Then, when at last she had persuaded Philylla, not suddenly but little by little over a long series of looks and words—snatched question and answer—and infinitely friendly kisses and touches, that she really might be trusted, she was shown the letter, and that did not help her to decide. It was Philylla at last who asked the decisive thing: would Erif lend her money, on no security beyond her word, to take her over to Alexandria, and, if so, would she help her to escape out of the house?

They were sitting close together on Philylla's bed; there was a pretence of trying on sandals. Erif said: 'My brother has the purse. I must ask him.'

'But would he? I couldn't bear—to be betrayed again.' Philylla, suddenly almost snivelling!

'I don't know,' said Erif frankly.

Philylla stopped and began to lace and unlace the new sandal. There was a charcoal fire in the room and she was naked but for a thin shift that rucked up over her thighs. Erif could see her breasts heave and harden under the tightening of shoulder and chest muscles. The unsaid thing about Berris stood like a crystal between the two women. Philylla raised herself and looked down critically at her sandalled foot. 'If he thinks he can get me for himself this way, he's wrong,' she said.

'Yes,' said Erif, 'yes. Shall I tell him that too?'

But Themisteas and Eupolia were beginning to speak to one another guardedly of possibilities. If Ianthemis were married off to Chaerondas and if Philylla—not at once, oh no, but after due formalities and presumption of death in exile—were married to this charming and certainly rich young man, who so obviously adored her and who could certainly be persuaded to take a Greek name and settle down, well—In the meantime they allowed Philylla to walk with Berris in the walled orchard, among the bare trees, half in sight, but not in hearing of the house. They did not know what Philylla was talking to him about so earnestly. She was re-telling him the stories Agiatis had told her as a young girl, at the same time soothing herself by speaking to someone of what was in her heart, saying often the name of the woman she had loved, and keeping alive in herself the flame of the revolution.

When she had told him the story of King Agis, Berris remembered the first evening when they had heard it from Sphaeros, and for a time his mind went back to Marob, and his sister, much younger, and Tarrik drinking from a skull-cup, and the paleness of Eurydice's hands, and himself seeing it, but still in those days not able quite to put it down. Then he began to make other pictures in his mind, rather deliberately childish and unplanned: the young and innocent King, the golden hair edged with sunshine against the red door of a house in shadow. The man, at the end, coming up to Agis in pretence of friendship and betraying him to the ephors with a kiss. A good scene. The dark betrayer. Done with sharp angles and zigzags and that violetish colour you see in a sallow skin, against Agis lighted up into squares and rounds, kind simple shapes, the shapes a child thinks of, looking at a rose. And he should have a blue tunic—probably did!—with the folds quite obvious, movingly common. Or it might be done as a crowd, dozens of tiny people seen from far off, and a rather steep perspective, so that the mere crowding and repetition of them should make up the weight and pathos of the picture. Not a pattern picture, a story picture. Not for himself, but for Philylla and her people of the revolution.

During the next week he was hard at it, first with one after another squared-up sketch, small and crowded and exciting, then with the big thing, on canvas. When it was done he rolled it and disguised it with some care as a bolt of linen, and he and Erif showed it to Philylla. When she saw what it was she looked from it to him and blushed and clasped her hands in rather a delightful and childish way, and threw down barriers and said in her old voice: 'Oh, Berris!'

She took his hand and he kissed hers. He kissed it softly up on to the wrist. At last she drew it away. He took the picture back to Sparta, and after that he made three more of the life and death of Agis, and under each, in careful lettering, he put the legend of which incident it was, exactly in Philylla's words. One of them was Agis in the mountains, suddenly knowing what was laid on him to do, a boy in the dawn, and lambs on the hillside behind him. Another was his speech to the people of Sparta, the gentle and earnest head among all those grim, specious, bearded, crafty heads: a picture of heads—the bodies were only flat patterns of colour. In the third Agis was dead: the hanged King cut down and lain naked across his mother's knees in the moment of her agony, before her neck too was in the noose. Berris told Philylla he was doing them, and that he would show them to her some time. In the meanwhile they were rolled up and put away in the room where he worked. As technique they did not interest him particularly, but whenever he remembered them, he was pleased.

Erif had hesitated for some time before approaching him about the money; when she did he smiled and said he would think about it, and then he said nothing more until he had finished painting the Agis pictures. Then one day he said to his sister: 'Do you still think I should give Philylla that money?'

Erif was planing down a wood panel for him. 'Why not?' she said.

'If you really want to be told, my dear, because I've got a chance of her myself.'

'I doubt it,' said Erif.

'What about Agis?' said Berris, jerking his thumb back at the rolled pictures. 'They're for her. She'll take them.'

'You surely don't think you've a chance of getting her for keeps? You know Sparta as well as I do.'

'Sparta now's not Sparta then. They'll have me.'

'But she won't, and what's the good of thinking you'll ever want to take her by force? You'd be bad at rape, Berris.'

'She can't go on staying in love with a shadow. She's always been half turned towards me; if he'd got killed decently instead of slinking off to Egypt, she'd want me now. She's holding out for her idea still, but it'll all crash suddenly.'

Erif saw, by his calmness, that he was really serious, and stopped planing. 'Darling Berris,' she said, 'I do want you always to get what you want, but she still is in love with Panteus. That is perhaps very silly of her, but I don't see what can be done about it yet. I'm certain she loves both you and me in a way, and you might work up a kind of glow in her with gratitude and friendliness which might do as pretence love before it was found out. I think once in a lonely winter night she might let you have her, thinking about the Agis pictures, and I don't see that she would be hurt by that because it wouldn't touch her marriage. But that would be all you would get and it might hurt you.'

Berris took up the planed board and rubbed his hands softly over the surface. 'You think I'm more easily hurt than I am,' he said, 'in these complicated woman-ways of yours. I'm just plain hurt at not having her at all. I'd sooner buy her than nothing. With the Agis pictures. I've bought women before!' He glared violently across at his sister.

Erif sighed; he was tiring to live with in these moods. But perhaps it was a possible way of helping him and Philylla at the same time. 'Well, go on,' she said, 'but try the pictures alone first. Keep the money out, if you can, till afterwards. But if she lets you be her lover you must help her to go to Alexandria afterwards. It's all very fine, Berris, looking like that, but after all, it's my money too, and if I like to sell one of my jewels—yes, and the ones you've made would fetch most!—I can get her away just the same as you.'

'Why don't you do it then, you devil, instead of sitting there looking at me!'

'Because we've been friends, Berris, all our lives, haven't we? And if we were out of Greece I would be able to magic you. How could I not give you the chance of having her once? You see, Berris, it might turn out to be all you needed. Then she could go to Egypt, and we could go to Athens or somewhere. Till the end of the four years. Why can't Hyperides write! I don't see that Panteus would really hate you, either. Yes, I know you don't care whether he does or not, but she'd hate you if he did. Oh, Berris, am I quite, quite wrong?'

Berris was calm again. He had begun to draw on the wood, a great tangly growth of elks and dragons—northern. He said: 'I think you may be wrong. She may have stopped being in love with that man after the letter came, only she hasn't found out yet, and she won't unless something shows her. Wouldn't it be odd, Erif, if she went out to Alexandria not knowing that, and only found out when she saw him! Or when she went to bed with him. She'd never be able to admit it to anyone but herself, and there it would be inside her all her life. Isn't that a funny thing to think of!'

Erif said in horror: 'I wonder if you can possibly be right.' And then she began to cry, but quietly, so as not to interrupt Berris.

He said: 'It's very easy to deceive oneself, and other people. It would be quite easy to deceive you, Erif, over this kind of thing. Yet it's a thin, flimsy bit of pretence, quite easy to break with the right kind of blow: a sharp tap would do it, Erif, a word if it were the right word. A very little force would do it—even I could use that amount of force! Even on her. And if it was broken there would be nothing left standing between her and me.'

'Oh, I wish you wouldn't,' sobbed Erif. 'You may be right!'

'Why shouldn't it be me who's right for once? And what a place we'll make for you, what a home for the four years! And I am sure, I've known this in my heart ever since I first saw her.'

'Oh, I do hate you all!' Erif cried at him, and threw the

plane on to the floor, skidding, crash, into the wall. 'I had it all plain in my head and now it's tangled, it's a bad magic! Oh, Berris, I've got this curse on me still, I can feel it, the seasons have turned on me, and all the proper things that go with the seasons, love and marriage and friendship! Oh, I make everything I touch unlucky, I spoil people's lives, I make straight things crooked! Oh, go away from me; I'm unlucky, I've lost Tarrik and Marob and my baby! Oh, take Philylla away if you like, I shall only hurt her! Oh, it's all my fault. Oh, Berris, let me go. Oh, don't hold me, oh, how shall I ever get free!'

But Berris wasn't frightened; he knew how these whirl-winds arise suddenly in the soul and then subside. He took her on his knees and patted her shoulder and arm and told her not to be so silly, and let her snuggle against him and cry down his neck. It would pass. She had this evil in her still; better to let it come out. Philylla was almost always, as he remembered her, calm and strong. He had just bought a squared and seasoned oak trunk with curious knots; in his mind it was already turning into a reclining woman with curious breasts. He hoped Erif had not taken the edge off the plane, throwing it about like that.

Chapter Six

NOW IT WAS NEARLY the end of the winter and very stormy. Once or twice a north wind had brought snow down on to the houses, but it never lay, and Berris and Erif had no chance of sledging. It was a cold ride out to the house of Themisteas, even for Berris with all the hot and hopeful eagerness of his body. Eupolia wished very much that they still had their town house, but that had been lost at the end of the King's Times, and she had quite enough to do salvaging their country estates; the house had been taken over by the ephors for the redistribution.

The classes were all in disorder now. During winter Dontas came home quite often. He was a silent, sometimes rather sulky boy, with tufty yellow hair and a blank face to his elders. He had been very much upset by the death of his Iren at Sellasia, but would not talk about it to anyone. He did not like Erif or Berris Der and went out quickly if they came into any room where he was.

During this time it seemed as though it were Erif who

was avoiding ever being alone with Philylla. She tried to go on making friends with Ianthemis, but the girl realised that Berris was not interested in her, and she spent most of her time coaxing her father and mother to take some more definite action about Chaerondas. Sometimes she talked to Tiasa. Philylla would not do that now. She would not speak a word to her foster-mother nor even go near the home-farm, where she used to be so often and where she would still have been allowed to go if she had taken someone trustworthy with her. She did not care that Mikon was there and sometimes one or two others who wanted badly to see her and get reassurance from her. She would have had nothing to give them. She was puzzled about her life; she looked forward very much to seeing Berris from day to day, but she could not tell where it was all leading. And unless her road led to Egypt she did not or would not know where else it might lead. There had been no more letters, or at any rate none had reached her. In the meantime she had stood beside Berris Der, looking at the Agis pictures, and his arm had gone round her and he had kissed her and she had thought for a moment that if only he would tell her what to do and give her reason, she would surely do it. For now Panteus was not here to tell her. Nor Agiatis. He had fought for the King and he had made the pictures, and his sister Erif loved her and would never let him do any hurt to the house of Panteus and Philylla. She would ask again soon about the money and help. She was sleeping better than she had done for weeks.

But as for Berris, he was being worse torn than ever Erif guessed. It was all very well to be violent and male and insist on getting what he wanted, but he did also want most deeply to be kind to Philylla and do what she wanted. The kindness of the brush: the violence of the chisel. He wanted to be liked. He did not in the least mind if people did not like his pictures, because he was certain of them himself, but he did mind that people should like him! That Philylla should like him. Why complicate one's life with women? Well, there it was: devilishly complicated. And she was so beautiful, so strong; she was not one of those little round girls one pummels and pulls the clothes off and takes by the thighs, squeaking. Some of her essential beauty would be lost if she did not come to him willingly and bravely, giving her hand in all honour with that piercing smile of hers, herself loosening the belt-clasp from under those lovely breasts, unhurrying, herself drawing him to her, down to her, to that incredibly tender and happy and all-satisfying meeting of the flesh. It did not do for him, though, to think of that much. His visual and tactile imagination was too good. For a little time the mere image filled his mind and body with deep joy, yet the joy held tension in it, ebbed and darkened away until nothing but the tension was left, an aching, stinging bodily tension that passed at last with other thoughts and other movement, but left behind it a terrible depression in which he could not work.

He wished Erif would talk about it more, help him to fix his mind, and, when that was done, help him to fix Philylla's. But Erif was less ready to talk than he had ever known her. She would not find out for him whether, for instance, Philylla was writing again to Egypt: merely said she supposed she was. Sometimes Philylla herself would suddenly begin to speak about her husband to Berris and he was never quite sure how to answer. For she might be doing it seriously as part of this marriage idea of hers, which sooner or later he thought he would be able to shatter, and, if this was so, he must always be on the look-out for the weakest point; or it might be that, unknown to him, the idea was already broken and she was only saying this maddening name, Panteus, Panteus, so as to tease him and stab him on; or she might be saying it to a friend she trusted—he knew she would not speak to her parents or sister as she did to him—and if so it would be both horrible and foolish to show himself as anything less than the dearest and most trustworthy friend.

Then, on the turn of winter, when already the sun was beginning to shine stronglier, and on southern banks the smaller flowers were out, two letters, forwarded deviously from Kirrha, came to the Queen of Marob.

One was from Hyperides, and the other was from Tarrik himself, and they were written after Harvest and the putting right of everything. It took her a little time to realise what had happened; she passed the letters to Berris without comment, for she did not trust herself to speak. It was he finally who said, trying to be as calm as possible: 'Obviously, there is nothing wrong in Marob any more. Tarrik has, as he says, stopped being afraid of anything, and the seasons are afraid of him! Yes, it's pretty complete, my dear. I'm glad.' He kissed her. Then he said: 'On this, do you think you can go back? It is—likely—isn't it, that this will have put you right too?'

Erif Der went very red and she said: 'Now Tarrik is made lucky, he will be able sooner or later to pull me home and make me safe and happy again. Oh, Berris, my marriage is not for nothing now! In spite of all the things which have happened and which will happen yet, in spite of pain and danger and separation, my marriage is real, and I shall see my husband and everything will come right in the end!'

'That is all true,' said Berris, smiling. 'Your marriage is a kataleptike phantasia, Erif wife of Tarrik!'

'And before this letter came,' said Erif, with her eyes fixed and bright, 'I was going to let you break a marriage and keep a woman from the husband she loves. Oh, if I go back to Tarrik, Philylla must go back to Panteus; and if she does not go, may I be stopped from going! Berris, do you hear, marriage is a real thing and the best thing, and I know it is the same for Philylla, and she shall have it again and make good come of it, and I shall sell my jewels and give her the money to go!'

Berris looked at her and did not speak for a time; he was rather white. At last he said: 'No, Erif, if anyone is to give her the money, it's to be me. But give me time—time—' He sat down suddenly, dropping the sea-stained letters from Marob, and held his head in his hands.

'All the time you want,' said his sister, and kissed him and stood there, enclosing in the circle of her mind Tarrik and Hyperides and her son and Essro and Disdallis and Kotka, and all the golden corn harvests of Marob, and at the same time her friend Philylla and her brother Berris and the beautiful things he was going to make.

For the next fortnight neither of them came much to Themisteas' house. Then one day Erif came with a pair of silver filigree ear-rings for Ianthemis, who danced away with them to show her father and mother and Tiasa. Berris had made them—not very well, but well enough—during the time he was thinking things out, so as to have something to occupy his hands. Erif found Philylla alone in her room, sewing; she looked up in the way she had, as though she were constantly expecting something, and shoved along the litter of needles and thread and half-made clothes so as to make room for Erif. She was very glad to see either of them again. Her hair had grown after the clipping at marriage, but she herself had cut it short again after Sellasia and had kept it short for mourning all this time; she usually wore a dark-coloured handkerchief stretched tightly over it and knotted at the back. She put her hands up to it now in an automatic gesture. Erif sat down beside her and in a low voice told her to be ready at such and such a time and place; she and her brother would have the money.

Philylla dropped her sewing and for a moment sat motionless with open hands. Then she turned sideways into Erif's arms and clung to her and sobbed against her neck with little funny bird-like shriekings of laughter between the sobs. At last she said: 'And then? You'll get me a horse?'

'Yes, we shall all have horses.'

'You'll come with me to Gytheum? You dears!'

Erif undid Philylla's arms from round her neck and held her steady, smiling seriously at her. 'As a matter of fact, we are coming with you to Egypt.'

The morning of the day came with a north wind slamming the shutters and making a grey flashing stream of each winter-leafy olive. Philylla put together the things she wanted, sewing them up into coarse, strong linen, so as to make two saddle-bags. She wandered about the house and was nice to Ianthemis and her father. She would not see them or it again until the King came back and she and Panteus had their own home once more. Then she would come and walk gloriously with her hair grown and perhaps, yes, perhaps carrying a child against her shoulder, a boy baby, through all the rooms and passages where she had been a prisoner all these months. Then she would forgive her mother for going Macedonian. Then she might begin to think of forgiving Tiasa! As the day went on, the wind, if anything, rose, but she was not afraid. She washed all over with plenty of oil, for she was not sure when she would have another chance. She visited the puppies. Berris had not taken his one away—he had said he would wait till spring when it would be easier to exercise and train it. They all came wobbling and scuttling up with tiny pretence barks, and licked her feet. It was beginning to get dark. She had a game of dice with her father and Dontas; they pretended all sorts of impossible wagers and all got excited about it and laughed a lot. Her mother brought in the lamps. About another hour.

She grew more restless now, and her heart beat uncomfortably. She found herself having to go so constantly to ease herself that she was a little afraid she had eaten something poisonous. Coming back from this, in that less well-lighted part of the house, she suddenly met her foster-mother, who stepped aside, bending her head, and then suddenly and imploringly stretched out her hands to her baby—who was hurting her so! A curious, sharp pain ran through Philylla, mixing with this spasmodic and nervous pain in her bowels, and she half moved towards Tiasa, as though on that bosom the pain could be cured or kissed away. But at this Tiasa sprang forward like a big, hot, soft tigress, and it flashed at Philylla that if she let herself be caught and touched and kissed she might be made prisoner again, and she hit out against Tiasa with one hand, not caring where it caught her, mouth or throat or breasts, and turned and ran. Her foster-mother did not follow her.

Berris waited with the four horses in the curious numb state he had been in ever since the letters from Marob had come and Erif had spoken about marriage like a priestess—like the Spring Queen. He was hurting himself and yet he knew he was also going through some experience as violent as any love affair, and which would ultimately set turning the wheels of his creation and make something solider and nearer reality than he had ever made before. There was a half-moon. The wind kept on tearing off piece after piece of cloud and sending them sweeping across its face; the stars were polished with cold.

Their fourth horse was laden with his and Erif's things, valuables of one kind or another, and some rolled canvases. It had not given him any pain to leave a great deal behind; he was done with it. In any case, most of his things were definite orders which were now with their owners. He had wrapped up the Agis pictures and given them to a man whom he knew to be on the King's side, asking him to pass them on, if he ever got the chance, to young Kleomenes, who was now with his mother Chilonis, slowly getting better of his wound. But he did not know whether they would ever get there. Erif had not made herself enough of a home to mind either about leaving most of her things behind and starting again.

With startling suddenness the two were beside him; he had not heard them because of the wind. Philylla threw up her bundles over the saddle and mounted. Both women rode astride—it was safer for a long distance, when they might have to go fast. Erif was wearing thick trousers, as the Marob women often did in winter, and a felt coat with loops over silver buttons that fastened it tight from neck to waist and hid whatever jewels she might have been wearing. She had soft leather riding-boots, like her brother's, that came up over the trousers. Her hair was plaited and tied, and she had a knife at her belt, which she enjoyed feeling with her free hand every now and then. Philylla wore a short woollen tunic, pulled up through her belt to knee height, an old one she had worn as a girl, and a heavy, dark-coloured woollen cloak. She tucked the flapping ends under her and sat back in the saddle and got a good grip of the reins. She had leather shoes, and inside them had bound her feet and ankles round with woollen strips to keep her warmer. She had grazed one leg climbing the wall, but she said nothing about it, and in the dark neither of the others saw.

They made a wide circle by sunk lanes and field-tracks to avoid the town of Sparta, and then came out on to the main way south to the sea, and halted to let the horses breathe, and stretch themselves; it was very awkward and uncomfortable riding in the dark on these winter roads. Impossible to talk much in this wind. It blew at their backs, every now and then whipping a gust of light sharp rain against them. When the horses moved on, the saddles began creaking again, the stumbling and jolting began again, the smell of the horses came up to their nostrils again if they leant a little forward to avoid the buffeting on their heads. Philylla's legs were very cold; they hardly felt the rain any longer. Only the inner sides of her calves next the horse's flank kept some warmth continuously with the horse, but her knees were already sore with rubbing, and her thigh muscles ached. All their hands, too, were bitterly cold.

The wind tore the handkerchief from Philylla's head. She grabbed and lost it; it was torn out of her fingers. Erif's hair-ribbons went too, and soon after that her plaits came undone. Then the wind got hold of her hair; it flapped the damp tangles with a noise like small thunder at her ears; it raised them off the scalp, sideways and forwards, with a

tug like someone pulling; it stopped her from being tired
and it was a flag. The same wind could make nothing of
Philylla's fair, close-cut head; it went straight through to
the skin in a cold streaming, with a prickle of hair-roots as it
brushed them across the way of growth. Berris' felt hat was
knotted firmly under his chin; it was still on. He watched
his sister's hair streaming out or standing away from her
like wild dark flames as the wind caught it one way and
another. When sometimes her horse drew level with his, a
cold lock might flick stingingly across his mouth or eyes.
But he did not look much at Philylla. All the same he was
not unhappy; it was almost joy that filled him. The sense
of action instead of creation excited him. He was going to
Egypt; suddenly he found the idea of that wildly thrilling.
He would see all manner of new things! He hoped he would
never see Sparta again, the house where he had worked, the
people he had worked for. He had done with Sparta finally.
Unless—But a great cold gust booming down on to him
swept the thought away.

After the first half-hour Philylla's thoughts were all
extremely practical. The most important one was that
if this gale went on blowing no ship would sail. Then
she remembered Neareta's cousins. Berris could ask for
them. They could shelter there; though somehow she was
quite doubtful whether she would be pursued—at once,
anyhow. She was almost sure her father and mother would
have an argument about it. Themisteas would like to think
of his daughter riding out into the storm! She wondered if
Ianthemis would miss her and be sorry at all. Yes, probably.
And even Dontas. And certainly the puppies. She wished
she could have taken one, but it would have been an extra
complication, one too many. Her legs were chafing most
damnably against the saddle; however tired she was by the
end of the ride she must be sure to dab them with olive oil
before she went to sleep. Her shoes must be greased too or
they would dry stiff.

But Erif was all tangled up with the weight of her wild,
mocking, inconsequent hair. Whenever she tried to think it
whirled her mind round and round. It got mixed up with
the idea of Tarrik being right and his own self again and full
of power. Tarrik leapt and charged like the wind. He was
the wind, coming down, breaking the earth, breaking and

tossing flowers and leaves and men and women! Once on a level piece of road she let go the reins a moment and tried to catch her hair and plait it up again, but that was no use; it danced and slid out of her hands up into the sky. The skin of her head was all alive and delicious because of the wind; the bright chill went down into her brain. It was wonderfully funny and delightful and splendid! She was not grown-up any more, not steady and responsible, and a person who had been hurt and might be hurt again. Oh for the time, for the time at least, she knew she was not unlucky! Tarrik and the wind and her hair. She laughed and laughed and laughed. The wind beat the breath out of her and stopped the others from hearing the loud laughter of the Spring Queen.

Towards dawn the wind lulled suddenly, flattening out into a mere steady breeze; the sky was clear of clouds. But they heard the sea roaring ahead, and it was plain to all of them that no captain would sail that day. They stopped and consulted; Philylla explained about the helots, and Berris rode ahead to find out about them. It was not a big town, he would probably hit on them quite easily, and he himself would not be recognised.

He cantered on and the two girls followed slowly with the baggage horse. Now Erif's hair hung over her shoulders, almost calm and tamed, but wildly tangled all through, and curly on its outer surface like a fleece. Her mind, too, was apparently calm again. She leaned over and kissed Philylla, who was white and in some pain. They smiled at one another; they were sisters. But they were very tired, and very wet, and very cold. At last the sun rose and almost at once they felt warmer and gayer; then Berris came back to tell them he had found the house.

They rode into the town and down two or three by-streets. It was too early for better class people to be about, but they went down to a poor quarter close to the sea. The man of the house opened the door and looked from Berris to the others, who dismounted stiffly and painfully, hardly able to stand. 'The gentleman was saying you were friends with Neareta, my woman's uncle's wife's niece!' he said, rather defiantly, 'but I don't see—' His wife came to the door and cried at them: 'Who are you, fine folks and foreigners?'

Philylla held on to the saddle and swayed. 'I am a friend to Neareta and Phoebis,' she said. 'We go their way.' She did not want to tell her name. But they still held the door. 'How do I know?' the man muttered, staring at her and from her to Erif with her trousers and loose hair. Berris came quickly to her side and held her up and whispered to her: 'Tell them!' She lifted her head and leaned back for support against Berris' shoulder and said: 'I am Philylla, wife of Panteus. Will you let us in?' For one moment still the man and woman whispered together, then the man ran clumsily forward a few steps and seized her hand and kissed it. 'I know you, I know you!' he cried. 'Neareta told us! Come in and welcome. You'll be safe with us. I'll take the horses round.' Then his wife came talking excitedly and took Philylla away from Berris, who went with the horses to rub them down and feed them.

While the woman of the house stirred up the fire and then gave them food and wine and put some special ointment of her own on Philylla's legs, they took off their outer clothes and told their story. By the end of it Berris had come back and the room was filled with men and women and children, some half-dressed. They were pressing round, mostly to see and touch Philylla, and she could hardly keep from sobbing with exhaustion. They were good people, she knew, but she could not bear their hands on her any longer! Her eyes groped round for help and found Berris. He made a way through and said to the woman of the house: 'Have you a bed for her?' The woman nodded. 'This way,' she said, and opened a door into the other room of the house, where her own box bed was. She shook out the blankets, which were still warm from her own sleep. Berris picked Philylla up in his arm; she crooked a hand round his neck to make it easier, and whispered: 'Thank you.' He carried her carefully so as not to touch her sore legs, and laid her down in the bed. She shut her eyes and then opened them again and looked up at him like a small child. He bent down and kissed her and came away.

After that Erif Der came in and took off her trousers and a great pile of necklaces, which she put underneath them in a corner, and she stood in the middle of the room in her long embroidered shirt, yawning and stretching. Then at last she plaited her hair again, and got into the bed with Philylla and curled up beside her. But Philylla was asleep already.

PART VII

Kings who die for the People

I'm sailing for California,
That far, foreign strand,
And I'm hoping to set foot
On some fair, fruitful land.
And in the midst of the ocean
Shall grow the green apple tree
Before I prove false
To the man that loves me.

NEW PEOPLE IN THE SEVENTH PART

Macedonians and Greeks
King Ptolemy IV of Egypt
His sister and future wife,
    Princess Arsinoë
His mistress, Agathoklea
Her brother, Agathokles
Their mother, Oenanthe
Sosibios, the King's minister
Metrotimé
Ptolemy, the son of Chrysermas
Leandris, a Spartiate girl
Monimos, a helot

Egyptians
Ankhet
Priestess of Isis

Jews
Simon and his friends

Greeks, Macedonians, Egyptians,
    Nubians and others

KING PTOLEMY IV WAS getting slowly and pleasantly
ready for his morning's official reception, and in the meantime enjoying the company of his friends. The room was
painted a warm yellow, with a flat, light frieze of great lilies
and sword-shaped leaves. One side lay open to a terrace,
a short flight of steps, and then a walled garden with a
square tank full of fishes and blue water flowers. Just now
it was the end of the growing-season outside in Egypt, but
here it was artificially prolonged, for the garden was kept
constantly watered by a criss-cross of small brick channels
and pipes, and it was all ramping with leaves and blossoms
and sappy arms of creepers that flung themselves in a night
from tree to tree. Agathoklea had just come up from it with
a branch of some very sweet-smelling purplish flower, still
wrapped about with the fat tendrils which had seized on it
only the day before. Turning back her lips, she nibbled
with her white teeth at a leaf with no vegetable chill but
warm from its own sap. She stripped a head of blossom and
ran it through her hand; it left faint purple stains on her
finger tips and the little rounded mounds on her palms.

There were niches at both ends of the room. In one was
a white marble bust of the young Alexander, with beautiful
wild hair and lips half parted; in the other was a bust of
the King's lately deceased father, the divine Ptolemy III;
this was in three different sorts of coloured marble, and had
silver lips and eyes. Both busts were wreathed hieratically,
though not with any formal laurel; they wore the Bacchic
leaves, ivy and smilax and vine, and young tufts of the
cone-bearing pine, rare enough in Egypt. On the terrace
there was also a small bronze altar which could easily be
carried about; satyrs and maenads and she-goats leapt and
fell about its three sides, none too decently. In the room
there were two or three light benches, gilt and polished,

493

with pretty, inlaid legs worked into elongated oryx heads and horns, and large, painted cushions; besides these there was the King's own lion-headed chair, and, of course, all the appurtenances of his preparation for the day.

He sat back in the chair, stretching out a leg for Agathoklea to attend to. He was wearing a loose vest of transparent muslin, and his long brown hair was not yet tressed up under the fillet. He was rather a beautiful creature, and by this time his movements, once a conscious showing-off, had become quite natural. He looked down along his own body now, gently and, as it were, modestly, like a decent boy. Thanks to Agathoklea's tickling and almost too pleasantly painful ministrations, he had no hair on his body-skin except such golden and attractive down as a child might have, and he was smoothly beardless. There was plenty of muscle everywhere, for he patronised the more exciting kinds of sport and exercise, and could dance as well as anyone in his Court, but in rest it was rather deliciously covered with a naïve layer of fat.

He was a youth, a Kouros. He lived up to his idea of himself. But also he looked intelligent, not with a mocking wave-quick Attic intelligence, but with the heavier Macedonian thing, the hill tribesman thinking practically and solidly, and then sometimes suddenly overbrimmed with some one terrific idea of politics or religion or love or hate. There it was in his eyes and his soft, heavy, Alexander lips, and the nostrils quivering occasionally as Agathoklea touched and laughed and bent forward, so that he could see down into the hollow of her breasts.

Agathokles was taller than the King, and fairer, with short hair and blue and shifty eyes. When no one was looking at him he made faces continuously; he could, if he chose, make such dreadful faces that small boys were terrified and ran away, or, if he held them, screamed and twitched and let him do whatever he felt inclined for. But when his face was still he was a beauty too. He had a light-blue tunic and a black cloak wrapped all round him. Just now he was standing in front of the bust of the divine Ptolemy III, screwing up his eyes and talking to himself, inaudibly to the rest.

Two little Indian boys held Agathoklea's perfume and ointment boxes, their dark, intent faces rigidly bent over the trays; they were naked except for tight jewelled collars and bracelets. They had been sold to her as kings' sons, and, as the price had been correspondingly high, she preferred to believe it was so, and took an extra pleasure in occasionally whipping them or setting her monkeys to pinch them. When asked whether it was true, they both said eagerly: 'Yes, yes,' and told long and more and more fantastic stories of their lost kingdoms to whoever would listen.

There was also a young friend of Agathoklea's, an incredibly innocent-looking Ionian girl, suitable Koré to the King's Kouros. Her great accomplishment was the discovery and reading aloud in the calmest possible voice, of all the most indecent books in Alexandria. She was standing now with her hands folded, gazing down into the garden. At the far end of the room were several young things, slaves and courtiers, it was not obvious which, but almost all Greeks or Macedonians, playing and talking and laughing discreetly.

The King lifted his head. 'Who is to be at the audience today?' Agathokles turned and clapped his hands; two of his secretaries ran out from the group at the far end of the room, handsome and clever-looking Greek boys, who were constantly quarrelling with one another. One of them jostled and pinched the other as they ran across, but got a look from his master, fleeting but quite remarkably horrid, that took all the kick out of him at once. Agathokles took the tablets from them and bought them over to the King. They read the list of names over together, while Agathokles stroked Ptolemy's loose tresses, feeling over his head a dozen times with hollowed palms. It seemed to soothe him entirely and his face went still and beautiful, while Ptolemy, cat-like, inclined his head into the caress of the long hands.

They read out name after name, and occasionally Agathoklea's girl-friend murmured some convulsing comment. Most were Greek, but three or four were Egyptian or Phoenician. 'And our poor clipped lion, as usual!' said Ptolemy, laughing a little as he came on the name of the King of Sparta. 'How he does hate you, Agathokles!' And then he checked at another name on the list, saying the syllables over with distaste, but holding up a hand to check Metrotimé the Ionian. Quintus Porcius. 'This, I take it, is the Roman who has been sent to make friends with Our Divinity. I suppose he will be quite too ghastly. I should like to know if these Romans think they are ever going to be anything—serious—to us. Sometimes it appears rather a pity that Alexander didn't have time to eat up Rome and Carthage in the same stew. However, they've never been anything but peaceable to me: stupid, flattering, peaceable, prize cows! Well, well, we'll have a show for him; turn out the barges. Yes, it's time I had the barges out again! Oh, Agathokles'—he half turned and flung up an arm round Agathokles' shoulders—'we'll have it at full moon, won't we? We'll go right up the river, a long, long way, with music, that marvellous, terrifying smell of the crocodiles—'

'Hush, hush!' said Agathokles, making his fingers strong and hard against the King's half-pretence shivering. 'You shall have all the barges. And the Roman shall see the crocodiles.'

'And you will arrange that there will be—something to show them off?' said the King.

Agathokles laughed and his upper lip lifted and twisted. 'Yes, yes; I'll make a scene for you. I'll find music that works in.'

'But you must do it yourself, yourself!' said Ptolemy. 'Heave him out in your arms. Or a woman! There must be someone in the prisons, some woman who poisoned her husband, but her lover betrayed her to the law!—throw her out to them yourself, my own Agathokles, so that you can hold me afterwards in the same arms. Be priest, be sacrificer to the crocodiles—'

'Do stop talking about crocodiles!' said Agathoklea. 'I don't like it!' And she spoke so exactly like a little girl, rather a darling pretty little girl, that Ptolemy was bound to turn round quick from her brother and give her a great smacking Macedonian kiss, as one would to a schoolgirl, and there were no more crocodiles for a time.

Ptolemy's body having been dealt with to his liking, there was a little to be done to his face, a heightening of colour, a smoothing out round the corners of the eyes. He held his mirror passionately in both hands, trying to stare right through it, to get closer to his own face, view it as close as a lover would. Could he be certain there was no sign of age? Sometimes it seemed to him possible that he might be one of the favoured, the ever-young. Through the grace of the slain and reborn god, the year-young, the life-giver, the northern Dionysos who had danced in the hills with Olympias, the mother of Alexander. Ever young and the King of Egypt! Agathokles had whispered to him in many close and lamplit nights that he did not age. They tied a diadem of linen sewn with golden lotuses round his head and looped the hair over it. Then very carefully they adjusted the Egyptian crown, the tall, swollen vase shape, a light framework of beaten gold fitting over the head, bulging at the top into a great round like sun or moon, and in front of it the darting head of the ruby-eyed cobra: symbols of Upper and Lower Egypt. His dress, on the other hand, was Greek, but in a wonderfully un-Greek material, something very thin and transparent, embroidered heavily with all kinds of snakes and birds. It tore if you looked at it almost, but what did that matter? Agathoklea saw that the royal wardrobe was always full.

Then the young things at the far end of the room stopped talking suddenly, and parted, and Sosibios, the chief minister, came in, wearing his full official armour, a great weight of gold and turquoise and carbuncles, with a deep-red cloak flung over all. His helmet was worked gold with a plume of ostrich feathers, red and gilt; he took it off as soon as possible and handed it to one of his boys. He was sweating slightly, especially on his fat neck. The old King had not minded his being bald, but the young King made him wear a wig, about which he always had a slight nervous consciousness. He rubbed a corner of the cloak over his face and began talking at once, telling the King exactly what he ought to do and what orders he ought to give about various military points. It was all sound advice, though rather irritatingly given.

Sosibios was an ugly man, with thick fingers and small bright blue eyes behind pale lashes, but not without charm of a kind, especially for those who thought him large and male and dependable, for when he was not telling people what they ought to do and why, with so many admirable reasons that contradiction was impossible, he could talk equally fluently about his many adventures in all parts of the Mediterranean world. They were actually quite numerous, and they developed still more in conversation, especially with women or young people. From time to time he turned on this talk to keep his hold over young Ptolemy, who was rather fascinated and flattered at the implied equality of erotic and political experience which Sosibios put in. It was also convenient to be told in detail how to deal with the duller part of his administration, or to have it done for him. Otherwise what was the good of being a king? Ptolemy did not, however, think that Sosibios' largeness implied that he was a great, strong male. He had done so at one time, when he was several years younger, but found, on experiment, that it was lamentably not so. His thin and comparatively frail-looking Agathokles was in every way far more competent.

The conversation went on to Kleomenes. 'He bores me,' said Sosibios, 'and, naturally, you. However, I think we shall do better to keep him with us for the time being. His tastes are not expensive, and it looks well, I assure you, as between kings. It is quite doubtful whether our friends in Macedonia mind either way, and we have, of course, to consider your divine father's late views on the matter. One has, unfortunately, also to consider the opinions, if one can call them that, of the mercenaries, of whom a growing number are Peloponnesians and ridiculously devoted, though one is not sure how permanently. Naturally, we shall take great care to be on the watch, and you can rest assured, sir—yes, absolutely assured—that the moment there is the least sign of danger, he will be dealt with. Yes, on the whole, my advice certainly is to allow things to rest as they are.'

'I can't help feeling,' said Ptolemy, 'that I shall be able to make use of him some day. If I go east.' His eyes flickered towards the bust of Alexander and he sat more upright.

'Yes, of course,' said Sosibios. 'But you would be rash to assume that merely because Kleomenes was once King of Sparta he would necessarily be of use to you in a completely different type of warfare. If we go east, as I trust we may sooner or later, when everything is settled, everything is as it should be here; if we go east, it will, I think you are bound to discover, be very largely a matter of diplomacy and out-manœuvring, possibly of protracted sieges at which these Peloponnesians are notoriously unskilled, and I think—naturally, I only say I think—that you might find Kleomenes and his Spartans not so very helpful.' He smiled in an elder-brotherly kind of way at the King; only suddenly, for a flash, the corners of the smile turned down into a horrid and devilish mark of disgust. Sosibios did not make such comprehensively nasty faces as Agathokles, but this changing grin was his special mark; any woman whom he had been jealous of knew it well, and Metrotimé could imitate it beautifully.

Ptolemy shut his eyes for a moment, and had a clear vision of Kleomenes and the Spartans, those outwardly calm, desperately earnest, bearded men. He suspected that below the calm and courtesy, Kleomenes was really a burning, raging creature. He suspected that if this King of Sparta chose to let go of his Laconic manner, really to appeal to him, Ptolemy the man—the boy—to appeal not with reason, but with deeper, violenter forces, he would be more likely—perhaps!—to get what he wanted. Or one of the younger men. What were their names? Panteus, that square, blue-eyed one by the King's shoulder. They were fiery too. They would have arms like steel, a grip you could not break.

Several more people had come into the room, among them the head nurse of his twelve-year-old sister, the divine Arsinoë, a tall, grey-haired woman with a strong Macedonian accent. She walked up to the King with an admirable disregard of Agathoklea and every one else except Sosibios, for whom she produced a stiff curtsey. 'Her Divine Highness, the Lady Arsinoë, asks permission to leave the royal city and go with her ladies to one of the summer palaces. And it's my belief,' she went on, 'that the poor little dear has been quite long enough cramped up in her rooms all this winter. She needs air—and riding. She's not looked herself since that nasty chill she got at New Year. If it please your Divine Majesty.'

Ptolemy had withdrawn into his chair, a peculiar look on his face; he did not answer. But Sosibios said: 'Of course I will see to that. The simplest thing in the world, certainly she shall have it. You see no reason against it, sir? No, quite. Well, she shall have which ever palace she likes. There, that's settled. She'll enjoy the country, of course she will.' He bowed the nurse out, with another exhibition of his special grin.

Ptolemy gripped the lion-heads on his chair and said low

and harshly: 'In three years I shall have to marry that! That poor little dear with a nasty chill! That sister-brat of mine. To please these filthy Egyptians.'

Sosibios had turned away and was talking hard to a youngish soldier, who attended to him meticulously. It was Agathokles who answered the King. 'She'll not be a child when the time comes. But a woman. Like other women.'

'That's what's so terrible,' said Ptolemy, staring across the room. 'Two children can play at King and Queen. A little straight she-child. But not a woman with breasts and—That bridal night! Mother bending over us both; straddling across us; naked. No shame. That place we've both been!'

'Why,' said Agathoklea, 'she'll be all dolled up, you won't know her. Besides, she's a sensible little thing; she won't expect much.'

'How can I ever get far enough away from her,' said the King. 'How can I ever separate my flesh enough from hers? I shall be tearing myself and my mother!'

'Why not?' said Agathoklea quickly. 'Why not, my King? Won't that be subtle enough? Won't that be a sacrifice? The god in his two halves reunited and spilling his own blood. Isis and Osiris.'

'Yes,' said Ptolemy eagerly. 'Oh yes! The two hawks. Dionysos torn and gleaming. If only I can in time get to think of Arsinoë as Isis. But she's not, she's only a stupid little girl.'

It was Sosibios now who had picked up the conversation, and interrupted briskly. 'Nonsense, she's no worse than any other woman. A little boring perhaps, but then they all are, even the most charming.' And he bowed to Agathoklea, who smiled back, hearing behind her a fairy giggle from her friend Metrotimé. 'Besides,' Sosibios went on, 'you Ptolemys are undoubtedly luckier than most kings: no embassies and treaties and fathers and brothers to be got round and given presents and all that. Why, my dear boy, think of the hold you have on her. Get just one divine son—a night's work, what, for a young man like you—and then the thing's done and you can live like the King you are. It will be time for the audience in half an hour, and then for tomorrow we are arranging a lion-hunt. You had better, don't you think, ask this Roman, he is sure to be afraid of lions; I shall see that one is killed immediately in front of him. You are certain that I am doing exactly what you prefer, sir?'

Ptolemy nodded a little gloomily, and got up and walked over to Metrotimé. 'You are finding the maenads for my feast?' he said, catching her round the shoulders and looking suddenly, deeply, into her eyes.

She leant away from him stiffly, her weight on one foot that slid against his, so that from one open sandal to the other, their toes touched. She nodded abruptly, once.

'And they are to be real,' he said, 'real! And believing. No actresses. No flute-girls. No paint. Only that colour of cheeks hot with wine—and him. His madness. Maddened virgins.'

Her eyelids flickered. She said: 'You shall have virgins. If we have to hunt Alexandria for them. I'll be your huntress. I'll be Artemis for Dionysos!' Her darkened eyes blazed at him with some momentary god-like quality and he felt himself divine enough not to need to kiss her. A warm wave of gratitude to that dear Agathoklea for her friend flowed and passed. He went on to speak to another friend, a poet. He had an idea for a marvellous play. Yes, he was demanding from the God inspiration as well as youth!

There was Agathokles over in an empty corner of the room; his black mantle flapped suddenly, like a wing. He had a young man pinned in the corner, a handsome, soft creature in a three-coloured tunic, his underlip sticking out between surliness and tears. 'I won't!' said the young man passionately. 'I won't!''

'Yes, you will,' said Agathokles. 'You will go back now, this minute, to my mother's room and you will beg her pardon on your knees and promise never to leave her till she sends you away.'

'But I can't!' said the young man, holding up his hands almost in prayer. 'I beg you, sir, as a man, listen. There's young women—there's one girl—oh sir, you don't know what the lady Oenanthe is! She wears a man out, she does truly. I'm all spent, I can't sleep, I can't live! Make her let me go for a week!'

Agathoklea came lightly over and joined her brother. 'What's this?' she said. 'One of poor mother's boys being silly? Buy her another and sell this.' And she flicked it with infinite contempt across the nose.

'This is the one she wants,' said Agathokles. 'God knows why!'

'Well, poor darling, she must have what she wants! Isn't she our own, only motherkin! He's being silly, is he? Well, if he doesn't stop, he'll do as well for mother like *that*, won't he!' And she made a downward gesture with her wrist, like an expert making some special cut.

The man looked piteously from brother to sister. 'I'm a Greek—' he said faltering. And then: 'Ai! I'll go back to her.'

He slipped past them, and Agathokles nodded and turned to his sister with a twitching screw round of his face which subsided while she spoke. 'We mustn't grudge mother boys or money,' she said. 'Where should we be without her! She brought us here first. And she's still useful, old sweet. She finds me little girls, little slave-girls that neither of us would have time to notice. She notices things, mother does.'

Agathokles assented, and then his eyes slid round towards young Ptolemy. 'Since he's been King I've felt differently about him. About being his friend. It seems a limitless thing. What I can do. Power!' His tongue tip flickered out and in.

'Yes,' said Agathoklea happily. 'It's lovely, isn't it!'

Then the King called over to them; he seemed excited. 'Agathokles!' he said, 'here's this good Battaros telling me of a young artist who's come to the city. What did you say his name was?'

'Berris—something!' said the courtier. 'A Scythian or God knows what, but, they say, talented. A quite young man who has been in Greece long enough to be civilised and learn his art, Athens, I believe. I'm told he does portraits.'

'One might at least see,' said Ptolemy. 'If I could get someone to do me some frescoes with enough life in them to stir me! Does he know Dionysos? But if he is an artist, he must. Under one shape or another.'

Agathokles beckoned over a secretary to note it down, then asked: 'Is he just over from Greece, Battaros?'

'Yes, he only landed a week or two ago. From Sparta,

I'm told; at least there were one or two more of these refugees on the same ship.'

'Kleomenes and his friends seem very certain of us! However, I shan't complain—yet! But supposing we suggest to this artist that he would be received at an audience?'

'I'll see his work first!' said Agathokles. 'After all—Scythians! Does he wear skins?'

'Only his own, I gather,' said Battaros. 'But I refuse responsibility! Still, if we could get a portrait of our divine King for the new coinage—But perhaps that's being in too much of a hurry.'

'Invite him, invite him!' said Ptolemy. 'Perhaps he can tell me of a new, a Scythian Dionysos. Perhaps he is beautiful. Perhaps—as he's an artist—perhaps he will think me beautiful. Invite him tomorrow!'

Now two Egyptian slaves came in carrying gongs, which they sounded relentlessly. The King lifted his hands, stayed still one moment, and then reached them down again slowly into a calmed hieratic pose. Six tall negroes had followed the gong ringer, and now they formed themselves up behind the King, a perpetually unused and grinning bodyguard, with enormous axes and jutting short gold petticoats, and iron rings between knee and ankle. They rolled their eyes at the women, and there was a general fluttering and heaving of breasts and thighs under thin muslin. Even Agathoklea giggled a little, but her friend Metrotimé most unfashionably found them not interesting. After the bodyguard went Sosibios, with his helmet on again, and his rather rapid short steps that would start him sweating before he got to the audience-chamber. Then the others, men and women courtiers, with Agathokles rather behind, whispering notes to one of the secretaries while the other one glowered.

They went along a cool, darkish corridor, painted with beneficent gods, labelled with their Greek names, so that no one should mistake them for Egyptians, in spite of their flat, expressionless profiles and tight draperies, and the curious beasts that followed them. Only at one the King hesitated, as he always did, and bowed his head slightly before going on. The bodyguard continued in step, but all the Court checked and bowed too, with the utmost solemnity. This particular flat god was labelled Dionysos. He held out a cup on the end of one stiff arm and he was followed by a pair of stalking panthers, and for some reason, perhaps merely to fill the space, three frogs.

The audience-hall was already full. As King Ptolemy came in every one rose and bowed, and such Egyptians as were there prostrated themselves completely, palms on the floor as for a god. The King bowed right and left and sat down on his throne, which was made like a Macedonian general's chair, but in ivory and zebra skin. The ceremonies of presentation began. The conversation was usually three-sided, including Sosibios. One of the earliest to be received was the Roman, very much muffled up in his long, thick, uncomfortable-looking robe with amusing purple edges. He spoke Greek passably, but was rather comically much on his dignity, and mentioned a number of persons and institutions with odd names, apparently of importance in his native town, but which neither Ptolemy nor Sosibios had ever heard of. He seemed delighted at the prospect of a lion-hunt.

Then there was the high priest of Bes, with whom the King was rather short, for he considered Bes a disagreeable and unimportant god who had better be got rid of as soon as possible. There were Alexandrians with petitions and thanks and demands for justice, and officers wanting promotion for themselves or friends and insisting on being fellow-Macedonians, which Ptolemy rather liked. There was a ship's captain just back from the Gulf of Arabia with gifts out of his cargo, spices and a cage full of whistling green birds, and something else which he whispered; if he pleased the King he could double his prices to commoners. There was a deputation from Aethiopia speaking through interpreters, which Sosibios took on. They were told to come back the next day for a private audience; it was something that would have to be attended to.

Among the petitioners there were several women, land-owners, or in business, but none of them were sufficiently young to be of interest. They were treated with as much or as little courtesy and justice as the men. There was a poor cultivator whose child was sick, and who was certain that if the divine King Ptolemy-Osiris, would touch and give back a piece of bread which he had brought, the child could eat it and live. He had spent all his money and wits on doorkeepers, and when he actually reached the King he fell flat with terror and wonder and excitement. Ptolemy raised him with his own hand: this man's faith had given him a sudden, wonderful feeling of security. He broke the bread and put into it several gold pieces from the purse Agathokles always carried for him.

Then there were more Alexandrians, a complicated divorce case, and a quarrel between inheritors over a big estate. There was a poet, a young protégé of one of the librarians, who humbly implored that the divine King would accept the dedication of his long poem about the phases of the moon. And there was, as usual, Kleomenes of Sparta, half a head taller than most of the Alexandrians, and with quite different eyes. He had that lame one with him this time, and the one-eyed man, ugh! But Kleomenes himself, yes, he was rather magnificent; he lifted his head and looked at one like some splendid beast that one had caught and caged. Not really a lion, not a cat-beast at all. Some antelopes have those proud eyes.

King Ptolemy was most courteous to King Kleomenes, rose from his seat and embraced him, spoke sympathetically of all the news. King Kleomenes must certainly join the lion hunt!—and any of his friends, of course. As to anything else, anything about lending him money to encourage the revolutionary party in Sparta, anything about promises for the future, well, he shrugged his shoulders. There was time. King Kleomenes had surely not found Alexandria dull! There were difficulties—yes, difficulties which even such an honoured foreigner could scarcely understand. King Ptolemy was, after all, only at the beginning of his reign. A little patience—Sosibios took the conversation over; he was still less encouraging, though even more polite.

After a time the audience broke up into informality, and King Ptolemy beckoned Agathokles over; he had another idea for his play; he wanted it written down before it escaped. The play was to be called *Adonis*. The little scarlet anemones, the blood-drops on the hills. Someone would have to see to the lyrics. A poet. Poets are easy to find. He held Agathokles by the arm, feeling the arm, smoothing it, reaching up under the black cloak towards the elbow, the armpit. What was the use of being a King if he could not

be and do what he chose, and when and where he chose?
Kleomenes and the Spartans had gone away again.

Chapter Two

BERRIS DER HAD done some Court portraits, but rather
reluctantly. He was bored with portraiture now; he had
come to the end of it. There was excitement for a time in
getting his effects more and more certainly and economi-
cally, and strengthening his drawing, but now another set
of problems was coming back into his head, old ones which
he had laid aside because he could not tackle them then,
but which by this time he felt, if once it were possible to
make the effort and lift the dead weight of beginnings, he
would be able to solve. They were again three-dimensional,
the thing beyond paint. He was unhappy and uneasy over
this new craving. Though he did not admit that the work
he had done lately was definitely bad, yet it did seem to him
valueless by present standards—and what other way had
he of telling? He got some blocks of sandstone and spoilt
two of them trying to find out what he was looking for.
They were not hard enough material, but he was still too
impatient to work on anything slower and less easy.

Erif, watching, thought that this unhappiness had more
direct connection with Philylla than he would admit. The
three of them had lived on the ship as one little, very close
group, trusting and loving. But in Alexandria Philylla had
just walked out of the group into her husband's arms. It
had been as simple as that. When they got to the city
they had asked for King Kleomenes' house and had gone
there. Kratesikleia welcomed them very warmly, though she
struck them as definitely older and more irritable. Gorgo
was a little shy at first, then climbed up on to Philylla's
knee and snuggled. Nikolaos shouted and jumped about
and kissed her hard and often. Nikomedes was almost
speechless; he sat opposite her for a time, and looked
at her and grinned softly, and then he went away to find
Panteus. They sat there, still all three close together, and
then Panteus came in and made a little movement with
his arms, and she got up and went to him like someone
at last going home, and they said nothing, and Philylla
did not once look back at her friends who had saved
her, and after a time they went away from the room,

never having let go of one another's touch since the first moment.

The next day they had both come to see Erif and Berris, and Panteus had thanked them simply and very deeply for what they had done for his wife, and said he would repay when he had the power: in the meantime here was his sword and his whole friendship at their service. Philylla had been infinitely friendly, but already a kind of vagueness was beginning to form between her and them. She did not belong to them any more. Berris had accepted this and tried to accept Panteus and his friendship, but could not do much with it. Erif, left alone, began to think more about her purification, and the meeting between mother and daughter, between Dead and Snake. She had written home telling Tarrik what had happened, but there could be no answer till autumn. She might easily miss a letter too, moving about like this.

Berris had not much liked any of King Ptolemy's friends, though he found them amusing. He kept Erif out of it for some time, but then she grew bored and insisted on accompanying him. However, when she got to the palace she was rather frightened, particularly by a rather charming girl who suddenly fell in love with her and felt no awkwardness about demanding her satisfaction there and then. Erif protested and finally ran out of the place, her ears tingling with every one else's laughter. She was annoyed with herself afterwards, thinking: why not? why be unkind? Yet she could not imagine she would have enjoyed the experience. And then suddenly it occurred to her: if it had been Philylla who had made love to her? Well, yes, she thought honestly that might have been different. But after this she only went back to the palace very circumspectly, with Berris.

He had discovered Metrotimé, or rather she had let him discover her, and they were both amusing themselves. She was exactly what Berris wanted now: her ironic and critical mind to deal with his sentimentality, and her practised and knowledgeable body to wake his up out of the calm it had been bullied into. But she did not help him to solve his aesthetic problems.

Erif made one new friend. This was the woman of the house where they lodged, an Egyptian of fairly good family, named Ankhet, married to a Greek corn-merchant. She was very shy and soft-footed, and a good housewife. After a time she asked Erif to her own room; almost as soon as she came in she saw a little image of a Mother and Child, and remembered the story of Isis and Horus, which she had heard first in Sparta from some of the Queen's girls. After much questioning and several weeks of patience, she found out from Ankhet that there were various temples in the Egyptian quarter of Alexandria, which, so far, she had scarcely been into at all. The woman was obviously rather afraid of having her gods misunderstood, if not laughed at, by the Greeks or those whom she supposed to be Greeks, yet at the same time she was intensely proud of them and longing to show them as powerful. At last she was persuaded to bring Erif within sight of some of them.

The Egyptian quarter was much more crowded, dirty and cornery, than the Greek or Jewish quarters, and quite different sorts of food were being sold on trays. Erif, enchanted, got her friend to buy quantities of it, and walked along munching and looking at the odd people. But Berris had seen a great smooth stone cat lying as guardian genius at the back of a shoemaker's shop, and he was thrilled to the bone. They went through low, covered alleys, and brownish people flimsily dressed in straight bits of linen looked at them over their shoulders. Then they went down a side-alley and through a square archway of limestone blocks.

Beyond that was a small courtyard, rectangularly planted with mulberries, and then a square, flat-roofed temple, painted red. They went through the outer row of pillars; Erif and Berris were rather startled to find that the inner row had curious, human heads, with stiff side-curls for capitals. They appeared to be staring in an unpleasant way. The temple itself was dark and entirely covered with small paintings, some bits of which were gilded and showed up inconsequently like pieces of jewellery. A priestess in a long white linen robe, pleated straight from the shoulders and ungirdled, walked past them very silently on bare feet carrying a dish. At the far end of the temple two others moved shuttle-wise across and across, occasionally lifting their arms with some musical instrument which tinkled sharply.

Suddenly the lady Ankhet said: 'Here is Isis,' and she

made one further pace and raised her hands forward and level with her shoulders, and stood still in adoration. Beyond her the other two saw a low altar and behind it the granite image of a goddess holding a divine child against her knees. Her head was small, her chin frail and pathetic under the great painted headdress. Her eyes were widely open, her lips heavy. The rounded conventional line of her dress was faintly marked, drooping from shoulder to shoulder, but below it the sculptor had left her breasts and thighs naked to her worshippers. The child had a funny, stiff kilt; his arms dangled. For some reason Erif was profoundly moved, her critical self stopped working. She lifted her hands in front of her as the woman had done, and remembered her own son.

At each side was another statue. One was cow-headed with a meaningless human body painted with symbols. The other was human, but had its arms stretched forward with stiff feathers growing down out of them, green and gilt; the mouth was quite straight, not smiling or drooping, and the eyes were elongated right along the top of the cheekbone in a convention which had quite ceased to be beautiful. Berris, fidgeted by the immobility of the two women, at last whispered: 'Who are those?' After a time Ankhet turned and said: 'These are Isis too.' Then she went to one of the priestesses and whispered for a few minutes. Berris produced what seemed to him sufficient gold coin to cover himself and his sister at the usual price of offerings. He was rather annoyed when Erif pulled off one of her rings and gave that as well to the priestess. Then they went home.

During the next few days they were both silent and excited, and both wanted to go to more temples. Few of the Alexandrian temples were very old, for Rhakotis, the old city round and over which Alexandria had been founded, was tiny and obscure, a shelter for goatherds and sailors. But some of the new temples had old-cult images in them, or very expert copies, and Ankhet herself had one or two rather beautiful small things which she kept to guard her home and children, for she did not think much of her husband's gods. She had inherited them from her own mother: the green beetle which meant life for ever springing newly from itself, the buckle of Isis in gold and rubies, and various small bronze and enamel beasts. Even her make-up box was a god-beast, the kohl-sticks long, thin goddesses, the protectors of beauty and the faithfulness of husbands.

Berris was extremely interested. He had not suspected that there was so much in Egypt that would jump out at him like this, promising a new series of problems, and perhaps solutions, of the same kind as those which were on him now. He met and argued with a father-priest of Osiris, a gentle formalist who, at last, took him a week's journey south, beyond the delta country, to see one of the ancientest and most famous temples. When he came back the whole outlook of his work was twisted over, mostly towards grimness, and a great interest in patterns, a defence of three-dimensional formalism. Erif did not like it much, especially for the first month or so while the interest was newest and most overbalancing, but he paid very little attention to anything she said.

Among all these things Erif had not found the ones she was seeking. Here, certainly, was the mother in many forms. Only the child was always son, never, so far, daughter. The Dead were here, even overshadowing the living in interest and importance; that was new after Greece and the insistence on life in flesh and art and poetry, most of all in the bodies and minds of the young. In Egypt the preparations for death began early, with youth itself, for who could escape? For the most part, both Greeks and Egyptians had the same fear and horror of death and lack of any confidence about more than a dim and almost worthless survival, but the Greeks faced violently away, while the Egyptians were all the time being drawn and fascinated towards that ultimate stiffness, that final formalising of the fluent body. Erif Der was by turns fascinated too, and then in a sudden Greek rebellion. As for the Snake, there were plenty, royal or divine, cobras, asps, small, horrible fanged creatures from the hot sand or the steaming marshes. There was no telling which make her own Snake was.

As summer went on it grew very hot, but there was usually a dry light breeze off the desert, not oppressive, that left pockets of cool air behind houses and in archways. It blew the sea into a strange glassy whiteness that looked as if it must stretch endlessly between here and Greece, and all the fishes came up and in towards the land. The nights were still fairly cool and all the households slept out on the roof, under the large stars, or in the afternoons in little shelters and bowers of stretched linen and vine branches. The native Egyptians went about their work much as usual, reaping their fantastically early corn-fields and setting oxen at once to tread out the grain. But the Alexandrians took more and more to the night. They had water festivals with lamps and barges, that did not end till dawn. The palace was shuttered and quiet during the day and every one slept, while King Ptolemy's brown and yellow subjects passed below his walls with tools and water-jugs and food-baskets, and speculated on how he was sleeping and after what delicious exercisings of the body. The King had many tastes; they were all catered for immediately. Parents of charming young people of either sex knew of one possible career for their children. Agathokles was usually willing to be approached or, failing him and his sister, the old mother did as well or sometimes better. The Egyptians laughed about the ways of divinity, and did not, on the whole, copy them.

Sosibios occupied himself less pleasantly. He put the edge on to his affairs, not through unusual and interesting activities and combinations, as the King did, but with ordinary cruelty. He was not nice to his wife. It was not always enjoyable to be his guests. The Egyptians, who held the housewife in a certain formal honour, and at any rate usually respected her as a business woman, did not like this in Sosibios. But it was generally agreed that he was devoted to the interests of the Ptolemys. Stories drifted about Alexandria, a continual consciousness of the doings of the Court. The divine Ptolemy with three boys at a time; his brilliant remark about the Roman envoy; Agathokles and the green pillar; Sosibios' curious idea of a pleasant evening with his wife; the poetry readings; Agathokles answering the philosophers; that rumour—surely not true?—about the intentions of King Antiochos of Syria; King Ptolemy's idea about an immense ship which was at the same time to be a temple of Dionysos-Osiris and to supply work for all the draughtsmen and carpenters in Alexandria; King Ptolemy and the elephant hunters; King Ptolemy and his plan for restoring the temple at Thebes with new scenes from the underworld, the Tuat. Sooner or later Erif and Berris heard most of it, but they wondered sometimes whether the Spartans were not so much out of the life of the place that the stories drifted by them and away.

Old Kratesikleia tried so hard to get into touch with high politics. She was a queen, she had been a great queen; what right had any palace to shut its doors on her! The old Ptolemy had been most gracious and encouraging, and so had many of his Court, but the new ones laughed at her openly, laughed her home to cry the bitter and uncomforted tears of age and widowhood. She stormed at young Ptolemy and his friends and the ways of youth in general, till she was tired out. There was no answering her.

Philylla came and sat with her, working on the same piece of embroidery, and tried to be hopeful and cheerful, though it was not always very successful. Queen Kratesikleia had three or four oldish women always about her, the generation between hers and Philylla's, widows who had been buffeted by life and joined her in lamenting, but on a lower tone. There was also a few younger girls, who had come over with her and the children at the beginning. They were less gloomy, but very discontented. They hated being kept in as firmly as she always insisted, and she thought it both unnecessary and undignified to use persuasion; she preferred the more Spartan method of force to make them preserve their painful integrity. Leandris, the eldest, was betrothed to Idaios and was going to marry him as soon as she had finished the weaving of her wedding sheets. She was a golden and upright creature, a distant cousin of Philylla, to whom she loved talking and confiding. Even after she was married she would be with the old Queen a great deal, but still it was comparative freedom, and some day, when the exile was over and they all came back to Sparta, she would live happily ever after.

Naturally, Sphaeros was the boys' tutor; but he was growing old. They missed their classes terribly, and were delighted with Gyridas, who was now being brought up with them. But he had been badly frightened and was too deeply a helot in his blood to recover very easily; he seemed to like playing best at make-believe games with Nikolaos. When Nikomedes grew suddenly earnest and violent it frightened him and drove him back to the horrible time when his brother had been killed and they had tried to turn him out of his class and make a slave of him! Sometimes he hated Nikomedes for doing that, for not staying part of the race of children, but going with the grown-ups, not only in words but with his whole self. But he did not know it was hate, and Nikomedes himself never suspected it, still less Sphaeros or any of the parents and grandparents.

Kleomenes told his eldest son about his plans and hopes, but even more about his disappointments, and the boy hurled himself from one peak to another of sympathy and indignation and love. He dreamt about it most nights and thought about it and talked it over with Philylla, who saw something of how things were, and, for herself, took great pains never to claim this love or sympathy, though, for that matter, the reason she wanted it from someone was too complicated to explain, even if she have could got it clear to herself. She told Nikomedes she was happy, and for three-quarters of the time she almost was.

Nikomedes went with his father occasionally to an audience. He stood there in a clean tunic, between Kleomenes and Sphaeros, silently watching this glittering, patterned man on the throne, hating him with a steady conscience for not helping them. He heard a good deal of Court gossip this way, though he did not understand it all. And he went down to the harbour with the Spartiates and hung about there, waiting, waiting for news. Ships would come in and he made up stories about them when they were still small, brown-winged things, just turning the corner of the island: how this was really at last the ship with news that everything at home had gone right, that would carry a great crowd of soldiers with spears and crowns and wreaths, shouting all together that they had put down the ephors and the Macedonians and were come to bring back their King to his rights—and they would all start that same evening! But when the ship had made fast and the captain landed, she was quite often not from Greece at all, let alone Sparta, let alone bringing good news.

They had heard one thing not long after Kleomenes had come to Egypt. Only a few days after Sellasia, King Antigonos had got news from Macedonia that there was a rising of the tribes against him. He and almost all his armies set off at once for home; there was work for the mercenaries. Gradually through the winter Kleomenes realised that if he could have manœuvred and retreated and put off the battle until that news came, he would not have lost Sparta. There were moments when the fresh realisation of this or some new disappointment from Ptolemy or Sosibios blackened the world for him. Then he was bitter to Panteus and Phoebis and all his friends, bitterest of all to Nikomedes, since it was over him he had most power, and he had to show himself that he still had some power, still could hurt someone, still be that much of a king.

Some of the Spartiates had got queerly involved with Egypt. There were none of them who had not had brothers or sons or dear friends killed. Death had moved nearer to them; they could not look away. They discovered Serapis first, because he was the most Greek, an almost deliberate invention, a liaison god between two hierarchies, taking for his kingdom that most elemental one to which all men journeyed. He was Osiris and Zeus and Hades, or, as some said now, influenced by the constant permeation of mystery stories, Dionysos-Hades. He had the attributes of all these gods. He was the Lord of the Gates. He held the keys.

The Spartans had lost their gods. Apollo of the market-place, who had also been the Guide of Souls, was left behind with the rest of the good things they had once been part of, being himself utterly and for ever Sparta. The little colony of Dorian strangers, too small to be spiritually self-sufficing in this many-templed city, began to be shaken by the new kinds of gods they found. Not all of them were touched, nor most of the King's best friends. Sphaeros was distressed; Kleomenes angrily ignored the whole business; Hippitas laughed. Panteus was just plainly troubled—one more difficulty added on to the burden of worries and anxieties and disappointments and petty, wearing schemes and rearrangements. No single thing was in itself unbearable, but the combination was beginning to split him up. It was not the kind of hardship he was bred to stand. Philylla watched him, laid herself open to his pain, so that it came directly and steadily on to her. He told his wife most things, and she guessed almost all the others. She tried to help him practically, wrote letters for him and ran his house with an economy which was very difficult for her. She went to the market herself; there was no home-farm to send down fresh milk and cheese and eggs. No horses to ride. She must not think of that; it reminded her of Tiasa. All she wanted was to help him and the King. If only she could have helped him better! She knew that even in this life it should have been possible to have intervals, moments of utter peace and happiness plucked out of danger, but, except for that first day of all, and a few rare and desperately lovely hours during the weeks just after that, it had not happened. She had not been able to put him right and give him what he needed. There was no sign of a child, but perhaps that was just as well. When this was over and they were home—then everything would be put right, and that too. She talked to him about his land and the little house; it was distant in the past and distant in the future. Neither of them could really talk about anything except this grinding present which was going on all the time. It seemed worse when letters came from home, as they were beginning to now. Deinicha had her baby boy, and they all had the fields and the hills and the air of home. It was difficult to write answers; every month the common ground of life which they used all to have together was getting smaller.

A little before midsummer, or so it seemed to Erif Der, everybody in Egypt began to get excited. Something was going to happen. Even the Greeks in Alexandria felt it. Then one morning a message came, ritually whispered from house to house along the waiting streets: 'The Tear has fallen.' And at once in all the houses men and women put on the clean white linen robes that lay waiting for them and heaped cakes and fruit into their flat baskets. Isis had wept and the Nile was beginning to rise, and all would be well with next year's corn.

The lady Ankhet and her two Egyptian maids came down the steps from the roof in white thin dresses down to their bare ankles. The maids carried food-baskets on their heads, and Ankhet had a lighter one balanced on her hip; she brought her elder daughter with her, silent and delighted. Rather shamefacedly her husband followed, half trying to look as if he were there by accident, but he was in a clean tunic too. Berris was working hard and Erif, rather bored because he would not talk, was kneeling by the window, leaning out, sniffing tentatively at the air to find out what this new feeling was. She saw them and called down: 'May I come too?'

Ankhet called up to her gaily to put on clean linen

in honour of Isis, the Year Queen who had pity on her
people, and Hapi, the Nile, who had answered her. Erif
jumped up, and ran and changed and came down to find
Ankhet waiting. They went on together down towards the
Sun Gate, the eastern gate of the town; just outside it
there were bullock-carts waiting, with straw and cushions
on the floor-boards and tasselled canopies to keep off the
sun. Ankhet pointed to a pile of rugs in their own cart.
'We shall sleep in the carts tonight.'

Erif wondered what it was all about, but was quite
content not to ask. There was a midsummer feeling in her
body. The bullocks grunted and heaved, the cart started
jerkily, hauling itself up on to the dry Canopus road.
One of the maids brought out large light veils; they
covered themselves at once, before the dust should have
got into their hair and eyes. Then they sat back among
the cushions, not speaking much, but chewing seeds and
leaves and little hard sweet cakes, and sometimes passing
round a gourd of water. In front and behind and at each
side other bullock-carts creaked and padded; through the
moving haze of dust they could see the backs of their own
driver, and Ankhet's husband, also veiled against the dust.
After about five hours they turned south off the Canopus
road, and fairly soon after that Ankhet lifted her veil and
knelt up, swaying in the cart, peering ahead. She signed to
Erif, who looked too. Not far ahead was the long line of
palms and acacias and close-planted fruit trees which marked
that branch of the Nile. The Egyptian women stretched out
their hands and murmured. In another half-hour the cart
jolted to a standstill in the shade of the first palms, and
they stepped out.

Everywhere other families were halting their carts and
getting out, and then the whole crowd began to move down
towards the river. Most were Egyptians, but quite a number
were Greeks or other foreigners. It was then that Ankhet
began to tell Erif of the summer flooding of the Nile and
how the flood-water brought down life with it for crops and
men. Far up the Nile this had started, and although down
here it was scarcely visible, yet they believed and came to
bless and be blessed by the waters. It was less immediately
important in the fertile delta country, but this was the way
of ancient days and ancient living.

They came down over the dried mud to the edge of the river, and then, in a soft, surprising rustle, men and women and children threw out from their baskets into the water, fruit and millet and cakes. The brownish, swift current took all the little things and swept them down and under. After that they all walked into the cool bosom of Hapi the Nile, ankle deep, knee deep, waist deep. Ankhet had led Erif by the hand, startled and yet not frightened, but glad to be one of a crowd again. She felt the warm mud oozing about her feet and as they got further out felt the soft tugging of the current about her legs and body. It was all very solemn at first, but soon here and there along the line came shrill, joyful cries, and people's hands stirred and then their arms, circling, plucking at the surface of the water, and the impulse came down on them everywhere, and they all fell to splashing and laughing and crying out of happy greetings and blessings to one another and to the dear and kind river. Some of the young men flung themselves out on to the current swimming and glad, shouting that they could feel the flood already. They circled down and back and were greeted with laughter and kisses and pelted with grain.

They stayed bathing and splashing till the late afternoon, and then came out reluctantly to let the sun dry their new linen dresses before nightfall. They played games on the bank and gave one another flowers and pottery tubes of scent. Then they went back to the carts to sleep, but Erif thought that the gaiety was deep enough into the crowd for the sleep to be best done in twos. She felt suddenly very angry and miserable that she—she the Spring Queen of Marob!—should have to sleep by herself with Ankhet and the maids and the little girl. She wanted to jump out and go down into the bushes where there were still lights and singing, and find herself a gentle, dark-eyed Egyptian boy to be her playmate and sleep-mate, but she did not know enough of the language and she did not think she could explain to Ankhet, who was, after all, her hostess and sponsor. It was all very well for Ankhet, she thought resentfully, with a husband any night, but for her it was long, long since last midsummer! She stayed awake till well after the others and then cried herself quietly to sleep. She woke just before dawn at a creaking and rustling, and, peeping through half-closed lashes, saw the two maids slipping back into the cart with flushed and drowsy faces. They at least had gone down into the bushes by the river and played midsummer properly!

Chapter Three

THE CHILDREN HAD all been allowed to come down on to the quays, even Gorgo, on the understanding that the boys should look after her properly. Every one was busy at the King's house, for Leandris was to be married that day to Idaios, and Queen Kratesikleia had set her mind on having a good show. She had asked a number of ladies from King Ptolemy's court, determined to overlook a great deal, though naturally she had to draw the line at Agathoklea! Leandris herself thought uneasily that probably none of them would come, though she did not quite know why, for she did not begin to question that her lady was a great queen still. But she felt from the beginning that it would be a failure and knew that Kratesikleia would end the evening in trembling indignation, and then she suddenly remembered that this time she herself would not have either to soothe or run away and hide till it was over. Because she would be with her husband. She would have the right not to think of Queen Kratesikleia all the time!

The children went down to the eastern docks, Gorgo in the middle, and bought themselves a half water-melon to share. By now they had got used to seeing the lighthouse on the end of the island, opposite them across the harbour; only Gorgo still stared. Last winter they had come down every evening about dusk to watch it being lighted, the yellow light bigger than the moon, which leapt and throbbed at first, and then settled down into a steady glare. The boys liked it, they would have liked to go up there and spend the night throwing on faggots, constantly stirring up the fire-dragon of Alexandria. But Gorgo did not like it, this great erect frightening thing with an eye on the top. She told Philylla about it, but Philylla did not understand properly. There ought to have been someone who understood.

Gyridas looked back over his shoulder at the palace with its high limestone walls and its own walled-off quay. Shiny green trees showed their heads over the white wall-tops, and there were red and yellow curtains in the far up ranges of windows. He said to Nikolaos: 'Ptolemy's in there. Suppose we made a sand palace and then put dry seaweed in and set it on fire?'

'Would it be fun?' said Nikolaos evasively, avoiding all implications and yet admiring Gyridas for suggesting them.

But Nikomedes was looking across the causeway to the big western harbour where most of the merchant shipping came. 'Come on!' he said suddenly. 'There's a new black-rig in! Let's see if there's news.'

But she wasn't from Greece at all; she was from the north, built and owned in Byzantium. She had touched at Poieëssa, Chios, Samos and Rhodes, then coasting south of Crete, and so to Alexandria. She was unlading exciting-looking bales. Nikomedes asked politely what they were, and was told furs; then came slaves, driven stiff and scared out of the hold, ducking and blinking at the sun-blaze. Then came the captain, all in his best, with rings and bracelets and a wolf-hound on the lead. He was carrying two or three sealed packets. Gorgo looked at him so adoringly that he couldn't help grinning back. He came over to the children and asked them if they could help him about the delivery of letters. One of them was for Erif Der.

She came back from the wedding fretted and jumpy with the thought of Leandris and Idaios together, while she herself must still sleep alone, and found that Berris, impatient, had opened her letter. 'What's the news?' she cried, running at him, and then, seeing his face: 'Oh, Berris—what? Not Klint?'

'No, no,' said Berris hurriedly, 'no one's dead. You read it, Erif. I'm here.'

While she read the long letter in Tarrik's black, hard writing, Berris watched her face. Her cheeks grew pink and her eyes looked bigger and bluer; she made a funny movement with her arms. 'The baby,' she said softly. 'Oh, the little baby! Oh, I would love to hold him!' She read on to the end. 'I'm glad it's a boy,' she said. 'I wouldn't have liked Tarrik to have his first girl except by me myself. Linit will have wanted a boy, too.' She rolled back the letter to look again at something in the beginning of it which made her smile. Then she looked at her brother. '*You* thought I'd be angry, Berris.'

'Well,' said Berris, 'yes, as a matter of fact, I did.'

'I'm not,' she said. 'I'm glad. I do love him! And she is my cousin; we were little girls together. I think I am them both, Berris. I know I am Tarrik, and because she has been so deeply kind to him and given him a child, I am her too. She would have been as kind to me; she became me at Plowing Eve to her own danger. She has taken away nothing from me.' She stretched out her arms and heaved up her breasts in a wide breath and thought very happily about Marob and her loves and the new little baby of the Corn King.

Then, of course, Berris laughed. What he said was unfair to her, but he was still rather annoyed about the loss of his property: 'It would have been nice for Tarrik if you'd looked so pretty over Sardu!' God, how stupid Sardu could be! And what lovely legs she had. 'Poor little Sardu, who hadn't hurt you either,' he added.

'I'm thinking of my equals!' said Erif grandly and rather tremblingly. Her brother did not appear to be impressed. Scarlet and purple rose viciously through her. 'Not little stinking worms, not your cast dirt—'

Berris laughed again loudly, mocking the spitting scarlet in his sister with something black of his own, determined to pull Erif down, to be King of the Castle himself!

But Erif refused the tussle. Someone else had come into her mind, following Sardu. Murr, who had killed himself just before midsummer, because of her unkindness. Now all the kindness he should have had came flooding up through Erif. She recognised the scarlet for the thing it was, her own jangled body that had been torn away from Tarrik and the sweet sucking of her baby and the life of Marob. She said she thought she would go and help Ankhet about the house. She thought she would be able to tell Ankhet about the new baby.

She went up to the roof. There, under a summer tent of palm leaves, Ankhet was damping and ironing the pleats of her best linen skirt. The little girl was doing the same with her doll's dress and an iron carefully not too hot; she talked to herself and the doll very busily all the time. Erif Der told Ankhet what the letter had said and what it meant in Marob, how every one would be glad that the Corn King had begotten a child on the Spring, and how she was glad with them. She made a picture in her words of Linit and the baby, and Tarrik's happiness, and the fresh springing of power reaching through his writing across the sea to Egypt. The strength of her imaginative well-wishing made her look beautiful to the other woman. Ankhet nodded and murmured. At last she said: 'It is full water now. Hapi, the great river, has risen and risen and brimmed and been kind to us. My husband says we shall have good crops. I am going to the Little Mysteries tonight. Will you come too?'

'To Isis? Isis and the baby? Will they not mind a stranger?'

Ankhet shook her head. 'She will be glad of you. She looks on the land now. She walks over the thirsty land and draws Hapi the river after her. She thinks of others. She thinks of their good. You and I will go to meet her; we will wash our hair and put on clean linen, and when the men go to supper we will not go with them. We will take offerings. She will accept us both.'

Erif said 'Yes,' she would go with Ankhet; but when she thought of Isis and Horus she thought of her young cousin Linit and a baby that was as like Tarrik as her own Klint had been.

To begin with, the temple was quite dark. Ankhet held her right hand and someone whom she could not see but knew must be a woman held her left. In front of them there was a row of little red lights and then curtains; the lowest five feet of the curtains were dimly visible with lotus stems growing up them, but the lotus flowers and the tops of the curtains were lost in darkness. A certain rhythm of grip and swing began to assert itself faintly on the worshippers; the curtains began to sway a little to this same rhythm. The sway gaining, at last the curtains parted altogether. One after another, on silent naked feet, priests in white with shaved heads came to the image of Isis and kissed its feet and offered it sweet ointment, head bands and shoulder hangings of painted linen, scent, butter, and pure water out of vases made in the shapes of flowers and animals. They bowed and swayed and passed on, leaving the image of mother and child more and more shining. They brought her a ship made of papyrus and fully rigged; she was Isis the Alexandrian, mother of the lighthouse, star of sailors.

Four of them brought in an altar and sacrificed an antelope, the wild thing of the desert, the suspect, the devil-ridden. This was done silently too, with no shock, for all closed on it at once with expert, choking fingers.

After this there began, to a tinkling music, a play of Isis and her wanderings as a forlorn widow, how the wicked rich woman who would not feed or house her was punished by a scorpion-bite on her child, but how Isis herself turned back and healed the dying child of her enemy. But Erif was not seeing the play properly. Because now that there was more light, faces were visible: the friendly face of Ankhet beside her, the fattish face of the woman on her left, and the face two beyond, which was not Egyptian, the unmistakable face of Tarrik's aunt, Yersha-Eurydice. She drew her own head back and down a little, so as to observe from behind. That face was still damp as though with a perpetually cold sweat, the pure linen of the mysteries clung damply about the neck. It appeared to Erif that Yersha's figure, of which she had been so proud, had collapsed a good deal. The breasts sagged; one could see that because of the damp stuff. And her eyes. Yes, Yersha had got the worst of it! This was the person who had come between her and Tarrik, who had tried to poison her and her baby, who had hated the true Marob people and thought and felt and acted against them. It was curious to see her. She looked very powerless now. Erif brooded on things that had happened and allowed her hands to swing to the tinkling tune of the Mystery Play.

Isis gave the rich woman her heart's desire, the life of her child. The woman knelt before her in adoration holding the child, and Isis stretched out her arms to her woman worshippers and bade them too ask for their hearts' lawful desire at this time when the heart of a goddess was warm from giving and aching to give again. Then the women spoke aloud, tensely, their desires, but as they spoke mostly in Egyptian it was hard for Erif to understand more than a word or two. She said nothing herself, till Ankhet tugged at her hand, saying: 'Speak now!' But even then she only murnured: 'Make me clean, Isis, Lady of the Lighthouse, send me home!' For she was listening to Yersha saying again and again in a voice she remembered so ridiculously well: 'Take the spell from me, Lady Isis, pitiful goddess; have mercy on me, give me peace at last; take away the spell that the wicked witch cast on me!'

That was, apparently, herself—and nobody knew. Unless the goddess knew. This was only a priestess dressed up as a goddess. If Isis had known she would have felt it; she would have felt an eye on her. But she did not. She laughed a little to herself in safe darkness, unrecognised. Yersha's Greek voice went on longer than the Egyptian voices, a priest had to sidle up and tap her on the shoulder. Yersha, with her wet, shining face. What had happened to the Rhodian? Had she lost him? It was enough to turn away any husband! She would not get another. Yersha, who had despised Tarrik and Marob!

The play went on. Those who had spoken loosed hands and settled again to watch and sway. What, finally, was the connection between all this? Marob went on too. It was not this Yersha who had done those things, but a younger, stronger woman, who would have been ashamed to cry in a crowd of foreigners. A woman a long time ago at the furthest end of the sea, back in Marob. In Marob where Erif had danced at Plowing Eve. In Marob where her dead baby had been alive and sweet for a little time. In Marob, where Murr had been alive among the pollen of summer. In Marob, where Harn Der had been alive and a great fighter. They were all going the same road to the dark house of Serapis, to the doubtful star of Isis, to dust and darkness. Why should this strange woman in Egypt be hurt because of something a long time over and past which had happened in Marob? Erif slid her hand down over the pure linen, feeling for Tarrik's knife, which would surely be the quickest spell-breaker on his aunt. But she was not wearing it. Of course not; she had left it at home; she seldom wore it here, seldom even looked at it, for what was the use in the too clear air of Greece or Egypt? It had not shone again since the day at Delphi. She said in Ankhet's ear, hurriedly: 'I have a gift for Isis—I must go—I am coming back.' Then she turned quick and rose and scurried out, keeping her face away from Yersha, who might have looked round at this disturbance of the line of worshippers.

Something rather trying happened on the way back. Erif thought she would not go by the main street, but would take a short cut she was sure she knew. But she lost herself in an odd part of the Egyptian quarter. Fortunately, the natives recognised and respected the white linen of the Mysteries, and put her on her way back, but she was flustered and distressed, and her hurry kept on breaking into little runs. All this time, whatever was going on went on, and she had not yet begun to alter it. Berris might have felt like that with an untouched block waiting for him while he shaved or ate or otherwise wasted his working time.

She came to the house and ran up the stairs to their room, thinking about the knife and exactly how it was to be used to cut the spell. She wanted to run quietly across to her bed and take the thing from the shelf above the pillow. But she found Berris chasing Metrotimé round the room; they had already upset various jars and stools and pulled a curtain half down. When she came in they stopped, laughing and gasping, and Metrotimé pinned up her hair. 'But how revoltingly chaste you look, Erif, my little angel,' she said. 'Come to the feast at the palace this evening and get a little splash or two!'

Erif twitched her skirt away, frowning. 'What feast?'

'But the vintage, the vintage; haven't you heard? Our divine King's direct inspiration. No, it's serious. Listen, Erif, it's going to be desperately exciting. It will be—yes, almost really—a return of the God. We shall get him down to earth if anyone can.'

'Catch any god coming to that palace of yours!' said Erif.

But Metrotimé held her wrist. 'It won't stay there. We shall go out—into the fields, into the vineyards. I think—we may get even the natives to see. It's an idea. A great idea. To bring the nations together under the youngest, the reborn God! Ptolemy said that himself.'

'An Alexander idea,' said Berris nodding. 'Right for this city.'

'I don't think the Egyptians will leave their gods for any of yours,' said Erif. 'Are you taking Berris?'

They both at once said 'Yes,' and laughed. 'He's to be a faun,' said Metrotimé.

Erif raised her eyebrows at him. 'He'll like that!'

'Well, why not?' said Berris, challenging her; and then: 'Come on, Erif, it'll do you good; make you come alive. This summer's too hot for us! Let's get the heat out of us somehow!'

'No,' said Erif, 'I'm busy. I—I have to get clear with Isis.'

'What a bore you are these days!' said Berris. 'You and your cow-faced females!'

But Metrotimé was rather shocked with him. She had been to the Temple of Isis herself before now. There was a stone image in a niche in her room; she had cooled a hot head against the knees of Her and the Child fairly often. If the Egyptians took Dionysos, the northern bull, she would gladly take the gentle, suffering and cow-shadowed southerner to comfort her when she needed it.

Erif fetched her knife and came back through the room. Metrotimé was watching Berris making loops in a piece of copper wire. 'What are you doing with Tarrik's knife?' he said sharply, looking up. But she jumped for the door and was running again. She could not explain. For a time the idea of her brother and Metrotimé held her, very disturbing. She liked Metrotimé in a way, but not Metrotimé with her hair down and dress slipping: let them have each other if they wanted, but not so untidily, not with all this silliness. She wanted it serious and honourable, a good magic, a hard, knife-edged delight to feel or think of. As he would have been with Philylla. As Tarrik was with her or with other women. The image of those two she had just left shook her thoughts of Tarrik; she could not feel the part of herself which had gone overseas to purr and smile at the new baby. These things she had thought beautiful and important reduced themselves grimacingly to something Metrotimé would laugh at. What was the use of love and generosity and magic? Why fuss about Yersha-Eurydice? Her pace slackened.

She thought that this time she would go by the great street of Sun and Moon, so as not to miss her way again. It was warm dusk now and crowded with men and women going slowly after the day's work. She walked quietly, her head down, the folds of her mantle over the knife. Very soon she came to the cross-roads, the centre of Alexandria, and had to wait a moment for a long string of potters' donkeys to go by. In the centre of the cross-roads was Alexander's tomb, the marble gleaming with extraordinary softness and brilliancy among the hard Egyptian limestone buildings. It was a great stepped sarcophagus, carved with eternal battles and perhaps eternal love between the Macedonians and their king. People brought offerings to it, barley cakes and cream and flowers; little snakes lived unharmed in cracks between the flag-stones and flickered in and out as though to show that life still faintly stirred there and might some day be roused. He had made Alexandria to live after him, and what else? Almost everything. But his only child had been killed. She believed all the stories she heard about him. He had magic. He had succeeded where Kleomenes of Sparta had failed. And now he was a kind of god. He had been fierce and serious and generous. He was like Tarrik, but not concentrated into one flame on one place and one small people, but spread about the world. As she thought of him, her heart calmed and lifted again and she went steadily to the Temple of Isis.

The play was over and Ankhet waiting for her, anxious and delicately questioning. But she said firmly that it was laid on her to speak to this other stranger, and found out after a time that Yersha was in a separate room with one of the chief priestesses, telling her wrongs and miseries. Erif found another Greek-speaking priestess and gave her the knife, saying with the utmost solemnity that she must make very sure to go at once to the room and tell the stranger that the knife was given to her to cut the spell. 'Then,' said Erif, 'it must be drawn very lightly down her face from brow to chin, and across from breast to breast. All this has been told me,' she ended, 'in a dream—fasting—and after having written the Names.'

The priestess looked at her and took the knife. 'Our Lady reveals herself in many kinds of darkness,' she said.

'Tell me,' said Erif suddenly, 'what happens to Eurydice the Rhodian.' The priestess nodded again, and Erif waited, shivering rather, behind a pillar, trying to understand the difficult pictures on it and knowing that she had given away Tarrik's knife. Ankhet had to leave her to go back to the children; it must be night by now.

After a long time the priestess came back and told Erif that the thing had been done and Eurydice's face and body wiped with new cloths. Then she had suddenly fallen asleep and she was asleep still; her skin was dry and healthy as a child's. 'She knew the knife,' the priestess said, 'for she cried out when she saw it as those do whose evil spirit is faced with a thing of power. And the light of the full moon walked for a moment along the blade.'

'Ah!' said Erif, 'did the knife glow?'

'Yes,' said the priestess. 'And now you had better tell me all about it.'

Extremely startled, Erif began to stammer, and suddenly found herself explaining it all to the uncommenting priestess—not very well, and constantly harking back to something she had forgotten. She dropped again into stammering and silence. She could not believe she had told.

The priestess said calmly: 'Then it was a lie about your dream.'

'Yes,' said Erif, 'but the knife glowed the way it did at Delphi! It shone then when I was helping Hyperides, who denied Apollo, and it shone here when I lied to Isis.' The priestess looked at her very gently. 'So there,' said Erif, but not in Greek. Some curious tide of security was mounting through her. Telling about Marob, she had become again the Spring Queen, the focus of the people, and she felt a quite definite sort of cousinship with Isis, who was a Year Queen too. This was only a priestess! As, in a way, Linit had been her priestess, and now for a time had taken her place and was acting it as these priestesses had acted the story of Isis. For a brilliant moment everything in the world fitted together with clashing and sparking in her head. All difficulties could be solved by an immediate and complete explanation. While that held earth and air were equally weightless round her. Then something came into her head: her brother and Philylla; and she was back in the temple, and it must be very late because she was so tired. The priestess had been saying something, she did not know what. She shook her head, questioning. But this time the priestess only smiled and gave her a long and elaborate blessing which she only half understood.

She went home through hot, dark streets, almost empty; because of her dress she was quite safe. She heard a certain amount of distant shouting, but did not heed it much. Berris was, of course, not in. She went into her own room, an alcove off the other one with a narrow window, undressed and fell asleep at once.

After some unmeasurable space of time Erif woke up to a noise and a bright spear of yellow light piercing through the crack of the curtains between her and the other room, jerking and sliding about. She turned over and put her hand over her ear; it was too hot for a blanket. But the noise went on, and even behind her shut eyes the light seemed to wobble drunkenly. She heard her brother's voice and Metrotimé's and others she knew; she came more and more definitely awake; her drowsed mind suddenly shook itself and began to race. She got up and slipped into her thin dress again; it was not quite cold yet.

For a time she stood in the crack of the curtains watching the other room. There were ten or twelve men and women, most of whom she recognised as Greek or Macedonian courtiers, back from the Feast of the Vintage. They were all dressed as fauns and maenads, with bunches of half-squashed grapes in their hair and dragging down on to their shoulders, and skins of leopards and antelopes and fauns. One of them was trying a pipe-tune, which kept on breaking down in the same place. Metrotimé lay back on a couch, one breast bare, staring and breathing and sometimes passing a long bryony garland from right hand to left. Berris was leaning against one of his own statues, grinning to himself; Erif thought critically that he looked rather well in his short faun skin. Two of the girls in helpless giggles were failing to mend a thyrsus; the big gilt pine-cone went rolling about, and finally landed by Erif's curtain.

She picked it up and came out into the room; they shouted at her joyfully, and two or three ran up and kissed her. They smelt of grapes and wine and the hot night; she pushed them away, but not really angrily. She put one of the torches into a safer place and then picked up the thyrsus and mended it with a piece of string. It balanced nicely; she held it across the palm of her hand. Metrotimé sat up with a long swing from the hips, and in the same movement flung her garland across Erif's shoulders. Bryony berries pattered on the floor. Berris leapt over and made it fast, over one shoulder and under the other. He stripped his own faun skin and tied it round her waist; it was hot and damp, and his naked belly and thighs when he took it off were stained with dust and grapes; there were little leaves and dry twigs caught up in his body hair; she reached out and pulled at them. He laughed and suddenly threw his arms round her and squashed her softly against him; the heat and excitement passed from his skin to hers; her throat and breasts and belly began to throb. He reached up a hand behind and pulled her dress loose from one shoulder. He let her go, staggering and laughing, the pure linen crumpled and spotted. She had left the people of Isis and gone over to Dionysos-Sabazios. So long as she was of some company it did not matter which. The evergreen things that had come down from Thrace with the plant-god, pine and smilax and holly, pricked her in Alexandria. She turned from her brother's arms into the arms of another faun. Dimly she saw him and Metrotimé together on the couch, locked and intent, but it was not really Metrotimé: it was someone full of godhead, as she was.

Once again that night she had a clear vision of Berris. She saw his mouth, hovering, kissing, biting a shoulder; and then he looked up and his eyes and the muscles of his face fixed themselves for a moment and quivered, so that she knew piercingly that he had thought of Philylla. At the same moment she herself thought of Tarrik; but Tarrik was well and happy with his new baby and his own harvest coming. And Philylla? She had not talked to Philylla for some time. They had smiled to one another at the wedding. Perhaps she was happy. The Spartans would not be sharing in the Vintage Feast. Then Berris dropped his mouth again hungrily and all her own thoughts were torn away from her and dispersed again into laughter and pleasure.

After quite a long time it seemed to be dawn and there seemed to be fewer people there. She thought she must have been asleep again. Finally, there were only herself and Berris and leaves and trodden grapes and single untouched berries that had rolled into corners of the room. He brought water and they both drank and looked at one another, and stretched and laughed a little. A cool air of sunrise blew through the open window and the leaves danced about the floor. She was sleepy again, beautifully sleepy with a soft, all-embracing exhaustion. 'I was thinking of Tarrik,' she said, out of the happy weariness. Berris did not answer for a time. He looked at a chip that had somehow been

made in a corner of one of his reliefs. He went over and
touched it. Then he answered her: 'And I was thinking
of Philylla.' But he did not say it in the tone that she had
used; it seemed suddenly as though after all no part of
him had been satisfied; he spoke not simply, but with
layers of complicated bitterness in his voice. But Erif did
not look up to see the stiff pain in his face, because she was
already almost asleep again.

Chapter Four

IT WAS ONE DAY later on that autumn that the King got
letters from Sparta in answer to his. He let Nikomedes read
some of them over his shoulder. While he read he would
every now and then feel the boy's breath against his cheek,
the tickling ends of his hair, and he would toss his own
head up and rub it against the young face. Then he went
off again to see King Ptolemy, and in the meantime sent to
tell the others to come the next day. Nikomedes was wildly
excited; he was suddenly certain that everything was going
to come right. The letters he had seen—though his father
was always folding them up again before he'd quite got the
last lines!—had been hopeful, promising all sorts of
support if only the King could come home with some
impressive backing, something at least to make a start
with. 'And why, after all, shouldn't Ptolemy let us have
it?' he clamoured to Sphaeros. But the old man said:
'These things don't go by reason. Try and keep steady.
You pitch up and down like a ship in rough weather!
How will you ever be able to face life unless you can see
it from one level? The bad with the good.' He sighed, he
found it difficult to tackle these boys; they had a kind of
formal stoicism, sucked up with their milk almost, a way
of abstracting themselves from their bodies. It was their
method of avoiding punishment. But he was almost sure,
though they wouldn't tell him so, that they went, not into
contemplation of wisdom, but into some play-world, back
to Sparta perhaps. He could not meet their eyes. Even little
Gorgo did it, copying her brothers.

Kleomenes came back in the evening, profoundly cast
down. To his mother's questions he answered that he had
not been able to see King Ptolemy at all, only Sosibios,
and he could get nothing out of him except this endless,

maddening talk! Had he asked for the King? Yes, but the King was busy—busy with one of his new boy-Nancies! The creatures Agathokles buys or bribes for him! Or boxers—nigger boxers with—But Kratesikleia, glancing at the listening children, hastily asked another question.

Nikomedes was directly unhappy through his father. It was as though he were completely the same person. Yet he found it painfully difficult to talk; any kind of pure sympathy was silly and useless, and he couldn't think of any reasonable way of helping! When Kleomenes was alone, the boys took it in turns to wait on him; tonight it was Nikolaos. He always managed to joke with his father, to make up some sort of game, even at the worst times. Nikomedes watched them and it made him feel unhappier still. He must do something!

He went to sleep and had horrid, confusing, tangled dreams, which settled down into seeing a long procession going past over and over again, with priests and oxen and his grandmother and all sorts of quite unbothered people, and in the middle his father, and he knew that at the last moment the beasts were just not going to be there and they would sacrifice his father instead. If only he himself could get into the procession he could stop them, but he was always in some way outside it. Then he dreamt about Ptolemy like an ogre eating boys, which seemed ordinary in the dream, and his father was mixed up in that too. He would have liked to ask someone about these dreams, but Sphaeros was always cross with him for dreaming or at any rate saying anything about it, and he was ashamed to ask the Egyptian servants who would have been delighted to explain.

The rest of the Spartiates came to the King's house; some of them had got letters from home too, by the same boat. They discussed them, getting down to the smallest possible amount of help that would allow them to try the adventure. They talked about Sosibios and the best ways to approach him. They were none of them cheerful. Nikomedes sat and listened. Panteus said behind his hand to Phoebis: 'The child oughtn't to be here. Can't he be sent away till we've got something better to tell him?' Phoebis hadn't noticed the boy much; he looked at him for a time and whispered back: 'He's old for his years; he can stand it. But I don't see why he need.'

It was beginning very slowly and yet with an odd effect of doing it by jumps, to take shape in Nikomedes' mind that he could do something to help. He could do it alone. He must. It occurred to him that if he was a Stoic he would not mind what happened to his body; if he was a good Stoic he could be a victim. It would be some use having been talked to by Sphaeros!

They went on discussing points, more and more dejectedly. There were long silences. Kleomenes sat with his head in his hands; he looked as if he had not slept much. At last there seemed to be nothing further to say. One after another they went out of the room. Nikomedes walked over to Panteus and said: 'Isn't there any way of getting straight to King Ptolemy?'

'I think we've tried everything,' said Panteus.

'If there was something he really wanted that we had! What does he really want, Panteus?'

'As far as I can see, he doesn't want anything honourable, anything a Spartiate has to give! We've offered him our swords.'

'And he wasn't interested. And father goes on being hurt. Have you noticed, Panteus, how his hair's quite white over his temples and a bit grey everywhere else?'

'Yes,' said Panteus, 'I've noticed.'

'Can I come and see Philylla one day? She hasn't asked me lately. Aren't you going to have a baby, Panteus?'

Panteus shook his head. 'Come any day, Nikomedes. We'd be very glad.'

Nikomedes went to Idaios who was rolling and tying the loose bits of paper. 'Idaios,' he said, 'before you married Leandris, did you love a boy?'

'Yes,' said Idaios. Then: 'He was killed at Sellasia. Praxitas. You knew him, didn't you? He was almost a man then.'

'I remember him,' said Nikomedes. 'I didn't know he was your love. Idaios, was that better than Leandris?'

'Why do you ask, King's son?'

'You don't mind my asking, Idaios? Well, I—I wondered what it was like.'

'You've got no love, Nikomedes, have you? And you should, of course, at your age. It's this damnable place. We're all too old for you, and no good to a boy anyway, and there's no one else. Bad luck, Nikomedes!' He put one arm round the boy's shoulder and kissed him on the forehead.

Nikomedes looked up at him and said: 'Tell me just this. If—everything were different—am I the sort of boy you could fall in love with?' Idaios looked rather startled, and Nikomedes blushed quickly and said: 'Please don't think I'm asking you to! It's not that. I only want to know. Do I look right?'

'I don't know,' said Idaios. 'I hadn't thought of you that way. You've been one of our council, one of the men. Yes, I suppose you do. Don't worry about it, Nikomedes. We'll get back to Sparta some day. At least you will, even if we've all got to die in these blasted sand-heaps!' He stacked up the piles of paper and went out.

The only one left now was Hippitas, who was always slow-moving. Nikomedes went up to him. 'Hippitas,' he said, smiling at him, 'do you think I'm beautiful?'

'Chtt!' said Hippitas, 'what are you after, imp? I'm not seducible!'

'Seriously,' said Nikomedes, 'am I?'

'Oh, you're well enough. Anyway, Nikomedes, you're a good boy, which is a less ordinary thing to be.'

'That's my own affair,' said Nikomedes.

'Isn't the other? That's news, if it's not. My dear, who's been making love to you?'

'No one, no one! Hippitas, *I just want to know*!'

'Can't you tell me what you're so excited about? No? Well, I think you look nice, as most decent, well-bred boys of your age are bound to do. Is that enough for you?'

But Nikomedes was away already, frowning.

He knocked at the door of his father's room. Kleomenes was writing letters to Sparta, grinding his teeth slightly from time to time, and getting up and walking about the room to get his sentences clear in his mind before he wrote them down. He frowned mechanically at the interruption. Nikomedes stood near the door, waiting, his heart beating violently with unexpressed and unexpressible sympathy and love. At last Kleomenes said: 'Well, what is it?'

'Father,' said Nikomedes, 'I want to ask you a question. It sounds stupid, but it's not. Am I at all beautiful?'

'Don't you know?' said Kleomenes, still frowning

because he wanted to keep the idea of his letter clear. Nikomedes shook his head. 'Of course you are!' said Kleomenes, 'the most beautiful thing I ever made. God help me, you're the image of your mother. Go away, Nikomedes.'

He went to the room where he and his brother kept their clothes. Gyridas and Nikolaos were playing draughts; they murmured to him but were too much interested in their game to look what he was doing. At last when he had washed and dressed again, Gyridas turned round. 'What *are* you doing in your best tunic, Nikomedes?' 'Did granny say we were to?' asked Nikolaos, vaguely certain that he was likely to have forgotten some occasion. But the eldest son went out without answering. 'I wonder what's the matter with him,' said Gyridas. 'Did you see—his hands were shaking and he had a funny look about his nose, as if he couldn't breathe?'

Nikomedes walked quickly through the streets of Alexandria to Ptolemy's palace. It was getting near sunset and the light coming down between the houses was very golden. They would probably think he was having supper with one of the others. He walked with such extreme certainty and carelessness through the gates that two sets of sentries let him by. When he was challenged he said: 'I am Nikomedes of Sparta and I have particular business with King Ptolemy.' He wondered what he would look like to them when he came out again. He had a little money, but he had decided when to use it. To the last guards who challenged him he said: 'Tell King Ptolemy that the boy Nikomedes, the son of Kleomenes, is here in his best clothes. Wait to tell him till he is alone. Sosibios is not to know. I think you will find that your master will be pleased.' He handed over his bribe, a small one as things went, and one of the sentries went off with the message.

The other one tried to talk to him and even to touch him, but Nikomedes evaded it with some skill. At last the man who had gone came back. 'I gave your message,' he said. Nikomedes took a step forward, suddenly feeling very cold. 'And now?' 'One nice kiss for me and I'll let you through.' 'You've had my money!' 'That! Why, that's what I give the old beggar women in the gutters! Now, don't be nasty—what's one kiss more or less to a pretty boy like you?' 'Very well,' said Nikomedes, hardening himself into a mere Stoic formula, and stood and let the guard kiss him. The man seemed rather dissatisfied, but he was allowed to go by. He went along a passage and pushed aside a curtain of painted linen, and then stood blinking for a moment, with his eyes full of the setting sun. A voice said: 'Come in, come in, Nikomedes; I've been hoping for a long time that you'd pay me a visit.'

It had been most startling for Ptolemy to get the whispered message. He kept the guard waiting while he turned it over and over in his mind. But he found he could not be rational about it at all. No amount of brain work brought him anything but the image of that silent and gracious and virgin creature who had stood sometimes between Sphaeros and King Kleomenes on the days of his audience, and had not seemed even to look at him. Nikomedes in his best clothes. So, he was at last going to get something out of the Spartans, in spite of Sosibios! He said the boy was to be brought in at once, and then, to one of the slaves: 'A little supper. Yes. I am not to be disturbed.' He mentioned the wine. 'And garlands. Something white, yes, pure white for both of us.' He glanced at himself in the mirror and decided not to wear anything more elaborate; it would only frighten the boy. The diadem? Yes, perhaps. What luck had he to thank for this? Was the boy bored with being shut up all day with a grandmother? Was he doing it merely out of curiosity? Or pique? Or to spite someone? One of those fierce, surly Spartiates who'd scolded him; his father perhaps. Or was it—had he come for the sake of the God—had he heard of the new wine? But while King Ptolemy was thinking this he heard light steps outside, not very fast, but quite even. Then the curtain was pushed aside and Nikomedes was standing in the Danaë gold of sunset. He raised his forearm to shield his eyes; he moved in beauty. He was all of old Greece that the Macedonians had ever longed for. Ptolemy went over to him and led him gently by the hand to the cushioned seat against the wall.

As he was touched, something went very quickly through Nikomedes' head; he only just caught and recognised it as being the same thing as the end of all dreams when a dreadful thing has been chasing you—the moment when it touches you and you dissolve into screaming, burning chaos. The

witch, the fury, the beast. Now he was touched and he had
not flinched. Although this touch, too, was chaos, although
he could not wake. He must speak now before his mind
had shattered under the touch like glass, for already it was
ringing, ringing, like glass about to break. He said:'King
Ptolemy, I want to talk to you.'

'Yes, yes,' said Ptolemy, 'and I to you, Nikomedes.'
He found it difficult to speak calmly. It was a long time
since any emotion of this degree of violence had come into
his life.

Nikomedes began: 'We have been in Egypt a very great
many months, hoping that you—' And then he broke
off, afraid of going too fast. Ptolemy smiled at him. The
Egyptian King was, after all, nothing to be frightened of
yet; he looked almost rather nice; only too smooth. Better
begin again. 'I know what you want of me, King Ptolemy.'
And then he stopped suddenly again, wondering, but did
he, did he know? Could he really be certain either of this
man, or, if what he had heard was true, about himself?

Ptolemy had taken his hand again. 'Do you know?'
he said. 'Do you, Nikomedes? I want everything, yes,
everything! I want your heart and body and mind, I want
your youth, I want to eat you whole—like new bread,
Nikomedes, new wine! And I'll give you everything; yes,
my crown and my kingdom, youth and life, you shall have it
all back, but changed, but coloured through me, but mine,
mine, mine!' He picked the hand up and began kissing it
bitingly, the funny, brown, untrimmed, square-nailed boy's
paw! The other paw reached up to push him away, push
away his biting, sucking kisses, he had both paws. No, no;
not too fast. He let them go again. 'Well, Nikomedes?'

Nikomedes looked down curiously at his kissed hands.
They did not seem to be his own any more; they were
apart from him, smarting a little. He let them lie. He said:
'If I give myself up to you, as I'm willing to do, you must
give my father all the help he asks for.'

Ptolemy stared and frowned and said: 'So you've come
to bargain!' Suddenly he leapt to his feet and hunched
himself over Nikomedes and shouted at him: 'Who sent
you?'

For a moment Nikomedes was choking back screaming
terror. Then he said firmly: 'No one! I came by myself.

I am a King's son and I won't be bullied or insulted, Ptolemy!'

Gradually Ptolemy's black look relaxed. He stood merely erect and said: 'Was I bullying you, King's son? Did I seem to you like that?'

'Yes,' said Nikomedes.

Ptolemy nodded. 'You see, I've got power,' he said, 'great power over all sorts of pain. Even over a King's son! Whips, Nikomedes, and licking fires and fish that eat boys and little, snicking knives. Don't let us talk of it. You want to bargain. You, not I, want that. I'm in a better position than you. I have, apparently, all you want, but I am not so sure that what you offer me is so good; that remains to be seen. Besides, you have come here to my palace, inside my walls. I am stronger than you, Nikomedes, even though you are a Spartan! Suppose I just took what I wanted? No, don't start so; I'm not touching you! Perhaps I don't even want to.'

They sat down again on the bench, Nikomedes at one end, his hands clasped between his knees, all at once feeling most unheroic and longing only to be home again with Gyridas and Nikolaos. Ptolemy, at the other end, sat and looked at him with the kind of eyes and mouth which might mean anything. He did not know what to do. The sun dropped and dropped towards the end of the world. The gold light in the room tilted and vanished. Softly the curtain was drawn aside and in came three lovely girls in blue with lighted silver lamps, which they hung here and there about the walls. Everything became kinder and vaguer and easier. While they were in the room the two on the bench did not speak. When they were gone Nikomedes found that Ptolemy was still looking at him as puzzlingly as ever. Suddenly and disastrously he found himself overwhelmed with tears. He got to his feet. He tried very hard to speak.

Ptolemy chose that moment to say: 'You want to bargain with me. Tell me exactly what you want.' He spoke in a new, a grim kind of voice. Nikomedes stretched out his hands dumbly, praying desperately for time, for one moment to recover. Ptolemy seemed to understand, to take that prayer. He was standing now, close to Nikomedes, so that those dumb, quivering hands just touched the breast of his tunic. 'You needn't tell me, then!' he said. 'Look,

Nikomedes, you aren't a very good bargainer! Hadn't you better trust to me? I'm not ungenerous where I love. You should trust me, Nikomedes.'

Something in Nikomedes said 'No, no!' If he could be the sacrifice he could and would make the demand! Only what was the best way? If only he knew more of the world! Was he certain he could save his father and Sparta? 'Ptolemy—' he said, 'I don't know yet.' It seemed to him that the moment to ask for money and soldiers was not yet quite come. He let himself be led a pace or two by the other King; his touched and breaking mind allowed it.

Ptolemy was sitting now on the raised end of the bench, and the boy stood beside him, shone upon softly by a lamp, his head bowed, his eyes open but veiled. Ptolemy lifted his arms and unpinned the brooch from the boy's right shoulder, a funny toy brooch of hammered gold with a quail on it. The tunic dropped forward and the young chin, too, dropped a little. The light fell straight on his shoulder and breast; the white tunic dropped in folds of shadow over his quivering belly. This innocent creature. This self-chosen victim. This March-bud beauty, this Spring God come at the turn of autumn for the mystery of the Vintage. He drew him closer to the bench, he began to turn him round with groping hands close against his hips, feeling down through the stuff of the tunic that would strip as a sweet almond strips. As the rough sheath from a crinkled poppy bud, a loose shaken white poppy.

At the far end of the room a little table was being laid for supper, a table of citron-wood almost covered with flowers, a foaming of blossom round the silver dishes, the faint jingle and glitter of the silver cups. Two of the girls and Agathoklea were preparing it under the farthest of the lamps. Between them and the bench there were great spaces of quiet shadow; they did not disturb King Ptolemy. Still he and the boy stayed as they were; still his bent palms waited over the flesh of Hellas. He was attending now to some ecstasy within himself which would surely come to a crisis and flow out towards possession of this beauty and of the whole world, the world which Alexander had died to possess materially, but which he, Ptolemy, would now possess spiritually through this little death, this agony of pleasure.

Agathoklea looked delicately and sympathetically across the space of shadow towards the lighted group and for a moment fumbled in her recognition of Nikomedes. Then she saw and was shocked in her every sense of expediency, and gave a slight scream of disapprobation. Only the most ordinary, small scream, but enough to alter everything. For suddenly Nikomedes lifted his head and said very clearly: 'Then you do promise me the regular subsidy and the soldiers and the transport ships?'

Agathoklea was not so much of a politician as her brother, but she could scarcely help understanding this. She bit her lip and began to walk across the room. But Ptolemy was rising from the bench. The young god had suddenly turned into a mocking imp, the victim was not a victim, the ecstasy had winked and shifted and become commonplace. His dream, his dream was broken! As he got upright, saying nothing, his grip shot upwards into a murderous one, fingers on throat, the only other way to take the victim and have the ecstasy!

Taken utterly by surprise Nikomedes stumbled back, choked, unable even to shout, clawing vainly at those fingers, his passion to save himself not for one moment equal to the fingers' passion to destroy him. The next thing he knew he was staggering, gasping and crowing for breath and in sharp pain, but his legs seem to have taken it on themselves to run, wobbling better or worse, in the wake of a woman who was pulling him along, stuffing him behind a curtain, rushing him down a passage, up steps into the open air, through a laurel thicket that whipped back sharp leaves at him, up some more steps, along—and plump into a small room with a girl at the end just looking up from a book with her mouth open to ask a question. Agathoklea let go. Nikomedes sat down hard and suddenly on the floor.

'There you are, Metrotimé!' stormed Agathoklea. 'Put him in the cupboard, into the book chest, hide him under your bed; I'm sure I don't know what to do with him!'

'Who is it?' said Metrotimé, getting up and delicately poking Nikomedes with her toe so as to disarrange his tunic still further. 'It looks rather nice. Bed, don't you think, not books?'

'It's Nikomedes of Sparta, devil fly away with him!'

'Oh,' said Metrotimé, waggling her eyebrows, and rather

obviously rearranged the tunic into complete decency. Nikomedes blushed and sat up rather more, patting his throat gingerly. 'A hot cloth?' suggested Metrotimé, and clapped her hands.

Agathoklea nodded. 'Is your woman safe?'

'Too dreadfully,' said Metrotimé, and when a large, kindly looking slave-woman came bustling in, ordered her to bring steaming cloths and a glass of wine. 'Now,' she said, 'what about it, dearest?'

'I came in,' said Agathoklea, 'and found the King, bless him, prettily busy with this young man in a corner.'

'How far?'

'Oh, the limit in another minute, wouldn't it, you wretch?' She shook Nikomedes, who was still rather too dazed to speak. 'Well, I thought, here's a nice business! For really I do think, mixing up politics and pleasure—! Don't you? Besides, I'll take my oath this brat knows no more about it than an idiot baby!'

'How amusing!' said Metrotimé. 'Is that true, Nikomedes? Haven't you ever enjoyed yourself with a nice friend?'

'No,' said Nikomedes, in some obscure way rather ashamed.

'Yes, quite too unsuitable! What happened?'

'The next thing was I heard the little devil say, as cool as a monkey, just what he thought he was going to get out of it—money and ships and goodness knows what all! Next thing, he'd have been dead in another two ticks if I hadn't got between them. And next thing, we'll have to get him out, and you'll have to go and talk to my poor ducky little King, and I only hope it's not too late to put things right!'

'Hmm. I gather the thing turned right over—the other side of the God! But what a fool the boy must be to speak just then. Who sent you, boy?'

'I came myself,' said Nikomedes.

Just then the slave-woman came back with hot cloths, which she and Metrotimé between them laid on Nikomedes' neck over the red bruises. 'I think, dearest,' Metrotimé said to her friend, 'that you should go back. I expect, you know, there's nothing to worry about. You should get him to sleep; he'll be tired. I've got some stuff here; just the thing. Tell him it's from me. It induces—dreams. Yes, very pleasantly.' She opened a chest, took out a small box and shook out a couple of blackish pellets. 'I take them myself from time to time. I'll see to this brat. Now, run along, dearest.' Agathoklea went out with a last, not perhaps absolutely serious, scowl at Nikomedes, and the pellets. Metrotimé sat down with her book beside her and began to polish her nails, glancing at the story from time to time.

At last Nikomedes said very shyly: 'Please, what do I do now?'

'I should get up off the floor if I were you,' said Metrotimé. 'That's right. Now come here and let me take those cloths off your neck. There! Now the bruises won't show. How old are you, Nikomedes?'

'Going to be fifteen.'

'Goodness, how old! Old enough to keep secrets. Do you think you can manage not to tell anyone at all about this evening?'

Nikomedes thought hard. At last he said: 'Yes.'

'Good. Now, how do you feel? Quite all right?'

Again he thought hard. Surprisingly, his shattered self had picked itself up again. The dream was ended; he was awake. 'Yes,' he said, 'I'm ready to go.' It was only then that he realised he had failed. But it was not, somehow, a bitter failure; it was blurred. He thought his father might be glad, after all, that he had failed. Only his father must never know. He liked Metrotimé. He thought it would have been fun to have an elder sister.

She said: 'Don't try this again, not for a year or two! You were lucky, you know. By the way, did you hear about the Vintage?'

'Yes, every one has.'

'What did you think about it?'

'Nothing much. I heard about the girls who danced and went mad and let the fauns have them in the open fields. I wish I'd seen that!'

'The God Dionysos had taken possession of them. I was one.'

'You! But I thought they were just common girls. Why did you do it?'

'It was as if each one of those men dressed as fauns had

been the God himself. They had got something divine into them by being part of the feast. One wanted that from them for oneself. Do you understand at all?'

'But you knew they were ordinary men all the time. One can't get behind knowledge, behind the real thing.'

'Yes, one can, and must. I suppose Sphaeros is your tutor, Nikomedes? You're a little Stoic, aren't you?'

'I try to be. But I'm not wise yet.'

'No, it takes time! But you haven't told me what you thought about the Vintage except that some of it was funny and perhaps shocking.'

'I'll tell you what I do think. I just think it's much too hot for running about and enjoying oneself here! And anyhow the vines don't do so well as they do at home, and the grapes are half the size, unless you fuss about all the time, watering them. They simply aren't worth having a feast about!'

Metrotimé laughed and told him to drink a little wine and eat some of the flat crisp cakes she brought out of the other room. While he was doing this she fetched a plain coloured girl's dress and head handkerchief. 'I'm going to take you out of the palace,' she said, 'and you must be disguised. It will be quite safe if you are. Come now, you can put this on over your own tunic.'

'But need I be dressed up as a girl?' protested Nikomedes.

'Yes, indeed you must. We've got two sets of sentries to pass. Here, let me fasten it. Silly boy, that's not the way to put on a handkerchief! Why don't you grow your hair long? It's a shame to cut it off, soft and fine as it is.'

'Spartiates used to grow it long in old days, but it would be silly now. Men don't, and I won't. Can't I hold this stupid skirt up more?'

'Not too far! You make the most darling girl, Nikomedes. Wouldn't you like to stay with me and be my sister? Oh don't scowl at me; I always do say things in the vilest taste! We'll just draw the kerchief forward an inch, so. And the end round across your chin. Now, keep your head bent like a nice, modest girl. One moment till I find a scarf for myself. There! Come along, Nikomedes.'

They passed the guards with no trouble at all, for they all knew Metrotimé; she was friendly and generous to them; though, for that matter, it was the only sensible thing to be. There were not many people about, and they took the smaller streets, hurrying rather, like respectable women getting home. 'Where are you going?' whispered Nikomedes at last.

'To Erif Der. She's the only rational one among you. You can tell her if you must tell someone, though I still advise you not. Berris can see me home. You can stay there for the night and have a good sleep and forget about it all.'

They came to the house and knocked. It was Berris himself who came to the door, a mallet in his hand and stone-dust all over himself. He stared at them, not recognising Nikomedes. Metrotimé walked past him into the house and whispered to Nikomedes to run along to the work-room and take his things off, which he was only too glad to do. Then she told Berris what had happened. He listened, leaning his chin on her shoulder and every now and then kissing her ear or neck. 'I didn't know the boy had it in him,' he said finally, 'after all this grandmothering. Well, I'm glad that divine lunatic of yours wasn't allowed to murder him.'

'Agathoklea is so sensible,' murmured Metrotimé. 'No, Berris, I will *not* have your nasty stone-dust in my hair! Go away! Well—wash!'

When they got upstairs they found Erif making a bundle of the dress and kerchief, and Nikomedes staring with some alarm at Berris' half-finished relief of hawks carrying off and eating little men and women. It was very horrid, with a curious stiffness and fatality about it, the stiffness of that same dream in which one cannot escape. 'Brr!' said Metrotimé, 'what a nasty, fascinating thing! It's like something out of one of these dreadful Egyptian temples, only worse, because it's now, not a thousand years ago. Do you know, Berris, I believe Agathokles would adore it! What's your price?'

'Depends on how many days' work I put into it. I'm not sure I shall sell it at once, either. I'm glad you don't like it, Metrotimé.'

'Well, I must be going back,' she said. 'Are those the things? How sweet of you, Erif! Good-bye, Nikomedes – ' She kissed him. 'You'll see me in, Berris?'

Berris looked at her and grinned. 'All the way!' he said.

Chapter Five

THE NILE ROSE more and more rapidly and flooded the land, though in the delta country this made less difference than in the valley itself. But there was a feeling of security and comfort about, even in the still, baking weather they were having now. The date harvest was gathered and every one in Alexandria went about the streets sucking the hot sweet things and spitting the stones into the gutters. But Kratesikleia had a theory that they were bad for children and would not let Gorgo eat them and tried to stop the boys. Neareta took to them; she kept house better than any of the Spartiate women, and Phoebis was fairly cheerful.

Not long after this the last of the season's letters came over from Greece. The chief news they brought was that Antigonos of Macedonia was dead, quite suddenly of excitement and haemorrhage after a battle. It was queer. King Antigonos was dead, and it seemed to make no difference! They were up against worse forces than Antigonos now, things that were out of the power of Spartan courage. The only real hold Kleomenes had was over Ptolemy's Greek mercenaries, most of whom had a great admiration for the Spartan King and his friends, half romantic and half practical, and would sooner have been led by them than by Sosibios. But that was a difficult power to use without letting it appear too much as a threat.

A month and a half later, when the Nile was sinking again and all the flooded land left with the soft, new mud, delicious to tread in and rich with the thought of the young growth, came the Festival of Osiris, the Corn King of Egypt, who is slain every year and broken into pieces and sown like grain over the long narrow valley of fertility. Last year Kleomenes had not known what was to happen that day, and woke in the morning and listened quivering to the wailing, for it seemed as though it had come out of his own mind into objectivity. Then the children, who had enjoyed it all the year before, came in and told him what it was: only the natives wailing for their God who was dead—as people at home in Amyclae still wailed for Hyacinth. But soon it would all turn right and there would be processions and songs and barges with lamps—could they go this year?—and the little troughs of barley, the resurrection gardens that every one had planted, would shoot up green, and the natives would say that Osiris was alive again.

This year Kleomenes knew it was coming and waited for it with an extra tension of nerves. Now it was too late for any more news from Greece this year. Though it was still fine in Egypt, there would be storms between him and his Sparta. How blessedly cold it would be on those mountain tops! Kleomenes sent for Panteus and rode with him to hunt in the edges of the desert till the wailing was over. Why not hunt? There was nothing else to be done. The palace laughed at them still! But there was pleasure yet in the swift air, in the sight of the hounds' bodies, in the skill, the sudden decisions, the alertness of the senses in hunting that did not leave the mind time to fret and jangle. It was marvellous to stop a quick, just glimpsed, galloping thing, to topple it over in bright blood! To run and shoot up overhead with the sting of the bowstring brushing one's cheek, to see the flying thing change direction, suddenly crash down through bright hollows and cliffs of air. Something in the mere check of speed sent the blood jumping through the heart. And the power, to bury one's fingers in warm quivering fur and feathers, to change it all in an instant to some other stuff. One found a wounded beast very still and close, and looking at one with bright bead eyes, as if one were a God, but with no wretched cringing or appealing, only accepting what God gives, so that one had no slightest twinge as the thin knife struck cleverly into the heart. They were very happy, those two, hunting, and sleeping at night tired out and full of the juices of toasted meat, on cloaks and saddles by some tree-shaded pool where they had drunk and would drink again in the morning. For three days they kept everything else out of their minds and hearts, while in Alexandria and all the cities of Egypt, folk wailed for the dead Corn God.

In Alexandria Philylla sat in her house and listened. Her servant had gone early, in delicious ecstasies of sorrow to the Temple of Osiris, that very old one, which had survived from Rhakotis, the forgotten city before Alexandria. This temple was squat and small, and now it was packed to over-flowing with kneeling, groaning worshippers, begging the

God to come again. Philylla went to their room and carefully folded up Panteus' tunics, and picked up and paired the shoes and sandals which he had scattered all over the room in his joyful scramble for hunting-clothes and boots. She had helped him, with gay looks; truly she did not grudge him his joy! He was very untidy; as a young Spartiate in the first years of the King's time, he had given up almost all his possessions except his actual arms and armour and the clothes he slept on, but lately he had accumulated more possessions, new clothes for palace ceremonials mostly, and Philylla had stopped him from throwing away three-quarter worn-out things. They would do—for something. There was enough good stuff to cut up for tiny shirts. If the time came. If. If. She sighed helplessly and patted the things down into the chest. For three days she would not have to fend for him, market or mend or think of new ways to try and make him look happier. She would live on the peasant grain which she never let him eat—it did not taste so bad, though!—and eggs, and he would bring back game with him. Philylla—Panteus. Panteus—Philylla.

What was wrong? Who would know? It went round and round in her head in time with the wailing. It was not the state of marriage, because that, after all, was what she had wanted and got, and Agiatis had been happy, and Deinicha and Chrysa had been happy, and Leandris was happy. Leandris was going to have a baby next year. Was that it? But Panteus did not seem to want children; he said he was glad they had brought no one into this terrible world. She wished he would not say that, when there was still hope for Sparta—oh, surely, so much hope! What else was wrong? Oh it was not, not the King! How could it be? She had known about that always, had thought it lovely when Agiatis had told her that first day when he had sent her the arrows and violets and her darling magpie. She had been right to see it so! It was the pattern of Sparta, and if Agiatis knew it for beautiful, then it must be beautiful too, for her, the other wife!

That was only right and logical. She thought of Sphaeros. He would say it was all delusion, a mere thing the disorder of her female mind had made. With age, Sphaeros was growing more and more formal, more apt to meet a difficulty with a stock phrase; she had not spoken with him much since

Agiatis' death, except about the boys. She wondered if the boys were getting out of life at all what Agiatis had meant them to get, and meant her to see that they should get. It was very difficult for her to do anything effective with Sphaeros and Kratesikleia, both firm that they knew best about everything; but she did keep up her deep friendship with Nikomedes and talked to him hopefully. He needed hope in that house. She thought he was very beautiful and was sorry that there was no one to tell him so. A little praise would not have hurt him.

Through noon the wailing went on; she could not eat, she knew the Egyptians would be fasting. She began to be frightened, though she told herself it was nonsense. She tried to read, then to embroider. She went through the movements of one of the Artemis dances which she had learnt in Sparta a long time ago, but that was more alarming than anything, all by herself. She began to imagine that Panteus might come back suddenly for something he had forgotten—or because there was no game—or because he had thought all at once how grim it was for her alone in the wailing city—because her thoughts had reached him and told him how she longed only for his arms and for one of those moments when he seemed really to be thinking of nothing but her. Could thoughts travel? The Egyptians thought so. They thought the Double, the Kha, could be sent out with messages. Well, even if that were possible, she would not spoil the King's hunting!

She went the next day to see Leandris, who seemed very happy and busy and not much disturbed by the wailing. And the third day Erif Der came to see her. 'I've just heard you were alone,' she said. 'Those two have gone again!'

Philylla answered back to the tone of indignation with a laugh: 'Yes, we shall have our larder full! I shall try to salt down some of it, for it won't keep long in this weather.'

Erif stared at her and said: 'Yes, but the next time they're away, come and see us.'

After that they talked very comfortably of this and that; the noise of mourning did not seem to penetrate so much. Anyhow, on the third day it was less loud, though perhaps more intense and spasmodic, after the fasting and prayer and saying aloud of many alarming names, to revive the dead Corn God. Erif had brought with her a curious little drawing of dancers which Berris had made lately, on parchment, some winged and others with animals' heads. Philylla said: 'I wish he would make some more paintings of King Agis. Those were wonderful. I hope they will have got to young Kleomenes now; he has written fairly often, but never about that.'

'Berris might some day,' said Erif, 'but he doesn't feel like it now. He doesn't want to think of Sparta.'

'No,' said Philylla. And then: 'I hear he's at the palace a great deal with King Ptolemy—and the others. He must amuse himself.'

'He does in some ways.'

'Is it bad for his work?'

'Other things would be better. Philylla, are yóu happy?'

Firmly Philylla said: 'Yes.'

'We want you to be,' said Erif, 'as we brought you. Is it the same as you thought it would be?'

'Not quite. What is?'

'It will be for me when I see Tarrik again. Different outside, perhaps, but oh—deeply the same.'

'After all, Erif dear, you're a barbarian'—she put an arm round her friend's neck, to soften the words, though as a matter of fact Erif smiled and didn't mind—'and it's simpler for you. I've got to deal with something much more complicated.'

'More complicated than being the Corn God? Tarrik does the things that these people are crying for now. Perhaps Osiris was a king like Tarrik once.' She rubbed her head down along the circling arm: 'But you'll come to us if you want us ever? Promise, Philylla!'

After the Osiris festival all the crops were sown and the colder weather came, making everything brisker and more alive. Young Agesipolis, recovered from his wound, made love, more or less, to his cousin Nikomedes, and they went riding and hunting and to see the crocodiles. Agesipolis wondered very faintly and occasionally what his baby son was like now. He and his wife wrote to one another regularly twice a year, very short letters which neither of them liked getting. It appeared the child was well. Perhaps when he was older—seven or eight—Agesipolis would feel he must take an interest in him and get him trained. In the meantime he had a mother and two grandmothers to look after him. Gods forbid that Agesipolis should come near that little nest! He did not want a wife; he wanted his brother, little Kleomenes, the brother he had loved and left at Sellasia. Failing his brother, he wanted Nikomedes.

But Nikomedes was curiously awkward and uncomfortable about it, as though any love-making carried some different and disquieting thought with it, and after a time Agesipolis, who was a reasonable and gentle young man, stopped any advances, but stayed great friends with the boy, who was grateful and enjoyed the companionship. Agesipolis was an important person, for his brother was the leader of the Kleomenist party in Sparta, the one most likely to be successful in any blow at the ephors. It was perhaps this feeling of the importance of Agesipolis, as well as his own uncomfortable memories, which held Nikomedes back; he would not be even the faintest shadow of a bribe to anyone now! He explained this a little to his father, who was curiously sympathetic. They did things together that winter, but not the swimming in Eurotas, not the wild-cat hunting among the crags of Taygetus. Panteus taught him and the others some of the more formal exercises, like disc-throwing; he was a better sprinter than Gyridas, but had less staying power for a long distance. Sometimes Philylla and Leandris came to watch them at their games. There was a good gymnasium near the house, belonging to one of the Greek clubs in Alexandria, which was always glad to give its hospitality to any of the Spartans.

Just after the New Year came another Osiris festival, the setting up of the Zed pillar, which was, some said, the tree in which the God's body had been confined, while others said more simply, 'No, it was his backbone.' The corn was springing now; they set up the pillar to show the corn how to grow. This was made into a great palace feast, and the Zed pillar was wreathed with plants of a different God—yet perhaps the same under another name! The divine Ptolemy and the enflamed Agathokles said it was that. They raised the pillar—and there were other things besides a backbone or a coffin which an erect pillar might signify!—for Dionysos-Osiris, and a song, written and composed by one of the poets from the Library, was chanted round it, in which a quantity of episodes in the lives of both gods were paralleled with great ingenuity, and sometimes with a certain tortuousness. It was a very esoteric, but a very decent song. Metrotimé wrote a much funnier version of it, which was neither.

A few weeks later, Philylla came one afternoon to visit Erif Der. That day Erif had been down to the harbour, asking about ships which would be likely to be sailing north for Byzantium that spring. She had a feeling that she was nearly free; she felt as though with all these festivals, she had taken over something from the Year Gods, Isis and Osiris. If they could do this strange thing in Egypt, every summer make the river to rise like a snake rising, surely she could do the easier thing in Marob! She could not be certain of having found Mother and Daughter yet, nor Dead and Snake, and she had not been five years—but supposing Hyperides were right about the Oracle, and she need not follow it? She told Philylla all this eagerly, wanting her to confirm those hopes. But Philylla only said: 'Oh Erif, don't go yet! I want you.'

After a little silence Erif said: 'You haven't wanted me much this last year.'

'No,' said Philylla. 'I thought I could make my own life. I was hoping it would all happen right. Erif, it hasn't! What shall I do?'

'Where is he just now?'

'At a council. The King sent for the twelve of them. But there'll be nothing new and he'll come back to me unhappier and further than ever!'

'Is that the trouble always?'

'That he's so far? Yes. It should have been a flame—it was, yes, truly, at the beginning, that would hold us both in its heart. But it never is now. Though I try so hard!'

'Marriage is the oddest thing in the world,' said Erif, playing for time, trying to decide what to say. 'I nearly killed Tarrik when we were first married. I wonder what would have happened to me. But I thought it always came righter and righter as people got deeper into one another's kindness, and now I see it doesn't. I suppose you know that Berris loves you still?'

'Does he?' said Philylla nervously. 'He shouldn't. Does it make him unhappy?'

'Yes,' said Erif Der.

Unreasonably, Philylla choked and began to cry. 'I do wish he wouldn't!' she said. 'It makes him make these stiff, unkind things.' And she hit out, bruising her hand, but shocking herself into tearlessness again.

Erif agreed. 'I wish he wouldn't either,' she said. 'But there it is. I believe he would flame with you, Philylla.' And after Philylla went home, Erif was occupied with this, almost to the exclusion of Marob. She wondered if her brother could give Philylla a child. But she doubted it; she had a theory that north and south did not mix well in these matters, so she had not been at all anxious about the result of her Vintage night. Not that it would have signified much; it might have been an interest and a pleasure, and she trusted Tarrik very completely to understand her now. She had sent back on an autumn ship letters and a sealed chestful of stuffs for her cousin Linit.

Philylla went home across the Jewish quarter. Some of the young men were beautiful copies of Greeks, regular at gymnasium and baths, admired musicians. But they seemed to get fat rather early in middle life. She thought some of the veiled women were probably beautiful too, but she had never been inside a Jewish house. They worshipped a God with many names, she had heard. He must have taken on the names of other Gods as they came to an end; some Gods seemed to live on the deaths of other Gods. She had been told a few of the names one time when Kleomenes had a scheme for interesting the Alexandrian Jews in Sparta. Adonai: that was Adonis. Sabaoth: that was Sabazios. So their God was Dionysos too; and Serapis was Dionysos. After Agiatis died nobody had the heart to dance for Artemis again. All the Gods were equally distant from men, equally unmoved by prayer or offering. She would not even have sacrificed a puppy to Orthia now. Sphaeros taught the boys that there were Gods, but they spent their divine eternity in understanding the universe. They could understand the growth of a grass blade or the workings of the human heart. And, understanding, they were without pity; they would not alter the tiniest part of their universe against the way of nature, which, supremely, they understood. What was the use of Gods like that to children? No wonder poor little Gorgo said prayers to the lighthouse. Well, let her, let her for a few years if it was any help to her! The old Queen did not know.

Panteus came home a little after she did. He was kind and unhappy and did not answer her questions at all at first. Then after a time he said that he and Kleomenes and Idaios had been to see various Alexandrians, to point out how the glory of Alexander's town was decaying under—well, not Ptolemy perhaps, but Sosibios and Agathokles. If an army could be got together privately and practised in a Spartan war under Spartan officers, with victory assured, how splendid it would be for the city to have later! The mercenaries could just as well be paid by private persons as by the Court. But the Alexandrians were not interested in armies. They had ink instead of blood in their veins. Or worse. It was horrible, horrible, to go tagging round the town, waiting in these rich stinking houses for the gentleman's leisure to see them! Kleomenes of Sparta doing that. The kin of Herakles. He beat with his fist once on the table and then fell silent. He never sang to her nowadays; it was as though the bird, the shepherd in him, had been killed at Sellasia.

She told him that she had been to see Erif Der. He said he was glad, but she must be careful going through the streets. Then he said that Berris Der was going with the Alexandrians; he had taken to the Court like a fish to water and they to him; he would be a rich man now if he were not spending it all on women. Barbarians went that way when they came in sight of gold.

After that Philylla went fairly often to see Erif, and once or twice Berris was there. He said very little, but kept on working and used that as a covert to watch her from. Towards the end of March there was a ceremony of blessing the land. The divine Ptolemy himself appeared in the crown of Egypt, and most of his Court in semi-Egyptian clothes and postures, except for Sosibios, who had a new and even more elaborate set of armour. The land was very beautiful about then, full of flowers of all kinds, and the corn was high and already ripening. Ankhet and Erif went out into the fields and brought in baskets of flowers and put them in jars all about the house.

One day Philylla came, but before she and Erif had time even to greet one another, Berris dropped his tools with a clang and clatter that stilled them both, and walked over to Philylla and threw himself on his knees in front of her and caught her wrists as she tried to push him away, and held them down to her sides. As he held her so she began to tremble; she felt his head jerking against her; she felt his tears coming wet and hot on to her skin; it was as if his open eyeballs were pressing against her thighs. She stooped over him; she loosed a hand gently and laid it on his head, trying to calm him. 'Don't!' she said. 'Don't cry, Berris. Berris, my dear, don't cry, I can't bear it!' It tore at her; he was like her child, the child she had neither conceived nor borne. Both hands were now cupped over his head, and his hands grasped, felt at her, pressed heavily like heavy birds on to her flesh. She was sobbing too, a little. Erif moved nearer to them; they did not notice her; she did not know what to say. She saw Philylla bending over him more, going slacker at the joints, and then suddenly springing away, tearing herself out of his arms. He slipped and fell forward, one knuckle on the floor. Erif put an arm round her. 'I didn't know,' said Philylla. 'Oh I didn't know I was really hurting him still! Oh my poor Berris!' And she turned and snatched up her cloak and went.

Erif looked at her brother. He was still on the floor, muttering to himself; he was suddenly very like Murr in the boat. 'You shall have her, Berris,' she said, 'only be kind to her.' He did not answer and she went on speaking, over his head, defiantly, at a squarish hound's muzzle, still unpolished: 'I won't make things worse for her than they are!' And at the same time she made up her mind that she must not go back to Marob yet.

Philylla was frightened at first, badly frightened for weeks, and mostly of herself; she had been so near doing whatever he wanted. A whole sleeping part of her had awoke; now she was Philylla who had embroidered the sort of patterns she thought Berris would like. She began to see a different side of life, something outside the hard, narrow pattern of lessening hope in which all the Spartiates moved stiffly. It disturbed her; it made everything else worse. And she was sorry, oh so sorry for Berris! Almost as sorry as she was for Panteus and Kleomenes. For them and their sorrow she could apparently do nothing; but she knew she could put Berris right. Her rational, woman's mind was haunted and teased by that. But at least she did not seem to be considering any possible good for himself. There was no one she could talk to; Leandris was too young and Kratesikleia far too old. She knew they would both be horrified at the mere possibility, though for different reasons. And Panteus had never liked Berris; even after they had helped her to Egypt, when he had been really grateful and sincerely offered his sword and friendship, he had never tried to have any understanding of Berris. So in the end it was Erif Der she talked to.

The barley was reaped and then the wheat and a little later the peasants' grain. The land lay half dead, veiled in dust and heat, waiting for Isis to weep her tear again and the Nile to begin rising. News came from Hellas, mostly of war between other states, with Sparta waiting and watching and patching up her wounds, and young Kleomenes gradually and cautiously gathering himself an adequate following and asking again why there was no help from Egypt. The Achaean League was helping Messenia against Aetolia, and old Aratos had been defeated but had talked it away. Antigonos' successor, the new Macedonian King, seventeen-year-old Philip, was going gently so far; no one knew what he was going to be like. It would be well not to delay action until the time when he was older. It all came in to the Council of Kleomenes and his twelve best friends, and was tossed and threshed round the table. Possibilities came up: Antiochos of Syria? So-and-so or So-and-so in Alexandria? Possible friends in Kyrene? No good. But what more could they do?

Philylla herself had one letter from Deinicha, a little hurt with her for not writing oftener, and one from Ianthemis, who had married her man that winter, a pleased and jerky letter with formal phrases and a good deal of small news. Her father was better and could ride, but was keeping out of politics. Dontas was as cross as ever and had taken to playing the flute; mother was well. She thought her own looks had improved since marriage; her complexion was better: didn't that sometimes happen? And how was Philylla and why didn't she write and had she got a son?

Philylla did not answer it yet, but one morning she went to Erif and did find Berris. He took her in his arms, and again pity overwhelmed her and she said she would do and be anything if only he would be happy again. She was almost as tall as he was; she did not flinch from his nakedness nor turn her eyes away. Through the narrow window sunlight barred her body with a white sword. When it was over she lay with his head between her breasts like a child; she could see her breasts quiver and stiffen at his touch; he touched the substance of her as an expert touches wood or stone, getting at the essential grain. Yet she could not quite become one with her own substance. Her mind hovered over her body as she had seen the Kha hover in pictures. Was she sure it was her own? He brought her water that had stayed cool in a porous jug, and fruit; he murmured in delight over her. Yes, she said, she would come back if he wanted her still for his happiness: why not? He asked her if she had been happy, if he had given her the pleasure he had taken. But yes, surely he had known how her body had answered to his! But happy, happy, happy? Philylla, are you happy? Are you all eaten up by a flaming softness as I am? Has the world suddenly grown bright, bright to you? Have you got peace at last? Philylla, my own, only love, tell me. Ah, Berris, don't ask these things. Be content with what I give you. Be content, my dear.

And when she came back again she would not speak of herself. Only, she drank in his happiness; she made him speak of it to her over and over again. He could not in any way find out just what he had done to her; always she evaded him, yet she would not ever let him think that he had done her harm. He was her child; how could he, how should he know just what was happening to her?

Not strong nor wise I, to support you
    And you'll not have me so.
I cannot tell if I have hurt you,
    Though at last I shall know.

I cannot hold my gladness steady,
    Giddy and mazed I find
Sweet the air and sweet my body
    And sweet my mind.

Oh this bright air! And this still kinder
    You, who would stop surmise
Of any pains drowned in the candour
    Of your wide eyes.

She wanted to tell Panteus; she wanted that more than

anything. But she could not do it because it would hurt him. She must not hurt her man. It could all be utterly secret. She trusted Berris over that; if he could keep the idea of a statue or a picture in his head, secretly for months until it ripened, he could and would keep this secret. And she trusted Erif. Now that the barrier between them was down the friendship between the two women quickened and firmed; one looking across to the other would make her friend smile and rouse a happiness in her heart that did not go completely into words. The touch of the one was very pleasant to the other; in the heat of the day they would undo each other's hot piles of hair and comb it coolly through; they needed to see one another every day. Philylla found now that she could remember Agiatis with less pain.

Berris understood that Philylla wanted to tell Panteus. He became full of the same kind of imaginative goodwill towards the Spartans as his sister had towards her cousin Linit. He worked hard and well. Suddenly he thought he would do some more pictures for Philylla, and he did them with a simplicity and clarity of colour and form that were far from Egyptian. They were lucid story pictures, and as he painted them, often with her beside him, it gave him a feeling of childish and delicious calm. He did not have to think, because there was no problem; he had solved it long ago. He was not even interested in the form; it was almost sleep-working.

He painted what she told him to paint, first more scenes from the life of Agis, or the old ones done again, among them the death-scene, the hanged King; and after that scenes from the life of Kleomenes. He did these tentatively at first, choosing those which had happened before he knew Sparta. First the marriage of Kleomenes and Agiatis, the very young bridegroom and the pale, unbridal bride. Then the King bidding farewell to Xenares, his first love, since already it had taken shape in his mind that the man who was not with him was against him. There were legends with all the pictures, often just one thing said by Kleomenes himself, words fitted into a pattern round his head. Then the killing of the ephors: the King's Times, which were to bring such strength and beauty, beginning not gradually or in peace, but suddenly and with a sword. Then the rich men casting away their goods and gold to follow the King, even the women plucking the jewels from their hair and breasts. For Philylla's sake he put in Agiatis here, and Philylla herself peering from behind her. He made another after that, but an imaged one, in which Kleomenes, frowning and with mouth set, and a whip of knotted cords, drove out Luxury, Usury and Greed, in the shape of snarling and fat old traders, from the Temple of Sparta. At each side Apollo and Artemis smiled stiffly at him. Then Kleomenes' good-bye to his mother before she went to Egypt.

By this time he had worked himself up into such an excitement that he did not need Philylla to talk to him. He wanted more subjects. He went himself to Panteus and asked him about Sellasia and afterwards. Philylla came home suddenly from her marketing and found them together. But she heard what they were talking about and then she was very glad. Panteus at first was embarrassed and did not want to tell anything, but Berris, with his new imagination spread wide to the Spartans and Panteus most of all, brought him at last to the point where he began abruptly to tell the thing which was still completely clear in his head, but which had never yet been put into words, not even to his wife. Kleomenes at the pillar, his utter silence and patience in the wrestling with bodily pain and still more painful decisions, and at his feet the beautiful woman with loose hair and weeping eyes. Berris went home and painted that on a great canvas, and all about in the background, among little houses and rocks and olive trees, he made the friends and followers of the King hurrying about their business or else snatching a little sleep. That was the best of the pictures so far.

Letters came from Marob again, and a drawing of Klint which startled Erif very much. She thought she had a baby at home, but the picture said she had a little boy. She rushed out—bought all sorts of the kind of toys which she saw little boys playing with and sent them back to him by a north-bound ship. Tarrik wrote very cheerfully and so did Hyperides who was still there. He said he thought he must go home the next year, and if so he would try and get Tarrik to leave Marob for a time and come with him. Every one there was now so well in awe of the Corn King that nothing would happen. That was exciting! Perhaps she could go to

Greece next year and meet Tarrik there and they would go back together to Marob.

In summer again came the Falling of the Tear, and nearly at the same time another festival, though one the native Egyptians themselves did not care for much, the feast of Adonis, yet another Year King to be killed and mourned for and to rise again. It was impossible not to see the likeness between these Gods, and many people agreed that they were only forms of one another. This year the Adonis festival was held in great state at the palace, for the divine Ptolemy's play was produced with intense enthusiasm and real wild boars. Two gods were honoured, for was not Dionysos Lord of the Theatre? Yet perhaps they both were one.

Metrotimé was surprised with Berris. He had stopped wanting her for anything, and his work had become dreadfully solid and unamusing again. She was hurt at first, but did not allow it to show, and consoled herself. After all, men were like that, Greeks or barbarians. Besides, she might easily have been the one to tire first! Though it had certainly been sudden. She still felt very friendly towards him.

That autumn Sosibios had arranged for a series of elephant hunts to take place in the far south. The beasts were needed for the army, and it would be just as well if Antiochos of Syria should get to know; he needed—discouraging. His spies were carefully allowed to find out about the magnitude of the elephant drives. And Berris Der, who was known to be fantastically interested in anything new, was asked whether he would care to go south and see the hunting.

The idea, of course, fascinated him. Real, untamed elephants among marvellously coloured flowers and butterflies and water-falls! He dreamt of them. But his love? He was torn between Philylla and the elephants. At last he asked her to decide for him. She looked down for a moment, steadying herself. One part of her was leaping with a queer relief that the moment had come; she could be done with this half-life and be fully truthful and herself again to Panteus; she would turn again and for certain make something good out of her marriage! But the other part was stunned and torn with the thought that Berris, her lover, was leaving her so easily and soon and seemed to care so little; and she shuddered away from the narrowness, the life without joy or colour that the Spartans led, against the whole spirit of Alexandria and the live, creating happiness of Berris! She looked up and smiled a little and said: 'Go, my dear! If I were a man I'd not hesitate once. Wild elephants!'

'But won't you miss me?' said Berris, suddenly not wanting it to be so easy.

She laughed as gaily as she could and said: 'I shall have Erif still.'

'I don't know whether to go!' said Berris. 'I know I want to see everything, but I do know that when I'm there I shall miss you far, far more than even I think I'm going to now! Oh Philylla, if I go, promise to be the same when I come back! You mustn't change. Dear love, whatever's different or unkind, in the whole world, ever, it mustn't be you!'

He went the next week on his expedition, and Philylla set about trying not to think of him. In the evenings, while Panteus and the King worked and worried over their plans, and wrote out lists of names, and talked themselves sick with their impotence against Sosibios and the Court, she would sew or weave, and deliberately not wonder whether Berris was at this moment in danger among horrible wild beasts. But when she and Erif were together, it seemed likely that things were all right. She could be certain for quite long spaces of time that Erif's love was, after all, the whole thing beyond her marriage which she needed for happiness. So long as Erif stayed with her and did not go. As Agiatis had gone.

Chapter Six

THE PALACE WAS a small elaborate city. Jutting into the great city. The wings were separated by gardens and steps and marble tanks and runnels; there were overhead galleries and underground passages, and stone lions and cats and great beetles. Now there was a light, clear wintry sky over it all and clouds blowing and a scattering noise of waves.

In one wing of the palace, the divine Lady Arsinoë would not play ball nor embroider with her companions, but knelt up against the window, looking out to sea and the white-caps dancing in. She wanted to be a man. She wanted to be in a boat. She wanted to be in a battle. She wanted now at once to gallop on a white horse at the head of a galloping army and cut off the heads of the Syrian generals. She had managed to hear how Antiochos of Syria had invaded Northern Palestine and plundered some of the Ptolemaic towns. She stood up and stamped. If only they'd let her go out! She could be a princess like the old princesses of Macedon. She would change everything. Yes, she'd hang Agathokles over the palace wall and shoot him full of arrows and cut off Agathoklea's nose! If only she ever got a chance. Perhaps it would be better after she was married to her horrid brother. They couldn't stop her then. Or could they?

She walked up and down the room, frowning, twisting her long yellow hair. Even the head nurse knew it was best to leave her when she was like that. Suddenly she made up her mind to do one definite thing; she would send to her brother and ask him to let her have a tutor. She was old enough surely! And she'd see it wasn't Agathokles!

This was the time of day for visitors. Sosibios received them and sorted out such as were to go further and actually see his royal and divine master. He had very definite views, and took care that Ptolemy should be sufficiently bored with the business of governing to allow his chief minister to do most of it. So now, for instance, a deputation of date-growers; it did not much matter what was said to them anyhow. A fantastic letter had come from the Roman envoy with the improbable name, saying that their Council of Elders would take Egypt under its protection—incredible what these barbarians thought of! Sosibios was composing in his head an equally fantastic letter back—perhaps even in rhyme?—which would leave them scratching their thick heads and mean absolutely nothing. Thinking of the letter he grinned; seeing one of the priests from the Serapeum, whom he disliked, the grin suddenly widened and turned itself down in disgust—and the divine Ptolemy too busy to see anyone. The priest bowed and left, without so much as a silver piece to the doorkeeper. Sosibios did not know why he disliked him and his slippers and his shaved head so much, but he did: it was his right to dislike people. It would, he thought, be pleasant to hire somebody to put a curse on to this priest. Yes, by and bye, when he had time; a pleasant evening's occupation.

Another letter came with fresh and worse news from Palestine, yes, decidedly, not so pleasant, but then, it was almost winter and nothing more could be done until spring. It would be better if his Divinity did not hear of it yet, not at least until the new elephants were back. And even more essentially not Agathokles and Agathoklea. Interesting news was not for women and —s. A deputation from the Jews of Alexandria, sent for by his Divine Majesty to discuss religious affairs? Certainly, certainly. That was the right kind of nonsense for the King. He'd had the Jews up before, several times, to talk all this God-and-water. Words, words, words—puff!

The three Jews bowed sweepingly before Ptolemy; two were oldish, bearded men in robes, carrying great rolls, and one was younger, clean-shaven and elegant with a short tunic. The two elders eyed one another and the room, but the younger looked gaily and defiantly at the King. Ptolemy approached the matter, Agathokles assisting. It was certainly a very brilliant idea, worthy of the successor and spiritual descendant of Alexander, an idea for the peace of the world, nothing less. All Gods are found to be the same God! Nothing was needed for this discovery but a cultured mind, ready to admit historical and philosophical truth, a careful study, and—yes, Agathokles, a touch of that same flame which I know in my own heart! All Gods the same God. The Egyptians have allowed that. Their Gods mingle like clouds. Yet there is one form of the God which is more potent and powerful than the others. I name him: Dionysos the Conqueror! King Ptolemy threw his head back, a hand on the base of his throat to still the leap of the blood. Agathokles made a curious sign with his fingers, and his face twitched. The three Jews were silent, waiting for the next step.

'The unity of the world under Dionysos Sabazios and me his chosen!' whispered King Ptolemy, staring at the younger man, who stared back with contracted pupils and a hardening mouth. He had been here before. 'You must give me your God too,' said the King, 'for he is the same. Acknowledge him as Dionysos, the ever young, the ever renewed. Even his name shows it. What is Sabaoth but

Sabazios? You, my Jews, who have always been loyal citizens, more industrious than Greeks, more cultured than Egyptians, you who have had privileges in Alexandria. Yes, privileges—which can be increased—or taken away.' He ended slowly, leaning forward in his ivory chair. There was a sense of power all about him, of orders written very quickly and sealed by grinning Agathokles.

But the two old Jews would not heed it. One of them pulled open his roll and began to read aloud, boomingly, in words which seemed as though they must mean something terrible. The younger Jew spoke with a peculiar, gentle restraint, as though he too were conscious of power, but his own: 'What is laid upon the followers of Dionysos, King Ptolemy?'

'I will show you, Simon,' said the King, at the same time loosening his belt clasp, while Agathokles, stooping over, unpinned the tunic. The King laid bare on his body the brand of the Ivy Leaf, pricked in and coloured. He looked down at it for a time, but Agathokles, watching, saw the shiver of horror on all three of the Jews. 'It was pain,' said the King softly. 'Yes, Simon, a burning pain, but now I am Ptolemy-Dionysos, and the pain has become a fire within me. He has been marked too'—the King nodded back to Agathokles—'and all those I love. Come, Simon, come and be marked with the Ivy Leaf and let me love you.' He laid a hand on Simon's arm, closing and clasping. 'You are marked already, Simon,' he said, 'for your own God. I know. Be marked for mine.' He pulled the hand forward till it rested on his own flesh, on the Ivy Leaf.

The two old men whispered to one another, glaring. Abruptly Ptolemy let the hand go and Simon fell back a pace, expressionless. After a time he moved his hand behind his back and rubbed the palm against his tunic.

'You are hard, Simon, hard as stone!' said the King, 'why do you go hard against Dionysos? He can be hard too. Dionysos-Ptolemy can be hard.' He fastened his tunic again, and his face changed alarmingly.

The young man said, speaking rather into the air: 'We are part of the greatness of Alexandria, the tall ships and the warehouses. You would not hurt your greatness, King Ptolemy.'

'Not yet,' said Ptolemy. 'Perhaps. Or perhaps Dionysos

will lay it on me to hurt—even my own greatness as my own flesh!'

From behind, Agathokles mouthed at the deputation to go. They bowed again with the suitable formulae of leave-taking. The curtains parted and then swung to behind them. Suddenly the King snatched up a full gold cup from beside him and flung it after them. It tumbled and rolled, dinted; the wine dripped down the curtains. King Ptolemy yelped once with anger and began to cry like a raging child. Agathokles comforted him. 'You shall have them all in a net one day, my master, my beautiful. Sabaoth will die in Sabazios. Their temples shall be our temples. Before that—we shall frighten them.' The names and powers of Dionysos twirled and shone in Agathokles, and through them tinkled a waterfall of gold, which was also power, out of the hands of the Jews who had been made afraid. A double music in his mind while King Ptolemy's rage burst and passed like a mid-summer storm.

After that there was something pleasanter to see. The design of the great Dionysos ship, which was to be ready in spring, to float the King and his Court, worshipping, along canals or coast, a marvel of lamps and flute song. Deep-nested in it was the shrine, the gold and jewelled bower of grapes where the fire of the God should light on his worshippers. Yet the designs for this were dullish; the King fretted and tossed them to one side. Agathokles had the good idea of getting the young Scythian, when he came back from the elephant-hunt, to design something newer—elephants among the grapes perhaps!

'Agathokles,' said the King abruptly, 'go down and see who there is waiting for me. Sosibios will send me stupid and ugly people. I can't bear that after the Jews! No, it would be too much. Send me someone young and new.' It suddenly came to him, if only Nikomedes would come again. Ah, he must come. He must come to his Ptolemy. Ptolemy would not be angry and cruel, would not try to hurt him. He would be kind; oh, oh, so kind and soft! How to get Nikomedes back? He called after Agathokles: 'If the Spartans are there, I will see them—whatever our dear Sosibios advises!' He leant across to the table beside him and began playing with an ingenious toy that was standing there, a thing that you twirled and little carved painted horses shot out and raced—absorbing!

After a time Agathokles came back, and, just as it was meant to be, King Kleomenes of Sparta and two of his friends with him. Ptolemy rose quickly, smiling, anticipating the moment when Kleomenes took his hand, the strong, slow grip on him. They began to talk, Kleomenes extremely glad that for once he had got beyond Sosibios and remembering the adder-flash in the fat man's eyes as Agathokles announced the King's pleasure. King Ptolemy asked most graciously about their comfort—the whole family, his mother and children. Would he not bring the boy to Court again one day? The eldest, Nikomedes, such a fine lad, a true Spartiate. His father must be proud of him. Why, yes, he should come again one day, said Kleomenes carelessly—oh, as if it did not matter at all!—and laughed. 'But the lad's no courtier.'

Then he began on what he meant to say, the thing which surely must move even Ptolemy! This fresh piece of bad news from Syria. Most fortunately Panteus had got wind of it that same morning and told him at once. He urged the King to act, to lead his armies against Antiochos and the invaders before they came any further. And he, Kleomenes, he would put his life and his skill—yes, and the life and skill of all the Spartans in Alexandria—at Ptolemy's service. They could drill the Egyptians. Yes, Kleomenes seriously thought that with Greek officers whom he trusted, Ptolemy could dare to enlist the natives, a thing which had not been done for three generations. Agesipolis joined in. Surely it was an offer worth taking! Surely King Ptolemy remembered still that Kleomenes of Sparta had been the terror and wonder of Greece, the one general whom the mercenaries wished to serve—yes, they had stayed with him even to the end when he could pay them nothing! Was not this worth something to Egypt? Even among the mercenaries they already had in pay, there were many Peloponnesians who would be worth twice their wages led by their own Kleomenes. He knew most of the captains already; they were fast friends of his. Yes, he could do almost anything with the mercenaries!

But Kleomenes, afraid of what effect even this slight shadow of a threat might have on Ptolemy, frowned at his nephew to stop. 'Let me help you against the Syrians, King Ptolemy!' he said. 'For no bargain, only for the hope of a little trust afterwards. I cannot stay here rotting like an old dog in the sun!'

Ptolemy was interested; he was so much interested in the bad news itself that he paid less attention to what followed it. Why had he not been told? But neither he nor Agathokles betrayed themselves. He said he would think it over carefully. He realised to the full what the offer meant. King Kleomenes must come again—and bring his son. He picked up the elaborate and lovely toy, and gave it to Kleomenes 'for Nikomedes from his friend Ptolemy.' Kleomenes took it gingerly, for it looked as though it would break. He wondered whether to try to get a definite promise at once. There was a little more talk. But Ptolemy was elusive and troubled. Yes, he seemed to be thinking about it seriously this time!

After the Spartans had left, Ptolemy and Agathokles looked at one another. One of the secretaries ran like the wind with a polite message to Sosibios, who came, wondering whether Ptolemy had thought of some wild-cat scheme about the Jews; if so, it should be put into practice—reasonably. With all this fighting in Palestine he was not going to estrange the Jews! But Ptolemy, sitting back in his chair with his legs crossed, produced the news: 'Now, what about it?'

'Oh yes,' said Sosibios, 'that news. Quite. Yes, we are taking measures. No use doing anything in too much of a hurry. We shall have the new elephants up from the south in a month or so. Nothing to worry about, I assure you. I have my eye on it.'

'Why was I not told?' said Ptolemy. 'Am I the King of Egypt, or not?'

Sosibios grinned once, in and out, as though to explain to the world that King Ptolemy must have his joke, then said: 'Naturally I was merely waiting to tell you until the end of your Divine Majesty's audience. I particularly did not wish to interfere with the flow of inspiration, yes, I insist, inspiration, while our friends the Jews were here. Naturally, I know my place.'

'Hmm,' said the King, dancing his foot a little. 'So you say, Sosibios. Now there's only one thing that seems quite simple and obvious, and easy enough for even me to understand, and that is, we should use the Spartans. They must teach, drill, get on with the job! We need an army, not just a palace guard.'

'Ah yes,' said Sosibios, 'that's one of King Kleomenes' phrases, of course. Very neat, yes, very neat and laconic. How clever of him to get the news so soon. One would think he must be looking out for bad news about Egypt.' He looked benevolently down on to Ptolemy, like teacher and child.

Ptolemy blushed and said violently: 'I will have Kleomenes if I choose!'

'Naturally,' said Sosibios, 'if and when you choose. But there are ways and ways of possession. In the meantime, Palestine is perfectly safe and nothing can be done until, first, the elephants arrive, and secondly, we get out a plan of recruiting. We shall have to consider the Treasury. Armies, unfortunately, cost money, which has to be saved from other objects.' He looked round the room and caught sight of a crumpled design of grapes for the new shrine. 'Your Majesty has certain rather expensive projects in hand at the moment. It would be more than sad if they had to be ended at once. The great ship, for instance. No, I am afraid you will have to put up with my advice and allow a month or two for revising the taxes, and so on.' He ended deferentially with his head bowed, but the bald patch seemed to twinkle with triumph. Ptolemy sulked and picked up a poem and pretended to read it. While he did this, Sosibios made up his mind quite definitely that, Peloponnesian mercenaries or not (for he was well aware of the position the Spartan King held among them), it was time Kleomenes of Sparta was got out of the way, before he either interfered dangerously with the King and his chief minister, or else became exasperated to the point at which he might—what? Perhaps go tale-bearing to Antiochos. Or lead a revolt of the mercenaries. Run amok somehow, as the elephants sometimes did: and had to be killed.

Kleomenes duly gave the toy to Nikomedes, who said he supposed it was really for Nikolaos and Gorgo, and gave it to them, to their great satisfaction. Secretly, Kleomenes was glad. Agesipolis had come to him that evening and strongly advised him not to take Nikomedes to the palace. 'Why?' asked Kleomenes. 'I think, my uncle,' said Agesipolis slowly, 'that it is a bad place for a boy to see or hear in, and if anything bad happened to this boy I think I would die.' 'Ah,' said Kleomenes, and looked at him with raised eyebrows and queer wide-open eyes, the flecked brown irises and contracted pupils, but did not seem to see him at all.

For several days after this Kleomenes and Panteus and the rest of the twelve waited eagerly for a summons from Ptolemy. It was the same wretched old game, played on them this much more cruelly. They dropped into bitter gloom and depression and did not go near the palace often. But all the same, a curious feeling of danger, made up of tiny incidents, began to grow on some of them, though not yet on Kleomenes himself. Philylla got this through Panteus, who was even more worried than usual and felt he was being spied upon, and she told Erif Der, hoping Erif would say it was all nonsense. But Erif had heard from Metrotimé that Sosibios was black angry against the Spartans, and no one now spoke of them in his hearing, and the King, though rather differently, had almost snapped off her head when she had happened to mention one of them.

Erif had been to see one of her friends of Vintage Night. He had been non-committal, and she was rather angry with him, but did not show it much, in case she might need him again later. She comforted Philylla as best she could, unable to suggest why danger had suddenly taken a step nearer. She supposed somebody had offended somehow; probably it would blow over. There was nothing for the Spartans to do until spring except keep quiet.

A month or so later Berris came back from the elephant-hunt, brown and lean, with a dimpled scar on one arm where some cat-beast had clawed him. The first evening he and Erif lay on their elbows on the floor, looking at all his drawings and laughing, while he told her one adventure after another. But the next day he wanted Philylla.

He wanted her, not so much to lie with her as to make certain of her continuous and constant kindness and faith. He wanted to tell her about himself and the things he had thought about his work, and he wanted very much to look at her so as to know whether he had her as completely as he believed in his mind, for he had an idea for a great carving and she was part of it. He went to Panteus' house and told him about the hunting, which interested Panteus very much. Philylla came in and listened too, only looking at Berris when she was fairly sure he was not looking at her. After a little time she found herself becoming desperately impatient; he went on telling Panteus—and her too, of course; and something important was being left out, some unasked and unanswered question. She did not know what it was. Only, as she sat there quietly, keeping her fingers to their sewing, this impatience began to bubble and burst in her like a boiling pot; abruptly, she got up and left them, with some kitchen excuse.

She waited four days, trying violently to suppress whatever she did not choose to have in her. Berris had begged his sister to wait too, and not go to her, and Erif did as he asked, though half-heartedly. Then Philylla came to see them, and to ask Berris whether he still thought of her—to ask that and go. Yet it was so lovely to be there, to have the other world again, the warm gold colour over the hard shapes of life, so perfect to have Berris added to Erif, that she stayed. That afternoon and evening after she was gone, and until the light was too bad, Berris was making his scale drawing of the statue of Love and Philylla, a thing from behind and above holding Philylla with hands across the shoulders, across the mounds of her breasts, which her own hands reached up to touch, a thing Philylla was accepting without expression except for the loving-kindness of her body.

He had bought a block of limestone from Carthage, beautiful close-grained stuff which would take a polish almost like alabaster. There were weeks of work to be done on it, but all the time he could be thinking out the final shapes. He could not decide yet what form to give to Love; he only saw him as curved and intersecting planes of the limestone, polished to a smoothness, an apparent tenderness, in some way cousin to flesh, but not remote from stone. He would not make a man's head on Love, for what man could stand as model for Eros? Not himself, and surely not Panteus. Not even Erif, hardened and thinned to a boy. He drew many strange heads, influenced by the sculpture he had seen lately, especially some of the ancient temples he had passed coming back up the

Nile from his hunt. He tried the tremendous heads of jungle beasts, and cat and bull-heads. The head which satisfied him best was a mixed one, a bird to start with, the curious, unhuman calm of a hawk watching and knowing its moment, the hawk of the soul, perhaps—what was it the priests said?—and then, branching down and away from it, the northern elk's horns, knotted and stiff and enduring, and in a strange way like a double branch of some northern tree in the cold months before the buds break on it.

For weeks Berris was absorbed in this, and in the presence and kindness of Philylla. He had brought a beautiful tusk back with him and liked to handle the ivory, but had not yet decided what to do with it. One day Agathokles came to ask him for a design for the Dionysos shrine in the ship, and after at first refusing to be bothered, he did three days' hard work on it. Erif tried very cautiously to find out from Agathokles how the wind lay now in regard to the Spartans, but got little out of the wriggling mask of his face as he looked from her to the new, linen-wrapped statue, and the stone dust all about the place.

The sense of danger grew and grew, but no one knew whether it was at all real or whether it was perhaps something in their minds which had not been removed, and so was going on growing there by itself. Erif had this to keep her awake at night, and also the puzzle of the relationship between her brother and her best friend, which must, she supposed, end somehow. If only she could make it end well!—or, for that matter, see any way in which it could possibly end well. She could not even tell for certain whether Philylla was more or less happy because of it. She was not happy herself.

In Marob now it was after the feast of the winter solstice and before Plowing Eve. The snow would be thick, caked crisply solid in the sledge-ways, wonderful echo-land for sledge-bells or bells on saplings or shouting, ringing voices of hunters and dancers. Berris had bought an Egyptian flute because it was beautifully carved. He played the beginnings of dance tunes, and the tunes they played in Marob at the end of a feast when the apples were thrown about the tables.

Apples in winter,
Apples and honey;
A noise like honey.
A flute noise, a drum noise,
Feet on the snow,
Fire on the snow,
Fire and dancing.

The Marob women dance
In coats of fur and gold.
They stamp their leather shoes
And the snow is not cold.
And I wish I was with them dancing
And the thing were over, were over, were over,
A story told.

The Marob witches dance
With ribbons in their hair,
Their plaits and skirts go wide,
Their white knees are bare.
And I wish I was with the witches
And this thing were over, were over, were over,
Oh I wish I was there!

Chapter Seven

ABOUT THE TIME of the royal blessing of the crops, ships began to come into Alexandria again, and Kleomenes and his friends began to hang about the quays, waiting for them. A big-bottomed merchant ship moved round the corner of the island, shipped oars, made fast and let down her gang-plank. In the hold were a dozen beautiful horses. Phoebis beckoned Kleomenes over to look, thinking it would please him to see the fine creatures stepping on to the quay and snuffing about them, then suddenly realising the air and space and whinnying and rearing and stretching themselves horse-fashion. One could tell they were Messenian horses, the small, flat-backed, wiry creatures they bred in those plains. The King and his friends stood watching them, going over their points, frankly envious. The owner of the horses came up and began giving orders to the grooms. Kleomenes did not pay much attention for a moment, then recognised him as Nikagoras the Messenian, to whom he still owed the price of a good farm and live-stock.

They met, however, with great affability, and no trace of this. The King commended the horses. Nikagoras pointed out the best six. 'They're for King Ptolemy,' he said. 'Then the rest are bound to go well! And I've other cargo I mean to get a good price for.' He slapped the flank of one of the horses. 'You don't happen to want one for yourself, King Kleomenes? I'd make you a special price for old sakes. Now here's a chap who'd gallop ten miles without turning a hair, and a heart like a lion—like a Spartan, what!'

Kleomenes laid one arm longingly along the tough, silky back, fingering the warm base of the mane, breathing in the smell of horse; but he shook his head. 'In a year or two, Nikagoras—perhaps. But not now.'

'Well, he'd be a bargain—to you. But I've no doubt I'll find a good market in Alexandria.' He looked at them proudly. 'Not a bad present, even for King Ptolemy!'

Kleomenes thought of the lovely, strong little Greek horses going to Ptolemy, and said with a quick bitterness: 'You'd have done better with a bunch of tarts: both kinds. That's the kind of riding King Ptolemy likes best!'

Nikagoras raised his eyebrows. 'So! I've not been here since the old man's time. He'd have liked my horses. Well, I must chance it now. Whoa there! See you again, King Kleomenes.'

Hippitas had overheard and was troubled. 'That was a stupid thing to say about Ptolemy,' he said low to Phoebis.

Phoebis nodded. 'It's hard to keep one's tongue off him.'

'Or one's hands. But we've got to. How's the boy, Phoebis?'

'Having a regular go of fever, poor kid,' said Phoebis. 'He'll just need to go through with it. We're not anxious now, but they say he'll be a two-three weeks longer at it. Then I'll get him out of the town if I can. Neareta's made friends with a woman who's got a farm by the river over Canopus way. She'll take him and feed him up. I wish the old Queen'd let those boys go too. This town's no good to man or beast.' He looked all round him, taking in warehouses and palace and lighthouse with equal and extreme distaste. 'Nowhere to stretch oneself!' he said.

Five days later Nikagoras called on the King at his house and went fairly straight to the point about the money which was owing. He took out the farm deeds and laid them flat on the table, and there, with a certain horror, Kleomenes saw his own name where he had written it. He remembered the occasion very well. He tapped with his fingers on the parchment: 'Who's on the farm now?'

'Why, your pretty lady, Kleomenes, or rather her husband. An oldish man,' said Nikagoras, with a trace of a grin and keeping firm hold of his deed. 'But they've got a fine boy.' He added: 'I shall be glad of the money because business hasn't turned out so well as I'd hoped. No. It would come in handy. Not much for a farm like that.'

'Maybe,' said the King, 'but I've not got the money to pay you, Nikagoras, and that's that.'

He and Nikagoras faced one another across the table and the deeds. 'It's a pity,' said Nikagoras slowly. 'It is sometimes—very awkward when debts are not paid.'

'You know as well as I do, Nikagoras,' the King said, 'that I haven't got the money now. If you choose to wait for a year, I may have it.'

'Or you may not.'

'As you say. In the meantime, there's nothing doing. I'm sorry, but I can't pay you.'

Nikagoras rolled up the parchment deliberately, the signature showing to the last. 'Kings' names—!' he said 'They're going cheap these days.' And he turned quickly and went out.

Kleomenes went out too, by the other door. He did not want to remember any part of this interview, either his debts unpaid or Archiroë married.

Nikagoras went straight through Alexandria to the palace without speaking to anyone. He asked for Sosibios and was admitted. He said nothing till Sosibios had sent away every one else; he supposed, and rightly, that there was a confidential secretary hidden behind a curtain taking notes, but he did not care about that. He told Sosibios the exact words which Kleomenes had used about King Ptolemy on the quay.

'Excellent, as far as it goes,' said Sosibios, 'but I must have a little something more. Let us consider.' He stared fixedly at a ring on his forefinger, then looked up, pinkish with pleasure. 'Supposing, now, that you were to find out

that Kleomenes had a neat little Spartan plan cut and dried
to get hold of the Peloponnesian mercenaries, and—yes,
he will find transport ships essential—supposing, my
Nikagoras, he had approached you about your ship, but
of course you would have nothing to do with it and loyally
informed me—and all this (here's what needs making
quite, quite clear!) has an object: yes. Instead of trotting
quietly home to talk to his friends, he plans to make a raid
on our Kyrene. That would be effective. But I shall want it
in writing, so that his Divine Majesty, who is occasionally
a little obstinate, may be convinced.'

'Letters are nasty things,' said Nikagoras. 'One signs
one's name—and it comes up against one afterwards.'

'Nothing shall be done until the day after you leave
Alexandria. By the way, I am distressed that you have not
found a better market here. Now I feel sure you will allow
me to do my best to induce you to visit us again. And of
course any information I get will have a certain value.'

Deliberately Nikagoras drew up a chair and sat down.
He took out his pen-case and ink and a square of paper.
'How much?' he said.

Three days later Nikagoras left Egypt, and at the same
time Sosibios gave orders that any Peloponnesian mercenary
troops still in Alexandria were to be sent at once to the great
camp which was forming east of the delta, ready to move
up into Palestine. The next day Sosibios brought the letter
and the remark to Ptolemy, who grew scarlet with anger
and stuck out his lip. 'Kleomenes must go! Not a day
more—him or his brats.'

'Go?' said Sosibios. 'No, seriously, I don't think he can
quite go. No, it would hardly be pleasant for us if he were
to go—for instance, to King Antiochos.'

'Not to King Antiochos,' said Ptolemy, 'but to King
Serapis.' He stared past Sosibios at a growing lily in the
sunlight of the balcony. 'A dark journey for this time of
the year.' And he laughed. 'A dark journey for a young
boy!'

Sosibios said: 'I doubt if we can be too precipitate.
One might create rather too much feeling among certain
fairly influential Greek communities in the city. No, if we
start with a modified imprisonment—oh, every comfort,
nothing to complain of, a mere misunderstanding—that

will allow me time to explain to the Greeks. Then it should pass off in the end—a month or so perhaps—without any unpleasantness at all.'

Ptolemy nodded. His heart was thumping at him heavily and thickly. He wanted Sosibios to go, and Agathoklea to come, and not make any fuss, or require any effort, but put his disturbed body right for him again.

All these days Berris was working on his statue of Love and Philylla. Waking in the morning he was often troubled, or going to bed unless he was properly tired out, or going out to buy things unless he kept completely overshadowed by his half-made shapes. But while he was at work he could see himself quite contentedly, watch his own fingers and his own mind, and he could watch with the same placidity the outside world and its joys or troubles. He remembered once in Athens seeing an old red-figured cup in somebody's house. He had not regarded it much at the time, but now he recollected that it was painted with a Komos scene, gay and frank young men and women with torches and branches and flutes, half or thoroughly naked, following and dancing and making love round and round the cup; but under each handle, sitting with his hands clasped over his knees, there was a little man who was watching it all quite calmly, and who would have watched in just the same way if the cup had been painted with battle or murder or witchcraft, not moved or shocked or excited, but just pleasantly influenced. Thinking back to that, two things occurred to Berris. One was that the little man under the handle was the real Greek doing for once the essentially Greek thing; and the other was that he himself, while he was at work and essentially occupying his body most fully, was also that same little man. So that he, Berris Der, the sculptor and painter, in spite of Epigethes and all of them, he was the Greek!

That made him laugh, and standing back from his statue, he noticed that the process of recollection and comparison had taken him the time of deepening to its full sharpness the groove between Philylla's arm and the Thing at her back, which was yet inchoate, only vaguely shaped into a great bird's head, and on one side the elk horns drawn on the surface with charcoal. He was puzzled as to how to make Love tender and gay while yet keeping the severe and unbroken lines. Philylla herself—the flesh Philylla, not the stone one—was a little frightened of this Love; she wanted him to give it a human head and attributes, garlands and doves and what-not. That was silly of her. He wondered what was to happen to the statue. He had seldom done anything big before which was not an order for a definite place in house or temple or market-colonnade, indoors or out; and since he had been in Egypt all his carved work had sold very quickly. Sometimes he had thought of taking in one or two apprentices to quicken up his output, but was bored with the prospect of training them. Then the outer door banged and there were feet running up the stairs, and his sister burst in, white and wild-looking. 'It's happened!' she cried. 'Oh, we knew it would!'

'What?' said Berris, turning quickly from his work to her, ceasing to be the little man on the vase, and snatching with his heart at Philylla.

Erif was sobbing with breathlessness and distress. 'King Ptolemy has imprisoned Kleomenes, and we don't know what to do!'

'Where?'

'In a house.'

'Are you sure he's alive?'

'Oh yes! But it's the beginning.'

'Very likely. Where's Philylla?'

'With the old Queen and the children. Sphaeros is there too.'

'Much good he is! Let me think. Do you know what they've charged Kleomenes with?' He began to wipe his tools and put them away. Work had been interrupted rather thoroughly by this time.

'It's all uncertain. Every one's trying to find out. Shall we ask Metrotimé? Oh, Berris, I'm afraid of something happening to Philylla! Berris, I do love her so.'

Berris at that produced a jerky laugh. 'So do I! Is Kleomenes imprisoned alone?'

'Just with a few servants. Of course, it may be the others any moment. Some of them are trying to get at Ptolemy and some have gone to Sosibios. The poor old Queen's terribly upset; most of the women are with her. Philylla was afraid she might try to do something stupid and violent, which would only make things worse. Berris, who's going to help?'

The last remains of the statue-as-it-was-going-to-be let go their hold and slipped out of Berris' mind. He said: 'We'd better find Metrotimé.'

'I suppose'—Erif hesitated—'Berris, I suppose you trust her still?'

'I've got to suppose so,' said Berris.

'We'll go to the palace, then. There'll be one or two others. What about that man—oh, what is his name?—yes, Ptolemy, the son of Chrysermas? He and Kleomenes have always been very friendly.'

'You go,' said Berris. 'I must wait in case Philylla comes.'

Erif said slowly: 'I saw her with the Queen. She didn't say she was coming.'

'What did she say?'

'Oh, Berris, she didn't speak about you! And she only told me to find out what was happening to the King. I think she's altogether back with Sparta. She was only thinking about Panteus and her own first friends. We're out of it now.'

Berris said nothing. He stood tapping with his fingers against the statue; then he picked up his cloak. 'Come on, Erif; we'll both go. The streets mayn't be too safe. Though I doubt if many people in Alexandria care. If she comes—'

'Berris darling, she won't. The old Queen needs her, and the children. At least, she thinks so.'

There was very little to be discovered at the palace. Metrotimé kept them waiting for some time, and then came in hurriedly and told them that Sosibios had found out that a plot was being hatched against the Divine King. She did not know, but Kleomenes might be implicated. 'You keep out of it,' she advised the two. 'Don't get muddled up with these Spartans, who've got no ideas beyond their own grievances. Make us something splendid again, Berris. We all believe in you. I hear from dear Agathokles that there's a new statue coming, and we're all longing to peep. I wonder if I can guess why it's kept secret?' But Berris was as dumb and unsatisfactory as ever.

Coming out from Metrotimé, they found old Sphaeros, also trying to get information at the palace and rather ashamed of feeling so much concern. He kept on repeating: 'He was my pupil,' as though it would be justified by that.

'Who have you seen?' asked Berris.

'I saw Lady Arsinoë's head nurse, a sensible woman, though she had little to tell now. You know perhaps that the princess has asked me to come to her as her tutor? But of course that is impossible, as I have told her, so long as I have charge of Nikomedes and the others.'

'Is Nikomedes very unhappy?' Erif asked.

'Yes. He appears not to be trying to face it reasonably. Even at his age I had hoped for better results, considering his training.'

'He's facing danger that may be real enough to his father.'

'So they keep on telling me,' said Sphaeros, with a queer little petulance. 'As though his whole life had not been one of danger!'

At first it did seem possible that there was some misunderstanding, but as day after day went by and nothing was altered, that possibility had to be dropped. It was very hard for the others to know what to do. Any action might endanger the King. The twelve were constantly together, discussing what was to be done. They were allowed to see Kleomenes, and could talk to him privately. They supposed the Egyptian servants were all spies or possible spies, but he was not guarded at all obtrusively. The house was comfortable, and his ordinary wishes were regarded. The head slave took the greatest trouble over his food and drink, saw that his bed linen was fresh, and even suggested the possibility of a nice little companion for it. Kleomenes' own two helot body servants were well treated too, and allowed to go in and out of the house, and bring him books or clothes, though they always had to report to the guard at the door. One of them, an intelligent youngish man, called Monimos, said he thought they were being followed. He had a mistress down by the docks, a brown dancer, and on his way there he often had suspicions. The King warned him fiercely never to say anything to the woman of what was going on, though Monimos assured him that she was absolutely trustworthy.

They decided that the best thing to do was to let the Peloponnesian mercenaries know what had been done to Kleomenes of Sparta and consult with their captains. But when Panteus and Phoebis came to the Sun Gate of Alexandria, the sentries who usually sat in the dust playing dice and eating sweets and joking with the market-women, shambled up and said politely but very firmly that this gate was blocked to them; the Spartans had been forbidden to take the Eastern road. That was the main gate out of Alexandria, but the others were forbidden too. They tried to hire a boat, but even at the most unlikely time of day there seemed always to be an official waiting to stop the boatman from taking them. The same thing seemed always to happen if they found a messenger whom they could trust with a letter. It was all extremely disconcerting.

Kleomenes began to think it very likely that he was going to be killed. He did not sleep very well, and most nights provided him with time to think it all out. Sometimes he was acutely conscious of wanting a woman, but he did not choose to be provided with Ptolemy's spies. It was, on the whole, merely a matter of the flesh and could be dealt with on Stoic principles. Odd, though, if—as seemed likely—he was never to have a woman again! Odd, to think of the ending of the body, its queer wants and habits. It was possible to think of dying, but impossible to think of never chewing a piece of bread or going to ease oneself again, those automatic actions which were more essential than thought or love, though utterly forgotten in memory and neglected in hope. He thought of Sparta. Over there Spartans were going on doing these things, though their lives—what he had always thought of as their lives—had been utterly altered by the rule of the Macedonians and the ephors. What had been altered really? What was there in man that could be changed by liberty or hope or friendship or a great idea? Where was it in the body? Sphaeros had never shown him. He had taken it for granted that he knew. Could one man alone have this part? He thought probably not, that it was only possible in a community. Then, could it go on in a community, apart from the individuals? Again, he thought not. If it could, it would mean—what? Gods, perhaps. Apollo of Sparta. Apollo real after all. Well, he had made the vows and sacrifices that a King must make. He had not neglected the Gods.

He had never considered the thing so deeply before. Always he had been interested in some immediate object, some future he was going to make and see himself. Now that had dropped away. And suddenly, out of calm thought, he would be seized with bitter resentment that he had thought and acted so violently and with such ambition. If he had been sensible and far slower, and placated more people, and compromised wherever it had seemed necessary, he might have another twenty or thirty good years to live—to live in Sparta with his children growing up round him—and their children—and Archiroë or some other soft and lovely she-thing to play with, and Panteus and his children, and all his friends, and the air and earth he loved! Then his eyes filled with tears and he twisted about and bit his pillow and, going from one evil rapidly to another, remembered that Agiatis was dead and he would never see her again or be comforted by her. Even though he died, too, he would not see her again even in a land of shadows, for all that was lies and unworthy of a free man's belief. The only thing that would happen would be that the memory of her which was still alive and real in his mind, would vanish too.

He talked of all this to Sphaeros, who agreed that it was so, and said that it must be faced and accepted, for who would choose to struggle foolishly and blindly when he might stand and look the Fates in the eyes? But Sphaeros was old; he could say these things calmly, meaning them, he was getting those extra twenty years which the King wanted so bitterly! It was time he did accept. But Sphaeros still did not consider the danger at all so certain. He had consulted with friends, yes, friends at the Library who went often to Court, and they were certain it would all be cleared up and explained away. All the same; it was as well for Kleomenes to have faced at last one of the realities, one which he had given to others, the only certain one.

Kleomenes spoke of it less to Panteus and the others, because they were still part of such hope and life as there still was. They had plans to make, conversations to report, the problem of whom in all Alexandria they could trust to help them if King Ptolemy decided finally to act—against them. He never spoke of it to his mother, and not to Nikomedes after the first time, because the boy had been desperately upset, Sphaeros said, for days. He would not speak, but went about looking as if he were not yet awake from some terrible dream.

One day Kleomenes sent a letter to his friend, Ptolemy, the son of Chrysermas, asking him to come and pay him a visit. The next morning the young man came, bringing with him a white kitten as a present; it managed to distract and dissipate the conversation a good deal. Kleomenes knew his visitor to be a great favourite at Court, good at playing any kind of game and admirably discreet at being defeated by his Divine Majesty; if the truth could be got at, he was likely to have it. He soothed Kleomenes a lot, producing all kinds of excuses and promises. The air of the place seemed to clear. Kleomenes began to take real pleasure in the pouncing grace of the kitten. The visit came to an end. They said good-bye very cordially, Kleomenes with the kitten on his arm; he was going to call it Lucky.

The visitor crossed to the door—the door which the King was not allowed to pass—and as he did so the kitten sprang and darted. Kleomenes grabbed at it, but it struck out with one claw, evaded him, and ran for the door with its tail in the air and Kleomenes in chase. The next moment it was sitting up in a corner, washing its face, and did not mind at all being picked up. But as the King began to fondle it again, he realised that his visitor was not yet gone, and with a curious feeling of impossibility, heard him say to the sergeant of the guards at the door, in a tone of extreme anger, that he would report him to Sosibios for their carelessness in guarding this wild beast, this danger to the State!

Kleomenes stayed quite quiet until he heard the door bolted again after Ptolemy the son of Chrysermas, and then walked back to his room, absently stroking the kitten. But for this accident he would still have thought the visit had been a most friendly and successful one, still have believed what Sosibios meant him to believe! He would have reported it happily to his friends. Now that was all finished. Yes, there was probably only one course open to them now. The Divine Ptolemy and his Court were moving to Canopus the next week; it was cooler and pleasanter there. Yes, that would be the time for them to do it.

Chapter Eight

WHEN KING PTOLEMY released a prisoner, especially a political prisoner found to be innocent, the custom was that he should send presents and garlands and the fortunate man would then hold a feast in honour of the King, his friend. That was well known. So when a quantity of fine things were sent to Kleomenes, robes woven with fine colours, jars of scent and honey, and ivory boxes of spice, there was no reason for the guards to disbelieve the message that all this came from King Ptolemy. They did not know that the last of the old Queen's money was gone, and Philylla had given Panteus all the savings she had put together in case—and Leandris had sold her silver combs and Neareta the necklace which Phoebis had brought her from the sack of Megalopolis. So Kleomenes and his twelve friends made a solemn feast in honour of King Ptolemy, who had set him free, and gave handsomely to the guards—wine mostly, heavy wine of Cyprus, spiced with a free hand, and meat from the sacrifice he made before the feast. The only at all surprising thing about it was that actually King Ptolemy and most of his Court were away at Canopus. But perhaps he had heard something new there about the conspiracy, and had sent back word that the wild beast, Kleomenes the Spartan, was to be freed.

It was hot in the courtyard; the air smelt of over-baked dust and dust-dry dung, as the air does in a city. The King's two helots brought bowls of tripe and ox-tail to the guards, seasoned with pepper and garlic, a good food smell to drown the other. They loosened their armour: no need to keep watch now. They had garlands of jasmine, cool over running sweat. In the shade of the trellis they stretched and belched and drank again languidly, and one by one went to sleep. The helots went back and reported, satisfied; their work was done; they could go. Monimos went off to his mistress at the docks, wanting to pass the hot hours there on cool pillows, watching her dance and shine and drip and wag her breasts at him.

But in the room the twelve and Kleomenes had eaten and drunk little. They had talked out their plan till it was clear. They were going to make one more attempt to rouse the Greeks in Alexandria against the palace—there might be a chance with Ptolemy away, the Alexandrians might be less in awe of the thing, they might remember they were men! Oh yes, it was possible. They would free the prisoners in the gaol. They would rush through the streets, storming, shouting people out of their houses; the Alexandrians might be fired by it, and if once they could get a foothold in Alexandria and send to the mercenaries—yes, it might happen! This might be the dark hour just before dawn—they would be able to look back on it and laugh—from Sparta. They had trusted their star, risked all, gained all. That was what they would say—in Sparta.

At first they were keeping themselves firmly into a group of planning and hoping, looking forward to material and solid things, the New Times again, the kingdom—in Sparta. Hippitas was best at this because he was the eldest and had seen many very unlikely things happen, and anyhow took the future lightly, as a good campaigner should. Idaios was hopeful because he was bound to have a very strong and sharp vision of the time when he and Leandris and his baby son were at last going to be home. Agesipolis said it was going to come right because he was the youngest, young enough to believe in the almost impossible. And Phoebis sometimes said the same thing, but there was a bitter taste of country irony perceptible behind the words, the mocking of the harvest people at the Spartiates, the mocking at death. The others were not hoping so well.

The King had seen Nikomedes the day before, but he had not told him or Sphaeros what was going to happen. He knew Sphaeros would discourage it, would say it was not only folly and violence and an animal struggle against Fate, but also impossible! And he did not tell Nikomedes because—if it was impossible, if all he was doing was going to his death a few weeks sooner than Ptolemy had meant—the less the boy knew about it the better. If he was not involved in the plot there was no reason why he should be involved in his father's death either. So young a boy. A child almost. A child he had looked that day, puzzled and kept out and terribly attentive to every word his father had said. No, no, think on across to the time when Nikomedes should be full grown, a young man, a kouros, running over the hills with a spear, the next King of Sparta.

As they ate and drank, helping themselves from the small tables set close to the couches, there were odd, sudden silences and then bursts of speech. There were curtains drawn across the windows, a half light. Their garlands smelt strongly, and so did the flowers strewn across the room; they were all still in the many-coloured garments of rejoicing that they had put on to show the guards. It was curious, but as the time went on, the same idea would seem to come into the minds of two or three of them at once, almost in the same words. They were being drawn closer and closer together. There were few enough of them for that to be possible, twelve and the King. They were all ages of strong manhood; they had known all kinds of different experience. Half of them were married or had been. Whatever happened, this meal, this meat and bread and wine, was the last of some series; either the last of shame and imprisonment and waiting—or the last of life.

Most likely the latter, Hippitas said to himself, passing a handful of olives to his neighbour, a scarred, grizzled man nearly his own age, and calculating their chances to himself. Well, so long as there was one chance in a hundred, it was better than leaving the King in prison to be butchered at leisure by Ptolemy and Sosibios. And, suddenly, that was just what his neighbour was saying to him, in a low voice, his mouth half full of olives. If one liked olives, one might as well eat them now, get the full flavour of them while the tongue could taste still. 'I've seen life,' said Hippitas, 'a good share of it, more than most. The thing's got to end some time. Whatever happens, we cheat Ptolemy out of getting the King.'

His neighbour nodded, bit on an olive stone and spat it out. 'It was the only thing to do.'

And at the same time, at the far side of the room, Neolaidas' neighbour was saying: 'It's the only thing we can do.' He looked down at his hands, spreading and clenching them. 'In a way,' he said, 'a pity to have to get killed yet. But we obviously must.'

Neolaidas nodded. 'Probably less painful than when I was wounded at Sellasia and lost my eye.'

'Yes, but—Here one is. A bore to be killed.'

'Perhaps. It will all be over before tonight.'

'Yes. And then—?'

'No more decisions to make. No more waiting. Responsibilities. Pain. This anxiousness all day and all night, what was it about? Life or death mostly. Odd and quiet it will be when that's settled for good.'

'Yet perhaps it won't be settled. Perhaps we shall succeed.'

'And have to face death thirty years on instead. Perhaps. Yet, of course, if we could get one of the gates or even part of the harbour and send to the mercenaries—'

'Yes,' said Phoebis, his neighbour on the other side, 'I was just thinking of the mercenaries. If only we'd got to them before. The bad business is that Ptolemy at Canopus will get the news before the camp does. Well, if so, we're done, even if we last out tonight. Unless, by some amazing piece of good luck we get Sosibios.'

'I'd sooner die now than in a week,' said Neolaidas.

'Die like a Spartan!' said Phoebis, with a queer little laugh. And then: 'My boy's down in the country getting well. He won't hear for a day or two that his dad's—dead like a Spartan!'

'You told Neareta?'

'Oh yes, she knows. She knows! Twenty years we've been man and wife. My eldest boy, who was killed at Sellasia—he'd have been almost nineteen now.'

'Mnasippos was a good chap,' said one of the others, thinking of the friends who had been killed at Sellasia.

'So was Hierax.'

'Odd, Xenares getting killed in the charge.'

'When we're cleared off, there won't be so many Spartans left.'

Phoebis was frowning. He said slowly: 'This is the Spartan thing, the Phiditia, this last thing, this last eating together. And I am only half Spartan.'

The King heard that; he said across the room, which was not after all, so big, and all held together by the smell of flowers and wine: 'You, my foster-brother, Phoebis?'

Phoebis looked at the King, who leaned on the edge of his couch with both elbows, Panteus behind him smiling at Phoebis too. It was Kleomenes, who had been a littler boy when Phoebis was a little boy, fantastically, incredibly grown up. For a moment Phoebis was busy with the flashing-by of thirty-five years. That image of childhood had persisted in his mind, in its old colours and proportions, and in the meantime this thing had happened! Then the room swung back, closed on him with the present. Panteus had walked across and taken him by the hands and held his eyes steady and restored the community. With a queer little grunt of relaxation Phoebis admitted it. Whatever he had been, he was a Spartan now. Panteus went back across the room to the King. He still walked with that peculiar springiness of his as though there were turf under his feet, and his hair was still thick and curly, but some of the colour was gone from it, as though promising that some day, in a few years, someone would look at him and suddenly see that it was all grey. He settled himself down beside Kleomenes and put one arm round his neck, and the King shifted his head imperceptibly into the strong crook of his love's elbow.

Three beyond Phoebis was Idaios. He said: 'This is the eating together, Phoebis, I know what you mean; this is the love feast. It is like something in a temple.'

And the man next him said: 'Yes, it is like something in one of the Mysteries. I was thinking of that.'

'It *is* one of the Mysteries.'

'Is it going to carry us on then? On across any threshold?' That was Agesipolis, three away from Idaios, 'for I had been wondering when I had felt like this before, and now I know.' He was one of the Spartiates who had been most deeply caught by the Gods of Egypt. He said: 'There is a feast before the rising of Osiris. I am not sure whether I should speak of it. No. I am sure. The God becomes corn, becomes bread. He is taken and eaten by the Initiates. They become one, through him. It was like this.'

Another man said: 'Some Gods become the beast that is sacrificed, the Bull. It is the same thing.'

Idaios said: 'But why is it like that now? Where is the God?' And nobody answered for a moment, but then, in that part of the room, they found that they were all looking rather intently at Kleomenes. He was the King. He was the focus of the feast. Idaios said sharply: 'But that's stupid. How can one think that? These things are not so.' And he began quickly to remember, first Sphaeros and the good, solid Stoicism which he had learnt, and then Leandris and his marriage, and the fact which he insisted on in his mind, that this was not the last eating together, because he and his bride were going to go home.

But Agesipolis only said: 'I wish Nikomedes were here.'

The King said quickly to Agesipolis: 'You did not tell Nikomedes anything?'

'No,' said Agesipolis, 'though I wanted to. I wanted him

to wish me luck. I wanted something—something special
to be said.'

'So did I,' said the King slowly. 'But we couldn't take
that. If we fail, we will not drag him after us. Or the
others.'

Idaios got up and came over to the King and knelt on
the floor beside him. 'You are sure of that, Kleomenes?
The women will come to no harm, whatever happens?'

'As far as one can tell, no,' said the King. 'Unless perhaps
my mother, because she is Queen and because she is sure
to say things to anger the Egyptians. I think she knew that
when she saw me last. She is old, you see, and there is not
much difference between an old man and an old woman;
she would want the things that happen to a man.'

'But the others—but Leandris—'

The King said: 'If we fail the women and children will
be able to live on as ordinary people, to live ordinary life
for its own sweet immediacy, and not be harassed as we
have been by greatness. Our deaths will at least take off
them the intolerable burden of kingliness.'

'But you will not die!' said Panteus, suddenly gripping
and shaking him.

'No!' said Idaios. 'No, we shall do it; none of us will
die.' And then he looked strangely round the room. 'How
can we—after this?' And he leant back for a breath or
two against the edge of the King's couch.

Kleomenes picked up a fold of the beautiful Egyptian
mantle from his shoulder and fingered it and then let it
fall, sliding from his bare shoulder and chest. He asked:
'What did Leandris say to you, Idaios?'

'She was making vows for me,' said Idaios softly. 'For me
and for you, Kleomenes. To Isis and Serapis and Any who
are powerful. The baby is—is very nice now. He always
wants me to pick him up and play with him. He'll grow
up. There'll be the classes again for him. Leandris—oh,
it wasn't good-bye we said!' He got up quickly and went
back to his place and drank a cupful of wine.

Phoebis said: 'Neareta and I said good-bye. We've
done that before. We did it before Sellasia. She thinks it
is—lucky. We shall need all the luck we can get.'

One or two others spoke of their wives, to whom they had
told much or little, and then Agesipolis suddenly thought of

his own wife, that rather stupid girl whom he had not seen for nearly six years, and the baby he had been so bored with, but who must now be quite a nice little boy. Kleomenes thought of Agiatis, how he would have told her everything, and how she would have made him see all the good or luck there was in it. Someone said to Panteus:'And you?'

But Panteus shook his head. There had been something queer and shadowy about his good-byes to Philylla. She had known everything, the plans and the chances. She said she would stay with the old Queen and especially the children, especially Nikomedes, till it was over—either way. They might need her. And he had talked to her about the King and how it had been driving him mad not to be able to help, but now at last he and Kleomenes would be doing something together again. She had understood and kissed him wisely and calmly, standing in front of him, a wise, strong woman, not a girl any more, but a comforter and helper of men. But neither of them had spoken of their own marriage, their own happiness or unhappiness, their own hopes and fears. It was as though that had been put aside to some later time when there would be infinite leisure, after all these serious things were past. But suppose that time never came. They had passed by some fundamental reality without looking at it. Because for now, he had to see all his realities in the King. And she? But he could trust Philylla. Even if he died with something unspoken, she would understand.

It was then that the two helots came in to say that the guards were asleep, and looked like sleeping till evening. The men stirred and glanced at one another. Another hour and they would start. Best not to do it too early, when most of Alexandria would be sleeping out the hot hours too. Spasmodically, they spoke of details of their plans, possible meeting-places if they got scattered, verifying objectives and catchwords. But there was nothing new to be thought of; it had all been talked out already. Then an impulse seemed to come to them all to talk about Sparta. They began to describe it in detail, places, the shapes of small hills, the springs among the rocks, the kind of crops, the very texture of the earth grown through with fibres of roots. They spoke of being young and in love, of racing and wrestling and hunting, of friends alive or dead. They spoke of the past, trying to tie the future down with it. They leant forward and moved eagerly; the coloured robes of rejoicing slipped off them, leaving half their bodies bare and strong and cool. Of these thirteen, there were several couples whose friendship was very deep-rooted. They were too old now to play the love-game as the boys and young men did, but however the thing had begun, it had left behind it now a most sweet and comforting comradeship. Those lovers turned to each other for strength and reassurance and perhaps remembered days they had not thought of for a long time. They looked in one another's eyes and touched one another tenderly. While the body yet lived, it served to show their love. A man, thinking of his friend as beautiful, could keep a beauty in him that would have gone otherwise. Yet the looks and words of these couples did not break through the closeness and community of the feast. They were completely included in it.

Kleomenes and Panteus turned towards one another, and it was as if they were alone in an island, and yet among friends so kind and so trusted, that it was no matter what they spoke of or who overheard. The King said: 'Do you remember the first time?'

'Yes,' said Panteus, 'I remember. It was during that early fighting towards Megalopolis. You'd praised me then, and given me the little dagger I lost afterwards at Argos. Then at Mess you bade me sit next to you.'

'Go on, go on,' said the King. He wanted strength and reassurance as much as anyone; his eyes were hungry. He trusted to his beloved to give it to him.

Panteus went on. 'You told me then for the first time the story of Agis. Simply what had happened, for those were the days when you could not trust even your friends to understand. As you talked I thought about what Agis had wanted, not very deeply, but yet I got a picture of that Sparta—ah, the Sparta we have had!—and I said suddenly: "I wish it could come real!" And when you spoke of his death I was angry not to have been there to stop it.'

'Will anyone be angry about our deaths, Panteus?'

'I am talking of then, Kleomenes. Listen. You said a little about Agiatis. I was very sorry for her, and for you both. I saw you as a young boy being forced into marriage. I know I put my hand on yours for a moment and then felt ashamed of myself and thought you'd hate it. After

that there was music. In those days you still used to have
somebody to come in and amuse us.'

'It was the custom. There were two Syrian jugglers. And
acrobats; I enjoyed that. Those flute-girls! How many
years since I've thought of them: good, honest girls. But
that evening it was the old man who recited. What was it?
Can you remember, Panteus?'

'I can remember. It was the sailing for Troy. Dull and
lovely! Most people were talking in whispers, but I didn't
dare, to you. I sat still, and sometimes I looked at you,
and sometimes, when I looked, you were looking at me.
When it was over you did not seem to want to break up
the drinking. You said: "Will anyone sing?" Hierax sang
first, something funny. We all laughed. Then Hippitas
said: "My cousin can sing." You nodded to me and I
stood up, very shy and rather angry with Hippitas. I tried
to think of something funny too, but nothing came into
my head. He said. "Sing: You Go my Way," and I was
glad, because what I wanted to sing was a love song. Yet
somehow I cannot remember that I looked at you while I
was singing.'

'You put your hands up over your eyes and sang so, with
your head thrown back. Didn't you know?'

'When it was over I walked back, being very gay, ready to
laugh with anyone if they wanted to laugh at my song. And
then you stood up. You put your hands on my shoulders and
I hoped you were going to say I had sung well. But you said
nothing. Only you looked at me and looked at me, and after
a time you bowed your head against my shoulder. I saw you
were shaking a little but I did not dare to touch you with
my hands. I said your name in a whisper, "Kleomenes".'

'Go on, go on; let us remember. Ah, what is it?'

'It is very bitter to think now of all that sweet!' Suddenly
it was Panteus who had lost grip, who had given strength to
the King, so that his own was for the moment shattered.

But the King took it up, smiling at him, seeing him as
he had been then. 'Not for us two, not bitter. Give me your
hands, Panteus, and I will tell you the rest. Every one went
away, and I back to my tent. I tried to read. It was a book
of Zeno's, but there was no sense in it that night. I wanted
poetry; but I had none. I went to Hippitas and asked him
if he had. He was in bed already. "Not a thing!" he said. I

almost asked him which your tent was, for I did not know. But then I wasn't bold enough. I went on to Therykion and asked him if he had any poetry. He had: old poets. He offered me Tyrtaeus, "War songs out of old days, King," he said, and I took the book and unrolled it, thinking this should have been what I wanted. I stayed and talked to him for a time. Queer creature, he was most nearly the one who might have understood me if he had chosen. I looked through his poets and at last found the Ionians I needed. I took Alkaeus and laughed and said he should have it back in the morning. I went to my tent and read, and then put it by and sat with my head in my hands. I took up my tablets and began to write myself. I tried again and again. "Dear, I would say you a word, Be gentle and stay and listen—" Oh, just echoes of Alkaeus, not my own love! And suddenly you came in, armed, and saluted me, with a message from the outposts which needed an answer. I took it out of your hands and tried to look at it. It was five minutes before I could see that it was just a simple question of communications the next day. I looked up and you were staring at me. I smoothed out the wax to write my answer, and doing that I made up my mind to speak. I said: "I have been trying to write a poem all this evening." You did not answer. I said: "It would have been to you." Then I shut the tablets and twisted the string round them, taking a long time, for I hoped you would speak. I had not the courage, myself, to say anything more. I handed you the tablets, not touching your fingers. You said: "I will take the message and then I will come back and we will speak more about this, Kleomenes." And you turned and bounded out.'

'I ran all the way there and back. I did not want to think, but my whole body was glad.'

'It seemed long enough to me. The lamp began to burn down and I poured in fresh oil. I wondered if you had been kept by anything. I thought there might have been a night raid from Megalopolis. I began to listen for it. And I heard your feet running, coming back to me. You came in, panting. I did not think I had ever seen your eyes as blue before as they were then in my tent in the lamp-light. I said: "Let us talk about this now." You came in and knelt beside me quickly on one knee and your right hand dropped and touched my foot; I felt it grip round my ankle. But your face was hidden, your head was against my thigh. I took your helmet off and laid it down on the bench beside me and I began to feel your head with my hands, tangling my fingers in your hair, pulling your hair, I think. I felt the bones of it under my hands, the way it juts out at the base of the skull. There were light hairs like fur on your neck, lighter than your skin. I pulled your head round to look at your face and I saw you were laughing. Why were you laughing, Panteus?'

'With delight, my King.'

'I did not know that. I thought you were perhaps laughing at me. Yet I thought that was better than anger or shame. You ducked a little as I lifted the sword sling over your head. I undid the straps of your breastplate. You kept very still all the time. I laid it by. I undid your shoulder brooches, pricking myself. You had a shirt of some very fine, soft, blue stuff—better than we've worn since! I pushed you away from me to arm's length, so that I could look at you. I thought then for the first time that you were square and balanced, like a statue by Polykleitos. You still said nothing, but your hands went up to me, and I knew what you wanted and took the brooches out of my own tunic. We must have seen one another often before, naked, but we had never looked so close. You took your tunic right off and laid it by the sword. I saw no blemish on you, Panteus.'

'Nor I on you. And I was glad that my body was strong and hard and clean. You were very brown all over, more than I'd thought. I put my hands on to you, on to your chest, and stroked down over your flanks and thighs. I stood up and we kissed one another. You said: "Tomorrow there will be fighting again. Stay with me now." So I said I would stay.'

'I think,' Kleomenes said, 'that after this we stood for some time only looking and being glad. I sat down on my bed and you sat beside me. Then I said: "What now? For we are neither of us boys, but grown men." Then you began to laugh. I had never seen anyone laugh so, your low and delightful laughter filling my tent. After a time you said, still with your mouth full of laughing, but very gently: "Now we will go to sleep, Kleomenes, and speak of these things again in the morning." So we lay down and I spread my cloak over both of us. We were close enough for each to lay his head on the other's arm. And it was a most sweet sleep we had.'

'Yes,' said Panteus, 'I remember that. A very sweet and deep sleep for both of us.' He sat half up on the couch beside the King, leaning rather forward on both hands, dropping his head between his shoulders, his eyes half shut in the thick tension of remembrance. The blue fringes of the Egyptian stuff lapped round his stiffened fingers. The others, who had been listening or half-listening, understood how he was thinking back to this thing which was within their own experience too. The King looked round at the twelve, calmer and happier than they had seen him for a long time.

Neolaidas was whispering to the helot servant. He looked up and spoke anxiously: 'Monimos has gone to his mistress. Are we sure that's safe?' The other helot assured him that it was, but Phoebis was doubtful and so was the King.

'I think we should get ready, my friends,' Kleomenes said. 'If the Alexandrians are not awake we shall wake them very soon.' Then he stood up and every one else stood up. In a way they were glad to have the time of waiting and remembrance cut short, the time for action come.

As they got up they shook those gaily woven Egyptian things off their bodies. They kicked them on to a heap on the floor, and while they stood naked, stretching themselves, someone in angry mockery threw a cup of wine over them to soak and blemish the fabrics of rejoicing. They could not come in armour to a sacrifice and feast of gladness, but they had brought their swords, and Panteus had brought a sword for the King under his cloak. The King's own sword had been taken, and nobody knew where it was.

Then they took up their ordinary town tunics, made, Alexandrian fashion, with short sleeves, but the King took his new sword and slit along the seam of his so as to lay his right shoulder bare, and the others did the same, in silence, with their swords. This was for two things. It would be a sign and mark to one another supposing they got separated, and a sign for those who joined them. And also it left the sword-arm and shoulder, for which anyhow the tunic was no protection, as free as possible. Then they went out into the courtyard. The guards were still sound and hoggishly asleep. They did not hear the bolts being slipped. Kleomenes and the twelve were out in the streets of Alexandria.

Chapter Nine

SEVERAL OF THEM were moving still. Idaios opened and closed his eyes slowly. There was nobody anywhere near. The Alexandrians had not dared to stay and look. Panteus shifted a little in the dust, sitting there waiting with his drawn sword over his knees, his sword, his sword waiting—So he shut his eyes again and counted steadily to two hundred. His wounds and bruises were too sore to let him think of much while he was counting. He looked up again. Idaios seemed to be dead now; his eyes stayed wide open and had begun to film over. There were one or two dogs slinking about, not daring to come near yet. Panteus was too hoarse to shout, but he threw stones at them and they disappeared again. He stared into the sky. Very high up still, a kite circled blackly against the dazzling blue; another joined it. The flies had come already.

The shuttle began to click in his brain again; the hours he had just been through began to repeat themselves. Three hours—two hours ago, there had been hope. Now he could not remember what hope was like. They had all gone charging down the street away from that house where the King had been a prisoner, shouting through Sun and Moon Street, calling on the Alexandrians to remember they were Greeks and join them for freedom! Hippitas could not keep it up—he had begged them to kill him and keep the pace. But they had found a man riding and thrown him off and put Hippitas up on the colt, and then they all went storming again through Alexandria towards the palace, shouting: 'Liberty,' and 'Down with the tyrants, down with Ptolemy and Sosibios, down with Agathokles and Agathoklea and Oenanthe!' It had even seemed as though that were going to work. They had looked round at the growing crowd, coming along with them, keeping up, shouting: 'Down with Agathokles, down with the palace!' They caught the traitor, Ptolemy the son of Chrysermas, coming out of the palace, and killed him. They broke up the city guard and killed their officer with his fine chariot and fine clothes. Every one cheered and shouted luck to them.

They got their first set-back at the prison. The keepers had been too quick for them; it was all hopelessly barred against them. And after that, when they turned back to the city, to try for one of the gates, or the docks, they began to see that it was all no good. They'd tried to organise this mob who ran with them, cheering and making a kind of triumph feeling for them, but it melted under their hands almost. None of the Alexandrians would help. Sphaeros was not in his house; they could not find him. They'd tried to get hold of the men they thought were friendly. Yes, they were friendly still, in a way, but there was nothing doing. Nothing, nothing, nothing. No use shouting: 'Liberty!' to men who didn't want it. The Alexandrians stuck to Ptolemy and Sosibios and Agathoklea. The cheering crowd dwindled, and they found themselves almost alone, then quite alone, in this little square, a deserted winter-market place with nothing in it now but the skeletons of booths, and broken baskets and crocks. It became obvious what they had to do.

They had risked and lost. But they were still, perhaps for an hour, free. There was one more action, and only one, which they could take. Hippitas had smiled a little and said he was the eldest and ought, by Spartan custom, to be allowed a privilege. He asked that one of the younger men should do it for him. Agesipolis did it; Hippitas had always been kind to him. And before they had quite understood that Hippitas was really dead, Agesipolis had killed himself too, falling forward cleverly on to his own sword, like a diver taking off. It was then that the King had moved a few steps aside with Panteus and told him to be guardian of their honour and to wait till they were all dead before he, finally, killed himself. Panteus had said yes, he would do that. He had not known it was going to be so difficult. He had not known how the thin icicle of loneliness was going to spike him through.

He remembered how he had felt sick with apprehension that Kleomenes would ask him to do it for him. He would have had to. But none of the lovers did that. They loved one another too well. Kleomenes had loved him too well to make him. They had fallen on their own swords, and most of them had lain doubled up on them, so that there was no need to look at their faces again. They could have been asleep. Only one or two had done it clumsily and struggled and flopped over.

He got up. Suddenly he found his head swimming. He put his hands up to his forehead. For a moment he got the odd idea that each one of these events had knocked away a piece of his skull, and now the whole thing lay open to the sun and vultures. Then he went round, doing what he had done once already. He pricked them each with his dagger to see if they were alive. This time none of them stirred. Then he went to the King. Kleomenes lay quite still on his face, his knees and elbows rather bent under him. He *must* be asleep. Otherwise. Otherwise. It was all impossible.

I would have supposed I had faced this. Faced it at the feast. Or before Sellasia. Sellasia was different. Different because I wasn't killed, because he wasn't killed. But I thought I had faced it first then, or earlier. First before this. Or not. Faced first at the feast. The blood has stopped creeping out from under him. It did at first. Crept first at the feast. No, there was no blood then. We were talking to one another. He won't ever speak to me again. He is not asleep.

At first Panteus could not do it at all, though he had his dagger ready. Then he bent and pricked Kleomenes with it at the back of the ankle. He could not help being certain that Kleomenes would wake up then. But instead something rather horrible happened. The thing jerked and heaved over and lay on its back. Kleomenes lay on his back. He was still doubled up over the red, slimy sword-hilt. His hands were clenched on it. Panteus looked away from that, at his face. His eyes were half shut, a line of white between the lids. His mouth was open and there was blood on his teeth; he had bitten his under-lip to stop himself groaning. Panteus leant over, closer and lower, staring and feeling; there was a faint breath in the mouth, a faint throb of some kind at the base of the throat. He crouched down till their cheeks touched; he murmured 'Kleomenes, Kleomenes.' But there was no recognition anywhere. He tried to take one hand, but they were clenched tight and slippery with blood. So he sat down on the ground again and waited.

He waited and counted and cried a good deal and called out people's names sharply, because he was alone and the flies were buzzing so. The kites and the dogs came nearer.

When he looked up next Kleomenes was quite dead. It was easier after that. He pulled the King's tunic straight so as to cover him partly from the flies. He began to do the same for some of the others, but a kind of blackness had begun to come down on him, a shutter of weariness. It was not worth while. He went back to Kleomenes and knelt over him and put the point of his sword against his stomach, just under the base of the breastbone, pointing up and to the left. He held it firm with both hands. He fell forward onto it, over the King's body.

By and bye some of the Alexandrians came tiptoeing out of the back streets to look.

PART VIII

Death and Philylla

Seine Leiche liegt in der ganzen Stadt,
In allen Höfen, in allen Strassen.
Alle Zimmer
Sind vom Ausfliessen seines Blutes matt.
  Der Tote Leibknecht

NEW PEOPLE IN THE EIGHTH PART

Kottalos, the Captain of King Ptolemy's Guards
Greeks, Macedonians, Egyptians and others

BERRIS WAS GETTING on well with his big statue, at least he thought so, though Erif could not tell much difference from day to day except a lot of stone dust on the floor. He had been at it all the morning and afternoon, stripped to the waist like an Egyptian, and sweating. Erif had been sitting near him, sewing and singing. She was making a dress for Philylla and embroidering it with all kinds of luck charms. She found her own clothes rather uninteresting to make and usually left them plain, but it was fascinating and absorbing to make something for Philylla to wear. All the same she was thinking that she must go home this summer. The five years were up and perhaps those unsolved meetings had happened without her knowing about them. Perhaps they had happened in Marob. Anyhow, whether or not, she could not be separate any longer. She had determined after long thought that it would be better to go back to Tarrik and Marob and perhaps die, than to stay here without them any longer. She had come to this conclusion quite happily, but also quite definitely. She was thinking of it now.

During the afternoon they had heard a certain amount of noise and disturbance in the streets, but that was often happening in Alexandria. Probably there was a strike or a murder or a procession or something. Once Erif had looked out of the window to see if she could see anything, but it all seemed to be a street or two away. She hadn't bothered.

Then, in the latter part of the afternoon, there was a knock and Ankhet came in. She seemed very nervous, and inverted the order of her Greek sentences, which seldom happened as a rule. She stood beside the statue without looking at it and told them just what the Alexandrian event of the day had been, adding that the bodies had now been collected by the authorities and would be suitably disposed of. Erif and Berris both listened without interrupting much, but Erif pricked herself with the needle and did not notice for some minutes. Even when Ankhet was gone again, soft-footed and apologetic, they did not say anything at all for a little time. Berris was thinking of those men whom he had known well and liked and lived with and worked for; the fighting up in Arkadia; all gone out of his life as though they had never been; all dead in some agony of spirit which he did not much care to think of. And then abruptly and dizzyingly he thought: do I get Philylla now? And almost at the same moment it came into his head that this death of the men was a thing past, part of the story of Kleomenes, and it shifted and stilled into another picture, a better one this time. But Erif was thinking almost entirely about Philylla and what was going to happen to her immediately. She put that into words. 'I wonder if Philylla knows yet,' she said. 'Yes, she's bound to. I suppose—Berris, I suppose she won't try to do the same thing?'

Berris was startled. He said: 'I'm going to her at once.' And he picked up his cloak.

'No she won't,' Erif went on, thinking hard, 'because of the King's children. But what's going to happen? Ptolemy and Sosibios will be very angry. And—you know, Berris, they may do anything when they're angry. I expect all the Spartans are in danger.'

'I'll make her come away,' said Berris. 'The old Queen can manage without her.'

'But the children?'

Berris shrugged his shoulders. 'Kings' children always find plenty to look after them. And there's the grandmother—what else is she for? They don't need my Philylla too.'

Erif was suddenly angry. 'She isn't your Philylla! She's—no, she's not mine either. Anyhow, don't be stupid. She'll stay if she thinks she ought to stay. We've no rights over her, worse luck. But you go to her, Berris, and do what you can. I'll go to the palace.'

Berris hesitated: 'Don't you want to see her, Erif?'

'Yes!' said Erif sharply. 'But I don't suppose it matters to her which of us, so you can. Besides, Metrotimé's at Canopus, so you won't find out as much as I shall at the palace.' She ran a comb through her hair and looked at herself in the mirror.

'Who are you going to see, Erif?'

'You know.'

'Oh, the faun. Probably you're right.' It was Erif's Vintage Night faun, with whom she kept up a certain spasmodic intimacy. He might be useful. Berris quite approved; he was a personable young man, good at games and hunting, and he took an intelligent interest in sculpture. Erif went to the palace.

She wasted at least half an hour with the faun before she could get him to find out anything. That was the maddening thing about men, one couldn't go straight to the point with them—or only to some points. And their stupidity! To go on kissing her and paying her useless compliments as though she wanted either at the moment. Tarrik would eat you up and not leave any bones at the end of it!—she thought savagely. But by and bye he did go to find out, and when he came back the news was that Sosibios was very angry and likely to do something quite unpleasant. 'You see,' said the faun, sleeking back the hair off his round, brown forehead, 'if nothing at all were done, they might go to Antiochos.'

'And what if they did?' said Erif. 'There's nothing to tell.'

But the faun said he was not certain. Kleomenes had known more than anyone ought to have known, things about the new camp east of the delta, various arrangements and surprises which the women might easily have heard of. 'Sosibios is so stupidly realist,' he said.

'Will they be imprisoned?' asked Erif, and then, after a little pause, in which she got no answer, 'or what?'

The faun said slowly: 'I am afraid—the latter. And if I may advise, my Scythian apple-blossom, you and your brother would do best to keep out of the way. Sosibios is in the mood to overreach himself. I am going to the Divine Court at Canopus tomorrow, by boat. Rather a charming new boat; I think you'd approve. Would you let your faun carry you off in it, out of all these unpleasantnesses which, after all, none of us can do anything about?—quite, quite gently, Erif, in between the blue ripples, so that you'd hardly know? This is the weather for Canopus; there'll be tiny breezes there. Alexandria is impossible. Don't you agree?'

'What?' said Erif, when he'd finished, and then, one hand on his shoulder, the other up to her own forehead: 'Oh—I'm sorry, my head's aching. The sun. No, not tomorrow, I think, but perhaps your boat comes and goes? Yes, Alexandria is unbearable. I think I must go home and—lie down by myself. No, faun, not again! Let me go!'

She went across the city almost running, as fast as a woman could without being noticed and delayed. She thought of the faun, whom she usually quite liked, with an extraordinarily violent mixture of anger and contempt. By the museum there were little agitated knots and crowds, discussing today's doings in the shady ending of the afternoon. It was said that one of the professors was going to make it all into a text for a Stoic lecture, which would be amusing. This Spartan King had been a pupil of Sphaeros, hadn't he? Sphaeros was rather out of date, of course; had lost touch during the years he'd been up north in Borysthenes, or wherever the place was. He was out of sympathy with the modern philosophic movements, the new *rapprochements* with the Mysteries, and all that. Most of these mainland Greeks were behind the times unless they'd had the sense to move. Their places were dead. Athens—Sparta—dead branches! The world was growing outward like a tree towards the sun. The green leaves and flowers were on the edges, Alexandria, Jerusalem, Carthage, even Rhodes, Macedonia perhaps, why, yes, Syria certainly, one must admit that one's enemies were civilised!—but Alexandria above all was the central blossom—wise bees knew that. It was to be hoped anyhow that these disturbances wouldn't lead to new police regulations. Such a bore not to be able to stay out after midnight!

But Erif Der was at Queen Kratesikleia's house. She heard that both Berris and Sphaeros were there. The servants knew her well and brought her through, but she could see that they were all terrified and on edge, even the old helot doorkeeper, whom one had never thought of as having any more sensibilities than a watchdog. Berris met her in the courtyard; she told him her news quickly. He nodded. 'They think so too, but they don't know what to do. And—Erif, I've seen her. She'd heard. The old Queen's crying and howling like a girl—listen!' They listened and shivered. 'But she—Erif, she was as calm and hard as ivory. Erif, do you think that perhaps she really doesn't care?'

'No,' said Erif. 'No such luck, my dear. She's being a Spartan. So will the old woman be, the moment she's got over the first shock of it. Is Sphaeros with her? Mmm, I expect they set one another off. We've got to get Philylla and the King's children away, Berris.'

'It will be harder with the children. If this Sosibios really does mean business.'

'She won't leave them. I know. Beside—Berris, it may be stupid of me, but I'm not going to let these three stay and be murdered. Agiatis was very kind to me.'

'Yes,' said Berris, 'you're right, we must get Kleomenes' kids out of it. That eldest boy particularly. I think we may have to run for it. If I do, I hope to God nobody will go mucking about with my statue! How much money have we got, Erif?'

'Enough for the passage money, and bribes. Where do we go? Oh, Berris, north!'

'We might. Erif, there she is. Erif, I don't think I have ever seen her looking more beautiful!'

He stood and watched her, amazed at the new strength and beauty of her face and bearing, but Erif went to her quickly and they kissed rather hard. Erif knew she could say nothing to help, either in love or magic. But the touch of hands and lips would talk. 'We are going to get you away,' she said, after a minute. 'Yes, I know what you want to say!—you and the children.'

'You think,' said Philylla slowly, 'that the danger is as certain as all that?'

'I've been to the palace. I know.'

Philylla shivered a little. She said: 'We did not tell them at once. It was—difficult. But Sphaeros said it must be done. He and their grandmother are telling them now.' She frowned. 'I wanted to tell them myself, but the Queen would not let me. It would have been better for me to do it—being nearer Nikomedes and perhaps hurt in the same way.'

It was the first chance Erif had found to say anything. 'Is it too bad?' she said. 'Dearest, dearest, can you tell me at all?'

Philylla said: 'I don't think I know yet. Only I don't think I mind whether I live or not, for myself. That was my real life. Now it's over.'

'But it's not over!' said Erif, and Berris was beside her, saying the same thing. 'You're younger than me. You're only twenty-one. You'll get free again—as I have. I'll make you a life, sweetheart.'

'You and Berris,' said Philylla, 'you two dear—barbarians. You don't begin to know what's happened. It's not my own single life, it's not—not Panteus.' She had hesitated, but managed to say the name without a tremble of the lip. 'It's the life I was part of that is gone. I feel—hollow. My God has left me. There'll be no more Sparta. I've tried to face it as possible before, all these three years, but I suppose I never could. This is the hour I had not guessed.'

Berris and Erif had each taken one of her hands. They tried to make her feel that she was part of their life, of their God. They told her their plans. Berris had been thinking them out. The best thing would be to get her and the children down to the harbour that evening—it would be dark in an hour—and embark on almost any ship that was due to sail at dawn. Berris could certainly bribe the captain and crew to say nothing till then.

'I've no money,' said Philylla abruptly, 'nor have they. You understand I shall have to get them secretly without letting Kratesikleia know. She'd never let them go. She'd rather they were killed under her eye like Spartans! As though one hadn't got to learn retreat too! But I can do that. They'll come with me.'

'You and they shall be the guests of Marob,' said Erif, a little proudly. 'Get your things, Philylla.'

'A small bundle,' said Philylla, considering, 'for them. I'll need nothing.' And she turned.

But as she did so one of the Queen's women ran out into the courtyard and caught hold of her with a kind of flustered, half-suppressed, throaty shrieking. Philylla shook her. 'What is it? What more? The Queen?'

'No,' said the woman. 'Oh—oh, Philylla—it's Nikomedes!'

'What is it?' said Philylla in a very queer voice.

'When he heard the news about his poor father, he didn't

say anything at first, but—but he went up to the roof
and jumped off!'

Philylla asked stonily: 'Is he dead?'

'No, but he's hurt—all over—and his head, his
face—oh, God save us, the blood!' And the woman
began to throw herself about again and shriek.

'That seems to end our plans,' said Philylla. 'I'm going
to him.'

She went very quickly into the inner part of the house,
from between Erif and Berris, leaving them to grasp at
nothing. Then they both turned on the woman and pulled
her to her feet and hit her till she stopped. They wanted to
know more. But all the woman could tell them was about
every one running out to pick the boy up, hardly daring to
move him, he seemed so hurt; and all he did was to cry
and curse them and say they must let him do it, they were
his subjects now and they'd got to let him kill himself!

Erif caught her breath in horror; she hated things happening to children. It seemed a quite unnecessary piece of
cruelty. The woman went back to the house sobbing. After
a time Berris said: 'If he dies I suppose she'll come with
the little ones.'

Erif didn't answer. She was also, in a way, jeal
ous of the King's children—of the remaining Spartan
idea—which kept Philylla from coming with them to
safety. But she also loved them because Philylla loved them.
In a way Berris did that, but not gently and deliberately as
Erif did, not as a mother separated from her child could love
other children. He sometimes turned his imagination on to
them and saw them beautiful—more beautiful because
of their danger—but other times he turned his feelings of
jealousy and ownership and need of Philylla on to them and
saw them only as obstacles in his way. He recognised those
last feelings and hated them, for they were unproductive,
they stopped him working, even. But he could not always
have the other thing, the imaginative well-wishing; that
was more than human; that was—yes, god-like. He
walked up and down in the quickly lengthening shadows,
thinking that, sometimes deeply sorry for Nikomedes, aching
with imagined pain, anxious and hurt with Philylla, and
sometimes just angry. But Erif stayed still, asking herself
if she had any possible magic which would take effect here

in this Greek household, but knowing there was none. And she became rather frightened at the realisation of how deeply she loved Philylla. If anything happened to Philylla—as it would, unless—unless—And then Sphaeros came out of the house, all grey and untidy and more distracted than they had ever seen him.

He said: 'What have I done? Why did he do that? Couldn't the child have waited and thought?' And then: 'It is—it is a very horrible mess, Berris. I helped to get him on to a bed. All the time he was angry, hating us for trying to help him.'

Berris answered, rather hardly: 'You taught him to be a Stoic, you taught him not to regard his body, Sphaeros. And now he seems to have thrown his body away very completely. Those beautiful eyes and straight temples of his!' he ended, suddenly furious at the waste, his anger at that mixing with his anger at the delay and danger to his love. Then he said: 'I suppose you realise that Sosibios will be after the women and children now?'

Sphaeros turned rather white. He said: 'I was afraid that might be so. Kleomenes should have known.'

'Known—or cared. Yes,' said Berris Der. 'But I've got to get Philylla, the widow of Panteus, away, and the two younger children.'

'Why Philylla?' said Sphaeros, with an old man's finicky panic at someone else's perhaps dangerous idea. 'Why not—'

'Because I choose!' said Berris.

'Because of Agiatis,' said Erif quickly.

Sphaeros seemed to understand that. 'Tell me how I can help,' he said. 'If there are any risks I can take—naturally, I should be most willing to die for them.'

'You won't get the chance, worse luck,' said Berris grimly. Then Philylla came out again; her hands were washed, but there was a fleck of blood on the front of her dress.

Berris said: 'Are the little ones ready to go?'

She said: 'I'll bring them. But you must take them, Erif—you and Sphaeros. I must stay with Nikomedes now.'

'You shan't!' said Berris, ånd caught her up to him and kissed her hard on the lips, regardless of Sphaeros, who stared, a little wearily, as though he had already seen too much that day.

She kissed him back once with an almost stinging violence, and then shoved him away with both hands. 'No!' she said. 'Take the two children. Take them back to Sparta some day. Tell them about the New Times. Tell them about their father and—and his friends. Only—don't make it too terrible, Erif. Little Gorgo dreams so. She ought to marry young—someone kind. Oh, Erif—Erif, my darling, I don't want to leave you yet!' And for a moment she ran into Erif's open arms and sobbed against her breasts and her hair was soft against Erif's neck and her body was soft and so much too easy to hurt. And Erif felt suddenly more like a sister than a friend, more like a mother than either. Sphaeros and Berris looked on, for the moment equally out of it. This was a woman's business, the she side of things suddenly showing itself to the men, a great fish leaping out of dark water. Abruptly, Berris felt his eyes prickly with tears. He knew that Philylla, his love, must do what she thought best. And Philylla raised herself from Erif's breast and shook out her dress and gasped and smiled and said: 'I'll fetch them now. And good-bye.'

Only, then, there was a very loud knocking on the outer door and men's voices, and all at once the courtyard was full of soldiers, forty of King Ptolemy's soldiers and an officer, with written orders in his hand, and two women marched along with them, Leandris carrying her baby, and Neareta with her hands tied and her face red with anger and her dress torn as though she'd fought. Philylla said to the officer: 'What do you want?' And the officer said he had orders from Sosibios to take out and execute the mother and children of the late Kleomenes and all the women who were connected with them.

'So,' said Philylla, and she looked the officer up and down. Then he gave an order in a loud voice, and half the soldiers marched past her into the house. Sphaeros and Berris both at once rushed at the officer and began to argue. Another order. They were both violently arrested, their arms twisted behind them and their mouths gagged. Erif had said nothing. She stood very quietly beside Philylla and she saw Philylla's hands clench and quiver with rage, and her eyes, when they took Berris, struggling blindly against four of them, and kicked and twisted him into obedience, were like a growling chained bitch's when men take her puppies away.

It was then that Leandris said, sobbing, the thing she had obviously said over and over again already: 'Don't kill my baby! Why need you kill my baby!' Erif went forward quickly to take it, but she was barred off with spears.

'Saves trouble,' said the officer. 'Clear out, the lot of you. Now then, you Scythians and you old dodderer, you Sphaeros, out you go or you'll be for it too!'

And at that all three of them were grabbed and gripped and frog-marched and pitched out of the house, and the door was clanged to after them. Berris got the gag out of his mouth and ran at that door and beat on it and yelled and turned again and seized hold of a man out of the crowd who had collected outside, and screamed at him to help beat down that door! But none of the crowd were in the least willing to do anything. They laughed or made helpfully helpless remarks, both to Berris and Erif and also to Sphaeros, who was appealing to them too, and they laughed still more when the two barbarians began to drop their Greek and shriek and shout at them in some fantastic and ridiculous language. Two red-faced Scythians and an old man, whose bottoms they'd seen kicked by the King's guards! It was as good as a show. And inside there—ah, there was a pack of women being killed!

Chapter Two

IT WAS NOON OF THE next day at Canopus, and very hot; the room faced north to the sea through square openings, and naked fan-girls, alternately black and white, created an artificial breeze, cooled by the constantly watered marble of the steps. In the room itself there was a fountain playing through silver swan necks, and there was a silver statue of Dionysos resting against a rock, while birds clustered at his feet with offerings of flowers and berries. Ptolemy and Agathokles were both naked to the waist. In some ways that was a pity, as Ptolemy was beginning to get fat. There were little rolls and creases all over his body that Agathoklea found it amusing to run her fingers along. She and Metrotimé wore straight dresses of Egyptian muslin, butter-coloured and completely transparent. Nobody ate much, but they drank snow-cooled wine and dabbled their fingers in the fountain and picked at an olive or two and a few nuts. 'When do you expect him?' said Agathoklea at last.

Ptolemy smiled and said nothing, but her brother answered: 'Kottalos? Any time. Sosibios will have sent him off at dawn.' Then he too was silent and smiling a little and breathing rather fast.

Metrotimé said: 'And after that we shall be sure it has happened.' And she stared in front of her between the two men.

'We're sure now,' said Agathokles, 'when Sosibios says a thing of this kind has been done—! '

'Dear Sosibios,' said Agathoklea mechanically, 'how well he manages everything!'

'I am not sure it was supremely good management,' her brother said, 'to have Kleomenes running amuck in the streets like a mad elephant. It argues perhaps a lack of finesse, of political foresight. I had ventured to warn him myself once or twice, but there—I'm not a general!' He glanced at Ptolemy. But the Divine King was squeezing and rolling a piece of new bread in one hand, and looking towards the door. Agathokles went on: 'And not very subtle to make amends by simply killing the women.'

'And the children,' said Ptolemy, in a sudden whisper, that showed he had been listening, after all, 'and the eldest son!'

Agathoklea glanced at Metrotimé; they both remembered the episode with Nikomedes. 'Try this Thera wine, dearest,' said Agathoklea; 'it's stronger. You're looking pale.'

Then there were quick footsteps and an officer in armour came in and saluted. He was the man Erif and Berris had seen in the courtyard of the old Queen's house. 'Ah,' said Ptolemy, stretching out a hand, 'ah, my dear Kottalos. You've come all the way from Alexandria?'

'At your Divine Majesty's command,' said the man, 'to report how—'

'But sit down, sit down,' interrupted Ptolemy, 'and take your armour off. Yes, and a cup of wine before you start your report. Yes, first. Positively, you make me sweat, you look so hot!'

The man saluted again and sat down nervously on the edge of the fountain. Agathoklea went to help him to unbuckle his breastplate. 'Your Divine Majesty wished to know—' he began.

But Ptolemy interrupted again: 'You are sure you are comfortable there, Kottalos? How did you come, by horse or camel?'

'On horseback, your Majesty. My report—'

'And no accidents on the road? Nothing to be seen?' The others stared and wondered what their Divine Ruler thought he was doing. Agathokles made faces vaguely in the direction of the officer.

But Kottalos had a firm notion of his duty; Sosibios had given him his orders. He looked away from Agathoklea and Metrotimé, whose clothes embarrassed him, and went on sternly with his story. 'I took my men to the house, your Divine Majesty. There was no opposition there, and there appeared to be no signs of discontent or hostility in the streets. I had arrested two of the women already, widows of the rebels, and brought them with me. I was met in the courtyard by one of the other women.'

'Which one?' said Metrotimé quickly.

'The widow of Panteus, I was told.'

'Ah, Philylla. Erif Der's friend.'

'There were also the philosopher Sphaeros, the Scythian sculptor and the Scythian woman.'

'And what did you do to them?' Metrotimé asked, leaning forward with a rather curious smile, and swilling the wine round in her cup.

'Them? Oh, I—' He hesitated, looking from Metrotimé to the others. 'They—mm—went. It was no place for strangers. I had the house searched and the women and children brought out. They came quietly. I decided that the execution should take place in the furthest yard, beyond the store-houses and the vegetable plots, as it is more remote from the street, in case of any noise. This woman I mentioned, the widow of Panteus, helped the old Queen along and talked to her. A very fine-looking young woman, as these Dorian women go.'

The King said suddenly: 'And the children? My dear Kottalos, what we are hoping for is detail. Vivid detail.'

Kottalos frowned. He was not at all a sensitive man, but he disliked thinking of that. However, kings must have what they want. 'The smallest child of the lot did not, probably, quite realise, but she clung to her grandmother or to this other woman. The second boy tried to fight my soldiers and had to be tied up; after that he cried a good deal. It was an unpleasant duty. The eldest boy had to be helped along. He was too much hurt to go by himself.'

'Hurt?' said Ptolemy, with a queer sort of grunt, and he and the two women all stirred and moved their hands and feet a little.

'Yes, your Divine Majesty,' said Kottalos. 'He had attempted to commit suicide by jumping off the roof earlier in the evening.'

'I did not know that,' said Ptolemy. 'Sosibios had not thought it worth mentioning. No. Off the roof, you say. Walking on to a gulf of air. And he was hurt—where?'

'His head mostly, your Divine Majesty. It had been bandaged up. He said nothing, I believe, or only in whispers. This woman I spoke of went to him once or twice. I allowed that. I am not sure how much he knew of what was happening. His eyes were blurred.'

'His eyes, his eyes,' said King Ptolemy, and for a few moments his body seemed to stretch and relax rhythmically, slower than breathing.

Kottalos went on: 'We came to the further yard, and I made my arrangements. The men with the swords came out of the ranks. Then the old Queen asked, with a certain dignity, to be killed first '

'And was she?' said Metrotimé.

'No. I had my orders. The children were killed first.'

'The children first,' said Ptolemy. 'Tell me more about that. Did they struggle, Kottalos?'

'Certainly not, your Divine Majesty. My executioners are too competent. Only one stroke was needed for each. Then we executed the Queen.'

'But did no one say anything?'

'Yes, your Divine Majesty. The Queen said: "Oh, children, where have you gone?" None of the women were violent. It was all—yes, if I may say so, it was a credit to every one concerned. One or two of them cried, especially a youngish woman with an infant, one of the widows; however, when it came to her turn there was no special unpleasantness. The infant was also despatched. That other woman, Panteus' widow, was most helpful. She said nothing and did not appear disturbed, but she looked after the others one by one, laying them out decently, so that we

had practically nothing to do afterwards. A great relief,
when dealing with the other sex. After the rest were all
executed, she asked permission to withdraw a little for her
own execution. I saw no reason to refuse this, so they
went rather further from the rest of the soldiers. She then
smoothed out her dress and wrapped it tightly about her, so
that she would be certain to fall with decency, thus giving
no trouble to anyone after she was executed. A most helpful
woman.'

Kottalos ended there suddenly, with a definite and
uncomfortable feeling that his account of yesterday evening
had left out something important: for the life of him he
could not tell what. But he was certain he would never be
able to arrive at it, especially to the Divine King. Perhaps,
he thought, one day later on, in a year or two, talking it
over with some friend, or a sympathetic mistress—He
had, as a matter of fact, been considerably disturbed and
moved by one or two episodes. But these four only took
it as so much juicy sausage-meat. He looked round. No!
The Ionian was moved too. She was dabbing at her eyes.

'But surely you have more to tell us, Kottalos? Drink
and go on. I have been waiting for this all the morning.'

'Well—' said Kottalos, and wriggled uncomfortably.
'Well, your Divine Majesty, I'll try. It was almost dark
before the thing was quite finished. Obeying instructions
I had the bodies removed at night and burnt, decently but
unobtrusively. There was only a very small crowd, and
that not at all hostile, so I did not risk unpleasantness
by dispersing it. The bodies of the other rebels are still
awaiting your Divine Majesty's orders.'

'Are they?' said Ptolemy slowly. 'Are they indeed?
But Nikomedes is dust and ashes now, dry ashes scattered
on the wind. Unpossessed. Ungarlanded.'

'If I had known you had wished—' Kottalos began
nervously, but Agathokles motioned him to silence.

The King sank into a queer brooding; the fan-girls
walked up and down outside on silent feet. At last Ptolemy
raised his head and spoke again: 'So it was Sosibios in
the end who made the sacrifice. Not I. And I do not know
what Sosibios had in his heart. I never know that. Perhaps
he was not thinking of the God. Or did the boy sacrifice
himself? Did he leap off the cliff of the house as Gods

have leapt into the air and vanished in fire? There is nothing left for me to sacrifice.' And tears began to roll out of his eyes and down his cheeks, down his chest and quivering, convulsed belly.

Agathokles' face twisted and he reached out a hand to the King and said softly: 'There are always the other bodies. They are waiting for you to act. Waiting very quietly and obediently.'

Ptolemy said 'Yes,' and his hands began to pull to pieces a slice of the new bread. He thought in violent flashes of Kleomenes; of the strength of his Spartan arms, which he had never felt crushing him; of the straight and wounded look in his eyes; of his voice which had not asked for mercy; the other King. He looked up at Kottalos and said sharply: 'My orders are that the body of the rebel Kleomenes is flayed and impaled at the cross-roads beyond the Sun Gate on a stake of pine-wood. Dismiss.'

Very hastily Kottalos saluted, picked up his helmet and breast-plate and disappeared out of the room. It would be capital to get back to Alexandria that same day, and, if possible, get drunk in the evening. One needed something to take the taste of the Divine King out of one's mouth.

Ptolemy smiled and looked round at his friends 'That will end it nicely,' he said. 'Dearest Metrotimé, what are you writing?' For Metrotimé was scribbling something on tablets at her knee.

'Do let me see, darling!' said Agathoklea. 'Or isn't it proper?' And she giggled with relief.

'It's quite proper,' said Metrotimé, 'but I haven't finished it. And I don't think I ever shall.'

'Why not?'

'Oh, it's not interesting or amusing. An old-fashioned kind of poem. Or might have been going to be. But this is all there is to it:

As for thee, as for thee, child,
With great joy begotten
On the hills of Sparta:
Thy name, thy name shall be forgotten,
Thy beauty and thy wild
Eyes. And no tears starting
Shall ever—

But I oughtn't to write poems about rebels, even bad poems,

ought I!' She laughed and made one movement with her thumb and rubbed it all out.

Ptolemy leaned forward and their eyes met, as they sometimes did, across the eyes of the other two. 'When did you see him?' asked Ptolemy.

But Metrotimé only laughed again and began to tell a new story of marital tit-for-tat which she had heard from her Egyptian maid the day before. And they all started eating and drinking and being an amusing party.

Later they had in a flute-player and two dancing dwarfs with fat childish noses and cheeks. They laughed and teased the dwarfs, especially Agathokles, who pinched and made faces at the male one till he screamed. And then the divine Princess Arsinoë was announced and came in, followed at a discreet distance by four of her ladies. She was a tall, rather fierce-looking girl with yellow hair under a fillet of silver leaves—a real Macedonian princess. They all rose to greet her, but she disregarded every one except her brother. She said: 'I have heard the news from Alexandria. Now that those Spartan boys are dead, there is no reason why I should not have Sphaeros of Borysthenes for my tutor. When can he start?'

Ptolemy looked at her with his usual dislike. She had no mysteries, nothing of the goddess; she was a tough mortal and there were freckles on her arms. However, there seemed no reason to refuse this. 'He can come in a few days,' Ptolemy said. 'Make a note to send for him, Agathokles.'

Metrotimé said: 'I expect he will be in no mood to teach for a few days, divine Arsinoë. He is not so young as he was and all this will have—upset him.'

'What's the use of being a Stoic if he can't stand that!' said the princess. 'Upset! If he is, I'll tell him what I think of him and his philosophy.' And then scornfully and bitterly at her brother: 'He's got to teach me to stand you!' And she turned and went out.

Ptolemy flushed deep red and then paled slowly. Agathokles licked his lips. 'It will be extremely interesting for you, later on, taming our divine little scratch-cat. A husband—and his friends—is usually able to humble a wife who starts with her nose in the air. Yes, Arsinoë tamed will have quite a relish.' And he laughed, and Agathoklea laughed, lying back, her breasts shaking merrily.

The conversation turned again to this and that, the other news of Alexandria. An Indian priest had wandered there lately; he could stick knives into himself. They must have him over. Trade was at its best; the great harbour crammed and magnificent with shipping. Someone had said that one of the latest arrivals was a biggish boat from the north with rather curious painted sails. There were rumours of rare furs aboard—and how Agathoklea loved a nice fur!—and hemp tablets to smoulder on charcoal and make an atmosphere conducive to dreams, and smoked salmon and caviare, and pale northern amber. The ship had come from some place with a ridiculous name. No, not Olbia or Panticapaeum or Tyras. What was it? Oh yes, Marob.

Chapter Three

ALL THAT DAY BERRIS had gone on with his statue. He wouldn't eat, though he drank a good deal, and by the late afternoon Erif could see what was happening to it. The thing behind had taken shape at last and it had the flat brainless head of a bird and eyes staring to its sides, and its beak was open to tear Philylla, and its wings were closing on her greedily. It had no elk horns; there was nothing northern left in it. It was the desolation of the south, the vulture of the sand, Love changed into Death. This was the Egyptian convention, the very forms of Egypt, dissolved and recrystallised into something more potent than Egypt had made for a long time. Looking at it, Erif began to cry again till Berris turned and glared at her with his red-rimmed savage eyes. He had not slept much the night before, either, not until dawn, when he found out for certain that he could not see the bodies, that he would never see even that still image of Philylla again. Then he had slept for an hour and woke screaming—that woke Erif, screaming too—and he had gone straight to work on the thing he had dreamt of. Erif had sat and watched him. The dress she had been sewing for Philylla lay on a chest where Ankhet had folded it; every now and then she could not help seeing it; equally she could not bear to touch it and put it away. A dull pulling seemed to be going on in her mind; it was the kind of pain of her twisted ankle that time Tarrik had raped her. She called to him softly: 'Tarrik, Tarrik,

Tarrik.' But nothing happened. Perhaps he was dead too. He and Klint. Perhaps everything had stopped. She held her breath, listening to see if there was still any life. She heard the chisel tapping against the stone. She thought of cooking something, an egg. Berris might eat an egg. She did not move. She watched the pain in her mind going on, steadily increasing. No use, nothing would come to birth, not even a statue of Death and Philylla.

In the evening, when it was beginning to get dark, exactly a day and a night after, Sphaeros came in. When she saw him, Erif screamed. There was no possible reason to; she could not have thought he was anyone else; he had not frightened her. But some tough layer had been stripped off her and under it she quivered like taut gut and screamed at a touch, as it does. She said she was sorry. Berris cursed her pretty foully and went on working. Sphaeros was kind and kissed her, a very odd thing for him to do. They sat together and watched Berris; he did not attempt consolation in words. Then something came into her mind. 'Sphaeros,' she said, 'there's just one thing we can do!'

'What?' he asked.

'Phoebis' boy. Don't you remember? Gyridas is down on a farm, getting well after his fever. They forgot that. We can save him.'

'We will,' said Sphaeros.

Then Erif said in a whisper which would not disturb Berris: 'Oh, if only I'd thought of it when I saw Neareta with the soldiers! I might have said something and she'd have known it would be all right. But they killed her and she didn't know.'

'You couldn't have spoken then,' said Sphaeros. 'It would have put the child in danger. I'll get him. His father and mother and elder brother, his playmates—all taken. Yes, he has been stripped to the soul. I wonder how, being mostly helot, he will stand it.'

'But oh,' said Erif, 'I might have made her a sign and I didn't!' And instead of being something saved from destruction, the thought of Gyridas turned in her mind into a new pain. She cried quite quietly, licking up the tears that ran into her mouth, as she had done when she was a child. Then she lighted the lamps, all of them, and the different light flickered and made queer shadows on the statue, and Berris had to stop with a grunt and a sigh. Then he lay down rather suddenly, giving from the knees upward, flat on the floor among the stone dust and his scattered tools, and for him everything dimmed out into a merciful swaying dullness of all the senses, and he rested for a long time.

Quite late that evening Ankhet came into the room, bringing them food she had cooked herself. Berris did not move or speak. Nor did the other two, but she laid it out on a little table in front of them, with wine and a single lily flower in a tall glass and her best fringed napkins. Then she said: 'There is an order from Canopus about—about one of the bodies.'

'Kleomenes.' Sphaeros seemed certain.

She flushed and nodded. 'It is to be flayed and impaled at the eastern cross-roads. That has not been done for a great many years.'

'I see,' said Sphaeros, and scarcely shuddered at all.

Ankhet said suddenly: 'It is like the thing that King Set did to King Osiris in the Mystery stories.' And she went out of the room and left them.

They ate a little, and then Sphaeros said: 'Now you must try to sleep, my dear. The worst is over. After this, we shall only have to accustom ourselves to accepting it. That is comparatively easy I think I can show you some exercises for it tomorrow. In the meantime I will see about Gyridas. There is no more for you to do. Try to calm yourself. Try to stand apart from the agony. Let it alone, do not touch it. Do not think of her till you can do it without too great disturbance.' And he kissed her again and went down the stairs by himself.

But she did not sleep that night, even though she stayed in the big room and lit the lamps again so as not to wake up in the dark and see Philylla fading into it with the kind of look she had at the moment when the soldiers came into the Queen's house. Every waking destroyed the rest and quiet she had perhaps been getting from the minutes of sleep. Her head and body ached, but not enough to stop her thoughts and imagination from racing. Towards midnight Berris began to talk in his sleep and that was very painful. He had not covered the statue, so when dawn began to seep into the room, she could not help looking at it. Without Berris to control it, the thing seemed to blur and waver in front of her eyes. The bird behind seemed to move closer with its tearing beak. She could not bear it, but she did not dare to wake Berris right up, even though she thought he must be having horrible dreams. She got up and dressed and tried to read, standing by one of the windows, where there was enough light already, but her eyes were too sore with tiredness, and none of the books made sense. If this kind of thing could happen, what was the good of the world, what was the good of magic, why go on at all, why think of going back to Tarrik or Marob or her son who would have forgotten her, whom she did not know now and therefore could not love? Why imagine there was any reality in having been Spring Queen?

She looked from Berris to his statue, the god or devil he had made. For the moment he was lying very still. She stepped out quietly into the street. Very few people were up yet; during the night the lanes seemed to have emptied themselves of smells and hurry. They were fairly cool, but with odd pockets of undisturbed warm air, left over from the day before. She came into the main cross street and turned left towards the gate that led out to Lake Mareotis. It was very wearying even to walk when she was so tired already, but she had to do something. So she walked on. The sentries at the gate let her pass, and she went down to the shore of the lake and walked along it, first under the walls of Alexandria, then past market gardens and spaces of straggling tufts where goats grazed, east away from the town. The sun had risen almost straight ahead; the glare was beginning to make it difficult to see. She moved her head impatiently from side to side. Everywhere the lake had shrunk and dried away with summer, leaving a series of crusted curves of mud; beyond, it lay still and patient, waiting for rain. Quantities of birds were feeding out there, a good many ducks and moorfowl and cranes, but mostly the tall rosy birds, the flamingoes of the African marshes, great flocks of them the colour of the sunrise that had almost faded out of the eastern sky, that was giving place to the thick blue dazzle of day. The rosy birds stood on one leg, jutting their long necks and crooked beaks, fishing the muddy shallows. They paid no attention to Erif Der.

She took off her sandals and began to walk out towards them. She remembered there were leeches in Lake Mareotis, but she did not mind. For a long way out it was little more than ankle deep, and there were patches of slimy weed. The birds began to move from in front of her; the cranes unfolded white wings and lifted themselves away to the far side; the flamingoes stalked slowly to right and left; the duck squattered towards the middle of the lake and settled again. It was cool underfoot. It reminded her suddenly of the salt marshes of the secret road; it reminded her of Murr, dead a long time ago, dead and forgotten as Philylla would be forgotten. She sobbed aloud as she walked out. The tears began running down her face again. She felt as though she had been used to that for years now. She remembered that she had once been happy. How was that? What did it feel like? And then she blamed herself and mocked herself for not being utterly happy in those impossible times. She had been frightened of happiness. Instead of taking it and accepting it, she had looked forward timorously to its inevitable ending—as though she could know then how it would end!—and used up her strength and thought in trying to ward off evil before evil was yet there. She had let herself be disturbed and driven away from happiness by countless things which were now not even noticeable. Even two days ago she might have been happy! She had been afraid of the jealousy of unknown powers, and had tried to propitiate them by spoiling her happiness, by cutting off a part of it to sacrifice to them. Today she was afraid of no power, not even death, now she knew what it was. She had doubted and feared and compromised and distrusted her happiness. So it was taken from her and it would never come back.

She saw now that she was a good way from the shore, walking slowly through water almost up to her knees, dragging her skirt in it. The rosy birds had stepped away with their long legs. There was only one left out of the whole flock. She was not at all surprised, because she suddenly remembered what bird it must be. She went up to it and said: 'I don't know what to do, mother. Please tell me.'

The bird said: 'I've been waiting for you, Erif. But I knew you'd come in the end, so that didn't matter. Stop crying, Erif. There, that's better.'

'Do you know what's happened to me, mother, all these

years since you turned into a bird and we cut ourselves and mourned for you?'

'Quite enough, Erif. You're Spring Queen, as your father meant you to be.'

'You know what I did to father?'

'Yes, darling, you had to. Men are so stupid sometimes, aren't they. And sometimes they're all one wants, for ever. I'm glad your Corn King is that kind of man. I always hoped he would be, even when your father was silly about him.'

'Yes, but he isn't here and I haven't seen him for six years. And I haven't been Spring Queen for six years either.'

'Oh yes, you have. You are going through the agony of the Spring Queen now. You have to do that, you know, before the really important thing happens.'

'Nothing more is going to happen to me now, mother. I don't see how it can. The important thing has happened and it has broken and smashed everything else, for me and Berris, so that we just can't move. I've got stuck, mother; my life has got stuck and broken.'

'That's part of it for both of you. You have to be broken before you can be put together again. That was what they did to King Osiris here, a long time ago. That was what happened to your father when he was made into the corn. It's curious, isn't it? Do you like my new feathers, Erif? You always used to like pretty things.' The bird stretched out its rosy wings and slid its neck admiringly across them.

'Yes, mother, they're lovely. But even if something's going perhaps to start again with me—and I don't see how it possibly can—Philylla is dead and I loved her and she was younger than me and so beautiful. And my first baby is dead too. Both those things are real, not just in my mind. Each of them is—a kataleptike phantasia. And an utter waste.'

The bird laid its neck caressingly on Erif's; its pink feathers were cool and soft, but with an odd pliancy, a pleasant roughness of texture against human skin. It said: 'I don't know about anyone except the people I love myself, and most of all you, because I love you best of all, Erif. And it's no good answering when one doesn't know. I expect somebody knows, or will some time. I wish you weren't so unhappy, my darling; but I think you've got to be, and I know it won't go on.'

'I'm not so unhappy as I was half an hour ago. It's funny.'

'When somebody one loves is dead, the worst time is just afterwards, when the final thing is done, when their bodies are buried or burnt.'

'Philylla was burnt, mother.'

'Up to then they have still some kind of reality. They are still in a way themselves. It's you who make me talk about reality, Erif, though it's a thing that always puzzled me. But when that happens there's a sort of thud, isn't there? Something heavy comes down on one. It echoes for a long time after that, but fainter.'

'Yes, mother. That's the worst time. I suppose it does get fainter. I suppose one does stop keeping faith with one's friends after they've been dead for a little while.'

'I don't think it's that,' said the bird. 'Keeping faith has two sides, and this is only in your single heart. Don't cry, darling; that's not as bad as it sounds, and it'll make your head ache. You've got something difficult to do still.'

'Have I? What?'

'Well, there's the other part of the oracle, you see. Hadn't you remembered?'

'Was it true, then, in spite of what Hyperides said?'

'Oh, Hyperides was right too. You may tell him I said so, not that he'll believe you. Oracles are a clumsy way of doing things and they often go wrong. It would be much more sensible if King Apollo saw to things himself rather more. He used to, so perhaps he'll start again some day.'

'Then what have I got to do, mother?'

'Don't worry, Erif. You'll do it. You see, you'll have to, because you're the Spring Queen. Now, darling, you'll catch cold if you stay with me any longer. Your dress is wet through. I don't like these Greek dresses you wear now nearly so much as the old ones, but you're doing your hair very prettily. Kiss Berris from me. I'm proud of him. And of you, Erif. It's much more interesting to be a woman, really. Good-bye till next time, my darling.' The bird lifted its long legs and stalked off to the others, keeping a look-out for any oddments in the way of fish or newts. Erif turned back to the shore and paddled slowly out of the water. She sat down on the bank, pulled the leeches off her feet and put on her sandals. Then she walked back towards Alexandria. She was not quite sure what had been happening.

She went in through the same gates and back up the street. Every one was up now, and busy and noisy; they jostled into her. She came back to the house. On the stairs Ankhet met her and said: 'They have done that to the body of King Kleomenes. At dawn today.' But she did not answer. In the big room Berris was at work again. She heard the knocking of the mallet against the chisel and the chipping of the chisel against the stone before she got there. When she came in he looked round at her once and then went on. 'I've been down to Lake Mareotis,' she said. 'I met mother there.'

'Lie down,' said Berris. 'You've been out in the sun without a veil. You don't know what you're talking about.'

'But I did,' she said, lying down all the same. 'She's turned into a flamingo. She said she was going to, ever so long ago, in the tent. This time she told me a lot of things.'

'Do stop,' said Berris. 'All this has gone to your head. I don't blame you, Erif, but it makes it difficult to work, so keep quiet.'

'She said I was to kiss you from her, Berris,' she said. 'Do come over and let me. I feel somehow as if I couldn't stand up.'

Reluctantly Berris came over and stood beside her. She looked up at him, pursing her mouth. He bent and kissed her quickly. He wondered whether he ought to send for a doctor; perhaps she should be bled. He put down his chisel. She seemed to be trembling rather. The edge of her dress was muddy. He heard Ankhet on the stairs, probably bringing them up some food again. He called to her quickly and even anxiously. She came in and stood beside him, but Erif did not seem to notice her. 'Berris,' she said once, in an odd sort of hissing whisper. Her hands clenched tight on the sides of the couch and her eyes began to blink heavily. He knelt down beside her, suddenly terrified. 'Erif,' he said, 'Erif darling, what's happening?'

The whisper sank lower, as though it were being dragged out of her painfully, the last remains of consciousness. 'The Snake to the Dead,' she said thickly, so that he scarcely recognised her voice. Then her eyes snapped tight and a hard shaking took her body as though she were in the grip of something invisible.

'Erif!' cried Berris. 'Erif, oh Erif, don't!'

But Ankhet seized him suddenly by the arm and pulled him back. 'Let her be!' she said. 'Let her be or you will hurt the khu. This will stop in a little.'

She kept hold of him for a few minutes longer, stopping him every time he made a movement towards his sister, and by and bye the shaking grew more spasmodic, slacking down for moments and then reviving, at last slacking down altogether. The body of Erif Der lay still, only breathing deeply at long intervals. The tension of the arms and face seemed to be relaxed. 'There,' said Ankhet, 'the khu has gone. It will come back. Only we must wait and not let her be disturbed.' She drew the curtain across the window immediately above Erif's head, so that no direct sunlight should come on her.

'But do you know what's happened to her?' said Berris, and then suddenly he sobbed: 'Oh, Ankhet, if she goes too—!'

'But it is all right,' said Ankhet slowly. 'Nothing will happen to her. I will try to tell you in Greek words, Berris Der, but it is very difficult, and I do not know rightly even in my own head how it is. The knowledge has been lost. But I believe it is like this.' She paused and counted on her fingers. 'There are seven, eight, nine parts of a man or woman. It is quite easy to say what they are called, but not so easy at all to think of them separately. But I will try. There are the body and the shadow. There are the heart, the soul, and the spiritual body, which is a different thing again, but does not get much separated during life. There is the name and the power. I do not know if names matter very much among you barbarian people, and I do not know if you have power, though I think she must have.' Ankhet slanted her head towards the couch. 'Then there is the kha, that is, the double, one's own image which is always separate, but yet it cannot be taken away, any more than a reflection in a looking-glass can be taken away. And there is the khu, that is, the spirit. And both the kha and the khu can go on journeys and do things, and the khu can enter into other bodies or make itself a body to do its will. Do you understand at all, Berris Der?'

'I understand the words,' said Berris, 'but not what they mean. And I don't see what they have to do with my sister.'

'She has split up,' said Ankhet patiently. 'People do that, you see, when something has hit them very hard, and some people learn to do it when they choose. I am not quite certain how she is split, but I have seen something like this happen before, and I think she has sent out her khu, her spirit, to take or make some other body and make it do something she wants it to do. Do you know what that would be?'

Berris said slowly, trembling a good deal himself: 'The last thing she said was: "The Snake to the Dead." '

'Well, that will be it,' said Ankhet, with a suddenly satisfied tone in her voice. 'Do you know what dead?' He shook his head. 'But that doesn't really matter. It is her concern. But if we hear of any snake during the next day or two, we may be certain that it is Erif. Now, all we have to do is to see that the rest of her is not disturbed or wakened before the right time, and that the khu is not hindered from coming back.'

'What must I do?' said Berris, for the moment at least relying on her.

'Do?' said Ankhet. 'I think you had better have some breakfast. I was bringing it up with me. It is a pity she did not have any before she started on this journey. However, it will do her no harm, though she may be hungry when she wakes. And after breakfast you had better go on working. And if anyone comes in, do not let them try to wake her, however much they may want to and however much they may say I have been telling you the thing that is not so.'

'I see,' said Berris. 'I think I quite understand. You are sure it will not disturb her if I go on working?'

'Oh, quite sure,' said Ankhet smiling, and she brought him in his breakfast.

Later that morning Sphaeros came in. He was very much worried when he saw Erif and wanted to send for a doctor or try to wake her up, but Berris would not let him. He said he had found out from the woman with whom Phoebis and Neareta had lodged where the boy Gyridas was, and he was going at once to fetch him. And then he said: 'You know what they did to my pupil Kleomenes? Well, a very strange thing seems to have happened. There is a great snake which has wound itself round his body and the stake. It keeps the birds from pecking at his head. I have not seen it yet, but I have heard on good authority that it is so. It is very curious. One knows that dead bodies breed worms and beetles, but I do not think that can be the explanation here. Berris, you are looking very ill! What is the matter?'

'Nothing,' said Berris, 'but I think I have heard that the bodies of heroes in old days were guarded by snakes or even changed into snakes. I have heard that a snake is the easiest thing a man can turn into. Or a woman.'

'Superstitions,' said Sphaeros, frowning. 'I did not think you would believe these old wives' tales, Berris!'

'All the same,' said Berris, 'I hope they will not drive off the snake or hurt it.'

'They are more likely to worship it,' said Sphaeros, and sighed. 'They will do that for Kleomenes when he is dead for the sake of a serpent, who would not lift a finger to help him when he was alive for the sake of his ideas.'

'I am going to make some more pictures of him,' said Berris.

'Are you?' said Sphaeros wearily, turning to go. He was not interested in pictures, even those ones.

So for three days the snake guarded the body of Kleomenes, and every day more and more men and women came with offerings and expiations. Sosibios was very angry and tried to drive them away, but they would not go, so he thought he had better acquiesce, and refused to concern himself with the affair at all. Word was sent to the divine Ptolemy at Canopus, and he sent back in return a very curious offering which was taken to the body by a solemn procession of Alexandrians. And in the meantime the flayed corpse dried and blackened and shrivelled, but it was so heaped with flowers and sweet leaves that no one saw it, but only the great bright-eyed snake above, coiled on the stake and weaving its head from side to side. For three days people came from town and country to see this and whisper and pray. And for three days Erif Der lay on the couch, unmoving except for the rare deep breaths that lifted and filled her body and then let it sink again. For the first day Berris worked and watched, taking long spells from his work to kneel beside the couch, staring. But the second and third day he worked steadily without

interruption, because other watchers had come, and it was
they who stood or knelt beside her, watching and waiting
for the khu to come back and Erif to open her eyes.

Chapter Four

ANKHET AND HER husband had gone early in the morning
with their offering to Kleomenes and the snake. She came
back hurriedly and called Berris to come down to her. She
seized hold of him and said: 'The snake has gone! When
I went, it was there, hanging on the cross-piece of the stake
and moving its head, and then in a moment it had glided
down and was among us. It was going somewhere, and it
knew where it was going, for its eyes were bright and fixed
like polished sards. We all gave way to it and blessed it,
and no one has trodden over its track in the dust. But
now, Berris Der, I think your sister will open her eyes
very soon.'

Berris ran up the stairs again. He looked at Erif; there
was no change yet. 'I wonder if I'd better shave,' he said.
For it was four days since he had.

'You'd certainly better!' said Hyperides. He was looking
at the big squared charcoal drawing for one of the new pictures. It was amazing how much better they often looked in
that state. Like one's own books before they were published,
he thought.

Berris found a razor among his paint-brushes. 'Let me
know when the change comes,' he said.

'Surely,' said Hyperides; but neither he nor Sphaeros
thought there was likely to be a change. He was resolved
to get a doctor in that evening whatever the others said. He
had made inquiries and heard of a first-class Greek doctor
who would have nothing to do with Egyptian superstitions.
The catalepsy had already lasted unbroken for three days;
it could not be allowed to go on much longer. If this had
been happening in Marob he might almost have accepted
the fantastic explanation, but in Alexandria, that city of
learning which he had always longed to go to—no!
Even Tarrik thought it most unlikely. What had his Erif,
his Spring Queen, to do with Kleomenes?

Gyridas was making a rush plait. It was rather terrible.
That was the only thing he had cared to do since he had
been brought back. He looked well enough and answered

when he was spoken to, but unless he was definitely told to do something else—and there were times when he had to be told two or three times before he seemed to hear—the only thing he wanted to do was to make elaborate rush plaits and knots. The woman at the farm had taught him. When they were finished he gave them to Klint, who left them about or undid them or used them to play horses with Ankhet's little girl. When the two children were playing, Gyridas used to stand watching them or following them about. Once or twice they tried to get him to join in, but he couldn't play properly, so after that they ignored him.

Klint-Tisamenos was already completely bilingual, and had now, in two days, picked up a good many Egyptian words. He liked being called by his Greek name here, and had escaped out of the house at least three times and been retrieved, talking to amused people in the street. He had begun bothering Hyperides and his father to take him to see the lighthouse, which the little girl had told him about. They made him keep quiet in the big room, and so he did, although by now he was quite used to that sleeping lady, whom they said was his mother, and not a bit afraid of her.

Tarrik was kneeling beside her, watching her face. Even still, it was horribly frightening that she breathed so rarely; he had tried to time his breathing with hers, but could not do it. He felt it stiflingly hot in the room, even with all curtains drawn and the floor sprinkled with water every half-hour. The smell of the paints bothered him too, but there was no stopping Berris. Berris would not cover the statue, either. And it was terrible, though in a way very beautiful. But it seemed larger than the room, so that there was no place for both it and several living people there; it seemed to be forcing every one out. Tarrik wore a Greek tunic, the finest linen Ankhet could get, but it was belted with the gold belt of linked fishes which Berris had made once. Round his neck he was wearing a curious jewel of gold and red enamel which one of his metal-workers had made for him. It was based on corn ears and a springing or dancing beast, some kind of tiger or wild cat. It made Berris suddenly want to try his hand again on metal-work; he could not allow some unknown man in Marob to do as well as that without doing better himself!

Tarrik called out sharply, and the others all looked up and dropped what they were doing, except Gyridas, who went on plaiting rushes in his corner, talking rapidly to himself under his breath, as he usually did now. 'What is it?' said Sphaeros.

'She took two breaths quickly,' Tarrik said. Disdallis came over and looked at her intently, passing a hand once or twice near to and in front of her shut eyes. Again Erif Der breathed, and there seemed to be a faint creeping of colour into her pale cheeks. When she saw that, Disdallis went to the head of the stairs and called Ankhet, asking her, in bad Greek, to bring Tisamenos up with her.

Disdallis was wearing a green and cream-coloured linen dress and no coat; her knife, too, had green shark-skin round the hilt. When she had heard that the Chief had become so certain of Marob and himself that he was going to bring Erif back and make her certain too, Disdallis had gone to him and said she must come with him. It was possible that they might have to bring Erif back against her will or out of enchantments; if so, he would need her. Tarrik had agreed and taken her with him, leaving Kotka and Linit to carry on his powers; but he had gone after Plowing Eve and meant to be back before midsummer. Linit's next child would be born by then, and while he was away she should choose herself a husband from the best of Marob, who would know that she was a well-ploughed and sun-blessed field, and honour her for it.

Disdallis had been very sick on the voyage, and found Alexandria a most alarming place, but she liked Ankhet. They had not been able to discover at once where Erif and Berris were. There had been formalities to go through, and the whole place was disturbed. Tarrik had asked for King Kleomenes and the Spartans, which, in the circumstances, had been the worst possible thing to do, so he and Hyperides had been put through a long cross-examination. The police had done their best to bully him into bribing them heavily, but by that time the King of Marob was rather angry and suddenly decided to be forceful himself. Even so, they were delayed a good deal and then they found the Spring Queen—as they did find her. Disdallis thought it was as well she had come with the men. She consulted Ankhet and went with her to see the snake. It certainly appeared to her that the snake had turned its head towards her and flickered its tongue. At any rate, she was fairly satisfied. And the wooden star on Tarrik's chest burnt and quivered.

Ankhet came up, bringing Klint-Tisamenos, rather cross at having been disturbed in the middle of a game and looking ridiculously like Tarrik. Berris cut himself and swore; he had nearly finished shaving. Hyperides and Sphaeros both came nearer. Hyperides had been very nice to the old man, and listened to him expounding Stoic doctrine without making anything but respectful and friendly comments. Already Sphaeros was more like himself, more pulled together, more able to smile and tell little stories with an obscure philosophical joke at the end; Hyperides had laughed and told Tarrik he was going to set up as a doctor. Now the two of them stood at Erif's feet and watched. 'Perhaps,' said Hyperides suddenly, 'there may be a force of some kind in all of us believing that she will wake. It might be worth trying, Sphaeros.' 'Yes,' said Sphaeros, 'it might become real. A very dear woman, Hyperides.' And Hyperides thought how little her face had changed in the four years since he had seen her last. The thing which definitely had changed was his point of view towards her and Tarrik. He had not wanted then to be in any way instrumental in giving her back to her husband. Now he wanted more than anything to see them together.

A perceptible tremor came into Erif's hands; it spread upwards to her body. Her breathing became irregular and quick. Berris said: 'Who should she see first?' and mopped the cut on his chin with a painting rag. Disdallis and Ankhet glanced at one another, and then Disdallis said firmly: 'Klint.' Tarrik agreed. 'Klint,' he said, 'you are to stand by your mother's head—here, this side. Understand?' Klint frowned, not much liking the idea. However, he went there and stood with his feet apart and hands behind his back. The others stood round, all except Gyridas. 'Quiet!' said Ankhet, 'it is coming back.'

Now tides of crimson began to flood over Erif's face and neck; the trembling became more violent and then ceased. She breathed short and hard; her eyelids twitched and so did her mouth. There were moments when she was almost smiling, moments when it looked as though she were playing with them, frightening them and trying not to laugh herself.

She seemed to round out, to look younger, and at the same time as though she had been through some solid physical exertion, for there were small beads of sweat on her neck and temples. She gasped and opened her mouth as though she were trying to speak, and every one leaned forward, eager to catch what she should say, except Klint, and he tautened and braced himself like someone in front of a big wave. He managed not to say anything, but he turned his head towards his father, and Tarrik put a hand on his shoulder, thinking suddenly how young he was after all.

Then Erif Der laughed low to herself like a bride laughing in her sleep at some delicious dream, induced by some yet more delicious touch. She laughed louder, as though it were irresistible: as the actor in the Corn Play must laugh when he wakes again after Death and Winter. Then she was still, but her eyelids flickered and came half open and then fully open. She yawned and began to stretch as a cat stretches, rippling every separate muscle and joint of toes and fingers, feet and hands, legs and arms; her body arched and relaxed; she breathed deep. She looked at solemn Klint and said: 'I suppose it's very silly of me, but I can't help thinking you're my baby.' Klint said, wonderfully steadily: 'You're my mother. I'm Klint-Tisamenos. I'm not a baby. Good morning, mother.' And he stooped and pecked at her nose with a small, funny kiss. She shut her eyes and then opened them again, as though to verify these curious phenomena. She said, mostly to herself: 'That seems to be a kataleptike phantasia.' Then she turned her head a little, and she was looking at Tarrik. It seemed to be a completely satisfying look between the two of them. As he moved, she swung herself up from the hips, her breasts and mouth towards him. Hyperides said to Berris: 'The Spring Queen appears to be saved too, but I'd give my ears to know just how it has happened!'

'She's changing,' said Berris. 'Hyperides, she's changing every moment. It's all dropping off her.'

'What is?' whispered Hyperides.

And Berris jerked his thumb back over his shoulder at the statue of Death and Philylla.

Then Gyridas came out of his corner and the rush plait dropped from his hand. He plucked shyly at Sphaeros and whispered: 'Did you see?'

'What?' said Sphaeros, looking at him a little vaguely.

'The snake!' said Gyridas, 'the great coloured snake. It came into the room and touched me. I think it was wearing a crown. But it was a real snake, Sphaeros; it felt real. Then it went to her. I would like it if she touched me as the snake did.' He was speaking louder now and had come forward, looking up at Erif.

She walked a step out of Tarrik's arms. She took the boy's right hand in hers and laid her left hand on his head. 'You're a Spartan, Gyridas,' she said, 'one of the rest of them. Take heart, Gyridas, stand up, look up, you are becoming one of the men who can stare the world in the eyes!'

As she said it, Gyridas did stand straighter, and stretched and smiled and seemed to be trying to adapt himself. He had a look of his father that none of them had seen before. 'Yes,' he said, 'yes! That was what I thought the snake said to me! I'm to be one of them for always. I'm going back to Sparta. Sphaeros!' He turned suddenly on the old man. 'My father killed one of the ephors at the beginning of the New Times. When the next New Times come, I shall take heart, I shall break the laws too!'

Disdallis whispered to Hyperides: 'Do you remember seeing this happen before?' 'You mean to your husband, by Tarrik, after his coming back?' 'Yes,' said the witch, laughing quietly in her throat. 'Poor Hyperides, you've got to believe it again!'

Klint-Tisamenos said to Gyridas: 'I saw a snake too. What snake was it? I don't like snakes—there aren't any at home.'

Gyridas said: 'I think it was the snake that guarded my King Kleomenes. I don't see what other snake it could have been.'

'Hyperides said that was silly and I wasn't to bother about it,' observed the smaller child, 'but this was a real snake. It went past me. I wonder where it's gone.'

No one said anything at once, then Hyperides asked: 'Did anyone else see the snake?'

Disdallis said: 'I thought I heard something coming along the floor.' But she was the only one.

Erif said: 'I can't quite remember about this snake. I think I've been asleep for a long time, and now everything is rather different. I half remember a snake. It hung in the sun, didn't it—somewhere?'

'On the pine stake. Over King Kleomenes.' It was Gyridas who answered her.

'Yes, and there were people all round making a noise, but the snake didn't understand what they said. It was afraid of them; it was glad when the night came, and they went, and the sun went. Poor snake, it was tired of coiling so tight. It was afraid of the smell of all those people and afraid of the great birds that swooped, and still more it was afraid of the thing underneath it. But it had to go on. For the sake of—of what? Who told me about the snake?' She looked all round her, frowning and puzzled. Then she said: 'Tarrik, you know King Kleomenes is dead? I can't remember how much you know.'

'Yes,' said Tarrik, 'I knew. He killed himself for his honour and for Sparta.'

Gyridas said: 'He died for Sparta. He died for the people.'

'But he did not save the people,' said Sphaeros with a deep sigh.

'I don't know,' Gyridas said. 'He must have died and saved something—mustn't he?'

Nobody answered him, but Berris said: 'Kings don't always save their own people. Not at once anyway. By the way, Hyperides, you notice that the oracle has been fulfilled?'

'In some respects,' said Hyperides, 'but I never denied that coincidences do occur! If it has, Apollo presumably knows what people Kleomenes died for.'

He and Berris and Tarrik were all standing together now. Erif sat on the couch, still dazed and smiling, and her son, who seemed to have decided that he rather liked her, sat beside her dangling his brown legs. Tarrik said: 'My Spring Queen has been given back to me. Also, I did not have to die myself, though I thought, when she went away, that I would most likely have to. Because death had been brought into the seasons. Perhaps Kleomenes of Sparta has died for Marob.'

'It is as the boy said,' Hyperides answered him. 'One doesn't know. Possibly it may become clearer in time. In the meanwhile the great thing is to preserve an attitude of scepticism.'

For a time none of them spoke. Erif had got Klint to come and sit on her knee; she was asking him questions and at the same time stroking her chin with extraordinary pleasure against the tips of his golden-brown curls. Berris said: 'I wonder whether she has quite forgotten Philylla.' And his face stayed for a time old and strained and bitter among the happiness of the others. For even Sphaeros was glad, because of what had happened to Gyridas. Berris had been glad to see his friends—very glad to see Tarrik—and for a time relief at his sister's return had filled him completely. But now again he was becoming blackly absorbed in the pointlessness of life.

For four days he had been at work almost solidly, exhausting himself of all other feelings. Or not, perhaps, even going through such a human process as that. Because feelings did not belong to what he was doing. While he was at work he had become again the little man on the vase, not happy, not hoping or loving, but in some odd way content and apart and observant. Now the other side of him asserted itself. He could see nothing but the terrible plain fact that Philylla whom he had loved for seven years was dead. Seven years of his life had been more or less steeped in the consciousness of her presence, near or far. Now they were wiped out, wasted; he could not think of them any longer. Reality and beauty had been taken out of past and present, and the substitute was this dull, hopeless pain; he saw nothing else in the future. Berris Der looked at the world and found it evil, and promised himself to return its evil with evil of his own. He looked at his statue and got some momentary satisfaction; that was a slap on the mouth for the kind and hopeful people who thought everything must come right in the end if only one waited patiently! He had made a portrait of what there really was at the end. But did anyone seriously hope? Yes, probably always the quite young. And the saved. He would have to make something worse before he could get at them. He would, some day. Once, a very short time ago, Berris Der had been innocent—not hurting, not wanting to hurt. Now he knew the innocence had dropped off him. He did want to hurt.

He went to his pictures and turned them over, so that

they faced out into the room. Two of them were quite finished. Tarrik came and looked with him; he had not done that satisfactorily before, because he had been so preoccupied about Erif. Now, for a time, he could leave her with the child.

The first picture was of the feast at the prison, the last eating together. Berris had made the two helot servants tell him about it, and he had kept more or less to the grouping, though he altered the room so as to get three windows across the back of his picture. The King was in the centre, with Panteus beside him, leaning against his breast. Berris had made Panteus look rather young, more as he had seen him in Sparta at the end of the first year, when he had wrestled with the King in the open field, the boys of his class watching. That picture was grave and balanced; the fringed Egyptian cloaks drooped heavily off the pale bodies of the King and the twelve Spartiates, in rich and sombre colours touched with gold and only lightened where the three windows threw a curtained shining down on to them. There was food on the tables, picking up the same colours. The Spartans drank wine and broke bread with curious fixed gestures which pleased Berris now, looking at them.

The second was a much smaller picture, less grave and static, and in a different range of colours. Hippitas riding on the colt, with the others round him waving swords and shouting, and the crowd behind them at each side shouting too and waving branches and coloured cloths. The one short moment of triumph before the end, yet too violently tensed to have any possible duration. The tension was expressed in a squareness and angularity of muscle and movement, and even in a sky strip heavily and threateningly blue between white houses.

The third was the picture of the death of the men, with Panteus fallen over Kleomenes. Berris had felt suddenly uncertain while he was doing it, and so only those figures were finished. The others were all sketched in, with crossed and twisted arms and legs, sometimes a foot or an elbow jutting into the foreground and meticulously drawn. Behind, sketched roughly, were the wooden skeletons of the market booths.

The next he turned over was the squared charcoal drawing

of the death of the children. It had been the hardest to do, and had been fidgeting him with its problems and implications even while he had been tackling the other three. The women were mourning over the dead eldest son, the boy Nikomedes, one older woman and one younger, Kratesikleia and Philylla. It was a curious parallel to one of his earlier pictures of the mother and grandmother mourning over the hanged King Agis, who had been only so few years older than Nikomedes. The figures of the women were beautiful, and the head of the old Queen was finished in exquisite and painful wrinkles, but he had not yet faced making that final portrait of Philylla. He had tried; his hand and mind had been willing; but some part of him had shuddered away and spoilt his craftsmanship. So far he had not been able to regard her too as so much material for his work—less now than when she had been alive. He turned that one back quickly with its face to the wall.

There was one more small sketch of the stake with its cross-piece and the snake coiled on it. The body was hidden altogether. Round the margin he had drawn the growing vine which King Ptolemy had sent, and the cup, and then the hammer which had driven in the stake, in through the flayed flesh of the King. Tarrik took this out of his hands to look at it more closely. He had commented a good deal on all the pictures, but though it was mostly praise, and intelligent praise at that, and praise from a friend, Berris had paid no attention. 'What are you going to do with all these?' said Tarrik at last.

Berris said: 'They are part of a story. I made them for—her. Anyone can have them now. The first lot are in Sparta, or should be. These had better go to them.' Then he called across the room: 'Oh, Gyridas, do you want my pictures?'

Gyridas said very quickly: 'Yes!' And then: 'I'd take them home. I'd show them to—to anyone there is. Berris Der, do you really mean me to have them?'

Berris nodded: 'In about a week. I must finish them off, Gyridas. Then you will have to tell me if I have made good likenesses of your father and Nikomedes.' He watched to see how much the boy would wince, but he stood it almost without moving.

Erif had been looking at the pictures too. She said:

'The charcoal one is wonderfully good of Philylla, Berris. One can almost see her moving. Why haven't you gone on with her? And why did you turn it to the wall just now? I wanted to look at it longer.' There was a queer, silvery quality about her voice, as though she were still not quite awake. Tarrik wondered how long that would last. He thought he would be able to wake her without hurting her; he thought he would be able to substitute some intellectual acceptance—the kind of thing he had got from Hyperides—for this magical one before it ended. He would be able to communicate his own certainty.

He said now: 'When you have finished your pictures, let us go home, Berris. The Spring Queen and I must be there by midsummer.'

'I'll come with you,' said Berris. 'I want to do some metal-work again. I think I shall marry Essro. I am sure it makes her unhappy not to be married, and she will be able to imagine I am like my brother. She will think of my pictures as she thought of the secret road. And I may as well have some children.'

'That is a very good idea,' said Tarrik, 'and then she will stop being frightened of me.'

'And the statue?' Sphaeros said. 'I know what I would do with that if I were you, Berris Der.'

'What?'

'I would break it. It ought to be broken. Things like that are only disturbing, and men are enough disturbed. It is not reality, but only an image distorted by pain. Break it, Berris!'

Berris grinned with hard lips. 'I might have done that five years ago, Sphaeros. I would have thought how right, how good Sphaeros is! But he isn't right. And my statue is meant to be disturbing, it is meant to break up all kinds of little realities which ordinary men and women have made for themselves, and little calmnesses which philosophers have made for them. It appears to be successful. I am glad you hate it, Sphaeros! Between now and then I will think of the right thing to do with it and the right place for it to go. Are you coming back to Marob, Sphaeros?'

Sphaeros shook his head. 'No,' he said. 'You go back to Marob and the future, Tarrik and Erif and Berris. I must stay here with the past. I am going to be tutor to

Princess Arsinoë, as I was to Kleomenes and Eukleidas, and to Nikomedes and Nikolaos. It all happens over and over again. But Gyridas—' He looked round uncertainly. He was thinking that Alexandria would be no place for that boy, even with the pardon he was almost sure he could get for him.

But Hyperides said: 'I'm going to Athens, which seems to be rather completely the present, because my play's to be acted there this summer. And I'll take Gyridas with me. Then he and his pictures can go back to Sparta when it's safe.'

'You won't find you can keep away from Marob,' Tarrik said. 'You know, Hyperides, you did better work there than you've ever done in your life. I made you!'

'Yes, Tarrik,' said Hyperides, 'and that's why I've got to get away from you, to see that I can work by myself. But I'll come back to Marob often in the summer, to ride through the future with you and Erif! Keep a good horse for me, Tarrik.'

'After I come back, there will be a good season in Marob,' said Erif suddenly, standing beside the witch Disdallis, an arm round her neck, 'and dancing and marriages and new songs and new things made. Everything will go on again.'

'And now,' said Klint-Tisamenos, 'can I go out? Will you take me out, mother, if no one else will? I want to see the lighthouse!'

Chapter Five

KING PTOLEMY WAS having a supper-party at Canopus on the night of the full moon. There were tables and couches set in the marble square of the garden, between the fountains and the statues, under the palms and holm oaks and bong trees. Dancers and flute-players wandered about from one group to another, in and out of the deep shadows; they caught fireflies and let them spark about in the dances; they carried heavily scented long garlands of jasmine and water-lilies. Agathoklea had brought her mother, and Oenanthe had brought a very special little dancer, a Jewess she had discovered and bought in the docks, who could imitate the sailors of every country in every stage of love-making. Oenanthe had taken rather a fancy to Kottalos, and Kottalos was divided between the

certainty that his fortune was assured if—And yet, on the
other hand—The divine Ptolemy and his friends made
life very complicated for a simple officer of the guards.

Sphaeros was there. He had said good-bye to his friends.
He must not regret them nor wish life had been otherwise.
He had new duties. He watched his present pupil, the blonde
Princess Arsinoë; she had received him with a fierce pride,
a kind of malice against the world; it was difficult to be
sure how to deal with that. What was she thinking now?
Glancing towards him with that same look of hurt malice
from between two of her maids of honour, girls not much
older than herself. He trusted they would withdraw before
the end of the party—if it was going to be like most of
Ptolemy's parties.

Something seemed to be amusing Sosibios. He grinned
to himself and ate rather fast and not very fastidiously.
Metrotimé sent one of her girl-friends to find out what it
was all about. After sitting on his knee and being rather
intimately pinched and tickled, she discovered the secret,
and shortly afterwards found her way back to Metrotimé.
'My dear,' she said, shaking herself, 'he pinches like a camel,
the fat old wretch! And all he's got to grin over is a silly
letter from Greece. The King's party in Sparta have gone
and murdered their magistrates, and he's laughing because
they're just too late. That's all! Dearest, lend me a pin.
He's torn my gathers right out at the shoulder. And his
breath! What he wants is a good wash—with soap.' She
laughed and stuck the pin in cleverly. She was thinking that
if this Greek news hadn't come too late, and if Kleomenes
of Sparta had gone back—well, there wouldn't have been
any snake or any processions or any new hero to whisper and
shiver about in the hot afternoons. But Metrotimé didn't
believe in that. Or said she didn't, anyway.

A new course was brought by ivy-wreathed dancers and
torch-bearers to the King's table, with a music of stringed
instruments, a low throbbing that caught oddly at the pit
of the stomach. One was put down before every guest;
the arms of the dancers reached over their shoulders;
flowers and breasts squashed for a moment lightly against
them. Ptolemy reached behind him for the unseen dancer's
thigh, and dug his fingers and polished nails into it. He
had ordered the course himself, so he knew. Every guest

had a marzipan crocodile about a foot long, dyed in natural colours and biting a naked man or woman made of white nuts appropriately stained with red in parts. The nut faces had all been carved separately by a Persian ivory-worker, each into a different and individual little mask of screaming horror. If you liked that sort of thing, that was the sort of thing you liked. Agathokles did, for instance. The throbbing music went on, as though to drown the tiny squeaking cries such tortured dolls must give. Agathoklea shuddered a little and pulled her crocodile to bits. She wanted a nice, strong man to snuggle against. Then it would be all right, then she'd be able to giggle at the crocodiles. She looked round for a nice, strong man—hairy.

King Ptolemy suddenly had a brilliant thought. He let go the bruised dancer and leant towards Agathokles. 'Next time,' he said, 'we will have an even newer sweet. We will have a staked body and a snake—yes, Kleomenes! This Persian is brilliant; he will get the likeness. See that he stays with us. Do you like my idea?'

Agathokles was a little uneasy. 'A marvellous conception,' he said. 'But—the effect? Some of your guests may take it too seriously.'

'Ah, but I take it seriously myself!' said Ptolemy. 'Kleomenes is mine now, my god that I have flayed and staked and done what I wanted with. His image must be made.'

Agathokles quivered and twitched responsively. 'For a small party, then. Just ourselves. As you say, to eat. That will be wonderful: better than this, even. We'll have a poem written for it.'

'Metrotimé shall do that.'

'Metrotimé,' said Agathokles, rather spitefully, 'has become quite incapable of doing anything one asks her since Berris Der gave her that new statue of his.'

'Not incapable of everything,' said Ptolemy, and smiled to himself. He had found her a particularly stimulating companion. 'She understands,' he said, delicately grooving along his crocodile's back with one nail.

'What?' said Agathokles, sharply jealous.

Ptolemy lifted his head. 'About kings dying. About sacrificing kings. Taking a living man and mixing him with pain and death—yes, mixing him—like a cook—and making a god. I have made a god that way. A new form of god. Dionysos-Sabazios has shown himself again on one man, a torn man. Like Pentheus in the play. By the way, Agathokles, we might have that acted again soon, before people forget. It was a pine-stake—his tree. And the growing vine. It was a manifestation. I made it appear.'

Agathokles looked away, his face working. He wanted not to believe in the thing at all; he wanted to laugh at it the way Sosibios laughed. But he had seen with his own eyes.

Princess Arsinoë and two of her maids of honour came to the table where Sphaeros sat, talking quietly to the man next him. The girls carried a basket of fruit; all kinds, heaped and fine in the torchlight. She offered the basket to him with a pretty speech. He was touched. The pomegranates were particularly large and rosy: he took one. There were interesting analogies to be drawn from the structure of a pomegranate, the tough though red-cheeked rind, and the multiplicity of seeds. He put his knife into it. The pomegranate was made of painted wax. All the fruits in the basket were wax. Arsinoë laid her hands on her hips and threw her head back in the torch glare and laughed in shaking fits. The other two girls laughed too, spilling the wax fruit, clinging on to one another with delight at their successful joke. 'You can't even tell whether a pomegranate's real or not,' said Arsinoë. 'You and your kataleptike phantasia!'

Sphaeros put the pomegranate aside gently, steadying himself against the mocking laughter of the girls. 'Pomegranates, after all, are not so very important,' he said, 'and perhaps I meant to take a wax one—how do you know?'

And Arsinoë stopped laughing and looked at him and said: 'Yes, perhaps you did.'

PART IX

They that Mourn

Dem Begriffe nach, einmal ist allemal.
  Hegel

Δαιμόνιοι τίνα τόνδε θεὸν δεσμένεθ' ἑλόντες
καρτερόν; οὐδὲ φέρειν δύναταί μιν νηῦς ἐυεργής.
  Homeric Hymn to Dionysos

NEW PEOPLE IN THE NINTH PART
THE EPILOGUE

People of Marob
Klint-Tisamenos as Corn King
Erif Gold, youngest daughter of
 Berris Der and Essro

Greeks
Tisamenos, a helot, and others

THERE WERE TWO people standing on the big breakwater of Marob harbour. One was the Corn King, Klint-Tisamenos, wearing the Corn King's crown of ramping beasts, and the other was his cousin, the girl Erif Gold, the youngest child of Berris Der and Essro. She had been fishing off the end of the breakwater, for she had a way with fish, and now there were a dozen in the heavy net slung over her shoulder. Her hair blew into her eyes, so she stopped and swung the net down beside her cousin, and began to remake her plaits. She laughed to herself, because the wind pulled at her hair and skirt and because she was standing beside the Corn King and because she had just discovered that, besides being a witch and able to catch fish quicker than anyone else in Marob, she could also make a peculiarly lovely green enamel, which all the metal-workers had come to see and admire, including the young man she was very nearly in love with. She had been telling Klint-Tisamenos about that, which had made it all suddenly realer, and it was spring, and the most exciting and the best-coloured spring she had ever lived through.

The ships from the south had been coming into Marob for the last few weeks. There was one moored near them now, her black, pitched bulwarks about on a level with them, but rising at bow and stern, so that the red-painted eyes looked out side-ways over the quay. During the war between Flaminius the Roman and King Antiochos of Syria, Marob had been cut off from the south almost altogether. Byzantium and the straits were deeply involved, and the merchants took their cargoes elsewhere. But now there was peace again and everything was cleared up, and the Black Sea harbours were filling with Rhodian and Cretan and Corinthian and Athenian ships, and Antiochos was beaten and sulking, and the Romans had gone back to their western place on the other side of the civilised world, and in Marob the midsummer market would be held again with the old magnificence and profit and passing about of goods and money.

This ship was a Cretan, laden with wine in casks and jars, and oil, and some woven stuffs. They had been unlading all the morning, and now three or four slaves were clearing up the decks. Sometimes one of them would begin some kind of song, or what had once been a song, but had now been reduced to something sub-human, an insect's drone; not encouraged, it dropped again. Otherwise they scarcely spoke; they worked dully. Marob was a harbour like any of the other harbours where they had strained and slipped and ached through days of lading and unlading between other and endless days of rowing. There was nothing for slaves to talk about.

Erif Gold and Klint-Tisamenos did not notice them. She picked up her fish-net again, sticking her fingers in among the firm, sticky bodies; their salty cold smell brightened the spring about her; the hair on her forehead and temples and the base of her neck curled and shone into tighter rings; she kept a grip of the hour, balancing on her airy happiness. The Corn King saw this and saw it as a part of the thing he did in Marob. He breathed deeply and steadily, and for him, too, time went as he chose. He thought of his cousin's marriage coming soon, the toughness and gentleness and pleasure of her body, as though that net weight she slung about so easily were already a child. She knew he thought this, and her skin warmed as it would have under kisses or a cloudless sun, and her mind went back to the forge and the praising circle of faces and the lovely colour she had made, and she began to picture a cup with lion handles and green inside, so that the lions should constantly be staring and straining down to a green, tiny lake. And then she saw that the Corn King had suddenly stopped thinking of her and was listening. He was listening because he had heard his own name spoken aloud, his rather curious Greek name, Tisamenos.

Earlier that morning the edge of a wine-cask had dropped on to a slave's bare foot, so that he screeched and let go of a rope that kept the gang plank in place, and he was properly lammed into by the captain, first with the rope's end and then more thoroughly with a stick that had nail points in it. However, he was quite unable for the time being to stand up again, in spite of this inducement to do so, and after a time one of the others helped him down into the dark of the hold, and tied up his foot with rags and left him. As his eyes got used to the almost lightlessness he turned his head towards them again, those drawings of the kings he and his friend had made on the planks in red and charcoal, after the pictures they both knew: the picture of Agis betrayed and dead, the picture of Kleomenes in agony at the pillar, and the picture of Nabis with a bloody axe. He talked to the pictures. He asked King Agis and King Kleomenes to come back and help him, to come back to their wretched and mourning people, but he did not say that to King Nabis because he himself had seen Nabis dead and stiff, murdered by his false friend, the Aetolian Alexamenos.

He lay on his side with his head on a bean sack, muttering and remembering, thinking sometimes of Nabis and the revolution which had made him a citizen and a soldier, but mostly telling the other two—the Kings who had died before his time—what had been done to him, to him and his friends and new Sparta; and it seemed to him that King Agis answered that he had suffered too, and suffered worse things, even the last thing of all when he was still young, and he understood, and King Kleomenes answered that he had suffered all that, he had died for Sparta, and he would come back one day and revenge it on Philopoemen and Megalopolis; he was the snake, the vine, the cup, the remedy, the king who remembered his people. So by and bye the man fell asleep, and while he slept his foot got better and his cut back almost stopped stinging, and when they shouted down to him to come up quick and help them scrub decks, he came without too much pain and with some curious kind of faint hope of something, some idea that he was not alone. And that one of the others who had been his fellow-soldier in the old days, called him by the name he had got then, Tisamenos.

The Corn King of Marob walked over to the ship and looked down into her, and Erif Gold followed him, because she wanted to see everything this spring day. The slaves looked up from their hands and knees and gaped at these glittering great ones, at the pure shining gold on the belt and knife and crown of the Corn King, and the blowing, brilliant hair of the young girl beside him. They ducked their heads down towards the decks and did not dare to think that these were barbarians. The Corn King said: 'Who is there among you called Tisamenos?'

And after a time one of the crouching scrubbers lifted his head a little and said: 'It was I.'

'Come here,' said the Corn King. The man looked up. He thought he had to obey that voice, but he also remembered pains and penalties if he disobeyed his master's and left the ship. 'Come here!' said the Corn King again impatiently, standing on the edge of the quay. The man got up and limped to the gang plank and up it and knelt on the stone in front of the Corn King and Erif Gold. He looked at the Corn King's boots, which were made of red leather with black-and-white lions sewn on to them. He heard the voice over his head say: 'Why are you called Tisamenos?'

The man said: 'I was given that name, Lord, when I was a boy, when King Nabis came and avenged us, the poor people of Sparta, on the rich. It means that we had been paid, Lord—'

'I know,' said the Corn King. 'It is my name too.'

The man looked up a little, not understanding, and saw someone older than himself, strong and crowned and smiling. Timidly he said: 'Lord, does it please you?'

Klint-Tisamenos said: 'My father and mother were in Sparta once. I have heard a great deal about it. But it was King Kleomenes who paid back the poor on the rich.'

'Yes,' said the man, 'but he died.'

'I know,' said Klint-Tisamenos, and said nothing more for a minute. The man felt he had no leave to speak again.

It was the girl who said: 'My father was in Sparta too. You aren't a Spartan, surely?'

The slave lifted his head and stared at her. It was terrible to say to this bright, free, half-scornful woman that he was a Spartan; it was more terrible to deny it. He said: 'I was.'

'And now?' said Erif Gold. But the man had no answer.

The Corn King sat down on a bollard and the girl curled herself up on the stones beside him, fingering her shining fishes. The King said: 'Tell me what happened.' He wanted to sit in the sun and be told true stories. He suddenly wanted to know all about these odd affairs of Greece. He himself had been there three times. Once it was as a child on the way back from Egypt, and there had been a bigger boy who played with him sometimes, but they had left him and Hyperides in Athens, which was a very hot town and he had been bitten by fleas.

The next time was when he was seventeen. He stayed with Hyperides, in Athens most of the time; he remembered how anxious every one had been, trying to make peace between Philip of Macedon and the Aetolian League, the northern Greeks, so as to get the Roman barbarians out of the way, back to their savage west. Every one was angry with the Aetolians for calling in the Romans, with their brutal but rather efficient ways of making war and plundering, but Philip was a savage in his way too, and a tyrant, and old Aratos who used to advise him was dead—broken heart or poison, it didn't make much difference which. It was a difficult time for Greece between Rome and Macedon, with Egypt and Syria in the background. As he remembered it, Sparta in those days was not much of a place. Machanidas was ruling as guardian of a baby king—constant chops and changes there—but no one paid much attention. Hyperides had once or twice spoken of that older boy—Gyridas, his name was—it was the only reason they ever thought about Sparta, for there'd been so much to do and see that summer. Yes, a wonderful summer it was! But Klint-Tisamenos had gone back to Marob very glad he was not a Greek, very glad he had not got to face those problems, above all that Marob had not got to deal with Rome.

He had not been in Greece again after that for more than sixteen years, though once or twice Hyperides had come to Marob, getting older every time, wanting less to do things and more to talk. It seemed to Klint that his father and mother were very happy talking to Hyperides. But Klint himself had gone out on the plains with his brothers and sisters and cousins and friends and they had danced and raced and made things, and hunted, and fought the Red Riders, and made love in the long grass or round the camp-fires, and the years had gone by and he didn't get to Greece again because of the troubles there: Philip of Macedon and Antiochos of Syria, and always more and more these Romans out of the west, fighting and looting and going away, but always, somehow, coming back; dark, stolid little men who never knew when they were being laughed at, and were quite amazingly dead to some sorts of ideas and wonderfully unwilling to do things on their own without sending back to consult their fantastic Council, the Senate of Rome.

But it was later that he had seen so many Romans, when

he finally did go in the last year before the great war with Antiochos—because his father, Tarrik, had told him he must go now, for it would be difficult later when he was Corn King—Tarrik knowing his hour was almost come on him. Tarrik probably happy. So Klint had gone out then, and he remembered now hearing about Sparta, and he frowned and fidgeted, still uneasy to think of his home-coming that time, and the feast, and the taking over of power for him and his Spring Queen. He frowned and breathed and relaxed, and became aware again of the man with his own name kneeling at his feet. So he repeated: 'Tell me what has happened to Sparta.'

The slave Tisamenos said: 'Lord, I was bidden not to leave the ship. My master will come back—'

'But this is the Chief,' said Erif Gold. 'He is the Corn King of Marob. If he chooses to have your master drowned off his own boat, nothing will happen. Don't be so frightened.' Then she got up and stood over him and said: 'Let me see your foot.' The man undid the rags quickly and fearfully; his foot was bruised and cut and ugly with scars and hardenings; she touched it and laughed and said: 'You aren't much of a Greek now, Tisamenos!' Then she tossed the old, stained rag into the sea and began to handle the foot; she seemed to him to be putting everything into place, laying muscle and bone rightly together. For a moment it came into his head that she was one of the women out of the pictures: Agiatis—or Agesistrata—or the woman of Megalopolis.

He shut his eyes; then he opened them and said: 'Where shall I tell from, Lord?'

'From the time Machanidas was your King,' said Klint-Tisamenos. 'He reigned alone, I think?'

'Yes. Because they had banished little King Agesipolis, as a child. I never knew why. And his uncle Kleomenes was dead. Not the real Kleomenes, Lord; his nephew. Then there was another king, who was only a child. But it was really King Machanidas. And he was allied with the Aetolian League against the tyrant Philip of Macedon.'

'With the Aetolian League. And Rome.'

'And Rome. Yes, Lord. But we hated the Macedonians. I was a young boy then. But nothing came of it that first time and the Romans seemed to go, and King Machanidas was besieging Mantinea and the Achaeans. And then Philopoemen who had been in Crete, learning fox-ways, came back and was made general of the Achaeans, and he killed our King Machanidas. But we did not know about Philopoemen then.'

'Know what?'

'I did not know I was going to hate him, Lord, as I hate him now.'

'What were you? A citizen?'

'No, Lord, I was a helot, the son of a helot. I herded pigs in the hills. But my grandfather had been one of King Kleomenes' citizens till Sellasia. He was killed then. We were slaves again after that. My father was dead too. But mother told us. And the others. And we had the pictures.'

'What pictures?'

'The pictures of the Kings. King Agis and King Kleomenes; and the twelve; and the Queens in blue. And the stake with the vine and the great snake. We made them ourselves on the walls. When I was a child they took me to see the real ones. They are hidden in different places from time to time, and only shown sometimes. Till the Kings come back.'

Suddenly Erif Gold laughed and said: 'Do you know who painted the pictures?'

'No,' said the man, hating her because she had laughed.

'But I do,' said the girl.

'And I,' said the Corn King. 'Go on, you with my name. Did every one think so of the pictures?'

'All of us. All of the poor. The rich did not know about them, or pretended not to know. And then King Nabis came and they renamed me Tisamenos. It was as though the thing we had asked for had happened.'

'What thing?'

'A King had come to the people. But we did not know then that he would have to die too.'

'I have heard,' said Klint-Tisamenos slowly, 'a good deal of evil of King Nabis.'

'Yes, Lord,' said the slave, 'because you heard it from the rich! They tell it their own way.'

'Perhaps,' said Klint-Tisamenos, thinking of that very reasonable man, Hyperides, who had such a dislike for torture or any artificial and violent form of death.

'He was our King,' said the man. 'He made the revolution again. They hated him, they tried to stop it. So he killed them and banished them. He took their land and money for us. He divided the land and made us citizens and soldiers; he built a navy and made an army, and Sparta was strong again. It was us. Us all together: no more rich and poor. The children of the first revolution were beginning to grow up. Every one was afraid of us because they saw us all together, all thinking of one thing. King Nabis was a kind of cousin of King Agis, but far off, and his wife Apea was from Argos; she thought like him. We did all the old things: the discipline and the eating-together. I was taken from herding pigs and put into a class and taught about the revolutions.' The man dropped silent for a time after that; he did not look frightened now and it seemed as though his foot were paining him less.

The girl said softly to Klint: 'We must tell father. He always said they were rather bad pictures. But I would like to see them.'

Klint said: 'Your father will laugh. I hate it when he laughs that way.'

The man went on: 'King Kleomenes started the New Times and died for them, but perhaps he did not go far enough. He left the rich too much power. King Nabis did not make that mistake. His New Times were ours, ours only. In those days we were strong on the sea; he filled Gytheum with shipyards and stores for gear and arms; he made us refuge places in Crete. He had a guard of Cretans; it was useful. They would do—anything. Every year in my class I got prouder of being one of the citizens. They treated us rough; we liked it—mostly. The captains of the class went off raiding towards Messene and Megalopolis; the Achaeans ran and our men stuck them like pigs. Philopoemen was away again. We hated him and we hated Philip. We used to get news of what was going on in the rest of the world: how Antiochos of Syria went to India and the dragon places and the lands of fire and snow, and stayed there six years in war and magic. How the King and Queen of Egypt died in a queer way, and how the people of Alexandria revenged them in the end.'

Again Klint-Tisamenos and Erif Gold looked at one another and nodded, remembering what they had heard about Sosibios and Agathokles, and how amused Erif and Berris had been at their singularly unpleasant deaths.

The man was speaking again: 'We heard about Philip's tyrannies, and we heard about the war between Rome and

Carthage and the great battles with ships and elephants. And after that we heard how the Rhodians had sent to Rome for help against Philip, just as the Aetolians had before. That was what it was like when I was a boy.'

'Were you a Stoic?'

The man shook his head. 'We didn't have time for all that. We didn't want it. We'd got what we wanted.' He went back to the telling: 'Then the Romans did come; they attacked Philip. The Achaean League was friends with Macedon; they always had been. But they couldn't help this time, because we were keeping them busy. I did my first raiding then and killed my first man. Philip couldn't help them against us either, so they had to change sides. The Roman, Flaminius, made them do that. Then Philip tried to make peace, but Flaminius wouldn't give him terms.'

'That,' said the Corn King, remembering it bit by bit, 'was when you changed sides too.'

The man shrugged his shoulders. 'Philip gave us Argos. It was Queen Apea's town—and, God, she did play with it too, later on, getting the revolution going! A proper little tiger bitch she was. But Philip was no good to us except for that, so he got the chuck and we made peace with Rome and even the Achaean League for a bit. Well, after that Philip was beaten, and Rome had it all her own way, and Flaminius went about making speeches about how they'd won the war and freed Greece. But we went on with our revolution. And in other states the poor people looked towards Sparta and they wanted a revolution too. So the end of it was that we had every one against us. All the rich, all the states that were jealous or frightened, and the Achaean League again, and Rhodes and Pergamon and Rome, and our own dirty lot of rich too, that we'd turned out earlier, instead of killing the whole pack of them as we ought to have. They came at us all at once, land and sea. We stuck it, though. He—he wasn't King of Sparta for nothing! We could do it for him. But they got the coast towns, they burnt the ships, they burnt the farms, they burnt the standing corn, they stormed Gytheum. They tried to storm Sparta itself— yes, Flaminius and the Romans did that—but we lighted fires—we burnt our own homes and drove them back. But in the end we had to come to terms. The rest of the states hated leaving us alive at all, but Flaminius didn't care. We had to give up Argos and the coast towns and the fleet and give hostages. Yes. Our King gave his only son as a hostage. But the revolution stayed and the eating-together and the way we lived. The next year the Romans left Greece again. Flaminius had plenty of friends among the rich, the ones who wanted things to stay as they are. But the poor hated him because of what he had done to us. I know that because men used to come from the other states to get what hope they could from us; we showed them the pictures sometimes; they prayed too. A great many of us were killed then, but for those who were left it was not too bad.'

'But then?'

'Well, then we joined with the Aetolians against Rome. We hoped Antiochos and Philip would join too, but they were afraid. King Nabis blew on the ashes and the flame broke. We got back our sea towns. But Philopoemen was with the Achaean League again. We defeated him at sea. But—' The man stopped speaking for a moment and screwed up his eyes painfully. At last he went on: 'He beat us, up in the hills, a little beyond Sellasia. We were driven back through Sellasia Pass into Sparta itself. I saw that old battlefield, looking awful and evil still. When we went between the two hills we made vows to King Kleomenes; we asked him to come back and help us; we sacrificed. In the end the Romans made peace again, but we were terribly weak, helpless, and Philopoemen just beyond the frontier waiting for his time. We knew that. But it was not the worst yet.'

'That was the time when I was in Greece last,' said the Corn King. 'I remember hearing about Sparta. Tisamenos! Was there a man called Gyridas? His father was Kleomenes' foster-brother, half a helot—'

'Gyridas!' said the man eagerly. 'God, yes! He was in it all, in to the neck! It was he who had the pictures first. It was he who was in command at Gytheum during the siege. He escaped then, but they killed him in the end. The Achaeans speared him clean. That was better than living on—as I did. Because the Aetolians saw we were no more use to them as allies, but they wanted to steal our State money. They sent the traitor Alexamenos with troops, as though they were bringing help; we let him into Sparta. And he murdered King Nabis in the King's house. But we killed him. We tore him into little rags and bloody pieces. It was all we could do. But we couldn't make our King alive again. And Philopoemen came and took Sparta and dragged us into his Achaean League. We were too badly broken to stop him. That was four years ago—more.'

'And since then? I thought nothing had happened in Greece, but the war with Antiochos. We've had little news up here.'

'We didn't matter enough to be told about, Lord,' said the man. For a time he had been half-sitting on the stones of the quay, but now he knelt again, stiffly, stiffening himself to tell this last part, only his hurt foot sticking sideways. He said: 'We stood it for two years. We kept things going somehow for the sake of the future; we thought they'd left us that. There were children. We told them. I got well of my wound, but most of my friends were dead. Dead as the Kings were dead. And there wasn't any woman I wanted much. Then all those exiles began coming back; they lived in the coast towns and laughed at us trying to live our way, and began to get back their land, for they were rich again now, richer than us. There were a lot in Las, near Gytheum. At last they made us too angry; we went for them, but a good many escaped. That was what the Achaeans had been wanting. They sent—yes, they sent to Sparta!—and said the ones who'd led the attack were to be handed over to them. There were even some in Sparta who were so afraid they would have done that; but not for long, because we killed them, thirty of them, and said we would have no more to do with Achaea. It was better to belong to Rome and the barbarians than that! But it was no good. Rome didn't care. They let Philopoemen in on us. He came marching over from Megalopolis, and the exiles came in after him. We couldn't begin to stand against them. He took all our leaders and made a mock trial and killed them. He pulled down all our walls and forts, Lord, and dismissed all the armies and—and he said we were not to have our things any more; the things the Kings had died for, the things Lycurgos had made first for Sparta. We were to be like any other state. He sucked the life out of us. I think he specially hated all of us like me, who had been helots; he wanted to wipe all that out. Some of us went away, to Crete or wherever we could. I had nowhere to go and no money; I had only my bit of goat pasture and three olives and my little knotty vines, up between the rocks. But I thought they would let me stay in the hills of Sparta, on my own earth;

they had taken away everything else. Oh, I thought I could stay when I loved it so!'

'But you couldn't?' said Erif Gold, very gently, trying to help him.

'No, lady,' he said. 'The League passed a decree. Then they hunted us down all over Laconia. All of us who'd been soldiers, who had shared in the New Times, who had pictures of the Kings. They took my land away and then they took me and sold me. They sold three thousand of us. And now there are none of us in Sparta, but only the exiles and the Achaeans, the men from Megalopolis, Philopoemen's friends. Lord, I must go back to the ship, or I will be beaten again.'

'You are not to go back to the ship,' said the Corn King. 'I will buy you, Tisamenos.'

The man ducked his head again and murmured: 'Lord.'

Erif Gold said: 'Are there more of you on the ship?'

'There is one, lady,' said the man. 'We were cheap beasts to buy.'

'My father will buy him,' said Erif Gold. 'Then you will be together. It is better being together, isn't it, when you have the same Kings?'

'Yes, lady,' said the man, staring, for he could not think how she knew that.

She asked: 'Is your foot well?'

Astonished, he felt it with his hands, and slowly got to his legs and stood firm on it. 'Yes, lady!' he said again.

She nodded, satisfied.

Klint-Tisamenos said: 'I think this is a story I half know. About the kings who die. My father told me that. I am the King here, and when my time comes I will die for the people. That time is sure to come for a king. Your King Kleomenes died in Egypt because he did not die at Sellasia. My father told me that too. And now he has turned into a god, he has become part of the year. But you are staying here now. And in Marob we have got the thing straight.' And then he stood up, too, and he took the hand of the other Tisamenos and led him, wondering and dirty, back from the sea and the harbour into Marob.

CANONGATE CLASSICS
TITLES IN PRINT